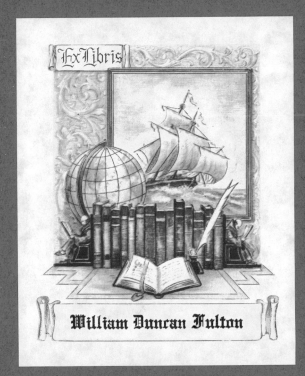

Ex Libris

William Duncan Fulton

ALSO BY

JOHN HERSEY

Here to Stay
(1963)

The Child Buyer   *The War Lover*
(1960)   (1959)

A Single Pebble
(1956)

The Marmot Drive
(1953)

The Wall   *Hiroshima*
(1950)   (1946)

A Bell for Adano
(1944)

Into the Valley
(1943)

THESE ARE *Borzoi Books,* PUBLISHED IN NEW YORK
BY *Alfred A. Knopf*

WHITE LOTUS

White Lotus

JOHN HERSEY

New York Alfred · A · Knopf

1 9 6 5

L. C. catalog card number: 65–11104

THIS IS A BORZOI BOOK,
PUBLISHED BY ALFRED A. KNOPF, INC.

FIRST EDITION

AUTHOR'S NOTE

This work is not intended as prophecy; perhaps it should be thought of as an extended dream about the past, for in this story, as in dreams, invisible masks cover and color known faces, happenings are vaguely familiar yet "different," time is fluid, and there is a haunting feeling that people just like us, and maybe we ourselves, have lived in such strange places as these. It is, in short, a history that might have been, a tale of an old shoe on a new foot.

CONTENTS

CONTENTS

The Sleeping-Bird Method

PROLOGUE

⟮ "Every Measure"

I MUST COMPOSE my face and push the fear and doubt beneath the skin. Nothing must show on my face today but white skin.

All that I have done and known must shine in this act. I am to stand alone out there, a solitary "sleeping bird," for on this day I have been chosen to make the symbolic individual protest that our movement has found so effective in recent months.

Our group of whites, about two dozen all told, is huddled on the near side of a large reviewing ground in the capital of Four Rivers Province.

Across the way is my "roost," the place where I am to stand—beyond a memorial archway, before the gate of the provincial yamen: a stack of masonry in the worst taste of the new regime's "popular" style, squarish, pink, false-humble like the bureaucrats it houses, a cartoon in bricks of the obdurate heavy yellow spirit that we whites have set ourselves in this campaign to break for good.

The reviewing ground is a plain space of unpaved dirt which is as nearly level as anything in this hilly city. A long, low swell of earth rises left of center; to the right the bare clay, mud-cracked and shoe-worn, slopes down to a brick wall.

Around three sides of this parade area a large crowd of yellows, mostly young and male, has gathered. So far these onlookers are

silent. Are they simply curious? Do they know that our weapon
is one that will prick their shame?

A thin old dog whose orange fur is molting out in ragged handfuls slinks along the open ground in front of the memorial arch,
its tail between its legs, appearing to think that the crowd has
assembled in order to humble a cur.

This dog reminds me of Grin's dream, so long ago, of the endless riverlike pack of runaway-hunting dogs on the way to "the
mountain" of freedom, and of Dolphin, who became a fugitive
shadow, it could be said, in that very dream, Dolphin who failed
his kind because of his utter selfishness; he wanted to go alone.
Then, looking at the squat yamen beyond the dog, I think for
a moment of Peace, standing with legs spread, looking up at
that exquisite sculptural palace of power, ice-whited by limewash
and the late-slanting sun, at Twin Hills—Peace who failed us
because of his inflexibility, the rigidity of his vision. How
many traits could I count as causes of failure for whites? No, I
must not think in this vein. . . . My face must show nothing today
but skin.

There is activity at the yamen gate. Some yellow official has
come out from within and is talking with a slouching group of
gate guards.

The official, who, though provincial, affects the ultra-plain,
quasi-military tunic of the new national regime, modest to the
brink of ostentation, starts across the reviewing ground, accompanied by three out-of-step guards. He is coming to us.

Rock takes me by the arm and edges me, or tucks me, back into
the center of our group; perhaps he thinks it best that I be somewhat hidden for the present.

The official has approached us, and he asks, "Who is your
leader?"

This is the invariable question, and always when perching en
masse we used to greet it with unanimous silence, and now some
instinct keeps us silent again. I suppose Rock is our leader, but he
is quiet with the rest of us. Or perhaps *I* am the leader today;
I remain half hidden.

"What is the matter? Is your leader afraid to identify himself?"

Now our silence is becoming effective. Yellow taunters have
always been enraged by the solidity, the thick imperviousness,
of our silence.

"I have a message for your leader from the Governor."

It is not easy to keep silent at this announcement. I want to shout, "What? What is it?" For we know about His Excellency Governor K'ung of Four Rivers Province. It is precisely his shame that we have wanted to stir by coming here—if he has any. He is my personal adversary for this day. We have heard about Governor K'ung from a distance. He is a former warlord who made an accommodation with the new regime, which accepted him for the sake of immediate stability in Four Rivers Province, and he is said to be a short man with a big belly and a thick neck. What concerns us—me—is his attitude toward the whites. He has publicly stated that the whites were brought here from foreign parts to be slaves; slavery was the proper station of the whites; through no fault of his they are no longer slaves, but in Four Rivers Province they are to remain, so long as he is Governor, subservient to the yellow population. He has openly flouted the decrees of the national regime, weak and vague as they are, respecting the universality and inviolability of citizenship. In his public speeches Governor K'ung uses the old epithets: "pigs," "smalls," "moonlights," "fogs." His is the voice of insult, provocation, hatred; a thin veneer of old-fashioned manners covers a hard core of pure hatred.

Governor K'ung is what his province deserves—this exquisite rain-drenched interior area of pyramidal hills which we can see all around, whose profiles are fringed with thin lines of trees; rice land of the Red Basin, once a sea floor, now a rich earth bowl of food. This region is backward, scandalously backward from our point of view, for the white farm workers are still held in an ill-defined state of villeinage—their bondage consisting not in legal arrangements but simply in a millstone poverty that they haven't the strength to lift off their backs. The worst of this thralldom is the vileness of the yellows toward our starving whites: Governor K'ung in his genteel nastiness mirrors his yellow populace. This is the valley of hate.

The official is angry at our utter silence, which he sees as sullenness.

"Excellency K'ung wishes to state that he will take every measure to prevent agitators from outside his province from causing any trouble here. Do you understand the phrase 'every measure'? Excellency K'ung knows your plan—to station a single so-called sleeping bird on public display. Excellency K'ung will not allow such a display. He forbids it. Please understand that any overt act on your part will constitute deliberate disobedience of his commands."

The official wheels away and returns to the yamen. His progress across the reviewing ground brings a half-humorous cheer from the watching yellows—they're glad something is happening.

We are quiet for some time after the official has gone out of earshot, then suddenly everyone in our party is talking at once.

Several of our group feel that we should call off the demonstration; I hear one man say that going through with it would be too dangerous for White Lotus, for me. Another advocates at least a postponement, taking time to work out a new technique, a surprise, some twist that would catch the Governor off balance.

Deft, our theorist, speaks. He is a man of slight stature, with a delicate chin and a receding hairline and flashing eyes which give an appearance of conviction and force to the words that tumble out of his moist little mouth. He says that we can't withdraw, we can't postpone. This would be the first defeat we'd ever suffered. We'd be giving in to a show of force that so far consisted only of commands. Besides, we'd be giving in to the worst yellow man of all those whom we'd attempted to impress.

Rock agrees to this but says that he feels that a man, not a woman, should take the risk of this demonstration. He volunteers his own person.

Deft says, "No, that's wrong. A woman offers a far greater reproach to violence, or to a threat of it, than a man. It would be a mistake to send a man out now."

Rock does not press the point. I think he believes that Deft is right. He has made his gesture of protecting me.

Through this exchange our friend Chang, pressing at our shoulders, has been studying the matter, peeking often at Rock to see where the man of action would jump.

Chang is a yellow youth who is on our side. He is one of a growing number of young yellows who in their zeal to help us, activated rather than paralyzed by shame, have begun to attach themselves to us, taking risks with us and often embarrassing us with their complex motives and naïve suggestions but also, in a few cases, and Chang is one of them, bringing to bear an underlying sweetness and generosity which, no matter how perverse its innermost origin may have been, lends us comfort and moral force when we face their so far untouched fellows. But at this moment Chang disgusts me.

A food vendor has just come to us, a white man, who carries on the ends of a shoulder pole a strange little kitchen in two parts —a cylindrical wooden canister at one end, which serves as a pantry for raw foodstuffs and utensils, and, at the other, another cylinder, this one of metal, containing a charcoal brazier and a boiler of deep vegetable oil. On a spike that leans out over the hot oil are crisp bean crullers, newly cooked.

The vendor is excited; he knows by hearsay what is about to take place, he will be a witness for the local whites—for no whites besides him have dared to come out to watch here in this province where brutal intimidation is still the rule.

Is it my imagination that makes Chang's demeanor toward the vendor, as he buys a cruller, different from ours? We whites are easy and direct with the man; good-hearted Chang, it seems to my eyes, is at a great remove as he takes a cruller in its wrapping of crude paper and drops a copper in the hawker's hand. His air is patrician, accustomed to servants, white servants. He snaps at the cruller with beautiful teeth, his lips are drawn back in a kind of snarl to keep them from being burned by the still-hot cruller. The vendor is already dismissed from his mind, not a man but a convenience.

Whereas, by contrast, the vendor lingers in my mind as I nibble without appetite at a cruller that Rock has put in my hand.

The vendor is one of those ragged creatures whose wild appearance should not be unsettling, for there is nothing mad or ascetic or haunted about it; it is a matter of calculation. His quilted coat is leaking dirty cotton, and his hair is long and matted. The man is cheerful. In his present excitation, he is inclined to talk too loud, laugh too hard. I am to be a sleeping bird for the yellows' shame, but he shames *me*. I feel in his filth a crafty deference to those who buy his wares—and this means, for the most part, to yellows. I am at one with him because we are both white, and I am sorry for him because he is poor, but I am also angry at him because he *wants* to be filthy; he knows that in this province it is good business for a white to be a low, beastly man.

Patting some of our volunteers and muttering words of encouragement, then lifting a new batch of cooked crullers out from the boiling oil, one by one, with a bent wire and hanging them on the spike, he seems to want to linger with us. But we have finished eating, and the lure of money takes him away.

From a side street, parting the crowd and coming out into the

open area, several bands of policemen appear, and they begin
to stroll about the reviewing ground by twos and threes, un-
militarily, like chatting philosophers. To keep whose peace?

We do not trust them. Everywhere our movement has gone,
rumors have accompanied us: that the quiet pose of the sleeping
birds is false, that a great bloody rebellion is in the making, and
that someday, in some demonstration, a signal will be given—
perhaps one of these human birds will flap its arm-wings—and
then all over the country the whites will flash weapons out from
under their clothing and attempt a terrible slaughter. We tell
ourselves that these rumors are a product of our effectiveness,
yet they disturb us. They fill us with dread of an opposite violence,
a fear that one wrong accidental gesture by a sleeping bird, perhaps trying to regain balance, flinging out an arm in what might
be taken for a signal—"Begin now!"—might cause the yellows to
descend on us to cut down our eloquent reproach by an even
more eloquent, because unanswerable, knife edge. So the appearance of armed policemen in increasing numbers at our perches
is no comfort to us.

The yellow crowd, however, reacts in a mischievous, inverted
way to the arrival of the police. The many idle young yellow
men begin to jeer—at the police. Is this because the police are so
casual, so ill-disposed, as it seems, to take strong measures? Or
is it a case of young men in a crowd responding to a show of
authority which they may think directed against themselves?
Or is it simply boredom, fun, anything for a moment's entertainment? I cannot think that any of these interpretations is good
for us—or, on this day, for me.

I have been chosen for this solo task today because in earlier
group perches I have shown endurance. I have been thought
stolid; some have called me courageous. If I have been courageous, then courage is quite different from what I had always
thought, for it must be something less than pure self-possession
in the face of clear danger, it must be compounded of misgivings,
anxiety, confusion, desperate and sinking efforts to master one's
doubts, and even uncertainty as to the meaning of one's actions.

I am physically tired. I suppose I will be able to manage the
long perch; something takes hold of me when I adopt that stance,
an inner strength, so that I do not feel wearied by it, awkward
though it is. But today I am tired. We have had a long journey upriver by steamer. For the first part of the trip we whites had

the run of the vessel, but on reaching the border of North-of-the-Lake Province, passing into this province, Four Rivers, we were firmly ordered by crew members to proceed to the filthy stern quarters, under the rattling steerage chains—familiar to Rock and me from our hopeful trip downriver, so long ago it seems, to Up-from-the-Sea. Not being able to see where we were going, only knowing of our progress by the constant thumping of some huge engine bearing and by the chatter of the rudder chains—this blindness made our trip exhausting. But even worse: the sense of outrage, of frustration, the wondering whether we would ever get anywhere with our painfully gradual methods.

Still, we *have* come a long way since that afternoon at the match factory. The Sleeping-Bird Method caught on after that with brushfire irresistibility as the one means we had in our power to disturb the yellows, to push the yellows, to shame the yellows into grudging change. It was so simple, so pure, an invention of genius by Groundnut's hawk-eyed friend, the priest named Runner: merely to stand on one leg, like a bird settled on a perch for the night, helpless as a sleeping bird, in a large flock of sleeping birds. It worked. For some reason this gesture reached to the very roots of the yellows' conscience, obliging them to face up to the intolerable conditions of our lives, wringing their guilty souls with that sweetest of all Buddha's teachings, "Harm no living creature." For as sleeping birds we seemed at last to have forced ourselves on their minds as vividly living creatures. At first the drive was confined to Up-from-the-Sea. We got jobs. We broke the back of the printeries; then papermaking, rubber goods, and enamelware fell. We began against cotton weaving. We were helped, it is true, by the unrest of the yellow workers themselves and the instability of the central regime. We perched precisely where the yellows were on strike. We began to hear that the Sleeping-Bird Method was being used in other cities, and our movement began to acquire theorists, strategists, organizers, a bureaucratic endoskeleton—and to the outlying provinces Runner began to send emissaries. We heard from a great distance that five thousand sleeping birds stood all one day in the plaza, where elephants once guarded the passage, before the Meridian Gate of the Forbidden City in the Northern Capital; and the regime must have wilted a bit with shame at that, because we began to hear of those vague proclamations on the nature of citizenship which were "for" us. Those documents, however, did not produce change in themselves, and our first reaction to them, of triumph and delight, shaded soon into a realization that we would see no *real* change that we did not bring about by our own efforts. Indeed, in the outermost provinces, in the backward ones like Four Rivers, we found that the secret police of the central regime, its "open" militia, and its high judges were playing an ambiguous game, making public declarations that seemed to support us but behind doors making agreements and judgments that tended, in the old phrase, to keep the pigs in the pen. This was the time when our movement seemed to be bogging down in a vagueness of its own, and this was when Rock, at that bicycle-wheel plant at Hankow, invented the individual protest that we have been using ever since: one sleeping bird standing alone.

I feel stifled. I break out of the center of the group. It is a beautiful day. The morning river fog has been burned away by a sun now high at our backs. The crowd around the reviewing ground is restive; we hear hoots, calls to action, nasty insults. The vendor of bean crullers is off to the left, selling his wares to some of these impatient yellows; he is apparently a local clown, for he leaps and dances about his portable kitchen, and I hear sallies of laughter from the yellows near him. I try to imagine a figure, my figure, standing on one leg beyond the memorial archway. Isn't that form very small? Does it make any impression at all? On either side of the pretentious yamen I see, in the far distance, fringed green hills steaming in the warm sunlight.

I turn now, and seeming to speak to the whole group I speak to Rock. "I'm ready. I think we had better start."

Rock says, relieved, "If you say so."

The knot of my companions seems to sigh as with one pair of taxed lungs.

My heart is beating violently, but I feel able to do whatever I must do. Rock comes out of the group and says in a low voice, "It will be all right. The Governor is bluffing. They can't stop us."

Ai, Rock! I hope you're right.

I turn away and step out quickly onto the reviewing ground.

❨ The Cruller That Fell

Before I have taken ten steps the crowd of yellows falls suddenly silent, and the hush seems to come at me like some sort of net. I am caught in it. My steps become awkward; it is as if I had forgotten how to walk. I have to instruct myself to fashion each step. Bend knee, carry right foot forward, deposit it. Meshed in this attentive silence, I feel something distinctly sexual in the interest this male crowd gives me, and I walk badly.

Yes, I have not gone ten more steps when the dog howls, the whistles, the mating hoots, the inactive-rapists' snickers break out and engulf me. I am shocked and refreshed. I am white, young, and more or less forbidden. This gives me strength I had not counted on.

Looking out at the reviewing ground from the side, I had not been aware of its expanse. I am having to walk a great distance, and every step thrusts me farther from my companions, yet I feel that *they* are in danger, not I. I enter my solitude as a refuge.

The ground is dry, cracked, and dusty. I have flickering thoughts of the marching displays that have buffed this grassless earth, the games, the ceremonies for war dead, the lantern festivals, the dragon processions, the public beheadings. The yamen is ahead, this is the heart of the province. The footing is shabby precisely because the place has been, for so long, stately. I hold my head up; my walking is a little better now.

The bleating of the lustful goats in the crowd, the sounds of invitation and mockery, are dying out, and I feel again that I am getting caught in a web of quiet.

I do hear, off to my left, a minor commotion of squeals and laughter. I don't want to turn my head to look. I have a feeling, but it is only a feeling, that the vendor of bean crullers is making fun of me, possibly mimicking my walk. Can this be? He is white!

I am approaching the memorial gateway. Its shafts are of wood; it soars delicately up over three arches to a splendor of seven narrow little tiled roofs flung out at three levels and bedizened with tiny stone lions, cranes, and peacocks. Under the centermost roof a tablet proclaims: VIRTUOUS WISDOM—GENTLE HAND. The usual lying praise of some villainous warlord.

Passing through the memorial arch I have to climb three stone steps, cross a platform, descend three steps. The blocks of stone are awry, the steps are worn.

Ahead I have an uninterrupted view now of the yamen. I see that it is really a vast bunker which was built to be held by force against artillery.

I feel weak. Facing this lumpish, cannon-proof building I feel the hopelessness of my position. How can I, just learning to walk, bring down those walls? What if Governor K'ung decides simply to hold his fort? What if he meets my attacks simply by staying inside? What if there is no reaction at all? My siege is broken before it starts!

But I cannot retreat. I must decide how near to the imposing triple gate of the building I am to approach. I do not want the memorial arch too close at my back, but I should stand off at a distance which gives due notice of a sense of proportion.

Is it an illusion that the yellow crowd is swelling, or at least pressing in from the two sides?

The silence now hangs on the air like an unanswered question. It is broken only by flurries of laughter off to my left. Is that the vendor, making a good money-thing of this affair?

I think I have gone far enough. I cannot pause and root around like an animal sniffing out its "safe" place. I must simply decide as I walk, and stop, and let the spot where I halt serve as my station.

All right. Now. I stop.

The silence is broken by a wave of next-to-silence, a murmur so quiet that it cannot be made up of words spoken to each other by the men in this concupiscent crowd. It is a mere catch at their throats.

I cannot hesitate. I raise my left knee and stand on my right foot. I try to make myself as comfortable as I can, working my right foot to make sure that its sole is well founded and level and unbothered by any pebble or tiny ridge beneath. I consciously ease my arms, I bow my head.

Finally I am alone, and I am a sleeping bird, to put the yellows to shame. My face shows nothing but white skin.

I am very excited, very proud.

But . . . but what is that? What do I hear?

The crowd is laughing. Laughter is spreading through the yellow crowd. Now the whole assemblage is roaring with laughter.

The white skin of my face is suffused with a hot blush.

I know that I must not look from side to side. I must stand still, my head bowed. The whole force of my posture is lost if I become dismayed.

The laughter continues. I am, in spite of myself, so upset by it that I cannot feel its precise tone. Mocking? Good-natured? Cruel? Prankish? Relieved? Scornful?

Can it be that some item of my clothing is disarranged? Is my gown torn behind? Are they laughing because there is such an incongruity between the walking girl for whom they felt a playful lust and this awkward, asexual, perching creature?

I even think: Have I soiled myself in my extreme agitation?

Then I wonder: Is it the vendor? Is he perching, too, but in an absurd way? Could it be possible that a white man would, for the sake of his own popularity or profit, make fun of a solemn protest on behalf of the white race? The vendor seemed so thrilled at the prospect of our demonstration, when he was selling us the crullers.

No, they are laughing at my standing here as a sleeping bird at all, at the Sleeping-Bird Method. They are laughing at the very idea of a white protest.

I cannot allow myself to think this. It must be less ugly than that. The vendor. Something awkward about me.

As I fight against the thought that the crowd is scoffing at the essence of our struggle, the laughter dwindles and dies out.

It is silent again, and I am alone and unsure of myself.

We can't be stopped. I have thought that, and Rock has said it. I say to myself that I still believe it, but this is a kind of incantation, or a prayer. At this moment I wish it, I try to push it into being by the sincerity of my thought.

I am aware of the yamen before me. The Governor is in there. But wait! He has said that he would take every measure to prevent my doing this. Yet here I am. Nothing has happened from the direction of the yamen. Even with my head bowed I can watch the yamen gate. Gate guards have seen me, and some of them have been passing in and out, and word must have gone in to the Governor's chambers about me. Nothing has happened.

Could it be possible that the yellow crowd got word of the Governor's threat to us—he had absolutely forbidden a perch—and that the laughter was *at the Governor,* at the impotence of authorities defied by a weak woman? This is just the sort of thing that young men would laugh at.

I clutch at this. If this is so, we really cannot be stopped. I feel safe in this thought, I wrap myself in it.

I hear another bounce of laughter off to the left. The vendor?

I want to look over there and see what he is doing, but I cannot. Another laugh.

All at once I am demoralized, as I think: The Sleeping-Bird Method has worn itself out. These yellows are right to laugh; this *is* laughable. I no longer believe in sleeping birds. I feel a deep absurdity in this act; it is just as absurd for a person to pretend that he is a bird as for whites to mimic yellows. The Method is a trick, and the yellows have begun to see through it. I remember an outcry of my own from long ago: *Only the powerful are free.* Perhaps Old Arm was right, who wanted violence, wanted to take open and honest steps toward revenge. *Only the free can punish.*

There is a tone of bitterness in our movement. I do not mean the all too natural bitterness at the yellows for what they have done to us, but rather at our own other selves, within our closest ranks. We are bitter over childish rivalries, jealousies—of which the principals seem quite unaware. We are bitter that our movement, once a surge of action which flowed from thought and feeling, is turning into an institution; the mark of the Sleeping-Bird Movement is now its professional careerist—its advance man, its distributor of membership chits, its collector, its theoretic tactician.

But doesn't the essential bitterness stem from the frustration, and isn't the frustration over our not partaking, in these months, of a satiating sense of *revenge?*

I do not face a yellow crowd. Instead it flanks me to either side, and I am only aware of it in the corners of my mind; I cannot see what is causing the periodic chugs of laughter at my left.

My full-face reproach is directed at a building. I cannot take revenge on a yamen.

It is true that I am in theory addressing my protest to a single man, Excellency K'ung, but I do not feel him, and he is certainly insulated from me.

I wish I could see him, and I wonder what has been reported to him about me.

I watch the gate now with a clearer eye. The regular gate guards are still trotting in and out and conferring, but now others are emerging. Several men are carrying staves with what appear to be banners rolled up under oilskin coverings—I remember the sentencing flag held in the background at Nose's trial; but there is an air of festivity here, and of military pomp, rather than of sinister judgment. There are as well numerous extra guards bearing rifles. They have not taken a formation but mill about at either side of the gate. Some of the policemen, who have been meandering about the reviewing ground, stop to talk; the effect is of a cluster of yellow schoolboys waiting outside the school gates for the handbell that will call them to recitation.

There is a strong volley of laughter at my left, and now I see the various guards—the regulars, the banner-bearers, the riflemen, and the policemen—all turn their faces at once to whatever is happening, and all laugh. But I see by the faces this is not the mirth of simple enjoyment but rather is a laughter of embarrassment, a crowing at something grotesque.

I have an idea, which makes my heart beat hard. Since the Governor is shielded from my protest by the thick walls of the yamen, I will turn and face the crowd to the left.

I will do this not simply to satisfy my curiosity about the vendor and the laughter, but rather to test what I have been thinking, for if the Sleeping-Bird Method is indeed spent, I will have no effect on the laughing spectators, whereas, if it still has meaning and power, I will be able to shame the crowd into silence and by a show of moral force prepare a stronger defense against whatever the stirrings at the gate portend.

So I put my foot down, face left, and perch again.

I see at once that the crowd has moved much closer than it was when I first walked out on the reviewing ground. There is the vendor. Yes, he is playing the part of a sleeping bird, facing the onlookers. His portable kitchen is a few paces to his right. He does not seem to me to be caricaturing my stance, and unless he is making faces or rolling his eyes he is not, so far as I can tell from behind, poking fun at our movement. In truth he seems in dead earnest.

Then why have the watchers been laughing from time to time?

They have now noticed me. I get a few halfhearted mock cheers and a spattering of laughter, but it *is* halfhearted. I feel a certain strength. Facing faces is far more rewarding than trying to shame a yamen. I now consider that I have come somehow to the rescue of the bean-cruller vendor.

Suddenly a young yellow man breaks out of the crowd, runs out to the portable kitchen, snatches a cooked cruller from the spike over the brazier, turns to the crowd, stands on one leg, and eats a cruller, flourishing its remains in the air between bites.

The barking of the laughers engulfs me. I feel the guffaws as gusts of cold wind against my cheeks and abdomen.

The young man has ended his performance and runs back to the crowd.

The vendor has stood in poise through this theft of his cruller and mockery of his stance; he has behaved like a veteran of our movement. But they have laughed at him. Why? Is it because his face is too familiar to them, they have paid him too often for his crullers, he is too everyday and well known to them to serve as a hero of reproach to their hoodlum ways? Or is it because of the mood of this backward province? Are we out of our depth here?

Another young man runs out from the crowd. The crullers are all gone from the spike. This ruffian reaches down, opens the door of the canister, takes out a large lump of the vendor's soybean dough, and plops it with a thump on the top of the container. Then he stands on one leg. He begins, with elaborate swinging of his arms and ducking of his head, to break off bits of the dough and stretch it and twist it to form the shapes of raw crullers. Now and then he loses his balance and has to hop a bit. He has seen the vendor mold the dough so often that he can caricature every movement. The crowd bellows. Finally he hobbles on one foot from the canister to the brazier, and with fastidiously pinched fingers he drops the flexible twists one by one into the boiling oil. Then he swaggers back to the crowd; he has had the biggest success of all the lampooners.

The vendor has not moved a muscle. I misjudged him; I let myself think that he was using our cause for his own profit. Look at him! How steadfast he is!

This is horrible. These young toughs of Four Rivers Province have chosen to ridicule the vendor—and me, and all whites—precisely at the point that matters most: a man's means of making a living. And my turning has made no difference. My facing the crowd has not been a deterrent to the hooligans. I must do something. It is clear that the pranksters intend to let the crullers cook, to take them out and spike them, and then to eat them (standing on one leg), one by one. I must try to forestall this somehow. If I do not, we whites will all have suffered a dangerous loss of face —at a time when there are stirrings at the yamen gate.

Yet I wait. Hai! What a comment on the life I have led—as a white! I wait until after the next move, I do not want to intervene while the crullers are cooking, for if I proved to be successful and turned the roughnecks back, the crullers would be overcooked.

spoiled; food would be wasted. And so at great risk to our cause I wait for some nasty young yellow to come out and hook the crullers out and put them on the spike. Then I will try to do something.

For a moment I wonder whether my resolve to "do something" is not mere bravado—a kind of inner noise I am making to drive away my own qualms, as if my qualms were nothing more than bothersome geese in a mud-walled yard. What can I accomplish against these young toughs? The Sleeping-Bird tactic does not impress them, they are shameless. They have gone over to counter-revolution: to ridicule. What have I learned in all this time that will do me some good now?

I have learned to live with fear. Ayah! The sound of the yellow mobs running past the orphanage in the Northern Capital, hurrying cloth shoe soles making sounds of wheezing, as though of a city's breathing in sickness and pain; the look on the broken-out yellow face of Cassia Cloud, as she leaned across the table in the tavern, calling me chieh-chieh, older sister, and telling me vile, vile news; the thought of Dirty Hua at the crest of the hill when Dolphin launched his too daring kite; the beheadings—my eyes fastened, in order not to see the swords fall on white necks, upon the peonies brocaded into the curio dealer's sea-gray gown in front of me. . . .

Yes, I have come to take fear of open cruelty for granted, I have learned how to stifle that fear, to push it down. But it is harder for me to deal with covert cruelty, implicit cruelty—with the massively threatening conditions of life that the yellows have imposed on us: the oppressive fitness, in the yellow scheme of things, of the conversion of the Peking elephant pens to a jail, where white men waited for capricious sentences with equanimity, betting on cricket fights; the rage and hunger that drove sturdy young men in Up-from-the-Sea to become "sweepers," stabbing rice bags on street carts and brushing up the spilled rice on the dung-dusty pavement and racing off with it. It is the generality of our existence that has filled me with a dread I don't know how to subdue. Not the specific bamboo blow, but rather the great accumulation of affronts, the taking their total for granted, even as the conditions of life "improve"—this is what is intolerable, because this seems to us whites to get worse, not better.

In this sense I made a mistake to turn left to face this petty disturbance surrounding the vendor. I am not afraid of the cruel

pranks of the young men in this crowd; I am afraid of the abstraction in the yamen.

The young man who twisted the dough and dropped the raw
crullers into the boiling oil cannot wait to savor more of his triumph of miming, and he runs out to the vendor's kitchen—I could
have told him that the crullers would not be done yet, for they
must be brought to a crispness so delicate that they seem to be
made of some delicious vapor—and he hooks one out. He is standing on one leg. He sees that it is not quite done, but he wants to
get a laugh from the crowd, and foolishly he squeezes the cruller
between forefinger and thumb, and he burns himself and drops
the cruller to the ground and begins to hop on the one foot and to
flip his hand, trying to shake off the pain as if it were a wetness.
This is in earnest, but it looks like a burlesque; he gets a laugh he
doesn't want. Then, when the hurt has drained away somewhat,
he gets another by hooking up the now dirty cruller and plopping
it back in the oil. Then he is satisfied and runs back to the crowd.
But when he turns around I see that he is flushed, and I suspect
that the burn hurts more than he dares to show.

My eye moves to the vendor. All this time he has not moved,
and I think: Our party has come from beyond the borders of the
province, we have nothing to lose here, for we are, as Excellency
K'ung spitefully says, outside agitators; whereas this poor vendor
is staking everything. Has he a family? What powerful emotions
he must contain in that still, still form of a sleeping bird! What
risks he is willing to take!

The sight of him stirs in me a familiar melancholy feeling, a
pity-sadness that is surely one of the most common sensations of
our depressed race—a feeling that does no one any good, yet one
in which I soak myself, almost as if it were enjoyable, a luxury.
I felt it powerfully that day long ago when Peace, Auntie, Mink,
Harlot, and I stood beside the show ring in the Scholars' Garden
at Twin Hills while the nearly naked white equestrian acrobats
hurtled in somersaults from the broad hips of their horses, and the
yellow showmaster came at us with his long whip to chase us
away; and at Provisioner Lung's, on our first visit to him, while he
kissed at his talented lark, and Rock and Groundnut and I stood
there knowing in our guts that this was a prelude to one more
vile cheating of whites; and at a contemplation of the long row of
frail white girls standing all day at the steaming copper basins in
the silk-reeling filature.

Yet there is anger at the heart of this melancholy. The sadness is a modulation of the anger. We can't stand the anger, so we run it off into sorrow. I must hold on to the anger that I felt on the vendor's behalf before I lowered myself into this emotion; I will need the anger to support the courage I will very soon have to display—display, I mean, to my own inner eye in order to finish my work.

A yellow youth runs out to the vendor's cookstove. I have no more time for preparation. Here it comes, whatever it may be.

Not the same young man as before, this boy has an elegant style; he moves smoothly, with dramatic understatement. He lifts a cruller out on the hooked wire, examines it, and sees at once that it is done to perfection. His job is to dip out all the crullers and spear them on the spike, and he does this with swift, neat, flowing probes. Incapable of slapstick, he seems serious and thoughtful, as if he realizes the gravity of these events. Then why does the crowd howl at him? Because all through this pensive activity he is standing on one leg.

Judging by the pattern of the pranks up to now, it is my guess that this young man will not eat any of the crullers but will go back to the audience as soon as he has fished them all up; that there will be a pause; and that then another will come out to eat the first new cruller. I will make my move in the pause.

Yes, the last of the crullers is on the spike, the young man stirs the hot oil with the hook to make sure there are no more. Then in his quiet mode he hangs the hooked wire on its loop and walks back to the crowd.

The vendor is as immobile, as serene, as ever.

How much time will I have? I cannot speculate. I must move. Now.

I put down my lifted foot, which prickles, half asleep, but I cannot linger to favor it. I walk forward toward the portable kitchen.

The moment I start the crowd of young men reacts. Such hoots and whistles! They greet my approach with a jubilee of air-kissing and obscene invitations. If noise could rape I'd be defiled a hundred times in the course of taking fifty steps.

I am more excited than I thought it possible to be. I can walk well, and indeed I have a bizarre thought, that I am beautiful—not because the yellow rowdies think I am, but because I have managed to hold on to some of my earlier anger. I think of the vendor. I am furious—for the vendor, for Rock when he had to pull rickshas, for myself with my fingertips in boiling water lifting out a cocoon when I was a reeler.

I did not realize how close to the mob I would have to approach. I station myself in front of the portable kitchen, between the spiked crullers and the crowd, not more than five paces away from the first of the yellows. The anonymities fade; each of these is a personality. Each man has a separate pair of lips that curl in a particular way, and I see pimples, broken front teeth, and laughter in one man's eyes.

Now I perch.

Ai! Was I thinking a few minutes ago that the Sleeping-Bird Method has passed the peak of its effectiveness, and even that it may be absurd?

I have not been standing here long enough for my racing heart to beat a hundred times when the shrill indecency of this whole crowd of hooligans has died out to utter silence. A sleeping bird has shut them up—or at least changed their mood so sharply that they have chosen silence. I have to be impersonal, my eyes are downcast, I cannot search their faces now, but I feel sure that they are all put down. Their fun is over. They are in for a period of meditation. Their pricks are subsiding. They may never have believed in the teachings they have heard since infancy—*the five aggregates of grasping are pain; hurt no living creature*—but they are at least now briefly gripped by those precepts as if the kind words were policemen or angry fathers.

In the midst of my relief and triumph I suffer a pang of doubt. Will it last? Will that hold on the crowd last? Will the hoodlums not recover their phlegm very soon? Should I not break the spell while I have the best of it—go back to my perch before the yamen? But if I do, what happens then?

The vendor comes to *my* rescue, in a sense. He puts his foot down and walks to his portable kitchen, behind me. I hear him checking it over. The little door of the pantry canister clacks shut. He makes the sounds of putting some charcoal on the fire. I hear him setting the shoulder pole, and there is a creaking sound, and he utters the understood grunt of everlasting weariness and submission of the poverty-stricken white underdog as he lifts his kitchen up. I wonder: Is he going home? The crowd is silent.

He is looping around to my left; I sense this. He comes now into my field of vision, and I see that he is really a brave man: He is going to pretend that nothing has happened, he is a cruller peddler, he is going to sell fresh-cooked crullers to any in this crowd who may be hungry. He is going to act as if he is glad a crowd has gathered; it is easy to sell soybean crullers when a crowd has gathered.

He makes a sale; money changes hands. A young yellow man eats. The vendor thinks now to take out some dough and shape and twist new crullers and drop them in the oil to cook. Another sale. There is an air of normalcy; quiet talk spreads like a moisture through the crowd. I still stand perched. The vendor is doing a good business.

It is time, I conclude, to go back out to my proper perch. I feel that my strength is renewed. I stand on both feet for a moment and look squarely at the vendor, and I see that he is even resuming his playful behavior of earlier. I turn and start out to the center again.

It seems to me after I have walked a few paces that the murmur of the crowd has suddenly swelled. Then almost at once I am struck by an appalling realization which must also, I think, be flying through the crowd.

The vendor is selling the yellows crullers made for him by yellows. Someone will buy and eat the cruller that burned the yellow youth's fingers and fell in the dirt and was tossed back in the oil.

The vendor knows what he is doing.

I have an impulse to turn back, to hasten back and resume the perch I have just left before it is too late. Still walking I inwardly hesitate; I tell myself that it would be a mistake to return, it might even incite the yellows somehow. . . .

Behind me I hear a rush. There are grunts, blows. I do not turn, I *cannot* turn now, I walk on. I hear thumps, wood splitting, a metallic banging, a hiss. Much scuffling.

Then there is quiet again. I am still walking. I cannot look back, but I know that the vendor's form lies motionless on the ground, his kitchen is broken to pieces and scattered.

The crowd is silent again. I have reached my post. I turn and perch, facing the brutal block of the yamen, my blood boiling in a need for revenge, revenge.

The elation I felt a few moments ago, the peace, the inner strength—all are flown. I will never know whether, by returning to the edge of the crowd and resuming my perch there, I could have averted this outcome, for it might be that the yellows would have attacked the vendor even if I had been there, indeed even if I had been standing there as a sleeping bird the whole time and had never shown my back at all. I will never know. I can only stand here in a helpless folk-fury that seems to burn my body.

With my head lowered I see the cluster of guards and policemen near the yamen gate. They are looking toward the place, to my left now, from which I heard the noises come, and they are animatedly talking; I realize that none of them has lifted a finger to intervene.

It is clear, as time drags itself unwillingly along, that nobody in this throng, either official or idle, is going to do anything about the vendor and his ruined kitchen. They are going to be left lying where they are.

I wonder if the vendor is alive. I wonder what would happen if he stirred.

Now a party emerges from the yamen gate. At its heart is a brisk fellow in the uniform of an officer—not splendid, rather drab, for the tone of the new regime, reacting against the pomp of the old court, is dun-colored and cotton-quilted.

The officer seems to be barking orders, though I cannot hear them, and he points here and there with a stiff arm.

The policemen have been waved off, and they disconsolately pull away, as if they have been told they cannot play with the other schoolboys. They saunter along the fronts of the onlooking crowd, still without formation or parade bearing; it seems as if they have been strictly drilled in awkwardness.

The military detachments at the gate drift into patterns, and slowly these rigidify into ranks. The regular gate guards are in squads flanking the main gate and its brick-checkered spirit screen; they are armed only with staves. The provincial militia, with clubs and revolvers, form a double line. The rifle-bearing troops make a square directly in front of the gate: directly in front of me. And now the banner-bearers remove the oilskin covers from their flags and unfurl them, and I experience a surge of relief, for these are not the unanimous white banners of death, such as I saw at Nose's trial in the Northern Capital; they are nothing worse than varicolored guidons of Excellency K'ung's military units.

Now we wait. I say "we." I have a feeling that I am an onlooker with all the rest of this crowd.

The forming up at the gate has caused a drowsy murmuring in the crowd, which is curious but not thrilled and horrified as it was a few moments ago, when they—and I—were participants; now we are all watchers, for the abstraction in the fortlike seat of power has taken some sort of initiative.

A sharp order rings out, which even at this short distance seems thinned by the dry air so as to sound not manly but falsetto.

The slapping of hands on rifle stocks, a presentation of arms.

Around the spirit screen comes a squat figure in brilliant blue. The sunlight is bright, the man's hand goes up to shade his eyes —or perhaps that is a disenchanted salute. No, he holds the hand there: he wants to see the enemy. Me.

He turns his head and says something. Three or four petty officers scramble to him with anxious faces. He waves a hand over his shoulder in a vague gesture of something left behind in the yamen. Two men run in.

The fat man chats with the officer in command. The latter turns at one point and with the throaty contralto of an aging actress puts his soldiers at parade rest.

The two men return helter-skelter from within. One is carrying a sword in a scabbard, which he hands to the fat man. The stubby man hooks the scabbard to his belt on his left hip. The two soldiers who have run the errand are panting; the officer flicks the back of his hand and they fall back.

The fat man draws the sword from its sheath with his right hand and steps out onto the parade ground, and he walks straight toward me.

❲ The Trembling Blade

His progress is a hybrid of a waddle and a march. Although he has a fat man's handicap of not being able to keep his feet close together in their swings from step to step, so they glide forward in little arcs around his center of gravity, nevertheless he also has a spinal erectness, a tucked chin, a tight rhythm of paces —a bearing of martial command. The sword is in his right hand, point forward.

Not for him the modest uniform of the new regime. He is gorgeous in the old style of warlordism—vivid blue satin, a touch of ermine at collar and cuff, gold cords and braids, metal buttons that glisten in the sun, as if to advertise many plunders, vaults of squeeze, a wealth that both derives from and becomes power.

I cannot tell anything yet from his face, except that he keeps it inflexibly aimed at me. He has not looked once at the crowds that flank him and me, and I doubt that he has even noticed the prostrate vendor and the debris of the kitchen.

I do not want to think explicitly about the sword, yet it keeps attracting my attention by sending forward to my eyes piercing gleams of reflection of the sun, as though the blade can project its stabbing power to great distances. I push the sword aside in my mind as just another accouterment, a symbol of authority—a fat creature's assertion of his manly power. I look away from it, but ai! It cuts me again with an upstroke of razor-edged sunlight.

He is approaching me with a rapidity for which I am grateful. I haven't much time to wonder what is going to happen to me.

He is wearing a conical hat of the old-fashioned mandarin style —even to the spray of red-silk threads that falls from the apex. He dresses out of, as he lives for, the past.

Now I begin to see his face: it does not look as fat as his torso. From this distance, bobbing atop his strides, it surprises me by its lack of harshness or brutality; I have the impression rather of a cool, complacent arrogance.

He is not more than twenty paces away. I suddenly see, as separate entities, his lips, his eyes. There is an illusion, grotesque as the seeming smile on a dead face, of some pleasantry unexpressed, a fleeting joke. The thin lips are drawn back (he's short of breath?), the eyes sparkle (so does the sword).

I feel my body tightening, as though, without thinking it through, I dimly expect him to lunge at me with that blade as soon as he is close enough.

He stumbles. He has failed to sense some minor unevenness of footing, and his left ankle seems to crumple under him. He falters only slightly, however, and I see that he is a man of unusual agility; he has that grace so often seen in the obese, who turn their hateful tonnage into a lovely weightless floating. His recovery is on the instant, and it seems to me possible that the crowd standing at distances may not even have noticed his false step. But I have. He knows I have. There has been a quick whipping of the sword, which he has used as the tightrope walker uses his long bamboo pole; he drops his eyes to the sword blade with a swift pout of his mouth, as if the misstep had been the sword's fault.

This incident, small as it was, has given me great encouragement, for I have had a glimpse, which Governor K'ung surely did not want me to catch, of fallibility. I feel my body, which had grown so tense, relaxing, and I am able to raise my left leg a little higher. (I have not the slightest thought of weariness.) I see that Governor K'ung, coming on, has noticed the movement of my thigh, and I believe I see a shade of surprise on his face, and it occurs to me that he has noticed for the first time, watching my leg move, that I am a woman. Had he not been told this?

By now, if he were indeed going to rush at me, he would have to be quickening his pace, leaning his stoutness into the start of the assault. But he marches still.

I make no pretense now of keeping my head lowered and my eyes hooded. I must see him, measure him. I am impelled to check on the forward-pointing sword.

Half a dozen paces. One, two, three, four, five. Now comes a dance of halting. It is the pure military stop: the right foot plunged into immobility, the left foot rising up as if with astonishment and then crashing down, *finis*, beside the right. During this maneuver, which was accomplished with an impressive jiggling of fatty tissue, I had the feeling that the Governor's eyes were not looking at me but were bulging with myriad lenses like the eyes of a fly, and that he was looking into every pair of eyes all around the reviewing ground watching him. I mean I had an impression of vanity of an absolutely staggering dimension. Whatever happens, I must take this into account.

Involuntarily I do now lower my head a little, pulling it down into my shoulders, for seeing the sword still held parallel to the ground I have a sudden fear that this supple ball of fat will whisk the sword through the air without a word and cut my head off. This is not too much to imagine; I have witnessed beheadings.

But what is that I see in the sun glints that are still on the sword? (I hear the man puffing.) There is a fine trembling. I might not have noticed the tremor on the bare steel itself, but intermittently the delicate shaking brings quick little darts of sunshine into my eyes.

Governor K'ung stands at attention in front of me. He is close to me, well within sword's reach.

At first he says nothing. He is sucking in air with his mouth open, and I suppose he is catching his breath. Vividly I see him.

He is exactly my height; our eye beams are entangled without an upward reach on either side. The pupils of his, under the puffy epicanthic folds of "good" yellow eyes, are dark mirrors in this light; the whites, pure white. Nothing clouds those clear eyes: never drugs, I would wager, no drink, no inner doubt. Could it be that an ascetic lives in this house of fat? To judge by the eyes, he is swift-minded, keen. My earlier impression, that his face is not as fat-looking as his torso, is confirmed, but his face is not for this reason haggard or drawn. His black brows are unusually wide and thick, his lips are wire-thin. Everything leads up to the brilliant eyes under the enormous brows; the mouth has to be abandoned, one cannot stay with that mean cut. The eyes speak to me, through their glittering, cheerful lenses, of filthy hatred, of haughtiness, of determination to hold me and all my white kind down in the dirt.

And one other awful feature: the thick neck. We have heard of this aggressive neck in distant provinces, and it is justly famous. The man's head is not small, yet downward from the ears there is a gross filling out—and not, it seems, to fat, but to a powerful corded lay of muscles which give the impression that they contain, like the bull's neck, erectile tissue for combat.

We stand and look each other over with frank, open stares, which would not be permissible in commonplace encounters: man and woman shamelessly stripping each other, to and beneath flesh, searching out with indecent haste the innermost core.

It must appear to the crowd (the vain Governor seems so aware of appearances) that we are talking to each other in low voices.

I look even more closely at the Governor's eyes, to try to see what he is thinking. I see his continuing surprise—he feels both cheated and titillated—at my being a desirable young woman. His gaze descends to my breasts, my hips. I believe I see him shaking off speculations, as if those glances had been little stumbles, like the one his foot made approaching me; agilely his eyes return to mine. He wants now to see how afraid I am.

Suddenly a thought comes into my head, as it were, from one side, and it almost knocks me off my one-legged perch: The vendor is lying off to my left. This is one thought the Governor cannot read. I feel sure he is unaware of the vendor. What will come into our relationship when the Governor knows about the vendor? I must weigh this.

The Governor's breathing is easier now. Those terrible lips lie together, he can manage through his nose. Yet he does not speak to me. What is he trying to do? Does he mean to stare me to death?

Or has he not made up his mind what to do? Has my unexpected girlhood thrown him off course?

He has a row of medals on his vast chest. The metal circlets overlap each other, hanging from their ribbons, but they seem to be identical, and the one that is fully exposed has in low relief an unmistakable (because of the neck) profile of Governor K'ung himself. Ai! The self-praising hero. Now *my* eyes move from breast to hip, right hip, where I see a revolver in a holster. He has modern means of doing away with me; he has a whole platoon of men with rifles at his back. Why then the sword? Is it (how I would like to blunt it with thoughts!) only ceremonial? Is it just for salutes? To remind of the past when we whites were slaves?

How effulgent the satin of his blue tunic! How many hours did it take how many white women silk-reelers to unravel cocoons for that tunic? With this thought—and remembering the vendor—anger has welled up in me, old white anger. I look in the Governor's eyes. I see the tiny veiled jump there when he makes out that I am angry. *He* is the one who is supposed to be angry. But I see plainly that he is not. He is a man with his own image hanging on his chest trying to make some calculations. I think I might prefer to find him angry.

He seems to exude cheerfulness and patience. His demeanor seems to say, "I have plenty of time. I have all day. I have all the time in the world." He has the good humor of the truly fat. No, it is more impenetrable than that: He has the good humor of the bigot. Bigots can be all too pleasant, for they have no doubts to worry them. Yes, something like a smile plays around those lambent eyes—nothing could be said to "play" around his lips; anything that trifled there might trip and maim itself. The Governor is definitely not in a hurry, and he has the look in his eyes of being in good spirits, notwithstanding that delicate shaking I saw on the sword blade.

But why doesn't he speak?

Hooo, I must keep my eyes away from his. I must not let him see the fear I feel. He must see nothing but white skin.

He is wearing a curious sash as a baldric from which the sword's scabbard is hung. I focus on it. A stretch of it shows, crossing his chest under his tunic, which hangs open at the front. The sash is a width of embroidered silk on which a story is told in frieze of gold thread, and of gray; a story of domination. Human figures, gold and gray, struggle across it. The gray are bent, they seem to be burdened. The gold are beating the backs of the others with rods. It is an awkward narrative of slavery! It is an old sash, made (no doubt by a slave woman) for a master who felt like boasting of his power. Governor K'ung has had it brought out from some musty box to wear today: to undermine me, to give himself strength?

His not speaking is very strange. I put it together with the impression I have had of his being at leisure: there is no hurry. Suddenly I wonder:

What if he has decided to wait me out? What if he has decided to stand there opposite me just as long as I perch here? What if he stands there motionless and speechless all day? All day, all night, as long as I last? Fat as he is, cannot he stand there on two feet longer than I can balance on one? Has he decided to answer our symbolic protest with a symbolic assertion? We never speak during our sleeping-bird demonstrations. Is he to remain silent the whole time while he demonstrates . . . what?—the tale on his baldric?—the old, old story of some men bending other men to their wills?

What shall I do if this is what he has chosen? How can I counter this tactic, if he has elected it? It would be an impressive answer to us, for I don't see how I could outlast him. What could I do?

The vendor comes into my mind; and Governor K'ung's vanity. The vendor. How could he help me? I cannot imagine. He is flat on his back, perhaps dead. I have not actually seen him prostrate, but I feel certain that he is. How could he possibly help?

I hear laughter. Laughter runs again like an eddying wind through the crowd, and I am made aware by this sound of the tense silence that had preceded it. I have been concentrating so closely on my adversary that I have lost all awareness of sound, or the lack of it, and now hearing the gusts of laughter I realize that a few moments ago I could hear the man breathe, so still was the noonday around us.

Once again I cannot imagine what the laughter is about. Something to do with the vendor? Is he alive? Stirring into consciousness? Have the young pranksters grown restless at the deadlock between the Governor and me, and are they playing new tricks? Would they dare, in the presence of Excellency K'ung of the bull neck?

I have been through the mystery of this crowd's laughter once before, but the Governor has not. I have to admire his composure.

What control! He does not take his eyes off me, but I do see minute starts and flutterings of his stare, reflecting what must be powerful temptations to look to this side and that. He resists them all, though he must know he could silence every guffaw and snicker by gestures of no more than his left forefinger.

The laughter increases. I sense a third presence; somebody or something is approaching. This feeling is confirmed as the Governor's gaze now does slide past me, to my left and rear, near the ground. His look is one of annoyance and contempt. I have the irrational thought that Rock is crawling toward us on all fours.

I am startled by a contact—something pointed yet soft—against the back of the leg on which I am standing; my scalp crawls, my buttocks congeal into gooseflesh.

Now appears in front of me, sniffing at my trousers, the same woebegone cur we had seen earlier. I cannot help looking down at it, and yes, it is the same one, with the raggedly molting fur. It is no longer a picture of terror, however; it fans the air with its moth-eaten-looking tail, it ducks its head in repeated invitations to petting and play. As it sniffs at me it pokes my leg with its nose.

The crowd is laughing hard.

The dog is bound to lose interest in my unresponding form, and it will surely go to the Governor and start sniffing and wagging at *him*. What will Excellency K'ung do then? He will kick the dog, send it hurtling away with a high-pitched yelp and tail tucked forward between its scurrying hind legs. He may even use his sword; I must brace myself against the sight of blood. Governor K'ung has been so contained, so controlled—rage must be boiling under the rashers of fat: rage, if at nothing else, then at the laughter of his yellow populace, and now at this insubordinate cur, and probably all along at me. The poor dog will catch the sword as my proxy; I wish I could give the creature a sign, keep him by my feet. It sniffs at my raised shoe, it sniffs at my crotch: gusts of hilarity right and left. I hold still.

There it goes, finally bored, toward His Excellency. Its head is lowered, its tail still wags but more discreetly, the whole form is lowered in a worshipful crouch, for even a dog can sense the august nature of the second figure standing here in the open. Authority must have its distinctive scent.

Governor K'ung's eyes flash now with a certain readiness, and I watch the feet to see whether the man's balance is being gathered for a swift and nimble dig at the gaunt ribs. I look at the sword hand, to see whether the grip has tightened, driving blood from the knuckles.

Something is certainly different. Ai, yes, the laughter has ceased. Utter silence, but for the snuffling of the dog's dusty, rubbery nose.

Governor K'ung, I realize, is not going to react. Not by so much as a hair. Neither kick nor whistling slash. Nothing. He is going to match my indifference. The mountain of flesh is frozen. What strength the yellow man has!

The wagging stops. The cur is mysteriously intimidated. It slinks off.

What does the poor dog know? I am frightened. Is there a K'ung Method, which may bring the defeat, for good and all, of the Sleeping-Bird Method?

A disgusting look of self-satisfaction seeps into the Governor's face.

What did the dog smell? Did it smell the habit of domination? Did it smell the power of yellowness?

We are back at the beginning of things. Excellency K'ung is a yellow man, and the essence of the K'ung Method is quite simple: *Have a yellow skin.* Even a dog knows that.

Governor K'ung is planted with a straight back, holding the sword pointing forward, parallel to the ground, and he seems willing to wait all day, or till I faint with exhaustion; he *is* yellow power, arrogance, contempt. I balance on the one leg, and I am white defiance. We are at an impasse. We stand. We glare. We cannot move.

BOOK ONE

The Coffle

❨ A Visitor

THAT DAY when it all began I was working with other young girls
at our village pottery shed.

I was near the wheel of Mrs. Kathryn Blaw, the senior potter,
who was also storyteller at our village library. Narrow parrot-nosed
face, hair drawn back in a bun, simple brown clay-spattered work
smock—she was in the shade of the tin roof of the wheel shop,
but the brilliant light of a reflected Arizona afternoon flooded her,
filling every wrinkle of her dry white skin with a juvenating liquid
glow; the wheel shop was only a roofed shed without walls.

Mrs. Blaw was building up from a lump of tempered clay the
sides of a large graceful urn of the sort our village sold, mostly to
California merchants, for the storage of grain and fruit. As she
worked on the earthen shell at the low wheel, her shoulders curving and her breasts pendent within the smock, the swift flapping,
paying, and wilting of her sharp hands expressed without doubt
her ferocity, her edgy temperament, the wild spirit that took hold
of her when she wound into a tale; she terrified my friend Agatha,
and me, and all of us who had lately been children.

She shouted for a new batch of worked clay.

The women at the kneading troughs started up like partridges
surprised in a thicket of greasewood, and their sudden flurry
stirred a fuss among the chickens, sheep, and goats that wandered

freely within the compound wall. Since our country's defeat in the
Yellow War we had lived a marginal life, subject to many dangers,
of drought, jealousy between states and cities, slave raids, brig-
andage, cow-stealing, and depressed lawlessness. For security our
village was divided into walled compounds, and all the compounds
together were enclosed in a single continuous hedge of impenetrable prickly growth: cactus, thorns, briers, brambles. My father's house was in the compound that also contained the pottery
works, and I never felt entirely safe outside its walls of clay pile,
which were taller than the tallest man, and except to go to the
clay pits by day I never ventured beyond the outer village hedge,
for Kathy Blaw had told us tales of carnivorous mountain bears,
yellowish in color, which traveled in herds of hundreds, swooped
down into the desert on hunters, seized their weapons, and made
prey of the would-be predators; and of men, unthinkably yellowy
too, who panyarred unwary wanderers and took them away to the
sea.

My mother, who was one of the kneaders, called out that it was
time for Agatha and me to go to the pits to fetch more raw clay.

We two scuttered like roadrunners in the dust of the compound
out through its gate, carrying a galvanized tin bucket between us.

A few yards along the unpaved village street, outside the gate
of the compound of the Church of Santa María de Felicidad,
among the many little outdoor shrines to various saints, I carelessly glanced at the porcelain figure of San Pedro of Chaco Rico,
a local patron of easy pregnancies, standing alone in his little hut,
which was like a birdhouse on a pole, with what seemed to me his
sensual gypsy face, and at once I crossed myself (though I was
not enlisted in his faith), for I believed he could alter the fate of
any young girl on his slightest whim.

Agatha's father was Mayor Jencks. Near the mayor's compound,
in a little movable booth shaded by a striped canvas awning, sat
sleepy Plimpton, who sold the villagers newspapers and magazines
that were dropped off outside the hedge by the Flagstaff bus, and
gum, shoestrings, cheap toys, and religious relics. Since the defeat
we had had a powerful revival of all faiths. Our village numbered
less than a thousand, but we had five churches, and Plimpy's
wares included a guaranteed lock of hair of Marcos de Zuza, the
first Franciscan friar to have explored our valley long ago; a speck
of gold said to be from one of Brigham Young's twenty-seven
wedding rings; slivers from the one and only True Cross set under

tiny magnifying glasses; and other "genuine" curiosa that Plimpton sold, mainly to children and gaffers, to attract good and ward off bad cess. I myself, though a Methodist, wore a locket he had sold me for a quarter containing a scrap of cloth from the robe of a Jesuit martyred at Guevavi; I had also slipped into the case, to fortify its beneficence, a used horseshoe nail and a tail thrown by a lizard.

"What's new?" I asked, scanning Plimpy's magazines and papers.

He yawned. "*Examiner* come in this morning, says the Syndicate's on the rampage again."

"Where?"

"Down beyond Jerome."

"That's pretty far."

"You never know," Plimpy said. By now his burdensome eyelids were sagging over the blue moons of his pupils, from which, they having perceived that no sale was to be made, the dim light was rapidly fading.

Agatha and I were girls of fifteen, and we could not help being easy-hearted. We ran on, giggling over Plimpy's delicious nodding, his news already gone from our minds.

We came to the gap in the eight-foot-high hedge that served as the main village entrance. The half dozen chevaux-de-frise at the opening—big spiked frames tangled with barbed wire—had been pulled apart by the pit tractor just enough to allow passage to people on foot. Four men stood sentry duty at the opening.

Edging outside, Agatha and I saw the sunlit world to the west —in the near foreground a sea of gold, where down a tipping tableland the chest-high rabbit brush was in full bloom, then the dusty ribbon of the unpaved highway, then a rock-strewn stretch, with the reddish massif of Dead Guest Mesa off to the left, and, all beyond, reaching up and up, cloaked with sagebrush and collared with pinyon pine, the great pale shoulders of the Chaco Rico Range. Elated by this wide sight, we sped to our right along the outside of the hedge, until, turning the village corner, we saw a landscape in a different mood: a curve of a brown river, feathery cottonwoods, a stripe of thirsty verdure meandering off southward in the general dustiness.

Here we came to the clay pits. We stood on the rim. The old half-track pit bulldozer was chattering and coughing, and the young men in the work gang, naked down to the belts of their jeans, shouted to each other over the engine's unsteady sputtering. They were cutting pile for a new compound wall as well as clay for the potters. The dozer was hauling an old-fashioned mud scoop, at whose handles four young men strained as the metal lip cut into the iridescent ooze.

Sitting like an easy horseman at the controls of the dozer was Gabe, the foreman of the village labor gang. Agatha and I had more than once whispered about his beautiful shirtless back at work, where manifold energies seemed to ripple like aspen leaves in languid air. Now Agatha struck me lightly on my backsides, and I knew what she meant: Look! Gabriel! There he is!

Our bucket having been packed with damp clay, we took it between us and started back with a fluent trotting straight-spined haste, for we carried half as much as either of us weighed.

As the path swung around a tall candelabra of giant cactus, not far from the main gate in the hedge, I was startled to see a convoy of three big autos turn off the highway and onto the bumpy spur up to the village. My first thought: They are some yellows. I had never seen a yellow man, but terror of the faraway victors had been bred into me and underlay every moment of my life.

Agatha and I dropped the bucket and started to run for the gate.

While I fleetly ran, soon leaving clumsy Agatha behind, I scanned the procession throwing up funnels of dust as it approached.

The first car was a blue Overland with a heap of baggage strapped into a rack on its roof; then followed, dusty but glinting in the sunlight with trimmings of brass around its headlights which curved up like cornets out of its fenders, a snazzy Pierce Arrow with wickerwork pants and a cabriolet top; and finally a long Packard touring car, in the back of which, behind an auxiliary windscreen, sat five men playing "Stormy Weather" with zany abandon on a tenor sax, two trumpets, a trombone, and a kazoo, while a man in the right front seat, who was evidently a drummer, thumped a beat on the outside metal of the car door.

Some sort of traveling show, I thought, as I scooted into the opening between the chevaux-de-frise. The guards were nervous. I was both elated and terrified. Our village never had casual visitors. California licenses!

I ran very fast all the way to the pottery shed, and I collapsed on my knees at my mother's lap, a piercing stitch under my ribs. I panted out what I had seen. My mother's alarm quadrupled mine.

She sharply told me to run and tell the mayor, Agatha's father, and at once I was on my feet again, running again.

I knew that my father, who was our schoolmaster—we were then in our summer vacation—was at the mayor's house "conferring"; otherwise known as having a beer. I ran straight into the mayor's office. Agatha's father and mine and two other men were in the cool room, playing cards. It was amazing how the mere sight of my father's broad face calmed me; my chest stopped its painful heaving.

I told the mayor what I had seen.

The mayor quietly directed my father to have the women prepare guest rooms in our compound and told all his companions to spruce up for the visitors; for courtesy was the basic law of our lives, even in danger, which was always presumed to exist.

I went home with my father, clinging lovingly by one hand to his belt at the back of his trousers.

The potters broke off their work; Kathy Blaw, fierce woman though she seemed to be, showed not a sign of emotion over the ruin, through incompletion, of her morning's efforts. By the time my father was finely dressed, in black coat and string tie, we could hear the visitor's musicians patiently playing outside the hedge. "Button Up Your Overcoat." "Mood Indigo." Most of the village went out to watch as the mayor strode to the gate to receive the visitor.

The band came first through the gap, six foxy-looking gents in sharp dark clothes, and then followed a large fat man in a crumpled white suit, with a white necktie and a Panama hat with a white band; his manner was benign and genteel, and he grinned with a corpulent man's irrepressible good humor.

Our mayor, my father, and other important men approached him, flourishing their pistols over their heads, whooping greetings and jumping around to make a show of politeness that was at the same time a show of strength, while the visitor laughed, bobbed his head, and gracefully waved his huge arms as if they were weightless wings; then removing his hat from a totally bald and perspiring capitol of a skull, he bent with some effort in a low sweeping bow, his Panama whooshing up a salute of our village dust.

Our compound was crowded all day. We girls had to keep our distance with the women, who stayed mostly out of sight—except for a few principal wives, who fed the men and shooed flies away from them.

Agatha and I crept out a couple of times and peeked into the house where the men sat, fanning themselves with folded newspapers, sucking at tall glasses with straws, and quietly talking.

After the worst of the afternoon heat the visitors left. The band boarded the Packard and played "Baby Face." The cars drove off in a whirl of dust.

Until evening there was a stir of talk; the visitor had set himself forth as a real estate speculator, looking for irrigable lands to buy and sell. The band and all was for auctions, he'd said. He was jovial, the reports went, a bottomless drinker, inquisitive beyond good manners, quick in his own answers, mendacious without a doubt.

Shortly after dark there was a fuss at our bolted compound gate. A messenger had come from the mayor to tell my father that two of the village men could not be found anywhere. Kid Schlepp and Johnno Pye, grove men. Were they with him? Father searched the pottery factory, the schoolhouse, and the eight homes of our enclosure with great zeal, but the men were not in our compound. They had vanished from the village.

⟨ Away Like Goats

I slept fitfully, starting up again and again from frightful dreams, in one of which, the worst of all, there was lightning. Early in the morning I burst from yet another, in which I had been pursued by all the potters, who screamed at me, and Kathy Blaw, with furious eyes, having howled louder and run faster than the rest, had hurled at my head the curved iron tool with which she scraped the drying clay of half-finished pots.

I awoke at that, but with a flesh-crawling feeling that the nightmare had not ended, because a ghastly faraway screeching persisted in my ears. I jumped out of bed. I saw that my mother, father, and sister—we all slept in one room—were not yet stirring. I was afraid that some evil presence had entered my head; I remembered my careless glance at San Pedro's porcelain smile the day before. I ran out into the compound. It was barely light. The shrilling was far beyond the wall. I had to see what it was, for fear that my mind was going, and clutching my locket of the Guevavi martyr which hung on a string around my neck, I hurried trembling in my nightgown to the compound gate, which was shut and bolted. I peeped through one of its judases, and wondered, with a new onset of tremors, whether I was still drugged in a bad dream.

At a distance I could see the gate of Mayor Jencks's compound, its stout boards splintered like matchwood, and back and forth through the gap ran strangers who seemed in the dim light to be dressed in ordinary dark suits, and they were dragging out limp shapes in white—could they be the forms of some of our villagers in pajamas and nightgowns? The shrieks I had heard were coming from within that compound.

I ran back and threw myself against my mother's body. She was awake and trembling; my father was getting out of bed. Mother clutched my sister and me in her arms. Father picked up his pistol and rushed out in his pajamas.

Cringing in our room, we heard my father and other men of our compound shouting and running, and later—time seemed strung out like an endless creeper of the thorn apple which Indians brewed to induce visions—many shots, cries, clashes, groans, and screams, of both men and women, and later still we heard the gate of our compound rammed and shattered, and four of the strangers bulled into our house and roughly hauled my mother and my sister and me outside. They drove us with other women of our compound in a pack toward the mayor's compound.

Not far along, near smiling San Pedro, I saw a headless body lying and, a few feet away, the head, its face shockingly at peace, of one of my classmates in school, Wesley Bane, who had been a shy, gentle youth, learning to be a weaver.

God, I saw then that some of these strangers in ordinary business suits were armed with swords—curving broad blades of the sort the yellows used.

We saw the corpses of a dozen men as we went—an ironsmith, old Shaughnessy the gravedigger, and several young grove men and stable hands.

The women and girls of the village, all in nightgowns, some of which were sheer and immodest, were assembled in the mayor's compound. There was not a sound, even of the terror we so amply shared. Not one of our men was to be seen. We waited. The sun climbed to heat our shoulders.

Led by the same small jazz band we had seen the day before, which was now playing a hepped-up "Halls of Montezuma," an important man, apparently the commander of this raid, dressed in a double-breasted blue pinstripe suit, came into the compound, and it was no surprise that by his side, whispering in his ear, obsequious yet always grinning, was our bulky white-clad visitor of the day before; and at *his* ear and beck stood our two village men who had disappeared the previous evening, Kid Schlepp and Johnno Pye, grove men, now complaisant to their kidnappers and sure of themselves. They must have led the breachers to the weakest stretch of the hedge; here they were giving information whenever it was demanded.

The commander sorted us into categories, the sturdy women in one crowd, the girls apart, and the weak, the sick, and the old in a group that was removed from us—to be beheaded, as we later learned to our horror. I was separated from my mother; I held tight to the fat body of Agatha.

In the noon sun we were driven away from our village like goats. The last I saw inside the hedge was the commander supervising the burning of our churches. A number of our village men marched behind us in chains. I searched in vain for my father.

We walked the dusty highway, having eaten nothing, until the sun was low. The procession was fairly long—the commander's party, in creeping autos, with the band swinging away in the open Packard; our able-bodied women, our flock of frightened girls; then the main force of the dark-suited raiders, many carrying cut-off heads and laden with looted belongings; and finally, under guard, our village men, whose progress in chains was slow, so we were all forced to halt often, letting them close ranks.

Near evening we arrived at an assembly station, a campground of a row of corrugated-iron roofs on poles. We girls were huddled under one roof, and were left, as dusk fell, to sleep on empty bellies on the bare earth while the raiders encamped in a hostile ring of fires around us.

Agatha and I clung to each other and wept. I had never in my life felt such dejection. I was torn from my village, which I had left no more than a half dozen times all told, to take the bus trip to Flagstaff and back; I was separated from my mother, and I was afraid I would never see my father again.

Agatha, exhausted from the day's march in her capsule of fat, fell quickly asleep, but grief and confusion made my head whirl. Sitting cross-legged, with one knee touching the hollow of Agatha's back for reassurance, I opened the locket of the Guevavi martyr and tipped out onto my palm the tiny fold of drab cloth, the rusty bent nail, and the shriveled curl of lizard tail. These, my only remaining possessions, had taken on a numinous importance in my mind; my only hopes, it seemed, as I put the luck items back in the locket, were housed in that little metal lozenge, and I lay down with it cupped in my hand and awoke in the morning gripping it.

As the sun climbed we were taken, all of us, chained men, able-bodied women, and sturdy children, into the shade of a grove of cottonwoods, and we were fed, and quite well, from camp kitchens, and the jazz band played for us. We were commanded to remain cheerful!

Agatha found her father. I hurried about looking for mine.

I came across my mother, in hopeless tears, her face and shoulders sunburned and her unshod feet bruised from the march of the day before (we young ones, having been perpetually tanned and barefoot, were not affected); she did not know what had happened to Father—she'd heard a rumor that a party of men had been kept at the village to raze it to the dusty ground with bulldozer, truck, and barrow, to remove every trace of it from sight and, in the end, from memory.

Running here and there to try to confirm this rumor, I saw Gabriel, who stood straight and somber in his fetters; and skinny Plimpton, hollow-chested and sallow-skinned, drowsing just as he had used to in his booth at home; and Mrs. Kathy Blaw, who took me by the shoulders and, eyes burning, told me that my boy friend had been killed, Arty Coteen, who used to take me to the movies and hold my hand. My breast was already so full of sorrow that I could not distinguish any new pain for Arthur.

The band blasted out an admonitory fanfare. A soldier shouting into an amplifier ordered us tinnily to stand still where we were.

Into the grove came the man in the pinstripe suit—Mort Blain, we had realized, a notorious front man for the Palm Springs Syndicate, whose pictures we had often seen in the papers over the years—and with him our portly, grinning, whited visitor, evidently Blain's aide, and our two villagers, Schlepp and Pye, their captive guides, who by now were strutting with self-importance.

We were counted. The fat man in the white suit held a clipboard, on which he recorded the tally. I was thrilled to be counted as a grown woman. When the enumeration was done the fat man and Mort Blain rode off somewhere in the Pierce Arrow, and we were dismissed. The raiders marched away, all but a guard.

We were kept at the assembly station for four days. Each morning and afternoon we were taken to the cottonwood grove for food and music. On the third evening a new large procession arrived, of captives from two villages far from ours, strangers to us; we made acquaintances with them easily, partly because of our common lot and partly because they, as we, were all in pajamas and night-gowns, so there was a shared intimacy, though a dusty one, to begin with.

The new captives were mustered the following morning in the cottonwoods, and again the fat man recorded the count on his clipboard.

As soon as this tally was completed, some of the dark-suited men began forming everyone into a procession, which circled our assembly area as its elements took their places in line, and to Agatha and me—we were only fifteen—this falling-in seemed, at first, an entertainment.

But then as the raiders formed up their line came the end in sudden nausea of our pleasure. Many of the dark-suited men were still carrying severed heads, to claim bounty for them from the Syndicate.

Agatha exclaimed: "Look! Arthur Coteen!"

She was pointing at a head that one of the first of the raiders had by the hair. I looked at it only long enough to see that Agatha had not been mistaken. Then I turned full away, my knees weak at a possibility that surged into my mind: what if I should see my father's head being carried along?

From that moment, and all through the march, I looked mostly at the ground.

We walked for seven days to horrible cheery music from the Packard. At night we slept under trees like ground squirrels. Agatha weakened; she leaned on me. She was hysterically fearful of all poisonous creatures—Gila monsters, tarantulas, scorpions—and during the nights her whispered fears seeped into me. Some days we passed many village hedges, and we trudged across wastes of mesquite and climbed through granite-ribbed passes. Our column crossed the Colorado on a bridge at Ehrenberg.

Mrs. Kathy Blaw walked much of the time with Agatha and me, and this fierce woman turned out to be sulkily protective of us; she was a barren woman and perhaps had an angry need for daughters. My mother cried day and night, apparently because her nightgown was sheer; I was ashamed of her and kept away from her.

We came to Palm Springs. On the way into the beautiful green town our procession had to move to the side of the road, once, to let the white Cadillac roadster of Gay Moya pass—the great movie star who had had the highest box office in the nation the year before. How often she had made me weep! In her car she looked amazingly plain to me, and rather cross at being delayed by our dusty file.

⟪ The Syndicate

Very early the following morning we were driven in a herd into and through the outer gardens of a vast estate on the edge of town. At the gate where we entered, and at each of the gates of the successive fences and walls through which we passed, pairs of human heads lay on the ground to remind all who entered of the limitless mountain-lion power of the Syndicate. We were urged into a corner of an enormous patio, along three sides of which ran Spanish arcades; under the central one of these a long curtain was drawn closed. Nothing happened for several hours. The sun climbed until it stood on our heads.

Suddenly doors at the far side of the great patio opened, pipe-organ music blared from speakers hidden in the palmettos, and at the command of our guards all of us fell to our knees and lowered our foreheads. Gabriel was near me; turning my head a little, I saw this proud young man, who had endured the indignities of recent days with such a grave, serene bearing, tremble now in his red-striped pajamas.

We heard the Syndicate's legal staff, which was like a flock of clerics, droning some kind of formal jargon with which "meetings" apparently always began. At length, under the direction of the guards, we raised our heads but remained kneeling. The curtains under the arcade drew back.

There they were, in a dazzling ambiance that I recognized at once, from Kathy Blaw's tales, as a striving imitation of yellow magnificence. This was the nightmare of our lives—that as shadows behind every event the yellows moved in ghostly ways, always the yellows. . . .

The five bosses of the Syndicate were seated under a purple awning appliquéd with silver devices, on ornate gilded sofas that were placed on a carpet of deep blue silk. Each of the five rested one foot on the back of a crouching woman, and a woman in a long silk gown held a golden spittoon for each, and other women in diaphanous pantaloons, with silver manillas all up their arms, fanned them, and still others kept flies away with long horsehair whisks that moved like curling smoke.

I wondered: Was this *really* what the yellows were like? Could they be so vulgar, so pretentious, so cruel?

I was astonished, daring at last to look at Themselves, to see that they were just men. Four out of five bald.

Of course I knew them from pictures in the papers: Gruenkopf, Shannon, Bink, Sammerfield, Rune. Bink, yes, pock-marked. Gruenkopf, Shannon, and Sammerfield sucking on cigars. All in business suits and horn-rimmed glasses—frightful crooks in respectable guise.

My alarm was intensified now by the entrance of Mort Blain, with his huge adviser, his lawyer, his bodyguard, and several of his dark-suited raiders, for their approach to the quintumvirate of the Syndicate was so abject that one could not help dreading the capabilities behind those five sets of heavy horn-rims. These raiders, so awesome in recent days to us their captives, crawled literally on their bellies the whole breadth of the paved patio, pinstripe and Palm-Beach no better than mop-rag and dustcloth, until they lay directly before the bosses of the Syndicate. At a snap of Bink's fingers they rose to a kneeling position, and attendants gave to them and, later, to others, including our own Kid Schlepp and Johnno Pye, who had served as all too willing guides, rich gifts as rewards for their roles in these raids.

Next, to a continuous tattoo of snare drums, raiders entered the patio carrying the heads they had brought back with them, to claim bounty, and at the sight of the first grisly burden I felt as if the heat of the sun were pressing on my own head like a flatiron; I thought I would die. I looked fixedly at the swollen feet of the woman kneeling before me; dust lay in cobweb lines in the wrinkles of her soles. The transactions seemed to take forever; I heard the telling out of dollars to each decapitator. I could think of nothing but my solid-hearted father, his broad benign face, his smile like food to me, and I wanted the sun's iron to press me into oblivion.

Now we went through a new sorting. We were driven on our knees in our filthy, dusty nightgowns and pajamas up a channel formed by lawyers on one side and raiders on the other, and we passed in review before the five men, one or another of whom occasionally raised a finger, at which a captive was set aside in a group destined, I guessed, for the farms of the Syndicate. Our thin newsdealer was taken out of the line just ahead of me. Poor, sleepy Plimpton!—would they send *him* to work on a farm?

The roll of the drums had now ceased, and there was no sound at all, except once when a small boy from our village whimpered with fear till his mother clapped her hand over his mouth.

I was unchosen. So was Agatha. We were driven back to our crowded corner.

When the selection was over, a noisy argument broke out among the five in the silky pavilion. I saw the mighty Sammerfield rail against Bink like a garage mechanic in a village row. Suddenly the great Mort Blain was thrust forward by soldiers, was stripped of his pinstripe and all his clothes but his one-piece shoulder-strap B.V.D.'s—presumably to reduce him to our level of shame—and he was unceremoniously thrust along on hands and knees, with a yellow-style sword pinking his Pierce-Arrow-softened buttocks, into our captives' corner.

Then we were led away to the movie-theater parking lot where we had been penned to pass the previous night under the open sky. Raiders who had leaped at Mort Blain's slightest whisper along the road from our village now treated him with no less, but no more, contempt than they bestowed on common captives. We settled down for the night. Agatha and I lay in each other's arms, exhausted with our daylong fright. We were told nothing.

⟨ The March of the Coffle

We arose with the sun, and some of us were strung in a coffle to march we knew not where. We were two hundred seventy-five captives, more or less, with a company of the Syndicate's special "police"—in robin's-egg blue and Sam Browne belts—to guard us, and a man, to whom the cops referred as Mr. Slattee, in charge.

The coffle was a series of strings of captives in single file, men first. I saw Gabriel in the line, his weight on one leg, a hip slung out, with his air of scornful indifference, his left ankle made fast by a length of chain to the left leg of the man ahead of him, his right foot fettered to that of the man behind. We women followed, tied to each other, a long pace apart, with leather thongs around our necks. My mother was left behind; we had no chance to say goodbye. Kathy Blaw was just ahead of me, Agatha next after me. Each of us, man and woman alike, was given a burden—some item of plunder for trade. Each man, besides, had to keep one of his loops of chain off the ground to make walking possible. Two Ford pickup trucks were loaded with foodstuffs for our journey.

As we were driven out of the Syndicate's winter resort I felt a sadness and fear deeper than anything I had known in the previous days, and I was forced to realize that despair is not like a well, which has a hard bottom at last. All my family ties—my living links with the golden Prewar Epoch—were torn away from me.

The citizens of Palm Springs scarcely glanced at us as we walked along, our only music now the rhythmic clinking of the men's chains, for the men were forced to keep in step in order to move at all. The festive feeling Agatha and I had had, the excited curiosity of our march toward Palm Springs, when we had had with us the Pierce Arrow cabriolet, the Packard as fecund with tunes as a jukebox, the raiders in their sinister suits—these, with their particular horror and thrill, were gone. Our guards, on incessantly puttering motorcycles with sidecars, were—robin's-egg blue be damned—surly men who did not hesitate to use their nightsticks; Mr. Slattee was a hard veteran who rode atop the cab of one of the pickup trucks surveying our line with jackal eyes.

Mort Blain, chief raider emeritus, who had ridden in curtained splendor to Palm Springs, was in B.V.D.'s and chains. His little melon belly bulged under the netlike material of his underwear. In the movie parking lot the night before, a report had hissed about that Blain's crime was that he had forgotten to film the beheadings in our village; this had caused Sam Sammerfield's peasant rage. The great Mort looked not only undistinguished now, but cowardly, servile, and unable to care for himself. He seemed disgusting. One of our desert proverbs said, "When children see an eagle draggled by the rain, they say it's a vulture."

Agatha would not speak; she seemed like a plant wilting of thirst.

Her father, the mayor, was with us; in the parking lot we had looked to him to procure some word of our fate, even perhaps some amelioration of it, but he had stared at the ground like a sick dog. He walked now with listless steps.

Beyond the outskirts of the town we tried to learn from the cops where they were taking us, but they, steeped in the prudent secretiveness of all of our people since the defeat—"never tell more than half that you know," said the gopher in one of Kathy Blaw's tales—would only say that we were going to have "a healthy walk."

Kathy Blaw called out in the raucous voice she had sometimes used at the climax of a story, chilling us to the marrow, that we were going to be slaughtered and minced and eaten with chopsticks in a sweet-and-sour sauce by men with yellow skins. A cop slapped her hard with the flat of his hand. Kathy Blaw glared at him.

We walked all that day, and all the next, past peaceful California hamlets, along the sun-drenched valley, with the San Jacinto range on our left and the San Bernardinos on our right. At night the soldiers chained the men's hands to necklaces of fetters. We slept in the open.

On the third day we left the highway—apparently our captors did not want the coastal Californians to see human beings in chains and thongs—and followed an unpaved truck trail into tiers of hills on the northern side of the valley. We left behind all signs of men. Over the clank of the chains and the muttering of the motorcycles we heard faraway barking—coyotes?—and now and then, during halts, we heard distant crashing in the underbrush— wildcats? mountain lions? Horrible lizards and toads abounded. That night we camped in a glade, with the terrors of the wild hills all around us. I tried in vain to shut out of my mind Agatha's constant babbling about hairy spiders and rustling scorpions. I clutched tight to my locket of the martyr of Guevavi, lest it be stolen from me. Many of the women, with sunburnt shoulders and lacerated feet, moaned awake and asleep.

Suddenly, in the dark, a flash of communal panic roused us all, and there was a hysterical chattering among our whole coffle, for the bizarre announcement Kathy Blaw had made from out of our postwar folklore (it couldn't be true but it could), that we were to be devoured by yellow-skinned people, caught among us, all at once, like a telegraphic epidemic sickness. The women all began to weep. We were desperately afraid because we felt we had no means of seeking safety through worship: our faraway churches were burned down, and we had no priests or preachers. Who could efficaciously lead us in prayer? The cops tried to whack us into silence, but our fears were not easily stilled in this hollow surrounded by looming shoulders of pinyon pine.

The next day was hard. We had slept little. The men were beginning to limp, lamed by their irons, even though the fetters were alternated from ankle to ankle each night. Now that we were in wild country Mr. Slattee removed the thongs from the necks of the women, for we were so fearful of our surroundings that we kept in a tight band anyway.

Here Kathy Blaw—such an irritable, sharp, and frightening woman back at home, the more terrifying to us who were young because she carried in her head the whole of the mythlike past from before the Yellow War—turned her reluctant attention to Agatha, who was so weak that Mr. Slattee had excused her from carrying a packet. My friend, who had always been so wily, mischievous, and self-interested, grew empty-eyed and pinguidly limp. Mrs. Blaw and I walked on either side of her, trying to support her while carrying loads of our own.

At dusk—and all through the night, I suppose—Agatha lay with her eyes open. At dawn she refused to eat. Halfway through the morning, as we began to descend from the hills through a fertile canyon in which ash-willows, stunted sycamores, and gnarled live oaks at least gave us shade, we women were attacked by a swarm of bees, and Agatha, indifferent to her surroundings, too feeble to dart away through bushes as most of us did, to get away from the frenzied insects, was severely stung. The coffle halted while Kathy Blaw picked out the stings and poulticed Agatha with the old remedy of cigarette tobacco, grudgingly granted by Mr. Slattee, and spit. Agatha refused to go on. She said with a sudden flaring up of spirit that she would never stand up again.

Mr. Slattee ordered soldiers to apply willow switches, and Agatha, though accustomed to the frequent disciplinary whippings that had been the lot of every post-defeat child in our village, soon could stand no more, and she struggled to her feet, and we moved on.

In the afternoon, when we had reached more level ground, Agatha uttered a single cry, as of surprise, and tried to run away into the undergrowth, but she was too weak, and she fell not far from the path. She was punished again, but this time she did not react. Mr. Slattee, who could not order Agatha to be carried on one of the pickups, because a dozen older women needed to ride nearly as badly as the fat girl and would surely have malingered if they had seen a single rider, ordered a stretcher made of willow splints, to which Agatha's body was lashed with some of the leather thongs, and she was carried by pairs of male prisoners in relays. Even this caused groans, feigned collapses, and exaggerated limps among the weaker women, but willow withes kept them moving.

At dark we reached a small clear stream at the floor of a pretty canyon. We had had a heavy forced march that day, under a hot sun, with only some dry biscuits to eat since dawn. Our people, even the strong men, were exhausted and demoralized, and some of the more desperate ones began to whistle in unison "The Drinking Song" from *The Shores of Barbary*. This gang whistling had a macabre effect of false cheerfulness and bravado that expressed, under the circumstances, a most insulting attitude toward Mr. Slattee. He ordered the men's hands bound, and he separated the most despondent a good distance from the rest of us. Agatha refused food. Lulled by the sound of the stream, I slept like a stone.

Most of us awoke with recovered spirits, but Agatha, who was roused with difficulty, was stiff in all her joints and could not, if she would, have moved. Mr. Slattee ordered her carried again on the stretcher, but our men grumbled at this, because the burdens of each pair who carried her had to be put on the litter along with Agatha's limp body, and we were still in hilly country where the trail was rugged.

When the sun leaned on our shoulders one of the men who was then carrying the stretcher shouted, "Cut her throat! Cut her throat!"

This cry was soon taken up all along the foresection of the coffle. How the Yellow War, the humiliating defeat, and the barren years of the New Era had debased us all! It was one thing for strangers to care nothing about a girl they did not know, but it seemed that our villagers remembered now only Agatha's spitefulness, vanity, and malicious gossip at home, and none protested the repeated shout. I myself made no sound, and though I suffered agonies of shame, kept saying to myself, "I'm tired, I'm tired, I'm tired." Even Agatha's father held his tongue.

Mr. Slattee off-loaded Agatha from the stretcher and tried to make her walk, but she fell more than once to the trailside and at last could not be stirred. Mr. Slattee ordered the coffle forward.

As we moved away we heard him arguing with a cop over Agatha's prostrate form on the ground. In a few minutes Mr. Slattee caught up with us and mounted a pickup truck.

Later the cop came running up with Agatha's nightgown over his shoulder. He told some of the women at the rear of the column that he had refused to kill her. His pistol was in its holster; we had heard no shot. He had left her in the shade of a thornbush, he said. I wondered only: Was she too far gone to be in terror of creeping things?

Kathy Blaw walked the rest of that afternoon with a hand on my shoulder—as if to suggest that I was the strong one supporting her.

Three days' march was blank to me. I dimly remember from our heights a view of a sloping plain, distant towns, a more verdant countryside.

Then we came down through the hills into a misty afternoon, and our guards, alarmingly compassionate all of a sudden, said that we were coming into the northern outskirts of Los Angeles, and that our fate would now be in the hands of a certain man on the Syndicate's payroll, known as the Executive Agent for Outgoing Personnel.

(Each His Price

This Agent, a man of sycamore stature and arrogant bearing, in a pongee shirt, light tan slacks, and open-toed sandals, wearing large-lensed dark glasses, appeared before us the next afternoon in the grounds of the abandoned Hollywood film lot where we had been billeted for the night. The Agent had with him two dozen men in white jackets with little black bags. We were lined up in squared formations, a pace apart each way, forty to a square. We were ordered to remove our pajamas or nightgowns, and when we had pulled them off, these filthy rags were collected by workmen with wheelbarrows. As we stood utterly naked in the great yard, the Agent's followers in white jackets, who proved to be barbers, came along the rows and shaved every hair from our heads and bodies. What a feeling of degradation! The Agent stood on the steps of what may formerly have been the set for some quiet Town Hall, and once, while we were being depilated, he sneezed, and all the barbers shouted blessings. He waved good-humored thanks. The barbers finished their work, and hoses were run out by companies of men who seemed to be firemen, and the desert dirt was emphatically washed off us. Then Syndicate "police" came along with buckets of vegetable oil and laved us from shiny crowns to the soles of our sore feet. We were dismissed. We were astonished, then outraged: No clothes, no covering at all, had been issued to us!

The following morning we were led, naked and freshly oiled, bald males and bald females together, the men's chains clinking but otherwise in total silence, to a walled-in area in an adjacent lot. At one side we saw men—and the sight stirred our deepest apprehensions—standing guard over a mass of Oriental treasures: Coromandel screens, stacks of scrolls, carved ivory and ebony balls-within-balls, little horses of stone in glass cases, fans, cloisonné vases, and many bolts of brilliant silks. We were told to kneel; the men were unchained.

The Agent was present, with a party of lawyers; he was in white flannel trousers, a blue blazer with black braid at the cuffs of the sleeves, and a yachting cap, and his eyes were again invisible behind dark glasses under the cap's patent-leather visor.

Suddenly through a gate across from us came a man in a long gown and a round black cap, his hands hidden in long sleeves that met in front of him at his waist, and at once we all began to chatter in terror, to bow our foreheads to the ground, to tremble, and to weep.

The skin of the man's face was a sickly jaundice-brown color, like the underside of the stretching foot of a desert snail.

I was flooded with feelings completely new to me. The thought crossed my mind that this was a monstrosity, some creature of frightful sickness, but I knew, of course, that I was having my first sight of a yellow man.

At once three more of the apparitions came through the gate. They filled me with fear and nausea at the same time. To be naked before them! They would eat white human beings—Kathy Blaw had said so. They were ugly: besides their sallow skin they had wide bulbous noses and eyes pulled down at the inner corners and long black hair gathered behind in braided queues, and one had a disgusting thin beard of no more than a hundred filaments hanging down like a moth-eaten billy goat's whiskers.

The Agent—how beautiful and naturally grand he seemed by contrast!—was ceremonious and gentle with the yellows, and obviously not afraid of them; this calmed us all.

The first of the men with skin the color of curds called forward porters with gifts for the Agent: a curious carved chair, a cane with a golden head, an embroidered lounging robe, a case of razors, flagons of brass, a roll of shimmering satin, and a red silk banner as tall as the Agent with what was said to be a poem praising him in black velvet characters.

Next this chief yellow man stepped forward, along with the one with lank hair at his chin, and one other yellow, and the Agent, and two interpreters, and they began taking us out into the sunlight, one at a time, alternating men and women, to stand before them, to be examined in total nakedness, and one of the yellows, evidently some sort of physician, inspected each of our people, looking into his eyes, mouth, and ears, inspecting his feet, even rudely handling his private parts, and the bearded one would command each person to turn and raise his arms to show his strength, and flex his legs, and then there would be a discussion, translated by one of the linguists, and finally the chief yellow man would call to his porters, and they would run to the piles of goods and get what he commanded and carry the things to the Agent's feet—and so of course we knew that we were being sold to be eaten by these monsters, just as Kathy Blaw had said.

I had not believed Kathy Blaw, but now I believed her.

Involuntarily, I guess, in a low voice, I began to call for my father. Kathy Blaw, next to me, pinched my arm and told me with vicious severity to be silent.

The physician turned away some of our people—an older woman from our village, Mrs. Carboot, for one, who, as we all knew, had the milky film of a cataract in her right eye.

But then Chandler Nott, a weaver from our village, a grandfather of several years, was bought without debate, and I saw why we had been shaved and oiled: Mr. Nott's hair had been gray as cobwebs and his skin slack-looking and dry, and now he passed for a man in his prime.

Agatha's father, Mayor Jencks, gave us a surprise, for he went forward in his turn with a manner that was eager, co-operative, and even obsequious to the yellows, and the monsters were pleased with him and paid the highest price they had yet given for any of us: a peck of Mexican dollars, seven braziers of hammered bronze, three bolts of Shantung, eight pornographic fans, six flutes, thirty-two brass cigar clippers, and an enormous bottle of rice brandy nested in woven rattan—and the curd-face with the scraggly beard, learning through his linguist that this was a village mayor, directed that Mr. Jencks be favored with a pair of underdrawers and ordered him to stand near the party of yellow men to tell them the real value of his villagers, which our mayor thenceforth did—lying, however, in our favor and to the yellow men's expense in many cases.

Gabriel acted in quite another way. He stood fast, when called forward, as if not hearing, and the Agent had to snap his fingers to some "police," who dragged Gabe forward. Gabriel then glared at Mayor Jencks, toady to the yellows, with a look of revulsion, and he would not even glance at the yellow men, and he stood as indifferent as a tree when the physician probed and kneaded his flesh with fulvous hands. Upon being directed by the chief translator to display his strength, Gabe remained as still and relaxed as a basking lizard. The Agent began to shout. Gabe was deaf. The highest-ranking yellow man became enraged, and his face turned from pale curd to wild bloody saffron, and he stepped forward and with his own hands wielding a leather strap he dealt Gabriel several unmerciful slapping blows, which Gabe took without a quiver of his body or so much as a murmur, though tears brimmed out of his staring eyes. As nothing could persuade Gabe to bend or stretch his limbs, the yellow cannibals, as we thought them, purchased him anyway—at a price almost as high as Mayor Jencks's.

Waiting to be called, I was torn between these two manners, the mayor's and Gabe's, of fetching a handsome price, and I tried to choose one or the other, imagining, in my immature way, that I could be valuable, but when I was beckoned forward by the head linguist I could do nothing but hang my head and try to still my knocking heart. The physician's clammy yellow fingers made me start, and the shame when he intruded on my privacy was unspeakable. Mayor Jencks, though he knew me well as his daughter Agatha's best friend, had nothing to say for my value. As I heard my insignificant price translated by the interpreter I could only think that I was worth even less: a brass incense bowl, three lengths of cotton cloth, a bag of pomegranate seeds, and ten dollars Mex. And that was all.

I thought myself dismissed and was turning away when the

man with the stringy beard stepped forward and snatched from between my young breasts my locket of the Guevavi martyr and whipped its chain over my head, opened it, took out the bit of rag, the rusty nail, and the lizard's tail, and hacking with laughter tossed them to the number-one yellow, who also laughed and dropped them to the ground, motioning me aside with the back of his hand. My terror at losing my luck locket, which had become disproportionately important in my mind, flared into a hope that its spilled contents would somehow bring disaster—smallpox, a bolt of lightning, a Gila monster's venomous fangs—to the bearded man; my eyes showed him my wish.

He turned and stepped on my locket where it lay in the dirt.

When the last of our people had been bargained for, the Agent ordered porters to carry off the goods our sale had earned for the Syndicate—Mort Blain, our captor, a flabby man, had brought but a middling price—and the Agent's party left.

Kathy Blaw had evidently been infuriated by the rape of my locket, and as soon as the Agent had left the courtyard, she pronounced out loud, in her queer, shrill storytelling voice, one of our bitter postwar proverbs: "The yellow man who lives in a palace like Sammerfield or Bink—when he dies he lies in the ground like anyone else."

The principal yellow directed the interpreters, who were white men, to tell him what the woman had said, but we understood the linguists to indicate that they had not heard. The yellow man grew excited, and the head translator, after commanding Kathy Blaw in English to repeat the proverb, which she did with much spirit, rendered to the yellow man what must have been an innocuous translation, or perhaps a complete invention, at which the yellows laughed uproariously, patting the linguist's shoulders. So we saw that the linguist, too, could lie for his own kind, even though he was the yellow man's creature.

An hour later we were crowded, standing naked against one another, into half a dozen large moving vans, Mack trucks, and we were driven for a long time, hearing incessantly the grinding of the trucks' chain drives, and when we stopped at last and the tail gates of my van opened, it was dark outside.

We were all put in a huge, damp, vile-smelling, cockroach-infested chamber under the ground, like a great cistern, already occupied by many naked strangers. There were only four small openings overhead, hatched with iron bars, and through these

stingy grates we got an occasional breath of air and saw the stars
of the open sky that we had always thought our own.

⟪ Gay Moya's Night

To me, a girl of fifteen, who had never been anywhere
outside my village except to Flagstaff on the bus six times in my
life, torn now from my beloved locket of the Guevavi martyr, that
little capsule with all my luck in it, this night in the pit at the
yellow men's fort on the outskirts of Santa Barbara was so full of
strangeness and terror that surely, had it not been for Kathy Blaw,
who held me tightly, my leaping heart must have burst my fragile
ribs to flee. All around us we could hear the sounds of prayers to
God, who must have been all ears in His heaven to catch the
many denominational shadings. Our plight—all of us naked, in a
dark hole, with creeping vermin supping at our bodies which had
been sold to the miscreated yellow-skinned men—made us all
equal, the once powerful with the once weak, so that the great Mort
Blain was nothing more than I. Once when I dozed into a hazy
half-dreaming state, I grew terrified that Mort Blain would somehow grow in stature and be transformed into a shimmering creature seven feet tall with a horned headpiece atop coruscating
masses of raffia strands, and that he would threaten to gore me
for not having shrieked and screamed and scratched to protest
Mr. Slattee's leaving Agatha on the hillside path to die. But most
of the night I was wide awake. Kathy Blaw beside me trembled
with the fury that had always been encysted in her, which had
often frightened me but now supported me, and I was astonished
to hear her rail, with utter disregard for her safety, against the
Syndicate and against the yellow men who seemed even more
implacable than that dreaded organization. I exerted all my will
to think about Gay Moya, not as I had seen her at the wheel of
the white Caddy, looking dumb and irritable, but rather in a glow
of her perfection in all her films, for I had always thought of her
as a gentle goddess of night and coolness who reigned over the
pleasures of the dark—over dancing, over kissing, over love-making in bed of a kind I had often tried to imagine but now would
never have from Arty Coteen, over the evening whispering of
an intimate (I would never hear it from Agatha again), over
music, calm thoughts, and sleep. But I could not, even with Gay

Moya's help, keep this horrible night from spinning, buzzing, biting. I could see a handful of feeble embers, stars as weak as I who would never be a star, in the grates above, and I heard groans and sighs around me.

❨ Fire on Water

Light seeped like a mist through the grates, and we were all taken out of the pit at last. We were formed in a courtyard into strings of sixes, men chained to men, women bound neck to neck with thongs.

The yellow man with goat hairs at his chin, together with the physician, a white linguist, and a troop of the Syndicate's bogus cops, appeared in our courtyard, and Goat-Beard said through the interpreter that he was our Big Number One, and that any slave—this was the first time we had heard ourselves called by that name—who caused the slightest disturbance would have his or her head cut off on the spot. That was all the yellow man said to us.

Many of us trembled, not knowing when we would be eaten.

I gave myself a moment's strength by thinking: I am not a girl, I am a brass bowl, three lungees of cotton, a bag of seeds, and ten bucks Mex. Let the yellow people choke eating that!

But my terror returned, wheeling back like a hopeful buzzard.

We were marched out of the yellows' fortress naked, and we made our way through woodland downhill. Suddenly we debouched into a wide, open glade, and ahead of us, beyond a further slope of the great trees and beyond a sandy stripe, we saw —new frights each day!—two atmospheres, one above the other, one lighter than the other, lying like layers into the unimaginable distance, where you could see their jointure in a perfect straight line. In my desert-village ignorance I thought the sandy stripe was the edge of our world of dirt, and that beyond lay nothing but upper and lower skies. But Kathy Blaw told me the darker sky was the sea.

I had imagined the sea to be a broad, sluggish, brown-watered river, the color of ours outside the village hedge, with a visible farther shore. I huddled against Kathy Blaw in a fear at this expanse of sumptuous blue. Where was its other bank?

We walked on until the sun stood hot overhead. As we approached the sea we could hear a steady roar, as of an overwhelming flow of traffic, and when we were close enough I saw what was making this clamor—lines, I imagined, of white fire coming to the strip of sand on the bank of the sea, rolling humps of dazzling white steamy fire roaring as loud as a thousand Mack trucks.

Along the strip of sand were tents, guarded by many white soldiers, which sheltered, as we could see, great stores of the yellow man's wealth, apparently recently landed here.

Out in the water, at a great distance, beyond the many flashing lines of the burning sea, lay a strange structure, black, with a white house on it and a metal chimney; it looked like some sort of factory—a yellow man's ship, Kathy Blaw said between chattering teeth.

Now squads of yellow sailors, in smart blue uniforms like lounging pajamas, came from above the tents dragging several metal boats down the sand, and they lay them in the lacy fringe of gleaming ashes that the lines of sea-fire threw on the beach. The bearded Big Number One, alone, leaving his physician and linguist and guards behind, stepped without fear into the first boat and crouched in it, and eight sailors, singing together, their trousers darkening at the touch of the fiery water, heaved the metal shell into the first line of roaring smoke, and leaped in, and began to propel it, fiercely slapping at the fire around them with paddles shaped like the fly swatters our women used at home. The boat rose and plunged like a bronco. I was stunned by the courage of the yellow man with his straight black goat whiskers blowing in the wind.

Then the "police" began to force our people, sixes of chained men first, into other boats. This was horrible. We were desert people. Our bravest men resisted. I saw Mayor Jencks trying to remonstrate placatingly with a squad of cops, but they menaced him with sheath knives, and I could see his bewilderment, after years of village authority, at these rations of threatening scorn. I myself was too frightened by the hot sea even to wonder how these white "police" felt about doing such work for the yellows, pricking at their fellow whites to drive them to God knew what destination. Gabe stepped into a boat without a flicker of fear. Mort Blain was lifted into one of the vessels as inert as a sack of corn meal.

The lifeboats went and returned many times. I saw that all of them shuttled safely through the lines of fire, but this did not slake my fear in the least.

Our turn came. My rabbit panic was increased many times over by the realization that Kathy Blaw—so stern, so positive!—was in terror, too. We hugged each other and crouched with our shaved heads bowed between the metal gunwales of the boat. Through all the pounding and crashing of our outward trip I had only one thought: that I was even more afraid of the yellow crewmen than I was of the horrible spumy fire through which they were rowing us.

Strong arms carried me up some stairs attached to the side of the ship. I stood on a wide floor of sun-hot steel in a crowd of naked men, women, and children, hemmed in by a five-foot palisade of bamboo stakes erected on the deck.

We saw a dozen yellow-skinned faces peering down at our nakedness from porches of the houselike white structure that rose at the forward part of the ship.

A long time passed while the boats returned twice more to the shore. When the last trip was done, there were more people in the enclosure than had lived in all our village; we stood body to body.

Big Number One mounted a platform near one of the huge masts with its cricket-leg lifting booms, and his white linguist translated his words to us:

That we were slaves, that we had doubtless heard lies about being eaten, that we would not be eaten, that we were to be carried away to his kinsmen's farms, that we would live, as we had at home, as tillers of the soil, artisans, laborers, and housekeepers.

Further, that if any yellow man on this ship abused us, we were to tell the linguist, but if any of us offered to strike a yellow man or made a disturbance of any kind, he would lose his life.

I, for one, did not believe what Big Number One said about not being eaten. Speaking of lies he lied, to stupefy us, I thought.

The men's strings were broken, and they were chained in pairs, and the thongs were taken from the women's necks, and we were sent down on ladders through two holes in the steel floor, the men into one, women and children into another.

Big Number One stood near the hole into which the women were being lowered. When Kathy Blaw and I, still clinging to each other, came before his eyes, the white linguist spoke to him, and Big Number One evidently remembered us, I because of my moment of defiance at the loss of my locket, Kathy Blaw because of her chanting of the proverb, which had apparently been given such a benign translation. Big Number One ordered that we two be put aside; the linguist explained to us, in a whisper in our American tongue that sounded so good, that he himself had suggested to Big Number One that we be chosen as two of the cooks for the slaves, and that we would therefore go down last. We were fortunate, he said. (So quickly I learned the value to a slave of behavior, even bad behavior, that draws attention.) The white linguist was a sleek animal, dressed in a long gown like the more important yellow men, firm-fleshed and prosperous-looking, like Mort Blain before his tumble, and he grinned at us with the condescending familiarity of a dispenser of favors.

Kathy Blaw and I, and two other women also chosen to cook, Baptists, were sent below at last. Belowdecks the air was hot, and there was a fetid smell of spoiled fish. The great space of the hold had been decked into several layers, like shelves, and we saw that all the women were laid out supine on these shelves in rows, heads away from the edges. Each shelf was less than three feet above the next lower, giving the women barely room to sit up in place. As in the pit in the fort, we saw the sky through square holes with steel bars across them. Kathy and I and the two Baptists were given places on the top shelf nearest the ladder. A wooden hatch cover was lowered with a clatter onto the opening, and we heard the clink of metal latches battening it down and then cloth-soled footsteps, evidently of a yellow man on guard, roundabout it. The whole ship slowly swayed. There were sounds of thumping, creaking, and clanging all through the vessel. The light in the barred holes dimmed; we were amazed that dusk had come so soon. We had had no food all day.

I must have slept, because I was next aware of the running of cloth feet on the steel deck just above me, and shouts in the yellows' undulous language, a rhythmic grinding of apparatus beneath us, a continuous thumping of heavy links of chain on heavy metal, and then a vibration, a stirring of the life of the ship. New light and sips of blessed fresh cool air came through the openings. The rhythmic swaying of the ship began to be mixed with a helical plunging, as of a great galloping slow-motion horse spavined in one hock. A strange sickish dizziness came over me, and when a child near me retched, I, too, became ill at the sight of its fear, and so did many others as panic spread among us.

The stench in the compartment became unbearable. We tried our best in the confined space not to lie in our bile.

Soon Kathy Blaw and I learned that the linguist had at least not lied about our own good fortune, for he himself opened the hatch near us and called us and the two Baptists above, and he led us to a huge open iron grate within the palisade on the deck. We revived at once. The motion was less than it had seemed below, the air on deck was keenly fresh, a dazzling light played on the white superstructure, and the sea was blue as the silken rug on which the powers of the Syndicate had sat in Palm Springs. Away to our left, backlighted by an early sun, was a silhouette of hills; we seemed to be creeping along the edge of the earth.

Our work was to prepare a large wood fire and to cook, in huge metal kettles, a paste of horsebeans and salt chipped beef—not a mere dish for a woman's household, such as we were used to fixing, but mess for more than a thousand.

The linguist was pleased to chat with us. I was constantly aware of my nakedness; I was ashamed before him. He was called by the yellows something that sounded like Shaw Funny-One, and we called him Shaw. (He explained to us later that his title was *Hsiao Fan-I Yüan*, or "Small Interpreter." But why "small"? He was six feet tall and must have weighed two hundred pounds.) Kathy Blaw asked him if we were in fact to be eaten, and he laughed raucously at her. But we did not trust Shaw, for he was after all the yellow man's contented donkey.

Shaw told us, among other things, that we had been shipped from a deserted beach near Santa Barbara because the yellows did not like to penetrate the principal harbors with slave ships for fear of arousing the Californians; that we were aboard a shallow-draft former mackerel fisherman and ship cannery belonging to a Tientsin merchant; and that the ship was not yet full of slaves, and that Big Number One was taking the vessel down the shore to buy yet more to join us.

Then what would he do?

Then he would take us "across," Shaw said, making an arching motion with his hand that seemed to encompass more than I could ever guess at.

Men with yellow faces, some with sparse goat beards like Big Number One's, passed by from time to time and stared at my scarcely nubile breasts and my hungry belly.

When the sun was high, the wooden cover of the companion-way to the men's compartment, forward from ours, was lifted, and two hundred wan and fearful naked creatures erupted from below, fettered in pairs. Each was given a ration of mash in his bare hands. The men had little taste for our rank and pulpy dab-a-dab. They were given water. Among them all Mayor Jencks alone guffawed and roistered in what seemed to me a most inappropriate way. Gabe, who was chained to a Seventh-Day Adventist, looked me squarely in the eyes as he passed the kettles with a glance that was deep, questioning, and profoundly sad. It was safest to look in the eyes; I was afraid of being caught glimpsing at a man's startlingly unnested sex, or of finding him scanning my poor bareness. When the men had been fed, they were sent to their hold again, and the women and children were brought up. They ate even less than the men, and they were returned below.

While we were cleaning our kettles the ship turned and went toward the land, in response to a signal of flags on a high pole that Shaw pointed out to us, a summons, he said, to trade for slaves near Ventura. The vessel approached a beach. The wind had died, the sea was calmer now; there were none of the burnings that we had seen at the Santa Barbara roadstead. A launch came out on the bay to meet the ship, a rope ladder was lowered, and some fine tall white men came aboard, and over the palisades we could see a ceremony at the rail; Big Number One offered millet liquor, a swallow of which made all the white men cough and redden.

We were taken below and did not see what followed. Some time later three terror-stricken women, High Episcopalians, rich before their capture, were brought down to us, and they lay near Kathy Blaw and me and wept and chattered.

The ship went along the coast this way for many days, taking on here two, here three, here a handful of frightened creatures.

(A Lump of Flesh

On the third morning the chains were removed from all the "Santa Barbara men"—slaves, that is, who had been embarked from the beach near that town; and on successive days new acquisitions, "Venturas," "Huenemes," "Santa Monicas," and so on, were also released. Shaw, who had grown confidential with Kathy

Blaw and me, for he had a huge appetite and we gave him extra food from the slaves' kettles, told us that Big Number One believed that when slaves had made three days' voyage they would no longer attempt to escape by throwing themselves in the sea. He added that Big Number One was angry, because the Syndicate's traders along the coast, knowing that he had a part-slaved ship and was anxious to be fully packed and away, were driving hard bargains and fobbing off less than prime men and women on him—some with teeth missing, others thin and probably old. One of the yellow sailors was sick of a fever. Big Number One felt that the Syndicate was spitefully delaying him. We would be well advised, Shaw said, to tell our companions to act docile, fawning, and cheerful.

So, pretending to be our friend, this hungry frog was trying to use us for his master's purposes.

Yet he allowed Kathy Blaw and me and the two Baptists great liberties; for one thing, on sufferance of Big Number One, he let us sleep on deck. We soon saw why. The very first night, not twenty feet from me, he shamelessly imposed himself on one of the Baptist women, who—how demoralized some of us were by the mere word "slave"!—submitted to him without protest, even with some enthusiasm, I thought. But Kathy Blaw next morning told him with spittle at the corners of her mouth that she would claw his eyes out if he put his hands on her or on me. He shook with pleasant laughter.

One day we were given some cubes of pickled pork to cook. It happened that on the chow line a woman purchased in Laguna, named Mrs. Taussig, a fervent practitioner of the Jewish faith, rejected her ration. Big Number One was standing nearby, and on seeing Mrs. Taussig's refusal he gave orders through Shaw that she must eat. Shaw bellowed in a portentous voice that slaves were not to try to escape by starving themselves. Mrs. Taussig steadfastly declined the food. The yellow man became enraged and ordered her flogged by a sailor, and when this quiet woman had been broken by pain she opened her mouth to Big Number One's sallow hand holding a lump of gelatinous fatty stuff, and in tears she gulped it down.

A seething silent fury spread among the women, not all of whom, I am sure, had been entirely clear in their minds, before their capture, as to just what they felt about Mrs. Taussig's co-religionists. They were unanimous now. Indeed, when they had gone below we cooks could hear through the barred hatches much weeping and moaning in the stifling fish-haunted hold.

Two days later Mrs. Taussig erupted with a rash, a revolting psora of her humiliation, sin, shame, and terror, and we had a feeling that this sickness of her defilement might prove mortal, that she was indeed probably doomed. There was no rabbi aboard, and no simple human hope.

⟪ A Hand Is Raised

We lay in the mouth of a river, near Del Mar, along with a dozen other yellow men's ships, taking on from barges and lighters many sacks of dried beans, potatoes, rice, cabbages, and cracked corn of a sort that had surely been processed as poultry feed—food for us!—in such large supplies that Kathy Blaw and I believed we were soon to be taken "across," as Shaw had expressed it with that hawk flight of his hand. The sun reached its zenith. The men were brought up for air and food.

At the kettles Gabe, who knew, I guess, that we cooks slept on deck, suddenly leaned forward and rapidly whispered that I should stay awake that night and, in the deep of the moonless darkness, I should closely watch the guard at the wooden hatch cover of the companionway to the men's hold, and if he dozed I should silently unhasp and lift off the wooden lid. Gabe took his food and moved away.

In those brief moments Gabe's eyes had flashed with the familiar arrogance I had so often seen in them when he had sat in the saddle of the clay-pit dozer.

I did not know why he wanted me to do what he asked, except that I realized the men had somehow learned about Mrs. Taussig; I did not know, either, whether I would have the strength to carry through his command without my locket of the Guevavi martyr.

In late afternoon, unable to keep my fearful secret, I whispered it to Kathy Blaw. Her face remained as blank as one of her own clay potlids: one could not see a single sign of the turbulent reactions she must have had to my words.

Night fell. Shaw chatted with us. The sounds of the small river-mouth town dwindled and died in the dark. I feigned exhaustion and lay down on a mat of burlap sacks on the steel deck, and Kathy Blaw soon settled near me. Shaw moved to the Baptists. Outside the palisade we could hear the four yellow sailors who were on guard on the deck talking and laughing from time to time; one was supposed to be stationed at each of the hatches, and two walked fore and aft along the decks. At last Shaw moved off by himself and lay down on a folding canvas cot that he set up nights near the stove.

The blood rushed in my ears. I could sense Kathy Blaw's tightness; she was like a cat poised to jump.

Shaw began to wheeze. The Baptists seemed to be asleep. I crept to the palisades and at a crouch watched the pacing guards through chinks in the fencing.

Half the night (Gay Moya! How that glimpse of your drawn face in the white Caddy disillusioned me!), which seemed like half my life, slipped away; the card of stars wheeled around. My joints ached; my head burned. The ship creaked and clanked at anchor.

The guard of the men's hatch sat at last on a great coil of hawser near the mast. The guard of the women's hatch, which was forward, was lost in blackness under an overhang of the bridge. I could hear the cloth-muffled steps of the other two. My man lay down his head. I waited.

Then I felt Kathy Blaw's presence beside me; she had evidently been watching from another part of the palisade. She touched my shoulder.

I waited for the pacing guards' footsteps to go far forward, then I crept out of the palisades and, sneaking along by the wooden wall, I moved aft to the vicinity of the men's hatch. Suddenly I remembered the clublike metal rods in the collar around the base of the mast, where net lines from the derrick booms were made fast, and on feet as silent as moth wings I slipped to within six feet of my sleeping guard, and with great patience I extracted one of the unused belaying pins.

Then, having waited again for the sentries to be walking toward the far end of the deck, I darted to the hatch, silently undid the latch, lay the bronze rod softly down, and as I began to put my strength under the edge of the lid, I felt its weight diminish as of its own accord—for Kathy Blaw was there, lifting with me. We raised the lid. It gave off one tiny snapping sound that was like a thunderclap.

I was barely aware of a form emerging from the hole in the deck. I picked up the metal club and reached it out till it touched the form. I felt a hand, in which there was a rapid tremor, cover mine, then it slipped the heavy rod from my grip.

Three more darknesses-in-darkness emerged and swiftly moved away.

Kathy Blaw and I stood holding the hatch lid off the deck, not knowing what was happening or what to do next. Then we heard thuds and grunts, a brief scuffle—and the pacing of cloth-shod feet stopped.

I could feel Kathy Blaw lowering the lid to put it on the deck, and I let my end down, too. I thought of the heavy iron spoons with long wooden handles that we used to stir our huge grumes of beans and potatoes, and I ran for one, but as I went the guard on the ropes by the mast, evidently having been roused by the sounds of struggle we had heard, cried out to his companions. At almost the same time we heard glass breaking, and a moment later the guard of the women's hatch shrieked.

There were shouts. A flood of electric light came from the mast-heads. The frightful crash of a gun sounded.

I stood in the gateway of the palisades holding one of the iron spoons, realizing it was all over. I heard moaning.

The two sentries were sprawled on the deck, their skulls crushed. The guard of the women's hatch had been killed with a fire axe from a glass case under the bridge companionway. Gabe, a big young man from one of the other Arizona villages, whom I had heard called Jiggs, and—I was amazed—Mort Blain were hemmed in a circle of sailors, their hands already bound behind their backs. A fourth white form, which I made out to be the corpse of a youth we had shipped at Santa Monica, lay in blood on the deck, a victim of the gun. I myself was being held by Shaw, and a crewman had one of Kathy Blaw's arms twisted behind her back. The two Baptist ladies cowered behind the stove.

I saw Gabe's face in the cold down-pouring light from the mast-heads. The insolent look of that noonday command was drained away to nothing: his purse utterly empty.

([An Exhibition

In daylight the men were chained again in pairs. We cooks were bound in thongs in the palisades.

Big Number One sent away a messenger in a gig to the other

ships in the river, and one by one their captains came to our vessel. There was a long palaver on the deck; the captains went away.

All of our slaves, men, women, and children, were brought above, and we stood in stifling sun-heat in the fenced area. We saw that naked white people also crowded the decks of all the other ships.

Our Big Number One stood on the bridge with sleek Shaw beside him. Shaw gleamed with sweat in his yellow man's blue gown.

In a pompous round-toned voice, which rang with the hollow potency of a powerful man's sycophant, Shaw bellowed down to us from the bridge a translation of Big Number One's words:

That we and all the slaves on all the ships were now to see what happened to a white man who raised his hand against a yellow man.

Sailors tied a rope around Mort Blain's chest under his arms, a clanking donkey engine started up, and the heavy man arose into the air dangling from one of the derrick booms. He seemed dazed, unaware of what was happening to him. Jiggs, chained to one of the masts with Gabe, recklessly shouted to Mort Blain not to worry—that if the yellow men wanted to kill him they'd have put the rope to his neck. But just then there was a terrifying roar; four yellows with guns at rear windows of the bridgehouse had shot Mort Blain dead where he hung.

Gabe and Jiggs were whipped and chained again to the mast, where they were kept day and night. Kathy Blaw and I were retained as cooks, but we worked bound to each other in thongs, and we were sent down to the foul-smelling hold as soon as we finished our tasks after the meals. Mort Blain's corpse was aloft three days.

BOOK TWO

Hawk Flight of a Hand

◖ Into the Blue

WE HEARD the thump of the anchor chain and the seaquake rumble of the engines. Our compartment was now so crowded that I could hardly turn over in my place beside Kathy Blaw. Mrs. Taussig, trapped in an envelope of raging rash, had begun to babble deliriously; her chattering all night had unnerved us. As the shelves heeled and dipped we heard intermittent hammering overhead and sounds of heavy objects being dragged on the deck.

It was late in the day before we cooks were led above. I saw four new things: that the palisades to prevent slaves from jumping overboard had been dismantled and stacked at the center of the deck; that Mort Blain's body no longer swung from a derrick boom; that Gabriel and Jiggs had been removed from the mast where they had been chained; and that—the realization threw me to my knees—we were out of the sight of land: all was blue except for our own straight carpet of spindrift pointing back toward our lost home.

Kneeling, I tried to pray, but I could get nothing of any value to God onto my tongue or into my head. Prayer belonged in church— my forehead on the smooth rail of the pew in front, looking down into the dusty hymnal rack, and at the tiny shelf with jigsawed round nests for the goblets from which we took Christ's blood

that tasted suspiciously like Welch's grape juice; and the little
cube of bread, His body, dry on my tongue as I thought carelessly
about Arty Coteen and the scene in the movie the night before
of the Saracens' camp at Monreale, when, after the battle, Francis
Huge lay his beautiful sweat-streaked face on Gay Moya's breast.
This queer snapshot of memory coming into my mind in place
of the prayer I needed so badly at that moment increased my fear
into panic: I was naked on an unfenced deck on a limitless sea.

At last I was able to creep to Kathy Blaw. I crouched trembling
near the stove, barely able to do my work.

When, under the sun's late slanting, the male slaves were
brought above, shackled in pairs, to eat, I saw my terrors re-
enacted many times over by them. Gabriel, double-chained to Jiggs,
did not fall to the deck, as many others did; his eyes were dull, he
seemed indifferent. Jiggs was forcedly jolly. . . . The screaming
among the women at the sight of the edgeless blue, their running
here and there in bursts like startled hares, their gibbering questions to Shaw—the signs of their terror somehow devalued mine,
and I grew calmer.

We sailed day after day on a measured following swell under
a hot sky. Each morning and afternoon the slaves were aired
for several hours at a time, men and women separately. All were
now dejected, and the discomfort of the fish-guts sleeping compartments grew greater as our spirits skidded toward despair.

Kathy Blaw became a second mother to me, bitter, testy, yet
tender, singing off key to me in the sleepless hours I had each
night, coaxing me to eat to keep up my strength, stinging me
with sarcasm out of depressed stupors of staring and dreaming
of home.

One evening the wind increased, and the shelves under us
began to lurch and heave and plummet. The shallow-draft fisherman was no match for an ocean gale. Rain and salt spray poured
through the barred hatches onto the unfortunates under them.
Soon half a thousand women were sick to their stomachs. Through
the singing of the wind in the rigging, the slatting of gear on the
ship, the sloshing of the sea, and the groans, kecking, and weeping
of our companions, we could hear a chilling monotone of Mrs.
Taussig's ravings. The stench of our vomit redoubled our nausea.

The storm continued two days. During it the crew dared not
take the slaves above, so on top of our seasickness we were without food, clean air, or water. I was sure I was to die. Occasionally

Shaw came partway down the ladder to look at us, and once he brought the yellow physician with him, but that tall, thin creature had scarcely stepped to our level when one of the once rich Episcopalian ladies from Ventura bit him on the ankle, drawing a profusion of blood; his face had already turned a greenish color from our stink, and he stumbled hastily up the steps grunting and pitching like someone in the last stages of drunkenness.

Then in the night everything seemed to stop but Mrs. Taussig's stream of talk.

As soon as it was light we women were taken above, all save Mrs. Taussig. The sun was shining as if through a sky of glass. There was not a sleeper's breath of wind. The ship was wallowing slowly in great humped swells; the surface of the water was silky slick.

Yellow sailors rolled several small kegs out onto the deck, and I was among a dozen women detailed to go down in our hold with wooden pails full of acrid malt vinegar from these barrels, and, weak as we were, to give our wretched quarters a cleaning with cloth swabs. Mrs. Taussig lay there the whole time, groaning and mumbling. On deck Shaw showed the women how to scoop up sea water over the rail of the ship in canvas buckets, and they bathed themselves. We had a meal, finally, and we breathed the air, and we thought we were better off.

But when, after feeding the men, whose chains had again been removed, Kathy Blaw and the Baptists and I were sent below, we found there was a new tense atmosphere on the women's shelves. I attributed it at first to the long, slow swells, the foul heat of the sun on the shell of the ship, the tart odor of vinegar and stale puke and vestigial fish, and the debilitation of our fellow slaves. I realized what it was:

Silence.

I felt I had to summon Shaw. I started up and, crawling over Kathy Blaw and the two Baptists, I climbed the companionway and pounded with my fist on the hatch cover. It was opened; a bearded yellow face leered down on my nudity. I urgently spoke Shaw Funny-One's name over and over. The face turned, and I heard a roar. Then Shaw was there. I told him that the woman Mrs. Taussig was dead.

Shaw said, in an offhand tone, as of one hearing an old, old, old story, that the body would be removed the following day, when the women's hold would be cleared during our airing.

All that night I lay awake wondering what it would be like, on one of these crowded shelves, to be Mrs. Taussig's neighbor, who after four days of the doomed woman's light-headed prating must now lie as close to her silence as I to Kathy Blaw's nervous warmth. What if Kathy Blaw should die? This sudden thought filled me with homesickness. I wept for my lost mother and father.

Daylight finally came, but it was many hours, celebrated by us with utter stillness, before we were taken up on deck. Under Shaw's direction six women on their hands and knees in the low place dragged the corpse, which had stiffened with thighs drawn up and hands clenched between the breasts, across the compartment shelf to the companionway. We saw yellow sailors refuse to touch the body. So it was that women slaves were made to lift Mrs. Taussig's crouching form out of the hatch, and to carry it to the rail, and to drop it, without a thought for the soul we had heard chanting its endless protests, into the sea.

(Kathy Blaw's Story

Like a fire slowly kindling, a formless communal dread began to burn among the female slaves. The ship was shuddering through flat calms. Heat lay on us like a breathing animal. Some of the women who had been under the dripping openings during the storm developed dysentery, which spread rapidly among us, causing, despite daily cleansings, a fetor far more wicked than that of our previous sicknesses. We breathed thereafter a miasma of vinegar and human discharge. When we were taken up for our daily airings some of the small children lay limp against the bulkheads and could not be stirred to take an interest in themselves. Four Lutheran women decided to starve themselves, and no abuse of tongues or thongs could make them eat. Our skins broke out in sores from lying in dampness. Roaches the size of frogs came out from the ship's crannies and made a festival of our filth. We were afraid of smallpox. But worst of all sufferings was the thought of Mrs. Taussig's unceremonious dead plunge into the sea.

In our religious revival since the defeat in the Yellow War, the funeral had in almost every sect become our most important American rite. Life had held scant hope; sweet death had become its goal. I remembered standing at the edge of the large crowd at the cemetery, only a month before, when old Joshua Benton's coffin, suspended on its slings, hung poised over the mouth of the tunnel (as I thought of it) that led to Paradise—a green garden where the petals of apple blossoms blew like snow the year round, where tigers were pets, and I would be Gay Moya, and soda fountains like the ones in Flagstaff stood in every rose bower. Preacher Honing uttered the final prayers for Joshua Benton, and the crowd was jealously tense. By and large we Methodists took no stock in formality—except at funerals, where each magic step had to be taken with utmost care and exactness. Like other American Protestants, we had turned away from the tradition of using the funeral to assuage the grief and shore up the morality of the survivors; our thoughts were for the dead. Atop Josh Benton's coffin, to be buried with him for his journey, were his Sunday clothes, the latest copy of *The Saturday Evening Post,* his wallet with fifty bucks in it, a fifth of his beloved sour-mash whiskey, and a number of other things his daughter, Mrs. Jart, thought he would want along the way. . . . The watchers by the grave, the six hired mourners that next week, the building of the cairn, the planting of the grave sycamore—none of it was really sad. Yearning, I think, was the village experience in honor of Joshua Benton. . . . But to be dropped without a single precaution into the sea!

My terror at this possibility for myself, as I thought about these things, reached such a pitch that I felt I must cry out, and at just that moment I heard a moan near me of a woman whose thoughts must have pushed her over the edge into sound, and then another wail far across our cavern, and soon, caught in a fever of common panic like the one our coffle had suffered in the mountains, we were all twittering and caterwauling like madwomen.

Beside me I began to be conscious of the weird falsetto whine of Kathy Blaw's tale-telling voice, which rose and dominated the voices around us, until finally all the women in the hold were listening to her words:

"There was a time when God took no interest in Arizona. Lizards gave birth to birds, and rams mounted women. One day a donkey and a jaguar went to Flagstaff to market. The jaguar had a suitcase in which he had collected all the wisdom of the world except for one last perception, which he thought he might be able to buy in Flagstaff. The donkey wanted to buy a human

wife—God, as I say, was busy in the Middle West and could take
no time to regularize Arizona. At the market the jaguar had no
luck; the perception was not to be found for sale. The donkey
bought a nice young woman named Helen. They started home.
The jaguar was beginning to find his suitcase heavy. Helen rode
the donkey's back. She wasn't light, either, being nice and plump,
and on the way she fondled one of his long ears and whispered
into it, 'I wish you were a man. If you were a man I would take
off my clothes and lie with you all night.' The donkey, who had
never learned to whisper, laid back his head and brayed, 'He-how?
He-how?'—meaning, as the wise jaguar understood, 'How can I
become a male human being?' The jaguar said, 'Are you mad,
you ass? Men are unhappy.' But Helen cupped the donkey's ear
again and said, 'You would be a handsome man, and a strong
one. I would remove my clothes and lie with you day *and* night.'
The donkey, filled with torment and delight, raised his nose toward the sky and trumpeted, 'He-how? He-how?' An eagle heard
him and flew down and said, 'I have flown long distances, and I
know several states where they have God, and everything is
orderly and just. Lizards beget lizards, rams mount nanny goats,
men and women lie naked beside each other whenever they find it
convenient, and dissatisfied donkeys are not saddled with their
lots.' 'Ha-where? Ha-where?' the donkey cried. The eagle said, 'It
would be a long trek for you with that fat girl on your back.
I will fly there and bring God to Arizona. Go home. I will bring
Him to your house.' The donkey was overjoyed. On the way
home Helen said, 'Jag! Jag! I see a perception in the top of that
cottonwood tree.' 'Which tree?' 'That one.' The jaguar began to
climb it, but he had a hard time, because he was trying to take
the suitcase up with him, and when he was halfway up the
donkey brayed in such a way that the jaguar understood him to
mean: 'You aren't wise, you're a fool, or you'd have had sense
enough to leave the suitcase at the foot of the tree.' One has to
look twice at a wise person to see that he is also a fool. The jaguar,
realizing the truth of the donkey's brayings, lost his temper and
threw the suitcase to the ground, where it split at the hinges,
scattering the wisdom of the world. The donkey went to his home,
and there the eagle was waiting for him with God. In his great
kindness God arranged for the donkey, after he had made certain
promises, to become a handsome, strong man, named Lion. God
then went to Ashfork, Parks, Bellemont, Riordan, Flagstaff, and

all along Route Sixty-six and told all the people to go to the sycamore tree and get on their hands and knees and gather up what
scraps of wisdom they could. This they did. And that night, when
Lion was lying with Helen, he asked her, 'What was that bit of
wisdom you saw in the tree?' Helen said, 'It was this, my beloved
Lion: *All the different forms Death takes are just the one Death.*'"

Save for the vibration of the ship and the slapping of the sea
against its metal flanks, all was now silent in our dark space.

(⟦ Our Prayers

The heat the next morning was like a bad breath in the
ship's maw, and for some reason the women slaves were not taken
up for their airing early in the day. When at last, near noon, the
hatch was opened and we were released, we saw why there had
been a delay.

We were going to be allowed to mix with the men slaves, who
were emerging from their hatch just as we were from ours. The
yellow men, our masters, may have sensed, or heard, the utter
desperation in our hold the night before, and no doubt the men
were despondent, too, and Big Number One must have decided that putting us all together for a short time, shamefully
naked though we were, might restore our spirits.

But we did not move to each other with pleasure. Because of the
heat and our sicknesses, our thirst was overwhelming, and perhaps the women thought the men would drink all the water we
were rationed, or the other way around. At any rate, there was
a rush for the barrels, by both men and women, and a riot followed, in which there was screaming, pushing, and clawing.

The disturbance was brought to a pause by a yellow man's
shooting a gun into the air.

In the slaves' gasp of silence after the gun's detonation there
arose a powerful sound from the throat of a Catholic priest who
had been taken aboard at Santa Monica: "'And now I exhort
you to be of good cheer: for there shall be no loss of any man's
life among you, but of the ship.'" This priest's name was Father
Principo, and he stood now on the hot steel deck with his hands
pressed flat one to another, fingers up, his eyes lowered, his
cheeks and mouth engraved with a habitual cheerfulness that even
our recent days had not erased, a look on his face so sweet and

removed that my imagination hastily and respectfully vested him, from a sharp white line of a starched backwards-collar at his jowls, down robes of black overhung with white lacy stuff, to the ankle-high wrinkled soft leather shoes of a dowdy small-town parish-house fussbudget. "'For there stood by me this night the angel of God . . .'" Around him gathered a circle of Catholics. From nowhere altar boys materialized. So vivid, so innocent, so booming was Father Principo's voice that one could almost hear a tinkling bell, smell incense, see mysterious glints of amber and cerulean stained glass.

At first a large crowd gathered around the priest and his flock to watch. Then across the way we heard another voice with the open tones of California—that of a Presbyterian minister; a knot of his faithful around him were soon singing: "Eternal Father, strong to save, Whose arm doth bind the restless wave . . ." Still another Californian—the soil of that state had been, for religious revival as for vegetables and fruits, far more fertile than ours in Arizona, and among the Californian captives there seemed to be numerous divines—called to his upraised hands all Methodists. And soon about the deck we were gathered in more than a score of clusters of worshippers, some standing with bowed heads, some kneeling (the women's buttocks trembled and were crimped as their owners shifted their knees on the hot, rough steel plates), some singing, some praying, and one rather exotic Californian sect shouting, jumping, barking, and speaking in tongues: Catholics, Presbyterians, Methodists, Lutherans, Jews, Northern and Southern Baptists, Episcopalians (I heard the good lady who had bitten the physician genteelly trilling: "Let the sea make a noise and all that therein is, Let the floods clap their hands . . ."), Congregationalists, Mormons, Quakers, Seventh-Day Adventists, and numerous sects on the near and outer fringes. The yellows thought we were all one, merely white, but we were many. Many voices, that is; the extraordinary thing was that we were of one mind. It was as if the entire force of all our postwar religious revival had culminated in one vengeful hope. Every churchlet on the scorching deck was, in its own vocabulary, calling upon God to bring on this vessel, which had the curious name *Tung Yüan* (*East Garden*), some vengeance of His cunning strength, hull-splitting thunder, typhoon winds, underwater rocks, or anything He might use to put us under, under, under.

A girl from a hysterical Californian evangelical sect near our mumbling Methodist flock, a large awkward creature three or four years older than I, showed signs of becoming possessed. Her neck jarred from side to side, and her fellow sectarians shouted for God to come down and settle on her head. Her naked breasts shook with her straining to receive God, and I could hear the yellow sailors on the superstructure laughing. (I gathered later from Shaw that the yellows thought that, males and females having been brought together after our long separation, we were carrying on some sort of sex rites; he said they were obsessed with speculations about the whites' sexual practices.) Suddenly the girl jumped up crying with a wild joy, and she tore around the deck as if she were some kind of disrobed heavy-fleshed storm, now holding in her hands delicate cords of shimmering rain, now raging in hurricane leaps.

This girl's sincere antics effectively broke up the other services. Eventually she calmed down. We cooks fed the men and women. And I—my chest was hot as the metal underfoot, with happiness —I felt, as I had not in my flash of defiance when Big Number One had snatched my locket, or when I was filled with anger and pity at Mrs. Taussig's death, or even in that moment when I had put the belaying pin into Gabe's trembling hands—I felt that *something* was possible, something could be done, even by one so small, so weak, so bare as I.

(On the Rim of the Night

But no cloud nesting thunder and steel-riving lightning came to sink the ship that night. We rode a smooth ocean with a favoring breeze for several days. All four of the Lutheran women who had refused food died and were thrown in the sea. A boy eight years old died and was thrown in the sea. A thin Baptist woman died and was thrown in the sea. For those who survived, it seemed as if this state of being that was not a life would last forever. The stench in our shallow compartment was worse every day. We felt as if the sun itself walked on the metal deck so close above us.

One night, when I had quite given up the crazy hope I had had that God might answer our multi-sected prayers and come to help us or drown us all, I heard, or thought I heard, a distant guttural mumbling. At once a number of our women murmured to

their neighbors. Soon, more distinctly, I heard what was undoubtedly a faraway roll of thunder. At once all five hundred of us were
stirring with a tense, buzzing excitement—the first flood of
emotion we had felt that had not the slightest tug of fear in it.

In a few moments the rectangles of the barred air hatches
overhead quivered with trembling light, then were dark again.
Much later, far away, we heard a new rumble.

The Methodist women among us struck up "Tossed upon the
raging billows," in hope, I suppose, of encouraging God to come
closer with some sort of holocaust. We were carried away with an
absurd, delusive happiness.

Suddenly we heard someone beating with his fists on the bulk-
head that divided us from the men's hold—one of the men unable
to contain his joy. Eventually his pounding stopped. Another
flash, another growl, another surge of our unrealistic hope. "Fierce
though flash the lightnings red . . ." It was strange: at home in
the desert I had feared lightning more than any other threat of
nature—I thought of its shriveling lick as a meting out of justice
by God; we could hear the thunder echo all along the Chaco Rico
Range. Yet now I sang, clapped, almost danced lying down, in
the hope that this distant lightning would come to the yellow
men's vessel, strike the bridge, crisp the captain, and somehow
cripple the ship.

There were a few more flashes. Slowly we realized that the
storm was passing along the rim of the night and would never
come to us.

The mumbling died away to nothing, and our blind joyfulness
crumbled to dampness, stink, sores, stiffness, and tears. We felt,
despite our knowledge that our prayers had issued from a distinctly unholy place, that the yellow men might have mysterious
powers, which lodged perhaps in their sneers and their derisive
laughter, that were greater than the whole constellation of our
faiths. We were weak in truth.

(Heavenly Stream

We lost count of the days. We rode through a calm that
seemed like its opposite—a limitless rage. Kathy Blaw and I were
cooking one morning when one of the yellow crewmen, who was
stationed in a crow's nest halfway up the foremast, gave out an

exultant shout. Shaw ran to us and told us that land, mountains, Shantung, had been sighted. The news gave me a lift; perhaps our long bad dream was to end. But I noticed that Kathy Blaw, who had been silent and dejected ever since the thunderstorm had evaded us, received Shaw's word with a face glummer than ever.

That afternoon, when we had just begun to see, off to the left, dark summits peeking over the edge of the glass expanse, two women died and were dropped in the water, and while we cooks were stowing our pots, Kathy Blaw, who had watched the crude casting over of souls with tears pouring down her cheeks, suddenly let out a mournful gasping cry, and she ran to the rail and jumped in the sea, where yellow men threw our dead.

I screamed, and a sailor shouted. We learned at once that while the yellow men thought that whites dead were worthless, they gave living whites an urgent value. To my amazement the tall, spiritless physician, who had had his ankle bitten by the Episcopalian woman, and who had been morosely limping around the deck ever since, now without hesitation kicked off the one shoe he was wearing and plunged over the side. The engines stopped, the ship swung into a wide turn. The physician, a strong swimmer, reached Kathy Blaw, who, apparently not knowing how to drown, was thrashing the water into an angry saliva, and he struck her a blow on the head which made her go limp. On the deck sailors were already swinging a long dory out on davits, and when the ship, engines backing, stopped near the pair in the water, the men hastily lowered the boat over the side, with a thumping splash, and four of them rowed to the doctor and lifted my naked unconscious friend and her rescuer out of the water and returned them to the ship.

When Kathy Blaw came to herself, Big Number One, his face above his whiskers wrinkled like a walnut with fury, ordered her given twenty lashes and directed that she be chained to the mast until we dropped anchor.

Kathy Blaw's bath in the ocean had washed away her melancholy, and the rest of that day and all through the night we could hear her tireless tongue, cursing not only the yellows but her own white companions, too, for their passive acceptance of their plight.

I shivered with loneliness on the shelf in the hold that night. Before we were taken above next day we heard the great anchor chain running out, the engines stopped, and there was a hammering on deck. Nothing happened for several hours. At last a hatch was opened and we were taken on deck, and there we found the shoulder-high palisades raised again, and over them we could see that the ship was lying at anchor in a broad bay off a flat land. Shaw told us we were waiting for high tide outside the sandbar at the mouth of the North River, which led to the *East Garden*'s home port of Tientsin, or Heavenly Stream, and in fact while we cooks were providing a meal the ship heaved its anchor and crossed over the bar.

We moved along the curving river through a green deltaic plain: fields of sorghum and millet bounded by flood dikes, clumps of yellowy willows, and villages of houses with clay pile walls startlingly like the compound walls of my Arizona home. Junks and sampans floated under patched sails in the almost windless morning, and I thought at first the river must have had a thousand mouths, for similar sails dotted the entire landscape, constantly tacking and bellying. They were wind wells, Shaw said. Apart from the distant barking of village dogs there was no sound but the plashing of our bow waves on the banks of the river levees. When the meals were done, women's and men's, we were sent below.

Early in the afternoon we heard much shouting; the engines died down; hawsers thumped and dragged on the deck overhead. All of us were taken above again from both holds, and we were massed within the pickets.

The *East Garden* was tied in a row of ships alongside a commercial bund. On the open embankment we saw—my heart turned over at the sight—a number of white men running about in dirty faded blue cotton trousers, obeying orders given by two yellows in long white gowns. The whites grinned, waved to us, shouted what seemed to be jokes to each other in the yellow men's tongue, and crackled with laughter like our hardened Jiggs. We saw that these slaves were not only uneaten; they were strong, brisk, rowdy, and tough.

Beyond the bund were warehouses and shops solidly built of bricks, with tile roofs; and the cries of a city.

Kathy Blaw was still muttering like someone in a tirade beyond the earshot of the object of the anger.

Under the constant bellowing of Shaw our thousand souls were sorted into groups—being graded, he explained, for sale, as prime men, prime women, boys and girls rated at two thirds of prime, and smaller children who counted as half prime.

I was not, however, put into any of these main groups but was set aside, along with Kathy Blaw, Gabriel, Jiggs, Mayor Jencks, the two Baptist cooks, the Episcopalian woman who had bitten the doctor, and about thirty other slaves, in one corner of the palisaded area.

Marked tags were hung around the necks of those in the graded groups. Then the dock slaves carried huge baskets up a wide gang-plank that spanned the ship's rail and the bund, and out of the baskets our crewmen took straight cotton pantaloons and long-sleeved tunics, all of the same medium size, and gave each of us a pair, and we clothed ourselves with a great deal of laughter—strange sound in our throats, expressive of our relief at having our nakedness covered at last, and our dismay at the awkward shapes of these tubed sacks; it was the fortunate middle-sized slave whom the coolie clothes fitted.

All the groups but ours were taken ashore, hemmed about there by a troop of yellow men with guns, and they disappeared within a huge gray-bricked godown. Big Number One, the tall limping surgeon, and Shaw, in a crisp white robe, went with them.

We few were left within the fencing on the deck of the *East Garden*.

❪ Four in One Hundred and Four

The captain's party returned to the vessel at dusk. Big Number One, flapping his goat whiskers about with wags of his obviously sotted head, was drenched in self-congratulations and some sort of yellow man's liquor. Shaw told us that the prices had been good, and as to us—we were Big Number One's own. It was now revealed to us that this Big Number One was not so big after all, for he was simply a yellow merchant's hireling, and of every hundred and four prime units of slave flesh that he delivered intact to Heavenly Stream, he could claim only four as his own. Why had he chosen particularly us? Because, said Shaw, our Big Number One liked extremes—either slaves who fawned on him (Shaw bowed his head toward Mayor Jencks and the Baptist cooks), as some were wise enough to do, or fought him (Shaw swept his eyes to Gabriel, Jiggs, Kathy Blaw, and the Episcopalian

lady with the keen teeth), as others had spirit enough to do.
Craft and courage he valued, Shaw said, adding in a low voice
that we mustn't expect this of most yellows, who liked best of all
whites who were—or had the wit to seem—stupid, tireless, craven,
obsequious.

Mayor Jencks asked Shaw: What would Big Number One do
with us?

He would take us to the Northern Capital, the linguist said,
where the retail prices were best.

For six days we worked at cleaning the ship, purifying it again
and again with malt vinegar; the yellow sailors followed us with
smoke pots whose fumes reached into every cranny till even the
gigantic roaches, with their shells as hard as the housings of
turtles, walked out and rolled over on their backs.

Then one morning we were taken ashore, and we were formed
once again into a coffle—the men were chained, the women were
tied wrist to wrist with hemp rope—and we were herded away
through the city streets.

So we had crossed, as the winged migration of Shaw's hand
that day had forewarned, to the other side of the ocean and the
earth, from the New World to the Old, from the domain of the
losers to that of the winners. And now I must tell of the weird
sensation we whites experienced as we moved, coffled, through
the yellows' city—of slipping, of skidding back across sheets of
time; a thrill like the half-hideous soaring of the pit of the stomach that a child feels when his end of the seesaw falls. To say
that we found ourselves in another era is exact. Not that the
yellows were "backward" by, let's say, two centuries, as we had
used to think before the war they won; indeed, we ourselves had
been "backward" since the defeat—making clay pots, sowing seed
by hand, training one youth to cobble and another to weave. It
was simply that the yellows, as we saw them now in the streets of
their own milieu, lived on another shore of time altogether, and
we had moved onto it with them.

Marching behind a large two-wheeled oxcart with an arched
hood of reed matting, in which Big Number One and Shaw rode,
we walked in three days the eighty miles to the capital of the
yellow empire.

BOOK THREE

The Chalk Circle

BOOK THREE

([A Loud, High Cackle

I BLINKED at the strangeness of all that I saw. We whites from the *East Garden*, thirty-four of us in rags, walk-sore and scared to the bone, huddled together on a wooden platform in the farmers' market of the Outer City. At our backs was the crenelated massif of the Tartar City wall, many times as high as the houses around us. Against the porcelain-blue sky we could see, atop a nearby gate in the wall, a rectangular, double-roofed tower of a suffocating grandeur: each of its faces had four rows of gunports, one above the other, high in the air, and on the wooden mantlets that shuttered these embrasures were painted, with a haughtiness that made me shiver, the mouths of cannons, as if to suggest that the yellows' powers were so vast that mere representation would repel enemies. The Fox Tower, Shaw called it, seeing us look at it; that name deepened my fears. A string of moth-eaten camels, a trader's caravan from Mongolia, stood a few yards from us; the stolid animals ruminated and stared with long-nosed, damp-nostriled contempt, it seemed, at our white skins. The market was crowded with two-wheeled carts of greens, melons, legumes, and fish; harsh cries echoed against the city wall, and schools of fish smells swam in the warm air, reminding me of the revolting slave ship's hold. In the square before our platform a bad dream of many yellow faces milled and squirmed, and, beyond, buildings of brick with curved tiled roofs hemmed in the marketplace.

Big Number One stood on the fore-apron of the platform hawking to the crowd the merits of each of his slaves in turn. Yellow men in ankle-length gowns, with flattish conical hats and braided queues, some carrying parasols to shade themselves from the sun, came forward, stepped up on the scaffold to inspect and prod, talked quietly with Big Number One, and bought or refused. One by one my companions were led away.

I had a glimpse of Gabriel's face for a moment as he was being sold, and the expression I saw was new to him—a look of incredulity. His face seemed a solid blank bruise of amazement.

Memories of that astonished stare were to revisit me often, as time passed, reinforcing my utter disbelief that life could take such turns as it did.

I was third from last to be put up for sale. Two yellow men came up when Big Number One had finished talking about me, and behind one of them, holding up his parasol, was a plump white woman in a slave uniform—a blue tunic with large circular emblems of identification, in red, on chest and back, and green trousers. The man without a slave pressed my arm to test its firmness and put a finger, which smelled of tobacco and had a long, clawlike fingernail, under my upper lip to examine my teeth. The back of his hand was glossy, like oilcloth. The more elegant man, who had crimson tassels and a large crimson button on his hat, and who wore a long gown of silk the color of the topless Peking sky, stood talking with Big Number One and with the slave woman. I heard a word that sounded like "Arizona," and the white woman asked me softly in English, with our beautiful straight-out Arizona accent, how old I was. She had been an Arizonan!

I fell on my knees and threw my arms around her thighs, and she bent down and raised me up and told me not to be frightened.

I could not help blurting out to her a question: "Are they going to eat me?"

She laughed at me, with a loud, high cackle, quite unlike her low speaking voice, just as I had heard Shaw cackle at Kathy Blaw when she had asked the same question our first day on the ship, and at once I mistrusted this slave woman; she must be, I thought, on the yellows' side.

I saw the man with glossy skin go down from the platform. The white woman's owner conferred awhile with her, then slipped from within one of his wide sleeves a velvet bag, and from it withdrew a single shoe-shaped ingot of sycee silver, which he placed

in Big Number One's wrinkled hand. Then he turned away down
the steps from the platform, and the white woman took me by the
elbow and steered me in his footsteps. She said I was his.

([New Words

Our master left us. He was going to his place of work,
the woman said, though I could not imagine his doing men's work
—hoeing a field, building a wall, picking fruit in a grove—in a
long silk gown with a folding fan in his hand.

The woman led me toward my new home. We went into the
inner capital, through the gate under the frightful Fox Tower.
All around the gate were many white beggars—filthy, ragged,
scabbed, and crippled.

The woman said her slave name was a yellow word that meant
Gull. The masters called her Small Gull. Every white slave, she
told me, was contemptuously called "small." They spoke of us
generically as "smalls." They also called us, when they wanted to
be more insulting, she said, "pigs," "hogs," "sows," "piglets."

Gull said she was to teach me the yellows' language. First I
must learn my master's name: Shen.

The houses were low-lying and presented cold, forbidding faces,
for there were no windows, only bare walls, fronting the streets.
We walked along a broad avenue in which there were surprisingly
few people. Gull said that twenty-seven years before, there had
been a great plague of smallpox, which the yellows called Heaven-
Flowers Sickness, as if one could keep a disease at arm's length
with flattery; the pox, unappeased by the pretty name, had seriously depleted the country's labor force. This had been one of
the main causes of the Yellow War, and this was why we "smalls"
were so much in demand.

I saw a pair of bare-chested white men between the shafts of
a sedan chair of rosewood inlaid with ivory; in it the slaves
were carrying at a trot a heavy yellow man, and their ribs stood
out from their wasted bodies, and their eyes bulged. I began to
cry.

A vast herd of goats—an illusion of a thousand Big Number
Ones—came charging at us along the street. Terrified, I ran to a
gateway of a house and crouched against it. calling the name of
Kathy Blaw.

Gull laughed at me, but she also ran to me and hugged me to her fat body and said in our nice flat Arizona accents that time would help me get used to the yellows' city.

While we stood by the gate and let the flock pass, Gull threw her hands over her mouth, as if she had just remembered something of vital importance, and she shouted over the chorus of bleating that she must teach me the two most odious expressions in our owners' language:

Ta Lao-yeh, the honorific title due a master from his white slaves, meaning, roughly, Big Venerable. *Ta T'ai-t'ai*, for the mistress, or Big Madame.

Gull said I must never, on pain of wicked punishment, speak to the man and woman who owned me without using these worshipful words. As whites were always "small," so yellows were always "big."

The goats passed. They were herded by vicious-looking yellow-brown dogs.

We walked on. I rehearsed the terms of respect. Then Gull said she would tell me the slaves' basic law:

No matter how frightened you are before a yellow person, no matter how angry, no matter even how happy, control your face and body; show no feeling; have a face as impassive as a figure painted on a china bowl.

Perhaps I would like Gull, after all. She was fat and cheerful, and good to me. She told me she had been abducted from her Arizona village, near Prescott, in a raid by the Sacramento Syndicate thirteen years before, not long after the defeat; that she had farmed eight years on an island off Kiangsi; that she had been shipped north and sold to our master five years before.

Big Venerable. Big Madame. I found that I could easily remember every word Gull taught me.

We came to an imposing gateway. This was our home, Gull said. Fierce stone lions flanked the approach; the male on the right was playing with a bronze ball, the lioness on the left fondled a cub. Over the entranceway, on a panel, gilt characters proclaimed (Gull told me): HARMONY IN ALL THE COURTYARDS. "Ha!" she barked, her only comment. A large double-leafed gate was flanked by two smaller doors, on one of which Gull rapped.

A gatekeeper, a hangdog-looking slave in a uniform like Gull's, opened the door. Gull said his name was Bean. He bowed to me in a sheepish way.

Gull led me around a carved marble spirit screen, along a veranda, through a passage hall, across a large courtyard, and into the main reception hall. I perspired in my thin slave-ship rags. Lacquered pillars, beams decorated with herons and dragons!

As we went Gull whispered that Big Madame would be waiting for us, and she would probably address me as her child, but that would not make me her child.

Off the end of the large room was a moon terrace, raised by several steps. There stood a woman. Having memorized the phrase "Big Madame," I was surprised at the tiny delicate thing our mistress turned out to be. She was dressed in a long straight gown of brilliant figured lavender, and her left hand rested on a waist-high lantern, on the horn faces of which were painted stylized hunting scenes.

I hated her at once. Her cheeks were rouged, her flat broad nose was caked with powder, her lips were like small caterpillars lying together. She spoke to Gull in a rasping voice.

Gull told me in our sweet Arizona accents that Big Madame had said I was a pretty child.

I could imagine it! My crown bristled with a half-inch stubble of light-brown hair.

Weak with fear, I sank to my knees, lowered my head, and softly said in the yellow language, as some sort of feeble plea that filled me with shame, "Big Madame!"

The woman came down the steps toward me with a curious stump-leg walk, and at each stair I saw peek out from her lavender gown feet so small as to seem deformed. She put her damp hands on my cheeks and lifted my head. She spoke again.

Gull, her face a chinaware image, said the Big Madame had named me White Lotus, and had called me her child, her new small child. But that, Gull added in firm Arizona tones, did not make me her child.

⟨ At Big Venerable Shen's

For a long time I was stifled by confusions; I could not have said what was going on around me.

In the courtyards, halls, side chambers, and verandas of the mansion, each of which had a name—Autumn Retreat, Peony Study, Pomegranate Court, Bamboo Terrace—everything was transacted in hushed tones, in an atmosphere of half-choked dignity and reserve.

One area, however, had no sweet name: the slave yard. There flies swarmed around a moist slop of melon seeds and vegetable parings, a shabby rooster mounted a hen and then flapped the dust of the yard with his wings as he boasted, and in one corner stood an astonishing knee-high heap of empty peanut husks.

My sleeping place was a frayed straw mat on an intransigent brick bed in a room I shared with Gull and all four of the Shens' male slaves: the major-domo, Old Bow, a silent, surly white-haired man who was profoundly courteous to the master and mistress before their faces but bitter and complaining behind their backs; the gateboy, Bean, a cringing nonentity; and two "runners," rowdy, stupid fellows, one very tall and thin, called On Stilts, the other a dirty, careless creature named Cock. Men and women slaves alike wore the Shens' blue-and-green pajamalike uniforms.

The Shens had a small son, eight years old, whom we were obliged to address as *Ta Shao-yeh*, Big Young Venerable; he treated the slaves as if we were mice or scorpions or lizards to stalk and torment. Vividly I remembered the swaggering rascal boys in the village at home in Arizona, skinning a measly gopher as if they were hunters who had been vouchsafed to shoot a powerful lion. Each such thought of home drove me to tears; each effort to silence my sobs gagged me so I thought I would faint.

I was haunted by Big Madame's hobbling walk and her queer, tiny, pointed feet. Gull explained, when I asked about them, that from childhood yellow women of the better classes had their feet bound, with the toes cruelly turned under, to make their feet small, for this was considered a mark of great beauty. Venerable called his wife's feet his "golden water lilies." My whole being ached at the thought of this torture every time the mistress peg-legged across my field of vision.

She carried a trembling little goggle-eyed dog in her sleeve to keep her hands warm.

I broke one of her painted vases, a gem of the T'ang dynasty, and rather than having me beaten, which I could have borne easily, she punished me, so that my heart felt empty as a gourd in my chest, simply by looking sadly at me, as if I were a brainless animal. Her eyes! Deep brown glittering pupils half hidden, seeming to *lurk*, under the epicanthic fold of skin that was the yellows' sure mark: they reduced me to jelly.

Venerable Shen moved about the mansion like a great cloud, edged and colored with the reverence that seemed to be due him. He was an official of the first class, a member of the College of Literature, which had had its one thousandth anniversary just the year before; its members were chosen from among those who had taken highest honors in the Triennial Examinations, and it supervised all new literature, instructed the Emperor, the Dragon Countenance, in the classics in the Hall of Literary Glory, composed prayers for ceremonies, gave honorific names to Imperial wives and concubines, and issued patents of nobility. Our master held the envied post of sub-curator of the Great Encyclopedia of Yung Lo, which consisted of twenty-three thousand volumes. Gull said, "He has the fragrance of books on him." He was also, somewhat less gloriously, a functionary of the Board of the Imperial Horse Department, in charge of processions, and of cleaning up after processions. All this honor, which had not come to him without considerable outlay of the Shen family funds, understandably made him nervous; he constantly rolled two brass balls in his right hand and wore a mask of sagaciousness on his face.

He called Big Madame "duck." Gull told me that the *yüan-yang*, the Mandarin duck, was the yellows' symbol of connubial bliss. This word "duck" he uttered without cracking his wise mask.

The master and mistress both had the disconcerting habit of laughing when they heard anything unpleasant.

There were tree geraniums and vivid varieties of chrysanthemums in the courtyards, and pomegranates were ripening; thrushes sang in cages in the side chambers. All the beauties around me, cultivated by the yellows with ritualistic self-consciousness, only made me the sadder.

The days were like Arizona's, hot and dry, but Gull told me just to wait, I would see Gobi dust storms and gray cold that would make me forget Arizona. Too bad, she said, that I had not been given a few years in one of the intermediate provinces to thicken my blood, as many of the slaves in the capital had been. Maybe I would be lucky and die of a lung ailment.

Gull explained my name to me: the lotus was perfection rooted in mud and slime.

When Gull took me into the city I fought off the whirling of my head at all the strange sounds: screeching hubs of barrows and carts, hawkers' wailing songs, bells and gongs shaking the air from towers, firecrackers in temple courtyards, hammers on anvils —and slaves laughing, slaves wildly laughing. Wherever I went I heard the bitter laughter of slaves.

The yellow man's language made my tongue so gibbous I felt sick all day, but Gull taught me well, and I was eager to learn, because this was the only way I could talk with other whites, all of whom used their masters' speech. Once I got the hang of the lilting tones I learned fast.

Gull inquired in the market about my friends. Their names, like everything else on earth, were changed. Kathy Blaw was now Old Pearl—a bad name, Gull said, because the word for pearl was a homophone for pig. Gabriel was called Nose. Mayor Jencks was Lapdog—humiliating!

At home a proverb had come into use, since the defeat in the Yellow War, which was ironic indeed now: "A free man's name is never lost."

I asked Gull what she had learned about Kathy, or Old Pearl.

A horrid master, Gull said. A carpenter, a morose man who lived alone. Old Pearl was his only slave. He gave her orders by means of furious gestures.

What about the one called Nose?

His master, Gull said, was Venerable Wu. She knew one of Wu's slaves, Wu's Moon Pot.

What sort of master was he supposed to be?

Gull shrugged—so-so.

Had this Moon Pot said anything about the one called Nose?

Yes, Gull answered, she had said the new slave was noisy, boastful, and wild, and she thought he would soon be a drunkard.

Gabriel? Was Gull *sure* this was the man who was sold in the lot with me?

He was the same one, Gull said.

⟨ Eelskin Bows

Time passed and my hair grew out. The mistress and master kept saying that I was a pretty child, that they wanted me to feel that I was part of the family. They said this to me often through Gull, and when I was far enough along in their speech they said it directly to me. "You are an agreeable little heathen, dear child," the mistress said to me once. The word she used for "heathen" was strange to me, and I had Gull translate it later. By stages I was led to the point of all this: the dutifulness, the submissiveness, the reverence for authority and for propriety and for tradition, that were at the heart of the yellows' beliefs. If I was the Shens' pretty child, I had the most profound duties toward them, even toward the whole hive of their ancestors, to whom incensed smoke constantly curled in the shrines in the Pomegranate Court. Venerable Shen was gentle in manner toward me, for, according to his beliefs, his wish for good treatment from his superiors required of him a corollary sweetness toward his inferiors.

Nevertheless, one day he took me, with Old Bow, On Stilts, and Gull, and three rented camels, into the groves to the east of the city, where many of the capital gentry with their slaves were gathering firewood against the coming winter. There was a celebratory look about the bright colors of the various slave uniforms. Bow, who was too old for it, chopped and split, with On Stilts; and Gull and I, who were too frail for it, made up the split logs into cylindrical bales and loaded them on racks on the kneeling camels' backs, while Venerable Shen stood and talked with other yellow slaveowners about—how smug they were!—their own vandalism: what a shame it was, they piously said, to cut down these ancient cypresses, these silver pines renowned in all the empire.

I was stumbling along with a bale of fragrant wood when suddenly I had a sensation of having been doing exactly this thing in exactly this place once before.

Then I saw why. Near the path a familiar pair of shoulders, dappled with trembling tree shade, was swinging to chop in a seen-before way. It was Gabriel, now Nose, bare to the waist. I called toward his back in a brassy tone that I did not wholly feel; I had learned to imitate Gull's two manners, which I took to be the accepted ones: ceremonious and noncommittal to the masters, and open, bluff, and a bit noisy to fellow slaves.

At once Nose turned, and I almost dropped the kindling to put a hand to my mouth, for I was barely able to keep from laughing (because of astonishment and chagrin) at what I saw.

Nose's forelocks were braided into four small plaits tied up with silky eelskin; his eyes were bloodshot and distant.

I had seen slaves in the market with their hair arranged in this bizarre way; Gull had said that those were the loud boys, the roughs.

Nose, speaking in the yellow man's language, asked me indifferently how I was. His voice was hoarse.

I wanted to stop and talk to him about our Arizona village, about the *East Garden,* about difficult questions of obedience and rebellious feelings, but all I could blurt out was a question about Kathy Blaw, now called Pearl—seen her? The bundle of wood pulled painfully at my arms.

He shook his head. The plaits shook, too. An irrepressible giggle at the sight of the wobbling of the eelskin bows came up like nausea in my throat, and I ran on with the firewood, and by the time I had reached the camels I thought my arms would break off, and I had a miserable heavy feeling in my chest, and I was on the edge of tears.

([I See the City

Gull took me with her on errands to get me used to the city. The capital was a nest of cities: at its heart, the Forbidden City, containing the golden-roofed Imperial palaces, with crenelated purple walls and a moat; around that, the red-walled Imperial City, with headquarters of the Imperial boards, and Imperial temples, and Imperial pleasure grounds along the shores of three lakes, called, as if all continents met here, the North Sea, the Central Sea, and the South Sea; and surrounding that in turn, the Tartar City, with its massive walls and huge gate towers, the living space of the nobles, the warriors, and the rich; and finally, appended in a great rectangle to the south, with a lower wall of its own, the Outer City, where lesser yellows lived.

One day Gull led me from the Shens' mansion, which was in the southwestern part of the Tartar City, not far from the Examination Halls, up to the Imperial Granary Market, near the Gate of Unmixed Blessings.

Everywhere in the streets whites were doing mortifying work: transporting yellows in ornate sedan chairs, carrying too heavy loads of charcoal or grain or bricks or tiles on shoulder poles, sprinkling down the capital's dust with foul-smelling water from the nauseating open sewer ditches. To right and left we saw in our frailty the red, yellow, blue, green, and purple glazed tiles, sparkling in the sun, of the roofs of the rich and the powerful.

I visualized as we walked that wonder-struck look on Nose's face when he had been put up for sale by Big Number One. Why did Nose upset me so? Every time I thought of him, I thought of home; thoughts of home became thoughts of Nose. As we entered the crowded market I searched the faces of slaves, yearning to see him.

As we came to the area where vegetable carts were hub to hub, a slave woman belonging to a farmer (for she wore plain blue jacket and trousers), with a basket slung from a halter over her shoulder, passed close to us, chanting shrill cries in the masters' language and stopping now and then to chaffer out a sale. Not understanding her chants, I ducked over and looked in her basket: peanuts roasted in the shell.

Gripped by a sudden craving, I begged Gull to buy me some, and she did, with coppers from the mistress's market purse. As we jostled through the press of hucksters and slaves, I opened peanuts and munched them and drifted into a memory: of rushing after school into our compound and to our dark little kitchen, getting down from a shelf a Mason jar of peanut butter that my own mother had ground, and lavishing a broad blade's load of it on a piece of the bread she baked herself; seeing out the window the sharp shadows of eaves on the dusty ground, the glistening skin of Sam Quill repairing the Carboots' loom shed across the way, a compound cat named Cal Coolidge watching a peewee in the scraggly locust near the wall.

Gull took some of my peanuts and loudly cracked them, and she laughed at my vacant look. "You've already got the peanut madness," she said. It seemed that every slave in the capital had a wild craving for peanuts, which, like some hypnotic drug, induced, on being eaten, thoughts of faraway homes and almost unbearable yearnings.

I remembered the peanut husks piled knee-deep in our slave yard at the Shens'.

Another day, early in the morning, under orders from Venerable and papered with long-winded permits, Gull and I carried some heavy books of his from his mansion to his place of work at the Hall of Literary Glory, within the Forbidden City. Here was a queer fact: yellows, other than mandarins of the Imperial staff and eunuchs, could not enter the Forbidden City, yet any slaves bearing credentials could. The key to this riddle: we slaves must not have been regarded as fully human.

Through Heaven Peace Gate and Earth Peace Gate we approached the fearsome Meridian Gate up a walled way. It was the hour of the entrance of mandarins of the Imperial staff—Venerable Shen was in the group of them waiting to enter ahead of us. Before the Meridian Gate stood six elephants, facing each other in pairs, their trunks intertwined and their tusks meeting. A bell rang. The elephants released each other's trunks, drew back, and knelt. The mandarins went through. We, and a handful of other slaves waiting to enter, were driven through the terrifying elephants' gamut at a run by guards shouting and waving bamboo beating rods. Then the elephants arose and locked the way again. At the gate itself stood four yellow eunuchs at least seven feet tall, bearing enormous curved swords, and overhead on the gate tower I saw batteries of brass cannons peeping out between merlons of Manchurian cedar.

Running into the awesome area within, feeling smaller and smaller as the weight of the books crushed my shoulder, I thought: our fearful Syndicate at home, whose power had overwhelmed our village, had used a handful of men in ordinary suits with pistols and swords. The yellow power was unimaginably greater.

Yet how Gabriel had cringed that day in the patio at Palm Springs, his forehead chalky with California dust where he had bowed it to the ground—and how insolent he seemed here!

After delivering the books we were shut in a dark room all day; we were allowed to leave the Forbidden City only at the evening parting of the elephants.

Late one afternoon when Old Bow was busy polishing the brass conch shells studding the Shens' gates, and On Stilts, Cock, and Bean were all somehow engaged, Bow asked Gull and me to fetch the family's tea water in place of two of the men. Carrying buckets on the ends of shoulder poles, we went eastward from our house to the so-called Jade Spring Courtyard of a yellow man named Yang, who, though rich, charged his townsmen coppers to draw from his well its sweet water, the least alkaline and puckery in all the Tartar City. Master Yang was a trading merchant, a familyless widower, Gull told me, away with caravans for long periods, and during his absences his well yard was a merrymaking place for men slaves, presided over by Yang's Otter, who collected the round copper cash with square holes at their centers, for the water. We found about twenty uniformed slaves in the courtyard when we reached it, in clumps chatting, laughing, shelling peanuts, pitching their masters' coppers to a wall. A boxing match was taking place off to one side, and men were shouting their bets.

Upon our arrival the slaves gathered around Gull and me making bawdy jokes and proposals, and Gull broke into quick mock-furious rushes at some of them. She seemed half pleased, half angry. Young as I was, I could not help knowing that much of their play was directed at me. Out of the crowd our Mayor Jencks, Tung's Lapdog now, stepped forward, dressed in a blue silk jacket and a black cloth hat, and he made a show of being familiar with me. He was rather grand, and he tried to condescend to me, yet I felt that I had an importance, bestowed on me by the ruttish slaves, to which he wanted to attach himself.

The slaves' remarks gave me strange feelings—my hands were too bony and narrow, my legs were crooked, my hair still stood out straight from my head.

"Leave her alone," Lapdog said in the yellow language, rubbing my shoulder as if it were a piece of polished hardwood.

I hastily asked him (giggling when I called him Lapdog) if he had seen any of our village people. Kathy Blaw?

Lapdog's speech in the yellows' tongue was stilted; pidginish yet flowery. "Old Pearl," he said, "is in number-one prosperity."

I asked about Nose, but I supposed I would get nothing of value from the old man; he was as pompous as ever, he spoke for effect, his eyes slid about to see whether the other slaves were listening to his words. Pearl—in "number-one prosperity" with her crabbed carpenter?

But Lapdog surprised me. He grew angry, spat on the ground, stamped in the spittle. "Nose is going the wrong way," he almost shouted. I waited, puzzled, looking an anxious question, I suppose. "I saw him drunk," he said, then he raised his voice. "That boy— I remember him!" And he rapped his chest, as if to conjure up a picture of a powerful young man who had somehow been *his* creature.

When our water pails were filled Gull and I trotted off with the steady jogging pace that the carrying poles required. I experienced rushes of feeling—anger at our old mayor's portentous manner, concern over what was happening to Nose, fury at the yellows' heavy tea water, and unfamiliar surges of elation at thoughts of the white men's eyes on me in Yang's courtyard, and of their harm-

less jokes that made me feel so gawky as the rope coiled around
the squeaking drum of the well.

❮[Boxing the Board

        One afternoon, while Gull and I were buying food in the
farmers' market in the Outer City, near the Fox Tower, we saw
that a sale of newly arrived slaves was in progress.

I had a moment's crazy hope that my father might be among
the prisoners, but the weak wish had faded before we could even
push close enough to see the faces of the whites cringing on the
platform.

Though I had been in the yellows' capital only a few months I
thought I could tell those miserable creatures in their trader's
chemises and drawers that their terrors were misplaced, that they
should not be afraid of what they feared but of what they did not.
I felt as if I had a wild hen in my throat that would fly out cackling if one of these trembling souls should ask me if "they" were
going to eat him.

There were no Arizonans announced among those brought
straight across the ocean.

Turning aside as the sale dragged on, we saw a crowd of both
yellows and whites gathered near a market godown, and we moved
toward it, and I heard shouts and ahs. Men slaves were boxing
for coppers on a wide plank in an open circle. The boxers, stripped
to the waist, feet bare and fists ungloved, were required to stay on
the great plank, four paces long and one pace wide, which slaves
at the four corners held in place on the ground. The boxer who
could knock his opponent off the plank with a clean blow would
win. Sometimes, when the sparring grew especially boisterous, the
four plank-holders, with started veins and excited eyes, would lift
the plank a span or two off the ground, and the boxers would
bounce and sway on their fluttering feet.

The yellows, who had no hand boxing of their own, and who
deplored naked competitiveness but seemed enchanted by the
sight of it, tossed coins, by way of applause, toward one end of the
plank or the other. I felt at first a disgust that the sport we had
called at home the manly art of self-defense should have been
turned now to beggars' uses.

Gull told me that these boxing slaves were from the Drum Tower

Boys, a gang of roughs and dandies among the slaves whose gathering place in whatever hours they could steal from their masters was the foot of the great structure, twenty times as high as a house, in the northern part of the Tartar City, from which an enormous drum sounded curfew over the whole city each evening.

I clutched at my breast with a reflex gesture of grasping for my lost locket of the Guevavi martyr, for I now saw Nose among the men cheering the boxers on the plank. Was he a Drum Tower Boy, or trying to be?

Ambitious Nose! My heart sank when I looked closely at him. His forelocks were done up in those plaits tied with eelskin; his eyes were red. He wore an old embroidered silk jacket that he must have wheedled from his master, which looked odd over short coolie trousers; his strong calves and his feet were bare. He was already some kind of dandy himself, and rough enough.

All this game of "boxing the board," as our men called it, was against the yellows' laws, I well knew. Gull had spent rich hours telling me of the two levels of the yellow man's laws—the laws for himself, and those for us. He could gather and loiter; we could not. He could game; we could not. He could vend food from a wheelbarrow; we could not. A yellow could slap a yellow's face, but twenty days in chains for a white who tried it.

Gull had told me of these distinctions not with resentment but simply as matters of fact; she shunned trouble.

But Gull had carefully shown me, too, that slaveowners could not maintain an eternal vigilance; there were times when the yellow man would wink his eye and times when his stare was averted—safe moments to cavort. His double standard bred our evasion, sometimes in the open, as with this bold boxing at the market, and sometimes where and when he never guessed.

Now a boxer fell from the plank, and another took his place. In the knot of slaves on the sidelines, Nose was aggressive, loud, and quite transformed from the eager, conscientious leader of work he had been at home. I knew that he had seen me, but he paid me no attention.

On an impulse I broke away from Gull and ran to the clump of men and straight to Nose, and I thumped his chest with my fist and shouted in his face in English, "Box, man!"

For a moment he looked at me with surprise and, I thought, distaste, but then with a scooping motion he swept me off my feet and began to jog around carrying me in a sitting position and chanting with bad grammar in the yellows' language like a pack-man, "Big Nose got big fish! Big fish! Big Nose sell. Two copper big mackerel fish! Two copper!"

I was mortified by the laughter I heard, and I could smell the acrid fumes of millet liquor on Nose's breath; I felt like weeping, yet I felt like squealing and laughing, too.

Still carrying me, Nose trotted toward the plank and jostled the two boxers from it, who gave him murderous looks, and he began to whirl on it with me in his powerful arms. I felt the jarring of his bare feet on the board under us. The slaves gathered around clapping. The yellows laughed harder than ever. I grew dizzy.

Out of the spin Nose threw me away, and I sprawled on the ground, and as Nose leaped from the plank a square ugly man and a tall fat one took his place, to box. I stood up unsteadily and dusted myself; Nose was strutting away. He would not look at me again, and he disdained the shower of coppers tossed toward him in the dirt. Other slaves scrambled for them on their hands and knees.

(Family Life

There came a chill on the air, and it settled in me. Gull said that the bad season had not begun; I waited in disbelief for the iron weather she described.

By day I heard my name called through the courtyards of the house: "White Lotus! White Lotus!"—or a tiny handbell rang three times for me.

The mistress, it seemed, could do nothing alone, not even dress herself, and I thought she must be weak, but one day she wanted to have a teak ceremonial table moved, to see how it would look at another side of a room, and, impatient at being unable to raise On Stilts or Cock with tinklings, she heaved on one end herself, with me on the other, and I saw that after all she was a plantain, having tough fibers hidden in soft little leaves. She was, however, utterly helpless in the presence of her little boy, Young Venerable, who tyrannized her. She spent hours with her favorite mocking thrush, teaching it to mimic a dog, a cat, a hawk, a rook, a crying baby, and a falsetto slave actor; and other hours combing her bug-eyed sleeve dog; and other hours with her collection of fans, opening one after another, blowing out the dust, gazing at the paintings on them. Once she showed me some fans with double folds—decorous peonies or peacocks if you opened them one way, but if you swiveled the blades the other way there were pictures of men and women who seemed to have taken leave of all sense of propriety, in various degrees of dishevelment, wrestling in strange positions like wild street urchins; Big Madame giggled over these. Often she was playful and tender with me and called me her sweet child and fondled me in ways that made me blush ferociously, but once I entered her chamber, the Pear Blossom Rest, on an errand, thinking her in another courtyard, and found her lying on her quilts weeping; when she saw me she started up and began to scream at me, calling me a vile, mangy cat.

The master was tall, like many of the northern yellows, and brilliant—at seventeen, in the Triennial Examinations, he had rated second of all the candidates—and in his brilliance he was cold and distant. Even his courtesies and gentlenesses were formal, and his flickering sense of humor was, whether he knew it or not, cruel. He played wailing music on a wooden flute at night, and sometimes leaned for hours over a board of a chesslike game called "surrounding pieces" with his friend the curio dealer P'an. One night, summoned by Big Madame's three jingles to the Pear Blossom Rest, I accidentally saw Venerable Shen ready for bed— an apparition. The front part of his crown was shaved, and in back his queue was unbraided and a cascade of black hair fell nearly to his waist; his long, curved fingernails against his pale gray sleeping gown gave me gooseflesh. He was fatherly toward me, and sometimes, manifesting his kindly feelings with a gesture, he laid a hand on my arm, and I felt his claws of idleness on my skin. Hooo! I was frightened by him. Under the yellows' unfailing courtesy and graceful motions lay a strain of implacability: Gull told me that they punished disobedient slaves by breaking their legs.

As I made rapid progress in the master's language, I was humiliated by his explanations to me of simple things, so over-patient and obvious. We had an Arizonan proverb, that a man ought not to try to show a child the sky.

Very grand was Venerable Shen; among the four classes of men —scholars, farmers, workmen, and merchants—he was undoubtedly at the summit of the highest, and there seemed to be an air of elegance in his mansion, and it was not until much later that I began to see the Shens as being rather seedy. Venerable Shen's paternal great-grandfather had been a Marquis, but in the yellows' nobility there was a descending succession of aristocracy, each eldest son ranking lower than his father; first-order titles had passed out of the Shen family. Their money was being wasted on clinging to what was left. Six slaves were not many; a curio dealer for a bosom friend!

Strange family life! At home in Arizona our village had seethed with active doings—chores for all, tales or games in idle hours. Here were three Shens and six slaves in a prolonged hush. Big Venerable and Big Madame and Big Young Venerable nodded, bowed, pressed their folded hands together. Some evenings the master would sit in the Peony Study and recite for his son the poems of Li Po, Tu Fu, and Po Chü-i, but the boy would fidget, and the readings often broke up with stiff lectures on etiquette.

The moment the master took off in his green sedan chair for work in the mornings, with all four of his male slaves on the shafts, even creaking Old Bow—at that moment the etiquette seemed to trickle out of Big Young Venerable like a bladderful of urine. Sometimes in a temper this urchin, in appalling breaches of the code of submissiveness, lifted his fist and struck his mother, who rewarded him for his blows with tearful hugs. Toward us slaves, he was like a coyote pup, skulking at the edge of cover, just out of reach, ragging us with nasty noises. He would lurk in doorways and jump out at me, and I would nearly die of fright.

The queerest sensation I had in that household was the feeling of *not being there.* When the three Shens were eating together at their low table, and especially when there were guests, the yellow people did not just ignore me as I served; they were simply not aware of my existence. They talked as if I were a screen panel. More than once *they discussed me* while I moved about the room, as if servitude and whiteness were deafness and dumbness. Had I been less unnerved, I might have heard, when the subject changed, incautious words.

The leaves slipped off the trees, and for many days rain fell, not a hearty spattering downpour on thirsty crops but a mizzling dampness that descended like choking wet smoke. I kept up an outward cheerfulness, thanks to fat Gull's example, but deep in my chest there lay a swamp, as if all the weeping drizzle of the yellow man's eleventh month had drained and settled there in the form of pure liquid sorrow.

⟨[Clapper and Rod

On Hata Gate Street, one afternoon, Gull and I heard a handbell ringing, and then we saw Wu's Nose, my childhood hero Gabriel now gone so fierce, tied to the tail of a donkey cart, bare to the waist, with livid wales across his back, accompanied by two yellow officers—a bell-ringer and a beater; Gull told me that this procession would stop at every corner along the street and the two men would give Nose strokes of bell clapper and bamboo rod. Neither of us wanted to see a stop, and we ran into a side alley.

Panting, Gull said she had heard that Nose had been caught stealing a length of Shantung silk. "This is not the first time," she said.

"How did you hear about it?"

"Moon Pot told me."

"Why did he do it?"

"He did it," Gull said, "just to do it." I had a queer feeling that she was praising him for his crime, but she turned on me with a stern expression and said, "If you steal, you'll follow the cart, too."

That night I was so homesick I had to bite the rotten straw matting on which I lay, to keep from sobbing. I remembered the cods on the cottonwood trees at home, nutlike globes that would burst open when ripe and suspend on the wind a whole bird flock of sunny white down. And then I imagined, as clearly as if the sun itself had intruded into our dark, stale-smelling room, Gabriel's slow, serene walk across the compound, his jeans closely encasing his moving thighs. He was coming toward me. His arms were spread wide.

⟨[Universal Yellowness

The mistress heaped clothing on me, and still I shook— with incredulity, fear, and chills.

Then one day a weird yellow cloud, as tall as a desert thunder-head, came down across a spotless blue sky from the northwest, and, just as Gull had threatened that one would, a three-day Gobi Desert dust storm descended on us. The wind blew, a dry yellow fog enveloped us, and dust—my enemy in the mansion—drifted into all the rooms, like mountain snow, under sills, through door cracks, penetrating the solid roof, it seemed, until we coughed with breathing the fine stuff, and it gritted in our teeth, and it scratched at our eyeballs.

Big Madame was upset: such storms usually came in the spring. This untimely visitation from the sky was, she said, an evil augury. A report came that at the height of the dirty blizzard the Dragon Countenance Himself had gone in secret to the Temple of Heaven to pray the evil away.

I wanted to go to my brick bed in our slave quarters and bury my head in cloth. The whole world yellow! Yellow to me was the color of terror, cannibalism, sailors leering at weak nakedness, goat faces, little snarling Young Venerable behind a door, the master in his gray gown with his hair loosened at night. This endless swirling gaseous cloud, seeming to challenge me, the poor duster of the Shens' mansion, to clean the whole sky, poured its dry issue on us until the ground was covered, the streets were drifted, the roofs were capped, the black bones of the trees were aged with dust.

On certain mornings Big Madame had the habit of going to worship at the Cypress Grove Temple, in the northern sector of the Tartar City, not far from the Drum Tower; she rode there in Venerable's chair, carried by two rather than four slaves, for she was a personage of less worldly importance than her husband, and she liked to have me run along behind, to fuss over her at starts and stops, to handle her wolfskin lap robe, to pick up her fan if she dropped it, smooth her cloak, spread her shawl. I soon understood that Big Madame Shen took me not because she needed my services but because my presence proved she had a white handmaid. Thus by her helplessness she showed her power.

The morning the dust storm cleared she summoned me from my hopeless task of cleaning the house to dress her for the temple. She wanted to help pray off the bad luck the storm had brought. I wrapped myself in one of her castoff cloaks and presented myself at the front gate for departure. Poor Old Bow, whose joints ached, was between the front shafts of the chair, and ineffectual Bean was behind, and when we started Bow jogged along, in a ragged Manchurian fur cap with side flaps bouncing against his head like a dog's ears, and he sang out for gangway to whatever blocked our way, and with every shout he seemed to breathe out a great puff from his brass-bowled pipe—though of course he was not smoking. I, running behind the vehicle, saw that my own breath condensed the same way; it was bitterly cold. I padded along in the universal yellowness of dust. There had never been anything like this in Arizona.

Tingling we reached the temple. It seemed that the mistress expected us to wait an hour for her at the sedan chair. My fingertips felt numb, and my ears burned with the cold. "Sit in the footwell of the chair and bundle up in the wolfskin, my child," she said with Confucian sweetness which did not warm me.

Once the mistress was gone, we heard in the street the snorting and stamping, muffled in Gobi dust, of horses in the traces of carriages that had brought noble and rich worshippers, and the shaking of harness bells, and the sneezing of sedan bearers. Bow said to me, "Go to Chao-er's. Fourth house on that lane toward the tower." He pointed. "Other smalls will be there."

"And you?"

"I have to stay with the Flying Commode," he said. This was his name for the green-trimmed sedan chair. Big Madame defecated in a close stool at home, which it was Bow's honor to empty after her every performance; it looked like the housing of the sedan, which Bow sarcastically thought of as her mobile toilet seat. He loathed having to carry it, yet he loved it, too, as a beautiful object that was under his charge. From a compartment in the rear under the passenger's seat he got out some linseed oil and brass polish to touch up the arabesques of fine bamboos and the shaft ends with wrought-brass tiger heads. "Go along, girl. It's warm in there. There'll be pigs and sows there. Take her along to Chao-er's, Bean."

I was timidly willing to go. I knew that Chao-er's tavern near the Drum Tower was a place where men slaves stole half hours when they were supposed to be running errands, and where some of the more daring women slaves also went on sacrifice days to pass the time while their mistresses worshipped at the Cypress Grove Temple or the Great Lama Temple or the Temple of Confucius, all nearby.

"Won't you come with us, Old Bow?"

"Later. Go on."

With silly Bean I ran into the lane, holding up the trouser legs of my uniform, along packed ruts in the drifted dust, past the cooper Chang's, to a gate on which was painted a rooster perched on a shoemaker's last—for, as I knew, Chao-er hid his tavern behind the pretense of being a mender of worn cloth shoes.

The moment I pulled shut, behind me, the large door of the high-roofed room in the main courtyard, I knew I had found some sort of home. A large dark room, full of slaves, heavy low beams, an acrid smell of charcoal smoke and pipesmoke and wine slops, a crude billiard table and a crap table, loud shouts and hearty laughs, cards and white hands slapping down; a feeling, at last, of a raucous corner of an Arizona compound in twilight, after work, after food, after a hot day. I knew no one, and no one knew me, but groups drew me to them. I moved in a species of whirling dance from one clump to another. Three yellow girls and an older yellow woman were serving drinks to the whites, and I saw a slave pat one of the yellow girls on her buttocks; she flipped a finger under the white man's chin. An arm hugged me, a deep voice growled in my ear. I spun away. I heard, amid laughter, the word "slanthead"—our secret name of contempt for the yellows. A taste of spirits from a stranger's rice-ware cup; I spat it out on the floor, because it made me think of the vinegar on the ship. Peanuts were cracking like a chorus of crickets. Old Bow came in; he stood alone by the central iron brazier a few minutes, with a down look, and then went back out to the Flying Commode.

I recognized some of the Drum Tower Boys, and once as I passed their circle I thought I heard the name Nose spoken. I leaned against a doorjamb near the men and listened.

"Which Nose is that?" (Quite a few slaves had that name; the yellows thought our prominent Caucasian noses a splendid joke.)

"I mean Wu's. The new man a few months ago. You know the one I mean?"

"I know him."

"Been beaten with the heavier bamboo."

"Truth? Ayah!"

"He did a mad-ride. His Big Venerable caught him on a mad-ride."

I had heard of these "mad-rides." Sometimes when slaves rode their master's carriage horses or mules bareback out to water them at one of the ponds within the Tartar wall north of the Imperial City, and back, they would gallop the horses fiercely through the city streets to show their own courageous bad blood.

"That Nose—he's all right. He's purely ugly."

"Small Wolf and him—did you hear about those two in a fight over at Yang's tea water?"

"Which Wolf? You mean Shih's Wolf?"

"Yes, that's the one."

"Ayah. That newcomer fight *him*? He's a bad one! Just bare-knuckle? On a board? How did they fight?"

"He's going to get cut," a new voice said. "This Nose, he'll get sliced. Wolf has a fish knife."

"No, no, no! Those two are soulmates now. Wolf loves a forward man."

I leaned against the jamb listening to this, my heart pounding. I wanted Nose to fight Wolf; I hoped Nose would be captain of all the tavern boys. I was thrilled by his badness. I had a moment of being tempted to swish my childish hips out to these roughs and tell them that Nose was from *my* village, and that I had a hot heart, too. I was giddy on the fumes and shouts in the tavern. . . . But I sucked my lip and moved on.

A slave in a shabby castoff Tartar greatcoat lined with fleece, with a cloth wound round his head and under his chin, stood in the door and shouted, "Ch'ien, Wei, Wang, Sun, Hsü, Shen, Lin, Feng—all out!"

I knew that this meant that my mistress, among others, was about to leave the temple; this man had evidently been a lookout. Bean and several other slaves hurried with me back to the sedan chairs and carriages. I wrapped myself in the wolfskin. Old Bow looked half dead with cold.

(At the Tavern

The giddiness persisted, and my mistress praised me twice that day for being a willing girl.

That night I lay a long time on the edge of sleep, whirling in my mind from group to group in the smoky tavern. Bow had lit a brief fire of chips in the oven under my brick bed, but I felt the warmth ebb quickly out of the hard surface. Gull was breathing her deep-sleep draughts, broken by sighs that seemed to vent all the misery her ample daytime cheerfulness masked.

Suddenly I was sitting straight up, shivering. I had heard in my ear once again the deep male growl—the sharp sand of a man's ill-shaved face against my cheek, a metal-band arm around my waist—from which I had spun away with a high laugh at the tavern. Now the words of that growl had come really through to me, I suppose, for the first time.

The voice had said, "Come over here some night, girl! When big master snores. We could play a game, eh?"

I was so excited I wakened Gull. I knew that some nights she had not come to our bedroom at all, and On Stilts and Cock were often absent, too. Shaking her, leaning over her, I whispered in her ear, begging her to tell me how to sneak out at night.

"You cold, child?" she asked in a mumble, still three quarters asleep.

But I shook her until her head was clear, and I asked her again to tell me how to run out.

"Big Venerable Shen will kill you," she said. "If you run out, he'll kill you."

I teased her to tell me. She pretended to fall back asleep, but I would not let her be, and I pleaded, and finally she told me what to do—quite gladly, I thought—and she said, "Getting used to the city, eh?" She dropped off in her sigh-rocked sleep, then.

I delayed three nights, lacing up my courage and waiting for a clouded sky.

In the end it seemed easy. We finished cleaning up, stretching out our work until the Shens had retired. After Bean had locked all three of the street gates with large beams held in place by crude bronze locks, and had gone to bed and fallen at once into his pathetic dog-sleep, with much smacking of dewlaps and running in his dreams, Gull filched the lock keys from his miserable box of belongings at the head of his bed mat, right beside his ear, and, going out with me, she showed me how to unlock and lift out the beam of one of the side gates. We returned to our room. I waited an hour in darkness. I heard a timekeeper's gong in the empty city streets: first quarter of the night. I cloaked myself and wrapped rags around my feet, and I let myself out the gate and pulled it shut. It did not matter to me—or to the other slaves who sneaked out, it seemed—that robbers could then have walked right into the mansion grounds.

The night was not as dark as I had hoped it would be. I ran across the deserted city, slinking along close to the walls, and I felt an alarming pressure of fear and ecstasy in the part of my throat where shouts get their impetus. The punishment for slaves being caught in the street after the Drum Tower's curfew was thirty strokes of the lighter bamboo on the bare back, even in winter, in a public place; and sometimes exposure in a cangue for a full day. Perhaps the master *would* kill me. My feet flew. My head cleared in the cold air. I saw no one. . . .

I leaned back against the door of the tavern hall, panting. The place seemed the same, yet not. Sounds—for safety at night—were subdued. Even the cracking of peanuts came in whispers. I was sharply let down. For a moment I was not at all sure whether I was child or woman.

A tall yellow man in a plain dun gown with an odd triangular mantis face on a stem neck, and thin shoulders, and an astonishing bump of belly like a slight-boned woman's pregnancy, came toward me, and I thought I was in trouble and I wanted to run home. But he was humble, stooping, soft-voiced, and he held his fists together in the yellows' gesture of appeasement, and he offered to bundle up my cloak and foot rags and place them on a shelf where I could find them later. He bowed to me and, with a look of one desperately eager to please, he remarked that I was "a new one." Who was my master?

I would not answer; my master was a potential killer, and I shook with fear in the presence of a yellow man who put on meekness and tried to spy out my owner's name.

The man said he was Chao-er, the cobbler, ha-ha. And he backed away.

Then I saw Nose, and I knew that the tavern was going to be home again, after all, but I did not go toward him. He was gambling over bamboo dominoes. Divination! What was his fate? What was poor mine? I moved with a cat's caution around the edges of the room.

Shih's Wolf, on a stool, had a yellow woman, whose slit gown of sky-blue silk showed half her thigh, sitting on his lap, and his hands swooped and fluttered around the girl's body as if they were swallows on the wing for a meal at dusk.

This was Nose's new friend, swilling a rancid brew the tavern served, made from millet and mixed with pigeon droppings to give it body.

I was asked to join a party. An old man slave was in this hushed carousal, Fang's Old Hammer, and he was foolishly drunk, but no matter how silly his words, the others showed him the gentleness and respect that was due the slave who would be soonest among us to die.

I was served a bowl of unheated *Shao-hsing,* a mild wine, under a surly impudent look, by one of the three yellow "foxes," as we called whores, whom I had seen on my first visit to Chao-er's, this one thickset and short, with high-colored cheeks but an unwashed look, and black hair in oily seaweed strings, and a grease-spotted plain blue gown. I banged a coin Gull had given me onto her wooden tray. I learned in due course that she was Cassia Cloud, a girl indentured to the tavern-keeper for four years at a low rate because she had been caught slitting purses in the marketplace in Tungchow. This stocky girl was said to be forward, saucy, bitter, and boring.

The yellow girl our people hated least was Peach Fragrance—a slave pointed her out to me, "over there sitting on what Wolf is proudest of"—for she was said to be open, freehanded, and kind, but deceitful.

There were, besides, two other slanthead women: Chao-er's wife, who was white-haired, with a face like an empty spoon, and his daughter Silver Phoenix, a timid, small, simpering girl. These two only cared about the tavern's money, I was told.

A slave urged me not to worry myself over cobbler Chao-er. That man was as soft as the down in one of our masters' quilts.

"If you tell that fellow he has a good heart," another white said, "he'll give you his house."

But, I thought, all the same, he's one of *them.*

I forced myself to drink the wine. It was cold. I had heard Venerable say one evening, "Wine is hot-souled. If you drink it cold, it will not evaporate from your body, and it will suck the vital warmth out of your organs." But we whites could not abide hot wine.

Nose's gambling came to an end, and carrying my wine bowl I joined his circle, with some of the Drum Tower Boys, named Fish Bait, Cabbage, Quack, and Fortune, and their white girls. Nose did not bother to look at me. He had developed a hoarse way of speaking. He was in a fine close-bodied slave coat of red felt piped with black silk; even in winter his calves and feet were bare, at least indoors. He could not move without seeming to swagger.

Various men told stories—bragged of fights, or sneered at their masters' foibles, or laughed down scrapes with women. Nose was loud, boastful, and thick-tongued.

I noticed that Wolf and Peach Fragrance went into one of several rooms across the courtyard, and later another slave named Card crossed to one of the rooms with the thickset waitress, Cassia Cloud.

Someone said, "Card will be sorry."

Another man said, "Ayah, she'll wrench it off him."

The crack of balls on the billiard table, the subdued dares of men shooting craps, the banging down of wine bowls. . . .

Nose boastfully recounted for his friends the execution of the great Mort Blain on the net boom of the *East Garden;* he did not mention the small part I had had in the hopeless mutiny. I could see that Nose already had a definite place among the toughs.

Rather soon the slave Card and stumpy Cassia Cloud came back across the courtyard. She was hotly rebuking the man, and he backed off, trying to quiet her. The tirade was not about money; we could hear that money was not in question. She stormed off to the kitchens. Card joined our group, settling down with an ostentatious wrinkling of his nostrils, as if he had smelled a bad odor. No one spoke to him, even in jest, because, as we had used to say in Arizona, when the hunter comes down from the hills carrying pinyon nuts, no one asks him for news of his hunting.

Someone plucked a muffled chord on a two-stringed instrument with a long pegged neck, like a guitar's, and a round body faced with snakeskin. Suddenly the man was playing "The Way You Look Tonight." I jumped to my feet, my heart pounding. My mind was full of rushing thoughts of a Halloween dance at the community center, back home, and then I thought of our gang's disfiguring village windows, late that witches' night, with pieces of soap, and being caught by one of our two village policemen, Officer Collard—and his earnest, heavy lecture on order and respect for property which made us children titter. And now, while the strummed music grew faster and faster, I became angry at Big Madame Shen's maddening talk of the virtues and proprieties— respect for the authority of all who were older, more elevated, more learned; prudence, fastidiousness, and abhorrence of roughness and cruelty; reverence for the past and for great exemplars of wisdom and moral rectitude; never-swerving sweetness to others. Only a master or a mistress, one who possessed the souls of others, could mouth such precepts and turn them to such shameless uses. What double meanings our life had! What could save one could kill another; nourish one, poison another; comfort, pierce; embolden, set to panic flight. This outlaw night in the tavern was neither good nor bad; it teemed with doubtful, ambiguous glimpses, pictures of frailty and hopeless hope—which the galloping, twanging notes of the fiddle, now in a fierce rhythm, had somehow set spinning around the room. I wondered if I was

drunk. The next thing I clearly knew was that the fiddler was playing one of the yellows' "sprout songs," at a slower pace, and Nose
was going through a besotted pantomime. He made a fairly
straight progress across the room: one heel out and up again, a
hand swinging low, pinched fingers snapping open, the same foot
arching high and its ball pushed rapidly down; then all with the
other foot and hand. Yes, planting! Planting corn! Nose was dropping seeds in heel marks in the furrowed ground and covering
them with swipes of his toes, as I had often seen him and others
do at home. I was filled with a stabbing delight of an order I had
never felt. In his bitter pain and maudlin drunkenness Nose was
using his mute body to speak of home to me alone in all the world.

⟨ The Emperor's Reception

I recovered some of my boldness. The mistress gave me
a worn-out gown of pale-green silk with a repeated pattern of the
formalized character *fu*, meaning "good fortune," which after
some patching I wore during off hours, and I walked in it as if
balancing a bowl on my head; my body was straight and the
pretty sheath clung to my moving hips—but to my disgust I
realized I had begun to imitate the elegant hobbling walk of rich
yellow ladies with bound feet. I stopped *that*. I caught up my hair
in multiple braids, which I fastened with throwaway ends of
satin bindings that a seamstress making undergowns for the
mistress had strewn on the floor. I did the work commanded of
me, and well enough, but I learned how to stretch it out, too,
and how to dissimulate. Once in a temper in the kitchen I dropped
and broke a platter with a willow so subtly painted on the china
that its long locks actually seemed to stir in breezes under the
glaze, and my mistress, who valued this piece, swooped on me,
and I pretended horror at my "carelessness," and feigned fear
(which to some extent, indeed, I felt), and my trumped-up
contrition was enough to make me laugh.

I found ways of getting around the town, and more than once
to Chao-er's; errands took time, after all.

One afternoon Big Madame Shen rang for me and ordered
me to bring her some buckets of hot water, and to help her bathe
and dress for a reception that the Dragon Countenance Himself

was to give that evening. . . . Her skin was a day-lily yellow, dotted with tiny goose pimples, and her breasts were soft. She sat in a teakwood tub and I bathed her, pouring dippers of water over her. It was my task, next, to stir into one of the buckets a great globe of elephant's dung, bought at a fantastic price from the Annamese keepers of the palace-guarding elephants, and to strain off the water, and to wash my mistress's hair with it. This was said to give black hair a brilliant gloss. I dried her and hung a satin undergown on her stubby nudity, and for an hour we dabbed, tugged, combed, patted, and smoothed, and when she was finally encased in a heavily embroidered court robe she was a middling sight. All through her dressing she nervously rehearsed the ritual kowtows and backings and bendings that she had been taught, in preparation for this event, during several visits to the Board of State Ceremonies.

At the spirit screen, upon departure, she said she wanted Bow and Gull to come and look at her; they over-exclaimed. She told me to wait up to help her prepare for bed.

The master smelled to the tips of the curving roofs with some smoky scent he was drenched in; he whirled around twice in front of his whites, enormously pleased with his appearance. He was so excited! Over a purple silk dress he wore a fur robe of sea-otter skin trimmed with ermine cuffs, and his Tartar hat had ermine ear flaps, and he had two waist-length chains around his neck, one of large amber beads, the other of red coral, from each of which was suspended a carved jade pendant. He was shod in new black-satin boots. What a jay!

The couple left in a rented carriage.

Later, when the other slaves had retired to our miserable bedroom, I went back to the Pear Blossom Rest to wait for Big Madame. All around me were the yellow woman's treasures. On her dressing table I straightened, with a growing agitation, the uproar of scent vials, paste pots, boxes of fingernail guards, jars of pomatum, pincushions in the shape of fat tigers, bowls of rouge, dishes of powder, mortars of unguents, cakes of washes, canisters of elephant dung, and small plates and spatulas for mixing and attaching all the touches of yellow-skin illusion. Then, trembling, I began an aimless rummaging on her shelves and in her drawers—put my coarse white hands on bone and coco-stick fans, on silk butterfly knots, on laced breast-and-belly aprons of the sort she used for modesty during intercourse, on

silk shawls and none-so-pretties, cauls and veils, tippets and
liripipes and lap robes. I was in a kind of rage. I threw open the
inlaid doors of her two great armoires, and suddenly I tore my
clothes off to my bare slave body as it had traveled across the
ocean in Big Number One's vomit-stinking slave ship, and I
dressed myself in one after another of this horrible Shen woman's
Shantungs, satins, pongees, habutais, tricots, lutestrings, sar-
senets, damasks, paduasoys, alamodes, calamancoes, ducapes,
poplins, soofeys, charkhanas, atchabanas, allapeenos. . . . In
each transformation I paraded back and forth before Nose's
imagined eyes: he lay sprawled on the bed in an otter gown
smelling to the borders of the province of smoky scent. . . .

Big Madame shook my shoulder. I started up in alarm. I saw
that I had been sleeping on the floor curled up around the warmth
of the mistress's brass handwarmer, in which charcoals were
dying away. I jumped to my feet and with a flood of relief saw
that before I had dropped off to sleep I had got back into my
slave uniform, and that all was put away, all the inlaid doors
were shut.

She babbled about the incursion into the Forbidden City. Her
eyes gave back the lantern glints that they had imbibed in the
Hall of Supreme Harmony all evening. She was truly happy, and
her heart was uncomfortably hot. She embraced me when she
was nearly naked.

"White Lotus, my child," she excitedly said, "our Big Venerable
was given the honor of drinking a bowl of wine face to face with
the Second Grand Secretary and the President of the Board of
Punishments. He stood less than an arrow's flight from the
Dragon Countenance. You would have been proud of him!"—
and she seemed to be granting me a right to such an unlikely
pride.

Soon this selfsame drinker appeared, in a long pearl-silk
sleeping gown, with his hair down, and he was rather abrupt.
"Send the girl away," he said. He evidently wanted to enter the
Pear Blossom Rest and exercise his rights. A certain imperious-
ness had rubbed off on him during the evening: he looked to
me like a gopher who had lost his mind and thought he was a
mountain lion. Fighting giggles, I ran out.

《 A Small, Dark Room

I lived for stolen hours, half hours, quarter hours, in the reeking tavern near the Drum Tower, for it seemed that the double-planked door of Chao-er's courtyard was strong enough to hold off the baleful, slave-nipping evil spirits with which every object in the yellow man's world appeared to be animated. Even the yellows who passed through that door seemed to shed, as they entered, these devils, elves, witch breaths. Lanky Chao-er, with his round gluttony affixed to his abdomen like a kitten clinging to a thin tree trunk, was a softhearted man, eager to please even us. He wanted especially to be thought a brave jack by our ruffians, Shih's Wolf, Ch'en's Fish Bait, and yes, Wu's Nose. How the checker stones cracked on the board when this senti- mental man captured an opponent's piece! His wife's function was to test whether coins were counterfeit by clinking them against true metal; beyond that she was nothing. The three yellow "foxes" in the tavern slept with white men for money— how could they be dangerous? Other yellows, worthless men and girls, joined the slaves from time to time; one Yü-li for instance, a slight, short, witty man, a professor of ritual swordplay, who kept saying that he loved to watch our men box and our women shell and eat peanuts, that he loved our innocent childish hearts and the way we moved. We wondered what he was really after.

We sat and talked, during one of these stolen hours on a cer- tain afternoon, of the unusual severity of that winter in the capi- tal. I asked a man, Tu's Sheep, if there would ever be an end to the iron cold, and he just banged me on the shoulder blades and laughed. There was famine in the outlying country. Chao-er said that wild dogs—the great lean long-haired creatures of which I was so terrified, *huang-kou,* or "wonks," as we called them—were running in packs in the frozen streets of the Tartar City, charging at chaise horses in broad daylight, and in the countryside these wonks were killing goats and chickens for a few minutes' lapping of blood. An old yellow with pitted cheeks, unpeeling the whites of his eyes, spoke of the way the pox had run, just like these packs of dogs, at rich and poor alike during the great plague, and had cut them down by thousands.

Wolf was there and, apparently stirred by the talk of wild wonks, he dared to change the subject and to speak, straight into

Chao-er's teeth, of a slave in Tsinan, in Shantung Province, who
had burned his master's house, and of several slaves on a ship
entering Tsingtao who had knifed the yellow sailors on the
lighter carrying them into the harbor, and of a slave called
Rocky who had collected a band of whites in Honan Province to
burn houses and kill yellows, and of the famous Hankow revolt.
Wolf stood as he hissed these subversive accounts and subtly
moved his hands and knees, as if he were boxing in the back of
his mind—but his eyes were righteous and severe. Yes, that was
it! The dissipated man spoke like a preacher. The tavern was
crowded with hints of our white God, and although nothing was
ever explicit or clear (if He came down, would He be Presbyterian, Lutheran, Catholic, Baptist . . . ?), we were nonetheless
bathed there in something like hope. This hope we bolstered in
every way we could. We drew lucky shapes in chalk on the floor.
A cob of yellow maize tied to a rooster's dried comb was hung
on a hook on the door.

My heart was thumping, and my mind fell, for some reason,
on San Pedro of Chaco Rico in his little birdhouse shrine at
home. . . .

Nose came in. He shook blown dust from his quilted outer
gown, blew on his hands, and came straight toward me. Perhaps
he saw the little porcelain patron of propagation crouching in
my eyes. He gave me a deep look and with a sudden single yelp
of exuberance he jerked his head toward the courtyard, and
when he turned to go I rose and followed him.

He led me across the courtyard into a small, dark room. He sat
on a k'ang and drew me, standing, close to him and buried his
head in my breast. When his face came up I could only see that
his eyes, though bloodshot and touchy, bloodshot, bloodshot, had
in them a flicker at least of his home self.

"I remember you, Gabe," I said, in English, in our lovely flat
Arizona accents, with a stuttering rush of not knowing what to
say or do, "I remember you one day in the clay pits . . ."—bare
to the waist, stretching every fiber of his broad back as he worked.
I meant to speak of the teasing way he had tossed bits of clay
at Agatha and me, but—

"No!" he said in the yellow's language with an ugly grimace,
and he made a gesture of throwing that memory across the floor
of the dingy room.

I was afraid to say anything else. It appeared that Nose did not want to talk—or to wait. I felt a peremptory tug at a cloth knot button in its loop at my throat, and as I stood still beside the brick bed, where Nose sat, the layers dropped one by one out of his fingers, which began to pay me the compliment of trembling: drab-colored padded winter gown, then the mistress's old green silk dress, a yellowish undergown ribbed with red, and another, of plain and patched slave cloth, next to my childish skin. He pulled me down. He drew a grimy quilted gown over us. I had not the slightest thought of right or wrong; all that mattered was: at last I was in a warm dark place in a cold yellow world. I said in a voice that seemed not my own—and tried to laugh—that Agatha and I had always been crazy about his bare shoulders. He shuddered, I suppose with distaste at this stupid remark. I knew in my too young heart that Nose would not be mine to claim, that there would be no relationship, but with my cheek I could feel the pounding, for the moment at least, of urgency for *me* in the arteries in his throat.

❴ On Fire

I believed next day that I was on fire with happiness, but it turned out to be a chest cold. I lay feverish on my unyielding mats for several days, with a cough that gripped me by the ankles and flung me like a whipthong against the wall. The master and mistress did not come into the slave quarters to see me; they sent word by Gull that they would have visited me but for the fear of carrying my contagion to Big Young Venerable, who was said to have delicate lungs in his body, which was in fact as rank and indestructible as a buzzard's. I gathered, however, that the master, though distant, was deeply concerned. After all, he had gambled a silver ingot on my surviving my first winter in the capital. He sent me a packet of ginseng and powdered deer antler to take with green tea to relieve my congestion. Gull took troubles for me that made me weep: Scouring the town to find what I needed, she made stews—of millet meal and pork, of chicken and rice—which were like home food and which, melting on my tongue, took me out of that drafty room into the full sunlight of my family compound at the hot heart of the dry season, with dust rising as Agatha and I ran in circles playing at owl and swallow.

(The Swearing

I was at work again, though not yet quite well—for the mistress was willing to endanger Young Venerable with my persistent barking because the house was falling down, as she put it, from neglect—when word came to our kitchen by the swift chain of whispers of the slave community that a white woman, Ma's Flax-head, had been horsed: driven around the icy streets of the city in a cart in which there stood a small wooden horse upon which Flax-head had been saddled to bring her public shame. This was a tour that was supposed to cure wanton yellow girls of whoring. Flax-head was the first white woman anyone could remember having been horsed. It seemed that Big Venerable Ma, trying to rouse one of his three slaves late at night to build a slack fire in his k'ang, had burst into their quarters and had found his slave boy Cricket mounted on his slave woman Flax-head without sanction of slave marriage—without, that is to say, the master's permission to couple.

Up to that time, news of a slave's punishment had inclined most of us to a short course of prudence, to a few days of sheepish industry and humility which infuriated us in the very moments when we displayed them, but for some reason the news of what had happened to Ma's Flax-head set up among us at the Shens', and among the Shihs' and the Changs' and other neighbors' slaves, a kind of giddiness and irresponsibility, a tendency to laugh too loud, to slur our manners before our masters, to act oafish, stupid, and clumsy.

I recklessly sneaked out to Chao-er's that very night.

It seemed to me that the smoky rooms were charged with excitement, perhaps on account of Flax-head's horsing, as if the whole crowd in the tavern were keyed up in some massive game of chance. I made my first skirting round. The slaves' clothes that night (the beholder's eye was like that of someone who had just stepped out into full sunlight, I confess) seemed bizarre, brighter than usual, splashed with declarative colors. Chao-er was tipsy. Yes, Nose was there—in a purple-trimmed suiting, his many braids tied up with gold ribbon. Wolf, Fish Bait, Card were there; and meaching-yellow Yü-li, the professor of swordplay.

At the door of the room where the table for the game like

billiards stood, I saw—gaunt, red-eyed, with the crushed look of
a lemon rind, all the tart juice squeezed away—the woman who
had been like a mother to me, Kathy, now Old Pearl.

Then she saw me, and she whooped so that heads turned all
through the room and the man about to shoot rapped his cue
butt furiously on the floor, and she ran to me, and I to her, and
we hugged and swayed.

We went in a corner and talked in English in our beautiful
Arizona tones.

How different this Pearl was from the Mrs. Kathy Blaw she
had been! That one whoop of recognition was all she contained.

"They call you White Lotus?" she said, soggy with cheap wine,
shaking her head.

I felt I must try to cheer her up. "Did you see Nose? See those
bows in his crazy hair?"

"Ftoo!" She waved away all that with a flap of her slender hand
riding down the spitting sound. "Lotus, I have a master. Big
Venerable Kao." She stretched out the name and spoke it with
a horrible rasp, and then she coughed. I coughed badly enough;
Pearl had a rattlesnake in her throat.

He was a carpenter. He had no woman. His woman had died.
He was bitter. He cursed all day. Today he threw a board end—
and Old Pearl put a hand on her hip and grimaced in tribute to
his aim.

Pearl's sadness, her helplessness, her lack of touch with me, or
anyone, or anything, were so profound that I wondered to what
hardpan depths all the wisdom of her numberless tales had
leached.

I took her with me around the crowded rooms, in which I could
feel an atmosphere of belligerency, muffled like the chatter that
other night, discreet where the yellows were concerned but nonetheless palpable. Men bumped each other in passing and took
offense, arguments climbed to the shouting stage, bets were heartfelt, and the old man, Fang's Old Hammer, drunk again, cursed
Chao-er to his face over some trivial brush. Some jack tweaked
Cassia Cloud, the stocky bad-tempered waitress, through her
gown as she passed, and being as usual out of humor she let
fly with a wine-slop rag across the slave's cheek, and *no one
laughed.*

The Drum Tower Boys were blustering, and when Pearl and I

moved to the edge of their circle, Nose, his eyes refusing to scurry for safety to his two villagers, suddenly began a queer tale of his first hunt at home.

. . . the older hunters took him up Chaco Rico for mountain lion, and at night by the fire he cleaned his gun, and in the morning, at the first weeping of doves, he cooked pancakes for the older men. Boss Carboot led the men out and placed them along a ravine, and they waited. A huge Mexican jaguar presently came under the crag where the boy Gabe was stationed, and he let fly, hitting the lithe animal's shoulder, and the animal leaped, fell, and died. Just as the boy shouted for Boss Carboot to come and truss the carcass, the hole of the wound suddenly grew larger, and a pocket gopher jumped out from within and ran away, and then another, and many more, and as each gopher escaped from the hide the corpse grew smaller, until, with the arrival of Boss Carboot, all that was left was the body of a thin, mangy goat.

Ch'en's Fish Bait, perhaps believing Nose had meant the story to be funny, did not laugh but scoffed, pushing a large rejecting hand toward Nose's face.

Nose sprang to his feet, his eyes wide, his teeth biting at oaths, wanting to go at Fish Bait's throat in earnest.

Others settled Nose down, but there was anger on both sides.

Wolf had a dozen bowls of a rotgut liquor, *baigar*, in him, and with Peach Fragrance beside him he began to mimic his master, the grain merchant Shih. No one knows a man so well as his slave. Wolf stood and in elaborate caricature showed us the prudish, straight-laced, thin-lipped man measuring out millet from from a storage box with a metal scoop, adjusting the balance weights on some scales with over-delicate finger flicks, greedily totting the price on an abacus, then bending over to make fast the bag, with his buttocks wiggling in the most expressive way. The performance was vividly comical, but—would he, like Nose, leap at the windpipe of a disbeliever?—*no one laughed.*

Suddenly the whole room was silent. A tall, slender slave woman was standing ghostlike in the doorway—Ma's Flax-head, the one who had had to ride the wooden horse. She was a new one at the tavern. She was said to be young; it would have been hard to tell. She had an odd face, all pushed forward at the lips and chin; we looked at her in silent fury, the personification of all our angers at our masters. She walked gracefully across the room to some friends, determined now to lose herself in sweet ruination.

Some clapping started up, and in one of the rooms there was boxing out of grudges by pairs of men. Two white girls got in a slapping scuffle. Nose went across the courtyard with some slave woman, and although I had known this would happen to me some-time, I was blindly furious. Old Pearl, quite drunk, grew ferocious in the way that had used to frighten me. Someone had a piece of chalk and drew a circle on the brick floor in one of the rooms; no one would go near it. A yellow diviner was throwing dried beans against a wall. Nose came back looking mean. It seemed to me that the whole room shook with rage.

After a few minutes Nose called with hoarse shouts for silence. He had a hand on Chao-er's shoulder, and the white man and the yellow man were standing beside the chalk circle. Several of the Drum Tower Boys were in a ring around it. Yü-li, the little swordmaster, was flitting at the outskirts like a gnat. Not a slave dared whisper.

Fish Bait, Wolf, and a slave named Unicorn each placed his left foot in the circle. Chao-er, in a pompous, thick-tongued voice, with sparkling eyes in his triangular face, which was purple with wine and agonized good will, said, "Do you swear, when the For-bidden City has been burnt, to set fire to your masters' houses and kill all the yellow people who come to see the fires? Do you swear it?"

The three slaves stamped their feet and bowed their heads. Nose annointed each man's plaited hair with a few drops of wine.

Now, as if ungagged, everyone began to giggle. The weird pair of drunk priests, one yellow, one white, ranged others around the chalk circle and swore them in, and little Yü-li ran back and forth to the kitchen, supplying *Shao-hsing* for the dousings. Soon we were all laughing; the tension was flowing out of us. This was a lark. What an incredible scene: the whole town in flames, the yellows in panic, the slaves turning into masters!

We howled when Fish Bait and Nose pushed dignified Lapdog (Gabe shoving our irreproachable Mayor Jencks!) to the edge of the dangerous circle, and Nose and Chao-er made this man, who had a towering character among the yellows for fawning on them, swear to burn their homes and kill their persons.

Eventually even I, my shoulders shaking with laughter inter-mixed with coughs, swore to burn and kill, and helpless Pearl, weeping with soggy laughter, swore at my side.

Our oath to act stood surrogate for the violence; as soon as we

were sworn we felt as if we had already done what we had contracted to do. We were masters and mistresses now. The rooms
rang with our happiness.

Then we heard Nose announce in the yellows' language: "When
we are done, I will be Emperor and Chao-er will be Generalissimo
of the Armies. We'll make a new Forbidden City for Emperor Nose
and General Chao-er."

But it seemed that mild cobbler Chao-er wanted to be Emperor,
not General. We began by laughing at the argument that arose
between the men, but the laughter quickly died out. Nose's hoarse
voice and Chao-er's tenor cries were deadly serious.

Chao-er almost shrieked, "No, you son of a turtle! I'll be Emperor, Nose. *I am the yellow man here.*"

Someone, having to run home, had opened the tavern door.
Icy air flowed around our ankles. The door slammed.

([Nose Climbs a Wall

Gull's counter to the master's power was to make accidental noises. In the kitchen, bowls leaped from her hand and
shattered on the floor as if inspirited by her touch, pans banged,
the pothook clattered, the poker drummed on iron kettles. She
never looked angry, she laughed and hummed, but some days it
seemed as if the master's house would collapse around his ears
from her catastrophic clumsiness.

It was one of the yellows' religious holidays. We had had a
thaw; the day was foggy. My cough persisted, and I sat hugging
myself by the oven as Gull tried to teach me the yellows' calendar,
with its animal years and local five-day market weeks, profoundly
confusing, frightening, and depressing to me.

I said I thought I would run over to Chao-er's.

Gull said I was going there too much.

I had a coughing fit, and finally managed to ask why too much.

Gull was a cautious woman. To tell the truth, I had begun to
despise her, for it seemed to me that she was finished with life;
resignation clung to her like a layer of fat. *She did not know she
banged the pots. . . .* She said the mistress was commenting on
how long it took me to run errands.

I coughed until there was a knife in my chest; then, feeling very low, I bundled myself and went out. The streets were muddy. I was suddenly in a panic about the dislocation of time that I felt the yellows' calendar entailed. Was I swept up in it? Would I evaporate like the two days from the week?

There was a queer still air in the tavern; only half a dozen whites were there, and I sensed that whispers were in order.

Stocky Cassia Cloud decided to befriend me, or perhaps to try me out. She beckoned me into the room with the crap table, where we were alone, and pressing down her chunky hands on the edge of the table, she leaned her unhappy face, whose once golden complexion had gone doughy and erupted into ranges of livid pimples, over the baize surface at me, and she spoke in a hoarse whisper. "Chieh-chieh," she said, calling me, with obvious sarcasm, her old sister, "you are a friend of Nose, yes or no?"

I hesitated. I supposed Cassia Cloud's eyes saw everything in the tavern; that she had seen Nose lead me across the courtyard that time.

"You are a good girl, Chieh-chieh," she said, in an affectionate tone that put me on guard. "You have the air of a guest."

I felt I had to say something hostile, but what came out was petulant. "Nose takes care of himself."

"Perhaps," she said. "But perhaps he's been trotting too fast for one pair of legs. Perhaps he has tied himself to Wolf and some of those other pigs with too tight a knot, huh? Ayah!" She leaned a few inches closer to me. "Nose has robbed again. Yesterday in the night. Ayah, the bastard. He climbed the rear wall and took the things into Peach Fragrance's room. I saw him there. I have no grudge against Peach Fragrance. I carry wine to her to open her eyes in the mornings. I carried the bowl in to her at dawn, and I found Nose naked there." Cassia Cloud's pink tongue shot out and back several times, like a lizard's. "How he boasts! He says, 'Come here, Small Cassia Cloud'—he speaks to me as if I were a dirty white sow—and he tosses me a piece of silver, and he says, 'Peach Fragrance,' he says to that drab, 'Peach Fragrance,' and waves a hand as elegant as a Big Venerable, 'cut the girl a gown from the cloth.' Ayah! I see this bolt of Honan linen on the bed."

Alarmed, I said, "You should be careful how you talk."

Cassia Cloud said, "Maybe Nose should be careful how he acts, yes or no?"

"What do you want to say?"

"You know soldier Ch'en? From the guard at the Meridian Gate of the Forbidden City who comes in here?"

I shook my head.

"You wouldn't. Not a white, him, he's a big flatnose—one of *us*." She laughed a deep-throated contemptuous gargle and pounded herself on the chest. "I will tell you. This fellow, soldier Ch'en, he played at dice with your Drum Tower Boys under the tower, and he lost a trouserful, but he didn't have it to pay. You hear? So he told them how to rob Mother Feng's shop and get plenty. He had seen it there in a chest, these silver pieces. There is a postern gate to the compound, never used, you hear, on Dried Fish Hutung, a simple bolt, you hear, and if three-four went in there to Mother Feng, some of them could keep her busy while one of them sneaked off and slipped the bolt from the inside. Then they could come back by night."

Cassia Cloud scanned my eyes for anxiety. I tried to hide everything.

"Which *he* did. Nose. With Wolf and those other hogs. You hear what I want to say, small girl? Nose came over the wall and slept with Peach Fragrance. He had nothing but cool air on his bare behind, this morning."

The lizard's tongue peeped out quickly twice. The whisper grew faint.

"You know what the bastard did? He gave the Honan linen to Mother Chao-er. She's keeping it for him. Behind the beam under the eaves at the kitchen end. I tell you, small girl! Old Chao-er, he took the silver pieces to the storage room, he has this hole to hide what those dirty white pigs forever steal, behind a cask, covers it over with a flat stone there. Ayah, the pricks, those men!"

Whom did Cassia Cloud hate the most, I wondered: her indenture-master Chao-er the cobbler, or Nose surprised with no clothes but complacent, or the man who had wrinkled his nostrils over her charms, or the long procession of disappointed whore-jumpers who must have preceded that one? "Those men!" I felt a new pain in my chest. I wanted to go back to Gull.

But Cassia Cloud would not let me go. She took my forearm in her callused hand. "Those devil bannermen were here an hour ago," she hissed. "Those devils know where to look."

"How?" I asked.

"Our flatnose, our soldier Ch'en. You hear? Mother Feng remembered his eyes like two lanterns when he got a glimpse of those silver bits in the chest there when she was making him change there. They fetched him from the Meridian Gate, and he says to them, 'Small Wine Mouth, he did it.' Know who that is, Chieh-chieh?"

"Yes, mistress," I said. I knew that this was a name Nose called himself at the Drum Tower. All the men slaves had off-hour aliases for the avoidance of trouble.

"Those devils came in here, and Nose sat in the stove corner like a lazy big dog, and those devils went around. 'Is there a pig named Small Wine Mouth here?' Nose—ai, he's a cock, all right! —he says, 'I am Wu's Nose,' he says. 'All these people know me. Wine Mouth, you say, big masters? I don't know anyone called Wine Mouth. Thank you, big masters,' he says. The devils walked out of there!"

Cassia Cloud laughed again, but there was something besides laughter in her eyes.

I was suddenly in a fury. "You bitch turtle, Cassia Cloud, leave Nose alone," I burst out. I thought she might tell the authorities some story. Then suddenly I realized the danger I put myself in by cursing this sullen girl, who was yellow even if indentured and little better than a slave.

"Who wants to get that pig in trouble?" she said with an air of innocence that covered a malicious delight she obviously felt at my loss of control. "Not I, Chieh-chieh!"

The tongue shot out at me, and I was afraid there might be more, so I turned away, ran to fetch my cloak and foot rags from their shelf, and hurried home more dejected than ever, and thoroughly frightened besides.

(Nose Thumbs His Nose

Now I learned what speed whispers can have, for when I reached home I found Gull in the kitchen carrying on her usual cannonade of awkwardness but also looking uncommonly wise and tickled, and she pushed me onto the ovenside bench and told me that Sun's Mink had come to the slave gate and informed her that my friend Wu's Nose had stolen from a yellow woman and given to a yellow woman. I pretended to know nothing about it.

Sun's Mink was a short, stooped young slave with something wrong with his spine—how cheaply he must have been bought!—who was said to be crafty at cards and dice. He was a member of the slaves' gang known as the Coal Hill Boys, who gathered occasionally at Chao-er's tavern; I had seen Mink there. He had a habit of appearing at our slave gate, and I wondered if he had some byplay going with Gull—for our chubby cook, who was so cautious, so accommodating to our mistress, would slip away to our sedan-chair shed and storage house for long unexplained afternoon sessions. Bow stayed away from his beloved Flying Commode then, I noticed, and I never followed Gull; I did not want to know her business.

"Mink says"—Gull spoke in the yellows' language with Mink's chopped style—" 'Any white man who gives stuff to a yellow whore that he stole from a yellow bitch, he has a stout heart—yes or no?' "

"Ayah, rich," I said.

"Mink says"—and now Gull seemed to shrink, and she hunched her shoulders, and she *became* Mink, with his demons of pain and malice in her flashing eyes—"Nose knows how to thumb his nose at the slantheads."

"He knows," I said.

Gull's mock Mink became even more deformed and said, "If a big master begins to worry whether he is master of his mistress, he is no master at all." Gull straightened up and was herself again. "Mink, he says that." She was obviously proud of the twisted slave. "They say Nose's Big Madame covets something about Nose besides his name-part. Once when all her maids were out on errands she had him carry in her bath water and made him scrub her back! He boasts about it. Says she has a body like a frog's. That's what Mink told me."

After the evening meal Big Venerable Shen told me that he and Big Madame would be pleased to receive the slave force in the Peony Study at once.

I led the way and lit lanterns, then ran out back to call the others.

As we marched in to audience, Gull had a streak of flour across one cheek, Bow limped on a winter-joint in his right knee, Bean and On Stilts and Cock rubbed their hands in an absurd unanimous humility, and I pretended to search the floor for some clue

to my unworthiness. The yellows sat, the whites stood. We slaves
hung our heads in the approved manner.

Master wished to know, were we acquainted with one Nose,
small slave to Wu, mandarin of the Board of Revenue, in the
hutung diagonally across from ours?

Bow answered, falsely, "Small slave called Nose, Big Venerable?
No, Big Venerable."

How could we not know a slave of such a near neighbor? Slaves
were forever banging at the gate and sneaking in to the quarter
past Bean.

"We have seen them saw timbers over in the other hutung
there. Maybe that was the small slave called Nose we saw there
with the other sawyer. Maybe he was one of those fellows who
was sawing."

The master turned to Gull. Had she ever talked with this small
Nose?

She said, "No, Big Venerable. I never."

"Are you sure?"

Gull swore an earnest peasant-slave oath which made Big
Venerable's lips purse in an ill-suppressed smile. "Let all the gods
and devils listen to what I say and afflict me with incurable fungus
scabs on my scalp if I lie."

The master glanced at me, as if pondering whether it was
worth his breath to ask a question of such an ignorant white sow
as I; he finally brought himself to do so. Had Small White Lotus
ever spoken to the man?

It came to me, as sharply as a knock on the head, that Nose's
trivial misdemeanor had been blown up by the yellows into a
grave affront precisely because he had stolen from a yellow
matron and given to a yellow whore. And I realized that by now
a good part of the slave population of the capital had already
heard whispers like Mink's, with a garlic whiff of sex on them,
and that to a man the slaves would lie, pretend, go mute, be foggy,
on Nose's behalf, if any questions were asked—for, as we had
used to say at home in Arizona, if God gave the swallow no riches,
He at least gave it swiftness in turning.

I said, "I know a small slave named Nose, he belongs to Magistrate P'an in Seventh Hutung, Big Venerable."

"No! No! No! The revenue mandarin Wu's, in the hutung right
across the way." Yes, my stupidity really impressed the master.

But now he threw a stone at us. This slave, he said, had been arrested late in the afternoon by the bannermen for robbery.

I am sure my face showed nothing, though the thoughts were running like a pack of wonks in my mind. The bannermen must have gone back to Guardsman Ch'en; perhaps they had taken him with them to Chao-er's. I was glad I had left the tavern. What would they do to Nose? Would they break his legs? This was not the first offense; I remembered the day we had seen him tied to the tail of a cart.

"This is not the first time for this slave," the master heavily said, and I inwardly laughed that my stupid white childish mind—as he considered it—had beaten him to the words.

We got off with a short lecture on thievery. The gate must be securely barred with double beams every night, our master said.

On the way back to our quarters I had a feeling of being hunted so queer and so strong that I felt compelled either to burst out the locked gates and flee through the icy streets or else to try to ease the sensation by confessing it to Gull and Old Bow. I managed to tell them about it. I started by saying that slaves were often caught stealing. Why were the masters so excited this time? Then I blurted out what had seized me: this hunted feeling. Gull, as sweet as she had been during my fever, put her arms around me and said that whenever the masters became over-exercised about a slave's wrongdoing, she, too, had the same feeling, and Bow did —didn't he?—and so did every slave in the city, because the whites knew that one day their yellow masters might not be able to contain their thrill of anger at us for daring to be their slaves, and suddenly a bolt of Honan linen would become a matter of life and death, of many more-or-less lives and unmistakable deaths.

I could not sleep at all that night. I coughed and rolled on my blanket pad. I had a sort of half dream of protecting Nose. The oven of my k'ang cooled fast, and chill drafts ran like rats' breathing around me.

(Nose's Sighs

Two days later, in the afternoon, I heard that Nose had been given thirty strokes of the heavier bamboo and had been released by the banner corps and been sent home, but that he was on some sort of parole. At a risk of appearing a fool in eyes where I would rather not, but unable to stand off the risk, I took time to run to the mansion of Wu, his owner, and there in the kitchen I found Nose propped in a corner, shivering in a Tartar cap with the ear flaps down, with a running catarrh and a bad cough, and nowhere to be seen was the proud, powerful leader of the clay-pit work gang he once had been; perhaps concentrating on pulsating bruises on his back and ribs, he seemed absentminded, and far from feeling me a fool for seeking him out, he appeared to think nothing one way or another about my being there.

For two days and nights I had had a childish idea of helping Nose somehow—of protecting him from his own badness—but all that was vague, and really illusory, for he cared no more for me than for half a bowl of lukewarm wine.

To Wu's Moon Pot, Gull's friend who cooked at the house, I said, "I cannot sit still. Staying home day and night makes my feet jumpy."

Nose said nothing.

Moon Pot said, "Now that they've beaten him, the whole thing will blow over."

"What about his parole? Other times when the masters have gotten excited, have they calmed down right away?"

Nose stirred and grunted.

"What's itching your skin, you little piglet?" Moon Pot asked me.

I told her I wanted to know how the yellows had come to identify Nose as the robber and arrest him—how they knew about his giving the stolen goods to Peach Fragrance; that was what really bothered them, wasn't it?

"The other fox told on him. Told the bannermen."

"Cassia Cloud?"

"That her name, Nose?"

"Yes." This was the first word out of Nose, and it was spoken listlessly.

"Did she tell the part about Peach Fragrance?"

"Why are you sniffing around that part of the story? Huh, you piglet? You wouldn't care what fox old Snot Nose here slipped in with, would you? Hah! Look at her, Nose, look at that pretty blush! Why, you bad little piglet! Hah hah hah hah."

"I care about my own back—it's the bamboo I care about," I said sharply. "That Cassia Cloud provoked me just after the robbery, and I gave her the dirty end of my tongue, and I don't want trouble. This isn't *my* trouble."

"Oh, baby," Moon Pot said, "you're wrong. This is *pig* trouble."

"Well, get off my behind," I said.

"Who's on it? Nose, tell this little girl to run home."

In a calmer tone I asked, "What did Cassia Cloud say?"

At this new mention of Cassia Cloud, Nose stood up with a groan and began pacing.

Moon Pot said that Cassia Cloud had spitefully reported Chao-er's receiving the stolen goods.

"Ai, the bitch," I said. "Paying off her bond! What did the old slanthead say to that?"

At first, Moon Pot said, confronted by Cassia Cloud's accusations, Chao-er had tried to discredit her. "Called her vile, said she had a wonk's temper, said she told lies all day." But on being pressed closely with a threat of jail, and therefore fearful of angering his accuser, he suddenly whirled right about and "declared she was a good child, long-working and faithful," and that in the hardest weather of the winter she had dressed herself in a man's clothes and had put on foot rags and had gone with Chao-er in his cart to the eastern groves to help him gather firewood.

Nose suddenly said, "I'll kill that bitch fox." His voice was harsh, and he slapped the back of one hand into the cup of the other with a high, wheeling blow. The force of the blow shook his flap-eared cap forward over his forehead and onto the bridge of his nose. Moon Pot and I both laughed.

To Moon Pot he was an everyday man. "Hah!" she said. "You! You *talk* them dead. You sit there—sneeze and sigh. You'll never kill a yellow man, or woman either, Old Nose. Your blood is thin, you turtle."

Already smarting over Moon Pot's teasing of me, I began now to run up some anger on Nose's behalf, but to my distress he acted out her rebuke: deeply sighed and sat down.

Under hard questioning, Moon Pot told me, Chao-er had finally confessed to having the stolen goods at his tavern, and had gone home and brought the bolt of Honan linen and the pieces of money and put them in the bannermen's hands.

"What about the Peach Fragrance part?"

"That again? Yes, sweetheart—all about it. Not a thread on

him; naked as a snake on her k'ang there. Hai! She spilled it, all right."

Now I did not know what to do with my anger. I turned and saw Nose looking at me with wide eyes. For a moment I felt that we did have a relationship after all. His eyes were limpid and tender. He was just a youth from my village. He was homesick, and so was I. His eyes said, Take my head and hold it against you, cover these bloodshot eyes! . . . But suddenly these illusions passed. He was absurd in his wobbling cap. He sighed again, and his eyes drifted dully away from mine.

(A Secret with Young Venerable

In the following days I felt painfully restless. On every errand I looked for Nose in the streets but never saw him. Had that brief shaftlike look in his eyes, that afternoon when I had run to his master's house, really been there, or had it been in *my* eyes, which printed what I wished on his? I was strangely comforted in those days by little Young Venerable, who had decided to like me, reserving, however, the right to torment me, too; he would lean against me while I sang a soft song from back home, mysterious to him, "Stormy Weather," or "For You," pressing his cheek to my arm. I responded to his sulky advances with an outpouring of tenderness which astonished and embarrassed me. We would peer, head by head, at the grotesque goldfish that Big Venerable Shen had bred, with froggy eyes, transparent scales, and waving calico fins. There was one called Celestial Telescope, with eyes on top of its head. Another, Five Shimmers Dragon, had double tail fins like two masses of shot-silk drapery which he sometimes folded forward so as to wrap his entire body in a trembling delight of vanity. On errands I filched Big Madame's coppers to buy Young Venerable foolish gifts. I found a street stall where one could buy tiny papier-mâché toys—farmers' carts, bannermen on horses, vendors with wheelbarrows—which, when tied with fine silk threads to the backs of big black beetles, moved about with funny frantic urgency; the boy greeted these with bursts of laughter that made his throat seemed lined with silver. But I did not want Gull or Bow to see me favoring the yellow boy, who could be so cruel at times, and I think that he sensed

that the intimacy between us was somehow conspiratorial. He
was only a child!

⟨[**Handing Buckets**

One noontime, in the yellows' second month, after a
thaw had made mud of the town, on a gray day, as the master
and mistress were at their midday meal, we heard the great curfew drum booming and then a shuddering bell sound—the Drum
Tower and Bell Tower in a daytime alarm!—and soon a clamor
of bells and drums and gongs broke out from the many gate towers
of the outer and inner city walls, all out of time and tune in a
way that hurt my ears. The Shens and all their slaves ran together
into the street, where we found many others, yellow and white,
asking what was being warned against, and then some man
shouted that smoke was to be seen going into the sky to the northwest of us, and shortly a yellow man in a leather apron came
riding crazily through the streets on a tiny bay Manchurian pony
which had lather all down its neck and flanks, and he was shouting, "Fire in the Forbidden City! Fire in the Forbidden City!"
It had been so long since I had felt a rapture that at first I did
not know what knot had been untied in my stomach and what
warmth it was that radiated from that loosened place to my breast,
my shoulders, and down my arms to my hands. The cobbled
street, and the people shouting back and forth from one house
gate to another, and the stripped plane trees whose closely pol-
larded crowns looked like upraised fists holding handfuls of
brown bones, and the gray brick houses with bluish curved
roofs—all blurred when the joy, dammed at my mouth, brimmed
in my eyes.
The Forbidden City was on fire!
I vividly remembered leaning into the chalk circle on the brick
floor of the tavern, laughing and coughing, as the oath to burn
and kill was intoned over my shaking shoulders in Chao-er's
crackling tenor voice.
When my sight cleared I saw that the tip of my master's queue
was whipping on his shoulders in the easterly wind, and his eyes
were—I must admit—like those of our Syndicate bosses that
time in Palm Springs, fierce yet bored, arrogant and frightful.
I felt for a moment I should fall to my knees. He roared above the

shouting in the street that Bow (whose winter-joint was stiff as a crab's claw) should stay in the house with Big Madame Shen and the boy, and that the rest of us should run for capes and then follow him to the gates of the Forbidden City to join the bucket lines that surely would be forming.

For a moment, as I ran through the Shens' courtyards to the slave quarters to fetch the faded red-lined Harbin wool cloak the mistress had handed down to me, I wondered how one set fire to a master's house—charcoals in a corner?—but then I lost all traces of the oath on seeing Gull's worried face, for she, though a cook, was terrified of fire, dreamed of it night after night with twitches and groans; together we ran out to the main gate, whence at once the master led us and Bean and On Stilts and Cock off at a jog with his long queue thumping and blowing like a kite's tail. Many others were running along with us, masters and slaves, and poor yellow workmen, and rounding into Meridian Gate Street we saw a huge canted column of smoke, pale blue against the threatening clouds overhead, blowing westward over the lakes of the winter palaces.

A large crowd of people were already gathered in the great plaza outside the Meridian Gate, milling about, shouting, getting in each other's way—hoping, no doubt, that this emergency would oblige the authorities to admit the populace inside the Forbidden City to fight the fire. The elephants were kneeling stolidly; the way to the gate was open. Our tall master stood on tiptoe in his embroidered cloth shoes, trying to see over the heads of the crowd; his face was like an orange-papered lantern in the cutting wind. We could see smoke breathing through the tiles of one of the highest of the golden-roofed buildings within the purple walls. The running had given me a pain in my chest, but I was so happy I hardly felt it.

The master, his eyes no longer calm, shouted down to Gull and me to edge toward the gate, inside which water lines would probably be formed, either from the Golden Water River or from the lakes to the west; and when the lines were made up, to fall in and work. He broke forward through the crowd and, waving his official credentials wildly over his head, he passed within the Meridian Gate.

Seeing the master swallowed into the smoky gateway, I remembered a surf of fire hissing through the dry rabbit brush outside our village hedge, once, and some of our village men beating at the flames with house brooms, and we who were urchins standing behind the chevaux-de-frise afraid either to look or to turn away; then for some reason I thought of a recurring dream I had often had, of a column, wide as I was tall, of black ants, like a dark stream of water, coming toward me, as irresistible as the sun's climb up the sky, across a newly worked field, I standing paralyzed until the pointed nose of the seething dark stripe was six feet away from me and then turning to run screaming into wakefulness. I huddled now against Gull. It had been a joke, the oath. The men were drunk. I did not want to be punished, either for burning and killing, or for not. Gull was right; keep a clean nose. The shrill voices all around me added to my confusion and anxiety. A sudden burst of flame leaped up from one of the golden roofs. Then a new bell rang.

This ringing, which came from the way we had come, caused me the utmost fear. Had some slave taken the oath seriously? Had Nose? Had I the courage to turn my head and see whether another tall subversion of smoke was leaning over the compound of one of the Imperial boards, or from the Imperial ancestral temples?

But the clanging was coming nearer, and the people around us began cheering, and to my immense relief—yet disappointment, too—I saw that the bell was on a huge water-pump cart pulled by six mules.

The crowd surged around the engine, and soon the mules were forced to stop, and the captain of the pump company stood on the platform of the engine beside the handles of the pump screaming for passageway, and the driver cracked his long whip again and again over the heads of those who were blocking the way because they wanted to help. We could see that flames by now capped the whole of the one roof, whose tiles had fallen through below, and had worked against the strong wind along the ridge of the next building, evidently from beneath. Slowly the wagon moved toward a ramp leading up to the Meridian Gate, and now the firemen and numerous yellow dignitaries were all shouting commands at once, and the crowd swayed and eddied to no purpose. The rapid spread of the fire and the danger that sparks might leap to houses in the crowded city made every yellow man feel that he was in charge, and slaves ran here and there trying to do whatever they were asked.

Gull and I were swept toward the gate in the wake of the pump wagon, and before we knew it we were inside the Forbidden City. Two enormous bronze lions frowned down on us.

The common yellows among us who had been pushed within to form bucket lines were awed by this sacrosanct refuge:

The chain to which the Emperor whose reign was called K'ang-hsi had used to tether the small black donkey he rode when he made his incognito trips out into the city! The carved marble box in which petitions to the Dragon Countenance were placed! The Hall of Proclaimed Intellect—on fire! The Pavilion of Literary Profundity—ablaze!

Two long lines were being formed. I saw Nose in one of them, not far from the fire cart. He was with Fish Bait. I tugged at Gull's sleeve and made her join me in the return-buckets line not far from those two.

When Nose saw me, he shouted, "Ai, White Lotus!" and he pulled off his mangy fur cap and made a low bow with a circling sweep of the hat. It was clearly a tease. I was annoyed. I supposed he had been drinking. He and Fish Bait were both noisy.

I myself felt a perverse joy at the sight of the palaces in flames, and I was inclined to giggle, talk loudly, and playfully jostle Gull.

At last the lines had formed, all the way from the engine, through gates in two walls, to the South Sea of the winter palaces, and before long hundreds of wooden pails were moving along the chains, one of which, all men, conveyed full buckets to the big staved reservoir on the cart, while the other, women and boys as well as some men, passed the empties back to the lake.

Teams of six yellow pumpers at a time swayed the great seesaw handles on the engine wagon, and soon narrow streams began to play feebly on the roofs from hoses held by yellows in uniforms.

I could not help glancing over at Nose, and I happened to be looking once when Fish Bait passed him a bucket of water, and Nose, with a clumsiness I could not believe, fumbled the handle so the bucket fell to the ground and spilled.

"Oh! Suffering Jesus!" Nose shouted in English with mock dismay, and he danced about in the most comical way, splashing up the water with his bare feet.

I tried not to giggle. I tried, indeed, to take my mind off Nose. Gull was on one side of me, and on the other was a thickset, apricot-cheeked yellow housewife, obviously too poor to own slaves, of a class that felt a need to be particularly contemptuous of whites, yet obviously a hearty and cheerful woman, whom I found, as we were drawn into the irresistible co-operative spirit of the bucket line, joking with me, jollying up my spirits—in condescending terms but in an undeniably endearing tone. (I heard a cackle from Nose.) We three women swayed in the rhythm of the chain, and I wanted to work harder and harder, yet I also wanted the palaces to burn faster and faster; I felt that I loved the yellow woman beside me—our hands touched at every bucket handle—yet I also wanted her to feel loss, humiliation, and bitterness, and I wanted some retributive power—my Methodist God or a Buddhist avenger, if there was such a being—to sear the condescending tongue out of her throat.

Hooo! Nose spilled another bucket. The same prancing. Fish Bait hooting.

We were working near a door of one of the burning wings of the palace, out of which, so far as we could see, the Emperor's chests and beds and chairs and lanterns and Imperial nightgowns and Imperial undershifts had been vomiting, and we saw yellow gentlemen running in and out of the doorway, gesticulating in their wide sleeves and shouting to others outside. Then soon the ones within began to throw out bundles of scrolls and books and records and papers, and the ones outside caught them as best they could and carried them off into heaps near one of the bronze lions.

At this time the wind sprung unexpectedly into a whirling gale, and documents that had been disgorged from the doorway were caught up like an enormous scolding of sea gulls, and they swirled into the sky, swooped around us along the line, and flapped along the ground.

Ever since Nose's first accident I had felt a swelling impulse to laugh, and now the gentlemen's faces—I saw Big Venerable Shen, who loved good order in his own dressing chamber, with his pigtail askew, watching the birdstorm of documents—were so grotesquely dismayed that I could barely control my throat, hard as I tried to be cautious. The housewife beside me began to chuckle. I heard Nose and Fish Bait loudly laughing, and I gave way. At first Gull angrily shook my shoulder and shushed me, but soon even she had started to snigger discreetly, and before long both lines, yellows and whites together, were laughing all the way to the lake.

In the midst of this Nose upset yet another bucket. The yellow man beside him sharply chided him, but Nose hallooed and flapped his feet in the mud he had made.

The wind remained gusty, and it began lightly raining; the fire still gained from peak to peak along the wings. The Hall for the Reverence of the Master, not far from our lines, caught fire, apparently from sparks that had dodged the sparse raindrops on the wind. Many were afraid that this fresh breeze would carry the fire into the city. There were shouts that we should redouble our efforts.

A bit later I saw the man next to Nose halt an Imperial bannerman, and this guardsman spoke to Nose, frowning and gesticulating, and for a while Nose was quiet. But soon I heard his laughter again, and that sound, too raucous, suddenly filled me with an inexplicable depression that stayed with me the rest of the day.

Then in the rain we saw a tall man, in a ferocious uniform as white as the documents that swooped around his head, and wearing a polished steel helmet with long ear lappets, standing on the pump wagon shouting to the people in the lines, and grinning in an unconvincing way. The yellow woman beside me said with great excitement that this was General Hsüeh of the Emperor's personal bodyguard. Men in the bucket chain began to shout for silence so we could hear him.

All that reached us was the word for gunpowder.

A gasp ran along the line in pursuit of the word, and toward the east from us, where the lines were closest to the burning palaces, they suddenly broke, and soon we had all dropped our burdens and surged away from the building, leaving two long lines of buckets on the ground.

Now bannermen came screaming toward us that General Hsüeh had been assuring us that there was *no* gunpowder in these wings of the palace, and slowly we began to move back into place. The lines had scarcely been restored when a series of explosions, rebuking the lies in the chief bodyguard's grimacing mouth, rumbled from one of the buildings that was on fire. This time all of us, and the yellow gentlemen, too, and his eminence General Hsüeh besides, ran away to the very wall where all stood uneasily watching.

A great *aaah* and a jubilee of sparks went up when the roof of the Pavilion of Literary Profundity collapsed. . . .

During the evening meal at home, Big Venerable Shen told

the mistress the story of the day. He could not sit steadily at the
low table, but arose from time to time and strode about, once
bumping straight into me as I was carrying a bowl of water chestnuts in my hands—as if he truly had not known that I existed.
The golden roofs of all the buildings in the Wing of Literary Glory
were down, he was saying just then, and burning timber ends
obtruded from the walls, and the high wind was blowing sparks
off them, and a nightlong watch had been set. His Ineffable Tranquility in person had been safely removed early in the day to the
winter palaces. The crowd was made up of fools; they had been
frightened away by some ceremonial fireworks exploding. And
General Hsüeh—a madman! so subject to agitation!—had beat
his Imperial bannermen to arms throughout the city, the master
said, to scout all the streets of every quarter the whole night
through: to what end?

The mistress asked, "How did the fire start? Do we know?"

I felt my hand, in the act of setting a dish of bean sprouts down
on the table, begin to tremble. The mistress poised her chopsticks
over the bowl, ready to dip some out, waiting for the master's
answer.

Oh yes, the master said, that was well known but would not
restore the wings of the palace. The Imperial household had that
morning given orders to a gutter-solderer, a stupid man, one
Ts'ui, to seal the drains on the roofs of the Hall of Literary Glory,
in preparation for the Feast of Classics, and the idiot had carried
up his firepot with charcoals to keep his sealing iron hot, *in that
wind*, and sparks had blown down between the tiles onto roof
timbers.

The fire had not been set by a slave.

I felt as if I had been struck in the midriff—as if the very last of
my pride had been stolen from me. I put a dish of salted goose feet
and duck gizzards that I was carrying down on the chest at the
side of the room and leaned for a moment's support on the solid
wood.

❨ Alarms of Bells and Drums

A fire, said to have been caused by an overturned brazier,
broke out a week later in the house of a wool merchant named
Hua, near the Imperial University to the east of the Forbidden

City. It was extinguished without much damage to the building.

Another week later, as the willows along the city's chain of lakes became fountains of yellowy green, a godown, an old structure storing deal planks, belonging to another merchant, Sun, in the Outer City north of the Temple of Heaven, caught fire, apparently because of the carelessness of a workman smoking a pipe while malingering alone. The building and its contents were lost, but great exertion in hauling water from the sacred fishponds outside the temple grounds saved the neighboring warehouses.

Three days later another alarm of bells and drums broke out— fire at the house of a Mandarin of the Bannermen, named Han, in our southeast quarter, not more than an arrow's flight from us, near the Examination Halls.

Later that same afternoon fire broke out in the mansion of a high functionary of the Board of Rites, Huang, and we heard that it had been discovered in his slave quarters in a straw paillasse on which a white girl slept.

Early the very next morning the bells and drums sounded yet again, but this turned out to be a minor blaze in an outdoor haystack.

We had not had a single fire all the winter through, and in these few days we had heard six alarms, counting that for the Imperial palaces. In all the excitement I had not dared go back to Chao-er's, and I remained anxious (who had no particular right to be) about Nose's parole. I stayed mostly at home, and I was starved for the warmth of the tavern and for a sight of Nose and of Old Pearl, and for gossip, for entertainment, for wine, for peanuts, for a boxing match; that morning, after the sixth alarm, I was moody and several times broke into tears over trifles. The yellows could talk of nothing but the fires. Our masters were convinced that they had been set by an organized gang of wretches who wanted to steal under the pretext of rescuing household belongings from fires—for after these alarms the victims and their neighbors had made many complaints of losses of goods, and even of large pieces of furniture, that had been carried out to the streets during the fires.

Up to this time there had been no suggestion that the arsonists were white.

I thought often, in fear, of the oath at Chao-er's, but always came back to these reassurances: the oath had been in fun; Nose and the other men had been drunk; we had laughed and laughed.

❨ Scorch, Scorch

That afternoon Venerable Shen's bosom friend the curio dealer P'an came to play a game of "surrounding pieces," and he arrived in a great flutter of excitement. I heard what it was about as I served tea and sesame cakes.

It seemed that a certain lady named Madame Liang, airing her sleeve dogs at her mansion gate and chatting with a cousin, Madame Ho, had seen three white men walking up Hata Gate Street.

One of the slaves, suddenly doing a queer breakaway dance with flashing eyes, had said to his companions in the yellow language with explosive stresses, "Scorch, *scorch!* A LITTLE smoke! Hai! Hai!"

One of the other two had answered, "A little *today,* but ayah! *Wait* till TOMORROW!"

Then the first had lifted up his hands and spread them with a wide vaporing gesture over his head, as if to encompass the entire city, and he and both the others had burst into loud laughter, bending at their waists, tossing up their fur caps, slapping the air, hugging each other.

The two ladies had been greatly agitated by this behavior, and they had run to the gate of a neighbor, Madame Fan, and had told Madame Fan what they had seen. All three agreed that these eccentric shouts must have had to do with the fires.

Mesdames Liang, Ho, and Fan lingered, chirping excitedly, at Madame Fan's gate. In about an hour the three slaves walked downstreet again, showing signs of having been drinking. Madame Fan recognized the two men who had uttered the strange lines: a man called Small Wolf, belonging to her friends the Shihs, she said, and one called Small Fish Bait, belonging to Ch'en.

Together the three ladies hurried to the nearest yamen of the Blue Banner Corps to inform of these ominous capers. News of them was now traveling around the city, said curio dealer P'an, with the speed of runaway horses, and causing great consternation.

Wolf and Fish Bait! Clearing away the cups, I anxiously wondered if Nose, their inseparable comrade, had been the third. He needed new trouble about as much as he needed a new ermine purse for the riches he would never own. Ai!

₵[The Whites Are Rising!

The following day—we were in the early part of the third month—three more fires sprang up, and the sky came down around our ears.

The first alarm was in midmorning, at a small house belonging to one of the officers of the White Banner Corps, opposite the Lama Temple; this was easily got in hand.

Shortly before noon a fire broke out in the eaves of the house right next to that of Mandarin Huang, which had burned two days before, and near a deep hole burned in a timber officers had found scraps of hemp tow that had been dipped in tar. A cry of arson was raised. Someone in the crowd shouted, "The Coal Hill Boys!"— the slave gang to which Gull's friend Mink belonged; it was dreaded in that neighborhood. One of its members apparently belonged to Mandarin Huang.

The bucket brigade and the onlooking mob took up the accusation. "The Coal Hill Boys! The Coal Hill Boys!"

Within an hour five slaves from the gang had been led to jail on suspicion of arson.

News of these arrests reached our street gate within minutes of their occurrence. Yellow housewives, their necks corded with excitement, were stumping on their bound feet from house to house with the reports.

One of these hysterical couriers told us that Wolf and Fish Bait had been arrested, on account of their famous eccentric behavior of the day before.

After the midday meal I was on my knees at the outer gate polishing the master's brass nameplate, which was embedded in a low stone monument at the base of one of the gateposts, and I was trying to scribe the gray incrustations of polish out of the beautiful characters, and I was worrying about Mink—when the bells and drums struck up their horrible clamor yet again. I crumbled into a crouching position, my head on my knees, and groaned out loud, "No! No! No!"

Big Madame Shen, who, I believe, had not enough excitement in her life (she talked so much at meals about this woman's pock-marked face and that one's warty hands), was out at the gate, with a heavy cloak around her shoulders, before the clanging and thrumming had spread to all the watchtowers of the city.

"Come, come," she impatiently said, reaching a hand down toward me where I was still on my haunches. According to her husband's strict orders, she could not venture into the streets without an escort, and she wanted me to go with her.

We saw the smoke toward the granary, and we sped in its direction without waiting for word just where it was. I was in my dirty work gown, my hands were milked over with dry brass polish, my wavy brown hair was wild. The mistress jarred horribly on her feet crippled for beauty.

We rounded from Hata Gate Street into a side street, and I saw with a flash of fear that the fire was in one of three large timber godowns belonging to Wu Li-shih, Nose's owner, some three blocks from the Wu home. The pump wagon was already there.

"Buckets! Hand buckets!" my mistress excitedly commanded me, and when I took my place in the line she stood beside the line giving me infuriating bits of encouragement and advice. The source of water was a miserable sewage-filled rivulet, and the buckets full of this liquid smelled of slave ships.

I saw that a chain of firemen was climbing up the roof at the end of the godown away from the fire, breaking out tiles to make a hole for the hose.

Suddenly one arose from a crouching position, waved his arms, and shouted words I could not hear; then, cupping his hands to his mouth, he called toward our lines, "A white inside! White man down there!" He was pointing down through the hole in the tiles.

Then I saw a flash of blue near the ground at the far end of the godown, and it seemed to me that a figure skimmed through the lacy shade of a locust tree and vaulted the low wall beyond the building and—yes, a swift wink of blue again, into the hutung beyond. The Wu house was in that direction—or was it? or was it?

My head was whirling. Like gunshots around me in the bucket lines, the single word *White!* was detonated again and again. *White!*

Then some man (*White! White!*) lost his head completely and roared like a braying donkey, "The whites are rising! The whites are rising against us!"

I felt the mistress's hand grip my arm. Women nearby were gasping. One shrieked.

Another man shouted, "Yes! The whites! The turtles!"

The bucket lines broke and the mob was in a frenzy of chattering and crying out.

A fireman ran toward us from the other end of the burning building. His swelling eyes were about to split his head. "I saw the bastard," he shouted. "Wu's hog. Wu Li-shih's white bastard hog! I know him! I saw the bastard!"

Had not the mistress been holding my arm with a clamp of bronze I would have fled. I think I tried to break away.

The man who had raised the first crazy halloo now bellowed, "Let's get him! Come on! To Wu's!"

A large number of men ran from the bucket lines toward the Wu mansion, and very soon we saw these men swinging down Hata Gate Street in the direction of the Board of Punishments carrying Nose on their shoulders. I could not see his face, but I could tell it was he; his head was bobbing loosely as he was jolted by his bearers. He was not in blue. His white tunic was half torn from his back.

(Why Did Nose Run Away?

After the evening meal—at which the master had reported that a mob of yellow men had caught, one by one, a score of slaves wandering in the streets after the alarm of an uprising, and had carried them off to jail; that Wolf and Fish Bait had been interrogated at the Board of Punishments; that General Hsüeh of the Banner Corps had ordered a perpetual night watch throughout the city—after all this the mistress complained of feeling faint and asked me to support her to her chamber and to help her get undressed.

As we made our way to the Pear Blossom Rest, I could hear, outside and overhead, the prolonged wailing of a bamboo whistle tied to the tail of a pigeon which, soaring over the city, was writing across the sky a melancholy account of its flight; this lament edged my fear with hopelessness.

When she was seated before her dressing table, and when I had taken a taper light from our candle and had lit a lantern by her face, I saw in the mirror over her shoulder that she had lost all trace of her weakness; she was in fact almost vivacious.

She whirled around with sharp eyes and said, "Tell me, small child, about Wu's dirty hog, this Nose, the one they caught at the fire. Do you know him?"

My stomach felt all at once as my hands and feet had been ever since autumn, bloodless and clammy. Might the mistress have heard somewhere that Nose and I had come to the platform in the farmers' market in the same parcel of slaves? Did *she* know about the dark room at Chao-er's? "No, mistress," I said. "I have never talked with Wu's slave."

Big Madame Shen drew a preserved litchi nut from a jar and after she had eaten its smoky sticky meat and spat out the pit she licked her fingers with loud sucking noises.

"Do you think he started the fire? Do you think that slaves have started all the fires, White Lotus?"

I fell to my knees, I think to plead in some way for Nose. "Ai! *No,* Big Madame," I almost groaned. "No, *no,* Big Madame."

I could not look in the mistress's glistening eyes, and my gaze turned to a dark corner of her room, where I saw in turn a dark corner of a tavern room, and a crude brick k'ang with straw ticking on it, and a pair of bloodshot eyes, bloodshot, bloodshot, and a strong trembling hand dropping an old green silk gown to the floor. My eyes, afraid of being flooded, fled to the flame of the lantern, and at first I saw a fire licking at a warehouse roof—but suddenly the brightness is sunlight itself, and I see a squad of men going across a compound, and Gabe is with them, telling them how they'll proceed. A truck stands beside the pile walls of the new Coteen shed, on which the men are working; we hear radio music from the open windows of the Coteen house, "Juanita." The lumber is cut and ready. Gabe is stripped to the waist, and he bangs a hammer on a mudguard of the truck to get the men's attention. . . . The wall plate and tie beam are up, and the face rafters. I hear Gabe's slightly off-tune voice now, *"We are watching, we are waiting, For the bright prophetic day* . . ." He is everywhere; now he runs from side to side on the ground; now he is at the ridgepole calling down to a man who is slow at tying in the purlins. His eyes are aflame. . . . Then it's all done. The villagers who are watching cheer as Gabriel climbs a ladder and nails a big leafy cottonwood branch to the king post which transforms the covered house into a living thing. It is a moment, for me, of soaring happiness. His shoulders as he draws back the hammer! . . .

"White Lotus, small child!" the voice of the mistress said. "Do not be afraid of me. You look so . . . feverish. Get up off your knees, small girl. . . . You have a look—*I think you know him.*" Her eyes had what seemed to me a teasing glint. "Is he *strong,*

White Lotus?" She spoke in a tone of some incredible mischievous-
ness.

I was afraid. I said I did not know this Nose. I said there were
numerous slaves called Nose or sometimes Big Nose. I said the
yellows complained of the ugliness of all white people's noses.
I did not know this Nose or that one, they were all the same
to me.

"But why would he light a fire in his own master's warehouse?
I trust you, White Lotus, *ai*, White Lotus, you have been like a
child to me."

Then I stood up. I said slaves lit no fires. I said the Big
Venerable had said a careless yellow gutter-mender had lit the
wing of the palace.

"But why did your friend Nose run away?"

"That was not Nose, Big Madame! The slave who ran away
was not the Nose you are talking about. That was not Nose!"
My voice had run away with me; it groveled and begged, over
and over.

"But why did the man run away?" The mistress's triumph
was so frank it seemed to spread like a blush of pleasure on her
face. She did not even have to say, "So you *do* know him."

How could I have forgotten Gull's very first warning to me?
Show nothing. Have a porcelain face in front of the yellows.

"Why do you think he ran away if he did not set the fire?"
the mistress insisted.

I said nothing to that. I thought of the chalk circle on the
tavern floor, and I fell to my knees again, trying with all my puny
draining strength not to weep.

"We will not tell Big Venerable we went to that fire this
afternoon, will we, small child?" the mistress said, standing to
dismiss me. "Run off, now. I see you are more upset than I imagined. Off to your quarters. I am quite able to get myself undressed."

(A Search

With tung oil I was polishing a wooden screen in the
reception hall in the first courtyard, some days later, when the
plunger bell at our front gate gave me a start. Since the series of
fires, the sounds of bells—even of the tiny finger bell that the

mistress tinkled here and there in the mansion to summon us—
caused me to tremble as if with an echo of the tower bells' jangling
alarms.

From where I stood I looked out at the gate for a moment,
half expecting some evil yellow spirit to float right through the
marble ghost screen and come and choke me; it would wrap icy
fingers of my own panic around my thumping neck.

An impatient hand pulled at the plunger, and the thin tocsin
pierced me again. Suddenly I remembered that Bean, the gateman, was out in the city, helping to carry the master in the
Flying Commode, and I ran to the gate with my rag in my hand.

Outside stood three bannermen. It took all my will to stand
ground.

My first thought was that the soldiers had come to question
me about Nose. Ever since his arrest I had felt deaf and blind.
We slaves dared not go to Chao-er's; we certainly could not
gather at the farmers' market or under the Drum Tower; even
visits to neighbors' gates seemed risky. I had heard nothing. As I
stood facing the three tall, stern men, the idea that the slaves
were rising up against the yellows, that I might be a threat to
these three brutes, seemed utterly mad, yet in that moment
before any of the bannermen spoke I was struck by a sudden
realization—that though the oath at the tavern had seemed
hilarious, it had perhaps not been a joke at all. Underneath our
peals of laughter had lain a desire for revenge that surged up
in me now and caused me, of all things, to giggle, as I bent in a
deep bow. I wondered, with my head humbly lowered: *Had* Nose
started a fire?

One of the bannermen asked for my mistress. Having straightened up, I stood staring at him, unable to believe he had not
come for me; then I turned and flew to the Peony Study, where
the mistress, with pursed lips, was practicing the lute.

I followed Big Madame Shen back out to the fore-courtyard
and pretended to resume my work on the screen as she greeted
the men in the reception hall.

Their spokesman said, with a strong flavor of memorization
on his tongue, that General Hsüeh of the Eight Banner Corps,
acting upon the advice of the Censorate, had ordered bannermen
to search the whole city, to see whether any goods stolen from
about the fires might be found, or whether there might be any
suspicious unfamiliar persons in hiding, or lodgers, or strangers,

who were perhaps the wicked instrument and occasion of the
fires in hopes of opportunities for pilferage, or plunder.

The soldier sighed then at having ejected that official verbiage
from his craw, and he added, "Shen T'ai-t'ai, we would be
honored to search your slaves' quarter—that is all there will be
of it. It's orders, you see, Shen T'ai-t'ai."

So this was the way of searching "the whole city": to look
in *my* miserable brick-bedded corner.

Glancing across the room, I saw that the spokesman, a tall
young man of Tartar lineage, with an odd squint in his right eye,
was standing before an exquisite painting by Han Hsü, a favorite
of my master's, the title of which was "Scholar Taking a Stroll
in a Light Drizzle," and which bore a couplet by a poet of the
Sung dynasty:

> *The mist touches his brow with the dream of spring;*
> *Beyond the mist lie ten thousand mountains of memory.*

The hypocrites—everything so delicate and sensitive that met
the eye! Would they find on my k'ang the pewter mustard spatula
I had stolen from Chao-er's tavern? How could I explain to them
that it was a remembrancer for a frightened girl of a half hour
she had had in a dingy room alone with Wu's Nose, who was now
in their not so delicate hands? It was a bent little dauber, worth
only a couple of coppers. It was in my reed matting somewhere,
along with a flea who had tided over the winter there. I hoped
this wretched insect would jump on a waxy yellow hand as the
hand fumbled in the dirty shredded matting, and that the flea
would ride off drinking at a bannerman.

I heard them troop away to the back courtyards. Soon they
returned—empty-handed, and without the flea, as I later found—
and I learned from their chatter to the mistress:

That there were better than thirty slaves in an improvised
prison at the elephant stables, and that the magistrates were
getting nothing from these white pigs about the fires save stupidity and denials.

My ears strained for the sound of Nose's name, but I did not
hear it.

I heard from the spokesman's voice that this brave winking
bannerman assumed for my mistress's benefit the airs of a mandarin, or even of a magistrate—the tones if not the true grip
of police power. Yet I also clearly heard in his voice, and in the

others', too, as they chatted on for a polite time, something that astonished me: namely, that all these official people, and my mistress as well, who was so mischievous and imperious and intimate and tender by turns with me—all were desperately frightened by the very ones they seemed to have most firmly in their fists, their slaves. The round ceremonial tones and the confident tapping of the bannermen's staves on the stone flooring had a hollow sound. When a ram is brave, Kathy Blaw had used to say long ago, its courage comes from its heart and not from its horns.

❨ The Master Dresses

The only mood that stirred Old Bow to a creaky buoyancy was one of sarcasm. We were in the kitchen. This was near the end of the fourth month. Big Venerable Shen had been impaneled, to his delight, as one of the some fifty so-called Ears of the Court who were to act as attendant authorities at hearings in the Board of Punishments on the recent fires, and Old Bow had helped the master to get dressed for the first of these hearings and had just seen him out the front gate; for tonic the master had decided to walk the short distance to the compound of the Board. Gull and I, seeing that Old Bow was determined to give us a full recital of the master's getting dressed, moved the kitchen chopping table without a word toward the cupboard away from the brick cooking cradle, to give Bow decent room for airs and graces.

In the middle of the brick floor Bow struck a pose, and by it we knew, somehow, that he (the master) was naked, bed-ruddy, and chilled, and before the old mimic had laid onto his canvas ten bold strokes we saw, breathing and blinking before our eyes, our double master: the man well known for probity, decency, liberality, and a sharp memory for aphorisms from the great teachers, explaining to a slave whom he considered boy-minded the nature of the hearings at which he was to assist; and, on his other side, the cranky, impatient, despotic owner of living flesh, commanding that flesh to fetch and truckle and button and pin. Old Bow caught, with all the malice of years of his bitterness, the inner tension of this contradiction.

"The Chefoo one, Old Bow, on the shelf above. Above, above! . . . Some might think, inasmuch as the hearings take place under a body called the Board of Punishments, that there is a pre-judgment here—that these prisoners are *known* to have set the fires, and *must* be chastised. Not at all. The Dragon Countenance is said to feel—hai! Turtle! Be a little more careful, Small Bow—those pins have points! . . . On the other hand, a great city can tolerate just so many frights and alarms, and then—the red velvet undergown, Small Bow—what? you forgot to brush it down?—you *are* a simpleton!—how *many* times?—all right, the camlet, then—and then the Emperor simply must find out whether there has been premeditated malice, for though we have the fortune of living under a majesty who exceeds all others in the gentleness of his laws and regulations, yet if those to whom —I think, let me see . . . yes, I'll wear the Soochow bow on my queue, with the matching purse; my corded-wolf's-paw bow is too *aggressive* for this particular occasion, you agree?—ayah, it is the *second* one, how many *times* have I given you the order of those bows?—one, pigeon's wing, two, Soochow, three, negli-gent, four, tiger's ears, five, wolf's paw, six, summer fountain. Can't you count to six, Small Bow? Let me hear you count to six. . . . I maintain only six bows at a time, Small Bow. . . . But if the authorities to whom is granted the power to discipline designing persons with wicked purposes—Minister Ts'ao calls such authorities the life and soul of the Emperor's justice—if these are not conscientious and adept—gray lining, Old Bow, gold will not do in the Board of Punishments, you know that as well as I. . . ."

Through all of this I laughed till the tears ran down my cheeks, yet I was also waiting for one small word, or a gesture, or a sniff about *us*. This was all about us, after all. They said we had robbed, we had lit. We were rising against them. We were the "designing persons," ours the "wicked purposes."

Then—whether just as it had happened or not scarcely mat-tered, for Old Bow gave the passage a conviction that froze my blood—the old man dropped the hint for which I had been hold-ing my breath.

With exaggerated gestures that themselves lectured on the grandeur of the Emperor's punitive system, Bow-Master tied the mouth of his Soochow purse and slung it in his sleeve, and he shook jasmine water onto his round hat as if watering a cabbage, filled his snuffbox, and then, with a decorous sneeze at the haze of snuff in the air, said, "I shout at you, Small Bow, I shout at

you all day, but I believe you would walk through pikes and
swords to protect me. You would" (the eyes were like those of
a bull terrier: vigilant, half-tamed, patient, famished), "wouldn't
you? You say, 'Yes, Big Venerable.' Five thousand times a day.
'Yes, Big Venerable.' But are you *sincere*, Old Bow, in your acquiescence? Are you *sincere*?" With the slave's assistance, he
slid into his wide surcoat with a silver-braided border and embroidered flowers on gray silk, and he shook out the inner sleeves
at the wrists. " 'Yes, Big Venerable! Yes, yes, Big Venerable!' I'd
like to know the truth of it today. Do you *mean* it? We have thirty
and more of your people locked up. I don't like these arrests by
simple seizure, I'll tell you that, Small Bow, I don't like the way
that was done. But—"

The old slave abruptly ended his performance on that word,
drawn out long, into which single sound he threaded a delicate
tremor of their terror, and of ours.

(A Matter of Being Rattled

Having served a dish of shredded pork with sea slugs
and bamboo shoots, I took my place behind the wooden screen
and overheard the master's account of the day. Before my eyes
on the screen was a dreamlike scene of ivory deer, jade clouds,
jasper rocks, agate trees, and ebony bridges—for even the backsides of the yellows' furnishings had this monotonous perfection
of sensitivity—while my ears took in a story of real life, ayah,
that was not so pretty.

The master confessed to his duck that he had misgivings. This
inquiry was being poorly handled. He had had, all day, "a bad
feeling." Partly it was ennui—the Ears of the Court, fifty distinguished men, had been kept on their feet all morning simply
waiting, and Secretary Wei had been such a bore with his everlasting games: "Come now, Elder-born Lu, silver spurs are just
for show, one wants steel, a fighting cock needs a lance, Elder-
born Lu, not a toothpick. . . ." Battledores, ritual swordplay,
horn-goring, whipping tops! All day, polluting the air with his
vigor that was as offensive as a beggar's pipe smoke.

But that was not the master's real worry. What troubled him,
he said, was that the authorities seemed rattled. Everything was

being run through on nerves. Old Hu, the Chief Mandarin of the
Board, was as skittery as a stung pony. "After all," my owner
said, "these white people are our slaves. We ought to be able to
be calm, at least."

The day's hearing had been taken up mostly with the slaves
Wolf and Fish Bait, the ones who had been caught boasting about
setting fires—*hooo*, how a vague supposition had grown into an
assertion! Behind the screen I trembled for those two—until
suddenly I heard the name for which I had been fearfully waiting.

"Toward the end of the day," the master said, "we took up
another case, and here was where Old Hu showed the rawness
of his excitement. This case concerned that ruffian belonging
to Wu of the Revenue Board, you know."

"Which one is that?"

"Called Nose, Wu's Nose: they thought they saw him at the
fire of his master's godown, don't you know, and some of our
self-chosen strong men carried him off to prison."

"Is that so?" says the mistress, innocent as a pussy willow.
"I had not heard of that."

"He, this Nose, was kneeling on the prisoner's stool there opposite Old Hu, surrounded by a handful of rapscallion deponents
—paid liars, I suppose, pulled in off the streets. This slave is a
vicious proud white, eye like a wild boar's—dirty torn tunic half
off him—glared defiance at the top men of the capital. But odd:
his speech was low, untrembling, respectful, and . . . yes . . .
plausible—though of vile grammar."

The slave, said my master, had sworn that he was at home—
three streets away from the godown—all afternoon, all through
the fire. Claimed he had handled buckets at the earlier fire next
to Mandarin Huang's that morning, and then he had gone home
and worked there till dark.

Now the deponents—all contradicting each other. A small
yellow boy, some indentured workman's spawning, teeth missing
in front, said he'd seen Nose at Wu's house sewing a long streamer
of red cloth bearing Old Wu's device onto a hame to mark his
master's carthorse, just before the bell for the fire. Then a neighbor, a yellow man, said he'd seen Nose lounging out at Wu's
gate shield shortly before the alarm. Another: *after* the bell,
when it was known to be a fire in Wu's godown, said he met
Nose in the street and asked him if we were not going to pass
buckets and the insolent turtle said he'd had enough buckets

that day. Worst of all, they next had an old gaffer, a yellow do-
nothing, who said he sunned himself daily near the Drum Tower,
knew Nose like a pet dog, yes, yes, saw him *watching* the fire;
asked Nose why no buckets—at which the slave had run over
and joined the bucket line.

But then it turned out the old ragbag was too nearsighted to
count his own fingers at arm's length. Blind as a mole!

The upshot, Big Venerable said, was that Old Hu concluded
and summed up—with total disregard for what the deponents
had said—to the effect that Nose had been *inside* the godown
at the time the fire was set.

"Do you see, duck, what I mean? This is not the way to proceed. This is a matter of being rattled. I don't like it."

There was a long pause.

"Are you thinking of taking the slaves' side?" the mistress
finally asked. There was a lacquered screen between the mistress
and me, but I could almost *feel* the slightest curl of an ironic
smile at the corner of that small mouth.

I heard the master's hand slapping at grains of rice that had
spilled on the table. "Misgivings, I only said I had misgivings,"
the master's voice said with some annoyance. "I trust the trials
themselves will be conducted in a more orderly way."

([Errand Within Errand

        The mistress sent me to the farmers' market, beyond
the Hata Gate in the Outer City, for some pork, and I had started
out at a trot, when, bewildered, scarce knowing what I was doing,
I found myself scudding like a leaf driven by the wind off my
course. I ran westward, to the elephant stables. I strode straight
up to a bannerman who guarded the gate of a section of the
stables, no longer used for elephants, that had been converted
to a slave prison, and I heard myself say, "Big Venerable, can
a woman see her man? Wu's Small Nose?"

The soldier, a tall, round-cheeked man, may have been tickled
to be addressed with an honorific title. He leaned down good-
humoredly toward me and said in a thick Honan accent, "What?
What you say, small sow? Want to see a prisoner?"

"Nose. Wu's Nose. My husband." I really did not know what

I was saying or doing; my heart was like a squirrel caged in my ribs.

"Ayah, did they snatch your man right out of your bedtick, small sow?" He laughed, overcome by his own jollity. Then he patted my shoulder and said, "Wait here."

In time the man returned and led me inside the elephant enclosure, where I saw six rows of large buildings, each apparently containing several stables, and he took me into one of them, through a timbered door in a brick wall as thick as my escort was tall. This building, which now housed the bureaucracy of the prison, had been divided into wooden-walled offices and cubicles, and in one of the smaller rooms, which had no furniture at all, I found Nose temporarily chained to a wooden post. He had been led out to see me.

He was astonished by my visit. Had the bannerman told him I had called myself his wife?

He spoke to me sharply: "Stay away from here. Why have you come here?"

I could not answer because I did not know why.

"Stay away," he said. "You can't do anything here." And he snapped out a succinct saying that was current among the whites in the capital: "A slave is guilty."

Suddenly there were a great many things I wanted to ask. *Had* he lit fires? Why had he turned himself into a rowdy? What had happened to him? Did he not care what the yellows did to him? Was the oath a joke? Did roughness, drunkenness, stealing, arson, and surly silence give any satisfaction? What should a white girl do with her life? Why was he so severe with me? Why could he not speak to me about what our awful days meant—if anything?

As if he could almost hear my mind crying out these inward questions, Nose modulated his manner and tone. He hooked a thumb under the filthy loop of rag that held what was left of his tunic up on one shoulder and said, "Fetch me a slave coat."

Without even answering I ran at once out from the elephant enclosure and, with a feeling of being tested and trusted such as I had not had since the errands of our village at home, I flew to Wu Li-shih's slave postern, and Wu's Moon Pot took me to the squalid toolhouse shed where Nose had had his k'ang, and she rummaged, and she handed me a blue coolie tunic, and I

ran back to the elephant stables. I think I expected, if my mind
was working at all, that I would run in and Nose would still be
waiting in the little room.

But at the gate my soldier was gone. Another—a thin creature
with several days' stubble of sparse beard—spread his legs and
barred my way. Absolutely prohibited per order General Hsüeh.
No matter husband.

"Please, Big Venerable! Give this to Wu's Nose, he's caught
in prison." I held up the tunic.

Disgustedly the soldier took the garment and went inside. I
stood dumbly waiting. He came out again still holding the tunic
and more annoyed than ever. "He is a nervy turtle, that smally.
Says it won't do at all. Wrong one, he says. Says it is no good
to him. Turns his bloody red pig's eye on me, he does, and says
it is no good to him. Here!"

But I had not the time. I turned and fled, leaving the tunic
in the soldier's hand.

As it was, when I finally got home, carrying some pork meat
wrapped in lotus leaves, the mistress said, "Where *have* you
been, you bawd?"

I said, as soft as Swatow silk, that the butchers had been
cutting the hogs. That I had no idea why they were so slow that
day.

❨ "One Night They Formed a Plot"

I stood behind the screen listening. Big Venerable Shen
could not bring himself to give an account of his day at the
Board of Punishments until he had put down five little bowls
of steaming tea.

"My tongue," he said, "is all dried up."

At last he told this story:

An informer, whom the master did not name, had whispered
to someone in the Censorate that matters of interest could be
learned from a certain prostitute in a mean tavern near the
Drum Tower—a disgusting swillhouse that catered to slaves.

As before, the hearing was badly managed. They sent bannermen out to fetch the whore, and the men were gone half the
morning. "So we stood there. They would not allow us to smoke,
or to leave the hall. We got to talking of the old war against the

whites just to keep Wei Lin-tu off dog-baiting. Tedious! These are busy men, the Ears of the Court, duck, you don't hang them out to dry on the bank of the stream like that!"

At last they had her in, a short, thick girl with a broken-out face and a sulk—a pout—as if someone was cheating her—tugging and wringing a greasy gown in which she had come. Her name was Cassia Cloud. . . .

And ayah! I had known even before hearing her name who it was. Cassia Cloud from Chao-er's. I remembered that malice-darkened face looming over the crap table to tell me about Nose's robbery, about Nose naked in Peach Fragrance's room; the pink tongue darting out again and again.

"She was extremely uneasy, yet brazen and defiant," the master said. "She swore by the Dragon Countenance himself that she would not swear in for us. You can imagine how this excited the magistrates—made us all think she knew more than the grimace on that dull face showed."

The Recorder read aloud the Emperor's proclamation offering fifty taels, good current silver money, to any yellow person who would discover to the authorities the arsonists of the fires. . . .

This stubborn girl appeared to despise money, and threats did no good; she simply looked bruised and put upon, and would not talk.

So Magistrate Hu ordered her jailed, specifying the elephant stables, and they led her off—the morning apparently quite wasted!

But hai! When the bannermen took her into the elephant enclosure and she saw boxfuls of white slaves there, she underwent a change—one of the bannermen said the rouge patches on her cheeks went the color of liver sickness and the rest of her skin turned shiny like a candle, and she said, have mercy, she'd talk.

Here she was kneeling again on the stool before the magistrates—and she went stubborn again! Like a tree stump. You could see under the bluff that she was terrified—of something to do with the whites, or with what she knew.

"Magistrate Han—you know him, duck—that giant with the long, narrow warrior mustaches drooping down on either side of his mouth? picture of the anger of war itself? upper arms big as oak barrels?—you do, but in any case, he turned, soft at first, then like an awful autumn windstorm, to considerations of Imperial vindictiveness: . . . the melting of the fat off your bones in a hot room if you remain guilty of the crime of with-holding knowledge of the fires we have had. Heat for heat: that would be His Merciful Presence's method. . . . Until those murrey cheeks of hers went sickly greenish again and the candleskin began to drip. I was a bit afraid myself!"

Whereupon she agreed to testify if they would only stop tor-menting her. It was hard to believe how agreeably, and with what alacrity, she warmed to her work.

She spoke first about her master, a miserable cobbler named Chao-er, and how he used to receive stolen goods from the dirty white pigs, and she reminded the magistrates of the case of the slave Nose—

At the sound of that name I leaned my forehead against the screen. It seemed to me that in telling the story the master was shouting at the little mistress; he sounded as fierce as the bark-ing wonks in the streets that wakened me each morning.

—of the slave Nose who stole from a yellow woman and gave his loot to a yellow prostitute: not this Cassia Cloud but another in the same tavern. And reminded the magistrates, too, that Chao-er had admitted to the authorities receiving stolen goods on that occasion.

"All right," the witness then said, and her eyes were now gleaming. It was clear that she had begun to realize that she might be a person of importance. "All right, now I shall tell it. One night they formed a plot, and this pig Nose and my master put twenty or thirty whites, turn about, in a circle of chalk on the floor and made them swear to burn and kill. They were going to commence with the Forbidden City, and they were to burn their masters' houses, and they were to kill yellow people. Some would gladly have avoided swearing but dared not refuse such powerful men. Wolf and Fish Bait, they were in it, too. My master, Chao-er, was going to help them. He wanted to be Em-peror, that's what he said, and Nose wanted to be the General. I heard this Nose declare and mutter that some people had too much and other people had too little."

Nose! Nose!

"My mistress, Chao-er's wife, she said she would poison me if I mentioned anything about those stolen goods, and those dirty white pigs were going to burn me under my gown if I breathed the plot. Now I've done it, and, Honors, you must keep

me close, you must. . . . The only yellows in the plot are my
master and mistress Chao-er. And—*ai! ai!*—I nearly forgot, the
one called Peach Fragrance was there. She was in it, the one they
call the Taiyuan Beauty, a whore. . . ."

The master said with mounting vehemence that Chao-er had
been arrested, and that this Nose . . .

I felt that I was . . . my left foot, in an old black slipper,
which was too large and was scuffed at the great toe, was in the
chalk circle, and I was bent forward, looking down at the shoe,
being sworn: If the Forbidden City caught fire, I, though small,
weak, and pierced with pain in my rheumy lungs, I would burn
and I would kill! I began to laugh! It was a lark! A moment's
manumission. It was a joke—a dream—an unbuttoning! Old
Pearl beside me was in tears from laughter, and I was laughing
and coughing. My shoulders shook with laughs and coughs as
I waited for the dousing of wine. . . . I perceived through my
heaves that there was no circle on the floor; that I was behind
the door screen, half choked with laughter and hacking coughs;
that I had just now heard Big Venerable Shen beyond the screen
shout at his gasping wife about a *plot*. Suddenly the end flap
of the screen, flying outward from the dining chamber, cracked
my forehead and caused me to take some stumbling backward
steps, and I saw over me the swarthy, ox-eyed face of himself,
my master. The laughter became a solid lump in my neck, and
I began to cough in earnest.

"Whatever possesses you, girl?" the yellow man barked at me.

Yes! For once the suave tongue in the whiskerless yellow lips
spoke with a terrible accuracy. I must have been possessed—like
that heavy-limbed girl on the deck of the *East Garden*. But not
by God. By some devil. Had some trickster devil come into my
head to make me swear the comical oath again, laugh again,
and cough again, as I eavesdropped in back of the pantry screen?
Had a devil come on me to show me—*but not the master*—the
enormity of the yellow man's belief in the story the disappointed,
stumpy, pimpled country girl had blurted out to the authorities?
Plot! Old Pearl, her tough vine strength gone brittle and crumbly
as if the vine shaft was nothing after all but bark—this ruined
Pearl in a *plot*? And I, White Lotus, scarce knowing the difference between a laugh and a cough—I in a *plot*? And Nose . . .
Nose!

The thought of Nose's danger struck me with such force that

my coughing was driven out of me as though by a thump between the shoulder blades.

"I swallowed down the wrong throat, Big Venerable," I weakly
said, tears in my eyes from having relived the absurdly funny
oath.

"What are you doing, eating now? You are serving at table!"

Had the trickster devil in my eyes told him that I had the habit
of standing behind the screen listening, listening? "Yes, Big
Venerable," I said.

He sadly shook his head and withdrew.

([Talk of Home

My fears for Nose grew day by day, and with them my
homesickness. There came a rainy morning; my chest hurt. Big
Madame Shen ordered me to go to the grain market to buy some
millet flour, and knowing that the carpenter Kao, who owned
Old Pearl, had his shop in Sixth Hutung, not far from the Imperial Granaries near the grain market, I ran all the way under
a torn oil-paper umbrella, spattering mud on my leggings, to have
some time to steal with my friend from home. I had never dared
visit her because of the wormwood character she had attributed
to her master, but that day I felt near the end of my resources
and I needed support of a kind that my fellow slave Gull could
not give me.

Asking the way of passing slaves I found the shop, and, having invented a false errand in case carpenter Kao, in a mood to
heave board ends, should overhear my arrival, I made my way
to the compound entrance and rang the pull bell.

A slave woman came to the gate. I almost turned away, thinking I had after all the wrong house. The woman was gaunt,
dirty, with a surly, peckish eye. She was not even the wasted
and discouraged Old Pearl I had seen at Chao-er's; this woman
seemed to be incurably ill. But it was my friend, or what was left
of her, and recognizing me she stepped forward in a sudden flood
of tears into my arms.

She drew me inside, assuring me that the carpenter was away
with his cart, delivering a chest he had made.

The carpenter's house, like his person, was mean, obdurate,
and morose. The kitchen was faced with smoke-darkened mud

plaster, the cooking pit was narrow, and Pearl lived in the merest lean-to shed, like some cold storeroom for cabbages, which jutted out from the kitchen into the shop courtyard. Pearl told me that Kao's hammering, his rattling of gluing clamps, his slapping of board on board woke her before each dawn and prevented her sleeping after dark; he worked late by lantern. His shop was his tavern, sweat his wine.

We were helpless; we talked of home. Old Pearl's voice, which at first was feeble and cough-jointed, like an old chair creaking, began slowly to gain strength, until, as she recalled incident after incident from our sweet Arizona past, it became something like her storytelling chant at home, and I had the eerie feeling that the commonplace events of our lives within the village hedge had been great fables, legends, stories not of limited men and women but of glorious, powerful, free spirits of the past. We began to laugh as she talked. She stood in the middle of the kitchen floor. I heard the richness of the bygone in her, and no future. Her eyes now had the ferocious tale-telling glint, and I thought of her leaning her hand on my shoulder that day after Agatha was abandoned at the trailside; I thought of her beside me on the deck of the slave ship calming the panic of hundreds of women with her story of the donkey and the jaguar. A flood of laughter poured out of me, and it tasted in my mouth like bitter spoiled fruit, because it stood for grief, horrible grinning grief.

I suddenly asked, "What has happened to Nose? Why did our Gabe turn into such a madman, so drunk all the time?" There was still laughter in my throat, but there was an urgency, too, that I could scarcely keep in control.

"No surprise, child. No, no. It was the direction in which he *had* to go."

"Why?" I was abruptly on the edge of tears.

"Would you want him to be a 'good' slave, child? That man has to be in *front*." But it was Pearl who was weeping! "Listen," she said, "being bad is the only revenge. They put a value on you, they buy you—the only answer you can give is to be worthless. That's the way to cheat them, girl! Be so bad that you're not worth a dirty copper. Ayah, I love Nose. Nose understands all that."

"Do you think he lit fires?"

"Hai, I don't know. I doubt it, child. The spirit of revenge is only a kind of make-believe. We're too weak. It's something we pretend. Do you know those poor white storytellers you see, just better than beggars, with the little shadow lamps they use? That's Nose. Nose is one of them. Make-believe—by being worthless, worthless."

"Why won't he do anything for himself? I saw him the other day at the prison, and he has lost all his spirit. What do you suppose has happened to him?"

"Ai, child, after you pretend you are worthless for a while you become so. . . . Fah! I don't want to talk about any of that. Look here, listen to this!"

My dying friend, her eyes like hot charcoals, began another tale. She chanted, standing with legs spread, arms raised, fingers clutching at the dense material of her story. . . .

A door slammed in the shop court, signaling the carpenter's return, and under my watchfulness this woman crammed with wild memories and vivid feelings suddenly shrank, became desiccated, and a senile voice and trembling hand sped me to the gate. As I ran down the alleyway I heard the old woman's feeble coughing behind me.

On the way home the pain in my chest felt like rage, and once I dropped the meal bag, and part of the flour was dampened.

❮ Good Swords

The mistress took me to the beheadings for the betterment of my soul. I think she felt I needed a spiritual purge; that she considered Old Bow too creaky and Gull too solid and Bean and the runners too stupid to be mixed up in plots, but Small White Lotus had an evasive eye!—or some such. She hired a street chair carried by two flea-bitten white freedmen, and I followed behind.

Wolf and Fish Bait were to have their heads cut off for what some yellow women thought they had heard the slaves say in the street about the fires.

The execution ground was in the Outer City, in the geomantically ill-favored southwestern quarter, and when we reached the Gate of Direct Rule, giving out from the Tartar City to that quarter, Big Madame Shen dismounted from the chair and paid off the bearers, who clamored bitterly for more money, but she waved them away with the back of her hand. We would walk the rest of the way. The crowd was too thick for sedan chairs. We were part of what seemed a holiday throng—a large press of yellow men and women, dressed as if for a temple or a reception, with many slaves in smart livery being taken along for an education. The crowd walked down the middle of the street, past the great factory where the exquisite glasslike tiles of gold, blue, green, and red were made for the palaces of the inner cities, and through a district of elegant shops, with gilded signboards, where paintings, scrolls, books, and curios were sold. It was a cheery bright day. The buds were swollen on the late acacias lining the street, while certain willows already had silvery leaves swimming in the air like great shoals of minnows.

Big Madame Shen greeted her many acquaintances with deferential bows and the gesture of humility—clenched hands placed together and pumped up and down. More than once she expressed herself to friends, with a sweet trill of laughter, as most apprehensive over what we were about to see.

The execution ground was a large area enclosed by a spirit barrier with a clear opening only on the western side, so that the ghosts of dead criminals would leave the city at once. With the help of our master's friend the curio dealer P'an, whom we met, and who had two slaves along to study the day's teaching, we found a place to stand with a fair view of the executioners' platform, near the mat shed where the officials of the Board of Punishments would sit when they arrived.

I stood behind the curio dealer and my mistress with P'an's Goose and P'an's Hairy Devil. We whites knew enough to remain silent and to take on a bullyragged look, as if to show that the lesson was striking deep even before it was taught. I thought at first that I could keep myself from being frightened; I had seen a troop of heads carried in soldiers' hands, so this was not much—two men to die. I had a brief glimpse in my mind of Wolf: sitting in Chao-er's with Peach Fragrance on his lap, his magician's hands fluttering around her slit gown, a grin frozen on his half-drunk, acne-scarred face—a man ferociously alive and careless of consequences. Fish Bait I scarcely knew; a large man, Wolf's hanger-on.

"Enlighten me," the curio dealer said. "Why are they chopping off only two heads, when I understand they have rounded up so many of the dirty pigs who were in the conspiracy to . . . *to burn us and slaughter us?"* The vehemence with which P'an spat out these last words made me shiver.

"As I understand it," my mistress began . . . and how she enjoyed being an expert! The master's friend was not deaf, yet she spoke in a shrill, firm tone, so ears all around could take in her special position, which her husband, engaged at the Board of Punishments, was fortunately not present to dim in any way. . . . "The magistrates themselves pushed the going ahead with these two executions, their logic being: these two men were of turtle-shell temperaments, either they were blockheads or they were resolute, and nothing, you see, had been, or ever would be, dragged from them about the plot—though the proofs against them were strong that they were parties to it"—yes, this was Big Venerable Shen's declamatory style; she had a nice little ear—"so it was urged that the example of punishment, through the immediate beheading of these two, might lead others to un-fold what they knew of the plot and recommend themselves for the clemency of the Dragon Countenance. So, at least, Shen says." In truth his pompous phrases turned stickily in her mouth, like a greedy bite of malt taffy.

Big Venerable P'an was well satisfied with this answer.

And I? I had the strangest mixture of feelings: of dread at the sound of this plodding, methodical, maggoty inanity that my mistress mouthed; of a self-protective conviction that all this had nothing to do with me; and of a righteous fury that gave me a queer inner quiet, a complacency almost, a feeling that these haunted people were at a disadvantage before us their slaves, for they were harried by a shame that drove them deeper and deeper into shame itself. At the same time I kept turning over in my mind the change in Nose. What had Pearl meant by his having to be "in front"? Were drunkenness and outlawry and purposeful worthlessness the essences of some kind of leadership? Could they lead anywhere but to this platform draped in crimson cloth? . . . I wanted to get away. Fear for Nose's safety was suddenly, vivid-ly, fear for my own. I looked this way and that, but I knew I could no more get away than if I were bounded by walls too thick for an elephant to butt down. I was quickly in control, sustained by that weirdly calm undercurrent of anger I had been feeling at the hypocrisy of which human beings seemed to be capable.

There were official delays, it seemed. There was no sign yet of the procession of the authorities and the condemned.

A yellow family near us took a picnic lunch from baskets and sitting on the dusty ground they ate it.

Now Big Madame Shen spoke to her friends in a murmur. I was standing directly behind her and could not but overhear— though "overhear" may be wrong, since to her I was not there, no more endowed with ears or sense than a rake handle, or a pole for bean vines to climb on. Can a broom standing in the corner overhear?

"There will be more beheadings, take my word," she confided. "So I am informed by your esteemed friend Shen." She passed a fan across her face with a sensuous look—which, though it may have had to do with her pleasure at being a knowledgeable insider rather than with the substance of what she was saying, was nonetheless disgusting. "He tells me they have tried the tavern-keeper Chao-er, and his wife, and this man Wolf's yellow mistress, Peach Fragrance, who also calls herself Hsia T'ai-t'ai—says she was married, but no husband has put in an appearance, *as you can imagine*—they have tried this miserable household—how could they be so *enamored* of white people?—for having a part in the slaves' plot, and *they* will lose their heads, too. Yellow examples, you see. To let our poorer sort of yellow people understand they had best not mix with whites. So Shen Lao-yeh tells me."

Friend P'an's delight at this news took the form of a stern, deploring expression.

"And after that, many whites besides. Many."

Nose! Nose! My rage now was at myself—that I could stand on the solid ground with a mask on my face and do nothing, nothing, nothing. The sighing of the crowd around us sounded all at once like the roar of the smoking breakers on the shoals of Santa Barbara where the slave ship waited, and I thought I might faint.

I fastened my eyes, to steady my head, on a side view of curio dealer P'an's wrinkled neck and face, as he digested what Madame Shen had been saying. Suddenly I had to fight down a crazy laugh. He was so tickled by my mistress's promises of more beheadings that his face had grown gray with a conscientious severity.

These people thought that we slaves comprehended little or nothing, but I could see all I needed to see; my fury, outgoing again, subdued my fears again.

P'an said to his slaves, "Now pay close mind, Goose! Hairy! I want you to learn a lesson today, and learn it well."

A small procession had appeared from our left hand and was now approaching the platform and the mat sheds along a roped-off passageway. Two mandarins led the way, in scarlet cloaks with voluminous cowls which were pulled up over their official hats; they had a strange, sinister appearance. Then, surrounded by a handful of guards and four executioners dressed in funereal white, came Wolf and Fish Bait, bare to the waist in the cool spring air—but what could a chill matter to them? Their forearms were tightly bound together behind their backs, and strips of paper three feet long, with large characters describing their crime, hung down their backs from their necks.

The party proceeded to the mat sheds, where the mandarins sat behind tables arranged in the shade. The condemned men kneeled. I saw some officials talking to Wolf, occasionally pointing up at the platform, and I supposed that they were trying one last time to extract from him, in the face of death, a full confession of the slave plot.

I saw Wolf clearly; we were no more than forty paces away. He kneeled upright and silent, not refractory or heroic in bearing, merely sullen—true to himself.

The palaver ended. Neither Wolf nor Fish Bait would open his mouth. With formalistic flourishes one of the mandarins wrote some large characters in vermilion ink on the papers hanging on the prisoners' backs—authority for the executioners to proceed.

Two of these white-clad men led the condemned pair up onto the platform, placed them on their knees, and began arranging rope headstalls under their chins, while the other two, wearing bloodstained yellow leather aprons, went to an altar beside the mat shed and took up swords, centuries old, having broad, short blades, like those of cleavers, fixed on long wooden handles carved with grotesque heads at the ends. They climbed the platform steps.

I had a shuddering moment of imagining Nose in Wolf's place, as an executioner began to stretch Wolf's neck by pulling on the rope halter.

"Eyes ahead, Goose. Sharp eyes, Hairy."

My mistress, falling back a little, reached for my hand, ostensibly to press home the teaching, as P'an was so boomingly doing, but actually, I judged by the fervor of her damp grip, to rally my sympathy for her—poor lady, so sensible of pain!

I could not watch. I dropped my eyes and studied the figures of peonies woven into Venerable P'an's sea-gray gown.

I heard dull blows, almost simultaneous, I heard the executioners each roaring, "I have killed!" Then I heard the spectators all shouting, "Good swords! Good swords!"—a superstitious warding off of the touch of those blades on their own necks.

When I looked up, the executioners were already placing the two heads in small wooden cages to be displayed at the tops of high poles at the gate of these grounds, to remind whites of their mortal duties to yellows.

My heart, though it pounded, was safe. I felt again a surge of that indignant fury which seemed to flow into a sense of moral advantage. Not we but these masters and mistresses were the transgressors—the mandarins in splendid crimson cowls, the magistrates, the men in yellow leather aprons freshly covered with blood, the crowd of spectators, these whispering yellow people. Not Wolf, with his drunken eyes and bird-wing hands, not stupid Fish Bait dogging his thick torso wherever Wolf might lead; not the slaves, not the white slaves. *Merely being slaves* gave us the advantage, though it might also give us pain, weariness nearly to death, and violent death itself.

I even felt that I was getting a little audacity, but I was unable to imagine what to do with it.

Yet . . .

There was a blaze of sunlight in my tight-shut eyes on my rotten mat that night. I was walking along an out-of-the-way goat path in the wilderness of chaparral and rabbit brush and greasewood at the far end of the village at home, daydreaming, and I was squirrel-small, no more than six or seven, I think. Turning a bend in the path dotted with goat droppings, I came on a group of older boys, over ten, becoming hunters, of lizards at least, and I could see that they had stolen a stray pullet and thought themselves brave, and they were secretively preparing to cook it over a small fire. There was a clamor among the boys at my arrival along that unfrequented path, for fear I would give them away and they would be whipped every one, and shy, gentle Wesley Bane—*I saw him decapitated outside our compound wall*

—was among them, and he urged them to give me a taste of the
pullet to glue my tongue to the roof of my mouth, but Gabe,
sticking out his chest, came toward me with deer eyes and told
me that I had not walked on that path at all, I had seen nothing,
I should run directly to the First Methodist Church and get on
my knees and pray to God asking Him to forget that foolish girls
sometimes straggled into the underbrush where dangerous hyenas
and man-eating bears lived. I turned to flee. . . .

I heard Gull sigh on her k'ang. I was awake. But had I been
remembering? Had Gabe, now Nose, denied me beside the path
in that way? Had he really turned me back, made me run? Or
had this simply been a dream?—a reinforcement of that sweet
self-preserving feeling I had had earlier in the day: that I was
not involved, that the happenings all around me had nothing to
do with me? I could turn and run away!

(A Walk with Mink

In the following days Big Madame Shen was unusually
gentle with me, and my audacity, such as it had been, sickened
and turned into bitterness, which I hid.

The mistress told me one day that she intended to pay me a
compliment: to show her trust in me she was going to leave Big
Young Venerable, of whose person she was wildly jealous, in my
charge, while she and the master went on an outing to Jade
Springs Hill with their friends the P'ans and the Suns. This, she
said, would leave Gull, who usually nursed the boy when the
mistress was out, free to prepare a meal against the party's return.

So I saw that the mistress's "trust" was simply her convenience.

My show of pleasure at this announcement of hers was one
of my best bits of acting, and my pretense filled me with as
much laughter as the news itself.

The day was dry and mild, and I took the child for a walk.
We headed southward. Something perverse in me wanted this
bloodthirsty child to feast his eyes on Wolf's and Fish Bait's heads
in their wooden cages; perhaps *he* might learn an unexpected
lesson.

Spring had fully come. Fragrant white blossoms like bunches
of grapes hung from the locust trees that lined Hata Gate Street,
and plane trees here and there were spreading out their shiny

leaves, bigger than human hands, which filtered a shimmering light on boles mottled with browns, reds, and greens. The boy skipped ahead of me, and I recklessly let him run. At Sun's house I paused, knowing that the yellows were away in the hills, and Sun's Mink, seeing me from the gate shield where he was lounging, came out to me. I asked him to join me in a stroll, and, grinning, he did.

He walked slowly beside me with his tense stooped-over carriage.

The boy came panting back and, seeing me with Mink, he said, "I shall tell my mama that you have been idling."

Mink said, "Do, and I'll skin you like an eel, Big Young Venerable."

The boy ran away with big eyes, laughing but scared. He began to throw stones, with a great show of bravery, at tree trunks.

I felt ashamed of my notion of taking the child to see the heads on display, and we bore right, toward the gates of the Forbidden City.

Mink said with a gentleness that startled me almost as much as the suddenness with which he brought the subject up, "Nose is as good as dead."

Did Mink, too, know about those few minutes in the dark room at Chao-er's?

Mink asked me if I had heard what Cassia Cloud had been doing. There was a lot of talk among the slaves, he said, about that bitch fox.

"I know that she told the magistrates about the 'plot,' as she called it."

"Worse than that," Mink says. "She has gone mad. She is telling them new things every day. She's inventing. The magistrates are off their heads, too. They keep asking her for more, more, more, so we hear, and she can't help herself—she *has* to give it to them."

At the Board of Punishments, the day before, Cassia Cloud had given a deposition which, in short, accused Nose of having enlisted a slave named Weasel to help set the fire in the Forbidden City; Weasel's wife was said to be a slave to certain yellow members of the Imperial household, and was supposed to be a cook within the Forbidden City, and was to be the men's accomplice, according to the whore.

Mink squatted in the dust to draw me a diagram of some of the palaces in the Forbidden City—the fires were *here*, Weasel's wife was said to have her kitchen *here;* then, half rising, Mink crouched partway between his tracings in the gutter and what passed with him for being erect, and he vehemently said, "Weasel is one of our Coal Hill Boys, and Nose belongs to the Drum Tower Boys, and you know, White Lotus, you aren't going to see any two such men whisper together. Milk and vinegar don't mix."

Cassia Cloud's whole tale had been a lie. Mink was in a fury, which had grown on him as he had paid out the account of Cassia Cloud's informing. He looked up at me from his stooping position. . . . Weasel had been taken up by the bannermen—good as dead. He had not been anywhere near the Forbidden City the day it burned, he had alibis that would stretch to the Western Hills. He and Nose hated each other—could not have plotted together.

"What do you suppose is the matter with her?" I asked.

"Some of the men say she's got ice at the root of her belly, and that's why they want to set fire to her down there to punish her."

"It can't be just that," I said. "She hates everybody—white and yellow."

"Maybe the bastard magistrates are paying her. Maybe she's doing it for money."

"Ai, no. Look, Mink. She has mandarins listening to her with their mouths sagging open. Don't forget she was trash—indentured for slitting a purse, wasn't it?"

"I think she wants to get back at our boy Weasel—he probably had her for a few coppers over there at Chao-er's. He's a brave boy with the pants-sword, I know that."

"What about Nose, then?"

"Maybe she wants to get back at him for *not* taking her."

"He wouldn't want her," I said, trying to be careful how my voice sounded.

"That's the point," Mink said.

I shook my head. "No," I said. "It's more than that. It's a chance for her. It's a big chance to be somebody."

The little yellow boy in my charge came running back to me on the dusty street. Something along the way—perhaps a snarl from a slave pulling a water cart along the street, across whose path the boy may have run—had frightened him. He clung to my gown and looked up at me, weeping, and my heart, racked beyond bearing, suddenly melted for him, for his childish terror of noth-

ing at all, and I ran my fingers tenderly through his hair and began to sing a home song.

❮[A Nest of Wasps

A woman slave we did not know came one morning to
our gate (harmony in all the courtyards!) saying she belonged
to the widow Fan, in Sixth Hutung close to carpenter Kao, and
that Kao's Old Pearl was lying badly sick on her brick bed in the
shed off the carpenter's kitchen insistently calling out for Shen
Ch'ing-wu's White Lotus.

When Bean, the gateman, reported this to us in the back courtyard, Gull dropped a ladle on the floor and said I had best not go.

This made me angry, and I said, "Best for whom? Best for
you?"

Gull said with a calm that enraged me even more, "Good time
to lay quiet, girl."

"When your friend calls your name?"

"Kao's Old Pearl is not a good slave. I saw her drunk in the
market."

Then I said bitterly in English, "Watch out! A witch is passing!
A witch!—But if you aren't a witch yourself, you don't turn your
eyes to look."

I left with the widow Fan's slave, having urgently asked my
mistress's permission to go. "For a very few minutes," the mistress had said. "You have the Autumn Retreat to clean."

Old Pearl was lying on a straw tick on her brick bed, talking
wildly in our old white tongue. Her skin hung like dewy cobwebs
on her bones. When I touched her and spoke to her, her eyes
glittered and with a rattling voice she said in the yellows' language, "Fetch Shen's White Lotus. Shen Ch'ing-wu's Small White
Lotus for me. White Lotus! White Lotus!"

I spoke loudly, "Old Pearl! I *am* White Lotus! I'm here."

But she looked through me and asked for me. I had a moment's
irrational fear that just as I often seemed nonexistent to the yellows I might now be fading from the sight of my own kind. I
shook Pearl's shoulders. She groaned and closed her eyes. Soon
she began to ramble again in our flat Arizona accent—gobbets
of supernatural tales, bits of magic recklessly jumbled—until
there began a series of deep coughs that seemed to shake the

whole flimsy lean-to. Then she lay still, and I knew she was dead.
I ran into the shop to tell the terrible carpenter Kao. Without
emotion he told me he had already made a box. Would I get some
men slaves to carry her remains in this box to the whites' burying ground? Then suddenly, to my astonishment, I saw grief on
his face, and he said the woman had cost him a hundred and
eighty taels and he had never got a decent copper's worth of
work out of her.

I went home and got the mistress's reluctant permission to
round up some slaves to bury my friend. I ran to Sun's for Mink's
help. On Stilts borrowed a two-wheeled cart from a vendor of
baskets he knew. Mink conscripted three ragged white men,
strangers to me, and got some shovels somehow, and in the
afternoon our little procession went down Hata Gate Street, into
the Outer City, beyond the built-up section, past the farms and
ponds at last to the slaves' ground in the farthest corner of the
southern city walls, with a cluster of potters' sheds and kilns at
the center and the many haphazard mounds now mostly covered
with knee-high grass and weeds. In two hours we put Pearl down.
The three ragged men spoke only in the yellows' tongue. I had
suffered agonies of superstitious fear and remorse at being unable to prepare the body properly for its passage to the company
of our white-faced God, and again and again, as the strangers dug
—talking loudly, cursing the hardness of the dry clayey ground,
and even laughing, for none of them had known, or cared about,
the dead woman—I remembered the firm voice of our minister,
Reverend Honing, as the body of old Joshua Benton was lowered
into the ground, with the preacher's assurances of rest, peace,
quiet unto the day of the sorting of souls for salvation. All that
could now keep me in one piece, as the dry clods thumped on the
box after it had been roughly dropped in its narrow hole, was
the memory of the *certainty* in Preacher Honing's voice. What was
the good of life if this barren field was to be its goal? Looking
around at the hummocked field, open to the sun except for one
pool of shade under a single ancient pine, I shuddered at the
sight of the crowded graves, unmarked conical mounds, like
yellows' graves but very small, in order to stress at the very last
our utter insignificance—a nest of hundreds of poor white souls
whose fleshly housings had been thrust underground without a
single word of prayer to God for repose, so that the spirits were
undoubtedly restless, damned, at large, and—remembering their

lots on earth—furious. I sensed their flying about me like angry
wasps.

❰ Names

In the following days, as Nose's trial approached, I
thought I might be losing my mind—such strange stories came
to my ears.
Item. Peach Fragrance, the yellow fox from Chao-er's, who,
so far as we had heard, had been loyal to her white friends, suddenly, stirred no doubt by envy of Cassia Cloud, vomited out to
the magistrates a weird story of *another* plot, sworn at *another*
tavern run by *another* cobbler, Han, who in a room with ten or
eleven whites, one night, with wine cups going around, said
Peach Fragrance, had churned the slaves up, observing how well
the rich yellow people lived in the Northern Capital, and advising
the slaves to lay hands on the money. "But how?" asked Wu's
Nose, according to this bitch. (This was a lie, a *lie!* I knew of
Han's inn; slaves did go there. But Nose was a Drum Tower boy,
a Chao-er man. He never went to Han's.) "Why, well enough:
Start a fire, burn the houses of those with the most money, and
kill them all," says Han. "We'll do it," says Nose, according to
her. "Yes," Han says, "we'll do it well enough. We'll send into
the countryside for more slaves, and they'll support us. The sun
will shine brightly, by and by, never fear, my smallies. But if
you tell any of this to the Emperor's men, I shall leave you here
to be beheaded, I'll run away to the seashore, or into the loess
country; I used to live by the sea. Anyway, no one can touch me,
I have friends, important men know me. The best among the
Emperor's household will stand behind Han." So Han said, according to the yellow bitch we thought we loved. Peach Fragrance
named names. Besides Wu's Nose, Tu's Sheep had been there,
she said, and Cheng's Spade, the late Wang's Monkey, Ma's White
Scholar, Chu's Spear, Ts'ao's Braveboy. There seemed no reason
in her list; it was sheer caprice and malice; these were not friends.
All were jailed.
Item. Cassia Cloud was infuriated by this upstart's informing,
and her imagination began to trot like a wounded boar crashing
into any obstacle in its headlong course. Oh, yes, she had often
seen this Hsü's Quack at Chao-er's gate in conversation with

Shih's Wolf, Ch'en's Fish Bait, and Wu's Nose. Lu's First Boy was
often there enjoying special favors of Chao-er's daughter, Silver
Phoenix. And around the chalk circle were the widow Kuo's Card,
Sung's Cabbage, also called Soldier by the whites. At the swearing of the plot, she saw in Chao-er's hand a set of yarrow stalks,
the diviner's shafts, and he made some passes and scattered them
on a table and studied their arrangement, and he said, "Now you
must keep secrecy about the plot; the stalks say that indiscretion
will lead to eye cataracts, stubbed toes, long voyages in storms."
And Nose said, "I won't lose my eyesight! I will not tell a word
of it, even if the yellow people put my head in a cage on a pole!"
   Item. Most depressing of all: The whites in their confusion began to inform against each other. Ch'ien's Shuttlecock, an elderly
slave who was notoriously "good"—we had never seen *him* in the
taverns, and the Imperial beaters and bell-ringers had never
convoyed *him* around the town—this Shuttlecock sanctimoniously
told how Hsü's Quack had tried to enlist his help in setting fire
to the Forbidden City, but he, Shuttlecock, had said he was a
dutiful man and would not run the risk of a sword at his neck;
that he had heard Wu's Nose say he was going to plant coals in
his master Wu's godown, and he would set some merry fires elsewhere in the city. . . . And he told tales on Lin's Strong, Tu's
Sheep, Captain Su's Jumping Stick, Captain Yüan's Whitehair,
Lu's Beetle, Ma's Stupid, Yeh's Heavenly Spirit, a fiddler, and
Wang's Fortune—all jailed at once. And no sooner was Wang's
Fortune jailed than he gladly told the judges how Weasel, a slave
of Hsü, the money-changer, had invited him to a certain kitchen
in the Forbidden City, where his wife cooked, to drink a few cups
of *baigar,* and how Weasel on his third cup had said we would
soon see great *alterations* in the Forbidden City. . . .

《 Scorpion

        I went on a day when Old Bow's muscles were knotted
with rheumatism to fetch tea water at Yang's well. Several slaves
were discreetly murmuring there. There was no laughter. There
seemed to be a heavy weight on our backs in the still setting. The
slaves at the well, who had used to pitch pennies, crack peanuts,
tell jokes, box, and flirt with any girls who brought buckets, now
seemed sluggish and surly. Every recent day had brought new

setbacks and amazements. Not satisfied with having found Chao-er and his wife guilty of receiving the goods stolen from Feng's, the magistrates had tried them for inciting our famous plot, found them in the wrong as a matter of course, and had beheaded them; besides displaying the tavern-keeper's head, the authorities had trussed up his truncated body in chains and left it hanging as a stern reminder, in an open place in the Outer City near the Temple of Heaven. Sixty slaves, all men save five or six, were in jail, named by the insatiable Cassia Cloud, by Peach Fragrance, and, alas, by their own fellow slaves in hope of mercy. Cassia Cloud's excesses of lying had become flagrant, but so hysterical was the entire city that it greeted each new invention of hers with new courtesies and honors. She had said under Imperial oaths whatever drifted into her skull: that Shih's Wolf had given Chao-er fifty taels of stolen silver to go up into the countryside and buy spears, swords, and pistols for the slaves to use in slaughtering their masters; that she had seen in Chao-er's tavern a bag of shot and a keg of gunpowder; that Chao-er had tried to bribe her to swear the plot, offering her silks and silver rings.

And now, as I stood waiting in the spiritless clump of slaves to draw water, I saw the men suddenly stiffen, as if at the sight of a scorpion, and I turned and saw this same Cassia Cloud running toward Chao-er's tavern, to fetch some belongings, presumably, for she lived now under the night protection of Under-Sheriff Wu. The slave Cabbage, sometimes called Soldier by his white friends, who had been named to the magistrates by Cassia Cloud but had not yet been arrested, burst from the group at the well and dashed into the street and blocked the bitch's passage. She looked at him with eyes that were like two little overturned thimbles spilling out their contents of brown liquid dread.

"You gave my name to the judges," Soldier said.

"No!" she cried, raising one hand and fluttering it back and forth, as if to dust Soldier out of her future. "No, no, I never."

"You said it. I know from Bone, the slops man at the jail."

"I never used your name, Sung's Cabbage," she said in a pleading voice.

"You female turtle!" Soldier cried. "It was not best for you. You're going to get fire in your crotch under your gown."

"No! No!" she wailed, and ran around him.

The next day Soldier was taken to jail. And Bone, a freedman

who swept the jail and poured out the prisoners' fecal buckets,
who had been manumitted by a dying master, a free man though
white, a slops-carrier though free—Bone, whom Soldier had inadvertently named, was in jail, too, to stay. They had to find
another white freedman to carry out the pails of ordure, for no
yellow man in the Emperor's city would do such a thing.

(The Ultimate Badness

        A seepage of hysteria spread through the yellow com-
munity. The yellows apparently believed every word of every informer, and the converted elephant pens grew more and more
crowded.

Our masters went about grim-faced and silent, but our mistresses, strangely exhilarated by the tension in the city, became
like magpies: sociable in alarm. The gentle ladies of the Northern
Capital had taken up with lively enthusiasm the education of
their female slaves, by herding them to trials at the Board of
Punishments—tutelage, that is, in docility, virtuous servility, de-
votion to owners, reverence of owners' ancestors, and respect for
"good swords." Big Madame Shen had long been saying that she
wanted to watch a proceeding, and late in the fifth month she
procured, in the name of precautionary instruction, her husband's
permission to take Gull and me to the Board of Punishments to
see a trial.

She had waited for the trial of Nose—who was, as every yellow
matron knew, "something special." I remembered the mistress's
glistening eyes, as she had asked me, that evening of my shame,
"Is he *strong*?"

The locus of the trial was a sumptuous high-roofed hall, with
crimson columns supporting a ceiling on which were pictured
reed-legged cranes and herons in effortless flight. The walls bore
gilded panels incised with willow leaves. Ai, that stifling sensitivity of our masters' civilization!

Big Madame Shen was ushered forward to a section of lacquered
armchairs where many yellow mistresses sat in their fine clothes,
while Gull and I were shooed like backyard fowl to the rear of
the hall into a barricaded area already crowded with slave women,
who were standing.

Three magistrates in embroidered gowns were seated cross-legged on a high dais draped in red velvet. A representative of the Censorate sat on a straight chair behind them on one side, and on the other stood an official holding a banner which was furled and encased in an oilskin cover—the insignia of oblivion, which would not be unfurled except to announce a death sentence.

At our right, in a thicket of gleaming columns, was a spacious pen, or enclosure, where the Ears of the Court, about fifty courtier-mandarins in splendid gowns, had plenty of room to stand and walk about, and Gull and I could see the head and shoulders, among the others', of our own master, Shen Ch'ing-wu, scholar and sub-curator. He was wearing his corded-wolf's-paw bow on his queue; evidently he thought it not too aggressive for *this* spell of justice. Barristers, chamberlains, clerks, and recorders in gowns similar to those of the Ears, though less grand, bustled about the forepart of the hall.

A high double door opened on the right side of the room near the Ears' pen, and four bannermen came in escorting—my knees suddenly seemed made of dry cloth—Nose, who wore, after all, the tunic I had fetched him, which he had said he did not want. He looked wan and listless. He was led to a low wooden stool before the magistrates' dais.

There ensued a flurry of kowtows, obeisances, nods, pumping of clenched hands, and salutes of infinitely subtle degrees of humility, involving every official person in the hall, which would have been irresistibly comical had it not been for the sight of Nose, at the bottom of the heap, knocking his forehead on the marble floor in every direction. How strangely eager to please he seemed!

I suddenly remembered the great Mort Blain and his retinue crawling on their bellies across the dusty courtyard in Palm Springs toward the Syndicate bosses, and with a shudder I realized that it had not been beyond whites to imitate (but rather badly) the hypocrisy of yellow power. It was the powerful man's love of his place and his fear of losing it that set the stamp of hideous falseness on this polite ceremony.

As the trial progressed I was more and more horrified by the elaborateness of the ritual before me, which seemed to hide, as the jewel-like enamel of cloisonné hides the base metal underneath, the ugly truth of the trial. Clerks cried, "Make proclamation for silence!" Chamberlains hinted at the unmentionable name of the Dragon Countenance. Bailiffs chanted formulas announcing successive phases of the proceeding. Mandarins shot their wide sleeves, the magistrates sipped tea.

What did this rigmarole mean? I saw that Nose was looking blankly around the hall, listening not at all to the drone of the proceedings.

At one point it seemed necessary to interrupt the depositions of witnesses and informers, in order that the Ears might erupt from their pen and present themselves, one by one, falling to knees and kowtowing, to the magistrates. How strange! When Big Venerable Shen kowtowed with his splendid wolf's-paw bow whipping uppermost, I felt some sort of disgusting pride, as Gull also apparently did, and we informed our neighbor slaves that *that* one, with the fiercest queue of any, was our master. Our neighbors nodded, seemed impressed by our connection with the corded wolf's paw, and passed along the word, and other white women leaned forward to look around at us, smiling and bobbing their heads. I felt important. I also felt slightly sick.

The catalogue of Nose's crimes. Lawyers' modulations! Wicked, malicious, willful, felonious, conspiratorial, voluntary . . .

"And so forth, and so forth." Over and over! The phrase in the yellows' language was *teng-teng-ti*, which pounded on my ears like physical blows. Was this chain of and-so-forths to be Nose's claim to be remembered?

Hai! Here was Cassia Cloud! She was kneeling on the deponents' stool, which was slightly higher than Nose's, and a fat mandarin was walking back and forth giving little verbal prods to her "memory." How she had changed in manner from the squat girl stopped in the street by Soldier! She was composed, chin-tilted, alert to her prestige—yet helplessly vulgar.

"Did the prisoner Nose ever threaten you in any way?"

Cassia Cloud wrung her hands in what must have seemed to her a gesture of delicacy. "Yes, yes. He. Wolf and Fish Bait. And all them. To burn me under my gown, in that particular place." She almost fell off the stool producing a prim shudder.

"Can you tell me of an occasion when this Nose imposed upon your person?"

"I remember there at Chao-er's one night after the swearing. The whites were talking about their plot, and someone said perhaps *she* would inform on them, meaning myself. But Nose, he said that no, *she* would not tell, not *she*, he intended to have *her*, meaning myself, for a wife, and he ran up to me with his hand out to grasp at my gown below and feel me. I had a dishrag in my hand, and I dabbed it very smartly in his dirty pig face. He backed off, believe me."

As she elaborated her story of Nose's leadership of the plot, Cassia Cloud invented many new details. Cassia Cloud was good of her kind. She was like certain natural gossips, who are unable to see, and so are unable to talk about, anything but the evil, the macabre, the stunted, the malicious, the purely diseased in their fellow beings.

A series of deponents gave various pictures, some of which burned my mind. An informer—a white man!—from the elephant pens, for instance, told how Nose "sits off in a corner by himself, won't speak to anybody, hums songs sometimes, weeps often." An Imperial pumper swore he had seen Nose inside Wu's godown while it was on fire. A guardsman told of Nose's spilling the buckets in the chain at the fire in the Forbidden City, slapping his bare feet in the mud he had made. The gutter-solderer Han, asked if his firepot could have ignited the roof of the palace, said, "I doubt that, Honors, for it was an enclosed pot, like a chimney lantern, with a little mouth *here*, you see, to put in my irons, and I was careful to put *this* part, the back, you see, toward the wind. It was not *my* fire that did it, Honors." Several whites told lies about the palace fire—for what? for money? for safety?—against Nose; stories that I knew to be lies.

Then for the first time I saw Nose's owner: Wu Li-shih of the Revenue Board. This mandarin was not obliged to kneel on the deponents' stool; a special chair was brought for him.

The fat questioner asked, "The day of the fire, Elder-born Wu, what were Nose's movements?"

"I set the man to sewing a pennant on a hame. That's all I know of it."

"As to his character in general, Elder-born Wu, what can you say?"

"I would best not speak as to that."

The loyalty of the master! I wondered just what Big Venerable Shen—or, for it would be more interesting, the mistress—would say about *me* to the magistrates. I was her sweet child; I was so good to her; her trust in me was absolute; dear child; sweet White Lotus! . . . *I would best not speak as to that.* . . .

And yet, come to think of it, Nose had dedicated himself to the cause of worthlessness. He *was* bad. How fiercely, for a moment,

I envied him!—for I had no answer to the yellows. Nose was at least, for good reason, bad all the way through.

And then, as if he were indeed so bad that he wanted to take away from me even these shreds of comfort, of admiration, of love of his nihilism, Nose, being questioned, turned out to be docile, abject, respectful, apologetic—all that a man with any sincerity in his badness would utterly scorn.

"Come, come, Wu's small slave, speak. What do you say for yourself? What have you to offer?"

Nose, in a low and civil voice: "I have nothing to say."

One of the magistrates, thunderstruck by this quiet tone from the tiger he had heard so much about: "You did all this that they've been saying? You lit the fires?"

Nose: "If you say so, Big Venerable Honor."

The fat questioner, suddenly seeming blown up to twice his former size, his cheeks and his grammar both ballooning with astonishment: "What? What? We understood you have been offering all along nothing but peremptory denials of the totality. Nothing to say?"

Nose: "I will say whatever you wish me to say, Big Venerable Honor."

The authorities were all furious at him, and I saw that Nose, shrewd to the marrow, had sensed that the ultimate badness might be gentle goodness. Beautiful man! How he had tricked them!

The chief magistrate, addressing a summary to the Ears, was venting his rage at Nose's submissiveness, though in a voice as flat as the Eastern Plains: ". . . this dirty white criminal on his stool has been indulged with the same sort of proceeding as is due to free men of our own yellow race, though the Merciful Dragon Countenance might well have moved against him in a more summary way. The depositions of whites, in the manner in which we have admitted them here, are warranted by special decree of the Merciful Dragon Countenance. . . ."

I saw the bearer of the flag of death lower its staff and begin to untie the oilskin covering.

"But, Worshipful Ears, the monstrous ingratitude of this white race is what exceedingly aggravates their guilt. Their slavery among us is generally softened with great indulgence and solicitude; they live without cares and are commonly better fed and clothed and are put to less labor than the poor people of most countries. They are indeed slaves, but under the protection of the impartial decrees of the Merciful Dragon Countenance, so none can hurt them with impunity, and they are really happier in this place than in the midst of the continual plunder, cruelty, and rapine of their native land. Yet notwithstanding all the kindness and tolerance with which these people have been treated, we see these heinous crimes, these proven plots to kill and burn. . . ."

The flag was unfurled—it was pure white!—and the bearer was slowly waving it back and forth. I partly wanted to cover my ears, because behind and under the words of the chief magistrate I had begun to hear echoes of a crowd shouting, "Good swords! Good swords!"

The magistrate was now addressing Nose: ". . . You, and the rest of your color, though called slaves in this country, yet you are all far, very far, from the condition of other slaves in other lands; no, your lot is superior to that of thousands upon thousands of yellow people. You are furnished with all the necessities of life —meat, drink, shelter, clothing—without charge or care, in a much better manner than you could provide for yourselves, were you at liberty. What then could prompt you to undertake so vile, so wicked, so monstrous, so execrable, so vicious . . ."

Nose's head was bowed, and my dread of the sword's blow on it grew and grew, until I heard the chief magistrate say: ". . . the sentence I am now to pronounce, which is: That you be carried from this hall to the place from which you came here, and from there, on the fourth day of the sixth moon, between the hours of noon and curfew, to a special place of execution upon the side of the Coal Hill, where you shall be chained to a post and burned to death, being paid for fire with fire, according to the explicit wish of the Merciful Dragon Countenance, and may your wretched soul go promptly to its destination."

(The Lists

In the days following Nose's trial I was gripped every moment by a feeling of *hollowness*. Twice at night, as I tried to flee into sleep, there flashed into my mind vivid pictures of the column of ants, a dark, seething stripe on the uneven ground, advancing toward me. My feet were rooted like cactus columns. If anything was fearful, it was that I felt no fear. I simply stood there. . . .

One morning after breakfast, the master, who looked more and more gaunt each day, as if his devout sweetness were gnawing at his vitals like a cancer, called Old Bow into the parlor and told him that the palace was to issue a proclamation that day promising the Emperor's pardon to anyone who confessed a part in the slaves' plot to burn and kill, and who named his confederates. Gently Big Venerable Shen advised Old Bow to take full advantage of this offer.

Old Bow was outraged. "I have been at home," he vigorously said. "Every night of my life. I never swore the plot. With my bad knee I don't run around. I never join those tavern lice. Big Venerable, you are talking to Old Bow!"

The master said, "I know you, Bow. You are a loyal man. I know you, and I think you are. I am only trying to say to you, it would be best for you to confess, be pardoned in the Emperor's behalf, and have a clean name."

"Big Venerable, I never swore!"

"I understand, Old Bow, I understand. Please open your ears. *It is too dangerous otherwise.*"

"Are you saying, Master, that I should confess to something I never did?"

At this our master blurted out what may have been an involuntary truth; a reflex of his own guilty doubts: "It is better to confess a lie and live than be accused by a lie and die."

Old Bow, his dignity falling off him like a husk from a seed, dropped to his knees and said, "Big Venerable, what must I do, Big Venerable?"

The master said he would tell him what to do. He should wait two or three days; the master would advise him.

When Old Bow told Gull and me in the kitchen of this scene, we wept—for him, for ourselves, for every slave; though for me the crying was dull and scant relief. Since Nose's trial everything had been flat, my emotions had seemed to evaporate away, I felt like a skinful of dust. Nothing mattered, and I was scarcely capable of indignation, sorrow, or even self-pity. I still had a withered bit of misery in me, though, and now I felt some of it for this crepitant, misanthropic Old Bow, whose only wrongdoing in life had been his keeping to himself.

That afternoon we heard of a public report of the proclamation, and within a couple of days we heard of its consequences: a rash of confessions, name-naming, and arrests. Women were now being named in large numbers. The slaves of the city were stampeding to save their own white skins at any cost.

Now each evening we had grim visiting to do at neighbors' gates: passing on lists. A slave would come to our kitchen and recite several times the lists of names—confessed, informed upon, on trial, arrested—and we would have to listen with utmost care, in order to memorize, to be able to spread the word.

Mink came to us one evening, and as he stood by the brick oven reciting the lists his round shoulders on his tiny torso seemed more stooped than ever; his look of craftiness and mischief had given way to a stare . . . into the pit of nonsense; at the dangerous absurdities through which we daily moved, waiting for worse.

"Confessions: Wei's Water Chestnut, Kuo's White Prince, Wang's Fortune, Chu's Mink—*he's* no Mink!—Cheng's Spade, Ma's White Scholar, Sung's Cabbage or Soldier, Tu's Sheep, and Yüan's Whitehair, some call him Ticklebowl. On trial today: Ts'ao's Braveboy—you know him, don't you, Old Bow?"

"He didn't swear," Bow said. "The turtles! Braveboy never swore the plot."

"Widow Kuo's Card, T'ang's Money . . ."

Mink broke off. He would not look at me. He said, as if to Gull, "Here's a list of names the bastard Ticklebowl gave them: Su's woman Snow Fig, Tung's Chairboy, Sun's woman Courteous Poppy—I think the turtle just wants some girls to play with in the jail there—Feng's Drum, Lü's Tallboy, and he gave Shen's White Lotus."

I was still trying to fix the names in my memory when I found myself in Gull's arms, realizing.

But why Ticklebowl? He was nothing to me, or I to him. He had seen me at Chao-er's, but I could not remember that we had ever even spoken to each other.

"The authorities gave the list to that bitch Cassia Cloud," Mink told us, "and she said, 'Yes, Masters, all of them were in it except Lü's Tallboy,' and she said, 'Shen's White Lotus was one of the first to swear in the chalk circle, and she slept with Wu Li-shih's Nose in one of the rooms in Chao-er's tavern.' "

So now. So now the minutes in the dark room belonged to whoever wanted to listen.

Old Bow said, "They'll come to get you, small girl." I heard contempt in his voice.

Gull said to Bow, "You'd better go spit it out, Old Bow, the way the master told you to. They're going to chop off all our heads, every one."

I could not tell at dinner that night whether the master and mistress had heard that I had been named. Big Venerable Shen's eyes were like attic windows back in Arizona—dusty, glassy, opening on an empty place. He was short-tempered, and the mistress apparently got hurt feelings over something and slammed her mouth shut. I made a hundred mistakes, and no one seemed to care.

❨ A Demonstrative Parting

It turned out that my owners did not know about my having been named, because when the bannermen came for me the next morning Big Madame had a wholly unrehearsed attack of crying, with some laughter intermixed, and she tore her hair and undid her coiffure without hope of my restoring it, for I was going to jail. It would do no good to try to hold off until the master returned from the Board of Punishments. The men had an Imperial order with a score of official chops on it. "Hooo!" the mistress wailed, with an underpinning of gasping that sounded like giggles; she was near breaking some things.

I went as I was. The mistress embraced me and, in a paroxysm of her avowals of love for me and dependence on me, scratched my neck with her fingernails. And then, as we were parting, I saw a secret in her perfectly dry eyes. It was only a glint, but I saw it. She was terrified of me. She was glad to have me taken off. She wanted me locked away. I was very much afraid myself, but I walked off between the constables with a feeling of exultation mixed with my dread. I was fifteen years old, and I was an object of great fear.

❨ A Game of Dice

I was marched up Hata Gate Street between two tall bannermen carrying staves, and I must admit I felt important.

Scarce anyone looked at us, for an arrest of a slave was by no means a scandal any more, but I do believe my two powerful escorts wore a foolish look complementary to my youthful swagger. So much brawn to fish for this tiny carp!

All my feeling of grandeur and jauntiness blew away like summer smoke the moment the elephant door banged shut behind me.

The thick-walled chamber had been a pen for a pair of elephants. Some twenty paces wide and thirty long, it contained two platforms, three paces by six, raised knee-high from the floor, on which the elephants had stood, chained by the legs to pairs of stone pillars. Tiny high openings gave scant light and air.

Men and women slaves were mixed together in the pen; there were about a dozen women among a hundred men.

These prisoners were sitting, squatting, and lying in tangled clusters on the brick floor in clothes for the most part rendered filthy by the dust of elephant dung clinging to the ill-swept bricks. The odor was foul, the air dark, the mood—despite a buzz of chatter and occasional hoots of loud laughter—was one of dejection and corruption more soul-drowning even than that of the women's hold on the *East Garden*.

I stood alone. My eyes swept the pen for a sight of Nose. I saw him at last, sitting against a wall with his forehead down on his drawn-up knees; I recognized his shoulders—in the tunic I had brought him. I wanted to go over and touch his back, let him know I had been taken up, but I did not.

A woman, Sun's Courteous Poppy, beckoned to me, and I went and crouched beside her, but soon I found her garlicky breath and simpering unbearable.

Near us on a corner of one of the elephant platforms four men were setting trained crickets to fight each other and betting on the outcome, and their group was the rowdiest in the pen, and thinking that Nose must rouse himself at some time, and that gaming and callousness would surely draw him, I crawled on hands and knees toward the men, watching them. These four —Lu's Beetle, Widow Kuo's Card, Ma's White Scholar, and Yüan's Whitehair, or Ticklebowl, who for reasons I could not fathom had named me to the magistrates—immediately haled me in and adopted me as a kind of mascot. They kept to their corner of the platform and made much of me. They ordered me to tend their little bamboo fighting-cricket cages, tiny jails within the jail, which had been smuggled in to them somehow, and they had me record in my head their complicated debts to one another, a reckoning that gave them an illusion of a future.

Gradually I felt, like a blast of damp cellar air, the real chill of the pen: a bitterness among the prisoners, not merely against the whites, but against each other. Within a few hours I saw the whole depressing picture. Each was for himself. So many slaves —at least a score—had now been condemned to death that a panic was on. The thing to do was to save one's own skin, and that meant confessing and denouncing in exchange for an Emperor's pardon. White was informing on white—yet ironically there was a currency passing around that one had to pick up, by guile or by goodness, before one could make a viable confession: the agreed circumstances. The slaves counseled together on the story they should tell and then used it to save themselves severally even if that meant abandoning each other to the sword. A detailed myth of the plot had been evolved for confessional purposes, and no one could safely go before the magistrates with admissions that did not interlock with the myth. Enmities were being paid off, but friendships were not being rewarded. The deadly game was disgusting and compelling, I could see that I had better busy myself at it.

The sight of Nose sickened me—so dreary, motionless, limp— though I kept up with my four patrons a show of wild cheerfulness. Once Nose raised his head, and he looked in the general direction of our noisy corner, and I was on the point of jumping up and threading my way across the crowded floor to speak to him, when down the head went again. His face—an old man's!

Bit by bit my four men endowed me with the great myth: who was supposed to have met whom by what slave postern to plan which fire, about the supposed meeting in Big Venerable Ma's kitchen, and how Yeh's Heavenly Spirit was supposed to have pulled out the two strings of cash he had earned fiddling and showed them to Tu's Sheep to urge the man to let him into the plotting. . . .

We slept curled on the bricks. We were like a pond of frogs at night; we put up a racket of groaning, unhealthy snorts, snoring, and starts from bad dreams, with cries.

For my part I fell into a deep sleep in the first hours but I awoke drenched in sweat and convinced that the end of the world was coming. I remembered, with a terrifying vividness, a half-mad, long-haired, barefooted Californian would-be prophet who had come to our village when I was seven or eight and had stood outside our village hedge screaming for three days and nights about the beast of the sea, marked with the number six six six, with seven heads and ten horns, and the angels pouring out the vials of wrath like the blood of a dead man, and men gnawing their tongues for pain, and the woman arrayed in purple and scarlet, *the mother of harlots and abominations,* and Babylon the cage of every unclean and hateful bird—and on and on to the binding of Satan for a thousand years. Finally someone threw a silver dollar over the hedge, and he stopped screaming and went away.

All through this night I yearned to be beside Nose. He was the one who was condemned, but I needed his comfort!

My second day in jail the weather was hot. A yellow doctor visited us; Ma's White Scholar said the masters were afraid we might die of some pestilence rather than by chopper or torch; hence their solicitude. Of course the yellows were obsessed with smallpox, which would not discriminate between the classes of men, slave and owner, and which might start in our filth and spread to the town. They did not clean our pens, however.

That day Old Bow appeared with a gloomy face, resigned to confessing lies. I tried to urge my quartet of rapscallions to take him in, but Old Bow was much too mechanical for their disenchanted club. He sat alone, staring. He would have a long wait, for since the Emperor's proclamation the list of applicants for confession had grown exceedingly long.

Nose remained listless, melancholy; I stayed away from him.

I laughed often, I must admit—what else could one do? The staple in our circle for crazy laughter was Cassia Cloud: how a confessor would think up a new detail to add to the myth, and she would follow with a grave confirmation, *Oh, yes, just so! I did indeed see Cheng's Spade there, gone soldierly on three bowls of wine and swearing to stab his big master in the liver.* Lu's Beetle was in particular a ready laugher. He would pummel his thighs and hoot with his head thrown back and his teeth gleaming like the rows of ivory "stones" in the game the Shens played often at night on an inlaid board.

For some reason I thought of Kathy Blaw's raucous shout in the coffle, long ago, that the yellows would devour us all. She had not been so far wrong at that.

On an oppressive night as I lay on my back awake, unable to sleep in the fetid, motionless air, I felt a hand grope on my thigh, then my dirty gown was pulled up to my hips, and some man took me quickly, entering with difficulty into my indifference and driving at my vitals, with what must have been a pent-up hatred of all mankind. For a moment, while it was happening, I had a wild hope that it was Nose—that he had crept across the room to me; but I knew that this was an absurd idea, for Nose was unaware of my presence in the pen, so far as I knew, and this man's importunity was different from his. I did not know which man it was, though by his goings-on next day, his plaguing me for his cricket-fighting standings, humming, assuming tigerish poses, I thought perhaps it was Widow Kuo's Card.

Every night after that at least one man, and sometimes two or three, mounted my fifteen-year-old body. I did not take to it. I did not feel either useful or desirable, and I did not offer myself to Nose.

One morning I saw five men led out of the pens to be beheaded: Fang's Old Hammer, the harmless old drunk, who had been condemned despite a dutiful confession, Hsü's Quack, Captain Su's Jumping Stick, Wang's Fortune, and Tung's Chairboy; and so I knew that despite the proclamation there was no hope for Nose. The magistrates were going ahead with the executions they had already decreed.

In callous voices some of our prisoners threw remarks at the suffering men as they were led out, all silent and compliant save one, Jumping Stick, who fought, dragged his feet, scratched, and pleaded.

My patron Lu's Beetle shouted, "This will pay you back, you turtle Chairboy, for giving my name and all."

Ma's Stupid, one of eight men in the pens who had been condemned to be beheaded a week later, lounged loose-hipped against a stone pillar and called out, "See you in the Buddhists' heaven, Fortune! Keep me a good place there, friend!"

Toward evening that same day, the warder called my name at the gate of our pen. Was I to go before the magistrates? I tried to neaten myself. Ticklebowl said, "Don't invent anything, small child. Except—try to give those crows some new names. They love new names. They're weary of those old stale names." Was this why Ticklebowl had given my name—for *novelty's* sake?

But my call was to talk with Big Madame Shen, who had come to see me, bringing clean underlinen and a pretty castoff day gown.

A warder put me in a cubicle, chained to a post, for our chat, and the mistress was tender with me. How she missed me! But after a bit I saw an irrepressible excitement creep into her eyes, and she lowered her voice almost to a whisper. She had not gone herself to the beheadings that afternoon, but P'an, the curio dealer, had. "A miracle has happened, White Lotus," she said. "Chao-er and Shih's Wolf, or their heads, at least, in cages as you know—they have exchanged skins! Chao-er has turned white, Wolf is yellow. Venerable P'an saw it himself. When they put up Tung's Chairboy's head in a cage beside Chao-er's they saw that Chao-er—his face, the skin of his forehead and cheeks— was whiter than Chairboy's who was a pale man, they said, and Chao-er's hair has become brown and curly, and his nose has gone sharp and narrow, the mouth wide, the lips thin; and Venerable P'an heard about how the other one had changed, and he joined a big crowd around the post with Wolf's cage on it, and truly, White Lotus, he says that Wolf, who was lifted earlier, is exactly the color of one of us, and his nose broad and flat, and his lips full. Some people believe they took a powder or potion before they were beheaded, by agreement between them, and that did it; some think it's the sun; some swear it's a sign. What do you think?"

I thought of a saying we had had at home in Arizona, but of course it did not cross my lips: *To the very end the hunter's name clings to the cougar's meat.*

⟨["Make Them Feel Young Again"

That evening there was a stirring in our pens. Reports had sifted to us through the thick walls—from visitors, from the warder, who was not a bad fellow, from the new slops-carrier, a freed slave named Honest, and from, it seemed, the very gnats that flew freely in and out the high slots of the pen—which made us feel, for the first time in weeks, as if a feeble, tremorous ebbing of hopelessness might take place. Men went from group to group, saying and hearing:

That the crowd at the beheadings that afternoon had been far smaller than at previous executions, for the masters were apparently growing sated on punishments;

That the magistrates and Ears were almost prostrated and were getting further behind every day; and that these officials were thinking of issuing wholesale pardons and transporting the pardoned slaves far away, to Ili and Turkestan, Nepal and Annam, places said to be warm the year round. . . .

Dusk had come, but still the pens buzzed. My four patrons sat on their corner of the platform letting the reports come to them. Through the shadows forms crept, and murmurs eddied like silt-brown water.

Just before dark the slops-carrier, Honest, came into the pens for his evening cleanout, and a few minutes later some electrifying whispers went around:

The entire madness of the yellows might be at a turning point.

It seemed that the Emperor's staff had received a letter from the warlord of a western province, saying that Islam was planning to carry a jihad to the realm of the Dragon Countenance, and that for this purpose had infiltrated many yellow Mohammedans from the outer provinces, disguised as barber-physicians, tutors, copyists, and teachers of swordplay, into the core towns, supplementing the sparse Mohammedan communities already there.

This letter was said to have had a sensational effect on the magistrates, who had widened their hearings to consider the implications of the letter. Cassia Cloud, who despite her churlish, thick-wristed manner bent like a cowslip to every shift in wind direction, had suddenly begun to accuse some of the guardsmen at the gates of the Forbidden City of being Mohammedans, and of having put their felt-booted feet in Chao-er's famous chalk circle. Little Yü-li, the yellow teacher of ritual swordplay, who had in fact supplied wine to be sprinkled on our heads during the swearing at the tavern, had had a hot hour of questioning, for Cassia Cloud had hinted that he was not a swordsman at all but an agent of Islam. And she was said to have scuffed up some testimonial dust that even left it unclear whether Chao-er himself, now dead, had been a practicing Mohammedan.

All this was wonderfully plausible to the yellows! The Mohammedan community in the Tartar City, in the undesirable southwestern quadrant, consisting mostly of camel-herding traders, petty merchants, small shopkeepers, and street vendors, was despised by the rest of the population. Besides being the victims of religious prejudice, the Mohammedans were accused of being clannish, over-thrifty, ill-natured, and tricky. Many were mercenaries in the Banner Corps, and they were notoriously good soldiers—a fact that made them objects of both contempt and suspicion. Indeed, it was well known that special officials were appointed by the Censorate to spy on them at all times. I had heard of a Buddhist opening a pork shop, out of undiluted spite, opposite that of a Mohammedan butcher; and in order to frighten away the sheep brought through the streets to the Moslem shop, the Buddhist had had a fierce tiger painted on the wall across from the Mohammedan's gate.

Suddenly I heard Beetle's voice crackling over the hum in the pen. "Someone tell me. What were the names of those two bully-boy sentries over at the Meridian Gate who used to sell off stolen vases and cloth goods for us? What were their names?"

"Chang," a voice shouted in the half darkness.

"Hsieh," another called out.

Beetle stood up. "Feng's Drum!" he called. "Come here to us, Feng's Small Drum!"

Poor Drum, who was to have his neck stretched under the sword the following day, came to our corner through the murk leaning on the shoulder of Lin's Strong, who was soon to be beheaded himself.

Beetle put it to Drum that his one hope of being spared the sword was to offer to inform on Mohammedans. "That is what they want now. Their ears are itching for it. Tell them Chang of the Meridian Gate was in it, and Chang's wife; that Chang used to wash his arms up to his elbows and bow to the west in a room there at Chao-er's. Tell a good story on them. Tell them Hsieh knew how to set fire to the palace wing, he told Quack to use cotton wadding that would make no smoke. Come on, Old Drum, tail up, small boy! Mix in some old slave names so they'll feel good. Make those yellow masters feel young again, Drum, give them some mutton-eaters, you give them Chang and Hsieh now, say they were mutton-eaters, and Chang's wife, too."

Weakly Drum said he would try that, he would try anything.

All this had stirred up in me a tumult of revived feelings. Could it be that in their hysteria the yellows might think the plot was deeper than they had dreamed—and not really ours? If one man could wangle being spared the sword, might not another wriggle

away from the faggots? I felt nervous and jumpy. I wanted to go
to Nose and shout to him, "Stir yourself, man! Go on to the
authorities and lie to them."

We were all restless, and within an hour we heard a strange
twanging music—a kind of Jew's harp!—and then some low
voices and, in the black closeness of our pen, the spreading humming of a hymn. "How Firm a Foundation." It was sung too fast,
with a crazy lilt, and someone beat a rhythm on the bottom of an
empty upturned shit pail.

("Leave Me Alone"

God, God, I had been in that damned hole five days before I even spoke to Nose.

The day after Feng's Drum was hanged—whatever he may
have said about the Mohammedans did him no good—a list came
to our pen from the Board of Punishments of forty-two slaves who
had been commended to the magistrates for pardon and transportation, when it could be arranged, to an outlying dependency.
One of them was Lu's Beetle. We celebrated on our corner of
the platform with a game of jumping sticks at merchant stakes.

At noon Honest, the slops man, told us he had seen the bannermen Chang and Hsieh led into the warder's gateroom and, later,
taken out in chains—so we knew that Drum's testimony had,
after all, had *some* effect, even if it had not saved him.

We later heard that for the magistrates Cassia Cloud had cor-
roborated all—and more. "Yes, yes, many times I saw the said
Chang, Meridian Gate Chang, at Chao-er's talking with Shih's
Wolf and those others of the plot. He bowed to the west four
times a day in the back room. Ai! Yes, Hsieh was there, and Fan,
Kuo, and Hu, all I think Mohammedans, all of the Meridian Gate.
Which Hu? I mean Hu Lin-fu, tended the Emperor's stable at that
gate, the hostler Hu, Masters. . . ."

Hearing this, Beetle slapped his legs, threw back his head, and
bared his teeth in hissing laughter.

In midafternoon I was slumped on the floor in our corner with
my eyes ranging the moldy ceiling, thinking: *Nose, with all his
badness, is more of a man in every way than this Beetle. Nose is
going to die; Beetle will go, a slave but alive, to a winterless country. How can I make sense of that?*

With this, confused feelings suddenly flew up in me like dry leaves in a smart twist of autumn wind, and before I knew what I was doing I stood before Nose and said, "Ai, Nose, why do you just sit there?"

His sallow eyes came up to mine. "White Lotus. What are you doing here?"

I laughed—ayah, I could be "worthless," too—and said, "What has happened to your blinkers, man? I have been here five days."

"Go away," he said.

No. This was wrong. He was not supposed to say that. I had come over to help him. I was suddenly trembling and felt short of breath. "You weak pig," I said. "You sit here and do nothing for yourself. Nose! Why don't you go around and lie to them? Lick their dirty cloth shoes! Save yourself, you fool!"

"Leave me alone," he dully said, not even looking at me.

I was in a sudden fury at his not having seen me all the time I had been there, while men had taken me night after night, and I began to abuse him. I called him a coward, a lazy turtle, a titful of goat's milk—back and forth from the old Arizona speech to slavey yellow talk.

Slowly, almost languidly, he arose, and with not even a flicker of the old fire in his eyes, he slapped me hard. "Go sit down on your elephant platform," he quietly said, "with your four pimp friends." And that, rather than the blow, telling me that he *had* seen me, all along, all along, set me to bawling in loud gasping sobs.

No one even looked up at our scrap.

Holding my cheek and fighting the sobs, only to have them triumph over me with ever more humiliating loudness, I was about to turn and flee back to the platform when I felt Nose's hands on my shoulders. Through the blur of my tears I saw that he was shaking his head.

I settled to the floor in a heap, and Nose crouched on his hams beside me.

"That man Beetle gets on my nerves . . . ," he began.

Stirring, I put my face near to his and whispered, "Did you light the fires—or some of the fires?"

But Nose was off on a gallop of his own. "Do you want to know the one who got us into all this? That bastard Chao-er. He pretended to be a friend. 'Yellow men and white men . . .' Ayah, Meimei, what a two-faced man! Maybe he didn't even know he was two-faced. Remember the night we swore? 'I'm the yellow man,' he says. 'I'm the yellow man here!' Remember that? Ai, there was a friend to the smallies! I hate to think what he told the magistrates."

"Was the oath serious, Nose? Did everyone mean it? Was it meant to be taken seriously?"

"Ai! The oath? Serious? Ha! Are *you* serious? What's serious? Listen, Mei-mei, this is a slanthead world. Everything in it is slanty. These turtle-shit fires were all *slanty*. This pen is supposed to be for *elephants*. Serious! Listen: Cassia Cloud is—*pfutt!*" Nose cranked a forefinger at his temple. "And she's not the only one, d'you know that? My master—Big Venerable *Pfutt!* Your master— Big Venerable *Pfutt!* You know what's the slantiest thing of all?"

"What's that?"

"Ai, Mei-mei"—the hoarse tone of wild, raving disgust had vanished, and Nose spoke now with a confidential sincerity— "it's me." He pointed to his own chest. "It's Shit-Nose. I'm worse than a yellow man. Ayah, Mei-mei"—his voice was barely audible —"I'm no better than a filthy bastard slanthead myself."

I was weeping again. I saw that Nose had come, in the end, not only to being worthless, but to the outer limits of hatefulness. He had turned his loathing of the yellows, at last, against himself— and now he called himself the worst he could, worse than a yellow man. Poor Nose! Poor Nose!

When I returned to the elephant platform, Beetle said, "What, baby fox? Won't that big fool promise to give it to you?"

I did not answer. I thought I had no anger, or pity, or love, or hatred left. I sat sniffling at the edge of the platform.

(What Was the Oath About?

Two days later Nose's time came. A bannerman swung open the high thick door of the pen and called out, "Wu's Nose! Are you ready?"

Was he ready? Was I? I saw him, down against the wall, raise his head and look toward the door, but his eyes were casual, incurious, as if he had heard someone else's name called, about whom he cared nothing. Soon he dropped his forehead again to his up-gathered knees.

The bannerman at the door nodded over his shoulder and four of his company, huge Tartar hulks, capable escorts, in Banner Corps uniforms, entered the pen. They seemed to know Nose. They made their way to him through the tangles of human flotsam scattered across the floor. They stood over him, and one of the soldiers spoke softly to him.

Nose looked up again, but for some time he remained crouching. A bannerman's leg blocked his face from my view. Was he going to defy them or was he simply detached from whatever was happening? Would the guards have to haul him out? I could not tell. I craned to see his face.

Prisoners who had been dozing stirred themselves and sat up, and the large dim-lit chamber fell silent. This gloomy hall, which for so long had echoed and re-echoed with our chatter, our desperate jokes, our nightmare grunts, our throat-clearings, snores, guffaws, and groans—the place was suddenly silent but for the subdued hiss of our breathing: the shush of the inside of a huge seashell. Nose was the only one condemned to fire; the prisoners were impressed by that. The peak of the yellows' hysteria had passed, and the danger was waning, yet they were going through with fire-for-fire; the prisoners must have been impressed by *that*, also.

Nose stood up, and the bannermen, not touching him but placing him in a box of their presences, started him toward the door of the pen. The four tall soldiers and the powerful white man high-stepped and tiptoed among the forms on the brick floor, murmuring and nodding polite apologies for the disturbance; even Nose in his extremity was excusing himself.

He would pass near our group. Would he speak to me? I raised myself on my knees. He had called me, here in the prison, Mei-mei, his little sister; yet I hardly knew if he thought of me as a dear person. At this moment every trembling nerve in me was alert, receptive, tender. Now he was nearby; I could almost have leaned forward to touch him. I felt I must not cry out to him, or I might choke. It was obvious that he was not even going to look at me. His eyes, fixed on his footing, were neither sharp nor dull; he did not seem to be inwardly stirred at all.

As the party picked its way to the great door, I became conscious of my patrons, near me on the platform, murmuring to each other.

Beetle, the cynic, the readiest laugher of all, destined for a new life in a faraway place, was deeply impressed. "That pig has a stomach! Ai!"

White Scholar, whom I had thought a timid man with a broadly sarcastic slave name, for he was both stupid and inelegant, said, "What's so special about him—except what they're doing to him?"

Card chimed in on that note: "Yes, what's so particular? That bitch made up a good story about him. He just sat here like a toad the whole time."

Beetle said, "I'd like to see you walk out of here like that—to where *he's* going!"

Ticklebowl said, "I was over there at Chao-er's, the night they swore. I didn't like the way he fondled that bastard yellow cobbler."

"What was that oath about?" White Scholar asked. "Did you swear?"

I missed Ticklebowl's answer, if he made one. Nose was at the door, which was swinging open, and he turned and looked at all of us who were watching him. I thought he looked suddenly startled; a vein stood out on his forehead. What was the oath about? What a question! Here we were all together in the pen of our utmost degradation, and there could be a white man who did not even know at what point, in what way, with what meaning, if any, it had all begun. What was the oath about? If Nose had any claim to being special, it had to do with his having stood by the chalk circle to swear us to that—that what? . . . He hesitated at the door, put his head down, spat on the bricks, and turned away. Was this our leader? Was this his farewell to us—a gob of spittle on the floor? No! Old Pearl had been wrong! He was *not* "in front." He did not have whatever was needed; thought of himself as a slanthead; was self-soaked; was not moved by the suffering of his fellows. What had happened to that flashing idealism, energy, zest—the real leadership he had shown in those long-ago days at home? I was filled with disgust and leaning over the edge of the platform I, too, spat.

Yet that afternoon, as time, which has no kindness in it, crept at its most contrary pace, I felt, at first, restless, then impatient, then angry, then—with a sudden flood of sobs—bitterly deprived, bereaved, lonely, love-starved, shattered by a loss I did not understand. I lay on the bricks and poured out my salt sorrow for hours on end. No one paid any attention to me.

When Honest came in to empty the buckets that evening he reported that nothing was known of the execution. It had taken place on the Coal Hill, in the Imperial grounds. The public had not been admitted.

([The Master's Pains

For four days officialdom seemed to be at a standstill, then a new list came to the pen, of slaves forthwith released to their masters' houses, and I, never even having been flattered with an examination by a low-grade mandarin, or mere bannerman, was on it. They led me out and turned me loose in the street.

On returning to the Shens' house I hurried into our quarters to get out of my jail-soiled clothes. Going headlong around a turn into our slaves' courtyard I almost collided with Old Bow, who was bent over carrying out the mistress's dirty bath water, and I half jokingly said, "You blind ass, you nearly drowned me." This was my new rough jail personality.

The figure straightened. It was the master! Buddha's flower! Old Bow was still in jail.

Himself was in a short tunic; in the dim place his face appeared to be greenish, covered with dewdrops.

"Excuse me," he said in automatic response to my rebuke, then, suddenly realizing who we respectively were, exclaimed, "What! You home?"

"They let out twenty just now," I said. "No explanation."

"Here," he said, beginning to sting from the greeting I had inadvertently given him, "take *this* out."

"Yes, please, Big Venerable," I said, the new harridan side of me in rapid flight.

"And control your tongue," he said, thoroughly angry at last.

"Please, Big Venerable, I mistook you for Old Bow, Big Venerable."

I found the master and mistress drained of their strength but plucky still. With two slaves in jail, and steadfastly enforcing a rigid rule that the gateman and male runners were not allowed to set foot in the Pear Blossom Rest, they had lived a sort of camping pioneer life. Madame Shen bravely dusted; the distinguished subcurator had dived intrepidly into chores. I dared not ask Gull about the disposition of the commode pots, always Old Bow's task, never Gull's or mine. Poor stiff Old Bow, in jail to please the master.

Lo, he was back at work the next day. Big Venerable Shen, having urged Old Bow to confess, but having seen me now set at large, spoke to his fellow authorities and maneuvered the man home, for the master could see that the mysterious tide was turning from flood to ebb, and that he could now recover his valuable property with some assurance of being able to keep it. As to any residual risks of a slave plot, it may have been that our good master would rather be killed in bed than empty the commodes.

But in truth the master was suffering; had lost five catties from his own waist, he said, and slept driftily at night. His face was drawn, his eyes searched inward. *Harm no living creature*, Buddha adjured; the Buddha demanded pity, gentleness, self-denial. My master's flaw was imperfect decency—for he was too kind a man to be wholeheartedly punitive, too halfhearted to be truly insistent on justice. He was sick of the city's sickness, but too slack to speak out. He looked haunted. He had been to the Coal Hill the afternoon of Nose's execution.

The master came home from the Board of Punishments one evening shaking his head, and it seemed he could not stop. At the evening meal it came out that he had assisted that day in the taking of a deposition from Hsu Wei-han, a mandarin of the Board of Rites—"You cannot question the veracity of a man like him, my duck. He told us that a good round month ago a white, K'ang's slave Small Number Two, had told Hsu and his own master—you know K'ang Hsi-lu, duck; that tall fellow we see strolling with a yellowish chow dog on a chain, from Seventh Hutung—this slave had told those two gentlemen that his confession to the court a few days before, touching on the plot, had all been false. He had accused Wang's Monkey on account of fear, he said. He had heard slaves saying in jail that the masters would burn anybody who did not confess. His charges against Cheng's Spade were lies. He had never been to Chao-er's tavern—did not even know where it was— had never heard of the man Chao-er until it became common talk among the slaves that he was the goat to blame for everything." One final time the master shook his head. "How many of these false confessions do you suppose there have been?"

([A Feast at Jade Springs Hill

Ten days later, as if nothing unusual had been happening, our gentlefolk took a summer's outing to Jade Springs Hill, and Gull and I were among the slaves who were chosen to help serve an afternoon feast.

We slaves walked out by the northwest highway in the morning beside a train of carts loaded with trestles and planks for temporary tables, utensils for cooking, baskets of charcoal, parcels of chinaware and chopsticks, hogsheads of sea water containing sharks' fins and fish lips, and hampers of mandarin duck and scallops and turnip cakes and water chestnuts and pickled bears' claws. A silver-haired man slave belonging to the wife of General Hsüeh of the Eight Banner Corps, named Old Velvet, who had presided over several such outings in past years, an old-style slave, courtly, proud of his yellow connections, contemptuous of the crude-mannered younger generation of smallies, was in charge of us all, and ordinarily this would have been a joyous, playful beginning of the day, until the time when our masters and mistresses would join us, but we were dragged down by the exhausting ordeal that had had the whole city in its grip. In the days since Nose's execution, we had felt sure that the yellows' frenzy was tapering off, yet it seemed that they could not stop. Huang's Cook, Chu's Magpie, Sung's Cabbage or Soldier, Widow Kuo's Card, Tu's Sheep, Ts'ao's Braveboy, Yeh's Heavenly Spirit—all these had been beheaded at a time when it was said that the masters had lost interest in the chalk circle.

Small wonder that on the way, when, as our party was held up by some fodder wagons belonging to the Imperial stables on the road ahead, one of the slaves spotted a squad of bannermen beside them, a wave of high-pitched chattering broke out among us, and many scurried to the far side of our wagons from these figures, as if for shelter—because in our minds bannermen meant arrest, and arrest seemed to lead straight to the executioner's sword. Even I, who knew that one could survive arrest, was caught up in the little panic.

And small wonder that when, several miles out on the highway, we came to a crossroads, where our string of carts was to swing left for Jade Springs Hill, each slave crossed himself, spat on the ground and stamped in the spittle, or made a sign of the devil's horns and aimed it back along the way we had come—for in our mythology from home days, crossroads had been well known to stand for Jesus' cross, and here in this land of idols and ancestor worship we felt them to be favorite ambushes of yellow trickster spirits, revenants, bogeys, and also (we could easily think now) of specters of vengeful dead bannermen, magistrates, Ears, bailiffs, leather-aproned executioners, kindlers of faggots.

But soon we had left the dull countryside of farms and entered, through a gate in a high wall, into a kind of enchantment—the Imperial hunting park known as Jade Springs Hill. We climbed through pine woods to the summit, and near the porcelain Jade Peak Pagoda, on a pavilion called Reflection of the Sun on Hibiscus Flowers, from which the city, with its core of sparkling golden roofs, looked like an exquisitely carved toy, we prepared the feast —set up the low tables, lit fires at a distance to cook hot foods, spread out the prepared dishes under dampened cloths, and arranged in their places pairs of old-fashioned ebony chopsticks tipped at each end with filigree silver.

I *was* enchanted! Try as I would to think with compassion or sadness of Nose, standing at the huge door of the elephant pen in his filthy tunic that I had brought him, spitting his valediction onto the bricks—try as I would to keep reality in focus, I was elated, overcome with the magic of this setting and of the yellows' superb artifacts. Once I was sent to fetch water at the spring gushing out through sluices from under the Temple of the Dragon King, and I gazed a long time into the water—like pure ice in a jade vase—in whose deeps every frond and stem of cress and water snowflake and floating heart could be seen. At last I shuddered, dipped my bucket, ran back.

In early afternoon, as tiny fair-weather clouds printed themselves on an enamel sky, the yellows began to arrive in a procession of two-seated sedan chairs, each carried all the way from the city on poles by eight slaves. The silk window curtains of these palanquins were pulled back, and the men in their conical hats with mandarins' buttons blinked and nodded at the tranquil views, the ladies were tightened into arch smiles and murmurs—for mixed couples, not husbands and wives, were riding together, and around the flirting pairs the Emperor's own air seemed soft as midsummer moss.

But when they saw us, and when Old Velvet and all the other

men slaves ran fawning at the sedan doors to hand down their
stump-footed ladies, a chill, a severity, a sense of falseness, a dour
habit overlaid now with recent perturbation of the nerves, settled
down.

Soon, however, as tea was served, as parties went off to catch
butterflies in the garden called Plucking Fragrant Herbs on Mountain Heights, or to sit conversing on outcroppings of rock that
overlooked the purple-and-gold toy city, the yellows seemed to
forget us, to wipe us out of mind, to root us in the landscape like
so many stones and shrubs—though now and then they called to
us, without however actually seeing us, to bring them mistress's
fan or master's long-stemmed pipe.

Old Velvet—I saw sweat on his face from the charcoal fire over
which he was bending, and I almost cried aloud, "Nose!"—was
presiding over an enormous caldron in which a shark's-fin soup
was bubbling. With a flourish and dancelike steps he uncorked a
bottle of herbal wine and dripped a few drops of it, as if offering
a libation of amber blood, on the earth in front of his rock fire-
place; then he emptied the bottle into the soup.

It was tasty, when served, so the masters said. They took dol-
lops of *Shao-hsing* with it, and when tiny gnats, chasing the
lowering sun, began to come up from the plain, the gentlemen,
mopping their faces after the work of overeating, grew itchy and
hot. Slapping at their own foreheads and cheeks, my master Shen
and his friend the curio dealer P'an, who was a bit out of his depth
in this company of mandarins, began to argue, and while we
gathered up the bowls and cups we could hear every word.

"Exactly what do you mean?" the curio dealer was asking.

"It is a matter of tone and shading," my master said, as if he
were discussing a scroll painting. "Be so good as to understand
me: I do not say that this turtle Chao-er was blameless. I say only
that his denials to the very end were firm, earnest, and—to me—
affecting. I cite you the day he sent a message that he wanted to
speak to the magistrates, wanted to kowtow and swear by the
Dragon Countenance that he hadn't been a party to any plot. I
thought him sincere."

"But what about all the circumstances brought out by that girl
servant of his?"

"Cassia Cloud? Chao-er's indentured servant, don't forget,"
my master said, "bonded to him for four years. Don't forget she

might have fancied she had good reason to weigh against her bondholder. . . . And listen, that other yellow girl from the tavern, Peach Fragrance—"

"A whore, laid herself down to white men! In heaven's name, Shen!"

"Yes, a filthy girl, perhaps, but stanch all the same, better-spirited than Chao-er himself, and what sticks in my throat is her taking it all back—did you hear about that? Two or three days ago. Said she'd lied in all her evidence about a plot at that other tavern, all of it imaginary, to try for a reward. I don't like our acceptance of her accusations but not of her recanting."

Two or three men in the group seemed to be with Venerable Shen, but most seemed to be shoring up the cinches of their trousers under their gowns to wade in against him.

"Ha! Shen Ch'ing-wu!" cried one of them, a certain Mandarin Ts'ao, as if he had a triumphant point to make. "Did you see that shameless Chao-er in the cart going out to get his neck stretched?" Several men laughed. "Did you see him, Shen? Standing up in the cart, looking around as if expecting to be rescued, with one hand raised as high as his pinion would reach, the other pointing forward. Ha ha ha! What a sight of martyred virtue!"

"His wife did well at the block," another man said.

"Did you see her afterward—like a short log?" another said. "I agree. She was brave."

Now the curio dealer P'an could not keep quiet in this party of his betters, and he said, "They should have held that burning in a public place—what was the name of that hog they burned?"

What was the name of that hog they burned? I almost fell with a stack of bowls.

"I disagree," my master said. "I witnessed that execution and I emphatically disagree."

"I say there should be more burnings—out in the open. What kind of a lesson is it in the Coal Hill grounds, where only a party of the Imperial household can watch?" Suddenly one could see that the curio dealer realized he had exposed himself: his bitterness stemmed from his being an outsider. But he could not withdraw, and he went on to further excesses of vulgarity; "What kind of lesson is that for the public—for the dirty white pigs?"

"It was a lesson for *me*," my master said in a quiet voice, and what he said now froze my limbs. "I think we got the wrong man. I don't think this fellow Wu's Nose was the chief man in their plot at all. The burning was supposed to be reserved for the master-mind. Let me picture it for you, P'an. The setting is private, a place steeped in the idea of punishment—on a shoulder of the Coal Hill, near the ancient sophora tree that is wrapped in heavy chains as chastisement for its allowing Emperor Ch'ung Cheng of the Ming Dynasty to hang himself in its branches—do you know about that tree?" (I saw that my master was not above rubbing it in that P'an was an outsider.) "A party of not more than fifty witnesses. They bring the man up—unshaven: you know how hairy the whites are: disgusting. Clothing caked in dust. They tie him to the post, pile chunks of wood around him. Then Magistrate Lin tells him that he can get himself off if he will give a full confession of the plot. Straightaway he begins to babble—'confess'— but it's gibberish! It is obviously all improvised. He doesn't even mention the Mohammedans' role. His details are at variance with the consistent story all the other whites have been telling. But there is more to it than that, friend P'an. On the basis of his bearing, what he shows in his eyes, this man is simply not at the heart of their plot. Oh, he's surly. Capable of whining and shirking— and stealing. *But he hasn't the moral force to defy us. He is not it.* . . . That's why a public lesson would have been a mistake, P'an. *Everyone* would have seen that we had the wrong man."

With the greatest of effort I continued the outward motions of some kind of work, though I could not have said what I was doing. I was absolutely crushed by my agreement with what my master was saying. Nose was not it. I knew no white man who was, but he was certainly not. And yet—how glorious he had been at times! Closing my eyes, I saw him for a moment that day in Chao-er's just before he led me off to that small, dark room—pounding dust from his quilted gown, blowing into his hands, approaching our circle: his eyes dancing with life, full of the best of himself, strong, cheerful, willing to make what he could of a very bad lot. A sob caught at my chest; horrified at the thought that the masters might have heard it, I quickly pretended to stumble; I dropped a small bowl and broke it. The masters' heads turned for a moment, but they thought nothing of a white girl's minor clumsiness. They went back to their talk.

"So you went ahead, even though you had the wrong man," P'an, shifting ground, sarcastically said.

"We had to. His 'confession' was a tissue of last-minute lies. He'd been condemned. We had to."

"I heard he was shouting something at the end in the whites'
old language—what was that?"

"I'm told the words meant: 'Water! Bring me water!' "

The palanquins were lifted, and the mixed couples left, the
curtains half drawn this time, so the flirting they began the moment they were seated had a kind of gravity to it. You could see
that the yellows were glad to ride away from us. Our masters in
that chat had almost spoiled the outing. Big Venerable Shen rode
with P'an's wife, and I saw his eyes glint as they started to sway
down the path, for he had passed his little agony of conscientious
doubt, like a bit of gas, and he felt much better.

❴ Dogs, Hawks, Owls, Lambs, Swans

We slaves should have been relieved, I suppose, a few
days later, to hear that little Yü-li, the professor of ritual swordplay, had been arrested.

To be truthful, however, we were exceedingly puzzled by the
way the wind was blowing, because we heard that Yü-li was in-
dicted, not for leading the slaves' plot to burn and kill, but for
"being," as my master said at table, "an ecclesiastical person, made
by authority pretended from Mecca in Arabia," who had no business, on pain of death, being in the Northern Capital of the
Dragon Countenance. Yellow witnesses were said to be giving
depositions that, while ostensibly teaching ritual swordplay, he
was training Moslems for the day when their holy war would
begin; that he maintained contacts with bannermen who were
Moslems, and with some who were not; that during one winter
month he fasted. He asserted that there was only one God. A
weird story was told that he had gone to the confectioner K'ung
and had asked for small rice-paper wafers in the shape of cash—
of a sort certain magicians of a black-art cult were said (this part
of the story was vague and often garbled) to place on their
tongues, or perhaps under them, while performing certain rites, or
while blaspheming against the Emperor, or while bribing—and
K'ung, thinking the teacher wanted sweets to give away to children, said he had malt wafers pressed in the shapes of dogs,
hawks, owls, lambs, and swans, but not of money, at which Yü-li
had insisted he wanted the little circlets with square holes in

them. The slaves, completely nonplussed by this drivel, as it seemed, rushed to the magistrates to be heard on the subject of Yü-li's fetching wine for the ceremonies at the chalk circle, but our masters the magistrates appeared bored with the scene at Chao-er's tavern, and they cut short all such talk, and they seemed weary of the whole topic of white slaves. They preferred now to listen to bannermen of Mongol descent, on what they had heard said about little Yü-li at Kuan's fighting cocks, and how the man was said by Ts'ai, a carpenter and house joiner, to be a muezzin in disguise, and how he had once been heard intoning the first sura of the Koran to a roomful of kneeling bannermen.

How strange the weatherlike terrors of the yellows were!

Little Yü-li was tried one afternoon and condemned to be beheaded.

❬ A Bad Smell

The day after the execution of Yü-li, in the early part of a still, hot, muggy summer afternoon with the barest suggestion of a southerly breeze, a horrible sudden stench passed like a patch of sick fog through the streets of the town. It caught me on my hands and knees washing the huge sill stone at our front gate, and I thought at first that I could not rise, feeling that the abominable vapor was in *me*, that I was putridly ill, but then I saw yellows in the street calling to each other, holding their noses, coughing, and making gestures of revulsion.

We heard that night that the stink had crept, as if the foul air knew where it wanted to go, into the inner hall of the Board of Punishments, and the magistrates in their robes had pressed their wide sleeves over their noses, and that this was what it had been: Chao-er's swollen corpse, exposed in chains on its gibbet near the wall of the Outer City, had burst, and many pailfuls of the inner fermentation that had blown it up so huge had erupted onto the ground.

The wave of nausea that crossed the capital that afternoon had a strangely curative effect. Yü-li was disposed of, and the tavern girl Cassia Cloud felt her queer inner aptitude stirring again, and she swore before the magistrates that certain respectable men— "some of your Ears of the Court, if you please, I can tell you their

names"—had tried to have her poisoned, and indeed these same
respectable men had put up the money for the slaves' and Mohammedans' plot. But the judges, glad to be breathing fresh air again,
stood her down and said they had had the last of all that.

She pouted and said they owed her fifty taels of silver.

What for, pray?

"The reward," Cassia Cloud said. "Ayah, the Emperor's proclamation. Your Honors took the pains to read it out to me in the
court here. Did you think I was not listening?"

They paid her the money and sent her away.

The madness, it seemed, was nearly over. Within a few days
the elephant pens had been emptied. The slaves condemned to
transportation were carried off on carts, and many others were
returned to their masters. The Emperor issued a proclamation
that thanks to his own divine mercy the city had been spared. The
magistrates petitioned the Emperor for funds to reimburse masters
for the loss of slaves that had been beheaded, burned, or transported. This was only fair, said my master to his wife. After all,
the masters had paid good money for these chattels that had been
removed from their premises by *force majeure* for the sake of the
common welfare.

Discussing this petition one evening at a meal with his friend
P'an, my own master fired a remark almost straight into my ear
as he ladled soup from a bowl I was in the act of lowering to the
table, and it was not until some days later that I understood that
the words had been intended literally. "Do you know, friend
P'an, I have come near to concluding that for us city-dwellers in-
denture is economically viable, and slavery is not. These whites
were farmers in their native lands, and they are good for only one
thing, P'an: agriculture. Not so?"

(A Parcel Is Sold

    And, accordingly, in about a month, when the master
had been able to secure and bond for four years' servitude six
healthy yellows, four men and two girls, Manchurians all and safe
Buddhists, I was sold. So were Old Bow and Gull. So, it happened,
into the same broker's hands, was Sun's Mink. The mistress
wanted back for her new girls most of the clothes she had, I
thought, given to me, and when we departed my small bundle,

wrapped and tied in an undergown, was easy to carry. We four were sent to Tientsin and were placed on an onion-carrying junk in a parcel, as they called us, of twenty-odd slaves—bound, we were told, for a somewhat warmer place than the Northern Capital. We were kept for the most part on deck by day, and we slept nights in the holds on sacking thrown over hills of pungent onions.

Peace's War

BOOK FOUR

((**On the Cart**

A WARM DAY in the eleventh month. Haze. The right-hand hub of
the crude two-wheeled cart needs grease, and half of each turn is
a living screech which sends groundlings ahead of us scurrying
away from the rutted earthen road into the forests, where leaves
are falling.

The morose agent, really a courier, a sapling boy in the shapeless black trousers of the local peasant style, who affects a pipe
with a stem nearly three feet long, at the end of which is a brass
bowl no larger than an acorn's hull, sits at the lip of the car between the shafts, shod feet dangling behind the donkey's tail. He
is armed. The donkey wears a bell at its neck to keep it awake.
Mink and I are the only riders on the flat-bedded cart, and, having
been told nothing, we can only assume that we are being delivered:
to the compound we now pass whose walls bear dazzling white-
plastered panels?—to another?—to an unknown farm cut from
the solemn forest, with wide fields of money crops lying all around
the landlord's walls? Mink laughs but is afraid.

We pass on, and at intervals we see other endless walls, and
we have glimpses of a river with barges and sampans, and the
ruts deepen, and the roots spreading in the track shake us. Mink
laughs again. I am afraid, too, and I laugh. Gull and Bow have
been sold away in a separate parcel.

What am I to make of my life? Whenever I think of the Northern Capital—the oath, the fires, the elephant pens—my flesh still
crawls; yet I am a girl of only sixteen, passing through new land-
scapes with wide eyes. Changes of scenery refresh and excite me,
and mislead me, perhaps. I have had my ears open, too, along
the way, and I have heard talk of flux. They say Emperor Yung-t'ai
is dead; long live Emperor Ch'ang-lo! The great dynast Yung-t'ai
had a long rule, during which he subdued the Manchu warlords,
so the northern part of the land massif has been more or less
unified. In the coalescing North, in the so-called "core provinces,"
into one of which we have been transported, the repressive measures of Yung-t'ai had prepared the ground for a rank growth of
liberal ideas. His successor, Emperor Ch'ang-lo, a scholar and
philosopher, has accordingly promulgated a set of principles by
which his prefects and magistrates are to conduct civil life; it is
called The Nine Flowers of Virtue. Despite this decree, real life
has not changed—everywhere are bloodshed and turnover, greed
and graft and injustice, disgusting cruelties in the name of progress; but the words of the Imperial edict are powerful, and hope
has leaped up in the hearts of the have-nots.

Ch'ang-lo's Nine Flowers of Virtue is a triumph of the enlightenment of sweet sun-soaked Buddhism, which perceives the causes
of suffering and the means of salvation from suffering. According
to this thrilling document, spiritual fervor and gentle reason are
henceforth to go hand in hand in every yamen, and as usual with
political reform, all must be turned to a practical end. Everybody
is to be in a better case. The only question in my young mind (remembering the white banner of guilt waved over Nose) is: What
is meant by everybody? Who is everybody this time? Surely slaves
are not included. We slaves are convulsed with a hope of betterment but, quickly seeing through the hypocrisy of The Nine
Flowers and comprehending that no one is to help us to a salving
of our pain, we know that we must help ourselves or give up hope.
But how strange! Hope meant to us, long ago, in our lives that we
called free, God in His heaven with a white face and a white
beard, and along the way, on the onion-carrying junk and on the
carts we have ridden since, I have heard that our old religion has
swept like a sweet rainfall across the slave population. God is a
secret we keep from the yellows; there are no more sects, only the
one white God of hope. And now, as I, a girl of sixteen, ride on
the cart with Mink to an unknown destination, my heart turns to

the fair-skinned God I thought I knew as a friend in Arizona. On the jolting cart bed I try to pray to Him, but I do not ask for much. "Give me, dear God, a mild master."

We travel another hour, and the donkey's hoofs pound on a wooden bridge over a brook, and beyond, as we pass a tavern where slaves lounge in the seats of their masters' sedan chairs waiting for their owners to come out tipsy and bad-tempered, there is a sudden high-pitched rasping of laughter from the row of chairs; and I understand that Mink and I are a joke to our own kind. We drive on some distance, partly through woods.

We arrive at our goal, and, "Thank you, God," I say out loud, addressing Him again in my relief as the squeaking of vexed wooden parts stops.

⟪ Unpainted Wood

My first impression within the compound wall, that day, was of the plainness of everything. The "big house," by no means a villa and not grand at all, was a brick structure of three court-yards, with unpainted jambs and eaves; it had a face of hard-headed shrewdness. A canopy of black walnut and of ill-smelling ailanthus trees, old watchman-trees, stood over the spirit screen at the front of the house.

Taking in the scene before I dropped from the cart, just inside the main gate of the farm, I had a glimpse of a pale figure, hurry-ing away as if for cover, under the darkest shade of the trees, a common blue gown, blurred face, white hair; this specter moved behind a tree trunk.

I had a senseless reaction of disappointment and even anger, as if I had been cheated at a bargain, thinking with something akin to pride of the elegance of the Shens' house in the Northern Capi-tal, the perfectionism of my mistress there—a glimpse in memory's eye of my thickened fingers on a polishing rag bringing out the creamy glow of an ivory figure, set in laurel-green lacquer, of a nobleman's daughter who is fondling a fawn; in the capital it had all been an inlaid story. But here: rude weathered wood, eroded bricks, straggling weeds, signs of peasant indifference and greed.

The agent led us to a shedlike building, in a side courtyard of the big house, the office of the place, unpainted and untended, too,

within which we found a yellow man about fifty years old, in heavy
work clothes, sitting with his back to us at a desk clicking an
abacus. His neck at the sides below the ears was crinkled like
the treated pelt of a woods animal. He turned and, seeing Mink's
bent back, cursed the young agent, in filthy terms, in the broad
Honan, or South-of-the-River, dialect.

The boy, in a crackling and suddenly cheerful voice, said, "The
same to your mother."

"This crookback is good for nothing," the man irritably said. I
took him to be our new owner. A cloth fastener had torn away
from the shoulder of his tunic, the cuff of his quilted sleeve was
frayed, and in his person he was bad-tempered, hoarse, and yel-
low-toothed, and I could not help comparing this wild wolf with
Big Venerable Shen, whose glossy queue was ever fastened with a
bow.

"The order said the cheapest pair, man and wench," the boy
said.

"Cheapest turtles!" the rough man said. "Old Yen would have
skinned you alive."

"It's not my fault," the boy whined. " 'Uncle' Ch'en made the
selection. You can send them back."

A white man came into the office, large, benign, grave, and
pompous, saying that "the Matriarch" had told him to inspect the
new girl—a possibility for seamstress; and as the yellow man
turned away with a shrug, the self-assured big white man came to
me, lifted my chin, examined my hands, and asked me if I had
had any experience sewing. I shook my head. "She will not do,"
the big white man said to the yellow man's back.

"Look at the prime hand they sent me," the yellow said. He was
leaning over, digging into a wooden chest.

The big white man looked down at Mink and laughed. "You
strong, small boy?" I was astonished at this white man's arrogance, for he behaved like a yellow master.

Mink, crouching in his fear, grinned and nodded.

"You can have the girl in the fields," the big man said to the
yellow. "Let the crooked one sweep out."

"Hah!" The man's bark was like a gunshot. He turned toward us
with his arms full. He threw the things he was carrying onto his
desk, and he counted out to me: two calico shifts, a drab coolie
gown, a shapeless suit of quilted cotton, and a pair of thick-cloth

shoes; and he ordered me to get out of my last castoffs from Big Madame Shen and to put on the coolie gown. He issued clothes to Mink and ordered him to change, too. The yellow errand boy stared at me, his mouth sagging, as I began to undress in the open room. The rough yellow man said, "Go, go, go, go," and drove the boy out, and the big white left. As I sat on the floor pulling on the shoes, I heard the cart's dry hub recommence its outcries. *Kr-r-r-e-e-e-e!*

When we were ready the yellow man told Mink and me to follow him, and he led us through the main courtyard of the big house. I was afraid to look about, for fear of seeing that disquieting form lurking under the trees, and I strode awkwardly, with a feeling that the shadow in the shadows was watching me. We went next through a large rear courtyard, around the sides of which were dingy small rooms and stables and sheds and storerooms. In the shade at one side a number of house slaves, somewhat better dressed than we, squatted on their hams in the peasant fashion and laughed cruelly at the sight of the frightened newcomers.

We went out at a postern gate along an orchard path by a well-kept vegetable garden, and then across a mowing lot, and at last, in a meager grove of locusts, we came to a shabby wall of mud and straw. Passing through a stout gate we entered a dismal courtyard. On two sides of this rude narrow enclosure ran long rows of mud-walled rooms, making the sides of a kind of street, along which, sitting in clusters, promenading on its pig-wallow pavement, chatting, passing an idle market-day afternoon, were a couple of score of slaves in clothes just like ours—the men in cotton shirts with elbow-length sleeves and rough shin-length trousers; the women in coolie gowns; children in tow shirts, their bellies and legs naked; and all without exception barefooted.

The yellow man turned me over to a heavy-set woman he addressed as Small Auntie.

This Auntie, wheezing and sighing, took me to her mud cubicle, which was also to be mine—a nest, she said, of unmarrieds. It had a dirt floor and two mud-and-straw k'angs, on which five women, counting myself, would now be sleeping. Auntie told me to take off my shoes and save them for the fields and cold weather. We sat on the high doorstep. She looked at me and nodded and said, with a wholehearted acceptance of me that made me want to throw myself in her arms and weep, "You're a well-made little thing, child." I was sixteen; I did not know what to expect. I began to ask questions and I learned:

This place, Auntie told me, was a tobacco farm, as big as—suddenly a phrase in our old language—"the Kingdom of Nebuchadnezzar." At that name from the Bible my heart began to pound; the white-skinned God was our secret. The owner's name, Yen. These people about us were field hands—plowmen, hoehands, wagoners, ox-drivers, cooks for the slaves; cowherd and hogherd; carpenters, masons, millers, smiths, spinners, weavers. Counting the house hands, Yen's slaves now numbered fifty-three. It was going to be a good year for the Yens, for the following reason: Many opium-smokers mixed their drug with tobacco, and last year there had been an Imperial edict condemning the use of opium, and this had had the perverse effect of greatly increasing the demand for the drug, and so for tobacco, too. . . . "Ayah, no, child! That was Li, the overseer. The young master is away today at Thousand Ducks Landing, downriver." The city from which the agent had brought us? Twin Hills. In the grove? The yellow Matriarch, the old master's widow.

Auntie said her own "Bible name" among the whites was "the Woman of Timnath." "Peace gave me my name."

"Who is Peace?"

"Let's see where Peace is," the fat woman said, and she leaned forward and looked up and down the street. "He will be along."

Soon Auntie said she must "be at Peace's side," and she left me with a thin, white-haired woman, who told me her man had died just a month before. A sour smell rode on this old widow's breath, and her eyes were full of a sticky fluid—some thick issue of grief?

There was an air of calm along the compound street, which gave me, agitated as I was by the shabbiness of my new home, a feeling of being caught and held. Slow movements. All being dressed alike, the slaves seemed to have one languid identity. I started up when a girl suddenly screamed, but the scream cascaded off into a squeal and a long tinkling laugh. The haze had burned away, and the afternoon light was sharp.

Then a moving clump of slaves, a kind of procession, slowly came along the compound street. I saw at its heart an astonishing presence, an enormous man, taller than the door lintels of the mud rooms, and as he came closer I jumped up again and held both sides of the door, to keep from falling, for I saw that the man looked something like Nose. It was Nose transformed, grown larger, coarsened; two upper front teeth were missing, and a scar arched over one eye, as if for that eye this man had two eyebrows, one light, one dark, and his hair grew down to his shoulders and was brushed out like thatch at sides and back, braided (a hint of the Drum Tower Boys!) into two locks over the forehead and in tiny queues at several points at the outer fringes of the stiff mass. And his eyes, yes, yes, were bloodshot. He looked twenty-five and brutal. Auntie walked beside him on one hand, and on the other a "mix," as the yellows called half-yellow, half-white slaves, a beautiful girl of about twenty; several other slaves strolled with this trio in a tight company.

Opposite the widow and me the big man turned aside toward us, and I heard him ask Auntie in a strong but gentle voice that reminded me, for some reason, of Preacher Honing reading the responses, "Is this the new daughter?" She nodded. He took some steps toward me. I must say that I had never seen Nose look at me in such a penetrating way. The man held his eyes on mine, unwavering, not blinking, and he seemed to be pouring some kind of power out at me through them. My heart was beating hard again.

"What is your name, daughter?"

I managed to say, "White Lotus."

His overwhelming stare moved to the widow, and he said to her —calling *her* daughter though she was more than twice his age, "Turn your thoughts out onto the ground, daughter."

"Yes, Peace," she said, but she shook her head sadly.

His terrible eyes turned back to me. "This"—he moved an open hand toward Auntie's cheek—"is my handmaiden, the Woman of Timnath. And this"—his hand swung toward the mixie—"my other handmaiden, the Harlot of Gaza." He spoke the "Bible names" in the old language. And he introduced a "brother," Solemn, whom he called his "maker of what I need," and another "brother," Smart, his reader and writer.

Auntie told him with a laugh that I had mistaken the overseer for the master.

Peace said the young master was away. He began to tell me about our owner. The father, the old master, Peace said, had died two years before. "He was a man with hard knuckles, he could stand any weather. He wanted to build—stole from the earth. He wanted to get it *all* in his own hands. Miser! Miser! You see this place—no plaster or paint, all rough. The boy—different: He sees the big places downriver, he wants kowtowing, he speaks of blood and breeding, silk sleeves, but he knows that his farm is unplastered brick and unpainted wood—do you see, daughter? The father came up here as soon as they built the canal across to the Yellow River and opium began to come in, he saw the chance for tobacco; the son sees no chance—he knows he comes from a line of clerks. The grandfather—a clerk in Twin Hills. You'll see what soft hands and long fingernails the boy has."

I was stirred by the fierce eyes into a boldness that urged me to say, "I saw a woman under the trees in front of the house. . . ."

The appalling stare was rigid, perhaps surprised, perhaps disapproving, perhaps furious. Peace did not answer this but moved on. Silence. My heart racing.

In the evening Auntie cooked a supper of cow peas with a chunk of pork for the unmarrieds—the widow; the young mix, Harlot; a girl about my age, named Bliss; besides herself and me. It grew dark and I was exhausted. . . .

A sad bellowing sound: it was Top Man, the white slaveherd, blowing the curfew on a water-buffalo horn. He stopped at our door a minute later and said, "All counted?"

"They're all here," Auntie said.

I could not sleep. The mud k'ang, which I shared with Bliss and the snoring widow, was uneven, bumpy, and damp.

(Stumps

No time at all had passed, it seemed, when the deep, mournful bawl of the buffalo horn sounded again. What alarm could it be? I jumped out of bed in the dark; the hard-packed dirt floor was cool to the soles of my feet. Auntie's husky voice: "All up. Morning call. Out! Out! Out!" Heaves and groans came from the k'angs; Auntie coughed and wheezed.

The children of the slave compound soon arrived, or were delivered in arms, for the care, during the day while mothers worked in the fields, of Auntie and the girl Bliss. Auntie told me that she had asked Top Man to assign me to the gang headed by Peace, who, though a blacksmith, worked "out," too; this was the old master's economical way, still honored.

At good daylight Top Man blew the carabao horn a second time, and we started along to the woods and fields. I was given a basket of millet meal to carry, and I put my shoes in it, on top of the grain. Harlot walked with me and explained what was in sight. I did not see Peace yet. There were three field gangs of about a dozen slaves each; Mink was not in mine.

We walked, speaking only in murmurs, along a foggy lane at first, past the great wooden tobacco house with slotted walls, a sweet odor drifting to us from within, and past the pounding and threshing mills on a dusty cart road, with now a pungent scent of crushed kernels of grain. The whole gang exclaimed almost in unison, a delighted shout, when we came over a rise and sud-denly saw the amazing sun, grindstone-size, made to seem as cool as the moon by the mists that came steaming up off a fallow field ahead.

Where *was* I? I had a sensation of being suspended in some vague moist midspace and of urgently wanting to get to a goal that was so far unnamed, unclear. All that life in the Northern Capital, those humiliations and bitter frights and losses—what had I learned? An uneasy craving stirred in me now as I remem-bered my arrival at this vivid farm the previous day, and thought of the huge man with the piercing stare. I felt young as a tottering calf; I had painfully much to learn.

At a crossroads each slave bent down, traced an X in the dust with his forefinger, and spat on it, and for my safety I did the same, pretending I had always done so.

Ahead we saw a train of three donkey carts and a pair of oxen being driven out in a double yoke, and there was Peace. I thought of his blazing eyes as he had stared me down; and then I thought of that voracious stare in Chao-er's the day when Nose had taken me into the small, dark room, and I was overcome by the dif-ference between those two glances. This man Peace looked as if he had just seen Preacher Honing's hell.

We arrived at our working place. For some days the gangs had been clearing a forest area to make new fields, and I saw a waste of fallen, untrimmed carcasses of trees, and stumps, and conical heaps of damp leaf mold. Following Harlot's lead I sat on a felled trunk and put on my shoes. Top Man set the gangs to work. The men cut logs with two-handled saws; the oxen hauled out prepared stumps; the women gathered brush. The sun climbed into a glorious morning. The ringing of axes and mattocks, the gentle protests of the oxen, birdsong in the woodlot, the slave-

herd's commands, the sweet voice of Harlot "encouraging" us with
song, bursts of laughter among the slaves—all these peaceful
sounds together gave me feelings, first of relief, then of unre-
strained celebration. Every time I turned my head I saw Peace.
The cooks, one for each gang, lit fires, and their kettles steamed,
and in midmorning Top Man called out the order to eat. The
warm cereal was like thick cream in my mouth, and now and
then a morsel of salted fish pleasantly stung away the blandness.
Back to our labor! Harlot began, in our old language strongly
touched with South-of-the-River tones, a hymn that almost made
me weep for the faraway life of our Arizona village:

"By cool Siloam's shady rill
How sweet the lily grows!"

The yellow overseer, Li, rode out into the clearing on a large
donkey toward our gang. He stopped beside Peace, who was fas-
tening the bullock ropes around a stump, the roots of which had
been mostly chopped through.
"Where are you heaping those stumps?"
Peace straightened up. "Where you said."
"Not where I said." Li knew the answer to his own question,
then.
"Where you said. We are hauling them where you said."
"Maybe the slaveherd said. Not I. I never said to haul the
stumps right to the place where we must clear a new field next
year."
"You said it last week."
"I never said such a thing."
All of us were silently going through the motions of work
but intently listening, for neither man would give ground, and
there seemed no way for this lock to be released. The yellow man
looked down from his awkward perch on the cloth-saddled
donkey; the slave stood with one foot up on the stump.
"Last week, when we came out here the first time," Peace said.
"What made you think I said over there?"
"The way I remember it."
I managed to notice, sweeping my eyes across the pair in mid-
motion, that Peace had not fastened his hypnotic stare on the face
of his adversary, and I could hear that he was not speaking in his
booming prophet's voice of the slave quarters, and he looked at
the ground, or at the donkey's flank, frowning, and in his voice

were notes of not very clever stubbornness, of deference underlying his opposition to the overseer's authority, of amiable stupidity, of a desire to please at odds with a servile self-defense—a tone surely far more baffling and infuriating to the overseer than frank contradiction would have been.

"Come along here," the overseer said, jerking his donkey's head. "I'll show you again where I said. Top Man! Get over here. . . . The old big one would have had you two bambooed skinless." He pointed out the proper place.

Then Li, his face livid with the frustrating moral defeat he seemed to be suffering, rode away to check on another gang, and our work took on a new willingness, Harlot's songs a wilder beat.

That evening in the quarters, when it was deep dark and time for our second meal of the day, Peace came to our hut to eat a supper of millet gruel, white cabbage, and persimmon wine prepared for him by the women he called his handmaidens, Auntie and Harlot.

In the midst of the meal Peace, seated cross-legged on a k'ang, facing the flickering fire of the open cooking pit, whose starts and surges, reflected in his eyes, made his intense stare seem to flash and burn, roared at the circle of cringing women his contempt for the yellow overseer, Li:

"I pity the man! *He* is a captive in Egypt himself. Must not be absent any night, or any daytime, either, without the son's say-so. Has to get a chit for absences just like a slave. We call him master, but he's no master. See the mules and donkeys watered! Rub down! Hay in the stalls! Doors locked up! Sheep. Fowl. Pigs. Watch out that the slaves don't steal anything! He's locked up by having to lock up. Keeps the keys in a safe place, but Peace knows where they are. I tell you, Peace knows just where the key to the master's gun box lies. *I tell you I do.* The *gun* box key! I pity him. No one but that man can unlock the smokehouse, vegetable cellar, stable door. Supposed to see us every one in bed—leaves that to the slaveherd—never comes down here in the hands' quarters at night; you notice that?—leaves all that to Top Man. The yellow Matriarch—she stands behind him in her fashion, but the old master's dead. It's the weak young Pharaoh now. I pity the man. Stumps! Haul Stumps, Here! No, no, no, over here, Small Peace! No no no no no, small boy!"

And Peace threw his long-haired head back and rocked off in a terrifying thunder-bellied bombardment of laughter.

⟮ A Laundering

I had been a Yen slave a whole month before I even saw
the courtyards of the big house again. On a market-day afternoon
I went up with Harlot to the laundering shed within the house
slaves' yard to wash my clothes.

I was afraid of the walled-in big house, and of the owner—the
invisible power, the more awesome because unseen. I had no
sense of the master except by hearsay. Big Venerable Shen had
been all too close at hand—bumping into me as I tried to pass the
bowl of duck; this young Yen was a figure in some sort of sorrow-
ful legend, and even in moments out in the clearing when I lost
myself in work (Harlot's thin swooping treble: *"Over the fields of
glory, over the jasper sea"*) I had a queer *empty* feeling of being
owned by a spirit with a floating misty mother.

Harlot ran with me through the orchard and past the garden,
toward the house slaves' postern gate. I was happy with Harlot.
She had been a house hand but had asked, for reasons of her own,
to be shifted to the fields; some said this mixie was the old man's
by-the-way daughter, and once the widow in our hut whispered
to me on a dank exhalation of garlic that I would never guess
whose sister Harlot was. My friend was playful and tricky, and she
delighted in teasing up my ignorant fears. Her singing voice drew
its intense emotional effect—its impression of a swimming gaiety
almost dragged under the surface by an undertow of pain—from a
swift, insistent trembling of the tones, a fluttering as of helplessness. When, along with Auntie, she was "at Peace's side," a
handmaiden, she was distant, stiff, and haughty, and she had a
hollow-eyed look, as if harking to inner voices.

As we hurried through the tall brown weeds with bundles of
soiled clothing in our arms, Harlot—building on her days of work
in the big house—fanned my superstitious fear of the figure I
had seen in the grove. The Matriarch! "She has a sharp tooth in
the middle that can make a hole in a person's neck!" Harlot
giggled and spurted ahead of me.

"Wait!" I pleaded.

We entered the house slaves' courtyard; this seemed to be the
heart of the farm. Along the postern side were a vegetable cellar,
a talkative poultry coop and a murmuring pigeon cote, a cowshed
and swine wallow, and a smokehouse for the curing and storage

of hams and flitches of bacon. Up one side stood a sheepfold, a cart house and stables, and storerooms for feed, hemp, flax, and tools. The house slaves' rooms edged the third side. At the far end were the kitchens, three or four rods from the rear entrance to the main courtyard, to spare the yellows' nostrils and ears, and, to one side of the yard, our goal—the well, with a pair of buckets slung from long bamboo levers, and beside it the washing shed, a roof on posts over a pair of stone tubs and stone blocks.

Harlot showed me how to draw water, and we half filled the tubs; we soaked the clothes and took them out and put them on the blocks and pounded the dirt out of them with battling sticks.

Across the way at an open stall of the stables we saw Peace and Solemn shoeing a horse.

I wanted to know from Harlot exactly what it meant to be a handmaiden to Peace. Where did she and Auntie go toward the forest with him in evening hours? Did Peace possess them there? On moss beds? Did that staring power of his release itself in some incredible gentleness? "Why," I asked, "does Peace wear his hair that way?"

Harlot balked—changed from a bubbling companion halfway to the rigid, vision-stiffened priestess she seemed to be when at Peace's side. "It comes from Smart's book," she said in a low voice. I was silent. "Peace," she said later, so softly I could barely hear her, "has another name. A Bible name. But it has to be a secret. Anyone who even whispers his secret name will get sick in the lungs. If you speak out Peace's secret name you'll spoil everyone's luck. It would be a curse on everyone." Harlot was pale; her whispers were rushed.

I was afraid, as it was, of the strange Biblical phrases in the old white language: Woman of Timnath, Harlot of Gaza. I had no more questions and pounded angrily at my soiled shift.

A circle of house slaves squatting outdoors on their heels around the compound entrance to the kitchens began to eat. We knew that they filched food from the Matriarch's stores, cooked too much, and ate the yellows' leftovers; three meals a day. They were better dressed than we—some wore castoffs from the yellow Matriarch and from the son. Several of them were mixes, for the masters liked slaves near them to have yellowish skins and folded eyelids. The house slaves had airs and manners; I peeked askance at them as I worked. Evenings in the hut Harlot had told us of our Yen house slaves' realization that theirs was a third-rate

aristocracy, for on pass days they had seen the high-style plantations downriver, and they knew that our Yen place was sketchy
and crass. The house slaves liked the young master's wanting to
show more. It was said that the yellow Matriarch, stubborn in
honoring the dead old man's ways, would not let the son have the
big house plastered or its wooden trim painted. The father had
tolerated "necessities"—cook, laundress, seamstresses, dairy maid,
gardener, handyman, hostler; the son had bought slaves to be
uniformed sedan-chair-bearers, body servants, coachmen, house-
maids, and houseboys. But this "elegance" was all halfhearted,
dissatisfied, lowlife, and unpainted; the hoe hands laughed at the
pretensions that Harlot made so vivid in the telling.

A young man, a mix, the young owner's body servant, Jug,
whom young Yen had won in a lottery at a party given for the
entire countryside at the Fan Tu-fu estate the previous spring,
strolled over to the tubs to tease Harlot. "Are you well, Harlot?"
he said. "How are your blisters, small girl?"

Harlot flapped her paddle at Jug as if to strike his buttocks.
"I'll show you," she said. "I have a strong hand now, Jug."

"I hear you've been promenading around with bigwig," Jug
said, pointing with his thumb backward over his shoulder at
Peace across the yard. I myself stiffened at Jug's condescension
to all field hands, and even to Peace. Harlot pounded her wash
with flat sharp smacks, and so did I.

"This the new chicken-biddy?" Jug asked, taking two or three
steps toward me.

"Go suck the yellow Matriarch's tit," I said, smarting.

Jug laughed hard, and he wandered away.

We drew fresh water and rinsed and wrung our things, to the
pinging of Solemn's hammer on the new shoes; Peace was paring
a hoof. The hostler and handyman were idly watching the work.

"Want to try to see *her*?" Harlot mischievously asked me.

I nodded, frightened but thrilled.

"We'll run through the front courtyards," Harlot said. With
deliberate care she lined up the twisted rolls of her wash over the
clean stone lip of her tub, and I put mine with hers. "She may
be in the trees, look sharp," she whispered, then pulling up her
coolie gown she sped away through the connecting gate to the
main courtyard, and I ran after her in a giggling panic.

At the spirit screen of the side courtyard I saw a figure, and

I almost tripped and fell: it was huge, I saw no face, something glittered on the form.

We had run only a few paces farther when this figure flew after us, shouting, "Harlot! You, Harlot!" We stopped. It was the big white man who had inspected me in the office—Duke, the yellow mistress's Number One Boy. He was wearing a wornout mandarin coat with dull, tarnished gold braid on it. "Where do you think you're running, you fool girls?"

Harlot was now deferential, humble. "White Lotus here said she was going to kill me," she answered, panting. "I had an accident, I spilled a well bucket on her—see her gown sopping there? She lost her temper, Duke. She's an ugly one, Duke. She said she was going to kill me, and I was just trying to get away."

It was easy to see that Duke did not believe this excuse.

In a pretended fury I said, "She *claims* she spilled it! She *threw* it at me!"

Duke came up to us and took us each by an upper arm and walked us deliberately across the main courtyard—and there, at the far side, under the trees, I saw the yellow Matriarch standing. I wondered: Had Duke understood the real reason for our running, and was he letting us see her? I even saw the yellow face: plain, long-jawed, wistful. At a steady pace Duke paraded back through into the house slaves' courtyard, and there at the stables he said, speaking smoothly as the owners' proxy, "These two are getting out of their place, Peace. Trying to spy on the Matriarch. See to them."

Peace's eyes suddenly seemed to go behind a shield of thought, and in a hollow voice he began to recite—in the yellow's language —a passage from "Smart's book," which was obviously a secret translation of parts of our white Bible: "So Esther's maids and her chamberlains came and told it—none might enter into the king's gate clothed with sackcloth . . ." And with a brilliance that took my breath away he recited more and more—the gnarled language of the prophets, strange in the yellow tongue, interpreting this yellow Matriarch to us, really to me, because I was new, so that I saw the Matriarch as a captive, a Philistine enslaved by her own enslavement of Israelites—pitiable, wandering in the grove in despair, or in her workrooms sewing endlessly at slaves' coolie-cloth gowns. Peace's manner was grandiose; his mind seemed to be in the grip of a self-steering clairvoyance; I began to tremble.

But Duke chuckled and said, "Small boy," using the yellow man's contemptuous diminutive, the more sarcastic for being thrown at Peace's powerful figure, "small boy, your head of hair is too heavy for your brains."

◖ Absences in the Night

As the weeks passed deep into the twelfth month I found myself increasingly troubled by a disquiet, a vague inner aching that I attributed at first to physical weariness, for the novelty, the sense of the festival release of our work in the fields, soon diminished, and I was often tired, but I began to understand that my discomfort was not washed out by sleep; it was rather a kind of persistent yearning. I had an impression something was happening beneath the surface of the life in the quarters. Auntie and Harlot—and several of the men also—would sometimes disappear after supper and not come back until very late hours. Awake when my hutmates returned, having waited for them with an alert heart, I dared not ask them where they had gone or what they had done. Their absences had to do, I felt sure, with Peace— but with more than Peace, too? With Smart's book? With sorrow, with anger, with the underlying pain of our lives? With appeals to our white-faced God to help us? I saw, and thought about, their gravity as they silently left the field hands' compound at night, their serenity in the fields in the morning after having been out to all hours.

I wanted to understand. Why was I a slave? I would go to any length of work to comprehend the meanings of the characters in Smart's secret volume I had heard so much about. This clandestinely translated Holy Book carried far more weight with me than the casual Bible of our Arizona days. I wanted to be able to read it myself. Trapped in my skin of a certain color, drifting through hostile days, I wanted to make sense of the world about me.

◖ The Turn of the Year

But now we came to the end of the yellows' calendar, and to their New Year, and in an almost craven spirit we faithfully observed the yellows' rituals, even among ourselves. Being

slaves, we played safe. Our white-faced God of whispers and furtive prayers might not suffice to relieve our many sufferings, and
so, on the twenty-third day of the yellows' twelfth month, Auntie,
Harlot, Bliss, the widow, and I gathered in our room about
the little niche in the mud-brick cooking range reserved for
Tsao Wang, "Hearth King," the yellows' kitchen god, and we put
honey in his tiny smoky palace, and smeared it on his mouth, to
sweeten his tongue, and we placed offerings of straw, black beans,
yellow paper, and fragrant punk before his tablet, and then we
took down his picture, and burned it, and bade him a happy
journey—for this little yellow god was said to be the chief of
secret police to the yellows' Supreme Being and was about to make
his annual trip to report on us, as on all the users of kitchens in
the whole land. We wanted the kitchen god to speak well of us—
in case the yellows' yellow-faced Supreme Being might prove,
after all, to be master of our white-faced Jehovah. Was our white
God Himself a poor slave? God help Him if He was!

What would the kitchen god report about me? That I was a
dutiful sow? Did he understand me well enough to speak of this
powerful feeling I had of wanting to know more?

(An Announcement

In the last light of one of those days I sat in our room
with Auntie, Harlot, the widow, and Bliss.

This was our home: one room, six paces long and four wide,
a wattle-and-mud affair built up of twisted branches of weed
trees, pignut and locust, as bones for a straw-bound plaster of
mud; a dirt floor; one window hole with board shutters, which,
warm or cold, we always closed at night to keep out bats and
errant spirits of ill-buried slaves; our mud beds and mud-brick
cooking range; one grain-seed chest for all our meager possessions
together; and a huddle of earthenware pots that held our weekly
rations of five catties of millet meal to each and two catties of
pickled pork. This was our bare home, which we furnished further
with stories, with songs, with grief, with bursts of laughter.

My companion Harlot had given me courage, and I was telling
stories of what seemed the far, far distant past: of Agatha in
the coffle when the swarm of bees came out, of Kathy Blaw chanting the tale of the jaguar and the jackass to the slave ship's hold-

ful of naked women, of the swearing of the oath over the chalk
circle on the floor of Chao-er's tavern (even now my shoulders
twitched with half-shaped laughter), and of "a man slave I knew
in the Northern Capital"—I could not speak his name!—his face
tumid and bruised from the carousal of the night before, his shirt
torn half off his back—the trembling of leaf shadows on that
broad back!—as he rode on the shoulders of yellow men off toward jail and the . . . *Water! Give me water!* . . .

My friends wept. Recounting the pain of two dim years, I was
perversely happy. I was among my own. I had no contact here
with yellows. The overseer never came near our quarters; the long-
jawed face in the grove of trees had been, yes, wistful; and where
was our young master, whom I had never even seen?—and on
this day early in a year that could hardly be worse than the last,
my tongue was free, my mind reached back, and I felt a marvelous lucidity . . . yet a pull, as well, of the uncomfortable, unformed
yearning of these last weeks.

The widow clapped the shutters closed. The evening air was
bitter cold.

There came to my mind, as I was talking of a wild, whirling
evening at Chao-er's—a flash of Cassia Cloud's wine-slop rag
across a white cheek—there came to me, as if a bubble were
bursting up into my mind, a shred of understanding that I had
not had before: that the dissipation into which Nose had willfully
plunged in the Northern Capital was not a way to be "in front"
at all, and that it was no answer to yellow power, yellow magic.
I saw that Peace here on Yen's farm understood this. I burned
with eagerness to know where he went late at night—where *he*
was leading.

Auntie and Harlot both spoke, with unaffected admiration, of
the clarity of my memory, and in the dull glow of the supper
embers I saw them look at each other as if exchanging some
thought I could not fathom.

Then they were gone. They slipped out without a word. Cold
air came across the earthen floor as they opened the door to
leave, and the widow put sticks in the k'ang oven to warm up our
bed.

At once I felt restless. The Woman of Timnath, the Harlot of
Gaza: they were the life of our hut. Bliss was a good-hearted girl
but lacked a will of her own; she moved as if someone else had
her by the shoulders and was guiding her gently here and there.

The widow wore a shawl of bitterness—everything was wrong.
I asked the widow, "Where do they go?"
"Pfaa!" she said. "Looking for men."
"They stay out so late," I said.
It was Bliss who spoke up then, looking into the waning firelight
of the cook-range as though she did not know what she was say-
ing. "They go to secret meetings."
The widow flew into a rage. "Close your mouth, you little frog!
What do you know about those two? You—a baby to take care of
babies—don't even work with your back—got a sheep's tongue—
ba-a-a! ba-a-a!"
They went to bed, Bliss and the widow, but I sat on the edge
of our k'ang, gazing at the dying glow of the cooking embers.
At last, before crawling onto the litter beside the other two, I
put some wood knots onto the k'ang fire, for a cold snap had come
—could the malign yellow blizzard of a Gobi dust storm be whispering at our stout shutters? I was unable to sleep. I thought
about this farm—the crude, unkempt "big house." What had the
old owner really wanted?
I was still awake when Auntie and Harlot returned; the fire in
the k'ang was out, and I was getting chilled. I sat up, shivering
with cold and with my desire to ask questions, but not daring to
speak, and they saw me stirring. Side by side they came over to
my bed. Auntie was wheezing. I could not see their faces, because
the cook fire was almost out. They leaned forward, and Auntie
whispered, "Peace and Smart, they're going to teach you, child.
We told them about the things you can remember. They want
to teach you."
*What had Peace said about my memories of Chao-er's—or of
the faggots by Coal Hill?* "What did you tell Peace?" I asked in a
rush.
"The things you told us," Auntie said.
"What did he say?"
"He said you had a good mind, Smart should teach you to read."
Now the yearning I had felt during these weeks seemed to be
building inside me to an almost unbearable pressure. "When?"
"Some night soon. They're going to start with you soon."
I began to sob. Sitting cross-legged on my mud bed, I covered
my face with my hands and wept with great heaves.
"Hush, hush, baby, you'll waken the widow."
No danger of that; the widow was sleeping on her back, with

her mouth open, making a creaking sound like that of big branches rubbing together in a tree.

Harlot said, "We told them about you, sweetheart."

Even as I sobbed I wondered why I was crying so hard. Would learning new things bring such sadness?

❨ In Peace's Eyes

For a time the ground was frozen, and the iron tires of the carts clanged on it as if the earth were one huge frigid sledge-hammer head. It did not snow. No use trying to dislodge stumps from cold steel: we were shifted to new work, carrying split rails of locust wood from the cleared land to a meadow half a mile away, for a new pasture fence. Two men teamed to carry a rail, or three women.

In the clearing and in the meadow bonfires burned, and we were allowed to warm ourselves a few minutes at each end of our shuttle. We almost ran with the rails on our shoulders, to keep warm; we traveled in trains of five or six rails in tandem, singing as we trotted. Despite the fire and the rush of our work, I was chilled through.

Now I was at the meadow warming my hands at the fire when Mink came along, sharing one of the long timbers with a slave named Tree, a tall spindle of a man, and those of us who saw the team could not help laughing at the sight of the rail sharply inclined from the straight thin one in front to the bent short one behind. When the pair came to one of the places where Top Man had told us to stack the palings, we saw them pause, and it appeared that Mink with his twisted back was unable to heave the rail straight off his shoulder to the ground. He and Tree, whose head was twisted around on his stalk of a neck to consult with Mink, stood awkwardly for some time. We laughed more than ever. At last we saw them ease the heavy rail off their shoulders into the crook of their elbows, then by another stage to their hands, and facing each other they swung the rail—counting, "One! Two! Three!"—and flung it out. It landed crosswise on the pile and cracked in two. How we howled!

Others joyfully tossed their rails the same way after that, and several were broken.

Li, the overseer, came on a donkey. He saw at once what had

happened and spoke to us collectively. Who had started this game? No one spoke. Li dismounted and strode straight to Peace and repeated his question. Peace shook his head, and his little queues jiggled; his mouth was open, and the gap of his missing teeth showed dark and disreputable. How stupid he looked! Did I imagine that Mink was trying to look larger than usual? He was actually strutting back and forth at the edge of the crowd around the overseer.

Li, seeing that he was up against our concerted empty-headed-ness, shouted at us with a rage-wrinkled face to straighten out the heaps and get on with our main task. Then he rode off.

We carefully heaped the cracked and broken rails alongside the whole ones, so the unsound pieces would not be discovered and discarded until fence-building time. Thus we trebled work that we had already doubled.

From the moment of the overseer's confrontation with Peace, the huge man had been muttering and shaking his head, so his massive thatch of hair swished about his shoulders. Almost all of us were back at work now, tidying the stacks, and at a sudden weird roar from Peace every face turned his way.

Peace appeared to be in a state of absolute calm, but for his eyes, which stared at something on the ground—at nothing I could make out. Then I realized he was gazing at a sight the rest of us could not see. I sensed this realization spreading like a hot liquid spilled among the slaves.

Slowly Peace moved forward and in a voice that sounded as if it came from deep in a cave he began to tell us his vision.

A lion. The carcass of a lion. It was lying on its side on the meadow grass, hollowed out, half opened out, the eater eaten, its flesh still red but tinged here and there into carrion, the bones in the basket of the great chest white against the meat. Great lion, hollowed out, on its side.

Peace stepped closer to this sight, stiffened, raised his hands as if to push back what he now saw as too amazing. I stood, as did all the others, in a thrill of awe and terror.

Bees! A hovering of bees over the hollow in the huge animal's chest. Ah God! A hive inside! A huge store of honey!

Peace took two staggering steps forward and dropped to his widespread knees, and fanning at the air as if to drive away the insects, he plunged both hands like dipping spoons toward the heart of his vision. But then he jumped and repeatedly started,

and he drew back, and his hands slapped back and forth as if he
were being stung again and again; his eyes showed his scorn of
the pain, his surprise at each pricking of his skin, his anger at
the pests.

"Ha! Ha!" he shouted as he beat at them.

Then resolutely he leaned forward again, and down arched the
hands into a single bowl, and they scooped forward, the fingertips
digging, and with a triumphant shout he raised his hands over
his head, and for a moment I really believed I saw the sweet
amber liquid and the clots of beeswax overflowing from the trembling cup of Peace's hands.

Harlot had begun a hymn; never had the tremor of her voice
been so sad. *"Watchman, tell us of the night . . ."* Others came
in on the second line—*"What its signs of promise are"*—and soon
a circle of women formed and fell on their knees around Peace
and his vision, swaying, singing with Harlot, calling on the white
God with heartbreaking cries. I felt with a sudden flood the bitterness of my life, the uselessness of everything, the emptiness of
the future. Apparently I had been crying, for I became aware of
a wetness on my hot cheeks.

Peace was standing now, shaking his head confusedly and looking at his hands, which hung down limply from his powerful
wrists.

A shrill voice shouted, "Top Man coming!"

The song ended abruptly; there was a scramble to the disarray
of rails.

(Into the Millet

Peace saw another vision a few days later. The cold
weather had continued, and a day was set aside for the cutting
and storing of ice. Men were taking turns on large-toothed hand-
saws, six at the same time in a far-stretched echelon cutting broad
strips of ice across the pond behind the tobacco house, and six
others, paired with the first six, cutting chunks off the ends of the
strips. A lane of black water was opening across the middle of
the pond. Men with gaffed poles hooked the floating cubes of ice
and with dexterous tugs flipped them up onto the solid ice, and
we women, bending over, skidded the chunks to the edge of the
pond, where teams of donkeys with stone boats were waiting to

drag the chunks to the sawdust-heaped ice pit at the rear of the house slaves' courtyard.

A huge bonfire blazed on the bank, and we worked in relays, those who were off duty standing in a circle around the wonderful fire, clapping the cold out of their hands.

By midafternoon I ached and shivered, and under my scarf my ears and under my foot rags my toes and under my improvised mitts my fingers stung from the cold. The gaiety of the morning had worn off. I wondered with each cake that was loaded on the stone boats whether that might not be enough. I yearned for another chance at the fire.

Li came down from the office on foot pushing a wheelbarrow with a wheel as large as a donkey cart's, bearing a large keg lashed to either side. I heard him say to Top Man, "Give them drams before you kill them."

"We're almost done, Overseer Li. About two hours more."

Subdued groans went up from all who could hear.

"Give out the drams now. I don't want the whole force down with bad lungs."

Li left the wheelbarrow near the fire and returned to his office. And so, to delighted rubbing of hands by the men, we gathered all around the fire, and Top Man began the passing out of drams in good big bowls, which lay in a rack on the wheelbarrow. Harlot had told me about precautionary drams in bad weather, but I had never had one, and when my turn came, and Top Man poured two measures of the millet liquor called "fire spirits" and one of water into my bowl, I was afraid to drink it, and I sipped, and everyone shouted, "Swallow it! Gulp! Gulp it down!"

I did, and the burning in my throat and the metallic, garlicky fumes in my nostrils—besides the flame in the liquor, there was a bite in the water, for the keg in which it was stored had strings of red peppers and lumps of amber asafetida soaking in it—made me clutch at my neck and cough and weep; the slaves laughed at me.

In a few seconds a wild release from cold and despair surged through me from the knot of heat in my belly, and I joined, still moist-eyed, in the laughter. There was a cheerful chattering all around me. I felt an ecstatic joy.

Peace, at his turn, swallowed his dram without the slightest shudder and stared deep into the flames of the bonfire.

All the drams were done. Top Man gave the signal for the

resumption of work. We were just turning away from the fire, in a little storm of shouting and chortling, when once again we heard that ghastly bellow from Peace's throat. Everyone stopped where he was and watched the big man.

This time Peace's eyes darted here and there, his hands, raised again in protest, moved in sudden defensive thrusts, and the deep, shaking voice began again to speak out what he saw. *Foxes. So many! A hundred, two hundred, three hundred. In all the field and the cart lot on the near side of the tobacco house, running around. CATCH THEM! CATCH THEM!*

Peace began to rush here and there in astonishingly agile dashes, and he would reach out with his hands and clutch and grasp, now lifting one of the invisible creatures by the brush, now seeming to have a weight in both hands. He put them all in one area—some kind of enclosure in his mind. Once in a while it seemed that a ghostly fox must have snarled and snapped at Peace, for he snatched back his fingers and grimaced.

Again I felt the rising wind of emotion in all the slaves. Women who had just been giggling over their drams were weeping; a look of alarm was on every face.

Peace's charges to catch the foxes of his mind's eyes were all near Top Man, and the coop into which he put them also held the slaveherd, who stood stiff and terrified.

Pine knot! Give me a burning pine knot!

Peace's shouts were hoarse and exultant. He ran to the bonfire and took up one end of a branch that was protruding from the coals and ran with it to his imaginary enclosure. He dipped the flaming torch again and again.

Go! Go on, fox! Go, you! The tobacco house! Ha! Hayah! The millet! The threshing shed! The walnut trees! Go on, fox! Go! Go!

This time we did not sing or pray. Top Man's terror tipped over into rage, and he came running toward us with arms flailing, shouting to us to get back to work.

The dram in my vitals had burnt itself out, and I felt cold in every part of my body.

(A Prizing

In the second month of the new year the weather grew mild again, to my relief, and on a rainy day, when the air was moist and the tobacco plants of the previous autumn's crop hanging in the drying house were pliable, the overseer ordered a session of striking, sorting, and prizing.

Along the center line of the tobacco house stood three great hogsheads, each with a man standing in it. Peace was in the hogshead into which the dark leaves were being prized, and as I and others ran with "hands" of this grade to his huge tun, Auntie and Harlot passed them in turn to Peace, who laid the bundles in courses within the hogshead, and then stamped them down with his bare feet. These three were joined in a kind of dance: Peace's acceptance of the tobacco from Auntie and Harlot was beautiful, his bending, rising, and rapid trampling, as his shoulders weaved, his arms flew and plunged, while his handmaidens, as he called them, pounded with heels and palms on the staves of the tun as they swung and turned.

In this work I forgot the stark, wrathful figure of the Peace of visions. Here he was playful, flirtatious, and graceful in his power. He rallied his gang to work faster than the others, and more than once he winked at me as I ran up with a bundle of "hands." His glances seemed to run all through me in a burning way, like drams. Nothing more had been said of the teaching Auntie and Harlot had whispered about, but I felt that Peace was aware of me, and that I was on the lip of some new phase of my life. I could only wait. I dared not speak to him.

I felt the next best mood to happiness—altogether lost in the headlong work.

"Handmaidens!" the spindly slave Tree, a sorter, commented once when I was nearby. "Look at Harlot's eyes. I call them bedmaidens. What?"

The other sorters laughed.

"What?" Tree said again, wanting to prolong the effect of his joke.

There was a sudden hush in the house; I could hear the rain on the roof. I looked around to see what could have caused the lull, and there at the bright-leaf hogshead I saw for the first time —my knees felt weak—my master, in a rain-wet yellow oilskin cape, Yen the son.

He was not much more than a boy!

It seemed he was showing a visitor around his holding. I saw in my first glance the whole of what I had heard: the tale of the father, just dead, a strong plain man; the yellow Matriarch, tenacious, domineering; the son's ambitions; the drive of a family of clerks at the provincial yamen, tavern-keepers, petty commissioners for the collection of the Emperor's rents, who wanted to be gentry. Jug, the young master's body servant, had whispered to Harlot, and she to me, of the young master's attempts to hobnob with the aristocrats of the estates along Favorable Wind Brook, the Hus, the Mas, the T'angs, the Shihs, in their rounds of quail fights, gambling on sending trained birds after seeds thrown in the air, foot-shuttlecock, and lifting of beams weighted at the ends with heavy stones—pastimes of yellow idleness. But young Yen had been snubbed. I could see that he was unsure of himself. Alongside his perfectly garnished companion he appeared somehow not quite right, in his too new scarlet pantaloons bound in white puttee tapes, his tunic with exaggeratedly long sleeves, and his peasant's oilskin cape. When the young yellow landlords went fishing, hunting, or trapping, Jug had said, young Yen did his part with great skill, for his rugged father had taught him from the age of eight all the lore of rabbits, wild quail, opossum, doves, snipe, geese, deer, bear, and fish of the brooks—but his very proficiency in these chases set him apart from the landlords of real quality, who were great parlor hunters, trainers of hawks, hard drinkers, but not, as was young Yen, truly at home in the wilds: Jug had seen all this himself in the forests. Yes, our young master had been snubbed, and he was pathetic trying to please this visitor.

The atmosphere in the tobacco house had suddenly changed. Work started up at an even more feverish pace than before. Harlot sang a hymn with a mad, incongruous speed. On one of the ladders Solemn, who was striking down stalks from the bamboo laths, began to wave each pair of stalks as he descended to the leaf-strippers and to fling his bare feet in semicircles as he scaled the rungs again. The sorters cut capers as they tossed the hands of leaves to the runners. Peace whirled in the great barrel, and heels and palms drummed on all three hogsheads.

I was caught up in the growing excitement. Would the young master notice me? I heard, repeatedly, loud high cackles of laughter that reminded me of the guffaws, so long ago, of Shaw the linguist on the *East Garden* and of Gull at the slave auction, at the question: Will they eat us? We ran for fresh burdens as if hard work only lightened our limbs.

Yet underneath my frantic gaiety, trying to keep up with the others', lay a chasm of bitterness. Yen the son wanted to show us off to his friend—as his docile, tractable, happy slaves. And we were doing as he wished. We wanted in spite of ourselves to please him. My shoulders weaved as I ran, I was more graceful than ever before, my arms and legs were liquid strength, and I wondered if the young master saw me. Horrible!

Then Top Man was thumping on Peace's hogshead with a heavy staff, and he held up a hand as a signal to us to stop our work. We stood panting: bursts of laughter kept spilling out, till Top Man thumped more, and we fell silent—rain and heavy breathing.

It appeared that Yen wanted to explain our work to his guest— a youth from Twin Hills, the provincial capital, a city dandy who had never seen a prizing before—and our owner had been unable to make himself heard over our exhibition.

The two young yellow men—how slender and delicate the Yen boy was!—walked along the center of the house, and they paused at Peace's tun.

"How is this for a specimen?" Yen said to his friend, tipping his head toward Peace as if the slave were a splendid oak.

I was standing near enough to hear our young owner's voice, which was reedy, low, and—betraying his eagerness to please— deferential. Was *this* the unseen power that had frightened me so many weeks?

"What is your name, small boy?" the fragile young owner asked huge Peace.

Peace seemed to hang back; he stood with his hands on the rim of the tun.

"He is Peace, Big Master," Top Man hastily said. "You remember Peace."

"Ayah, of course," Yen said. It seemed to me that he had known Peace's name all along, and that his offhandedness was a show for his friend. "The strongest man in the province. Yes or no, Small Peace?" A thin yellow hand patted Peace's upper arm.

Peace's face broke into an agreeable smile, split by the black gap of his missing teeth.

"Tell me, small son," the master said, "tell this gentleman here what you do when you have filled the hogshead."

The smile on Peace's face gave way to an absent look. His chin sagged, and now the blank of the lost teeth reinforced the vacuity of his expression.

Top Man began an answer for Peace: "We hoist another hogshead on this one . . ."

"No, Small Top Man, I would like to hear what Small Peace has to say."

"Yes, Big Master," Top Man said, and stepped back a pace.

Yen stood waiting for Peace to speak.

Peace appeared to be undergoing torture: forgetfulness and embarrassment. It was clear enough to us slaves that his sudden stupidity was a pretense. At last, with a great effort, he grunted out the words "The way the slaveherd said" in a wretched accent, and he poked a flat hand through the air at Top Man.

"He may be—I believe he is—the strongest man in the South-of-the-River Province," young Yen said to his friend, "but he is not the wittiest, would you say?" The master's friend laughed, and Yen said, "Ai, Liang, you Twin Hills men with your Peach Mountain ideas!"

Every nerve in my body was strained to receive impressions, and at the words "Peach Mountain"—the name of an island off the mid-coast where slaveowners, taking The Nine Flowers of Virtue at face value, had treated their slaves with unprecedented liberality, only to be rewarded by a bloody uprising led by a white fanatic who called himself The Saint—I noticed that Peace shifted his stance in the hogshead; Auntie's head turned and her eyes met Solemn's: no more than that.

"Can't you see," our young yellow master was going on to say, "that these creatures are just children? Look at this big beggar! He will never grow up—likes to jump around and clap his hands. Hai! It's a marvelous naïve gaiety, isn't it? Delightful! But it vanishes unless you take care of them, Liang. You know?" He had formed a fist at the phrase "take care of them."

Top Man said, "Prick the Ditcher, Big Master T'ang's ditchman, he's another strong one here in South-of-the-River." We knew that this slave, whom we called simply Ditcher, had been hired by our master to come and repair his drainage ditches in the third month.

"I've heard of him, Small Top Man," the master said.

"Quite a nest," Yen's city friend said of Peace's hair.

"Fill the second barrel," Peace suddenly blurted out, as if the procedure he knew so well had just come to him, "mash it all down in the under barrel."

"I see, Small Peace," the master indulgently said.

"Tackles and levers," Peace said in something like cleft-palate grunts, and he pointed at the pressing equipment lying at one side of the floor.

Then Top Man said, as if to cut Peace off, "Big Master, I told you about those rails. I have found out the one who started it. He is right here, Big Master." The slaveherd had a hand on Mink's shoulder.

The master slowly examined Mink. "Where did *that* accident come from?"

"He is one of the new ones," Top man said. "Uncle Ch'en, the slave dealer, shipped him out to us."

"Give him—"

But before the name of the punishment could come out of the lemon lips Peace's hands had begun to thump on the edge of his hogshead, Harlot's thin trill of a hymn promptly began, and the work was whirling around us again.

The master and his friend left us soon.

At once the work slacked off to a much slower tempo, and Harlot began a new hymn, in the old language of the whites:

> *"When I fall upon my knees*
> *Within the Camp of Dan . . ."*

The cadence was slow, but now the excitement in the room was greater than it had been as our feet had flown in the yellow man's presence, and I shared fully in it, for I understood that this song was a call to a secret meeting in the woods in the night.

(Lines in Cinders

Three weeks more passed, and I had begun to be resentful of Auntie and Harlot, for making promises that were not kept, when, one evening, as I turned away from the dying cook-fire in silence to drop onto my bed, Harlot came to me and whispered, "Tonight, baby!"

I knew, of course, what she meant. I lay down on my k'ang and covered myself, without, however, undressing, and I waited, staring at the flickering reflections of the fire on the crude ribs of the roof.

Anticipation danced with just such shimmering lights in my mind. How impatient I was to go!

At last Auntie came to my bed and touched my arm, and we three left the hut.

I could just make out the two forms walking ahead of me, and underfoot I could feel the cold, sandy hardness of a cart track. I had no idea where we were going. I was aware that woods loomed on either side of us. I shivered at the thought of spirits of the ill-buried dead that might be out walking their weary paths, but I was reassured by the soft, steady steps of my escorts.

I heard a click. A crack of light. We were entering a mud-walled building; a lamp was hung high on a joist.

"Welcome, handmaidens," Peace's deep voice said, and then, as my eyes adjusted to the dim light in the room, I saw him: enormous, his hair wildly fanned.

He saw me, too, and coming forward he said, "Welcome, daughter, to the Camp of Dan. Smart, Smart, the new daughter is here."

It was a blacksmith shop. I saw under the lantern an anvil glistening aloof and solemn, like an altar, and beside it a fire pit, and a leather-chested bellows like a huge bullfrog, and gradually, as I stood waiting for Smart, who was huddled in conversation with Solemn and a slave I did not know, I made out a heap of iron hoops for hogsheads; new spades and hoes, their raw handles like shocked sheaves of maize; mule shoes hanging on pegs, and smaller donkey shoes; a shining plow point—in a soot-blackened room, an atmosphere of dimness and grime, cinder-darkened, reminding me of thunderstorms and spiders' traps. I was still shivering.

I made out three or four of our field slaves, and two or three strangers, all men; they were murmuring in pairs and trios.

Then it began. Smart, gentle and soft-voiced, tall as Peace but thin and fragile-looking, took me to a bench. My fears drained away, and I was so excited that everything seemed to whirl around me: dim light, hints, snatches, undertones, men coming and going, great Peace's deep oracular voice, and the quiet, steady urgency of Smart's words. . . .

My heart is beating so hard, my eyes are turning here and there so fast, that everything seems confused. At one point Smart reaches down behind the bench and lifts a book for me to see— black covers—soot, soot—Smart's book! I see Peace under the lantern; a man leaves the shop. Smart is speaking to me in a low voice. Peace comes to our bench.

"Beginning at the beginning? '. . . without form, and void; and darkness upon the face of the deep . . .'?"

"No," Smart says, "I was telling her about the slave poet of

Ningpo. Wang's White Peony. To show this child what she could do."

Peace spreads his big arms and starts to recite. " *'Some view'* " —his voice is sonorous—" *'our pallid race with scornful eye . . .'* " He turns away.

Smart takes a rod of iron from a heap of scraps and traces in the cinders on the floor two lines:

"Man," he said. "That's where we begin. Man."

I understand, and I repeat the word "Man," and I make the two lines of the forked animal and tears come into my eyes.

Chao-er's tavern: the wild relief of seeing white slaves let themselves go—but here, in this somber room, the delight is of a wholly different order, and runs far deeper. Perhaps those two lines are all I can bear to take in. They seem so fateful; two simple lines for "man." A kind of picture, torso and legs. Will I be able to remember *everything*?

Smart has all too gloomily impressed me with the appalling task I am undertaking. I must learn a different character for each word. I cannot call myself even rudely literate until I have mastered three thousand characters. There are, he tells me, forty thousand characters in the Great Dictionary of K'ang Hsi. What a wild thicket I am stumbling into!

We will start, Smart says, with the Trimetrical Classic, which every yellow schoolboy learns to shout at the top of his lungs by heart. He draws the characters of the first pair of tripodies:

> *Man at birth is good;*
> *Men seem alike but differ.*

He makes the sounds, and the shapes he traces in the black soot burn into my mind as if they were lines of live embers.

Tracings in ashes. Smoke-darkened beams. This room stirs a strange uneasiness in me. ". . . our pallid race." Am I a slave for no other reason than that I am white?

I hear Peace's voice rising as he talks to men near the anvil: "Remember this." He speaks slowly, as if pressing words one by one into ears, about a recent provincial edict entitled "Pulling

Weeds," having to do with the disciplining of slaves. His voice
canters now. "Ayah! They shouted this order down three months
ago. Magistrate Chiang, Magistrate Ma, the South-of-the-River
liberals, most of all. But here's Magistrate Kuo Lin-tu in jail: they
use the order when they want it, these yellow liberals. Smart,
Smart, read this to our friends."

Peace comes to the bench waving a document. Smart stands
and reads the yellow characters aloud. It is a copy of a letter
written from the Twin Hills jail by Magistrate Kuo, and it raises
a question which gives me a queer feeling in my stomach: Is the
institution of slavery consistent with The Nine Flowers?

Later Smart sketches more wisdom in the cinders, and gives
me the names of the characters he draws. Can I fasten my attention to them?

> *Uncut stones are worthless;*
> *Illiterates ignore the proprieties.*

Men come and go. For a moment Auntie is beside the bench,
her hand on my head. I stand and hastily whisper, "Is this a
meeting, Auntie?"

"No, no, child," she says, laughing at me. "They're teaching
tonight."

Some time later an enormous man comes in—he is three inches
taller and even more massive than Peace, and he is loud and jovial; the others urge him again and again to tone down his voice. I
hear someone call him Ditcher. His hair is long, like Peace's, but
the effect is different. Peace's head seems majestic, prophetic;
Ditcher's hair falls low on his forehead, almost to his eyes, and
he looks like a playful bear, a buffoon. He slaps men on the back
and constantly laughs.

Peace is showing him something, and others press close. Then
Peace raises the object high in the air in one hand, as if to strike
or chop with it, and it is close under the lamp, and I see that it is
a slab of bone with teeth set in it—the jawbone of a horse or a
mule.

Smart traces new figures and makes new sounds.

It seems to me that Peace is speaking, now, for Ditcher's benefit,
and with a great show of authority, of the occult uses and powers
of snakes, lizards, frogs, scorpions, snails, worms, and rats.
Ditcher's eyes roll—he is impressed.

Smart's foot wipes out a tracing in the cinders. I remember

every shape he has made, and its sounds. I have waited so long for this chance that my mind is like a pure glass bottle. I take in every detail: a mattock head, whose tongue has been broken on a rock, hanging on a nail on a beam near the lantern, waiting for its turn to be mended.

I am amazed at Peace's memory. He cannot read the yellow characters—Smart is his reader—but it appears that every word that Smart has read aloud to him has lodged itself in his head. He is a mimic; he is transformed. Just now he stands with arms folded, his face modulates from pity to wrath as he gives back, like an ancient cliff throwing back echoes, the very tones of Smart's careful reading from a clandestine scroll: ". . . *There were several white brothers, blood brothers, who were sold in different lots, and it was deeply moving to hear their cries at parting. Ayah, you nominal Buddhists! Might not a white wretch ask you, "Did you learn this from your Buddha, who says to you, 'Harm no living creature'?" '* "

" 'Harm no living creature,' " Smart repeats, nodding. The sound of Smart's voice from Smart's own lips is startling when it has seemed to be coming from Peace's.

Peace goes on with the narrative. Ditcher's eyes are absurd—like those of a boy watching honey being poured.

Thrilled as I am, I nevertheless feel disquieted by a quality I sense in Peace—a stiffness; he is like one of the straight iron blanks for mule shoes I see lying nearby. Is there any heat that could bend him?

When Peace is finished Smart tells me in a quiet voice about the recklessness of the tobacco farmers along the canal. They are ruining the soil, he says. The good soil is a mere crust over clay, and it is exhausted in three years, and new fields have to be cleared from the forest, as I have seen; and besides, there is too much tobacco, they can't seem to sell it all, it gluts Twin Hills warehouses. And he begins to tell me—but it is getting late, I am rattled, I cannot absorb any more—about the Peach Mountain slaves' uprising.

"I don't know what you mean!" I protest.

"That is enough for one night, child," Smart says, patting my hand. "Don't you worry," he adds with great gentleness. "You are going to be a fine reader."

Now I openly cry.

Peace leads the way home. The Woman of Timnath and the

Harlot of Gaza walk arm in arm with him, and I hear a thin, delicate humming from Harlot.

We are accosted by Top Man, the slaveherd, at the rear gate of the field hands' quarter. I hear him hissing to Peace, "I told you before, Peace. You have to be here for the counts. I cannot stay up all night for you to take your girls to the woods. I told you. One of these days Overseer Li is going to hear about you." Peace is standing straight and stiff, and Top Man's voice begins to trail off into a pleading whine. "I can't help it. They are going to take my skin if they find out the count is wrong. They are going to skin me alive."

Peace walks past him through the gate without a word. Someone makes a spitting sound.

❨ Peace

So my life was turned inside out. I felt that I had a purpose, but I did not know exactly what it was. My growing curiosity about the secret work being transacted by night matched my growing sense of the pain of life by day. Auntie swabbed with herbal tea the bamboo welts on Mink's bent back—earned at the game of rails. Harlot's songs at work, even when we skipped through our motions with apparently weightless hearts, had a haunting sadness to them, of recollection: Egypt! Auntie brought Egypt to South-of-the-River Province by telling me that the Pharaoh of the songs lived so long ago that none of the great trees had been here, only a waste of sand, and some mean little bushes, one of which burned beside a path when God sat in it, and rushes on the bank of the canal. Sometimes at a teaching Smart opened his black-winged book to let me examine a character I had learned. The translated Bible, yellow ethics, dark superstitions—all spun together in my head. Once in a while I saw Peace under the hood of light from the lamp in the blacksmith shop, surrounded by whispering men, holding up in a grip of anger the animal jaw-bone: What was his threat?

Peace was indeed at the heart of the puzzle, and Peace was in my thoughts when I lay on my straw mat unable to sleep.

He was nothing like Nose. How had I seen Nose in him that first day in the slave quarter? My memories, my grief, my desire.

. . . Perhaps it had been a flash of prevision, an instantaneous grasping that this man would have, as Nose had had, an incalculable importance to me. These days I was obsessed with him. I yearned to be near him all the time, yet what I felt was less love than awe. He was far too austere to figure in daydreams of touching, embracing. I think I felt that my only hope for some vague rescue lay with him, but at the same time I felt a latent danger to me, to all of us, in his unbending iron straightness.

One day in the third month we were building fences, along the line where we had thrown the stacks of rails askant. The sky was overcast, the air was clammy. There were white patches on the ground, for a sleety snow had fallen the day before, but the ground was unfrozen and muddy. Top Man was pushing us hard—kept saying that the spring rampage would be on us soon. Peace was digging a ditch for the high palings. I was one of those who carried the stakes to the fence line, after Solemn and Tree, working with adzes, sharpened the upper ends.

Mink was in our gang that morning, and he, too, had been assigned as a carrier. Mink was already well liked by many of the men, for he was a daring gambler, and he had the hand of a master craftsman at pitchpenny; the coin would soar from his fingers, without a spin to steady it such as other men used, and it would hit the ground flat and slide no more than its own diameter and stop within a hairbreadth of the wall. He was sharp-tongued, and since he had been bambooed he had carried on a satirical cringing and sniveling before the slaveherd that made us all laugh behind our hands. During a wait for a rail, Mink picked up one of the wood chips that had fallen from Solemn's adze and pretended that it was a stale piece of *man t'ou*, and, stooped and doubled with the effort, he gnawed at the pretended bread with one side of his jaw and then the other, sighing and moaning grotesquely at the deliciousness of the morsel. All of us who were nearby broke into laughter.

Top Man, seeing the horseplay, walked up behind Mink and struck him a token slapping blow with an open hand on the round of the head, not so much to hurt as to surprise.

Mink whirled. A malevolent look on his face gave way at once to an obsequious pleading expression.

Top Man stood over the twisted figure, on the point of letting out a roar of frustration and censure, when, from behind, Peace, towering over Top Man precisely as the slaveherd dwarfed Mink, slapped the slaveherd's after-crown with the same force, the same dusting contempt as Top Man had applied to the bent jester.

Now Top Man spun around. "Peace," he said. He suddenly began breathing hard, as if from the running of his thoughts. "You are about due."

Peace said, looking at Top Man with a piercing Judas eye. "Would you want to be a crookback, Top Man? You don't have to be *born* crookbacked. You could get that way—sometime, late, dark night, a lizard could climb down your wall, jump on your bed. Think about it, Top Man. Would you like to shrivel up?"

Top Man's lower jaw was trembling. I myself was shaking. I believed in Peace's mysterious admonition. I did not like Peace's manner; his warning had been too merciless, his magic too sickening. Yet I felt relieved. Peace had put a hand on Mink's shoulder, and the hand had run down the bowed spine between the still-cringing Mink's shoulder blades.

From down the line Li had seen a cluster gathering where we were, and he strode toward us. Peace said, "Overseer coming. Best way to keep your back straight—keep your tongue straight, Top Man." He picked up his shovel and turned to his digging.

When the overseer asked the slaveherd a few moments later what we had been doing, we saw, with a satisfaction that was also heartsore, that Peace was surely Mink's avenger, not only for today's slap but also for the wales on his back, for Top Man said, "We were just seeing if there are enough rails along this stretch, Overseer Li. There are. It's all right."

Another day I saw a more compassionate side of this frightening man. We had begun to prepare the tobacco seedbeds—plots of deep forest mold on which the brush from the new clearings had been heaped and burned for a dressing of wood ashes. We were set one day to forking the seedbeds with special care, turning in the ashes and kicking up the leaf mold so it was as mellow as our master's steamed bread. Our gang was working by tasks; stakes had been driven in the ground to mark each hand's section, full tasks for the men, two thirds for women.

I was digging hard—when suddenly the widow who lived in my hut, the sour, sarcastic, defeated hag whom I had come to treat with a young girl's contempt for a gloomy old chawbacon, threw up her arms, fell to her knees, and began to scream the name of her man, who had now been under the ground five months. It was a frightful sound. Her shrieks semed to express, to the limit of desperation, the question I had daily asked myself: For what am I working?

Run away! I must run away! I looked at the edge of the forest beyond the seedbeds, and for a few moments the impulse to fly almost took control of my limbs.

I saw others looking at the woods, turning their heads jerkily this way and that, and I realized that the widow's terrifying breakdown had laid bare for all of us the utter hopelessness of our slavish life.

Then Peace was kneeling beside the howling, frail figure, and I heard his prophet's voice boom out, "Let us pray, daughter."

Behind the widow's back Peace was beckoning to Smart, and Smart ran across the soft seedbed and stood before the pair. I could not hear what Smart said. Peace put a vast arm across the old woman's cricket shoulders, and the two began to rock back and forth. The widow was catching at her breath, like an infant after bawling. A couple of minutes of this, and the old woman was calm, and, roaring, Peace summoned all the men of the gang, and with forks flying they completed the old woman's whole task for the day as she stood by shaking her head.

A few days later T'ang's Prick the Ditcher was hired on, as contracted at New Year's, and one afternoon we were hauling stones for his lining of a drainage ditch and a culvert. This slave must have weighed as much as a large donkey, and his strength and endurance were as gross as his joviality and optimism. It was extraordinary how he took the great rocks handed down to him by pairs of men in the supply chain—we women were handling smaller stones for chinks and gaps—and with one thrust drove them into the mud of the ditch so their flat faces were flush; and how he stood hour after hour up to his knees in the chilly water of a third-month day. His game was woman-chasing. His prowess was famous in three provinces, and it was said that his master was thinking of taking him off ditch work and hiring him out as a slave breeder; Auntie had told me with a straight face that fourteen babies had been born at one of the down-canal plantations nine months after he had stayed there on a two-day ditching: he had stopped at the farm, she had said, holding up her hands as if scandalized, only one night. The great satyr did not care about age or looks, it was said, anything female would do. This made for a day of squealing on the part of our entire force of women. Even the old widow got out a snigger when Ditcher chucked her chin. Once in a while Ditcher would leap from the water and run up the bank after a woman who had brought him down a little stone; she would scramble shrieking uphill, her foot slipping now and then in her hope of being caught. Ditcher would clamp his huge, wet, muddy hands on the woman's buttocks, give them a good shake, and slide back into the ditch roaring with laughter.

Once Ditcher made a sally after Harlot, and I could not help looking at Peace's face to see how Peace took this byplay with the girl he called his handmaiden. Peace seemed unperturbed— seemed, indeed, not to have noticed that anything unusual had happened. Peace heaved at the cracked rocks, passing them down to the giant in the ditch.

Later, during a pause, I glanced at Peace and saw that he was staring at the mud at his feet with a blazing, inturned fervency. I thought he was about to see another of his visions. Then—perhaps roused myself by the rutting high spirits of Ditcher—I had a moment of thinking Peace had gulled us all, for I doubted whether he had seen those awful visions: Had he *staged* them? My doubt was feeble, however, and it fled in panic as Peace happened to raise his eyes—they might meet my own!

Drams were given in midafternoon to Ditcher and a half dozen men, Peace among them, who had been working down the bank of the muddy run. When Peace was served he turned and reached his mug out to Ditcher. Ditcher looked suspicious. "Here," Peace said, "you could use it."

Ditcher did not like this. "Who's chilled? What are you trying to do?"

"Take it, brother," Peace said. He spoke softly but looked angry.

Ditcher glanced around at the other men's faces, to see if he could read their feelings. He wanted the dram, one could tell, but he did not want it at the cost of a humiliation. "Are you trying to put the phoenix eye on me?"

Peace held the cup steady at arm's length.

At last Ditcher could stand the temptation no longer, and he seized the cup and put its contents down his throat in one gulp. Then he belched grandly.

Peace, with a look less of triumph than relief in his eyes, said, " 'Out of the eater came forth meat, and out of the strong came forth sweetness.' "

As if with one voice Auntie and Harlot said, in the old language, "Amen."

At the women's tones Ditcher snapped his head this way and that in distress, but no one now was paying any attention to him. Harlot had started a hymn, and all joined in the choral praise of a loving God we could not really picture. Several women were suddenly in tears, for somehow, in a gesture of kindness—undertaken from who knew what motives—and with his deep-voiced words from Smart's sooty book, Peace had suddenly reached down into our deepest recesses and pulled out the yearning, the deep sense of having been cheated, the helpless anger of all of us who seemed to be the accursed children, not of that white-faced God who never showed mercy, but of a puny yellow man named Yen.

◀[Rememberer

A warm day—spring had arrived. The scene: a spring cleaning of the quarter. I was listless, distracted by sensuous thoughts, lazy in the sunlight, and dissatisfied. The catkins were out on the walnut trees; a weeping willow over the pond behind the tobacco house was a cascade of yellowy green. The tobacco beds had been seeded, the millet fields had been planted. A market day in the fourth month. All things topsy-turvy. We had turned every chattel, rag, and pot outside the mud wall of the compound, and in the groves and plots clothes and quilts and straw screens were spread out to the sun; the men had built at the compound gate a vast rick of rushes from the swamps near the canal, and we wove fresh matting for our mud beds.

I had cleaned the rude chicken house outside the wall where we unmarrieds raised fowl and eggs, and I had spread the chicken manure on our garden plot. Now I was to sweep our room, walls and floor, and sprinkle lime about, but I was obliged to wait, because an infant, who had been left in Bliss's care while his mother stripped her room, was asleep inside on some sacking in one corner, and I dared not sweep for fear—according to one of our superstitions that we had perhaps picked up from the yellows— of knocking the broom against his soul, which we supposed was out of his body while he slept, and perhaps sweeping it right away into the aimless breezes outdoors.

The men lounged in the street of the quarter, harassing the busy women with remarks that suited the voluptuous day.

Mink was sitting beside me on the door sill, chatting with me. "You can't just stand there and *see* a dead lion. One that isn't there. Hundreds of foxes running around! You can't just see things if they aren't there."

"Some can," I said. "Some people can."

"Is that really true?" Mink said. His shrewd face was pulled into a skeptical knot; one eye seemed to be higher on his face than the other. "How do you know that?"

"I saw it in Smart's book."

"Can you read that thing?"

"Beginning to." Yes, this was my happiness. Smart said I excelled. The beautiful characters moved like processions of memories in my mind, as vivid as sagebrush, clay pots, Gay Moya on the screen, and my father's walk. Yet in this setting and in this language, the book did not seem to be Preacher Honing's mild Bible, this was a book of burning hopes, of wild promises.

"You're a clever one," Mink said, "but I notice you have no man."

"Jacob," I said, "he was one who saw things: a ladder, he saw a ladder. He saw a man come and fight him . . . *touched the hollow of his thigh, and the hollow of Jacob's thigh was out of joint as he wrestled with him.*"

Mink looked afraid, but he said, "Why haven't you a man? You're old enough."

The sun was warm on my skin; I stretched my arms over my head. "What makes you want to know?" I asked.

"Ayah!" Mink said. "It's nothing to me."

I looked around and saw, approaching slowly from the lower end of the compound street, Peace, with Auntie and Harlot walking a pace behind him. There was something unnatural, formal, about their little procession; they were walking stiffly, and Peace was not turning to one side and the other to greet the flirting slaves. For the first time in months Peace was in his lightweight, elbow-length coolie tunic, and his strength seemed to be stirring under the cloth like a new season in the ground. I jumped up and gripped my broom, and I stuck my head in the door and saw the baby was still asleep; Bliss dozing on the bare k'ang beside him.

Peace came straight up the street of the quarter toward me. His eyes burned. I felt the rough, sun-heated jamb log of the doorway between my shoulder blades; I wanted to sink in delight to the warm earth; Harlot and Auntie were singing softly.

The trio stopped in the center of the street opposite me. Mink stood up and moved away along the wall of our room. I was in the doorway full in the sun.

Peace took one step forward, and he spoke to me in the old white language, "Peace sayeth, 'Blessed art thou among women.'"

I shivered, my scalp crawled. Auntie and Harlot were looking at the ground.

"Come with me," Peace said, "from the valley of Sorek. Your name?"

I stood frozen, wondering what he meant.

"Your *name*, daughter." His voice was impatient.

"White Lotus. Small White Lotus," I said as the yellows would say.

"White Lotus means something else—a secret name, dweller in the valley of Sorek. You are chosen to be Peace's third handmaiden. Peace needs a rememberer—getting so much to remember."

His speaking in the third person confused me. I was afraid, and I asked in the yellows' language, "Are you really Peace? Who are you?"

He answered in the old white language, " 'Why asketh thou thus after my name, seeing it is secret?' "

I had seen those words translated; Smart had gone out of his way to show them to me.

Peace spoke now in a low voice, still in the old tongue, "One command, daughter of the valley of Sorek: Thou shalt not touch these locks." Peace raised a hand to his hair; his eyes were boring through my head. " 'For it is given unto me to deliver Israel out of the hand of the Philistines.' "

I thought I would dissolve with fear and pleasure at the big man's dizzying words.

"Come with me, handmaiden," Peace said, turning away down the street.

I stepped out and took my place between Auntie and Harlot. The huge shoulders were directly before my face. We walked slowly, and I was aware of heads turning to look. I still had the broom in my hand.

《 "Kill! Kill!"

The seedlings in their beds were little inches. On a fine
day in the fifth month we were drawing the new fields into hills
with hoes, to ready them for transplants. The boy master was
away, gone to gamble on the quail fights at the Spring of the
Precious Bushel, on the Twin Hills road, though he had not, we
had heard, been admitted to the rich young landlords' secret
society that presided over these and other sports; we were forced,
humiliating as it might be to ourselves, to picture him as a
bumpkin hanger-on—in whose weak, uncallused hand, however,
our fates lay like careless dice. He was as powerful to us as God
—a hateful pariah god. My own life had changed, from root to
leaf. I attended Peace with Auntie and Harlot every hour away
from the fields, and sometimes at work, too. New thrills each day!
Smart's teaching had been intensified; I was reading well already,
and Smart gave me many passages to commit to memory. I knew
plans. I knew as I hoed in the afternoon that Harlot would in
time strike up a hymn which would call certain men to a meeting
with other owners' slaves that night at Yen's water hole, a teaching, and that a line in the old-language song would announce the
place:

"I met dear Joshua down by the water . . ."

And after dark that night, to be sure, some of us set out, looping around through the millet fields to the track to Twin Hills
that the yellows called Favorable Wind Brook Road. Peace's massive, work-shelled, ascetic hand was on my shoulder, and under
one arm I carried three large scrolls for Smart. To no sound but
the whispers of skin on sandy dirt, we made our way by the light
of a greenish rind of the moon.
Here was the spring—a black water hole in a basin of cattle-
trampled ground on a sidehill, with a backdrop of twisting trees—
honey locusts?—and, gradually densifying out of the murk, some
sort of low plank walkway set up on stakes and laid out to the
center of the pool for the dipping up of water in buckets; a long
scar on the edge of the open area—a ground for the yellows' game
of pitchpot, perhaps; a dozen men squatting on their hams.
"Have they come?" Peace asked at large.

"Sheep Wu is bringing the fellow out from the Canal Bund," a voice said.

"We can go ahead, then," Peace said. Auntie, Harlot, and I, the only women present, were tolerated, I sensed, as Peace's appendages; he snapped his fingers, and Auntie drew out from her sleeve a small chimneyed lamp, and Harlot struck a flint and blew up a taper to light it with, and I handed Smart his scrolls. Then we three drew back as Smart and a freed slave, named Fan, a mix, gathered the others around them and read to them from scrolls, handbills, broadsides.

I made out Ditcher; grunts and jokes. Some, too, whom I had seen at teachings at the smithy in Yen's woods: Wang's Judge, Ch'eng's Candy, and others.

The tiny light was poor; Fan, the free mixie, faltered reading the words: "Slavery—lives—in the—house—of—force. The white —the white man—the white man descends—therein—to the— state—of a—domestic—animal. . . ."

The slow, awkward diction burned in my ears. I had come to know long since that none of this was a drunken joke over a magic circle; that what seemed to be a kind of madness in Peace was, if seen in a certain dark-night way, rather an absolute clarity, an obsession, a gradual shaping of our energies. Helpless as we were, we were going to . . . going to . . .

"Here! Look!"

A hand picked up the little lamp, and the effulgence soared up toward a face: Wang's Judge, I recognized him, though the face seemed to lop out in the uneven lamplight—till the lamp, a tiny star glistening on its chimneyside, moved across, and I saw that one cheek really was swollen, and that the round of the cheek had been burned with a branding iron: the character *tsei*, meaning "thief." This was new, unhealed. I heard Auntie's wheezing shocked intake of breath.

Ditcher made a growling show of indignation. Peace hung back.

Smart read, with greater facility than Fan, the freedman, from the famous Secret Scroll of the South Island Colony. A certain philosopher, Hsieh Fu-tzu, had advocated in this document, an aide-mémoire to the Emperor of an oral proposal Hsieh had made, that the whites be set free, colonized to South Island, off the far-southern coast, "with arms, implements of household and of the handicraft arts, seeds, pairs of animals . . . a free and independent people . . ."

The plan had been summarily suppressed, but far from being hanged or beheaded, Hsieh was still a loud voice in the Emperor's ear. A man in our cluster by the water hole said he had heard that Philosopher Hsieh might be elevated to Minister of the First Rank, in charge of the writing of new laws on agriculture. *Might he help us?*

Then another slave said that his owner had called Philosopher Hsieh a coward—said he had put his tail between his legs during the sack of Tatung twenty years back. Let nine hundred Mongols simply walk in. Did nothing beforehand to mend the breach in the Great Wall. Sank the cannons in a lake. Left the slaves to flounder. Packed up and rode off with all the yellows.

At this Ditcher rose to his feet, fists clenched, growling, as if to say in his stupid mute way: Who dares to slander this friend of the white man?

Peace's voice, severe and sharp: "Don't count on Hsieh!"

Peace's omission of the minister's honorific title had the most startling effect—of audacity, of authority. He seemed to be speaking directly to Ditcher, and the giant sat down, discomfited and grumbling.

"Hsieh owns slaves," Peace said. "Fifty. A hundred. It's all talk. Set the whites free! If his heart bled for slaves, why didn't he manumit his own? He could have done that. Like all their 'scholars,' their 'good men.' They talk one way and act another."

Now a voice at the edge of the circle said, "We're here, Peace."

"Is that you, Sheep Wu?"

"We've been here some time."

"Bring him up to the light."

The small lamp had been placed on the plank walkway, and now a slender white man, a sailor, to judge by his clothes, came and crouched on his knees and bare feet on the planks, the lamp between his spread legs. The light cast upwards showed the hollow of his thin chest, and veins serpentining on the drawn muscles of his neck, a cleft chin, cavernous nostrils, and deep black shadows where his eyes should have been.

Sheep Wu, a free white who lived as a beggar in Twin Hills, with a mass of fleecelike curly hair, said in a hushed voice that the man on the planks was a free man of Peach Mountain Island off the mid-coast of the southeast, who had come to tell us of the whites' successful revolt there, and of The Saint.

" 'White brotherhood under God!' " the sailor began, using The

Saint's slogan. "I am glad to come here to you." He spoke in an
odd, broad dialect, which we could barely understand. "I was a
sugar slave." He started the story. "Nine years ago . . ." Sometimes
his hands flew out, and shadows, as of scattering birds, flapped
across his face—and I shuddered, seeing for the first time, as
he went deeper and deeper into horror, what I was involved in,
and how far. If only I could have seen his eyes! . . . A torch touching a silk screen in the Yew Ah plantation house. Men running
with cane knives lashed to the ends of staves. A wall of flame in
the dry sugar fields. Drunkenness: Kill! Kill! A yellow landlord
bound between two boards and sawed into sections. Fire! A snow
of fiery fragments of cane leaves carried on the wind and falling
on the thatched roofs of the North Cape City. The gruesome
cruelty of The Saint's lieutenants—one of them had had a banner
showing the corpse of a yellow infant impaled on a pole. . . .
Then a word picture of The Saint: fierce yet humane, the short
figure, pale pale pale face, huge eyes, upturning nose, long
stained teeth, a man nearly sixty years old, master—yes, that
word—*master* of a small island where slavery has been over-
thrown and the white zealot is king. . . .

When the amazing story was finished, Peace, in three or four
short, blunt sentences, proposed to these men whom he called
his brothers a war *here,* in South-of-the-River, against our owners,
the yellows.

"Yes! Yes!" A moanlike assent.

"When?" A sharp tenor voice asked.

"We will discuss that when we meet next time."

And that was all. That was all.

We stood around after Sheep Wu took the Peach Mountain
sailor away. I heard Ditcher muttering discontentedly; he was not
fond of being put down as Peace had put him down about Philosopher Hsieh. I moved nearer. "I don't take such things from any
man! Does he think his secret name is The Saint? How many
secret names does he think he has?" I sensed among the others a
furtive sympathy for Ditcher, a shrinking from Peace's fanaticism
in the moment of being overpowered by it. Shaken to the edges
of self-control by the sailor's tale, and appalled by Peace's word,
"war," I was now seized with a panic fear that Ditcher might blurt
out Peace's secret name and ruin us all. But did he know it? Could
he? Would he dare if he did?

On the way home, as the piece of moon fell low in the sky, we

stopped by the road while Peace, to my terror, in a sphere of lamplight, prepared, in the name partly of our white God of wrath and
partly of some horrible yellow witchery, a conjuration against
Top Man—a piece of shed snakeskin, spit, a knot of the vine
called devil's shoestring—to be placed in a chink of Top Man's
hut, to prevent his reporting our absences at night, on pain of
losing his manhood. Maybe the slaveherd would see the charm
jammed in a crack in the straw-bound mud; maybe someone
would help him by chance to see it! Then, in hysteria, Top Man
would hold his tongue.

(Men of Valor

The preaching, to slaves from the farms along the canal,
the farms of Chao, the other Yen, Chi Kuo, Ma, and our Yen, was
held in an abandoned tobacco house on the Chi Kuo place, near
Lü's tavern; Big Master Chi Kuo had given permission, thinking
our superstitions harmless. The long shed with vented walls was
crammed with slaves sitting cross-legged on the brick floor.

Smart was the ostensible preacher, but he seemed to speak with
Peace's tongue, and the tongue spoke obliquely of the one subject
that had been on my mind day and night since the meeting at
Yen's water hole. War. Peace's war.

With wheel-like motions of his hands describing the contours,
Smart cast up before our eyes an allegorical picture of Twin Hills
with its two eminences divided by the deep gulley of High
Thoughts Creek: "And the white God stood with His two feet that
day on the Mount of Olives, and the Mount of Olives divided in
the middle toward the east and toward the west, so there was a
valley, and half the mountain removed toward the one side and
half toward the other, and the white God stood with one foot on
each side, and He looked down and saw His white children all
around the divided mountain hauling and hewing and digging
and planting and transplanting and being bambooed and being
cheek-branded and lifting and chopping with hoes and walking
on the ice and carrying and striking the leaves and prizing the
leaves and plowing and hacking at stumps and ai, white God,
suffering, suffering, suffering, suffering. . . ."

The illusion of Smart's turning into Peace was astonishing.
Peace stood directly behind Smart, moving with Smart's motions,

his gestures precisely Smart's; it was as if he were manipulating
Smart's lithe body, and as if Smart could only choose words Peace
wanted him to use. Smart's voice fled more and more from the
mild, sweet tones of his own throat toward the deep, commanding
sounds of Peace's. Harlot had whispered to me once that Peace
could change himself into a cow, a cat, a horned owl—why not
into his slave companion? I was standing with Auntie and Harlot
behind Peace, and I could see his left cheek pushed out, for he
had in his mouth a translucent quartz pebble, taken from
Favorable Wind Brook, "of the sort that David used to kill
Goliath."

"Behold! The day of the Lord cometh in the city of two hills and
thy spoil shall be divided in the midst of thee, for the city shall
be taken, and the houses rifled, and the women ravished, and
half of the city shall go forth into captivity, and the body servant
shall . . ."

My blood was pounding in my ears. I had come to the preaching desperately tired that afternoon, because it had rained the
day before, and we had been put to the frantic work of drawing
the finger-length seedlings of tobacco—"Chekiang fan-leaf" and
"sweet-breathed"—from their beds and rushing them to the fields
and setting them out in their mellow hills, and Overseer Li and
Top Man, the slaveherd, nerves frayed by the insistent need to
finish the transplantation while the ground was damp, had
cursed, shouted, and openly struck blows. I had ached from
running, bending, concentrating—but now my limbs began to
lighten, my heart raced, I felt giddy with a trembling joy that
was mixed with dread.

". . . Jericho straitly shut up, locked up: 'I have given into
thine hand the mighty men of valor,' saith the Lord—"

I could hear a stirring, a kind of sigh, move through the
gathering.

"—and they utterly destroyed all that was in the city, man and
woman, young and old, and ox, and sheep, and ass, with the edge
of the *sword!*"

There were moans now among the listeners. With a growing
understanding of Smart's call to act, a kind of frenzy, which was
appallingly reckless, spread through the crowd.

At the height of this emotion, this burst of realization, there
came a roar from Peace's throat much like those we had heard
at the beginning of his visions.

But it was from Smart's throat!

Smart's hands were stretched upward, his fists were clenched, his eyes were lifted to the joists above—and behind Smart stood Peace in exactly the same pose. Each slave in the whole house seemed rigidly frozen in mid-breath. Smart's voice, indistinguishable from Peace's, cried out, "He will smite them hip and thigh!"

In the midst of the fiercest exultation I had ever felt, I had a moment's thrust of panic: Would Smart, unhinged by this houseful of excitement, say Peace's forbidden name?

But then Smart's lips were closed again, and again the same voice was heard—this time from Peace's own mouth.

"Yea! Yea! Yea!" the voice shouted. "The spirit of the Lord moves in me."

Now, with a sudden settling to earth that was startling in itself, Smart, his body relaxed, his eyes on the faces before him, spoke in his own gentle, quiet tones. "All those men who are with Peace," he said, "stand up. All those who are not with him yet, stay seated on the floor where you are. Women remain seated."

A rustling. Murmurs. Enthusiasm and doubts almost visible, like mists. Just what did it mean to be "with Peace"? Changes of mind. One by one the self-elected stood, until there were about a dozen men on their feet.

Smart said to them, "Come over to Yen's water hole. Peace has some drams for you men that are *men*." At this four or five more were emboldened and stood up.

The preaching was over, then, and there was a sudden stirring of talk in the tobacco house. We left with Peace and his volunteers, and as we walked away the building sounded like a spent pork barrel thrumming with bluebottle flies.

Auntie, Harlot, and I carried the jugs, with finger loops of porcelain at their stout throats, over to Yen's water hole. Solemn had a bucket and a dipper, and Tree a basket of bowls. When we arrived it was nearly sunset. I had not seen Yen's water hole by day; the scale was smaller, more intimate, the trees less grotesquely twisted, the plank walk less a pier, than they had seemed in the hollow night.

Peace himself poured the spirits from the jugs; Smart diluted the portions with water from the spring. Peace spoke to each man as he handed him a bowl, and he touched every one, putting his big hand on a shoulder, or a forearm, or an unkempt head of hair.

The excitement of the preaching carried over, and, indeed, as the men drank, it grew. They gave little yelps of what sounded like astonishment at their own boldness.

After a time Peace said, "We need captains. Whom shall we have for captains?"

Voices shouted: "Peace!" "Fan the mix!" "Ditcher!" "Judge!" "Candy!" "Sheep Wu!"

Nothing explicit was said about the war at any time. I tried to imagine its shape, its beginning—but Peace left everything to the slaves' own minds, until, when the drams were all gone and the slaves had abandoned themselves (at least I had, and I supposed they had) to wildest inner thoughts of insolence, valor, retribution, revenge, *revenge*, Peace began to give himself over, as I had never heard him do, to puffing and gasconading; he was talking like a master. I intercepted some looks between pairs of the men who had been named as captains—careful glances that meant headshakes. Those looks frightened me.

"You're going to see Peace walking around in there." He had begun speaking of the beautiful yamen, designed by Philosopher Hsieh, which housed the Emperor's provincial governor and his mandarins in Twin Hills. "Listen! Peace is going to step through the red-flag gate there, and you'll hear Peace's heels echo in the Hall of Obeisances, bare feet slapping on the stone floor! And Peace is going to sit at a long silk-covered table, with silver bowls, and silver chopsticks, and incensed candles in the lamps, and wine, right at the same table with Warlord Sun, and Brigadier Chang, and Ts'ao Hsi-kuei, and Third Minister Hsieh, and Feng and Li and T'ang and Wu and . . ."

The moment of appalling vanity was saved by Peace's beginning to laugh. He bent over and raised up and began to howl, hoot, snigger, bay, snort, shake, guffaw, chuckle, slap, gag, bellow.

The others caught it. I caught it. The woodland cove echoed with our bloodletting seriousness leaking out in helpless laughter.

Until we realized that it was dark.

"Captains come over to the Camp of Dan," Peace said.

Now this was the summit of recklessness: to go along to a secret meeting just after dark, without a discretionary wait for the deep of night, to walk along outside your own place without an overseer's pass when you knew patrols were sure to be ranging —the half-drunk squads of poor yellow farmers, hired for this prowling by landowners; resentful, bloodthirsty, bored, on the hunt for night wanderers and gatherings of slaves.

Auntie hung back, and Harlot and I were with her, for it seemed clear that women should not go to the smithy at this risky time, but—

Peace called out with a loudness that made me shiver, "My handmaidens!" He wanted us near him. He wanted Harlot to hum as we walked. . . .

Someone lit the lamp in the blacksmith shop, and before it was hung on the joist, Fan, the mix, said he had something to show us.

A ring of heads. A hand holding up the lamp. At the center a torn piece of paper from some unimportant official document, with the chop, or printed seal, a stylized picture in a red as dark as dried blood, representing the authority of Sun, the warlord of South-of-the-River Province.

"What is it? Smart, what is it?"

Smart bent low. "Sun Hou-tzu," he said. "The monkey who became a god."

I had had only a taste of the liquor, but I felt a slippage of restraint. Smart's (or Peace's?) wild allegory of Twin Hills, the pebble in Peace's cheek, the men volunteering for the unclear war, Peace's visionary boasting, and now this blood-red hint of transcendence—it all made me giddy with confidence in myself and in these men who were going to fight a war of which I could not see the shape. For me the room whirled with something like hope. The men were milling about, praying and laughing.

The next I knew Peace was standing at the center of the sooty room, holding up his teeth-edged mule bone, booming in the old language, "With the jawbone of an ass, heaps upon heaps, with the jawbone of an ass will I slay a thousand men."

Smart was on his knees praying softly.

Peace threw the bone down on the ground, his lips drawn back in a grimace. "This place is called Ramathlehi!" Then he put a hand to his throat as if he were half choking. "I am sore athirst. Now I am going to die of thirst, and I am going to fall into the hands of the uncircumcised." He fell, at any rate, to the ground, and groveled there, and reached for the bone, and seemed to drink

from it, and as he did, he gradually rose up on his knees like a
man renewed by decency, forgiveness, good food, honorable treatment. "This place is called Enhakkore! Enhakkore!"

❲ To Twin Hills

Early one morning a few days later, the first market day
in the sixth month, Peace went up to the office and procured from
Overseer Li five passes to go to Twin Hills to sell eggs and fowl
that we unmarried women had raised—passes for himself,
Solemn, Auntie, Harlot, and me—and we set out on foot toward
the Yen landing on the canal, through a landscape glistening in
pure sunlight after three days of rain.

Little skies of rainwater still lay in the cart track; I loved to
break their mirroring with splashes of my bare feet.

Auntie, Harlot, and I carried baskets of eggs; Solemn had half
a dozen pullets, their feet tied together, hanging upside down
from one hand, and the same number of cockerels in the other;
Peace carried four fat brown hens.

Peace told us as we walked through the woods that he would
be talking during the day with many key men, and that no matter
what was spoken he wanted all of us to cling nearby him, as if
we were a group engaged with him and his men in commonplace
gossip.

At Yen's landing Peace hailed, as it passed along the far bank,
a train of four shallow-draft cargo barges, each carrying twenty
or thirty hogsheads of prized tobacco, being towed in file by a
pair of donkeys and under charge of four white bargemen, slaves
out on hire. At Peace's call the men halted the donkeys, and a
couple of them poled one of the boats across to us on the landing,
and for one copper cash each we went aboard, and we floated
along the canal that way, to the harsh cries of the donkey-drivers.

Peace, his long, matted hair swinging as he turned his head
this way and that, the scar that rode his eyebrow seeming unusually prominent under the luminous sky, pointed out to Harlot
and me pretty sights along the way—a heroic willow, the Chi Kuo
big house, the ferry for towing-animals across the mouth of the
canal where it debouched into the river, and then, going down-
stream on the river, the landings of farms more famous than
ours, the bare-ribbed wreck of a barge, an island's upstream

prow mustached with snags of driftwood. The huge man was calm, sensitive, and tender with us.

The world seemed new-made under the rain-washed sky, and, feeling the warm sunlight soak to the pit of my stomach and watching the play of Peace's powerful arms, I thought for a moment of that small, dark room at Chao-er's tavern in the Northern Capital; suddenly I was overwhelmed with a sensuous aching. I was young, I tilted my face up to the sun and closed my eyes, and I imagined a strong hand slipping between my thighs to spread them wide apart. . . . Then I opened my eyes again and I looked into Peace's, and I saw not merely single-mindedness but something more that sent my daydream flying in disorder across the riverscape: a steely stiffness inside him, a control, an unwillingness to deviate by a hairbreadth from his set way, an absolute inflexibility of mind and spirit.

"What about the bargemen?" Solemn asked. "Who will enlist them?"

"Sheep Wu is speaking to the best of them," Peace said.

The city's edge was abrupt on the left bank; crowded trees and small farms gave way to crowded houses all at once.

The bargemen carried us to the far end of the town, to the Canal Bund, which looked like a fortification from a distance, with its tobacco and grain and timber and merchandise landings and its severe godowns. We disembarked. Peace asked around for a certain leader of the godown boys whom Smart knew, and we finally found him cleaning out the furnace in which tobacco unfit for sale was burned.

Peace spoke to the man's bent back. "Are you King?"

The man straightened up; he smelled like Overseer Li's foul pipe. "My name is King. They call me"—he smiled—"Mandarin King."

Peace set his hens down in the dust, and Solemn his young fowl; the creatures flapped their wings two or three times but, finding themselves helpless in their fetters, subsided, lying on their sides, heads up, seeming to swallow and blinking their waxy lids over their astonished eyes.

"I often heard my friend speak of you," Peace said. "Yen's Smart."

I saw this slave arrogantly eying Harlot. "I know Smart as well," King said, "as I know my hand fingers and foot toes."

"Would you like a dram with me?"

To my surprise Auntie, chewing her tongue with carefulness, pulled a bottle of millet liquor—it was nearly empty—out from under her eggs.

"I can't drink it unless you have water," King said.

"We'll get some. Harlot, get me some water."

Harlot went shooting off to ask for a well. Peace and King remained silent the entire time until she returned cautiously balancing a rusted tin pan of water.

The men drank. The sharing of the spirits seemed to be a kind of bargaining and dealing between them; they shook hands after it.

Peace said, "Are you a true man?"

"I'm a truehearted man. Yes. I am. Your friend Smart knows me if you don't. What business is it of yours?"

"I'd like to take you to a Lamaist temple down our way."

"No," the other said, "not King. Not Mandarin King. They say Lamaists never get to yellow heaven."

"Well, I don't really mean a Lamaist temple. Listen, Mandarin King, if that is what you call yourself. Smart says you can keep a proper secret."

"I can do that."

The two big men reminded me of boys bristling on the edge of a fistfight.

"You going to swear to me you'll keep your word?"

"I don't know. Depends."

"Can you keep a close mouth?"

"You are talking to a fox," King said. "Fox doesn't talk, he bites."

"I like that," Peace said, looking as though he did not. "I am going to tell you something."

"How many drams have you had?" King jeered.

"I tell you this, you godown boy: The smallies are going to fight the yellow people. We have captains. We are going to fight them and get free of them all. Are you willing to be a captain, King?"

The most violent storms flew in an instant across King's face, for he saw that Peace was in homicidal earnest, he grasped at once the danger in those short sentences, his heart must have leaped with hope and hatred, he was terrified by the importance of the secret and by its despair—all this in a blink, a twitching pull of one cheek.

Then, with a too grand coolness that made Peace frown, he said, "I never was so glad to hear of anything in my life—why, son, they ought to have taken that consideration a long time back. Oh, I am, and I will be—I *am* ready to join you any moment. I am *ready*, son. I could cut the yellow peoples' throats like sheep for meat."

"My name is Peace, not 'son.' Don't you forget my name, Captain." Peace's face was sullen.

"I rejoice you came along here, Captain Peace," King sunnily said.

"I am going to send you messages, King. Maybe you will get to be a captain."

The men shook hands again, and it was clear that both were now bound by an iron contract, a good faith squarely based on the misery each had seen in his time.

"You can hold your tongue," Peace said. "If you know any sound or steady-hearted men, you can speak to them about this, King. But know them well first. Don't speak a word of this in the presence of any house slave or any woman." King's head turned in surprise and protest toward the three of us. Peace said, "These are not women, King. They are Peace's handmaidens." And Peace's eye was suddenly so clouded by his dreadful prophetic look that even this arrogant King seemed to cringe.

So it went all day: Peace seeking out reliable slaves he knew, or had heard about, and, with a directness that took for granted whole volumes, whole preachings, night meetings, drafty hovels, seas of millet meal and rancid pork fat, years of yes-venerable, lifetimes of aching—plunging right in, and leaving all details to later "messages," he proposed the general fight against the yellows, and one by one the men, after nothing more than brief breaks in the weather of their faces, took in the thought and promptly agreed to go wherever it would lead them.

From the Canal Bund we went up East Dragon Street, the main thoroughfare of the city, with Hsing Temple Hill ashine on our right, sloshing and squidging up the middle of the muddy, unpaved street, picking our way in single file at certain bad crossings along dikes of ashes and cinders that merchants had put out for pathways, which pricked the soles of our mud-caked feet and made Harlot and me giggle as we quick-footed along, until we came to the market, a great open shed, crowded with poor yellows and country and city slaves buying and selling and bartering.

Here we sold our eggs and fowl, and bought a bottle of *Shao-chiu* spirits with the proceeds, and here we spent the better part of two hours as Peace, moving through the crowd with narrowed eyes, found men he wanted to see and took them, with his retinue always following, out for privacy of talk into the open field that sloped beyond the market shed down to High Thoughts Creek. This green pasture, considered a common, was a dazzling patchwork sight, for women, both yellows and slaves, washing clothes in the stream after the several days' rain, were spreading out their clothes to dry and bleach on the grass; we could hear their open-air shouts and laughter on the one side and the contained hum of the market on the other as Peace put drams and the war to man after man.

Peace drank with each one, but there was no change in him, unless it was a deepening of his obsession in his throat, a surer note of authority with each successive proposal as he became invisibly drunk, more, it seemed, on astonishment at the universal acceptance of the risk he asked than on raw spirits.

From the market we went down to the Rock Landing, a wharf built around a broad, flat rock at the mouth of High Thoughts Creek, where scores of small craft were tied up, and where Peace spoke to three cormorant fishermen's slaves, and then we went back up to the Creek footbridge, and across it, and along West Dragon Street, and to the prisonlike bulk of the Ho Ch'in Silk Company godown, where Peace knew a gateman slave, and then a block further, across a freshet that ran shamelessly across the face of the street, to the Swallow Hostel, a series of courtyards forming four sides of a square around a cobbled inner plaza, with an entrance for palanquins and carriages through an archway on the south side of Dragon Street. Peace boldly led his barefoot party of country whites into the plaza, past a number of yellow men, dressed in a new fashion of blue pantaloons and black tunics and with buttons on their hats of the nine official grades, walking in and out in pairs and trios, and Peace drew aside the inner-gate porter, a big man perspiring in a braided coat, shabby silk breeches, and muddy cloth boots, and the Porter, accustomed to hiding his emotions, nodded gravely at what Peace proposed, even without a dram. "Indeed," he said, unwaveringly genteel, "I am in accord. Kindly maintain contact with me."

So we moved through the city. I was dazzled by Peace; by the headlong thrust of his obsession, by his passion, by his strong sweetness as he proposed the slaughter of all that was not sweet. I loved him, I belonged to him, I was his handmaiden with all my heart; in short, I was hypnotized by him, as every white he approached was.

At the bulge of the afternoon, with the sun at a three-quarters slant, by which time I was footsore, hungry, and thirsty, we found ourselves at the corner of Dragon Street and Eleventh Hutung, and following Peace we started up a deep-rutted cart track that climbed at a meandering angle across an unfenced common onto a hillside gashed and marred with ravines and weedy patches and goat-galled places, sparsely tufted with scrub pine and chinquapin, and brightened in the most improbable way with white trumpets of datura, which practical Solemn said would brew into a kill-a-man tea, and the yellow disks of may-weed, which he said would set a woman to bleeding when she was late.

Then, as the track turned, and a big cart came down with its oxen mud-stockinged to the knees and its wheels solid between the spokes with oozing reddish clay, and we came around a lone white oak, I looked up and gasped as I saw, beyond a row of brilliant flags, shining like a carving in ice in the full flood of the westering sun, the most beautiful building, surely, ever built— so it seemed to me; the whited yamen with many curving roofs, cap on cap on cap.

Peace was now well ahead of us, striding with powerful steps uphill, almost running, his head lifted to the breathtaking seat of power.

Along either side of the great building was a long horse rack, and numerous horses were tied there now, and carriages were standing under the charge of well-dressed slaves, and a pungent steam of horse urine drifted our way; I hurried, not wanting to be seen in my field-hand clothes. In the distance, within the yamen, we heard mournful blasts of ceremonial horns, and deep gongs, and drums: officials, Solemn said, in the Courtyard of Advisers.

We came up on Peace from behind. He was standing on the open ground, near a rude belfry, or gong house, which looked absurdly like the Yen's dairy, with his legs spread and arms folded, gazing up at the soaring lines of the yamen. A narrow, winding stone stairway led up to the awesome portico with its huge purple columns. Clumps of goats stood ruminating in the

shade in the gateway near the glowing shafts; a broadcast of
their droppings trailed up the steps.

Peace stood there, just so, staring, for a time that seemed
endless.

Finally, at a grunt from him, and a sudden start away, we
tore off to High Thoughts Hill and the patrician end of town,
where famous men lived in beautiful houses, and Peace was
truly and dangerously drunk now, and it was all Auntie and
Solemn and I could do to hush his murderous shouts and steer
him along.

We walked out Favorable Wind Brook Road toward home, and
I thought often of my having ridden out that way the first time
on the cart with Mink and the agent.

There were certain stout men Peace said he wanted to speak
to at the villas along the road, and he made an effort to hide his
drunkenness when he approached these men—but he fed it, too,
offering and taking yet more drams. Either the country slaves
were more suspicious than the town whites or they sensed Peace's
state. The first three said they would think about what he said—
ponder it—turn it round.

Peace was disgusted; wanted to see no more cowards that day.
We went straight home. . . .

The next morning at Top Man's second blast on the buffalo
horn we started out, men and women alike carrying scythes to
cut a meadow's hay, and we saw that Peace had not yet come
out of his room. Auntie told me to hurry and rouse him.

I ran to look for him first in the room where he lived with
Solemn and Solemn's wife and two children.

He lay asleep on his pallet, loudly snoring. Frantic, I shook his
shoulder with my hand, again and again, to try to waken him. I
called him, dug my knee in his side, lay on him and rolled on him.
The smell of spirits on his breath made me giddy; my heart was
beating wildly.

All at once he lunged upward, with a kind of growl, and I
slipped aside, and on his knees on the k'ang he ripped his long
gown from the throat downward almost to his groin. He pulled
me to his chest with a pitiful moan, and he drew me down—
but he suddenly fell asleep again, groaning and snorting.

Then he seemed abruptly to waken, and he saw me through
swollen eyelids, and he said, "What are you doing here?"

I leaped up and stood by his k'ang, and I said, "You're late,

Peace. Top Man has blown his second horn. They're going out."

"Thank you, my dear handmaiden, Sorek woman," he said, in his usual formal tone. But he was still drunk.

([The Fish Feast

Late in the sixth month came the summer lay-by, and a time of light work after the tobacco had all been transplanted and the hay was in, and the weather came on fine, and word was passed around that there would be a fish feast for all the slaves of all the owners out our way, organized by the slaves themselves.

Peace took me fishing alone for the common supply the afternoon before the affair: Auntie was to mend his ripped gown, Harlot had planned to do some wash.

As we set out Auntie sallied after us and threw a child's worn-out shoe at Peace for luck in his fishing; it struck him on a buttock, and he picked the ragged shoelet up and roared that he would knock her ears together so they would lay side by side like two millet cakes, but she was running toward our quarter and would not look back at us for fear of snapping the luck. Peace laughed hard.

There were many whites out fishing along Favorable Wind Brook, but we found a fair place by the lower end of a pool. Peace was plain, jovial, playful, and boyish, and I was unusually spirited. Peace warned me not to bad-luck the poles by stepping over them, and he went off to catch some baby grasshoppers. The tall, thin slave Tree, who was fishing a few yards upstream, began to eye me and tease me, and I had a wild warm feeling, as if my loins had drams sloshing around in them, and when Peace came back and sensed what was happening and in good humor called to Tree, "Young man, plow not with my heifer," I laughed, as Peace himself did. He baited my hook, and I spat on the tiny green machine of a grasshopper and dropped my line into the pool, but I pulled it out often and fished poorly. Whatever Peace needed, I got or did for him.

"See that rock, Sorek girl?" he said, pointing to a round boulder with green skirts at the center of the pool. "That rock is called Etam. That rock is Etam rock, daughter. *My* rock."

Peace's eye was suddenly clouded, and I was afraid.

But at once Peace resumed his lighthearted manner and cub

gestures, cuffing at the heads of weeds and, once, tickling me in a grandfatherish, poky way.

We caught no fish, and Peace went to the water's edge and waded half up his shins and pulled up the long shafts of seven reeds, and he came up to me and offered them to me, and said, "Bind me, woman. These are strong. Tie me up. Just try and see."

Something—the fierce look in Peace's eye, his calling me woman instead of daughter, or perhaps a rushing feeling that I wanted to be with Tree, who was never baffling—something undid me, and I was suddenly sobbing, with my face in my hands and my elbows bracketing my knees.

"Come, daughter," Peace gently said. "No fish in this pool around Etam." And we went home.

What colors at the fish feast the next afternoon! The field hands must have borrowed from the house slaves, and the house slaves must have wheedled new wornouts from the mistresses. I had a patterned red silk cape that Auntie had thrown over my shoulders. We paraded in a clearing by the brook in yellow people's hateful leftover clothes—and such graciousness and kindness!

"Evening, White Lotus, sweet child!"

The men bowed. Friends were arm in arm. The day was as fresh and smooth as young Chekiang fan-leaf. Slaves playing pitchpot —arching arrows from a distance toward a narrow-necked jar— whooped at successes. Everywhere the talk was brisk, argumentative. My mind was whirling, and I could not make head or tail of the absurd chatter.

"If a snapping turtle grabs you, he's never going to let go till it thunders."

"Ayah!"

"Crayfish all get poor on a night when you have a big moon."

"Tee hee hee!"

Solemn came up and reported to Peace that Ditcher was going around asking the captains to give him their votes for general in the war when the choosing came.

Peace took this calmly. "Let him," he said; and then, with a smile, "Ditcher has a powerful frame."

Auntie was carrying a bottle for Peace, and he enlisted several men, Mink among others ("You're bent over, but you're *strong*"), and some came to him, whether for drams or for a chance to fight the yellows I could not have said.

"White God in heaven, you're too old," Peace said to Ma's Mule

Foot, one of these volunteers. "You're too old to fight the yellow people, Mule Foot. Go along now."

"I tell you this, Peace: I can run you up some bullets. I know where to get a mold. I can keep you in bullets."

"You do that, Mule Foot. That would be good."

Peace met one of the slaves with whom he had talked on the way out from Twin Hills. "Have you pondered this business?"

"I have. I'm going to be in it."

"You have a sword, friend?"

"My master has one, hangs up in the house. I'm going to get that one when the time comes."

"You're a good man," Peace said.

Peace was all practicality, and again I had a moment of doubting his prophetic side. He gave me the name of each recruit to remember, and he drank hardly at all.

The fish was delicious, but there was not nearly enough, and the men began to accuse the women jokingly of having eaten it all.

Peace shouted out at the top of his voice, "Captains to meet by Etam rock. Follow me." He nodded to Auntie, and we three knew he wanted us. He led his party to the bank of the pool where he and I had caught no fish.

The meeting was at first disorderly; all the captains had ideas. One said an oath of secrecy should be sworn. Another said a man practiced in Lamaistic charms should be found to make conjurations that would kill any white who talked about the war. Ch'eng's Candy said, "We're going to kill all the yellow males from the cradle up, but we're going to spare all ages of females." Sheep Wu said, "Ai, yes, that's the way it has to be." There was talk of arms, and Solemn said the men should steal scythes from their masters' toolhouses and bring them to Yen's smithy; he knew how to make swords and pikes of them. During all this Peace held back, silently smiling and nodding. Wang's Judge said he was going to enlist at Kaifeng market—could easily get fifty men there. Candy was to go down as far as "the singing tree" to enlist downcountry slaves; there was a diviner down there who could warn of difficulties and hazards with jumping sticks. Sheep Wu laid claim to the bargemen on the canal; another said he would get the copper-pit men; another, the godown boys; another, the dike-menders; another, the slave masons and bricklayers building the new prison. Sheep Wu said he was going all the way to the province of Anhwei to enlist, he needed money to hire time off from his mistress, and Ditcher said Sheep Wu would also need money for liquor to persuade the Anhwei men, and Candy said they would have to hire a donkey for Sheep Wu to ride down there. Solemn suggested going around to all the slaves at the fish feast gathering coppers for a treasury.

"Slow down!" Peace's voice was sharp. "Not so fast. We have a decision to make."

"What is that, Peace?" Sheep Wu, full of his trip to Anhwei, said.

"This army is not Tou Mu."

Ditcher said, "Talk plain."

"Remember! Tell them."

The idea of Tou Mu had terrified me, one night when Smart in the dark smithy had instructed me in a line of ancient yellow nightmares: Shen Kung-pao throwing his own head into the sky from Unicorn Precipice; the demon Hsü Hao, Emptiness and Devastation, gnawing at the vitals of the Emperor Ming Huang; the dragon with the head of a camel, eyes of a devil, neck of a snake, belly of a huge cockle, scales of a carp, soles of a tiger, claws of an eagle. It thrilled me to have Peace call on me for my small part in the war. Yet I was shaken by a demand like this, for it made me feel the icy breath of the fanatic in him; it reminded me of his unbending hardness like that of a hoe head. My voice trembled as I said, "Tou Mu, goddess of the North Star— three eyes and eighteen arms, that's the point. All around her, hands, hands—holding a spear, a pagoda, a dragon's head, and so on. *Eighteen arms.*"

The brave captains of our army which would set us free, sound and selfless men, suddenly looked as if they might faint or vomit: perhaps not so much at the thought of this horrible female creature as at Peace's way of dealing with them.

Peace raised one clenched hand and blithely said, "Time to pick a general. One pair of eyes and arms."

Now there was much bickering as to how the selection should be made, and finally Sheep Wu suggested that each man should place a pebble down, according to his choice, on one of a row of flat stones that would represent the several captains.

But then we heard Peace's cavernous voice, saying with a force which simply brushed aside all possibility of contradiction, "You can choose your second-in-command that way if you want. And treasurer, we'll need a treasurer. As for general, there will be only one general."

There was no doubt what Peace meant; there was no question in our minds who our general was. With subdued voices and cautious gestures, the men chose Wang's Judge as second, and Solemn as treasurer.

I was afraid to glance at Ditcher, the pretender; I heard him muttering and rumbling.

Somehow the news that Peace was general swept ahead of us through the fish-feast crowd as we returned into it. "Evening, General," men and women would respectfully say.

A thin man slave of Chi Kuo came up to Peace and said, "I want to fight the yellow people, General, but I can't move my hip down here, on this side, I have a crippling pain in my shoulder socket joint, and it seems as if I have ants creeping under my skin down my eating arm. . . ." And he went on with the catalogue of his miseries, and finally asked Peace if he could help him get well so he might fight.

Peace fixed his harsh charismatic eye on the man and grandly said, "Brass and copper, they're great enemies of bone aches. Tie a ribbon of brownsnake skin around your arm where it hurts. What is your name, anyhow? You can stew down some grease from a marsh hen or a good fat owl and rub it on the joints that hurt. When you put your shoes on out in the field, wear a cash out in the toe of one shoe one day and the other shoe the next. Fried grubs, they make a good ointment for pains like these. You see, these pains come out of the earth. Remember, tell this man about brass from Brother Smart's book."

I had to struggle to think what Peace wanted, for now that Peace was general it seemed that a thawing change had come over him, and I was carried away by the power of the emotion which, beneath the grandiose manner and the humble remedies, shook Peace's voice and hands—his great concern for a slave in pain, his trying to convey, without saying it, that all these pains came from being a slave.

"And the Lord," I lamely said, "sent fiery serpents among the people, and they bit the people, and many people of Israel died. And Moses made a serpent of brass, and put it upon a pole, and it happened that if a serpent had bitten any man, when he gazed at the serpent of brass, he lived."

All around, men and women gravely nodded. "General, I give you ten thousand thanks," the man with rheumatism said, bowing and backing away in the yellow manner.

❲ Summer Evening

Those seventh-month days were panther days, the heat was enough to drown one, and all we did the day long was hoe, hoe, hoe, keeping the tobacco mounds clean and the soil open and friable.

After dark one evening Peace took us to the blacksmith shop, the Camp of Dan, where, this night, the only eerie thing was the absence of eeriness. Everything was downright. Solemn had the fire going; he was cutting scythe blades in half and making swords. Peace set himself to woodworking the buckthorn handles. Men kept coming in. Ma's Whippoorwill gave in two scythes, and applied for a captaincy of the foot, but Peace said he stuttered too much to give commands, he could be a donkeyman: Hai! did not Big Master Ma have a sorrel horse? That horse would be earmarked for Whippoorwill. Lü's Gallant, too, wanted to be a captain, but Peace sniffed and said he was too trifling a fellow. At this Gallant stamped up and down the smithy shouting curses. "All right!" he finally said. "If you will make me a captain I will get you thirty, forty small arms, by Buddha's belly. By which I mean pistols and matchlocks, it's the truth! My master has twenty-nine right there in the tavern. I know where."

"I will go look at them," Peace calmly said, and they set the following market day for this project.

Various men, on the sly, stooped and made away with pinches of anvil dust, the shiny black flakes that scaled away from hot iron when Solemn pounded it; for that stuff would give strength.

Late in the night several captains were present, and in murmuring tones Peace said that in four weeks the business should commence. "Too soon," Ch'eng's Candy said; we would need more arms and better plans.

Peace was angry; his voice bounced among the roof joists. "We *have* plans!" Solemn and he would have twelve dozen swords made by then.

But, Candy said, we might have five hundred men.

Fine, Peace said, fine, fine, Chou's Tinsmith was arranging with Ku the Usher to let us into the yamen to get the arms out that were stored there.

To do *what?*—Candy wanted to know.

Well, the plan was to fire the lower part of town, around the Canal Bund, where the godowns were packed with inflammable goods and the houses were poor and thatched; the yellows would go to fight the fires; we would seize the arms and ammunition and commence the attack. But first we would meet at the bridge on Favorable Wind Brook and send a company to Lü's tavern to capture some arms that were hidden there.

This arguing made me nervous, and the sight of a forehead—it was Sheep Wu's—with drops of sweat gleaming on it increased my trembling. The room was suddenly charged; the dry air of practicality was gone. The smithy fire was low. The lamp was flickering, its wick smoking. I saw that Smart, his eyes rolling, had taken over. He broke a rain crow's egg in a rusty basin of water, and he directed each man to wash his face in it, and I wanted to bury myself in the heap of scraps in a corner, because I knew he was going to call in a ghost.

And then, yes, it was there, I knew it from the men's faces, though I could not see it myself because I had not washed my eyes with the mixture. Lord! Lord! Peace's guttural grunts and muttering told me it was the yellow Matriarch. I could only imagine her as a dim figure in the gloom of the grove. Mercy, God —a spirit of a living person.

Peace was standing, facing her—and now *his* forehead was bathed in sweat.

What could I do to drive her away? I could not run. Sprinkle salt in the fire? A glass button on a dog's neck? Burn an old shoe? Rice brandy on the ground? Put a knife that had not touched wood in my hair? I had nothing on me for exorcism; I could only die.

Peace said in a steady voice, "I am going to kill you, Old Matriarch."

"Amen," Smart said, as hollow as a pitcher.

Then Peace said, "Get rid of her, Rememberer."

I was paralyzed. I had no idea what to do.

"Book words backwards," Peace moaned in the old language. "Hurry."

" 'Light be there let, said God and,' " I began, and at once I

saw Peace's huge arms relaxing. "'Waters the of face the upon
moved God. . . .'"

She was gone.

([A Legion

A sweet-sour pork roast at the bridge of the brook. A
market-day noon at the far edge of the seventh month: too hot
to eat the sauced meat. A game of pitchpot under a big mimosa
tree. Women are sitting on the bank of the stream, their cotton
gowns tucked up around their hips, feet dabbling in the cool
water, while some men angle and argue below the bridge, their
shouts surely driving off the few puny sunfish and pickerel left
in the brook after so many weeks of its having been fished over.
In the shade of a willow Mink is at dice with a handful of friends.
We stroll. Peace is unusually grand, even for him; his tunic,
soaked, clings to his shoulders; he half nods to those who half
bow to him. Sheep Wu is at Peace's side. A slave named Joker,
Tu's man, who has a fair start on being drunk, accosts Peace, and
he swaggers and asks when we are going to begin the big business,
meaning the war.

"You turtle, Joker," Sheep Wu says, "you look so poor and weak
and miserable, you couldn't even kill a man."

"Ai!" Joker squawks. "Don't be taking me by my appearance. I
can do it. Don't worry, you Shee' Wu. I can and will kill a yellow
man as freely as eat."

"Good," Peace grimly says, nodding his great thatched head.

But here is Ch'eng's Candy, looking worried. "I know when we
begin it, my master and mistress will have to be put to death."

"Among the first," Peace says. "You know that."

"I have to have one of my lieutenant boys do it for me, Peace.
I can't do it myself. Those two raised me from a baby."

"You must harden up your heart," Peace says.

"Don't worry about me," Candy says, hitching up the cloth
cinch at his waist. "When the time comes, I'll be a knife edge."

"That will be good, Candy," Peace says; his voice is mild, but
his eyes are furious.

Now we are sitting on a grassy bank—I am ringed with hairy
dock leaves, which I tear along the juicy veins—and the responsible men are reporting on their enlistments.

First, Sheep Wu on his trip to Anhwei: "I was down there last market day, to a preaching at the Fragrant Hill of the Three Ox Legs, at a godown there. I have a good account for you, Peace." But Sheep Wu could not get to the point. "You see, the morning of the preaching I stopped by at the yamen in Pochow, and I came on an old friend, Lin's Thorn. I knew him as a boy, and he said he would help me. On the way I told him what you said, Peace, that we would meet at the brook to kill the yellow people in four weeks' time. Thorn says to me, 'I'm glad to hear it's going to take place so soon.' He says to me he's heartily glad about it. We got down there, and it was still too early for the preaching to commence, so I proposed to old Thorn we could go into a tavern and buy some liquor to melt the men with, when we'd speak to them about the war, and he agreed to it, and we did, we bought it—the money you gave me. There was a lemon-yellow in the tavern, there, she let us in through the slaves' postern, and we said, two jugs spirits, and she said, 'Are you smallies going on a spree?'

"And Thorn, he says, 'We're going on the grandest spree the yellow people ever saw.'

"She says, 'You boys be careful, now.'

"And Thorn, he says, 'We're going to be *most* careful, Big Mistress.'

"She could not understand why we laughed almost to bursting, and she shook her head at us.

"Thorn bought some malt taffy from a vendor in front of the tavern there, and then we went up to the preaching, and after the preaching we began it."

"Well, Sheep Wu," Peace said, "and how many?"

"I told you I thought I could get a hundred and twenty men down there, didn't I? Peace, I stayed three days, and I think we got, Lin's Thorn and Chang's Full Bowl and I—Full Bowl wanted to be a general, but I told him about that eighteen-arm bitch goddess, that we could only have two arms on our general, so he said he would go by the name or title of Colonel Tall, and he was going to make his men obey him."

"But how many, Sheep Wu?"

"In three days we got near five hundred."

A gasp among the men on the grassy bank. A rising excitement as one after another gives his report. Wang's Judge—enlistments in Twin Hills city, among the slaves building the new prison, and godown boys at the Canal Bund—has not brought his list with him, but he supposes it is four hundred fifty by now. Fan, the mix, has been as far as Tsining to enlist men, a good number, almost three hundred. Bargemen on the canal, over two hundred. Candy had been to the singing tree. Totals from the tips of the provinces of Shansi and Hopei; a large band from the Yellow River.

I see Peace swelling up with his thrill. "Hai!" he says, standing up, towering over us. "I have reports on a thousand men in Twin Hills proper. We have nearly five hundred at the copper pits. I wouldn't be astonished if many of the poorer yellows—when they see us in triumph—many will join us. We'll have every slave in Honan—and Anhwei and Shansi and Hopei, too," Peace says, punching a huge fist into a great palm. He is completely carried away. "I already have a cavalry of four hundred donkeymen from right around the brook. Six hundred foot from Ground Squirrel Bridge, four hundred from around the Peach Temple. I tell you," he says—and then a long pause; absolute silence; the eternal washing of stones in the stream. "I tell you, my dear brothers, we will have *ten thousand* men. Now shake hands all around. Give me your hands! We'll wade to our knees in blood sooner than fail in this thing. Hayah! Whoooo! Give me your hands, my strong boys!"

The men, who have leaped to their feet, are hugging, pounding backs like drums, and crying as they laugh.

❰ Velvet Pleats, Pink Codpieces, and Plums

Off we went again, on a market day, the third morning of the eighth month, to Twin Hills, ostensibly to sell the water chestnuts, bean sprouts, cowpeas, and white cabbages we had grown in our spare-time patches outside our quarter, baskets on our arms, trudging this time along Favorable Wind Brook Road, which was dusty under a haze-huge sun that had relentlessly sweated us for a fortnight, with Peace walking ahead leaning one hand lightly on Mink's shoulder, and the three handmaidens behind. Yes, Peace had taken a fancy to Mink, whose gambling sharpness and twisted back had made him an ideal doubter; he pricked at the General with skeptical questions that Peace said he needed to keep his toe at the line.

One question that Mink occasionally asked bothered me. "General, why can't you ever change your mind?"

The baskets were heavy, the air was humid. I was in the grip of an unspeakable disgust. The tobacco plants had been attacked by the midsummer glut of hornworms, and for days and days we had been stooping down, turning back the broad leaves, and picking off their undersides the sap-fat, segmented, wiggling creatures with their stubby middle legs like walking teats, their foul arching horns sticking out of their back ends, making them seem waspish, poisonous, and their ugly hard-mouthed button heads which reared up belligerently when they saw a hand approach. Their thick bodies, with pretty patterns repeated all along, writhed under my closed eyelids when I tried to sleep at night, and my dreams were washed in lakes of their spattering juices. I had moments now of imagining that these sphinx worms were squirming on my hands and in my baskets. This—to give the yellow man a little brass pipe-bowlful of sucking pleasure! Oh, I was ready for Peace's war.

Thump, thump. We looked back. Here came a ribbish donkey drawing a cask of prized tobacco, which rolled on its own fat-stomach staves, axletreed on wooden spikes at the center of each end to split saplings that were joined together behind the keg with a hickory withe. On a seat of bamboo lashed athwart the shafts in front of the tun was perched a wiry crab-eyed yellow man, his mouth drawn down in what must have been a long habit of misanthropy. He joggled past us without a nod.

Peace knew the man; said, when the rolling tun was well away, that his name was Yang, a small tobacco farmer from along the branch of the brook above Lü's tavern. Had a thin time of it. The agents at the Canal Bund would give him short shrift, would most likely cheat him, buying this keg that he had held until out of season hoping for a better price. A pitiable case—but we would have to kill him, Peace said, because yellow Yang was the owner of three slaves.

I suddenly hated this miserable cipher of a yellow farmer. I could see the sharp shoulder blades sticking out of the loathsome bent back as the keg bumped on stones going down a hill ahead.

Before the edge of the city we turned down a path until, nearly at the canal, on a high airy rise across from White Heron Hill, we came to the formidable quadrangle of the new prison, which was almost finished; indeed, a few white criminals were already locked away—and so was a large supply of arms of the Emperor's provincial guard.

By prearrangement Peace met, near the main entrance, Widow Chou's Heaven-Loved, one of the several hundred slaves who had been hired out to Warlord Sun by their owners to build the fortress. Heaven-Loved, who had been enlisted at Sunken Rock on the Yellow River, was lazing on his back with his head and shoulders against the building, half asleep in the sun. At a touch of Peace's foot on his leg he jumped up.

We walked down into the gulch toward White Heron Hill. For a long stretch nothing at all was said. At last Peace asked, "How are your boys? Are they ready?"

"I have thirty-two to kill the guards and get us in," Heaven-Loved said. He was quiet, earnest, tense, and very young: only a year or so older than I.

"How many guards?"

"Six by night."

"That should be easy."

"More guards inside."

"We will see to them. Where are the arms?"

"All my squad know the storage hall. They can lead the way." The sober eyes searched Peace's face, and almost down to a whisper Heaven-Loved pushed out a single word: "When?"

"The last market-day eve in the month. Listen to me, Captain. You can see the Canal Bund from here. Watch for the fires, wait half an hour after you see them, then begin it."

Heaven-Loved looked like a man who had taken a huge gulp of raw spirits. He who had been all restraint, murmurs, discretion, suddenly threw up his arms and bellowed, "Ayooo! So soon!"

Peace said, "Hush, son. Don't begin it unless you get a message the night before; it will be a confirmation. Don't begin it anyway unless you see the fires."

The young man was under tight control again. "I understand you, Peace." The mumbling voice, now strapped down with iron bands, added, "Thank the Lord for you, General."

We went into town, to West Dragon Street, which began as a narrow path of used tanbark through a boggy stretch, where lay the tanyards of Chu Yü and Ch'en, and then became a dusty street, and as we walked deeper into the city, and under the market sheds as we sold our wares, every slave we met greeted Peace as "General." I was astonished at the universal knowledge among the whites of the plan.

We climbed to the exquisite yamen up the cart road, and where once there had been deep mud, hard ruts now ran, and puffs of orange dust stirred, and beside the track thistledown blew like a snowstorm.

Peace boldly walked between the flags up the portico steps and waved us along behind him, but Mink would not go up; he was afraid. I looked to Auntie, who shrugged, coughed, and started up; Harlot and I, giggling, followed.

In the empty reception hall, where murmurs echoed like distant lowing of cattle, Peace was greeted by Ku the Usher, a non-agenarian white freedman who since long ago in the reign of Emperor Yung-t'ai had been caretaker of this yamen. Opposites— the huge slave in a field hand's dirty cotton gown, his feet bare, with his long hair knotted into seven braids, confronting the plump, white-haired, courtly man in black satin breeches and coat, all flaps and skirts, and blue shoes braided with gold, holding a brass ring of keys in one hand and a feather besom in the other.

With the manners of a mandarin, Ku the Usher presented himself to Auntie, Harlot, and me, and he led us on what appeared to be a tour for country cousins. "This throne, my dear friends, was formerly a seat of state used by the first Manchu governors. You can see where the emblem of the Mings has been scraped off. . . ."

He showed us every room in every courtyard. Harlot's eyes were as big as brimming wine cups, and she and I kept tittering in our terror of being surprised in these echoing stone vaults by a yellow man. Ku treated Peace with what seemed to me a faint contempt.

At last we came to a room where, before unlocking the door, Ku looked both ways, and listened. A key rattled, the door swung back, and in the dim light we saw many, many conical stacks of snaphaunce muskets. Peace's eyes!

Ku quickly drew the door to, and locked it, and in a whisper that rebounded from the walls he spoke to Peace, his white face suddenly contorted from that of a benign old statesman into a twisting, snarling grimace: "I'm glad to do it, General. The night itself, you'll find me near the governors' chair, and I'll give you the key to the magazine by my own hand, and I hope you slaughter them every last one, General, and I'll thank you to my dying day, and I'll bless you, bless you." The last shred of dignity was gone; the old man began to blubber. We hurried away, leaving him weeping in the dark hall over his years of kowtowing to yellow men.

Now we went to the postern gate of a public tavern down in the town, the Siskin Bird, and bought a bottle of spirits.

In our coolie rags and bare feet we strolled along the yellow people's fashionable promenade, on an elevated bank of the canal shaded by willows, to the Scholars' Garden, where Peace said he was to meet Reed-Mat Su, a free white man who had been enlisting among the Twin Hills slaves; he was employed in the garden's entertainments. Peace led us boldly down the sloping parade ground. We circled the many-roofed temples and came on the far side to a breathtaking view of a series of gardens running in terraces down to the canal, which here was artificially broad and contained several islands feathery with sycamores. Hundreds of yellows in leisure-day finery at open-air tables all around us sipped tea and nibbled at almond cakes and persimmons. We were intimidated and ducked behind some huge cork-spindle bushes and took each a heavy pull at the bottle; then, hot-throated, we walked daintily on bubbles of self-importance straight down to the show ring.

There was Reed-Mat Su, in yellow tights and a puffy-shouldered jacket, skipping about on errands—anchoring the posts for the slack-rope dancers, putting out colored tubs for the tame bears to posture upon. Reed-Mat was himself part of the show: an embodiment of all that the masters believed white men to be, for he stumbled and played stupid, shook his head over the simplest of duties, shuffled lazily, kept his jaw hanging slack, fawned in front of the equestrian acrobats, white men who were naked except for pink codpieces tied on with twisted cloths, and made secretive obscene gestures behind their bare rumps. He was an artist of self-abasement; we, too, laughed at him in helpless fury.

We stood in a good-sized pool of avoidance: the long-haired giant, the crookback, the three rustic women clinging to each other. There were no other slaves in sight.

The pink-pricked bareback riders leaped onto the heaving white hips of the horses going round and round and did somersaults in the air.

Reed-Mat came to us. "You can't come here," he said between his teeth to Peace.

"We are already here," Peace said.

"You are going to get me in trouble."

"You turtle," Peace said.

"I can't talk to you now."

"Do not talk, son. Give me the list."

"Here?"

"Do you have it?"

"I have it. But not here. What if they took it off us?"

"I'll kill any man that touches me." Peace's voice was rising.

Mink knocked a fist on Peace's chest, as if asking to enter. "Not you talking," he said. "The bottle talking."

At this Peace suddenly became reasonable. "Where can we meet you?"

"Up there, in the slaves' enclosure, after the magician's act."

The riders had finished. The showmaster, a yellow man in old-fashioned warrior costume, with mustaches dripping in narrow lines on either side of his mouth, and holding a long-tongued whip, came stamping over to us. "Send that garbage away from here," he furiously said to Reed-Mat.

"I am just shooing them," Reed-Mat said.

"I will give you ten breaths' time," the showmaster said to Peace. "Or this." He raised the whip.

Peace was abruptly servile, apologetic, stupid, slow, honeyed; he spoke with the thickest of country accents—Reed-Mat Su's caricature in true life, it seemed. And this served the purpose. We retreated. The showmaster and Su exchanged glances and broke into guffaws.

We went to the slaves' yard, fenced in with palings to hide the waiting smallies from the sight of the carefree yellows in the gardens. Here were carriage boys, hostlers, body servants, in elegant clothes, and they gathered about Peace, who looked like a rough, stinking cowherd beside them, and they gravely shook him by the hand, one by one, and called him "General." At last Reed-Mat Su came and gave us his list: Auntie tucked it in her bosom, where the bottle was already warmly cradled, supported by her crossed arms.

On the road out to Yen's we fell in with a company of men on their way home from a day's pass in town. They were mostly drunk. One had a basket of plums, and Peace reached down and took one. A drunken slave, who had said he was from Anhwei, and who did not know Peace, belligerently asked, "What business have you snatching the man's plum?"

"We are dear friends, son. He can spare me a plum. He is one of my society."

But the Anhwei man had an argument in his craw. He grasped

Peace's shoulders and spun him half around and fairly screamed, "What society, now?"

"A society," Peace said with a profound meekness, "to kill the yellow people. He and I, and all these men, we are bound under a pledge to fight the yellow people until we die, for our freedom— and yours, too."

"O Lord, have mercy," the drunk from Anhwei said, falling to his knees. "You the *General?*" Like Ku the Usher earlier in the day, this man broke into sobs.

❨ A Sense of Mink

Our young master Yen was away, over in West-of-the-Mountains Province, formally courting a girl his mother had chosen for him, and a secret meeting was called.

The meeting that night was pervaded with a sense of Mink. The crookback was not in the smithy himself, but the dark room was filled to its sooty peak—or so it seemed to me—with his perverse, heavy indifference, and with that appalling stiffness of Peace's that Mink kept poking at: his unwillingness, or inability, to swerve, to adapt, to improvise if need might be.

Peace and his "brothers," Smart and Solemn, were the only ones who seemed not to have lost their inner fire.

Someone asked, "Are there enough arms?"

Wang's Judge said he had been trying to make crossbows, but this was the season for topping the tobacco plants, he was a topper, from dawn to dark he was out there pinching back the flower buds and the stems of the tobacco plants to the proper number of leaves, and pulling out the sucker growths, and he simply did not have fingers or forearms left for night work on the crossbows; he had brought eighteen over this night, the best he could do.

Ch'eng's Candy said he was ready with his pistol, but it was in need of repair; could Solemn fix it?

"Give it to me, indeed I will," Solemn said, but the feeling in the room was down.

Then there was a bad question from Ditcher: Did we have enough military knowledge for this war?

"There is a good old man from over in West-of-the-Mountains Province," Peace said, "who was at the siege of Taiyuan. He has promised to come over and meet me at the brook when we begin

it. He is going to advise me. Sheep Wu, you went over there enlisting, you met him, I suppose."

But at first Sheep Wu was silent. "I'm afraid they may find us
out before we begin it," he then suddenly said. "There were two
men down in Pochow, I forget their names, they said they did not
like it, they would communicate with a master down there. Well,
Lin's Runner and some others pursued them, had the intention to
put them to death with a hog knife in the slave quarters, teach
all the others a lesson, but those two were all smiles when they
were cornered, never had any idea of communicating—so they
said—and Runner let them off. It's the truth! How many others
may have had such thoughts?"

"You have house servants all over that know about the war,"
Ch'eng's Candy said. "And slaveherds. And women. A man told
me your own slaveherd Top Man knows all about it. Some idiot of
a slave tried to enlist him."

"House servants, that's bad," Ditcher said.

Then Fan, the mix, asked in a complaining tone, "How are
we supposed to do it, Peace? What's the whole plan?"

"You know your orders," Peace said.

"I know what I am supposed to do, but you never told your
captains the whole war."

"Why, here it is, then." And here it was: Three thousand slave
soldiers, foot and donkey, were going to meet at the bridge of
Favorable Wind Brook the following market-day eve, at midnight.
Divided into three columns, whose officers had already been
designated, these were all to march on Twin Hills in the dark. The
right and the left, armed with sticks and staves, were to head for
the new prison and the yamen. A party of fifty, under the warehouse boy, Mandarin King, was to set fire to the godowns and
houses in the district of the Canal Bund, and at the sight of the
fires, Widow Chou's Heaven-Loved at the penitentiary would hand
out arms to the right wing, and Ku the Usher at the yamen to the
left wing. The center column, armed with scythe-swords, scythe-
pikes, pistols, and muskets, would meanwhile descend on the
town by way of the tanbark paths into West Dragon Street and
begin the slaughter. The city slaves would convene with the left
and right columns. Every unit was ready. A blockade would be
thrown across the canal bridge. A thorough massacre, street by
street, would be carried out after dawn. Then proclamations would
be issued calling all friends of humanity to our standard, and

in a week we would have fifty thousand. Ai! The capture of Tsinan was already planned; a slave named Hsiao's Gong was the colonel over there. We aimed to have Honan, Shansi, and Anhwei in a month!

But the sooty cavern of the smithy was dead. No one cheered or hugged or wept.

"I'll show you our standard," Peace said, and he went into a corner and fetched a shredded old banner that had belonged, he told us, to a secret society on Peach Mountain Island during the uprising there: a purple square with gold fringe.

I felt torn. I was shocked by the apathy of these trusted officers; yet the iron automatism of Peace, his stiff way of telling of his set plan, troubled me even more. Peace seemed inwardly deaf; nothing these men said reached him.

Wang's Judge said, "I'm not ready in my mind. I say wait. I say let's delay."

What a frightening calm on Peace's face!

"We scarce can wait," Solemn said, in his dull, practical voice, almost as if it did not matter.

But Sheep Wu, too, cast for a postponement. "I heard at a preaching that in the old days, when Pharaoh held the people down, so their backs were chafed, they were finally freed away from him by the power of God, and Moses led them away. But look —God gave him an angel to guide him. I can see nothing of that kind here, Peace. I have seen no angel. Do you have a sign?"

Peace's eyes were moving from face to face.

It was a sign they wanted, but Smart, in the same leaden voice as Solemn had used, tried reason. He said that the summer was almost over, the thing must be done before it got too cold; that the Emperor's warlords had stood down the provincial militias for the season, and this was why all the arms were propped in little haystacks in the new prison and the yamen—and what if the yellows should call the troops out again?

Then I saw the jawbone in Peace's hand. It was slowly rising. His hand was shaking.

Smart's voice moved at a faster pace. "Sheep Wu, speaking of angels, I saw in my book where it says, 'Delay breeds danger.' And where it says, 'Worship God and you shall have peace in all the land.' Where it says, 'Five of you shall conquer an hundred, and an hundred a thousand of thine enemies.'"

The roar that now broke from Peace's lips was one of such

agony that I wanted to run, or hide, or die, and the reason it
terrified me so much was that it released in me an impulse to
violence which I did not feel I could control.

"I will not wait!" he shouted. "Rather than bear any longer
what I've borne, I'll turn out *alone* and fight with this . . . this
stick in my hand!"

He shook the jawbone high above his head.

But Wang's Judge said in a dead level voice, "It would be better
on a market day. Our people can move about on a market day.
Why start the day before a market day?"

Peace bellowed, "We will go ahead! We will go ahead! Everyone
has his orders! Do as I say!"

I felt the heavy care-naught spirit of the crookback lurking in
the room. The men were silent and gloomy.

(The War

The morning of the day of the beginning of the war
was sullen. A solid dry-cloud cover of an extraordinary darkness
moved, or appeared to skid, too fast (for there was little wind on
the ground) low across our sky, almost brushing the limp treetops,
it seemed. The air was oppressive, hot, electric, still, like the fur
of a huge dark cat waiting to pounce. My eyes were sticky, the
cap of my head felt heavy, I was dull and uneasy. I had slept
scarcely at all. We had been up late at the blacksmith shop,
dispatching messages to Widow Chou's Heaven-Loved, Ku the
Usher, Mandarin King, and the other key men, to confirm the
start the following night; counting weapons and assigning them
to captains; making some last desperate prayers to the white-
skinned God. All of us in the dark room except Peace had been
tense and irritable; he had maintained his astonishing meekness
and sweetness, which, exuding like a fragrance from his gigantic,
muscular body, seemed to emphasize, to multiply in our minds
almost beyond belief, the impression of his inner strength—and
of his immovable stubbornness, too.

Peace had at last sent us all to bed and had stayed in the
smithy alone, to meditate and pray, he said.

I had lain down naked and thrashed on my straw mat all the hot
night; if I dipped into sleep it was only to waken twitching and

bathed in sweat. I was not afraid of dying; no, it was more shameful—I was afraid of audacity. This was the deepest horror of
having been a slave: I had lost the capacity for impudence, I was
willing to let life happen to me. A hundred times in the night I
pictured myself standing, a scythe-sword in hand, face to face
with the master's mother, who was defenseless, and I would raise
my arm, and she would look sternly at me, as if from behind a
pane of glass far too thick for my blade to smash, and the strength
would trickle down out of my arm, and the arm would go flaccid,
and it would fall, and the sword would clatter on the floor, and I
would drop to my knees and beg for forgiveness, forgiveness. Was
I asleep? Was I awake? Over and over the picture repeated itself,
until my self-loathing was so profound that I had to sit up in bed
to stop my nausea and dizziness.

What a relief the mournful squall of the slaveherd's buffalo
horn had been!

Upon hearing its first flatulent moan I had leaped to my feet—
only to find that Auntie and Harlot had already started up like a
pair of deer.

"Guh! What a witch night!" Auntie groaned, and all three of
us laughed crazily, as if the whole mare's nest of darkness had
been some kind of bad joke.

With the second deep bleat of the horn fear swept back into
my body, as I thought of our worried talk at the smithy the night
before about our slaveherd. Top Man had indeed been enlisted by
some fool from another place, and he had been asking questions.
Some thought that he wanted ferociously to be with us—that he
hated himself so bitterly for being the master's and the overseer's
tongue and eyes, and rod hand, too, that he would be the very
one to kill those two yellows; others thought that he loved his
measly power too much to jeopardize it, and that he might inform.
"Stay away from Top Man," Peace had finally ordered. "Tell the
fellow not a word, do you hear?"

I ran all the way to the blacksmith shop to make sure that Peace
had heard the horn. My breathing came hard, the clouds pressed
so low that I almost felt I had to stoop as I ran.

Solemn and Smart and two captains from other farms who had
bought their hire for the day were already at the smithy; and also
a city slave, Ma's Brass. A messenger, as he said, from a captain
of foot in town, Brass had come for last-minute instructions.

Solemn was asking Brass as I entered whether, on his way out
from the city in the night, he had seen any provincial guardsmen.

"Yes, a squad of six drinking at Lü's tavern."

"Did they have horses?"

"Yes, inferior ponies."

"But not paying mind to their duties?"

"It was late, awfully late, Solemn. Nearly morning."

"True."

Peace calmly said, "Don't fret, Solemn. We'll do away with all
of them."

Brass's eyes were big; I dare say he had never seen General
Peace before.

"The only worry," Solemn said, "is if they double the guard for
any reason, or put on extra men."

"No matter what you say," Peace said, "our plans are so far advanced that we are compelled to go ahead, even if they find us out.
. . . You have four swords to finish, Solemn."

"They'll be done," Solemn irritably said. "I told Overseer Li I had
hoops to do today, and he said to go ahead." Solemn stooped to
build a fire; he angrily clattered the grate.

Brass left, and I was able at last to say that the second horn
had been blown.

"I am coming, dear handmaiden," Peace gently said. "This will
be our last day in the fields—think of that, child."

But what a long day!

It was a hoeing day. Such a miserable claw is a hoe. Head down,
back bent, arms forever pulling the same way; broad snout strikes
a stone, and the jar of the unyielding handle runs all the way
through to the top of the skull. The only relief is time: crut, crut,
crut, the blade chips away at the morning, at the hump of the day's
heat, at the long afternoon, at the slanting shadows, crut . . . crut
. . . crut . . . crut . . . crut . . .

We tried to sing ourselves along, but Harlot could not find the
right hymn; we dared not be mournful, we were agitated and out
of tune.

I felt a kind of numbness all day long, perhaps from having
slept such shallow naps the night before.

Peace worked as on any other day—steady, patient, strong,
enduring. His eyes were veiled. I heard him humming once when
there was no gang hymn going.

The dark plate of cloud semed to push down lower and lower;

the wind rose from the direction of the Yellow River until the woodlots hushed at us, and the broad leaves of Chekiang fan-leaf, in the field where I was working, began to bow and clap. But the wind was not a relief, it simply revolted one, like an old person's bad breath.

Mink talked away as if it were an ordinary day, until we were all annoyed with him and tried to dam him up, but he kept overflowing where we least expected; he did not care.

Overseer Li came by. I thought: You are going to die tonight, we are going to kill you. He walked close to my task, and I hoed hard, because even though I wanted him dead I also wanted to please him. Yes, I would have this one last chance to show that I was a good worker. When he had passed, not even having looked at me, I was humiliated, furious with myself, and therefore quite at peace with the idea of killing this yellow man, and every other one.

My master. As the overseer walked away, I felt a surge of blind hatred for Yen the son; I had seen the young owner, over the months, not more than six or eight times—only once close at hand, that day in the tobacco house, otherwise crossing a field on horseback at a distance, or on a round of inspection with Li. He used my existence but denied it. He did not know me at all.

At our eating pause Top Man came to Peace and in a quiet voice said, "Will you tell me your plan, friend?"

Peace turned vacant eyes on the slaveherd. "What plan was that, friend?" Giving back "friend" for "friend," he set Top Man off his balance.

"I heard you were ready to begin it."

"Begin what, Top Man? You mean, begin the new pigpen in the back of Solemn's room?"

"You know what I mean."

"I am an ignorant hand, Top Man. I do *not* know what you mean. Be a kind man and tell me." This was obviously a dare.

"I mean," Top Man said, nearly weeping with rage, "the thing you mean to do."

"What thing is that?"

"You know."

"I am at a loss. Brother Smart, you have a better head than I. Do you know what this mystery of Top Man's is?"

"Why, I can't fathom it," Smart said.

"I can be as good as any of them," Top Man said.

"You are a fine slaveherd. As slaveherds go, you are excellent."

"I mean the other. For what you intend to do."

"Top Man, you're a riddle. I give up to you. I cannot puzzle out what you mean." A sudden gust blew at Peace's hair; the seven queues shook.

"I mean that I hate them just as you do."

" 'Them'? What is that, Top Man? Hornworms?"

"I could have told them. I have known for weeks. I could have informed."

"I believe that. Anything could have come to pass. You could have been found stark chilly dead in Favorable Wind Brook Swamp any night, Top Man. A slave hardly knows what to expect these days."

"You could be making a mistake," Top Man said.

"My soul, I think I could. I *know* I could. My body is big, Top Man, it's as big as a maize crib, it could hold a whole harvest of error. I make no claim to being without error. I'm full of it, Top Man. My bones ache with it. I'm a very mistaken man. Everyone knows that. But I swear I cannot see what you are trying to say to me."

"Ayah, Peace, you turtle," Top Man said. "I've never seen you bambooed. I'm tempted today."

"Today's your best and last chance," Peace said, pushing out his chest and advancing toward the slaveherd.

Top Man clutched his horn, which was slung over his shoulder on a length of twine, and raised it to his lips and blew a blast, the mournfulness of which was enough to drag out the spirits of the dead in the daytime. "All right," he hoarsely shouted, and I thought there were tears in the red rims of his eyes. "Hoe out! Finish your tasks and you go in. Brisk now, you hands. Hoe out! Hoe out!"

Crut . . . crut . . . crut . . . the day was so *long!*

Late in the afternoon there sounded a single, deep, distant rumble.

Every hoe hand's head came up; eyes darted to eyes. My heart began to pound—at the edge of my mind a distorted picture of the clumps of slaves praying on the deck of the *East Garden* for a cataclysmic storm, the yellow sailors grinning down on our nakedness. . . .

For the first time all day, after that faraway growl, Peace

showed signs of feeling. He chopped harder with his hoe, his locks bounced, his eyes were—afraid!

Ayah, white God, this made me nervous.

As each hand completed his task, which was marked out with stakes, he was excused; some, who finished early, helped others to get theirs done, and we walked back to the quarter in groups of half a dozen at a time, at about an hour before dark. Peace had gone ahead of the group with which I was working in one corner of the field, and I felt uneasy at his going off without Harlot and me in train—Auntie was with the children in the slaves' compound. He had walked off alone.

When we came into the street of the quarter, we saw Peace out in it, chopping at the hog-wallow earth with an axe. At each stroke he would hop to one side, so the next cut in the ground would form a cross with the last. There was a wildness about his looks that frightened me even though I saw at once that he was acting out one of our superstitions—driving the threatening storm away with a pattern of crosses of Christ, the white Son of the white God.

At each stroke, as he raised the axe head, Peace lifted himself on tiptoes and then brought the blade down with the ferocity of one splitting fire logs of twisted locust—throwing far more strength into the work of chopping the ground than it seemed to need.

He is already killing, I thought, hup, *kill*, hup, *kill*, hup, *kill*.

So for the first time I faced the real nature of the slaughter that was so soon to begin: that it would not be an abstract holocaust but rather a series of blows on separate human bodies, one by one. I heard Peace's deep grunts as the strokes went home, and then I heard two men in the circle of onlookers grunting in unison with Peace, and I saw that their lips, like Peace's, drew back in agony at each frightful crash of the flying iron wedge. I was torn apart. I was terrified of the idea that the killing, once started, might not stop, and might even turn against me, yet I myself felt, in my neck, under the gag of surprise and horror, beginnings of sharp, sweet exclamations. Hah! There! Our turn! Hoo! At last! There! . . .

The axe bite pulled away, and two big chips of earth crust flipped on their backs, and Peace swung the helve backward and upward, stretching his legs and torso and arms until the head of the tool was higher than the huts—and at that moment there came a single, short, flat crack of thunder.

The axe was already on the way down, but the force was out of the blow.

Before the thud of the head in the ground, a pelting of enormous drops of rain began.

I saw the axe fall out of Peace's hands, and he raised and spread his arms in a great Y. Waves of fearful disbelief washed across his face.

There ensued, for me, a moment of shock—not because the raindrops had been able to march so thuddingly over the line of our white God's crosses, but because Peace, in whom I had reposed so much hope, did not seem able to believe that our deity might abandon us. I myself had felt since early morning that our God was looking the other way; all day I had wanted Peace to change the plan while knowing that he would not, could not. Peace seemed now as if he wanted to split all humanity, of whatever color, with the axe.

He stooped for the handle and redoubled his efforts. The onlookers scurried for cover and watched him from doorways. The flakes of earth that he had shived up turned dark, then soft, and soon he was standing in mud hacking at mud.

But there seemed to be no more thunder, and the huge splats of the first downpour gave way to smaller and smaller drops, until the shower seemed virtually over, and Peace, his back glistening, runnels of water streaming out of his hair down his face, stood away, axe handle at hip, and looked at the sky, and seemed satisfied. He strode to Solemn's doorway.

The rain, however, did not stop, but continued first as a drizzle; gradually the wind, which had fallen still during that first loud spattering, increased, and the raindrops drove slantwise harder and harder as darkness fell.

The rendezvous at the bridge had been set for midnight, and I now hoped that the rain would prove to be only a prolonged shower, and would abate, for though I was prepared to risk my very life—insofar as I understood that concept—it was nevertheless hard to think of risking my life and being wet, chilly, and miserable, too!

Just at dusk the sky broke down on us.

There was enough light left to see the frightful black swirling edge of the new torment, pressing low on the terrain, coming swiftly from the river's direction, yet it was dark enough so that when the lightning came, in a hundred fitful licks from cloud to cloud and down to trees all around us, we were shattered by the light even before the thunder reached us. I dived on my bed and hid my face but could not escape the bombardment. I felt that it was seeking *me* out—and then I thought: No! It is after Peace. He is the one who brought this on us. Their magic is stronger than his. God's crosses didn't break the storm. Peace refused to postpone. Mink was right: Peace can't change his mind. The masters' yellow gods know the plan, and our God with a white skin is not strong enough, or cares too little for us; or perhaps it is His will that we should remain subservient, we should accept our tired backs, we should be, like His son, humble and forgiving. God has abandoned Peace because Peace is an upstart. Peace really has wanted to overthrow, not our masters, but our God Himself. He was trying to chop God with the axe. And this is why Peace cannot change his mind: He aspires to omnipotence. He wants to make and stop storms, enslave and set free, give and take life.

The thunder pounded these thoughts into me.

The wind was soon at a gale, and a wooden shutter at our window banged back and forth as if trying to flee, and when it crashed open sheets of water poured in at the square hole; when it flapped shut the deluge abruptly stopped.

I heard Auntie weeping. She had lit a lantern; it flickered a feeble counterpoint to the almost continuous lightning.

Peace came roaring into our room. He wanted to leave. He shouted that he was ready.

I saw him for an instant in the sputtering light of our lantern, then suddenly he was bathed to the seat of every pore by a flash so close at hand that the sharp crackle of sound, riding the brilliance, seemed to come from him. He was dressed in his ordinary work clothes, and he had tied around his forehead a fillet of red flannel, to keep his hair from plastering down on his face, and in his hand he held his huge jawbone, the yellowy teeth of which sparkled like jewels in the lightning. His lips were drawn back in the grimace-smile of his chopping in the earth. Then the lantern blew out, the lightning stopped for a few moments, and there was only his voice.

"Come, daughters! Call out the people. Time to leave."

"In *this*?" Auntie said. Her voice itself seemed to cringe.

"We have to get out there. My men are coming."

"Not till midnight, Peace. The storm could pass."

"The storm is safest. They will never see us."

"How are you going to see your own soldiers?"

Again, as he had at the smithy the night of the last meeting, Peace lost control. "OBEY ME, you turtle women," he shouted.

We are beaten, I thought then, we have no chance. If God were in him, he would not shout like that. He is incapable of changing the plan in the slightest detail. It is not that God has abandoned us; it is that Peace is not godlike enough.

"Yes, Peace," Auntie said, but her voice had a hair-raising too careful tone, as if she were speaking to one of *them,* saying, "Yes, Big Master."

"Go from room to room and call out the men," Peace shouted over the wind. "Solemn has a storm lantern. Light it in the cabin there and then meet me at the big-house end of the quarter."

"Yes, Peace."

I was drenched before I had run two steps. Going into the wind and rain I could hardly breathe, and I had to turn my head aside and gulp at the air. At each cabin, though I spoke with all the force I could manage, the men were astounded that Peace wanted to go out in the storm. As I ran from door to door, lightning seemed to trip me; each time it winked I would fall to my knees and cover my ears with my hands, but I heard the ripping sounds of the thunder all the same. The night, between flashes, was utterly black. Some cabins had lamps going. Many of the women were weeping, and when I appeared with Peace's unbending summons, the wails soared, and the wives threw their arms around their husbands' necks, and the men, tearing themselves out of the hysterical embraces, cursed both their women and Peace.

We met at the head of the street, where Peace, insisting on a count, found that four men had refused to leave their cabins. Bellowing, Peace went after them himself.

Then we set off roundabout through the fields for the smithy, to get our weapons.

The raindrops were coming so hard on the hurricane wind that they seemed to have been maliciously hurled, like handfuls of pebbles. We groped our way on foul footing, leaning into the wind. Now and then a fork of lightning would reveal the party in an instant's light-frozen tableau: tentative steps, wet clinging clothes, a strong man straining into the force of the storm, a hand at a forehead, a crookback bent to the gale, two men with arms about each other, a mule jawbone gleaming shoulder-high—then total blackness, save for what seemed a globe of solid water glistening around the muffled storm lantern in Auntie's hand; and a roar of drops hitting the ground and of wind lashing the trees.

We crowded into the smithy, where, though the whole shed shook in the wind and the rain drummed on the roof, it seemed we had found everlasting calm; but Solemn and Tree had a violent argument over the allotment of swords and pikes to our Yen slaves, and before long we were out in the storm again. Peace left Solemn at the shop to hand out arms to other contingents as they arrived.

If possible, the downpour was more vicious than ever. We made our way along the Brook Road as far as the bridge.

I thought we would be the only ones there that night, our dozen men and three women, but soon, to my amazement, the soldiers began to come, in pairs, then in handfuls, then in scores, then in companies.

The hooded lamp was the only light; the storm's flashes were less frequent now, though the rain and wind continued hard. Faces, streaming with water, swam into the small effulgence of the lamp, and now and then a scythe-sword glinted.

I heard Mink, his nihilism as vigorous as ever, shout in Peace's face with a wild glee, "Those fires at the Canal Bund are never going to burn."

"Hah!" Peace shouted. "The tobacco will burn. There's wood like tinder inside the godowns." He pushed Mink away with the side of his hand.

The brook was rising. Men were milling about in great disorder. Donkeys brayed at the thunder; in the lightning their huge eyes took fire, their dark noses glistened, their manes looked like blowing smoke.

A frantic man was pushed forward into the lamplight. He had come from Twin Hills, having run all the way; he gasped for air and rolled his eyes.

Brass and True, Ma's slaves, he said, had informed! They had shut themselves in their master's office and told him everything, and Ma had warned his cousin Ma out here on the Brook Road and had alerted Warlord Sun at the yamen. Sun had posted thirty guardsmen at the new prison, and fifteen at the yamen gate, and he was sending horsemen out along the Brook Road.

Peace held the jawbone high and shook it and shouted, "TOO LATE! They are too late! We have already started the thing."

But this cry, which must have been meant to rally the wavering, was a terrible moan, a bursting of frustration and inflexibility in Peace's massive chest. I knew we were lost; I hugged Harlot and wept, and I could hear her sobs, too.

I felt the ceaseless rain as a heavy, clammy texture weighing on me, like a wet shawl on my shoulders.

By now the brook was rising with alarming speed, and in the lightning, beyond the curtains of glistening beads of rain, I could see its pocked black surface licking at the timbers of the bridge.

Still men gathered. Smart called out that we had passed the count of a thousand. The confusion was frightful, and men argued in screams. Donkeys and mules tossed their heads.

Someone shouted that we had better leave, the bridge would soon be covered.

But Peace called out that the plan had been made, we could not abandon it, some of his captains were still on their way, the old man from West-of-the-Mountains who had been at the siege of Taiyuan had not arrived yet. No! No! We must wait!

Now the water was over the level of the bridgeway. Some city slaves, evidently fearful of being cut off, made a dash for the bridge, and then there was a surge. I heard the railings of the bridge cracking, and there were screams and splashes in the darkness.

I heard—I was sure I heard—Mink laughing.

All semblance of order was gone. Men were tearing at each other, starting off every which way, cursing, howling, and shouting into the swirls of wind.

I was seized, as if by a group of hands at my shoulders, by a feeling of helplessness, a sense that I no longer had any control over where and how my own feet would be planted on the ground, to say nothing of my destiny. Then I realized what was happening: A surge of the tight-packed mob around us was bodily carrying me—and Peace, and our whole group—away from the roadway and along the brookside. There was sloping leaf mold underfoot. I was indeed helpless and might well be stampeded into the stream.

Then I heard Peace begin to shout, "O God, God, God, where are You? White God, where are You?" I wanted to take up this cry, for I had very strongly the feeling of having been abandoned by Him. Why don't You help us? Can't You help us? We need You! Where are You? . . . I could not have said whether Peace was roaring these questions or whether they were reverberating,

hollow and wind-rushed, in my own head. It occurred to me that
Peace might have experienced, as I had, that slipping sensation,
that helplessness of being heaved over the loam footing by the
pressure of the crowd which had lost its mind in the storm. Such
helplessness would be the one thing an omnipotent being simply
could not stand. Yes, I did hear Peace shouting, his speech sounding thick and trembling as it was torn from his mouth by the
wind. The bridge washed away with terrible creakings and
splittings. I wondered for a moment if all this could really be
happening to me. For what was I being punished? I heard the
sopping tatters of Peace's shouts—some sort of raving about the
fountains of the great deep and the windows of heaven . . .
the rain was on the earth and the water prevailed exceedingly.
. . . Smart's dark book! I sensed the mob thinning out. It was as
if the men around us were recoiling from the sounds they heard
coming from Peace's mouth, and were scattering, getting away
as fast as they could. Had they found Peace out? Should I run?
The storm seemed to blow away snatches of the hollow chanting
that was now coming from Peace's throat, and to magnify words
here and there: ". . . FIFTEEN cubits . . . waters prevailed, and
all *flesh* DIED . . . fowl, and of cattle, and of beast . . . CREEPING
THING THAT CREEPETH . . . in whose *nostrils* was the BREATH of
life . . ." I felt such a bitter sadness. All my hopes of all this
time! I thought I heard a bewilderment in Peace's outcries, as
if he were losing his sense of power and could not understand why.
"GOD! GOD! WHERE ARE YOU?" The crowd was rapidly breaking up. I had no idea where the men were going—perhaps to hide
(from whom? from the yellows? from Peace?) in the woods. I
thought of the betrayal of our plans by Brass and True, and it
seemed to me for a moment that perhaps it was their unthinkable
treachery rather than the storm that had addled and routed Peace
and all his army. Peace was chattering about killing the yellow
Matriarch; he was moving along the brook, and I followed. I was
strongly affected by a need to be obedient. Somehow Peace,
Auntie, Harlot, and I drifted off by ourselves and were crashing
through a thicket. "Every living substance was DESTROYED on
the face of the ground . . ." We were at the big house; in a flash
I saw it looming there, asleep in the typhoon under the walnut
trees. But Peace did not approach the gate, and I felt a wind-gust
of relief, for my own weak aim to kill had vanished long since.
I wanted to hide; I was afraid of being caught. Peace led us

away. I felt the mud of tobacco fields under my feet. It now
seemed to me that God had abandoned us not by sending a storm,
or by failing to fend off a storm sent by the yellows' deities, but
rather had decamped from within each of us, from our natures,
from our worthless white souls. Ai, yes, I felt godlessly worthless.
. . . And ahead of me, indeed, I heard Peace shouting self-abasement. No longer the Flood; he was talking about himself—the
final loss of his secretly named inner genie, the powerful hero
of the war that in the end had simply been rained out. "—is *not*
my name. I am—O God!—not strong. I CANNOT take up the
doors of the gate of the city and the two posts and the bar and
carry them up the hill before Hebron the green withes GOD GOD
GOD they're tying me tight they have me pinned to the beam by
the web on my locks RAZOR RAZOR—my hair! . . . I'm weak, weak,
blind, blind. Fetters of brass, GOD, they've harnessed me—the
mill, the prison-house mill! . . ." We were in deep woods. The
despair in Peace's voice was worse than thunder: I had my hands
over my ears as we moved, but nevertheless I heard him reach
the bottom of the well of his hopelessness when he bellowed
three times, in an agony of uttermost surrender, the name of
his hero-self so long unspoken: "SAMSON! SAMSON! SAMSON!"
Then he fell sobbing to the soaked earth.

("Like the End of the World"

At the first thinning of the night we wakened. The rain
had stopped, and our four bodies were wrapped in a sort of ball on
a bed of leaf mold in the forest—we three women had curled
close about Peace, nesting him in what warmth we had left. The
trees, black figurations against the gray, were motionless above
us, and the woods around us were as yet birdless, sleeping, silent
—until Auntie began to cry with a small girl's catching whimper.
    Peace lifted an arm and drew Auntie into an embrace. "It's all
right now," he said in a gentle, calm voice.
    In a few moments he sat up, looked about us, and said, "I had
better move along now. I want you girls to go back to the quarter,
get in there before Top Man's horn."
    No more talk of handmaidens, daughters.
    "We are going to see you safe, Peace," Auntie said, "and no
argument. It's market day."

Peace accepted that. "Forgot about market day," he said. It was not yet really light. He said that the other side of Twin Hills was the place to be, they would never look for him on the far side of Twin Hills. We could not tell yet from the sky where the east was. A scythe-pike lay on the ground; Harlot thought she might have been carrying it during the storm. Peace took it up. The mule jawbone was half buried under old leaves. He did not touch it.

There was moss on one side of a beech-tree trunk, and Peace took our direction from it—northward toward the river, rather than eastward as I had expected. We ran across some unfamiliar tobacco fields—"Should be Wang's," Peace said—risking the open ground because it was still half light and we thought no one would be awake anywhere yet.

In woods beyond the fields, we came across two slaves sleeping on the ground, who were wakened by our footsteps.

One of them jumped up and said, "Where are you going, Peace? Where should we go?" No more "General."

Peace said he would go northward for a day or two and then loop around toward East-of-the-Mountains. "Can we go with you?"

It would be better, Peace said, not to make up into a party.

We moved along, and when we crossed a swollen drainage ditch I realized why we were not going straight toward the city: there would be no way yet of getting over the flooding brook, and Peace, indeed, soon said he aimed to find a small sampan such as would usually be tied up in fair numbers against the pilings of most of the tobacco growers' landings along the river. That, in due course, we did, and for an hour we poled ourselves and floated down the swollen river, and then, as it grew full light under dry clouds that were now scudding seaward, we abandoned the sampan on the far bank of the river and went into the forests there.

Peace, still carrying the lance, was quiet, soft-voiced, non-committal. Now and then there came into his eyes a flicker, just a flicker, of a dreamy speculative look; he blinked it quickly out, but I thought I would die of pain in my heart at the sight of those momentary, shuttered abstractions. I felt, as we went through the unbroken forests, checking the river from time to time on our right hand, that I, and we, and all of our kind, could never have any hope at all, never. Auntie was somehow cheerful, perhaps for Peace's sake, but I could not lift my spirits.

We saw the city once; we had to swing far around some farms, and a settlement on our side of the river.

The sun came out. The day grew bland. Could there have been such a typhoon?

Well beyond the city, in a stretch of the river called Tiger's Fan Narrows, we saw ahead, once as we came out onto the bank, a seagoing junk, a lumbering Ningpo trader, its three great spars slightly canted, so it was evident that the ship had grounded itself on a bar. It was only about fifty feet from our shore, and we worked along the bank toward it. The towering blue transom with red facings was ill reflected in the muddy waters of the river; her brown and yellow sails and their bamboo battens were furled and lashed upright along the masts. Peace dropped his pike in the river. As we drew abreast of her, the junk appeared idle, asleep, though we could hear some sort of bleating aboard. We saw a white crewman fishing with a handline in the shallow water over the near rail.

"You will never catch a fish there," Peace called out to the man.

"Might catch a river pig."

"Run onto a bank?"

"Yes. Blew like the end of the world last night."

"Waiting for a tide?"

"Yes."

"When is it due?"

"When it comes." The sailor shrugged.

"Where are you running?"

"Home. Ningpo."

"Can you take a man?"

"And *three* women?"

"Just the man. These women are taking the day off."

"You are a sight!" Yes, our clothes were muddy. "All right, son. *He* is sick." The sailor pointed with his thumb over his shoulder at the cabin on the high stern, and obviously meant the captain. "We have nine billy goats on here, might as well have you. You hold on there."

The man came off in a skiff that was tied alongside and carried Peace out to the junk.

Peace said nothing in parting, save, as the water widened between us, "You tell Solemn, now."

We turned upriver, and I could not bear to look back. Around a bend we took off our clothes and washed the mud out of them

in the river, and they dried on us as we went on. This being a
market day, we were bold. A white riverman carried us across
the river to Twin Hills. "That *was* a typhoon last night," he said,
as he sculled us over. "Had to haul this cockleshell a half a li up
the field so it wouldn't wash away. Had to do it alone. Our other
slave, Sinner, he skipped out, don't know where he's gone."
    The city was quiet. We walked out the Brook Road, and a slave
ferried us across the still-swollen stream near Lü's tavern. We cut
around through the fields to the quarter, and neither Li nor Top
Man saw us arrive. The men were all in their rooms, sleeping.

(Yellowing Leaves

        Now it was the ninth month, and it all began again—
informings, slapdash trials, beheadings, the feeling of nausea
every day. The young master came back from West-of-the-Mountains Province on the double, and we saw more of him in a fortnight than we had seen in nearly a year, saw that he was afraid,
and that his overseer was angry and frustrated because the work
was disrupted, for the crop was beginning to yellow, and it was
time to cut the stalks off close to the ground and let the plants wilt
and then take them in and hang them on the laths in the tobacco
house; but Top Man, the slaveherd, was exceedingly busy at the
yamen in Twin Hills, telling the provincial magistrates that he
had heard this, and that, and Overseer Li had to go and testify,
and provincial guardsmen infested our place. How Top Man swaggered in the quarter! He was a person of importance to *them,* and
he had the same fear that they did, that he would be murdered
in bed, so he swaggered to hide his terror. The first prisoners,
about twenty of them, including Solemn, and, we heard, Ch'eng's
Candy, Fan the mix, and Wang's Judge, but not Smart, were
locked up in the new prison. A unit of the provincial guard was
posted near Lü's tavern, not far from us on the Brook Road, and it
was said that War Lord Sun had asked the Emperor for reinforcements from North-of-the-River. Peace and Ditcher were missing.
    On the twelfth day of the ninth month, on a knoll at the edge
of the city, five white men were beheaded.
    Tree proposed to run away, and he began measuring himself
for a description to go on a pass he wanted Smart to forge for him.
    Fan, the mix, was tried in the Chengchow yamen, and he was

discharged for want of evidence, because he was a free mixie, and the provincial justices, keenly protective of the natural rights of men under The Nine Flowers, had decided that men who were slaves could not give testimony against a freeman, even though he might be partly white. Hearsay was fit enough for slaves, however, and five more were beheaded on the fifteenth, with the entire force of the yellow provincial guard commanded to watch.

⟨ A Firm Stance

Some days we worked in a more or less orderly way, and one afternoon toward the end of the ninth month, as we were cutting the plants in gangs, Harlot sang a hymn, slow and sad, and to my amazement she improvised a pair of lines that were an unmistakable summons to a secret meeting in the smithy after dark—though she no longer used the phrase "Camp of Dan," but sang "sword into plowshare."

As soon as I could I whispered a question to her about the call, and she said she knew nothing, only that Smart had told her to issue it.

Rumors ran around the rest of the afternoon—that Peace was coming back to see us for an hour, that he had been killed by a slave for the reward, that we were going to start the whole thing up again without him. I shook my head at the report of his return; I shook my head at any hope at all. . . .

Nightfall. Had Auntie, Harlot, and I any right to go to the meeting? Woman of Timnath, whore of Gaza, Delilah of Sorek— that fevered imagination! There was no more of all that now. Auntie crept to a whispered conference with Smart; and Smart, sorrowing for his "brother" Solemn who had been beheaded, whispered with tears in his eyes, yes, yes, yes, he wanted us to attend. . . .

The familiar lamp hung from the smoke-blackened joist. Our group was much smaller than it had used to be, and I was more conscious of the faces that were missing than of those that were there. On Smart's bench, where Smart had so long ago traced in cinders for me the first two-lined character, "man," a stranger sat, whose face was vaguely familiar, and as we three women entered he nodded to us in a jocular way, as if he knew us, a loose-jointed, slow-moving man, and when I saw him shrug his shoulders while

answering a question of Smart's, I knew who he was: the crewman on the Ningpo trader who had rowed ashore for Peace. He
was called Bow Steersman; perhaps that was his job on the vessel.
When he began his story I sensed that he was carefree, airy, far
from our mood—perhaps because he had never been enlisted in
the war, perhaps merely because he was a homeless, anchorless
crewman.

"I saw him throw that stick with a knife lashed onto it in the
river water; he thought I did not but I did. Captain Ts'ui, he was
down in his bunk with an earth fever. Queer man, that one. Moody
—no, not moody. You just cannot tell. You look in his face, and
he has a grin on it, but his eyes are mourning, or sometimes it is
the other way—sour mouth and those eyes lighted up like the
Scholars' Garden in Twin Hills there. He doesn't pay attention
to what's moving around outside his head—or in it, either one.
Has little crinkles all around his eyes—from laughing? I doubt
it. Used to be an overseer, won't talk about it. Before we got off the
bar there, Dogface, one of our men, he'd been asleep in the crew's
mat shed forward, he waked up and came on deck, and he says,
'Ai! Aren't you Peace?' But *he* says, 'My name is Steady.' When
the tide came in, Captain Ts'ui got up, groaning and aching, and
he set us some sail, and we moved off the sandbar. Two days later
we all got wind about the reward, when we stopped at Lu P'an's
landing, and Salt and Dogface—Salt is the longest one to have
been a slave to the captain there, and Salt claims Captain Ts'ui
set him free, but he didn't give Salt any papers, it was during a
time the captain was a Lamaist that he said Salt could go free,
but then he gave up being a Lamaist—he's a man like that, never
rests on one spot—and Salt was scared he'd changed his mind,
because the captain never said another word about it, sometimes
gave Salt some money, other times shouted and cursed at him like
a turtle. Anyway Salt and Dogface told him they suspected the
big man that came aboard on the bar, that he was the one the
reward was for, but Captain Ts'ui says, 'He came aboard as a
free man, I can't touch him.' Salt says, 'Where are his papers?'
Captain Ts'ui says, 'He left them.' Captain Ts'ui had been an overseer, he knows you don't have a white man running around without a chit or *some* kind of *proof*. All right, we were eleven days
on our down passage, and Captain Ts'ui said nothing. We could
have put in at Thousand Ducks Landing, or at Round House Landing, we could have hailed twenty vessels that were up-passaging.

One did hail us, Captain Yang boarded us, wanted to know whether it was safe to go up, with the slave revolt and all, but Captain Ts'ui said not a word about this man Peace or Steady that he had aboard there, two teeth missing, long hair, cut on the brow—exactly the man. Sometimes you would swear that Captain Ts'ui was walking around in a dream. We coasted down there to Ningpo and tied up on fenders alongside a big twenty-five-man junk, and Captain Ts'ui still said nothing to secure this man Peace, wrote his forms for the customs and said nothing in them at all about this runaway, sends Dogface ashore for some short-ration provender at the market and no orders to Dogface about trying to secure the man. All right. Dogface sniffs the reward. He goes to a yellow man, Chiang, whom he knows, Chiang goes straight to the constables, and at two o'clock, here they come, Constables Tung and Hsü—I know those bastards, just try to get slavey drunk and they're on your neck like a pair of dirty ospreys—so they came on board and took him, and they asked Captain Ts'ui how it was he had not reported the man Peace all along the voyage, and he says, 'Look, teachers, look at my writing tablet and brushes here, I was just this second writing to Captain Tu, at the Emperor's admiralty, to ask what to do with the man.' Well, those two dirty bastard ospreys came back later and bound Captain Ts'ui over, to appear at the yamen and answer to the Emperor for doing nothing all that time."

"How did Peace seem when last you saw him?" Smart asked.

"I never saw a man so stiff before the constables, especially those two turtles. I tell you, he smacked all over of stubbornness, he stood there *stubborn*. They tried to get him to confess it down on paper, and he said, 'I will speak to no one but Warlord Sun, in the yamen at Twin Hills, or else the Emperor himself.' He wouldn't, either; he pressed his lips *tight*. Those two hungry bastard ospreys were not used to pride in a white man, they shook him up hard, and he just looked as if he pitied them. I don't know what good it did, though, they just ran him off in chains."

⟨ The Spirit of the Accused

On eleventh month, seventh day, Peace was beheaded. We heard that his fortitude and dignity and inflexibility held up to the very end—that he had refused to make a confession that would implicate anyone else, that he had said to *them* at his trial, "I know you set your minds on killing me long before you laid a hand on me—so why this look-like-a-trial, which isn't a trial at all?" And that he had gone to the platform silent, calm, but hard to recognize as the terrible Peace, for his one request in jail had been granted: that his long hair be all cut off and his head be altogether shaved.

Three days later Ditcher gave himself up to the Twin Hills yamen, saying he wanted the reward of three hundred strings of cash, of a half catty each, that had been offered for his capture, to be given to a free white friend of his, Dirty Chi, who had persuaded him to surrender. The authorities decided that, being white, Chi was entitled to but fifty strings. Ditcher was beheaded.

On information from Top Man, the slaveherd, the guards arrested Smart, and he was tried and beheaded.

Brass and True, for their loyalty in discovering the plot to their master, were purchased by the Emperor's treasury and set free.

Altogether thirty-five slaves were beheaded; four, who had been arrested, escaped and ran away; one killed himself in prison. So we heard. The reinforcements of the Emperor's guard were returned to North-of-the-River. The cost to the Emperor of the entire disturbance, the treasury announced, was four ingots of gold and five thousand eight hundred twenty-nine catties of copper cash, so at least our war had cost them *something*.

One day toward the end of the tenth month, a woman came back to our quarter from a day in the city—young Master Yen would issue no more passes to men—with a sheet of rice paper tucked under her gown that had been passed, hand to hand, from old Ku the Usher in the yamen down through the town, and that was, they said, an exact copy of official minutes, destined for the Emperor's eyes, of a speech First Minister Hsien was said to have made in the beautiful yamen in whose hallways the light slaps of my own bare feet had echoed one afternoon many hopes ago. I, who had learned to read from dead Smart, went from room to room along the street, reading the paper in whispers: "The accused," the First Minister had said, "have shown a spirit which, if it becomes general, must swamp the five provinces in blood. They had a sense of their rights, a contempt for danger, and a thirst for revenge which portend the most unhappy consequences." When I had finished the rounds, I was able to throw myself on my k'ang and sob out my heart, in mourning, at last, for our stiff, obdurate, compassionate seer and general, who had died with the locks of his strength and decency shorn. The paper had spoken of a spirit among the whites that was still dangerous. All *my* fire, it seemed just then, had been put out with Peace's life.

(A Conference

The Yens waited to make their move until the dust had settled—and the crop had been largely laid away.

One day in mid-tenth the field hands were led in a body to the rear courtyard of the big house, the house slaves' quarter, and we were formed into a line. One by one our people were admitted to the back door of the main courtyard, and later we saw those who had been taken inside walking singly across the far side of the quarter, returning by way of the gate from the side courtyard, whence they had apparently been let out under orders to return to the field hands' quarter without speaking to those still waiting in line. By and large the women were discharged from the house very soon after having been admitted; men were kept longer. Auntie, however, who was ahead of me in the line, was kept an age, and when she finally left I saw her almost running toward the refuge of our mud huts, in great agitation.

My turn came. Top Man, the slaveherd, appeared at the gate and beckoned to me. I was so nervous I stumbled and fell over the high gate sill; a crackling laugh ran down the waiting line. Inside, an impression of darkness, heaviness. Top Man walked ahead.

He led me into the side courtyard and to a room that seemed to be a tailor shop—where slave clothes were made, no doubt. Bolts of cheap cloth lay in a heap along the inner wall. Across the room at the far end ran a trestle table, on which numerous books and papers were spread, and behind this—my heart tripped —the yellow Matriarch was seated. The young master was standing to one side, beyond her; he leaned against the wall picking his teeth with a quill, and he seemed to me even younger and more delicate than I had thought him that day in the tobacco house. Overseer Li was seated at one end of the worktable. Top Man stood beside me.

"Name?" the Matriarch asked.

"Small White Lotus, Big Mistress," Top Man said.

"Yes," the woman curtly said, and she leafed through a large ledger. "Ayah, yes, White Lotus. Let us see." She was far smaller and slighter than I had thought her, and her voice was mild and soft, and I kept thinking, Could her gods be more powerful than Jehovah? Peace had said over and over that he was going to kill her. "Purchased eleven eleven," she said, running her forefinger down the notations in the big book, "from 'Uncle' Ch'en, seventy-two catties of cash. Eleven twenty-six: Reprimanded by Duke for chasing around big house after laundering." The eyes, dark as the night mists on the ice pond, turned up to me. "Ai, yes, I remember you, I wanted you in the house the day you came, but Duke said you would cause trouble among the domestics, among the men. Has she, Small Top Man, down at the field quarter?"

"She is one of those three who messed about with Peace."

"Yen!" Addressing her son rather sharply by his patronymic, the Matriarch did not turn her head but seemed to be listening for the young man's whereabouts, as if she thought he might be tiptoeing out of the room behind her back.

"Yes, T'ai-t'ai."

"I believe Duke is getting senile."

"If you say so, T'ai-t'ai."

The two, and later the overseer as well, talked for some time about the Number One Houseboy. I was too agitated to take in what they meant, but I sensed that both the son and the overseer were helplessly bored, that the yellow mother was one of those plodding, thorough, domineering women who want to do things in an orderly way but cannot help running off into endless digressions.

I had, very strongly, the feeling I had so often experienced in the Shen dining room, in the Northern Capital, of *not being present*.

Above all, I felt that the three yellow people in the room were carrying on their business, whatever it was, with a wholly inappropriate flatness and dryness of feeling: I was rigid with fear; they had been in mortal danger; they were planning, I sensed, to assert with utter finality their mastery over their rebellious slaves —but it was all bored, congenial, distant, punctuated with sighs.

She was reading again from the ledger in a dull voice, and before long I was overwhelmed by her words—the most minute

observations about my movements and behavior: seen talking
with Mink a few days after the rails were badly piled; good work
as a runner in the tobacco house (someone *had* seen me!); first
night visit to the smithy; other visits, with hours of departure and
return; to Twin Hills with Peace; idle, joking, and snickering
during a haying; constantly on Peace's gown-skirt in market-day
pastimes—fish feast on six twenty-four, pig roast on seven twenty-
eight. . . . Mostly from Top Man but much of it from some other
informer or informers, because several of the entries were about
actions which Top Man could not have known—all neatly noted
down.

"Were you intimate with Peace?"

"What, Venerable Matriarch?" I asked, startled.

"Did you know his plans?"

"No, Venerable Matriarch."

"You went everywhere with him, didn't you?"

"No, Venerable Matriarch," I said. "Never."

She spoke over her shoulder to her son. "They tell lies like
little children."

"They don't know what the truth is, T'ai-t'ai."

"Well, what do you think, son? Li, what do you say to this one?"

The overseer waited, seething with dutiful respect. The son put
a hand over his eyes and said, "Come, T'ai-t'ai. You had your
mind made up about this girl before we started. Can't we move
along? How many more, Top Man?"

"I'll go and count them, Big Master."

"Stay where you are," the woman said. "Li?"

"Sell, Mistress."

"I think so. Get the next one, Top Man."

Top Man led me to the house slaves' gate.

([The Pleasure Garden

It could not be done all at once, for we were a glut on
the market. All the masters were selling slaves whom they did not
trust. The Yens wanted to sell eleven slaves, field hands—and
with all the little notations in their books to go on, they were
right about some and wrong about some. There were nine males
and two females on the list, and seven of the men had indeed supported Peace beyond others. But Mink was on the list, and Harlot

was not. I suppose Mink's bent back recommended him for sale; and we all guessed that Top Man, the slaveherd, had for some time fancied having a handmaiden himself and that he may have eased the reports on Harlot, who was, besides, of the sort that the yellow people considered intelligent—yellowish skin and "good eyes" of a mix; had been a house slave; was, maybe, the old master's back-courtyard whelp. The idea of parting from her made me weep every night.

On an afternoon early in the eleventh month a large wagon, with a high wooden fence set on its bed and braced with metal bands, came for us. The same green boy that had carried Mink and me out from the city, so long before, was driving, and two other men, armed with pistols, were along as guards. Mink and I recognized the boy at once, but he looked right through us. We set out. We could see tops of trees over the fencing as we lurched along and, much later, the roofs of city houses. When the tail gates of the tall box were opened and we jumped down, we saw that we were in an area enclosed by a high brick wall; in the foreground we saw a small pleasure garden—round stone tables, lanterns, fish pools; beyond were two large buildings with ominous iron bars in their gates. We were led to one of these, men and women together. The following morning the commission merchant who owned this big slave jail, "Uncle" Ch'en, came to inspect us, a fat man, all smiles, carrying a canary on his shoulder, one leg of which was attached by a delicate long silver chain to his little finger. He made a wry face when he saw Mink, and he pinched me under the chin. As he left, he said, "Cheer up, small boys and girls, I'll get you settled comfortably. I'm going to find you each and every one a sweet master."

We waited six days. They fed us meal and salt fish. On the afternoon of the sixth day we were led out of the jail building and were filed past a storehouse, and yellow attendants handed us bright clothes to dress ourselves in: I was given a curious blue capelike smock with yellow figures on it, which fastened around my neck on a kind of drawstring; I was not allowed to wear my dirty shift under it. Some of the men had brilliant pantaloons: crimson, orange, purple! We were taken into a yard surrounded by a fence of bamboo palings. It grew dark; lanterns were hung in our enclosure, and the place seemed cheerful. We heard sounds of laughter and applause from the direction of the pleasure garden. A pair of yellow attendants brought a bucket

and some tin cups—and we were given drams! Strong drams!
Suddenly a white man dressed as a rooster, short, paunchy, with
a cockscomb cap on his head and arching feathers attached to his
buttocks, whirled out among us, and he began to juggle burning
batons, and he spun china plates high on balance sticks, and his
fingers like blowing ribbons made a coin appear, disappear, come
from his ear, sprout from a slave's nose. We laughed! We laughed!
Someone put a hand on my shoulder: It was the poor-yellow boy
with the fuzz on his chin who had driven the cart out and the
wagon in, and he beckoned to me. I followed him out of the enclosure. I was charged with two drams' heat and the wild images
of a suddenly enchanted world; I wanted to whoop. We made a
turn around a small building and were suddenly in the pleasure
garden. Circles of yellow men—not a single woman—sat around
bowls and bottles at the many tables; bright lamps shone down
from the trees. "Uncle" Ch'en in an elegant braided gown was
standing before the assemblage, and with a silver-headed stick
he waved me toward a kind of fence stile, a set of wooden steps
leading up to, and down from, a platform. He smiled patronizingly
at me, and with the residue of confused joy in my throat I smiled
back at him. "Ai," he cried, "gentlemen and alley thieves!" The
crowd laughed. "Look at her. Happy child of nature. Strong,
supple, cheery, willing, young . . ." Hooo! A queer sensation. I
felt as I climbed the steps as if I were walking downward into
icy water. "Come forward if you are interested. Inspect. Satisfy
yourselves fully on any purchase you make of 'Uncle' Ch'en, my
jolly boys." Have pity, white God! I was for sale. O God, O God,
if you have any power, but I know that you do not, give me a
bland master. A pair of hands reached round my neck from behind
and loosened the drawstring of my smock, and it was pulled open,
like a pair of curtains. The faces began to swim before my eyes
—grizzled traders, some of them, to be sure, but also many young
men, hardly more than boys, out for a night's adventure. I saw
moisture on lips. My head began to cloud; I thought I would
collapse. "All right! All right! Seats, gentlemen! That's all, that's
all. Down you go, my champions!" The hands were at my throat,
the curtains were drawn, the string was bowed. Then at my very
ear a sudden chanting began in a twangy voice: an auctioneer,
standing beside me and a little behind me, crying me off. I heard
bids pounded on the stone tables with stone blocks in a code of
stone sounds. The auctioneer's voice rose in tone to an operatic

falsetto—a maniac's singing. "Riding high, riding slow, time is short, life is short. Bid her now, now, now, now. The sun high, the sun hot, ride my donkey home tonight. Now. Low moon, cold moon. Bid her now." With each "now" there was a rumble of stone on stone before me. Then suddenly it was over. "Next, next, next," "Uncle" Ch'en was saying. "Move her off of there. Look sharp!" I was given a shove down the steps, and the boy led me back to the jail.

But who had bought me?

(Beyond the Bridge

We were carried out of Twin Hills next day in six open wagons, still in our festival clothes. Bystanders stopped and looked at us, and surely they were thinking: How humane! Not many slaves are treated so well as *that!*

We rode over the canal bridge and two miles into the country. The caravan stopped. We were unloaded. Men stood in a ring around us with pistols in their hands at half cock. We were ordered out of the pretty clothes, and we were tossed old field-hand outfits in exchange; mine was much too big. Our forty-odd men were chained by the wrists, alternating left and right, into two coffles. Ayah, now we knew that we must have been bought by a slave merchant from the terrible outer provinces. Auntie and three other Yen slaves were in our caravan. Mink was not. The empty wagons turned back, and when a wagon loaded with provisions and six yellow men on muleback came along the road from the city, we began to march. We covered fifteen li that day and every day that followed, for twenty-three days. The riders carried bamboo rods. Nights we spent in slave jails, paddocks, godowns, and pens. I wept in Auntie's arms.

BOOK FIVE

Going to the Mountain

([The Sunken Road

I WAS BOUGHT in a small-town slave sale by a man who was out
at the elbows. He turned away after inspecting me, and I saw the
holes in his sleeves and the horny pads of yellow skin over the
sharp bones. He was a young farmer, in his late twenties or early
thirties, thin as a grasshopper.

He told the slave merchant that he was ginning at Sun Lao-
yeh's place, he would have to go back out to his farm for the
money; he would send a hog in later with the cash for the girl, and
to carry her out, he said.

My owner in rags! But his face was like the surface of a lake;
he had bought me at a bargain.

I waited in the packed dirt courtyard of the inn where the merchant had staged his sale. Yellow men came and went, laughing
and cursing; perhaps there was a gambling room inside.

In the afternoon an elderly slave came to fetch me. He was
wearing a woven reed hat which bore a paper notice, written in
inelegant characters:

DO NOT TOUCH THIS HOG
OR TIGER WILL EAT YOU

"Where did you get those filthy bags?" he asked me, looking
scornfully at my clothes. "Hua T'ai-t'ai will give you a gown of
louse bedding." This was the cheapest cotton cloth.

He took me on a two-wheeled cart drawn by a donkey whose ribs showed. My escort sonorously announced his name as Chick Fu-ch'in or Daddy Chick. He boasted about his own trustworthiness. "I don't even have to carry a chit to leave the farm. See this hat?" He tapped the oiled paper on his hat with its warning. "Hua looks out for me." Hua was our owner, apparently the tiger of the hat notice. Daddy Chick made himself sound astonishingly familiar with our master. Daddy Chick said he himself was a number-one fiddler; he was fifty-four, a pious man, he told me. "I never complain. I bear everything. I am a good servant and I am affectionate to others. Hua gives me money and sends me after rice up at the town. They bring the rice in oxcarts from Tsingtao, the rice carters blow horns all night when they camp along the road to scare away the rats. Look, we have rats the size of wonks in Shantung. Listen! Hua lets me carry his money off any day of the year. I came up here with a cash belt stuffed like a meat dumpling to buy you. What's your *name*?" He affected sharp behavior toward me.

Daddy Chick said that the old mistress took the hogs and sows and piglets right into the house. You would think that Jasmine's piglets were her own children!

Hua—he used to be an overseer, Daddy Chick said, quite off-hand. Old Sun, a rich cotton-planter, fathered Hua along and set him up as a farmer. "We," Daddy Chick said, as if he were one of the proprietors, "we have twelve hundred mu of land—not enough. Right now we are picking. Ginning. Baling. Good year this year. Hua is happy as a canary. He hasn't used the bamboo but once in the year, when Lank stole a swine. Lank hid the meat in Grin's k'ang.

"He got you cheap," Daddy Chick said, tossing a glance at me, like a gob of spit, as if to confirm my worthlessness. "Hua is building on a slow plan, ha-ha! Buys a young sow, and maybe she'll have a piglet, one this year, one next year, one, one, one, one. . . ." The old slave's hand chopped out a whole generation of new Hua slaves. "He's young. He can wait. . . . Our Moth is pregnant at the present time."

The country road was like a great continuous ditch; myriad wheels had compressed its bed far below the level of the fields. Once when we were mired Daddy Chick said, "We say around here, 'A daughter-in-law sours at last into a mother-in-law; a road in a thousand years becomes a river.' "

This depressed track was crowded with carts and barrows, and we were forced to stop often. Carters contended in an endless warfare of fake haste; Daddy Chick was insolent to whites and like silk with passing yellows. We pulled out of the ruts at a precarious angle to let a cart pass that was stacked as high as a house with little split-bamboo cages of singing birds. Slaves, their heads shaved shiny, jogged along with heavy loads—of melons, night soil, raw hemp, sesame oil—on shoulder poles, trailing strong smells behind them.

All around us were cotton fields in full fruit, blowing in the dry wind, glorious green seas with a billion whitecaps, flecks of froth, foam, spindrift.

We came to a cornerstone with a lion carved on its head, and Daddy Chick jumped down from the cart, climbed out of the road's gully, and with his hub-oil brush daubed the lion's face, which was already black with carters' oil. This was to propitiate the guardian of the road, in order to ward off accidents. "Ai," my escort said, remounting, "I lost an axle near here last month."

Soon: "Here we are."

In the flooded pits beside the road, from which earth had been taken for the building of the new master's houses, there was now a little congress of his ducks, geese, pigs, children, and slaves' children swimming and playing with an uproar of splashes, giggles, wing flaps, oinks, honks, quacks, and shrieks; a holiday bedlam that jarred on my grief, bewilderment, and weak hope.

Daddy Chick shook his head like a patron at the sight. With a finger cracked and slashed for many years by the brittle dry calyxes of cotton bolls, he pointed at the yellow and white children playing together like brothers and sisters, and he named them for me: "Hua children: Barley Flower, Cart Tongue, Stone, and Little Four. Grin and Jasmine's children: Perfection, Bargain, Tale, and Tender." All were naked, save Perfection, a big girl on whose gently swelling promises a cotton-sack shift glistened, white on white, more immodest than skin.

(A Poor House

This man Hua was barely scraping along—gourd pots and pails in the house. For a broom, to sweep the uneven dirt floor, someone had taken sage twigs and bound them to a buck-thorn stick.

Hua owned, nevertheless, ten souls: Daddy Chick, Grin and Jasmine and their four children, a man named Lank and a girl named Moth, and, now, me.

The main house, made of mud from the pits where I had seen such jubilation, was on the north end of a walled courtyard, and it was a dirty box-shaped hutch of only three "spaces," end to end, a space being so much as could be covered by timbers of a certain length, perhaps twelve feet.

The entrance door was double-leafed, just two worn wide boards hung on pins. Inside the door, in the middle space, was the mud cookstove with its thin metal boiler in the shape of a shallow bowl. Slices of eggplant were sizzling in it, and the house was full of garlicky smoke. Above the range, fat, sooty, and seeming to laugh at man's endless strivings to fill his belly and ease his loins, was Tsao Wang, the kitchen god, on a cheap print tucked in the mud niche.

At the left was the Hua's sleeping area, a huge k'ang spanning the far end, stacked with rolled-up quilts, wooden boxes, baskets of all shapes; upon it, I supposed, the entire family slept.

The third "space" was a work place, with a spinning wheel, a loom, farm implements, jars of grain, carpentering tools, and a bats' cave of miserable hoardings hanging from spikes in the rafters: sieves, scythes, old shoes, an abacus, a teeming wealth of poverty.

Why, this master's house was no better than the slaves' quarters at Yen's!

Six mangy wonks panted and snapped at flies in the shade of the wall in the courtyard.

⟪ Eating All Together

Hua's wife, who was at least fifteen years older than he, took me into the sleeping space and drew out of one of the baskets on the big k'ang a gown of gray louse bedding for me. She said I could use what I was wearing for work in the fields.

My mistress had a deep vertical crease between her eyes; the axe of worry had nicked her unmercifully there.

"Are your bowels clean?" she asked me.

She jogged on her bound feet as if on stubby stilts.

"Turn the eggplant," she said, and my work as a slave began.

Before long Hua and his little force came in from work. They were covered with lint from the ginning, and the man called Lank could not stop sneezing.

The master seemed to me cheerful, sturdy, and phlegmatic. "Where is my sun hat? I'll need it tomorrow." His wife told him, and he got it down from the rafters with a hooked pole.

Daddy Chick, Grin, and Lank all had shaved heads, and I soon learned that men slaves in Shantung, or East-of-the-Mountains, were called, besides pigs, hares, because the words for "bald" and "hare" were homophones. Women slaves, if good breeders, were, I learned, sometimes called rabbits. Perhaps the girl Moth, who was in the early stages of pregnancy, and was apparently unmarried, would be such a one.

The children rushed in, excited, reverberating still with their squeals of the muddy-watered pit, and famished. One warning from the mistress silenced them all. The naked ones, yellow and white alike, were tossed plain shirts that came to their navels.

We ate all at the same time, the Huas with their children sitting cross-legged on their big k'ang, we slaves in the workroom, squatting on our hams. Jasmine kept slapping her smaller ones, Tale and Tender, who were still brimming with giggles, into silence.

In the bustling about in the smoky house, and during the meal, when comments on the day's work were shouted back and forth between spaces, Daddy Chick maintained an uninterrupted flow of affirmation of the yellow man's thoughts and wishes, "Yes, Master! Hai! Imagine! Number-one certain. Yes, yes. Ayah, I believe it. No doubt. Ai, ai! Ha-ha-ha, yes, that's good."

He who on the cart had spoken curtly of Hua-this and Hua-that now seemed quite lacking in any sense of self at all. The master treated him like a shuttlecock to bounce on his heels, and the old man flew into the air at each kick gaily and even eagerly.

The eggplant slices that I had carefully tended were reserved for the master alone.

I had an impression of Hua's wife's strong will. Her voice cut like a cleaver, but I must say she was polite to us all.

"Old Sun's muskmelons are bad this year," the master, maliciously happy, shouted from the distance with his mouth full. "Like round stones."

"Hayah!" shouted Daddy Chick back again. "They are! Ha-ha-ha. That's good, Master! That's wonderful! Like nothing but stones. Did you hear that, Lank?"

Lank, chewing slowly and moistly like a camel, nodded.

⟨ My New Home

After supper we slaves retire to our quarter. If Hua's house seemed poor, ours is dangerous. Upon worm-eaten king and queen posts there hangs over the single room a grid of rotten timbers and rotten purlins holding an enormous weight of sodden earth spread over a matting of kaoliang stalks. When will it crush us? Here there are two k'angs, one for Grin's family, the other for the rest of us. No windows. A moldy smell. A blackened interior which points to a stove whose chimney is built of timber in the body with a funnel of mud stacks.

A cloth hangs down to set aside privacy for Grin's family.

At the very first glance I see a sign of dissension: a shelf with two gourd water buckets and two gourd dippers.

And yes, shortly Moth and Jasmine quarrel, at first over the hanging of a washed gown and then over Tender's urinating on the floor on the wrong side of the cloth drop.

Daddy Chick says, "Be quiet, or I'll get Hua to sell you both."

This warning does not bring anything like peace.

Peace! That word—that name! In the coffle on the way to this place we have heard strange reports. The Empire, following its ancient cycle of unification and disintegration, has begun to divide into two great parts: the core provinces around the Northern Capital, loyal to the gentle dynasty; and the periphery, the lands of the coast and south of the rivers, restive under the central rule with its feminine principles yet at the same time groaning under numerous warlords, each of whom, it is said, whirls on his bed at night in mad dreams of usurpation and coronation. In the Northern Capital, Emperor Ch'ang-lo's early liberalism has been followed by a sudden series of swings from meticulous tyranny to riotous benevolence. We slaves now yearn for the Northern Capital, where, we hear, slaves have been set free! In the most recent flicker of enlightenment, slavery itself has been sentenced to death by a few strokes of a soft brush tracing

Ch'ang-lo's command on the red paper of happiness. And following upon this decree, the white-skinned slaves in the core provinces have been bought from their owners out of the revenue coffers, and they are said to be making their way, though with great difficulty, as a caste of unskilled laborers, servants, and farm hands, beasts of burden but free beasts. Out on the periphery, where I am, we are no less slaves than ever. God with a white face has proved to be of no practical aid to us; prayers to Him fell to the hard ground. I have gathered that the whites in this area are now inclining to yellow idols, yellow kowtowing, yellow incense braziers, yellow rituals, yellow dreams—to yellowness itself, a moiety of which we can, by being raped, achieve. Our life here is the pursuit of a false syllogism: *The yellows are free; we will imitate the yellows and liken ourselves to them; we will be free.* Ha! And I? I am eighteen. Exhausted after the long march in the coffle, huddling in this rude slave shack, I am eager to conform to the yellowing tendency among all the slaves, yet I am also anxious to take my life more into my own hands, if I can.

It is not quite dark. I manage, by the most careful maneuvering, to lie down on the k'ang, where we are going to be rather crowded, between Moth and the place against the back wall reserved for Daddy Chick. Moth has tried to get me to sleep next to Lank, but I suspect that her pregnancy has to do with that proximity, and I appeal to Daddy Chick.

"Sleep next to me, little cat," he says, with a creasing, something like a smile, around his lips in the half light that makes me wonder if I have chosen wisely.

Before the cheap lithograph of Tsao Wang, the kitchen god, plastered above our stove, Daddy Chick kowtows on the dirt floor, and in a singsong like that of a paid supplicator he prays for grace and fortitude to help him and all of us to overcome our trials, and for self-denial, humility, patience, obedience, and, good Tsao Wang, the capacity to forgive.

Lank gives one last sneeze and begins at once to snore. In the doorway Daddy Chick plays, mostly off key, a sad song on his snakeskin-faced Tartar fiddle. When he stops I can hear Grin and Jasmine making the two-backed animal on their earthen bed beyond the cloth drop.

⟮ Moth

We picked in pairs, and Moth, my partner, working along the opposite side of the row from me, taught me what to do. The plants, which lightly interlaced their outer branches across the middles, were nearly as tall as we, and I could see Moth's expression—the face of one who was puzzled by life, yet cheerful; rather stupid, yet wily, too. She had a thin high-pitched voice and a lively interest in accidents, bloodshed, danger.

"Have you ever seen a 'boar'?"

"What is that?"

"Do you not know about the 'boars'?"

"No."

And she explained in an excited voice, holding down its sound so Hua, who was teamed with Perfection three rows away, could not hear her, and poking her face forward among the beautiful splashes of white lint, that "boars" were runaway slaves who lived in groups, like packs of wonks, in the hills and forests. Running away, Moth said, was called "going to the mountain."

"Why mountain?"

"T'ai Mountain."

I had heard, even in South-of-the-River, of T'ai Mountain, the sacred mountain of the eastern provinces, to which pilgrims from all over the Empire made their way in the second month of each year, and where, if he reached it, a runaway slave could not be touched by a yellow hand and could purchase the papers of a freedman and go under safe conduct to the core provinces.

Suddenly, with a sinking spell, a softening of my knees, I saw a picture from the immeasurably distant past—of a Sunday-evening playtime dash across an Arizona courtyard from a hiding place behind a wheel in the pottery shed to "safe home," a diamond space marked with a stick in the dust, and squealing (had the sight of Perfection in her glistening sheath at the mudhole stirred up such a memory?), "Free in! Free in! Free in!"

A sack for the lint I picked from the plants hung by a strap from my neck, its mouth at my breast, its foot bouncing against my feet. I was terrified. My hands were clumsy. Master had assigned me a task, for this first day, of seventy catties—the "standard" for a woman being a picul, or a hundred catties. Moth had whispered with glittering eyes that Hua would beat me with a bamboo rod if I did not complete my task.

"Daddy Chick said Hua had only used the bamboo once this year," I whispered through the branches.

For answer Moth, after glancing on tiptoe over the rows to make sure that Hua was not looking, quickly lifted off the loop of her lint bag and, turning her back to me, suddenly peeled up her louse-bedding gown over her bare back, where I could plainly see many long welts of scar tissue. Swiftly she lowered her dress again and put on her bag, and her fingers flew to the bolls.

Whom was I to believe? How long ago had this happened to Moth? How could I tell how much I had picked?

Hua worked hard! He had struck a gong to waken us in the morning, and he had done chores and had burned paper money and set off firecrackers for Shen Nung, the god of farming, and Ch'ung Wang, god of insects, and T'u Ti, the local constable god, and had been getting out the picking bags and baskets before we even reached the house. Now he and Perfection had finished a row; Moth and I were barely a third done with ours.

I asked, "What is he like?"

"Hua?"

I nodded. (I already thought nothing of our calling this man, who could do anything he wanted with us, plain Hua.)

"One good thing: He never drinks."

"Good. *Never?*"

"Never even sips it. He works hard. You see how he works."

"How can Perfection go so fast?"

"She keeps both hands flying, the little whore. Hua can last us all out. Endurance! I'll tell you something else. He's grateful. If you try hard, he is thankful, very courteous." Then a kind of pout formed at her mouth, and she said, "But he lies, and he can be very cold, very cruel." There was a teasing look in Moth's eyes that confused me. She leaned toward me, parting the branches with her graceful hands. "Masters in East-of-the-Mountains are famous for their cruelty. They cut off noses, use the branding iron, chop off the legs at the knees." Her voice became so confidential as to seem warmly friendly. "I knew a hog, named Fairhead, his master cut his chestnuts out." She stood on tiptoe and looked toward Hua, then leaned forward again, and hissed, "This Fairhead could still do it." Moth giggled, and I lost sight of her as she ducked to pick the lower branches.

Some of the bolls had been blasted by worms; the top crop was touched with dry rot. How long the row already seemed, and the day had scarce begun! At the ends of the rows were the huge split-bamboo baskets, one for each picker, into which we would have to empty our bags many, many times; my sack was not yet full once. The tips of my fingers were getting raw; my neck and upper arms ached.

"Wait," Moth said with a sudden note of tenderness toward me in her voice, "it's not bad. You and I will have a good time over at Old Sun's place some night. Lank's not the only one. There are plenty of nice fat hogs over there. You wait, sweet child. We'll get them to stand up." She made an upthrusting sign of a man's lust with her middle finger, the back of her pretty hand toward me. (But what of the swelling in your belly, Moth?)

"How big a place is that?"

Moth opened her arms in a great arc of immensity and joy. "A hundred slaves," she said, but I could not tell whether she was merely using the round number in the yellows' manner, to express a plenty, such as, "enough for you and me." "Old Sun is rich," she said. "Look!"

On tiptoes yet again, she pointed off across the fields, and, craning myself, I saw a tall structure, and at its peak two great wooden arms reaching down and out in a vast possessive embrace, as if to grasp at the whole countryside, even at us. These were the turning arms of Old Sun's cotton press. Moth said the old miser allowed Hua, who could not yet afford a gin and press, to store and process his crop on the big place; the old turtle, posing as Hua's bene-factor, extorted one bale in ten for this "kindness." We would carry our pickings over to the Sun place at the end of the day and put them in Hua's lint stall. Then, said Moth, I'd see some of those fat hogs over there. "Ayah!" sighed Moth, as though the service of those delightful pigs at Sun's were a heavy, heavy burden.

When the sun stood high, Hua's wife, with Barley Flower, Cart Tongue, Stone, Little Four, Bargain, Tale, and Tender milling around behind her like puppies, brought food and water out to the field on a slide pulled by the skin-and-bones donkey Daddy Chick had used the day before to cart me out from the district town.

I noticed this: Hua's wife treated Jasmine as something like a beloved friend, but toward Moth she was stiff, reserved, and

even hostile. If I was to get on the good side of the mistress, I
could see that I must not be intimate with Moth—at least, in
Hua's wife's presence.

When we went back to picking, I brazenly asked Moth whom she
would claim as the father of her baby.

The only answer I got was tinkling laughter. I could not see
Moth's face; she was low on a plant.

Shortly afterward she said fiercely, "Be careful! You are breaking some of the branch ends. Old turtle Hua will beat you dead."

But she meant no harm. Soon she was joking and giggling
again. She was like an autumn day, when a brisk wind blows
little rainless clouds rapidly across the face of the sun; the bright
intervals are warm but somehow melancholy, for the summer is
surely over.

Each boll had four or five compartments. I had for a few moments after the meal seen Perfection's deft fingers pluck out the
entire contents of a boll at a time with a single snatch of either
hummingbird hand, and she kept the lint, as she pulled it out,
quite free of the trash of the dried calyxes. I had frequently to
pick several times at a boll to empty it, and Moth told me that it
took ninety to a hundred good bolls to make a catty. I was often
on the edge of tears. What kind of life was this?

"Tell me more about the boars," I said.

"Ai, they're filthy, like badgers. Sometimes they hide around
Limestone Hill Generous Temple, I've seen some of them there.
They want salt and kaoliang. Some hogs steal fowl or cuts of pork
from their masters and slip it to them at the temple. Why, they
live in caves, ten, twelve, twenty together."

"Are they ever caught?"

"Ai, those turtles are hard on slave-hunters. You see, they all
have knives, and some even have guns they've stolen. You know
what they do?" Again Moth was leaning forward, her confidential
mouth a blossom among the leaves. "They stab the slave-hunters'
wonks and"—her voice fell to a harshly aspirated whisper—"*they
skin them and eat them.* That's what Lank says."

"Do you believe Lank?"

"Ainh, he's harmless."

"Is he the father of your baby?"

The face withdrew from the bower of cotton leaves; no giggle
this time; no temper, either.

"Two months ago the boars raided a farm five li from here,

Big Cheng's place—and they stole three sows." Moth waited. "I
mean slave women, sweet child."

"Would you like to live like that?"

"Ayah, don't even think about it. This is a cleaner life, child."

"Moth."

"What?"

"Is Hua the father?"

This time the silvery laughter ended in an explosive obscenity.

"You ask questions like a virgin, small baby."

"I'm not."

"Who is?"

"Why did you call Perfection a whore?"

"Oh, no, dearest! Don't take Moth seriously."

(Storing the Lint

In the evening we jogged with the baskets of lint on
shoulder poles, teaming in pairs to carry pairs of baskets, through
fields of cotton, kaoliang, millet, melons and squashes, sweet
potatoes, hemp, and sesame, to the big place. I was terrified,
because my basket held so much less than anyone else's.

What prosperity we came upon! Everything built of bricks. The
outer wall of the workshop yard brightly decorated with patterns
of brick and painted plaster. Glints of china and glass at the
crown of the wall, to keep out robbers for sure. The wonks fat
and glossy-coated. Carts with well-greased hubs. Slaves in uniform
tunics and pants.

The storage godown was next to the gin house—a brick structure on stilts, where, underneath, a pair of blindfolded mules
went round and round, turning the cogged iron pinion of the gin,
while men slaves, above, fed in the raw lint, and others, at the
foot of the chutes, bagged the clean cotton, and the seeds, and the
trash. I was ashamed of my foul slave-trader's clothing. We went
in the godown. The master weighed the baskets. My yield was
less than fifty catties; my heart pounded.

Hua turned to me, with a mild and even gentle expression, and
asked, "Have you picked cotton before, child?"

"Never." I could barely hear my own voice.

"You must do better."

So much for my beating! I glanced at Moth, and I was unable

to suppress a titter at her mischievous expression. At this Hua gave me a deep look, of interest rather than reproach, which chilled me to the spine.

Hua, Lank, and Grin emptied their baskets into the bins reserved for my master's crop, and we left for home. I felt elated at having been let off so easily, and at the light weight of the empty baskets. We trotted. Crossing the courtyard I looked up once more at the gin, and there, on the highest platform, feeding raw lint into the chutes, wearing a clean uniform of the Sun force, stood a man who seemed to me to be Peace.

I tripped and fell. The shoulder pole broke. One of the baskets struck the backs of Moth's legs, and she turned and shrilly cursed me.

From my crouch on hands and knees I looked up at the big man, who, with a bare head, bright-eyed and relaxed, was raucously laughing at my clumsiness.

(The Oil Brush

Day after day, row after row, boll after boll after boll, I could think of nothing save that man laughing on the dizzying platform.

I had the impression—perhaps because of the height, the foreshortening—that this man was not quite so huge as I remembered Peace to have been; that he was not gap-toothed, but seemed to have a full set of unclean teeth; that the scar on the brow, with the look it had given of displeased astonishment, had faded, and so had the prophet's stare; the shaggy braided cone of hair had given way to a shiny clear-shaven pate. The face, against the evening sky, with a glow of the sun on it, had been sly, canny, cynical, selfish, ruthless—all that a slave's face should be. I melted at the thought of it. On the k'ang at night I felt illuminated like a lantern; once I awakened from desire-fuming sleep with my cheek against a hard rib cage, and I pressed myself to it, only to start up with shame and disgust—Daddy Chick. Moth's suggestive talk stirred me to lewd answers such as I had never given. I was apt to swing my hips right before Hua's eyes. I stroked the fur of flea-bitten wonks with great tenderness. All the time, at every moment, I was thinking of that figure on the gin-house platform.

My life was unquestionably horrible. I was eighteen—ready for harvest. Except for flashing thoughts, in moments of utmost frustration and rage, of "the mountain," there was no hope of any kind in my world. I was in a frame of mind, like all the slaves around me, to take what I could from each rotten hour as it passed.

Several days passed before I saw him again. We had filled Hua's lint bins, and it was time for a day of ginning and baling. When we went to work that morning, the man I had seen was in the squad of four Sun slaves detailed to make sure that Hua's worthless riffraff, as Old Sun regarded us, did not ruin his beautiful cotton press.

When I first noticed him he was again on a raised platform, brushing vegetable oil onto the massive wooden screw of the cotton press. He was singing, but he seemed surly. I saw him dust off a fellow Sun slave who tried to joke with him. But when I caught his eye for the first time, he immediately lost his footing and mockingly sprawled on the loading platform at the top of the long oblong box of the press; he threw his arms around the screw as if to save himself. It was all to make fun of me for the fall I had taken in the courtyard that day. I could not, however, catch him looking at me for a long time afterward. But at last I did. From then on my eyes were often on him, and he knew it.

I was assigned with Grin to the task of laying out the strips of hemp bagging at the foot of the press, to be wrapped up over the bales after the landscape-grasping wooden arms, moved by blindfolded mules on a circular track, had driven down the huge wooden screw and packed the feathery ginned lint into a hard hexahedron. And with a huge curved steel needle and hemp string I swiftly sewed the edges of the sacking while Grin made fast the ropes that kept the bales confined. (Pompous Duke at Yen's had said I "would not do" as the terrible Matriarch's seamstress! But look at me now!)

I had had the sense to rip my slave-trader's bags, as if accidentally, one day, beyond repair, so I could wear my louse-bedding gown. Now my self-conscious body moved freely in the clinging sheath.

Grin was obsessed with hunting. Hua loaned him his awkward, heavy gun, from time to time, to shoot rabbits, weasels, and ground foxes, which Hua's wife cooked for all of us to eat. In the manner of limited men with one-track minds, Grin could remember, and gladly recited, every detail of every pursuit in his entire

life, and now, as we waited for the huge screw to worm down, he
was telling me about a certain weasel whose habits he had studied
in a long, patient, delicious savoring of the moment when he
would finally shoot it—how it would slink along the edge of the
upper kaoliang field, pause in the shade of the lion-headed marker
beyond the irrigation well that we called Big Lizard, and dart
toward the duck run with its low mud-brick wall. On and on Grin
went with his tedious working out of his perverted lust—until,
suddenly, an interruption came to my relief.

The tung-oil brush, with which the man on the platform had
been lubricating the squeaking ridges of the male wooden screw,
fell directly at my feet.

"Hai! Turtle! Down there! Throw me up my brush." These
shouts were addressed to Grin, but I had already bent down and
snatched up the brush, and I looked up, to see the shouter leaning
over the edge of his platform. Hua was in the gin house at the
time.

When he saw the brush in my hand, the man unveiled his dirty
teeth in a smile that made me wonder whether he had dropped the
brush at my feet on purpose. "Ayah," he called, "there's little Fall-
Down. Throw it up to me, you sweet little sow. Let's see if you can."

I shook the brush at him, in a little threat. What a glorious man
he was! He had all the power of a Peace who had shed, as a locust
sheds its taut waxy skin, the saintly, ascetic, dedicated stiffness
that had made him so untouchable, unreachable; and he had
Nose's abandoned, disenchanted air without the awful melancholy
of those bloodshot eyes; and Arizona Gabe's fresh, unspoiled physical strength, too. But there was a new quality, close to the surface,
visible in his frank face and manner, a trait which seemed to me
perfect in a slave—utter selfishness.

I coiled myself, with the brush hanging down from my fist behind my back, to try to throw it up to him on the platform, knowing in advance, with a warmth of inner laughter, that I would fail.
But before I could unwind he sharply shouted down, "Watch out!
Don't trip yourself! Be careful! Don't fall down!"

Now I was laughing out loud. I threw the brush. It arose end
over end but had not half the force it needed; it plopped against
the box of the press, leaving a fan-shaped stain of oil on the dry
wood, and fell again to the ground.

The slave on the platform guffawed, and so did the other Sun

slaves. Grin joined in, but faintheartedly. Moth, feeding Grin and
me sacking from a heap in the corner, slapped my rump in playful
rebuke.

"Try again, little Fall-Down! Throw it again."

I ran and picked up the brush. Now all work had stopped in the
press as everyone, with cheerful face, leaned to watch. The great
screw groaned; Lank was outside leading the mules. I bent even
lower than before and let the brush fly; it went higher this time
but arched far away from the platform.

Everyone laughed. "Ayah, what a dangerous sow!" the man on
the platform called out. The other Sun men up there with him
roared and punched each other.

I ran again for the brush. I laughed as I ran. I was tightening
myself for the greatest pitch of all when I sensed a sudden silence,
renewed activity. I straightened. Hua was standing directly behind me, his face a typhoon edge. "What game is this?" he roared.
I was astonished at this mild, henpecked yellow man's sudden
fatherly severity. Daddy Chick, who had apparently come into the
press with our owner, stepped around him toward me and took
the oil brush out of my hand and looked up toward the platform.
"Who was using this?"

My teaser pointed at the man beside him and gravely said, "Bark
is the one who oils the screw."

"All right, man," Daddy Chick said, "come down the ladder and
get it."

The hog called Bark snapped his fingers in my man's face, but
willingly, with a stylized agility in the manner of yellow-trained
slave acrobats, he spilled down the ladder, took the brush from
Daddy Chick, made an ironic little kowtowing crouch to him, and
squirreled up the ladder again.

Hua, in the meantime, had moved facing me. He gave me,
again, that deep look of curiosity, of interest, that was far more
harrowing than chastisement.

For an hour we were all strenuous, servile, engrossed. At last
we became more natural in our timing, and everyone was chattering, and I asked Grin, "That Sun pig with the oil brush—what's
his name?"

"That's Dolphin."

"Is he troublesome?"

"Look, child, that man is bad-disposed. Lank says he's probably
going 'wild' one of these days."

" 'Wild'? To the mountain, you mean?"

"Hold your tongue," Grin said in a low voice. Daddy Chick was walking toward the base of the press, not far from us. "You stupid little sow," Grin said, when Daddy Chick had moved out of hearing again, "you can kill a man with your loose mouth."

But I was not frightened by Grin. I was wondering: Would Dolphin *always* be on platforms? My heart was still dancing; laughter still pressed at my throat. For the first time in my slave life I had a clear-cut goal.

¶ An Old Uncle

An old uncle, a distant relative of our mistress, from a nearby village, was always hanging about the Hua house and courtyard. For a yellow man he was a pathetic figure, nervous and irritable, dry-skinned, a kind of beggar, one of those worthless derelicts of whom it is apt to be whispered, to account for their broken spirits, "He was disappointed in love when he was young, and he has never been the same since." Such was not, in fact, his disappointment, but another, as I learned to my benefit one market day.

I was idling alone in the courtyard, surrounded by the Huas' pack of wonks. These mud-caked, scurfy dogs, who usually slunk about with their bushy tails between their legs, dodging cloth-shoed kicks, their eyes alert for flying stones, had, ever since this selfish Dolphin had dropped an old oil brush at my feet, seemed to me touching creatures, themselves something like slaves: the smallest sign of kindness raised their hopes to the skies. Old Uncle came into the courtyard. As usual recognizing this visitor as a fellow outcast, the dogs swirled about his legs, fanning the air with their tails, and he, poor man, feeling that even curs were against him, tried to drive them off. The dogs took his feeble thrashings for loving play, and they frisked all the more.

I had learned how to calm them with a sedative clucking sound, and I did, drawing them off Old Uncle. He was as grateful for friendliness as one of them, and he began to chat with me.

Soon he and I were seated side by side on the beam of a harrow, and somehow our random talk settled on Daddy Chick, and I happened to speak of the "touch-hog–tiger-eat" sign on the old slave's hat that he wore on errands to town, and Old Uncle, with a sigh that seemed to come from the bottom of a water well, nodded and said he had written it for Hua.

I remembered the crudeness of the characters on the hat sign. "Forgive me," I said, "I did not know you could write so beautifully."

"Do not have the air of a guest," Old Uncle said. "Write? Hai!" As a boy he had been chosen by his family to be a scholar, he said. Scholarship, as I knew, was the path to yellow power and influence, because civil servants and officials of the Emperor's court were chosen by competitive literary examinations. He had applied himself, he said, and he had "soared like a hawk." He had memorized the great classics and had combed and caressed the art of essay writing. "I was the highest of seventeen selected from four hundred after the terrible four-day examinations at the perfectural town. Out of two hundred perfectural survivors I stood fourteenth in the examinations at Tsinan, the provincial city. The examinations lasted a fortnight. The hall was dark, and when it rained the roof leaked onto our essays. Four scholars died of cholera at their desks. One man, after writing for eighteen hours, stood up for a moment to stretch his limbs and for this the literary chancellor beat him a hundred blows on his brush hand, and his characters then showed the pain, and of course he failed. In four years I passed the grades of *hs'iu-ts'ai, lin-sheng, kung-sheng.* I wore a brass button on my hat, and I was entitled to a semi-official robe and a title of respect. Then as a Selected Man I went to the Northern Capital for the ministerial examinations. The morning essay was on a theme from Mencius, 'Like climbing a tree to catch a fish.' I was aflame with ideas. The characters flew off my fingers like crickets. I would be a minister of the third rank, the second rank, I knew it. I had come from an East-of-the-Mountains village, and I was going to live in honored robes in the Forbidden City—I *knew* it. My poem in the five-character meter—the sounds, the tones, the meanings were all interwoven like brocade! I transcribed exquisitely a passage, as required, from the *Sacred Edicts.* Midnight was the deadline; I finished just after the last quarter-hour gong. I went back to my lodgings and slept twelve hours. I was not afraid. I knew I was among the best. We had to wait two days. Then all the candidates went to the Examination Halls and waited and waited. At last they 'hung the boards.' Of fifteen who passed, my name was fifteenth. I thought I would die with joy. I drank wine until I could not see. It cost me eight thousand cash to send a messenger to my father's house in East-of-the-Mountains Province with the strip of red paper announcing to him that his son had achieved all that he wished. I had six hundred Joyful Announcements printed from woodcut blocks, proclaiming that I had placed fifth—everyone who passed exaggerated, most announced they had come out first. At the very moment I was paying for my lodgings to leave for home, where I would wait for my high appointment, whatever it might be, an Imperial constable came for me, and he took me before the literary chancellor, and that official announced to me that I had committed a terrible crime—cheating against His Imperial Blessedness. Not only had my name been removed from the boards, he said, but also all my ranks, down to *hs'iu-ts'ai*, were stripped from me, at the Emperor's command. All my work, all, all, all! I felt that I was in the grip of a nightmare, then the dream turned to utter madness. My protests were disallowed, and I was thrown out into the street like one of these yellow dogs. My repeated appeals for hearings were turned away. I could not believe this calamity. How could I go home to my father? I lost my appetite. I never slept. I became as thin as a leper, and I shuddered and shivered morning and evening. I knocked daily at the chancellor's gates, and always the watchmen set on me with staves. Then by accident, after four years of this deranged life, I learned what had happened. The youth who had stood sixteenth, just behind me, on the examinations, and so had not passed, was a son of a rich Northern Capital merchant, and it was he who had brought the accusation and the "proofs." Now. Do you know the world? I'll tell you something. Some scholars did cheat. Oh, come, you little sow, did you think every magistrate was a pure scholar? Look, there were three good plans. First: the 'little-box' plan—the candidate padded his white silk vest with prepared essays. They were written on small sheets in fly-eye characters, you had to be keen to see them! Or carried them into the examination in a false bottom in the basket of provisions he could take into the hall. Second plan, 'coin-honor.' Buy essays from essay brokers. You could smell those men, they were like pimps—got posts as inspectors in the hall for the literary chancellor by graft. Third plan, 'transmission.' Ayah, this was sporting! Theme is assigned. Subject is thrown over wall to courier. Courier runs to eminent scholar outside. Scholar writes essay. Courier wads it carefully. Runs to wall. Gives signal—dog barking, or maybe peddler's drum with a certain beat. Throws wad over. Inspector catches. Enters hall. Drops at candidate's feet in passing. Candidate copies. But listen, little sow. Those vultures picked my bones dry! I had 'entered' honestly! I had never experienced such inspiration as during the examination! I was innocent! I was not a cash scholar! The young number sixteen, the failure just behind me, who would replace me if I could be eliminated, had gathered 'witnesses': inspectors who could be bribed to sell essays could be bribed to slander. Even the literary chancellor had spoken against me and had ridden in a new carriage within a month. Ayah, listen, little sow, life is a cheat. Evil men connive against good men. It is all useless. Utterly useless. You are a slave, small sow. You know what I am saying. Don't you, now? Don't you?"

A desiccated yellow hand patted mine, and silt-laden tears were flowing like the Yellow River down the dirty leathery cheeks, but I had a conviction that the old man had in fact cheated on every one of his examinations, from district town to Imperial Capital—how he had *relished* telling the three "plans"!—if, indeed, he had ever been a scholar at all.

Yet my mind was racing. I saw a chance, and I knew its value.

I asked the broken old man some questions to keep him prattling and, idly, as he talked, I took up a stick and scratched in the dust right at his feet the three-peaked character *shan,* "mountain," which Smart had traced deeply into the cinders of my mind in the blacksmith shop at Yen's:

$$山$$

Old Uncle's eyes fell on this meaning in the dust, and I thought I saw a flicker of surprise—but perhaps he thought that I had simply chanced upon the shape of this rather symmetrical character. I therefore drew then one of the marvelously expressive characters, *ma,* for "horse," mane flying, feet in motion, full tail swept downward.

$$馬$$

The old man stood up, his hands spread and patting the air as if to press down two impossibilities in one. This from a woman and a slave!

I looked up into his eyes, and I whispered, in tones halfway between those of an imploring child and those of a seducer, "Will you be my teacher?"

He sat down hard on the tongue of the harrow, and I thought he would begin again to weep. To be a master of the classics! For one who had gone for so many years from gate to gate of distant relatives to eke out a millet cake here and a bowl of bean curd there—to teach!

Swiftly there passed across the old uncle's face, like the shadow of a crow flying between him and the honest sun, a brief look of such hate-laden craftiness that I was all the more convinced that he had been a many-year fraud; but at once he mastered this look of self-betrayal. "We will have to get Hua's wife on our side," he said, speaking secretively and looking over his shoulders.

Thus in one sentence he took cognizance of the strict laws against teaching slaves, of the basic gentleness of my mistress's nature, of Hua's rigidity, of the illiteracy of both master and mistress, of his own mendicant caution, of his passionate desire for a revenge on society, and of a sow's best chance for safety in cheating the yellows.

And so we worked up yet another "plan."

(Hua's Wife

It took us three weeks to win Hua's wife. We proceeded against her by what the old uncle called the "patient rice" method. "He has the longest meal who eats one grain at a time." Act by rice-grain act, I gained her trust. Obeisance by minute obeisance, the old uncle reinforced her pity of him.

Hua's wife was a sturdy woman who, had she not lived in a slave economy, might have been a kind soul. Like her husband, she worked long hours, striving to rise above both self-pity and an ugly marginal life. I learned that her being more than a decade older than Hua was not remarkable; generally in Shantung wives were older than husbands. (Perhaps the Great Plague had taken more men than women from the province.) This difference in age put a strain on her vanity and on her husband's temptations—I had seen that look of interest in his eyes. Hua's wife was outwardly subservient, compliant, obedient, yet she steered him as surely as if he were a plow. She smoked a brass-bowled pipe. Her feet had been well bound (i.e., ferociously)—and she bore her ambulant pain and their great "beauty" with an excess of pride. This, from the beginning, was her triumph over me—my enormous feet like dirty river sampans. Stray wisps of her stringy hair, which was supposed to be fastened in a bun behind, fell across her face, and a thousand times a day she shoved the tickling strands aside with the back of her hand.

I was careful. Moth was my friend in the fields, but I shunned her in the house. I flattered Jasmine, Hua's wife's favorite, who was fond of herself. I put a strict end to the exultant swinging of my hips before men, before Hua himself, that thoughts of Old Sun's Dolphin had induced.

At last I found out something surprising: that Hua's wife, too, wanted her revenge on life. When the old uncle asked permission to teach me some characters, on the grounds of giving him one last reason for being alive and giving me the capacity to keep Hua's planting and harvesting records (he having heard from the pigs, he told her, that I had already some rudimentary reading and writing), she responded by joining the conspiracy—we would trick her husband; he should not know of the lessons until the girl was ready to be useful. I wondered, all of a sudden, how much she despised him.

So we began a regime of carefully scheduled meetings. Every trip Hua took to the district town was an occasion for a visit from the old uncle and for my being assigned to some "miserable work" on the loom or the wheel, while the other slaves were in the fields, for Hua's wife thought it best to keep my lessons from the other pigs, for fear they might be envious of me (and perhaps betray her to her deceived husband).

For me, the thrills of a minor subversion!—to say nothing of the pure joy of preparing myself for a larger one. Among the yellows, learning meant power. I would never have power, but only by means of this wealth could I diminish, at least, my utter weakness.

And my sips of the wonderful texts: *The Four-Hundred-Names Classic! The Thousand-Character Classic,* in which not a single word was repeated! *The Analects, Great Learning, The Doctrine of the Happy Mean!*

The old uncle possessed the books, he brought them strapped to his thin chest under his gown. His method at first was to tease me with a glimpse at each masterpiece, then he started me on the more solid work of memorization. It was astonishing how much he himself could remember, and although I was convinced that most human beings cheated their way through an unfair world, I could not explicitly tell whether Old Uncle had used "plans" to get through his examinations.

He was in a way a fine teacher—he was *enthusiastic*. The promises he made for my future! *The Classic of Filial Piety! Songs! The Book of Changes! Springs and Autumns!*

But I was too excited and almost spoiled it all. With Hua's wife's knowledge I practiced writing in secret, whenever there was a chance, and one day I left my inkblock lying on the dirt floor beside the loom. Hua found it. Deeply stung perhaps because of his own illiteracy, he rooted around among us like an enraged wounded wolf; he asked each slave many questions. I denied everything, but I felt that my uncontrollable trembling gave me somewhat away.

"If I ever catch you with a book, you filthy sow, or with an ink block and a brush, I'll give you five hundred strokes of the heavier bamboo. I'll cut you in two with it. I'll have no pigs learning characters on my place! If you give a hog the span of your hand he'll steal the whole distance to the horizon. Don't try to learn in my house, you turtle-spawning."

Hua's wife moved calmly about while the farmer screamed at me. Her poise was terrifying. What treachery! Wearily she swept the ends of hair from her face and said, "That baby sow hasn't the brains to learn. I'm sick of her. Get her out of here."

At once Hua puffed up his cheeks and then blew out the air— and with it, one felt, his rage.

"It is probably Old Uncle's inkblock," I heard Hua's wife placidly say as I was leaving. "He is losing his mind, the poor old 'magistrate.'" This, in honor of his famous failure, is what people called the old uncle behind his back.

"I'll give that louse-bitten beggar the toe of my foot where he won't lose it," Hua said, suddenly recovering his bad temper.

◖ At Limestone Hill Generous Temple

The eighth day of the twelfth month was set aside by the yellows for worship, and Hua gave leeway to his slaves to go to Limestone Hill Generous Temple.

In the slave hut Daddy Chick praised our master for his liberality. "He is an old-pious," he said. "I know slaves here and there who have to put their heads in jars in order to pray."

"Ayah," said Lank in a cautious low voice, "you forever suck the master's tit, Daddy Chick. When will you learn that it's dry?"

I walked with Moth. The temple was on a hill six or seven li from Hua's farm. The sunny day was chilly but not as cold as some we had already had. Hua's wife had supplied me with a quilted cotton tunic and trousers and a set of ankle bands. Along the road Moth and I were noisy. Daddy Chick said from his rearguard position that our cackling was objectionable—it was the kind of behavior that would give the whites a bad name.

"Pigs," Grin said, meaning we already had one.

I enjoyed Moth. In the fields we were fast friends, and she accepted as a matter of course my being cold to her in the presence of Hua's wife. She took delight in talking about Dolphin, sometimes teasing me and sometimes gravely coaching me in his seduction. With a fickle, undependable, arrogant man like him, Moth said, the best strategy was to alternate throwing oneself at him and scorning him. Stir up a cloud of dust!

We had finished picking and ginning, and Hua had twenty-eight bales; a good year, he counted it. The last few days we had been picking in the early mornings with frost on the bolls. My fingers had cracked open and bled. The men had kept a small fire of trash going in the fields, and when Moth and I had been unable to stand our tender fingers any longer we would run and warm our hands awhile. Some days on the way out we had stolen turnips and when no one was looking had slipped them in the coals and on trips to the fire we had stirred them out and taken hasty bites of the hot black-encrusted turnip flesh.

We could see the temple ahead on a hill scarred on one side by a quarry from which farmers took limestone for their fields; two or three commonplace buildings within a wall. The exalted feature of the temple compound, as seen from the roadway, was an enormous weeping beech tree, which must have been hundreds of years old. It seemed to brood with animate sorrow over the follies of the temple—over the false promises given by idols and the credence given them by men and women with only a moment's trot to death.

Looking at the tree, I was suddenly frightened by the flimsiness of the high spirits I had been enjoying—reading and writing would only earn me whip wales on my skin, and if for an unlikely moment I should catch selfish Dolphin he would slip from my grasp to that of another woman or to the mountain from which no slave returned.

Yet when we climbed the hill and I saw, as we approached more closely, knots of slaves idling outside the temple walls—chatting, gambling, boxing, for all the world like the carefree groups at Yang's tea-water well in the Northern Capital long before the oaths were sworn over the chalk circle—and when I noticed several men in the uniforms of Old Sun's force, my cheerfulness returned with an actual physical surge, like a pang of acute hunger; I rejected the weeping beech, as it were. I saw Dolphin! He was waving his arms at some summit of narration, and he was wearing bright red trousers. Of the tactics Moth had urged on me, I quickly chose, for this day, the far easier: throwing myself at his feet.

We of Hua's went inside to worship. This temple, crowded now with both yellows and slaves, was shabby. Gilt and paint were peeling from some of the divine images. We were herded into the special enclosure for slaves, behind a wooden partition taller than men, so that worshipping yellows would not have to look at us. The priests and monks considered us slaves a nuisance; we had no coppers to spend on incense or paper money to be burned to the idols. A sweet smell of burning punk hovered in our slaves' box.

I was floating in a strange many-leveled mood: impatient to be finished with our worship so I could go out to Dolphin; stung by the disdainful droning of the yellow-robed yellow monk with his wheel of supplications praying for us pigs from a platform in our enclosure; frightened and awed by the grotesque figures of all sizes looming before us in an array of divinities banked up to the very roof beams of the dirty building; inclined to skepticism but prudently hedging my doubts with kowtows and murmured requests to certain gods that I thought I could trust; filled with vivid feelings of youth, eagerness, receptivity, fervor; aware, as if of a weight on my back, of the huge mournful tree resting its arms on the tiles over my head.

How transparent the monk's warnings! We must remember that Yü Huang, the Jade Emperor, was the author of slavery and the protector of the obedient. That Confucius (a tuft of the philosopher-idol's horsehair beard had fallen away, leaving a sore of pitted clay in the compassionate face) taught the duty, above all others, of respect. That running away was an offense concretely against the San Kuan, the three causes, rulers of heaven, earth, and water; that the T'u Ti, the local constable god, would punish runaway slaves; that the hog's hard hands and white skin were marks of the displeasure of the three mythical emperors, Fu Hsi, Shen Nung, Huang Ti.

And I? I struck my forehead on the brick floor in honor of many-armed Tou Mu, the goddess of the North Star, who was said to have a kind heart for the sufferings of humanity and could lead a slave to the mountain, and to certain of the Niang-Niang, the woman goddesses, who granted babies and protected a woman's eyes and gave her regular periods, and to Ch'ung Wang, god of insects, praying that he would send blights and worms to Hua's crops.

While Moth and I were in the very act of kowtowing, close beside each other, she nudged me with her elbow and whispered, "That's enough. Let's go."

We slipped out together, knowing that Daddy Chick would stay in the enclosure bowing and murmuring for nearly an hour.

We walked straight toward Dolphin's circle. Moth had her eye on a Sun hog named Quart. "When a man has a big nose," Moth had said to me one day, talking of Quart, "you can be sure he has other big things, too."

When we had gone about half the distance to the group a slave woman stepped in our path whose appearance made me grasp Moth's upper arm. Her hair was matted, her face was long unwashed, her quilted jacket and trousers were torn and the filthy padding within was leaking out, so she seemed a frightful old stuffed doll that was losing its insides. But worst of all were her eyes, which had a piercing stare so like the prophetic one that Yen's Peace had used to have that I immediately began to tremble. She was, I knew, a witch woman, a follower, in the face of strict prohibitions by the yellows in our province, of our old white-faced Jehovah. One or two of these fanatical witch women were forever lurking around temples rebuking the rest of us for accepting yellow gods, abusing us, laying down spells on us; stirring in us, for all their absurdity, disquieting echoes of past beliefs and fears.

The woman, her eyes glittering, said, " 'And I saw three unclean spirits like frogs come out of the mouth of the dragon, and out of the mouth of the beast, and out of the mouth of the false prophet . . .' "

"Seven, eleven, go to heaven," Moth said in the old language of the whites, to drive the witch out of our path.

"Erh-lang will bite your arse," I said, using one of the yellows' exorcising curses, in the name of the Jade Emperor-god's nephew, who was in charge of ghosts and spirits.

Moth and I both sounded lighthearted, and we crowded past the awful woman. All the same, she had, like a whirling wind, lifted up a flying funnel of fallen leaves inside me. Slavery had long since seemed a triumph of the yellows' many idols over the whites' one God, and in the temple, shut away behind a wooden wall, even as I kowtowed, I had felt, through a deep unease and dissatisfaction, the essential hostility of the yellow-faced figures towering over me. On the one side of the wooden fence the yellows were thanking these figures for keeping things as they were; on the other the whites were pathetically begging for change. For a moment I yearned for the deity of my dim, distant, tranquil Arizona pillow:

> *Jesus, friend to little children,*
> *Be a friend to me!*

But I saw Dolphin ahead, and all that distress promptly went under the surface.

There were now about twenty slaves in Dolphin's group, both men and women. They were standing a few paces from the lip of the limestone quarry. A thicket of juniper bushes and scrub pine straggled off down the hill behind the temple. There were other clumps of slaves all around the compound—so many!

Moth and I pushed our way into the group, until she was beside Quart and I was next to Dolphin; my shoulder jarred against his arm, and he looked down at me.

"What's going on?" I asked him.

"Ayah, it's little Fall-Down!" he said, and he put an arm around my waist and pulled me to his flank, tucking me under his armpit. I could feel the hardness of his chest through his quilts and mine. "Have you learned how to walk yet?"

"Have you learned how to hold on to an oil brush?" I put on as impertinent a face as I could manage.

Dolphin laughed, but then he turned his attention away from me and back to the exchanges of the group. Dolphin, Quart, and three or four other men were arguing about something or other.

Dolphin kept his arm around me but seemed to have forgotten that I was there.

Shortly a hog of the Sun force pushed his way into the group, which was growing all the time as the quarreling voices rose to a louder and louder pitch, and he tapped Dolphin on the far arm and whispered in his ear. Dolphin grunted, removed his arm from my waist, and started to turn away. Then, apparently as an afterthought, he turned back, swung his arm over my head, and pulled me with him in an embrace. "Come on, baby," he gruffly said. "Something a little sow ought to see to help her grow up."

So, tightly held, I was swept along across a hump of the hill into a smaller band of slaves, perhaps six men and three women, who were standing at the edge of the low-lying thicket of evergreens. When Dolphin came up some of the others exchanged with him several rapid whispers. I heard Dolphin ask, "Where?" A woman made a motion with her head and eyes, indicating that whatever they were discussing lay hidden within the thicket. "Let's go," Dolphin said.

One, two, or three at a time, the slaves in the little party broke off, with looks up the hill toward the back of the temple to make sure no one was watching, and ducked into the cover of the pines. Dolphin released me, but when he started in, he flapped his hand, commanding me to follow him.

Fifty paces within the thicket we came on the others. They were standing in a circle next to a large juniper bush, and when I took my place beside Dolphin in the ring I saw the object of the quest.

On his hands and knees, taking cover under the bush, was a beast of a white man—bearded, long-haired, tattered, foul, thin, and hollow-eyed. Yet at his lip curled a smile and in his eyes lurked a jewel-light so serene, so contemptuous of all of us, that I suddenly felt a catch at my throat and found that I was weeping—for what? For this miserable fortunate man? For all of us? For slaves? For myself—noticed by Dolphin but not really seen by him? For worshippers, idolaters, God's witch women, anyone who hoped for anything?

Dolphin reached under his quilted jacket and pulled out three cakes of millet bread and tossed them on the ground between the boar's hands. Another slave reached down with a flitch of bacon. A third placed a small earthen jar, presumably of salt, on the ground. A fourth undid his waistband and, reaching down into his trousers as if to scratch his private parts, instead pulled out with a guttural laugh a cloth bag of flour that had been hanging within from his cinch; holding up his pants with one clutching hand, he put down the small sack with the other.

The boar's dirty claws scooped up the pieces of bread that Dolphin had tossed on the ground, and settling back on his hams the wild free man began to gnaw at one of the hard cakes. His hunger was like a dog's. He trembled as he ate. We waited until he had finished one of the cakes. Then three of the men, including Dolphin, knelt and murmured confidentially with him. He nodded. Under the ferocious, wild, unkempt outer face of the boar there was a look, which tortured me to the edge of tears again, of intelligence, tranquillity, and compassion for us who were slaves.

We left him there. Perhaps Dolphin and the others had planned future rendezvous with him. We emerged by the temple, and I rejoined Moth.

Walking home, I was in a daze. Moth, who was thrilled by the thought that Dolphin had taken me into the thicket for interesting reasons, teased me all the way. I did not tell her what I had seen; I tried to play up to her gossipy excitement.

At the Huas' we all dined on *la pa chou*, "winter-sacrifice congee," the delicacy reserved for this day of the year—dates, chestnuts, jelly, fruits, good things to the number of eight, mixed into a kaoliang gruel. Hua's wife had decorated the bowls with designs of birds and flowers made of bits of fruit. We slaves were given each a taste, and as the delicious mixture melted on my tongue I closed my eyes and saw again the tattered free man under the juniper bush gnawing like an animal on the dry millet cake.

(Hog-Kill-Hog; Pig-Eat-Pig

At the first series of days with heavy frosts, the Huas held a swine-killing.

Grin and Jasmine, whose daily extra chore had been the feeding of Hua's swine, were in charge of this routine of slaughter and feasting. So skilled was Grin at the split-second work of slaying and cleaning the animals that Hua himself remained in the background, and at times, if a big hog got loose when we were catching him to kill him, or if a piece of hoisting equipment appeared to be on the point of giving way while a carcass was being lifted, we

were treated to the spectacle of a slave giving urgent commands
to his master, which the owner obeyed with alacrity.

But Grin was no threat to our master. Grin's temperament was
lax, and but for the strength of Jasmine he would have been a
shiftless man, or a drinker, or simply a groveling shame of accommodation.

Grin had, however, certain specific skills, which were developed
to a high degree. Swine-killing was one of them, and under his
direction the two days of this work became a festival—or so the
entire household except for me seemed to regard it.

Every moment of the festival was, to me, a horror.

In the first place the swine themselves filled me with revulsion.
I loathed the very words "pig," "hog," "sow," "piglet," meaning
slave, meaning creature with white skin, meaning myself, Dolphin,
Moth, Perfection, even defenseless Tender; connoting our skin,
our filth, our disgusting greediness, our degradation, our grunting
speech and clumsy feet, our "bad eyes," our light and often curling
hair, our hopeless single fate: to fatten our owners.

The men hauled out two enormous caldrons, filled them with
water, and placed one of them over an ogre-throated fire in a pit,
and erected above the pair of kettles a tripod of bamboo poles as
thick as thighs.

Now the process of catching and killing began, and Jasmine,
Moth, and I had to help. We were within the mud-walled swine
wallow; the footing was slime. The swine seemed to know what
was in store for them, and they ran here and there at hurtling
speeds, grunting with effort and fear. Grin bounced around with
the grimaces of an all-or-nothing athlete. With each lunge or dive
we made, muddying ourselves like the animals we were trying to
catch, Moth flew into cascades of laughter. But my only inclination
to laugh was at a bitter incongruity: I was a devoted student, at
the time, of *The Doctrine of the Happy Mean*, and I was reduced
to tackling swine in their own element—playing at pig-catch-pig.

Yet hog-kill-hog was far worse. Once caught, the swine com-
menced a screaming that mimicked the extremities of human terror. Grin with flying fingers roped the kicking knuckles, and Lank
and Daddy Chick hoisted the creature, who kept shrieking for
sympathy from any who might be called pig in this world, onto a
shoulder pole and jogged around to the blood pans in back of the
swine hut, and there Grin would cut off screeches and life with a
single perfect axe stroke. Relief and pity. Fellow pig!

Each time new squeals for help arose I thought, for some reason, of the boar under the bush near the temple. He had needed our help, his silent eyes had pleaded for help; but *we* had needed *his* help, because he was free, and I thought I had seen a kind of scream in selfish Dolphin's eyes! Yes. Dolphin wanted to run away. I knew that. I was in a desperate fool's race. Try to win him in time to lose him.

When the prime animals were dead and bled, Grin attached the carcasses, one at a time, to a hook at the foot of a system of blocks attached to the bamboo tripod. By this time the water in the great caldron on the fire was boiling. Grin would hoist each body over the caldron, let it down into the scalding water just long enough to loosen the bristles, raise it again, and drop it into the other kettle of cool water beside the pit.

From there Hua, Lank, and Daddy Chick lifted the corpse with grappling irons and hung it from a crude bamboo frame, under which Hua's wife, Jasmine, Moth, Perfection, and I worked with scrapers to remove the bristles. These, of course, were kept—to be sold for hairbrushes for fine ladies in faraway splendor. I thought of Big Madame Shen's table of cosmetic marvels—and of the night when I tried on her exquisite clothes; I was caked now with the mud of a wallow.

But mostly, as I scraped and scraped at the tough pig hides, which had gone from pink to deadest white in the scalding water, I thought about skin. White skin. My fate in the color of my skin.

I looked more than once at the skin on my arm, and the sight filled me with an impotent spirit of revolt; I raged, for want of a more suitable target, at the swine, and I clawed at the stubborn bristles with an energy that brought a quiet word of praise—increasing my fury—from Hua's wife. "You are an industrious small child," she said, belittling me as she applauded me, having the right to do this because the skin on *her* arm was yellow.

After the pallid skins were cleaned the men brought big gut trays and they slit the carcasses and cleaned out the vitals; and as the afternoon waned Jasmine, Moth, and I were submitted to the final indignity: we had to clean the bowels of their feces for the sake of the chitterlings and casings. This was too much for Hua's wife, who did the less nauseating work of separating out hearts, kidneys, livers, and lights. All these parts we placed for the time being in tubs of salt water, and, still stinking, I rehearsed in my memory the tranquil opening passages of *The Happy Mean*!

It grew dark, and we carried the carcasses into the courtyard, where, behind locked gates, we laid them out on bamboo racks through the freezing night.

The next morning Grin, wielding dangerous knives and cleavers as if they were sources of delight—as if they were fiddle bows, gong beaters, and tappers for jade sweet-sounding tubes—cut up the bodies, and the rest of us salted the meat. On trays and salting benches we laid out the leaf lard, the hams, the shoulders, the heads, the twinkling feet—no shred to be wasted. The bones were set aside to be boiled. While the men rubbed salt onto the large cuts, we women sat at wooden blocks with hatchetlike choppers, and we diced the inferior meat to be pickled. Hua's wife tried the fat out from certain portions, and the fragrance of the sizzling lard hung about our heads. The children flocked around us begging for mouthfuls of crisp, for pigtails to roast in the ashes of Hua's wife's fire, and for bladders to blow up as balloons rattling with a few beans inside. They ran about, white and yellow, pounding each other over the heads with these blown-up bladders and squealing at their fun. Did the little whites slap the little yellows with an extra force of childish revenge? I thought not. It was I who applied with my white-skinned hand an extra vicious push to each clop of my small hatchet, in honor of my frustration.

When all the meat that mattered was in salt or in barrels of brine we were offered a feast of bits: of spare bones and backbones, jowls and feet, tripe and chitterlings, with a gruel of kaoliang and white cabbage. It was a rare night when so much was set before a slave.

"What is the matter, small child?" Hua's wife asked me. "Why don't you stuff yourself?"

"I'm too tired to eat," I said. I was, once again, on the edge of tears, at the thought of pig-eat-pig.

(The Seed-Catching Bird

Yet ten days later my heart was as light as a thrush's voice. It was the day before the yellows' New Year, and Old Sun had invited masters and slaves from the entire district to a celebration, and I knew that I would see Dolphin.

The morning flew. Hua was talkative; he was pleased with his crop, and in general we were not so far behind as usual in the care of the farm. He affixed new couplets, rather grand for our style of life, to the doorposts, in black characters on strips of red paper:

PEACE TO THE COUNTRY ESTATE;
TRANQUILLITY IN THE MANY CHAMBERS.

Hua's wife pasted up a new picture of the kitchen god, to signal his return from his annual report to heaven, and she spread sesame stalks in the courtyard on which the old year could secretively tiptoe away. She gave each slave a pair of new cloth shoes.

We were excused to the slave hut to dress ourselves for the celebration at Old Sun's. I had nothing but my quilted field coat and trousers to wear, but Moth drew from her poor bundle of possessions two new cotton scarves, brightly printed with patterns of butterflies and cicadas, and she threw one over my shoulders. "If you don't wear something new on your back on New Year's," she said, "the wild birds will shit on you all year long." Then with great ingenuity she fashioned headdresses for herself and for me, by folding red, black, green, and gold papers, which she had somehow acquired, in intricate patterns, cutting designs into them, and then unfolding them—lace, combs, jade earrings, gold flowers!

Seeing us decked with these cheap jewels, Lank sourly commented, "Two whores—one's a fool because she let herself get pregnant." All the same, I could tell by the way he looked at us that we did not appear quite so hardened as he said.

Going over to Old Sun's, all of us, even Hua and his wife, walked barefoot, cold as it was, with our new shoes clamped under our arms to keep them clean, and our hands tucked into our sleeves— as if having one set of extremities warm would prevent the others from getting too cold.

On the way our path passed through the humped barren field where dead slaves from all the estates of the countryside were buried under paltry mounds—like sea waves, the meaningless tombs of the dead we had thrown in the ocean from the slave ship *East Garden,* unmonumented, unmarked, indistinguishable one from another; I thought for a moment of the burial of poor Kathy, killed by her bondage to that mad humanity-hating carpenter in the Capital. This moment of dark thoughts, however, passed;

Moth, sensing the chill I was having, took me by the hand and broke into a run, and she pulled me with her out of the graveyard. We waited beyond for the others to catch up.

Outside the wall of Old Sun's main courtyard we all stopped and put on our shoes, and then we were ready.

The road before the compound gate was crowded with guests, yellow and white, who were arriving on foot, on carts, on mule-back and donkeyback riding double and triple. There were three carriages by the gate in which rich men must have brought their families. The slaves were all wearing whatever scraps they could set their hands on that were new and colorful—red-paper hats, multicolored ribbons, paper birds and flowers. Children wore good-luck necklaces of a few cash interwoven with ribbons into the shapes of dragons.

We entered the gate. The yellow guests were bidden to cross the verandas and enter the central hall; the whites were relegated to the large back courtyard, where they were to be left outdoors in the cold. On the lintel of the gate into this courtyard was pasted a New Year's inscription: THE BOND SERVANT FINDS HEAVEN-JOY IN DUTY.

No matter! Three hundred slaves, or more, some in the uni-forms of prosperous masters, others, like us, in threadbare quilts, were assembled in the open space, and there was much raucous shouting and uncouth loud laughter. Trestle tables had been set up, covered with sheets of red paper. Crude paper flowers and decorations were displayed on the window grilles and door frames. Here and there characters on red paper proclaimed all those things that slaves would never have: happiness, wealth, good fortune, longevity, and peace of mind.

Moth found Quart, in a runner's uniform, and I went with her to him. Quart threw his arms around Moth and lifted her off the ground, and then he hugged me, too, pressing me hard to his body. Thinking that Moth might not like this, and finding that I did, I was embarrassed, and I blushed, and my blush made me furious.

I was in the midst of this confusion when Dolphin came striding up, in a tunic like Quart's but again sporting his red trousers, which he apparently wore on festive days, and he said, "Hai! Fall-down! You look like a magistrate's concubine! Have you a little mouse for me?"

(Now "mouse," as I well knew from Moth, was the expression white slaves used at that time for the dark, hairy thing at the base of a woman's belly—as well as for the co-operative use to which she could sometimes be persuaded to put it.)

For Lank to call me names was one thing; from Dolphin this rude talk came much harder. I thought he was going to embrace me, and I spat at him the one word "Rooster!" because of his crimson pants and rutty tongue, and I bit my lip, turned my back on him, and on an impulse (at the root of which Moth's advice on tactics my well have lain, though I felt angry) I walked swiftly away, losing myself in the crowd.

But then I was at a loss what to do. I knew no one. I stood awkwardly among chatting groups. I tried to pretend that I was paying close attention to this and that. I hoped Dolphin would not see me floundering this way.

I was rescued by a loud gong at the courtyard gate. Here came Old Sun in a crimson hat and brocaded robes! All the slaves in the courtyard fell to their knees and kowtowed. The old man kept nodding and flapping his hands to us as if dripping water off his fingertips. He spoke a few words, which I could not hear, in a cracking voice, and all stood up. Slaves lifted him into a carved chair on a raised platform, and he presided over the giving of cheap gifts: shoddy hats, fragile pipes, bits of ribbon, trashy scarves like the one Moth had given me—so this was how she had acquired hers in the first place!

Near Old Sun's feet, besides, were several huge clay jars, as high as a man's waist, full of spirits distilled from a millet mash, and this liquor was dealt out indiscriminately to the slaves as they came forward for their presents.

I received a cow-horn comb and almost choked on a single sip of the drink; it reminded me of "Uncle" Ch'en's nightmarish pleasure garden, whence I had been sold out of South-of-the-River Province.

During the giving of gifts various slaves, who were thought, or considered themselves, eloquent, stood up and made florid speeches, squealing in the falsetto tones of itinerant actors, in praise of the senile miser sitting on the throne at the top of the yard. Old Sun nodded at each hypocritical flattery, obviously gripped with a conviction of the truth of the praise.

Dolphin came up to me with a bowlful of the millet liquor and offered it to me, and like a fool I gulped it all down, cupping my hands tenderly over Dolphin's in a pretense of steadying the bowl. The brew burned me right to my belly as it went down, and I felt

wild, and wildly I turned once again and strode away from Dolphin.

This time he followed me; I soon felt a strong hand clamped to
my upper arm. "Not so fast, you little sparrow. Come on. Let's
go up near the platform; they're going to have games."

I was dizzy from the liquor. I shook off Dolphin's hand. "Leave
me alone," I said, "you . . . you centipede!"

This wooden epithet from the traveling slave-players' stock
roster of villains made Dolphin throw his head back and roar
with laughter. My silliness vexed me; I was filled up with false
emotion, and with tears in my eyes, firmly believing that I was in
the act of stalking haughtily away from him for the third and last
time, I flung myself on his chest. His arms closed tightly around
me, and I heard him laughing in my hair, "You stupid little sow!"

With his arm around my shoulders Dolphin pulled me up into
the thick press of slaves around the platform. Old Sun had been
carried off, and two jugglers were hurling and swinging five fire-
tipped torches back and forth; the flames somersaulted and caracoled.

For the better part of two hours I leaned, half drunk, in a paralysis of tongueless bliss, against Dolphin's side. The noisy crowd
forced us against each other. Dolphin's hand was at my waist,
and now and then, at the sight of an acrobat's masterful passage
with a foot shuttlecock, or at the sudden lifting of a weighted
beam, on the third desperate try, by a strong-man slave, or at a
conjurer's making an entire living pheasant disappear into thin
air, converting it into a sudden brilliant flutteration of paper birds,
the pressure of the hand palpably increased. All my slave's life
melted into the mind-numbing contentment of this unreal place,
this unbelievable pressure.

In all the time he spoke to me only once. "So you belong to
Dirty Hua?"

Was this what Sun's slaves called my master? I nodded.

Then suddenly there was a commotion, some shouting back and
forth, and he was gone. I felt a panic. Dolphin was going to be
exactly what I had judged—selfish, ruthless, and indifferent to
the feelings of others. He would pick me up and drop me, like a
twig, whenever he wanted.

Now bareknuckle boxing began, and Dolphin appeared in the
fourth bout. I was relieved: he must have been called away from
my side.

He fought unshod and stripped to the waist, in just his red trousers, and all across his back I saw long ugly welts.

He won his match and was given a dipperful of millet liquor as a prize. He came back to me, red-faced from the drink. A bruise on his cheek was turning dark. "How was I?" he asked, with a conceited leer.

"They have beaten you," I said.

"Ayah, baby," he said, facing the platform and putting his arm around me again, "I'm not going to let them do that to me any more."

A slave gave a demonstration of sending a bird into the air to catch seeds that the man tossed up. The bird's foot was tied by a string. I felt very close to the bird, as if it were another self of mine. Its feats were miraculous! It had learned to turn right over in the air (did the slave jerk the string?), to glide, to catch three seeds at one attempt.

The whites in the crowd cheered, whistled, and hooted with pleasure, and the bird seemed to nod and bow at the applause.

Yes, the slaves made all sorts of joyful noises—and yet, and yet: What was the heavy atmosphere, like a layer of smoke, that hung over all our heads? The applause was false, the laughter was false, my own melting luxurious warmth of contact with this man who was always on my mind—that, too, would play me false. This was a celebration in honor of a new year, which could bring us nothing but worse. How strange it was that we could express our sorrows through cheers, our utter hopelessness through gales of mad laughter!

"Baby, baby," Dolphin said, "this is no day for that." I realized I was weeping. Then, evidently understanding my pain-in-pleasure, showing a hint of bottomless grief himself on his face with its now livid bruise, Dolphin said in a soft voice, holding me tighter than ever, "Bastard sons of turtles!"

Darkness fell. Sun slaves lit lanterns all around the courtyard. Old Sun gave us a stingy feast—pork meat, kaoliang gruel, white cabbage; what we called white man's slops. Horrible feast for the New Year's eve!

"What can you expect from Venerable for three hundred hungry bellies?" Quart said, rising to the defense of his master.

When it was time for us to go home, Hua bought for a few cash from a peddler at Sun's gate a handful of pine splits with big knots at the top, and we lit the sap-filled knots, and our procession of smoky flares made a long sulphurous glowworm going through the fields. I was light of step. I felt that in the easy flow of my feelings toward the man I had begun to think of as mine I had found at last the secret of survival for one who was white in a yellow world.

We stayed up in the slave hut till the arrival of the New Year, talking about the many colors of the day. When Hua struck a gong at midnight, we went up to the house and removed the sesame stalks from the courtyard, to avert bad luck from the family, and yellows and whites together kowtowed toward the east so we would not be stung by scorpions all year long.

⟨ Dragon's Head

Hua felt complacent about his crop, stacked in the safe godown of Old Sun, and he honored the traditional period, from the new moon of the New Year to the full moon that followed, of a thorough suspension of work. But for the daily chores to keep the animals and fowl alive, and to get the cooking and washing of the household done, we were relieved of all labor. Grin hunted; he shot his long-watched weasel. Jasmine mended her family's clothing. Daddy Chick sat all day in the door of the slave hut playing his fiddle and dozing. Lank, armed with written chits authorizing visits to nearby farms, spent whole days in the traditional pastime of the New Year layoff: gambling, mainly with dominoes made of bamboo; he grew thinner and more morose than ever. Hua's wife's mei-mei, her younger sister, visited us, and our mistress wanted to show how aristocratically one could live with ten souls in the slave quarters. "Mei-mei wants a foot-warmer." And I would have to heat a brick and wrap it in cotton cloths and carry it to the mei-mei and kowtow after I tucked it under her tiny blood-starved feet. But several days Moth and I, wearing cedar twigs wrapped in our hair in the belief that they would protect our bodies from lice, got chits from Hua to visit Old Sun's. Moth was tired of Quart and had taken up with a humorous hog named Second; her pregnancy was by now thoroughly noticeable, but nobody seemed to be put off by it, and men still sought and enjoyed her company. And I? I spent the whole layoff softening Dolphin's heart by devious means.

For instance: Moth told me that a pinch of dust from a woman's footprint sprinkled in a man's food would make the man's private parts itch unbearably in desire for that woman alone.

It took me three visits to Old Sun's and a great deal of fatuous byplay to get a few grains of dust from one of my own footprints into a bowl of cabbage that Dolphin was about to eat.

From a peddler in the crowd of itinerant salesmen that was forever milling about the side gate of the Sun compound, where Sun's housekeepers did their buying, I bought, with two cash I had stolen from Hua's wife's bag of kitchen coppers, a piece of root from the plant called never-shame-weed, and I kept a small piece of it in my mouth and chewed it whenever I was near Dolphin, for this was said to provide an irresistible magnetism.

I played, as well as I could, Moth's game of offer-and-snatch-away.

I had no inkling how my efforts were succeeding until the holidays came to an end, on the evening of the full moon, with the Lantern Festival. We had learned that the Sun slaves had organized a procession that would go from farm to farm that night to entertain yellow masters of the countryside; we supped early and cleaned up and waited.

In the distance, at last, we heard, coming across the lanes in the fields from the direction of Old Sun's, a confused noise of gongs, peddlers' drums, sweet timbrels, and short strings of firecrackers, and running outside Hua's walls we saw a sparkling celebration creeping towards us—lanterns held high on poles and flaming pine knots weaving about, and at the heart of the beautiful train, a long, writhing, cloth-backed dragon with many capering and dancing human legs. Barley Flower and Perfection wanted to run into the fields to join the thrilling parade; Hua struck his oldest child a flat blow on the head to give her better sense. Cart Tongue, Stone, Tale, and Tender jumped up and down and squealed with excitement at the magical apparition, and in this they acted for Moth and me; we wanted to leap and chirp, too.

As the procession came near, we fell into our proper places— Hua and his family in the front rank, to be entertained, we slaves behind, "in attendance."

The dragon, the light-bearers, and the accompanying noise-makers and performers stopped on the worn, grassless square of ground between Hua's gate and the road, and under the many swaying lanterns and torches a group of slave athletes performed, wheeling around a female contortionist, whose knots of limbs and grinning glances at us from between her own legs made me slightly queasy, as at the sight of a double deformity—body and skin both unacceptable. There followed, to the beat of the timbrels, a *yang ko,* or sprout song, in the haunting whole-tone scale of the yellows, to which its performers soberly danced charades—and I thought of the mute planting in the Arizona manner danced for me, and for me alone, by that red-eyed tipsy man in Chao-er's tavern so long before.

The performances were over. The dragon, which had been standing by in a drooping condition, now heaved up its cloth flanks, and its head, built up in fantastic lacquered intricacies of ferocity, began to waggle, and the noisemakers all began to bong and rattle, and the long form—thirty men's worth, at least—resumed its twisting dance. The lanterns and the dragon were going to leave us.

The dragon, having described one full circle, seemed all at once to hesitate. Then it turned toward us of the house of Hua. Its head dipping and yawing, it advanced in our direction. It came past the Huas. I began to have the strangest feelings. On one side of me Moth retreated toward the gate with little feminine half-laughing shrieks, and on the other side the squad of Jasmine's children also fell to rout. Rooted in I-knew-not-what audacity, I stood ground alone.

The dragon came to me. The noise seemed deafening now. Confronting me so closely, the huge paper head, trailing spiral paper snorts out of its nostrils and blinking its warrior eyes with lashes of pig bristle, seemed not fearful but buffoonish, clumsy, playful, and charged with overwhelming lust.

The head dipped before me. It bowed to the ground. Abandoning all ferocity, it nuzzled its cheek in the dust toward Hua's wife's consolation, my ugly slave feet.

I believe I was blushing all over my body, from head to foot.

The dragon's face, constantly rocking and nodding, lifted up, and waggling its fang-studded lower jaw up and down in a dragon's chomping grin, it began a series of marvelous leaps into the air.

With these leaps I saw that the legs under the head were encased in bright red trousers.

My feelings, as the dragon crawled away to the ditchlike road, were in a swirling confusion like that of the procession itself. Dolphin, human engine in the dragon's head, had singled me out

before the entire gathering, and I should have felt, I partly *did*
feel, the keenest delight I had ever known. But beneath and
within the delight, I felt disgust and anger. Why should this man
upon whom I had fastened my hopeless self submit himself to this
indignity, to entertain a few yellow masters, cavorting through
the countryside wrapped in a papier-mâché bestiality? Yet . . .
Better to be the head than a meaningless segment farther back!
Yet . . . What had happened to us? How had our natural white
courtesy turned into spineless humility? I had seen Dolphin taking
his cheap gift from Old Sun's hand on the day before the New
Year: humble. How had stiff backbones become so flexible: moral
strength became a willingnes to kowtow? No, no, what had happened to this Dolphin was insupportable. He worshipped, as we
all did, in the yellow temple, and his faith, if he had any, was
fatalistic, and fatalism brought out strange traits—selfishness,
lasciviousness, and an urge to martyrdom. I felt a struggle within
me, at the very moment when I might have burst with joy, a
struggle between submission and rebellion, giving and stealing,
resigning myself and hardening myself. Death of the soul, or the
mountain! Take the easy way with Dirty Hua, or—or *what*? Why
did the dragon not carry me off?

Moth was whispering and giggling about my ears. "You've got
him," I heard her murmur. "Take him out in the fields some
night."

(Dirty Hua

On the day of the resumption of work, the sixteenth
of the first month, our master went off with five carts, four of
them rented from skinflint Sun, taking Lank and Grin as extra
carters, to carry his twenty-eight bales of cotton to market. As
they set off, with a basket of food for four days cooked by Jasmine, and with two of the donkeys in their cart shafts tied by
their bridles to the carts ahead, so the three men could manage
five carts, Hua was in high spirits: this was the best crop he had
ever raised, and his wife's mei-mei, whom he clearly disliked, as
an extra mouth for both eating and talking, had gone home, and
—ayah, he was fifteen years younger than his dry-necked wife,
and he was going for an unsupervised sojourn in the district capital.

Lank and Grin were excited, too—Lank by the prospect of having the measly cash that he had won from country card players eased away from him by city gamblers with drooping eyelids and honeyed fingers, and Grin by the idea of loosening his tongue at the taverns and telling townsmen of the low-bellied, razor-fanged beasts he had stalked and bagged.

How brave, each in his own vein, those three seemed to think themselves!

In their absence Daddy Chick was in charge of us. He loved his flimsy authority so much that he grew befuddled, and went around clearing his throat and shifting us arbitrarily from task to task—knocking down and burning the dead cotton plants; bringing in the kaoliang stalks, which had a hundred uses, from fencing to fuel; hauling out rotted cotton seed, ginned from the old crop, for fertilizer; marking out the plow lines; and patching the walls of both houses with straw-bound mud, which we dug from the pits where, on the day of my arrival, I had seen yellow and white children playing like blood kin.

In these days I saw something remarkable: Hua's wife at a wooden plow, listing the kaoliang fields for the new planting. In the absence of her man, who had been so glad to leave her, she was grim, powerful, stone-jawed. She ripped the bowels of the earth in lines as straight as bees' flight. . . .

Moth and I were alone, storing kaoliang stalks in a drying rick hung from the rafters of the work space in the Hua house. She was in a confidential mood.

"Do you know why they call him Dirty Hua?"

"Why?"

"I'm telling you this for your own good. He's like all the yellow men. Don't let him touch you. Listen, small flower, never let a yellow man touch you in that way. Hua has this curiosity—he's like the rest of them—this curiosity about us. He thinks we're different—better—when it comes to . . . you know what I mean. All these yellow men want a white woman—do you know why? They have heard about the romantic idea that the whites are supposed to use—they think we *use* it—like some sort of tickler—something like that—when we lie down together. Or like a fascinating position. Hush, dear; Dirty Hua—I call him that, too!—why shouldn't I?—he told me all this. Shhh! He says he can't help himself, he says he *has* to learn about this Idea that is

supposed to make the white people almost explode—down there
—you know what I mean—when they do it together—the Idea
getting into that place and making it different—better. Listen. I'll
have to whisper. He's quite cute. He's very polite when he tries
to find the Idea inside there, only he's *scared to death*. He's afraid
he won't have the Idea in—or on—his own—well, you know—
and so he won't be as good as the white men. And, being afraid,
he isn't. He just isn't. I swear he isn't as good. And then he
gets in a terrible heat to show that he *could* be. I *told* him that
the idea of the Idea was nonsense—we don't do it with our *heads*
—it's just that slaves have no other way to be wild except that
way: he won't accept that. He won't let you alone. He also thinks
we're *made* differently—you know where I mean—and he wants
to investigate. It gets disgusting. He *is* dirty. Listen, my mei-mei,
keep him off you. Treat him like a biting fly. Slap him hard. I'm
telling you for your own good."

Both Moth and I were blushing like two angry girls.

In a shocked voice I said, "Then he is the father."

"I don't know." Moth was suddenly wringing her hands and
appealing for help no one could give her. "That's the worst of it.
I don't know."

It made no difference anyway, because a white woman's child
was always her responsibility. The Imperial courts had long since
held that nothing could be expected of a white woman's baby's
father, whoever he might be. Moth must have known this; probably she was terrified of Hua's wife.

"But that's not why they call him Dirty Hua," Moth said, recovering suddenly and solidly from her discomfiture.

"Then why do they?"

"Because of this," Moth said, opening her arms to the squalor of
the crowded work space. "Those Sun hogs are used to satin and
lacquer. Second says to me, 'Do you have good mud in that wallow
you Hua pigs live in?' "

"But Hua works!" I said. "He works in the fields."

"I know, child. But that is no reason not to call him Dirty."

"I'm not trying to defend him," I said rather sharply—though in
truth I had a feeling of protective anger on our master's behalf,
and this had made me disgusted with myself, even a little alarmed,
and short with Moth. "It is only that the Sun hogs' calling him
dirty means that they think you and I are dirty too."

"Ayah! We are!"

There was no answer to that. We were. I felt bad-tempered all the rest of that day. Everything Moth had said about Hua upset me.

(The Glut

Five days passed and Hua did not return. Six days. Seven. Eight.

As if bad weather had set in, we gave up all pretense of hard work and huddled nervously in the main courtyard.

On the evening of the ninth day we heard carts drawing off the road in front of the courtyard, and Daddy Chick, Jasmine, Moth, and I rushed out and gave our master a welcome the warmth of which was wholly false. We kowtowed, rushed about helping with the donkeys, and gave Hua many flowery expressions of our gratitude at his safe return.

Hua and his two men had empty carts and long faces. We had expected Hua to bring provisions and gifts back from the city.

I heard Jasmine say aside to her husband, Grin, "You stayed long enough. What kind of game were you hunting, man? Mice?"

When we entered the house I saw that Hua's wife, too, was furious with her husband over the length of his sojourn in the city. She and Jasmine seemed to attribute their husbands' gloominess to shame and remorse. But our master soon set the women straight as to that.

"It's a disaster," he said, with haggard well-pouched eyes. "You should have seen the cotton! Every man in the whole district was out on the road with the best crop in a thousand years. Carts piled twice as high as ours, till half of them overturned when they tried to get out of the ruts. Pole boats on the rivers stacked with bales twelve tiers high. Every man in East-of-the-Mountains Province was suddenly a planter, merchant, comprador, factor, all talking cotton, cotton. Suffocating! The godowns were vomiting cotton before we even reached the city. I thought we would never sell our lot. And when we did, it was for a price that ruins me. Last year we got forty-eight taels of silver for a four-hundred-catty bale. This year the official price is twenty-six taels. I got twenty-two. Ai! It costs me eight taels a year to feed a pig."

The last word he spat out at us, his slaves.

This was the beginning of a change in our master.

([My Chimney-Head

I was as happy as a slave could ever be. Day and night, daring thoughts of Dolphin pushed much that was evil and ugly out of my mind. I saw him one morning at Limestone Hill Generous Temple. He was brusque with me, but I perceived in his eyes and around his mouth telltale signs which gave me all I needed for encouragement. I was determined, for his sake, not to be a dirty pig of Dirty Hua—to be as close to satin and lacquer as louse bedding and tung oil could make themselves. Some of my efforts to become attractive were, as I came eventually to realize, extreme and bizarre. The yellows had conveyed to their slaves the idea that the black, coarse, and straight hair of yellow women was "good" hair, and anything unlike it was "bad" hair. Mine, being brown, fine, and inclined to curl when damp, was "bad," and I now bought from an itinerant vendor at Old Sun's side gate one of the many hair dyes for white women that these scoundrel peddlers foisted off on us. It consisted, I am afraid, of lard and soot perfumed with a few petals of nicotiana. This stuff made me exactly what I wanted to avoid being—filthy. It came off on my clothes and on our communal k'ang. Daddy Chick called me a chimney-head. When I perspired in the fields the preparation ran down my neck and forehead. But I was sure that I was more attractive than before. Lank said in his sour way, "Do you have a 'good' little mouse, too, baby?" I had a traveling barber pierce my ear lobes; Moth had showed me how to make earrings of shiny black beans and silver thread. I wore tight shoes and hobbled like a woman with bound feet.

([A Spreading of Lard

We had a common saying that a white man who would not steal had jade toenails.

One day Dolphin went into the woods on Sun's place with Quart, and they waded into the walled swamp where Old Sun kept a herd of half-wild swine, and they stole a fat shoat, killed it, and hid it in the woods under some dead leaves. At night they went out and found it and carried it behind the wall of the slave village on the great estate, and they dressed it there, burying the offal. They put the salted meat in earthenware jars, and they buried them, too, and marked the place.

This much Dolphin told me—whispering in my ear as Moth, Second, he, I, and several other Sun slaves were seated cross-legged on Dolphin's own k'ang one evening. Moth and I had slipped away over the fields without a chit, and I was too nervous to enjoy myself. Dolphin and Second wanted us to stay the night with them, but we were too afraid.

A few mornings later, on the second day of the second month, when, each year, the water dragon, who controlled insects, was supposed to rouse himself from his winter sleep, Jasmine, Moth, and I were instructed by Hua to propitiate the dragon, so he would not infest us with crawling insects, while the men went to break out and back-furrow the remaining balks in the cotton fields, and to begin planting kaoliang.

To pacify the dragon we dusted cinnabar under the folded quilts on all the k'angs, and we carried cooking ashes and placed them in rings around all the wells, both that for drinking and those for irrigation scattered about the farm.

It happened that one of these irrigation wells, with a long canted bamboo lever for a lifting arm, was in a field adjacent to one of Sun's, and a squad of Sun hogs was planting there. Second was among them. He saw us and hailed Moth. To control his slave force, Old Sun had a kind of private militia of armed yellow supervisors, and we saw Second run across the field to the one who was in charge of the planting squad. The slave and the militiaman talked a few moments. Then Second broke away and came at a loping run toward us.

He was out of breath when he reached us. Gasping, he said, "I have only a moment—White Lotus—come over here." He drew me aside.

Jasmine was alarmed and suspicious. I heard her ask Moth, "Who is this pig?"

"Ai!" Moth said. "He's an old turtle. Don't bother yourself. I know him." And Moth made that middle-finger gesture of hers, of a man's readiness. Mischievous girl, she was trying to make Jasmine think that Second was after *my* mouse.

Second, his chest heaving, leaned down to me. "Dolphin—he has been asking for you—he's in the sick-house."

"The sick-house! What's the matter?"

Second was still gulping air. "Bambooed—bad."

"When? What happened?"

"Later—the bastards'll give it to me—have to go."

"Tell me!"

"The son of a turtle said he'd skin me—said run over, run back."

"But you could be telling me—"

"Old Night-Soil Basket"—so the slaves called Old Sun—"he took charge himself. Pepper—you know that bastard pig?—he told on Dolphin—about the shoat—Dolphin beat Pepper up boxing once. Old Night-Soil Basket sat in his sedan chair—they had Dolphin's hands tied up to a tree—Old Night-Soil Basket threatened branding—sat there talking while the turtles gave it to Dolphin. They took him down—laid him in a cart. Old Night-Soil Basket said, 'You're one of my best hogs, what's-your-name, or I'd have given you a number-one bambooing—but you are such a good small pig —I like you—I thought I would just dust you off this time. You be a good hog now. Behave yourself. If I ever catch you again, I shall be obliged to give you a proper pounding with the heavy bamboo—not just an easy one like this. You understand, what's-your-name?' Old Night-Soil Basket never knows our names."

"What about Dolphin?"

"They took him in the cart—sick-house. I have to go. It'll be me next if I don't go."

Second ran off.

I was agitated all day.

With the help of Moth, who was adept at plausible excuses, I concocted a story, which I whispered to Hua's wife, about having irregular periods, about being afraid that the water influences of the Number Six Field to the east of the slave hut had affected the fire element in my lower body; I wanted to consult the old yellow monk, a mendicant physician, who treated the inmates of Sun's sick-house.

Hua's wife whispered to Hua, and within a few minutes I had a chit to go to the sick-house.

During the hushed conference between our master and mistress, Moth stole a scoopful of pork lard from one of the jars in the "cool corner" of the work space, and she wrapped it in some dried kaoliang leaves, and as I set out for Sun's she slipped the package into my tunic and whispered, "For his cuts—the best help." I remembered, from the sight of her naked back, that day in the cotton field, that Moth was not a stranger to bamboo rods.

With one exception the buildings at Old Sun's were sound,

clean, and made of bricks. The exception was the slaves' sick-house, which was in fact a pesthole. Set off at a far corner of the slaves' vast compound, out of sight and mind of the master's family, it was one large room, its walls of mud and kaoliang stalks; its floor of dirt; its roof leaky; the oiled paper pasted on the grille of its one window tattered and flapping. There were two huge communal k'angs, in whose ovens inadequate fires were lit once a day, only to flicker out before the damp clay of the beds was dried out, to say nothing of warmed, and on these k'angs lay the slave inmates. As I entered the open doorway I felt the beginning of an anger that was to grow during the next few minutes to an almost uncontainable pressure. An old man, nearly eighty, covered with a tattered quilt, lay staring with glittering eyes at the roof beams as he waited for the end; a multitude of flies crawled about his mouth, which sagged open, for he was snoring, though awake. A handful of women (complications of childbirth, fevers, rheumatism) sat with crossed legs near the window stoically passing the time with talk. And in the dark far corner, with a cloth over his head, and the back of his tunic stained with dried blood, lying prone, was a form that must have been Dolphin's.

I crawled across the k'ang toward him on my hands and knees. My anger now was a hard knot in my throat.

I knelt beside him. Perhaps he was sleeping. Should I touch him on an arm?

After a time I leaned forward until my mouth was near the cloth over his head, and I murmured in a voice so quiet that it would not rouse him if he was asleep, "I brought some lard for your back."

With a suddenness that startled me, one of Dolphin's hands snatched the cloth away from his head, and he lifted his mat-printed cheek and turned his eyes enough to look up at me.

This was the first time he had seen me with my sooty hair and bean earrings.

"Ai!" he said, his mouth curling in a bitter smile. "Who let in the magpie?"

"I brought some lard for your back," I said in a voice shaking now with two angers.

"I don't have a back," Dolphin roughly said. "Old Shit Basket has my old back."

"Would you like me to spread the lard?"

"Listen, little Fall-Down. I wouldn't give a turtle's dropping to have a potful of hair dye spread on my cuts. Why don't you go home to Dirty Hua?" He pulled the cloth over his head.

My anger was dissolving into a nameless and bottomless heat that was far worse. "It was not easy for me to get here," I said.

"I'll tell you the easy way," the voice under the cloth said, blowing out part of the cloth in small puffs. "Steal a shoat."

Something now took hold of me, and with firm hands I lifted Dolphin's near shoulder, reached under his chest, and undid, one by one, the cloth-knot fasteners of his tunic. He did not resist. In fact he rolled a bit to his side to make my task easier. But as I did the horrible work of pulling the tunic away from the long scabs, he threw a stream of abuse at me for trying to make myself look like a yellow woman. By now my pulsing anger—not at him, but at *them*—had surged back again, and I did not care what he said. I took the cloth from his head and spread the lard on it with my hand, and applied the whole compress to the broad place at which I could not bear to look, and Dolphin stopped railing.

The old man with the flies swarming around his open mouth suddenly started to groan. The sick women paid me no attention.

I leaned forward to Dolphin's ear again and in a low furious voice said, "I am your sow, you terrible hog."

Dolphin said, "Go away."

An ancient yellow monk, in filthy yellow robes, with a shaved head and a black spot on his forehead, was sunning himself against the sick-house wall when I emerged. I went to him, kowtowed in the dust, and said, "Old Worshipful, sell me a paper saying that you must treat me here a few minutes every day for a month." I held up for him to see the coppers that Hua's wife had given me for medicine.

"What is your trouble, small sow?" the old man said.

"My trouble is the man who was beaten."

"Ayah," the monk said. "You are a very sick pig." He fumbled in a greasy bag, then took out inkstone, water jar, brush cylinder, and a scrap of thin paper. He wrote what I wanted. I gave him the coppers.

⟨ The Money Belt

My "sickly" month was the best time I had ever had under yellow dominion. I visited the old monk at Sun's sick-house

—or, in other words, Dolphin—every afternoon. I continued my secret lessons with the old uncle. I feigned a weakness which completely fooled Dirty Hua and which earned me light work part of the time. I kept wheedling coppers from Hua's wife for powders and pills the old monk never administered to me, and I gave the money to Dolphin.

Spring was now well advanced. I entered the sick-house carrying a branch of pear blossoms. Dolphin was able to sit up; his industry was a surprise to me. He was weaving a mat. Day after day he wove baskets of bamboo splits and mats of kaoliang splits, made brooms, sewed canvas mule collars stuffed with kaoliang leaves—and all these products he sold to Old Sun's militia supervisors. He kept the money from these efforts and the coppers I gave him in a money belt that he wore at all times. His hands were flying.

"Are you going to buy me a beautiful sedan chair?" I asked him.

"I am going to buy you a beautiful nothing to wrap your most valuable nothings in," Dolphin said.

I knew well enough why he wanted money—to help get himself to the mountain; but this knowledge I pushed to the back of my head.

We were planting cotton. Some days I worked between Lank on the fore plow (who often asked me openly and crudely to lend him my mouse; I was sorry for him, and he knew it) and Grin on the after plow. Lank, up ahead, behind a mismatched team, a donkey and a bullock yoked together, lightly opened the crests of the back-furrowed beds, and I, walking behind him, drilled the cotton seeds, and Grin came along behind me with a concave board on a plow stock to cover the drills.

The air was soft; redbud, black haw, and jasmine were in bloom along the edges of the fields.

"How long are you going to keep up this sick-house game?" Grin asked from his plow behind me.

"Until I am well," I called over my shoulder.

"Ai! Do you mean well the way Moth is well?" She was so far along in her pregnancy as to be excused from field work; she had only about a month to go.

I held my tongue. My silence spoke of my happiness, which teasing could not ruffle. But as we came to the end of a furrow I had a chill; I had imagined for a moment in my rhapsodical eye, against the blue horizon, a frightening faraway mountain, its brow blood red in a sunset.

⟨ My Certainty

It was a season of watching and waiting—the seedlings appeared in spite of a chilling rain in the first week, and I felt sure, with anticipation blind to consequences, that Dolphin would soon ask me to help him make good use of the warming up of the spring nights. He was healed and back at work.

A tiny toad hopped out from under a seedling once when we were chopping weeds. "Watch out with your hoe there!" Jasmine sharply said. It was bad luck to kill a toad; it meant you would stub your toe. She clucked her tongue and shook her head over my absent-mindedness.

"What is the matter with you?" the old uncle peevishly asked me one day during a lesson. He was seated on the stool of the spinning wheel; I was cross-legged on a kaoliang mat on the floor. "Have you lost interest in our work?" I burst into tears; I could not tell the broken old man how full I was of delight and hope.

The third day of the third month was Ch'ing Ming, the spring festival—a day when the yellows visited their ancestors' graves, offered a feast to the spirits of those who were gone, and directed their slaves to repair the graves. Now Hua's wife was distantly related to Old Sun, and on Ch'ing Ming all of us save gravid Moth went to the burying ground, our owners to worship at, and we to repair, the graves of Hua's wife's grandparents and parents.

For me the trip into the Sun family graveyard was a thrilling curiosity, for Moth had long since told me that the Sun graveyard was a favorite trysting place for white lovers. It afforded perfect safety; the yellows were known never to set foot in the burying grounds at night.

Where would Dolphin and I lie? Between the grave mounds on that gentle slope, under the great willow? Near the artistic wall, its designs of studded bricks and blue-plastered spaces now so brilliant in the sunshine?

Squads of Sun hogs were working all around us. I felt that I was in the grip of brassbound certainties: Dolphin was among the uniformed men, I would encounter him, he would command me to meet him here in the graveyard—not on this night, because there would be too many other white pairs copulating among the mounds on a night when so many hogs were reminded of this safe place, but two or three nights from now. I did not even look for Dolphin; he would find me. He would ask me. And when the time came . . .

These certainties in my mind caused a piercing pain of anticipation and longing in my chest.

Yes, there was Dolphin. Yes, he was coming with sure strides toward me. I was calm. I knew what was to happen. I thought I would melt from that hot melancholy pain in my chest.

According to the custom of girls on third third, I had my hair done up in spiral coils as a sign that I was available for marriage —at any rate, available. Would he notice?

"Fall-Down!" he said, coming straight up to me. He looked around and saw that Hua and his wife were busy several paces away setting out the propitiating foods. "Listen to speech. I want to ask you something."

"Yes." With every fiber of my being I was ready.

"Look. You've got me in trouble."

"How trouble? What trouble?"

"The old monk at the sick-house, he says you owe him money, he says you owe him a hundred cash, he says if you don't pay him he's going to tell Old Sun I had a Hua sow come and lie with me every afternoon while I was in the sick-house."

I had not yet even realized the inappropriateness of my facial expression. Dolphin seemed thoroughly annoyed. Yet I still stood receptive, face tilted to accept.

"I'll pay him," I said, with asinine eagerness. "As soon as I can get a chit I'll pay him. . . . But, Dolphin. I didn't lie with you."

"He'll make it so. The yellow people always believe a monk."

"But I didn't, Dolphin." With a rush I was telling myself, but not Dolphin, that I owed the monk nothing, that he was an extortionist, and worse—he used his holy calling to suck slaves. Yet I wanted to keep my mind on the invitation Dolphin was surely . . .

"You'd better get the money to him. Before they skin me again."

At last I was beginning to mobilize myself. I saw a passage of uncertainty in Dolphin's face. He appeared to want to turn on his heel and walk away, yet something held him—a moment's vacillation. In all my days of visiting him at the sick-house he had never spoken an endearing word to me. How had I become so certain then of his wanting me?—that he would ask for me, today? I had become so certain, I now imagined, because of my reading of just such moments of hesitation as this in a man to whom decisiveness was the only valid pose. There was that hint of tightness around his mouth.

I moved close to him and said in an urgent voice, "I'll come here day after tomorrow night, I'll wait for you."

Dolphin said nothing and showed nothing, unless possibly a draining off into his eyes of some of the feeling, whatever it was, that had stiffened his mouth. He began to turn.

I delayed him for a moment by saying, "Under the willow."

Now he turned away and I said to his back, "After the time-keeper's gong for the first quarter of the night."

The selfish man was walking quickly away.

❰ Figures in the Dark

Under a cuticle moon I could barely make out the nearest grave mounds. I stood beneath the willow, my hands on the trunk to keep, through its rough touch, some sense of reality. Willow! Symbol, in the yellows' tales, of frailty and lust.

The cemetery wall was at my back. My eyes, adjusted to the night, strained up the hill toward the main gate. I felt gloomy. The night air was damp, and walking alone among the newly weeded graves in the dark had been quite a different matter from our social outing on Ch'ing Ming in dazzling sunlight. Dolphin had by no means agreed to meet me. Slipping away from our k'ang in the slave hut had been a strain. Would Daddy Chick waken and miss me, and if he did, could he be counted upon not to report me to Hua?

Near me, a grave of some important Sun ancestor was surmounted by a huge marble tortoise bearing on his back an inscribed tablet. Why a turtle—the yellows' most insulting curse word? I felt all about me forces I could not understand, and over me the ragged willow seemed to have stars clinging like aphids to its leaves.

I was shivering. I spat, to exorcise evil spirits that might be near me.

A motion on the hill! I gripped the tree trunk harder, unable to decide whether to run toward or away from the apparition.

I had said I would wait for him under the tree. I would try to stay where I was.

The moving thing came closer and closer. It paused, divided into two, and sat on the great marble turtle and laughed in two drunken voices—man's and woman's. Then it folded into a tight ball and rolled down the ancestor's mound and fumbled in a draw between graves, not ten paces from me, and I began to hear grunts, sharply drawn breaths, moans, and suppressed cries.

In the midst of this I saw a new figure swiftly approaching. It came down the hill toward the willow and straight through the draw, and I saw it go down, stumbling over the drunken fornicators; then I heard a woman's horrified gasp and a man cursing, then guffaws—more than one voice. Then Dolphin was with me under the tree. He was shaking with laughter. The other forms were scrambling uphill; I saw them drop down several mounds away.

I did not know, beyond a flood of relief, what I felt. Anxiety, awe, hope, fear of the dark, a slave's inchoate longing, a feeling of the rawness of life that came from eavesdropping on the drunken lusts of others.

"You decided to come," I said in a voice whose trembling I heard indifferently, as if it were not mine.

Dolphin did not speak or move for a long time. Then he took my cheeks in his palms and lifted my face.

Never, until that moment, had Dolphin, by word or act, showed me the slightest sign of outgoing tenderness, but now I felt in his hands, which shook like my voice of a moment ago, the full force of a strength-and-helplessness that must have been a male slave's lot. I did not know whether this force had anything to do, really, with me. The endless passivity of his days; this blundering, wild, unstoppable assertion by night, its power expressed in its very gentleness. This touch of the cupping hands was far more intense than anything I had been offered in those few minutes long ago in the small dark room in Chao-er's tavern.

Now explicit feeling began to pour into me. All my hopes and daydreams of so many days had shaped this flood of—why, there was nothing to call it but desperation. The warm hands on my cheeks filled me with a blind and boundless desperation.

We lay together in the very draw where the drunken pair had made those unbridled noises. A grave to one side looked to my distracted glance, in a moment of transport of an order that was

new in my life, like a—could I bear to think it?—like a distant
mountain. Did I make sounds like that drunken woman's? I
do not know. We stayed in the draw until the sky began to lighten.
I did not sleep all night, because of my beliefs that moonlight and
starlight, no matter how pale, could paralyze a sleeping cheek,
and that if a glowworm crawled across a sleeping eye, that eye
would never see again.

⟨ A Fatal Greed

       I was in the clutch of a fatal greed—fatal, I mean, for
a two-legged sow. I wanted to possess Dolphin. I wanted him for
mine alone.
    We slept together often in the graveyard and in the woods and
in the open fields, always now at Dolphin's urging. He enjoyed
me; he spoke, at last, some tender, almost abject, words of promise to me. I came second with him: himself came first.
    But I was greedy. I determined that we would be married,
knowing perfectly well that slave marriages in the yellow dominion were meaningless. They consisted of owners' permissions, and
they lasted until an owner's convenience required the moving of
one partner to another farm, or until a master sold husband or
wife away—or, indeed, until one or another slave tired of the
arrangement. All a sow's owner cared about was that she should
breed, increasing his wealth.
    In those days I began to wear a charm to help bring this deter-
mination of mine to pass—a pair of mole paws on a cord around
my neck. This talisman, which I bought from a peddler with
stolen coppers, restored to me a feeling of confidence that I had
never felt since the owner of the East Garden had snatched my
relic of the Guevavi martyr from my neck when we were first
sold.
    How fitting!—the spadelike tools that a blind creature used to
make his way through the endless sod of this world.
    Yet how perverse the charm was, too! Moth had whispered to
me of something secretly called the Kingdom of the Mole—a place
beyond "the mountains," beyond the borders of the slave provinces, where, though the territory was supposed to be free, Imperial laws still required the return of slaves who had escaped
from the slave lands; it was said that there certain yellow "moles"

led the runaways through their "runs" to safety far from the borders. And so my charm presaged both getting and losing. . . .

First, before I even opened the way for Dolphin to ask me to marry him, I had to make sure that Hua and his wife would give their permission. I thought that this would readily be granted: all they could wish was for me to be pregnant, to give them a gift of another piglet on the place.

Two events now took place, however, which forced me to postpone my plan.

Before dawn one morning in the fourth month Moth began to suffer birth pains. Jasmine, who was to serve as midwife, prepared for the delivery, and I did whatever Jasmine told me. I had never seen a baby born, and when the labor began in earnest I was afraid, partly for Moth but indirectly for myself, imagining myself in Moth's place on the straw mats on the mud k'ang in our slave hut—pale hands gripping a plow handle, forehead running with sweat, teeth clamped on a twisted wet cloth to curb the unearthly cries.

Jasmine anointed her hands with lard. She made poor Moth between pains drink some tea made from the clay of a mud-wasp's nest, to ease her labor, and for the good influences of iron we placed the head of a hoe in the k'ang oven under her. Jasmine sent me out to collect cobwebs to stem hemorrhages, and to steal some sugar from Hua's wife's jar to put on the dressings afterward.

When, hours later, a strange object, cheese-covered and blotched, emerged at last to my terror from a struggling Moth, Jasmine lifted it upside down in her firm hands and with hard blows knocked breath into it. It squalled! It had tiny fruit in its crotch! A noisy boy! A great value to the Huas!

Jasmine, overjoyed, cleaned it up. She put a greasy bit of half-cooked pork fat in its mouth "to clean out the insides," and she made me light a fire outdoors and burn the afterbirth—else, she said, Moth would be a long time recovering; a chore that made me ill. When I returned, the baby was still crying, and Jasmine was murmuring over it. "Look!" she said to me, pointing at his tightly clenched fists, so perfect and delicate, like secret scrolls of fern in earliest spring. "He's going to be a thief, he'll turn out a thief—that's what it means when they grip their hands like that." This seemed to delight Jasmine.

Hua's wife came and inspected the baby. I saw the mistress's face cloud over, her jaw set up hard. She swept out in a wild fury.

Then Jasmine showed me the awful trouble that had come into our house: The infant's skin was yellowish, its hair was black, its still-squinted eyes were "good"—there were the telltale vertical folds of the inner canthi, drawing down the skin to prove who was the father.

We moved in fear. Stealthily the second morning we washed the baby in water in which a branch of acacia had been boiled, to make the child immune to the diseases that killed white infants.

For days Hua's wife spoke to no one. Hua, who had been increasingly morose since the sale of his crop, lay low; he got out of his wife's way like a wonk with its tail between its legs. How unlike a master he was! In small ways we slaves were rude to him, but we kept our distance from the seething yellow woman. Moth, recovering, fondling her doll-like infant with all sorts of cooing and murmuring, was oblivious of the storm that was raging in the main house.

A few days later, the second deterrent: One of Old Sun's private militia discovered, buried under sacks in the old miser's seed house, some literature from the so-called Uncage-the-Finches Society in the Northern Capital.

A large number of Sun hogs, Dolphin among them, were shut up in a bamboo palisade and were questioned for days on end about these documents.

We were dimly aware of an unaccountable fervor among some of the yellows, mostly Buddhists, in the faraway core provinces, who wanted all slaves throughout the Empire to be set free. But this fervor was remote; the harsh, exhausting routine of our daily lives dulled our minds, and apart from a persistent aching consciousness of "the mountain," toward which we could struggle one by one if our individual lots drove us to such a mad risk, we gave little thought to the vague rumors.

Besides, we mistrusted yellows who wanted to help us—what did they *really* want?

The discovery of the literature, however, terrified the masters and impressed the slaves of the entire district. It was, indeed, the violent reaction of the slaveowners rather than the broadsheets themselves that stirred us to endless whispered conferences out of the yellows' earshot.

Even Daddy Chick made our hearts beat wildly by playing tunes on his Tartar fiddle which, without his singing at all, acted on us like thrilling messages in code, for we knew the unsung words of the songs:

> *The finch in the pine tree was sighing,*
> *The sky was an ear for his voice.*

And another—about "the mountain":

> *Ten thousand stones, the path is a place to stumble.*
> *From the high crag the path cannot be seen.*

It was certain that Daddy Chick had no thought whatever of running away, yet he played these "away songs" on his soughing fiddle with a melancholy that made us, as we lay on the k'angs, grind our teeth.

For a week I lost track of Dolphin. We could not get any word back and forth. There opened before my eyes the abyss that life without him would be.

When Moth's little mix was nine days old, it was time to name him. On Moth's first rising at dawn she carried the infant three times around the slave hut and then, at the door, Jasmine loudly pronounced the name Moth had chosen: Apple. We all kissed Moth, who wept with joy.

Jasmine's children had all survived, and Moth felt that Jasmine understood the magic that was needed to bring a slave infant through the trials of the beginning of life as a chattel. One night the baby was fretful. We were all up. Jasmine made Grin light his pipe and, drawing on it, she blew smoke on the throbbing fontanel of Apple's head. "It'll make him drunk," she said. The baby was soon asleep.

Apple had a pale birthmark on its chest. Jasmine directed Moth to lick it for nine successive days to make it go away. She said it would fade in a few months.

Jasmine had endless advice. "Feed a child out of the cooking pan, and he'll go to the mountain when he gets big enough. If he turns out to stutter give him a drink of tea out of a bell. Don't show him his face in a mirror until he's a year old, or he'll be tongue-tied. When you take him out in the fields, Moth, don't shade him with a hat belonging to Hua, or his teeth will be slow coming in, they might come in snaggled. Wash his limbs in the water we've used to cook rice if you want to keep him from being bowlegged. In the fields don't put him down and then forget and step across him; he won't thrive if you do that, he'll be stunted.

To dry up when you're weaning him, hang an old cash that's been worn smooth around your neck, hang it down between your breasts, then take it off and put it on an anthill, and when the ants go down you'll dry up. You can rub camphor on your breasts, too."

Moth said, "Stop, stop! You make me dizzy."

Moth now returned to the fields on a suckler's status. She left the infant in charge of Hua's wife, whose face puckered daily, as if she had been chewing hot ginger root, at the sight of the little master-begotten bastard. Moth was excused to the main house at brief intervals during the day to feed the child at the breast, and she was allowed rest periods "to cool her milk."

Hua's wife made no secret of her continuing fury at Hua, and her sarcasm against him, in our presence, made us laugh when we achieved the privacy of the slave hut. Moth seemed not the least bit ashamed of the paternity of her baby; in fact, she spoke of "opportunities" that might open up to a little mix, and I thought she carried herself with an almost insolent pride before Hua's wife, who, surprisingly, now that the baby was born and the half-suspected truth was out, behaved towards Moth with a forbearance that verged on tenderness.

Hearing that the grillings in the bamboo stockade had been brought to an inconclusive end, and that Dolphin and the other suspects had been set at large, but still having heard nothing more from him, I decided to set about getting what I wanted.

One day I helped the mistress clean the floors of the main house. We spread dampened charcoal ashes on the caked dirt and left them there some time "to draw the smells out," then swept them up and threw them out in the courtyard, where I scattered them with the back of a wooden rake. I went in the house and abruptly told Hua's wife that I wanted to marry a hog belonging to Old Sun.

I saw at once that she would accede; I thought she seemed relieved.

However, she said, "It is bad for slaves on separate farms to marry."

"May I ask Old Venerable?" We slaves used honorifics only when we begged for favors.

Perhaps she saw my appeal as a chance to punish her husband in some vague way. She said, "I'll take care of it with him."

Two days later Hua's wife took me aside and said, "All right.

You may ask his permission now." Why the half-formed smile? Had she brought it home to Hua that my marriage would place me out of bounds to his itch? What had she put in *my* lips as she quoted my appeal?

I asked him, and he—responding to whatever had been behind that smirk of hers—was bad-tempered. "I have no objection," he said. "But I'll wager you will never get old Night-Soil Basket's permission." How undignified for a yellow man to use hogs' epithets! "And if you do marry this pig, don't ask for a chit every night. It is no good to marry a pig on another farm." Hua walked away from me. Had I not been completely absorbed by my sweet greed, I might have been frightened by Hua's manner.

Now Dolphin.

I thought of using the policy Moth advised—suddenly refuse to go out in the fields and lie with him; drive him to distraction with desire; make a bargain—*that* in exchange for marriage.

But I decided to do just the opposite: give myself to him altogether. This was easy. Was I not a slave to begin with?

Within a fortnight he had, without a word of prompting, asked me to become his wife. I could not refuse him! He said he would ask his master's permission.

At work at Hua's I waited anxiously for three days for some word from Dolphin. Then one of Old Sun's militiamen came to Hua with a curt message that Sun Lao-yeh intended to buy the slave girl White Lotus from Hua for seventeen taels of silver— a despicable price, an insulting condescension, which only a patron could offer a man who was at his mercy.

Hua blew up. He saw himself driven to ground—his wife and his patron after him like vicious wild dogs. Hua railed; the militiamen remained calm and over-patient.

"Sun Lao-yeh is doing this for the sake of the two pigs," the militiaman said with infuriating serenity and obvious hypocrisy. "The permanence of the marriage depends on their living together, working side by side, being drawn together by common experiences."

"Turtle shit!" Hua screamed. "The old squeeze-purse wants the girl because pig offspring follow the condition of the mother."

"Lao-yeh would not be happy to hear that he had been called a squeeze-purse."

The upshot was that Hua went himself, in his tunic that was out at the elbows, to plead with Old Sun.

Hua came back with permission to keep me—and with permission for me to marry Dolphin. Hua exulted before his wife and before us all at having pulled off this result, but there was something unconvincing in his pride. What had he yielded to make this bargain? He made it amply clear to me that I was in his debt. I saw this; it was Moth who pointed out to me that his wife saw it, too.

We chose the holiday of the Summer Festival, fifth fifth, as our wedding date. Hua's wife was suddenly like an aunty hen to me. She gave me three louse-bedding gowns, and Moth, who was childishly excited by my prospects, showed me how to dye them in bright colors.

We boiled hickory bark and bay leaves, and strained the brew, and let it stand a day; then we heated it again, wet one of the gowns in cold water, plunged it in the boiling dye, let it soak awhile, and took it out, dried it, then set it with urine. That was my yellow dress. We dyed another in bamboo and set it in copperas, and that was my red. We dyed the third in pine straw and set it with vinegar, and that was my purple. My old dress that I had been wearing in the fields we dyed in indigo and set it with alum, and that was my blue. The colors were uneven and streaked, but they were at least colors.

Hua hovered about these activities with a surly expression. "What courtesans!" he sarcastically said.

We gathered petals of jasmine and leaves of sweet basil, and we stole some cloves from the kitchen, and we folded these things into my colored gowns and let them stand three days, and then my clothes were good-smelling.

The entire day before the wedding Hua's wife kept me shut in the work space of the main house, hidden behind a sheet of bamboo matting that she propped against the loom. "A bride must not be seen," she said. She handed food to me around the edge of the screen in a bowl.

In the afternoon a cart came from Old Sun with gifts for the bride's "family"—meaning the Huas: two dozen hunks of bread, a box of noodles, a penury of rice, some salt from the sea, and the carcass of a pig. Obedient to custom, Hua cut the pig in two and sent half back.

"Look at this skinny animal," Hua bitterly said.

(A Spirit of Irony

I felt that the entire Summer Festival was meant for Dolphin and me. The Huas hung willow twigs and artemisia on the door lintel of the main house, and they pasted red papers cut in gourd shapes on the walls—all for us, I felt. The yellow and white children wore five-colored long-life strings—for us? Hua's wife, Jasmine, Moth, and I pinned paper cutouts of the character "tiger" to our gowns. (I was in my red, for happiness.) Jasmine cooked triangular rice puddings called *tsung-tzu,* and we ate them with warmed wine in the morning. Feeling that the wine was for me, I drank too much.

At midday Dolphin's procession of drunken hogs came for me. It was all shabby and cynical, but I was wildly happy. I was tipsy myself. Two Sun hogs led the way with strings of fingerling fire-crackers hung from poles, and when I showed my face at the Huas' gate I was greeted with their seemingly endless snapping. Savory blue smoke of their exploded powder hung about me, and it mixed with the sweet perfume of my dress to brew a pungent scent like that of litchi nuts. Behind the noisemakers were two men waving lanterns on rods, though it was a bright day. Then came crude banners, made of red paper and bearing characters, some of which were traditional luck-words but some of which were merely obscene—a semi-literate hog's bad jokes. Drums and gongs shook the air. Then followed an oxcart bearing Quart and Second, Dolphin's best friends and attendants, quite besotted. And last came two seedy sedan chairs—obviously long discarded by the Suns—one trimmed with green paper, one with red, and in the latter, borne by four hogs, sat Dolphin, rocking and roaring with a neckful of brandy.

Daddy Chick brought out a jug of cheap wine, donated by Hua, and three bowls, and offered drinks where they were least needed, to Dolphin and his two attendants.

I stood at the gate, suddenly paralyzed by disappointment and a feeling that all this was utterly without reason or meaning.

Lank and Grin took bellowing Dolphin by the upper arms and tenderly guided him, as if he were somehow wounded and delirious, perhaps blinded, into the Huas' sleeping quarters. Before Hua, Dolphin suddenly fell silent, but his bearing was so insolent that I became deeply frightened.

With a dignity I could not help admiring, Hua's wife poured a bowl of tea for this Dolphin.

Without waiting for it to cool, perhaps thinking that it was hot wine, Dolphin took a gulp. It burned his mouth, and he spewed it out on the dirt floor, sputtering and spitting. Hua stood up in a fury, but I saw Hua's wife touch the master's arm, and she picked up a pair of paper flowers and firmly pulling down Dolphin's head pinned them to his hat. Dolphin began wagging his head in a stupid way, to make the paper flowers rustle. Hua's wife draped a square of red cotton cloth over Dolphin's shoulders. Lank and Grin turned him around and marched him out.

He had not once looked at me. Was he too far gone to know that he was getting married?

Now Jasmine and Moth, my attendants, led me to the red sedan chair and seated me in it. Dolphin was steered to the green-trimmed chair. A Sun hog handed Jasmine a small square mirror, donated to the bride, he said, by Old Night-Soil Basket, and Jasmine slipped it under my gown—to ward off evil spirits that might be lurking along the way to the Sun farm.

I was now fighting back tears of humiliation, fear, and anger.

Four hogs lifted me off the ground, and I sat swaying while Daddy Chick tied a teapot of water to my sedan chair, in order that, dripping along the path, it might insure a long, happy tie between the bride's and groom's "families."

Sore and dulled though I felt, I could not help giggling during the slow ride along the path where I had so often run in my haste to be with Dolphin. I jounced up and down on the springy poles of the sedan chair; my bearers were comically drunk; the mere fact of being carried in honor and supposed joy was bitterly funny.

The Huas followed in a cart.

When we arrived at Old Sun's ornate main gate, Quart, with a great deal of sarcastic pantomime, set fire to two bundles of wheat straw, while Second, dancing around like a monkey, at last wound up and threw a small cake over the gate. All the slaves were laughing now, because these acts were supposed to mean that "the groom's household," signifying really Old Sun himself, would grow richer on account of the wedding. Ha-ha-ha!

I was at last beginning to enter into the real spirit of my own wedding, which was irony.

Yes, I got a huge laugh from the crowd of slaves at the gate, when, stepping over the cloth saddle that lay on the gate sill—for the yellows' characters for "saddle" and "peace" were homophones —I squatted momentarily over it in the awkward crouch we sows had to use relieving ouselves in the open fields at work.

I was led before the tablet of Yü Huang, god of heaven, Jade Emperor, and I kowtowed before it with no hope of any kind that the god would bless my marriage. Then I was led before Old Sun, and for the first time I saw that the old man had cataracts in his eyes; he could not see me. He did not remember the name of his own slave, the groom.

Old Sun had killed a sheep, and we had a "feast," which is to say that each slave had a tiny taste of mutton. During this affair I was oppressed by a constant tinkling of small bells—for the bells were on a high metal rack that was locked to the back and shoulders of a hog who had tried to go off to the mountain, but who had been caught; he was forced now to wear the rack of bells day and night. This was one occasion at which I did not want to think about the mountain.

Dolphin was now too drunk to recognize me.

After the feast Old Sun and his entire family, together with the Huas and their Barley Flower, Cart Tongue, Stone, and Little Four, led a procession to the slave quarters, where, in the bare room in which Dolphin lived with five others, a nuptial chamber had been prepared; his fellows would sleep elsewhere for one night. There Sun and Hua bowed to each other and exchanged congratulations, and pledged eternal friendship. Then interminably the slaves of Sun trooped past him, kowtowing on the floor and congratulating him.

It seemed that in this way I was married, for when at last this endless process of adulation of Dolphin's master was finished, I was simply pushed into the nuptial chamber and Dolphin was half-carried in and stretched out on the k'ang, where he began at once to snore.

Slave musicians started a racket at the still-open door, and I shrank back against the k'ang as I saw that one of the percussive instruments being pounded for a clacking sound with a small wooden tube, was an animal jawbone—and I remembered that other jawbone of futility held high under the lamp in the smithy in a trembling white hand.

Someone shoved shut the two leaves of the door of the room. All night, drunken-hog pranksters howled and cat-meowed and donkey-brayed outside the door, and now and then pushed a lit firecracker through the crack between the leaves.

One of these firecrackers wakened Dolphin. He clamped his hands to his temples; he had a throbbing headache and was bad-humored. He sat up for a time, however, and tried to talk about the day with me. He nodded off now and then. We kept the oil lamp in the wedding chamber lighted, because we had been told that whichever put out the lamp would be the first to die.

At the dawn gong I had to flee, without benefit of procession or sedan chair (in fact, Sun's gate guard stopped me on the way out to ask who I was and why I trespassed in the Sun compounds), back to Hua's farm, to scrape cotton. In the fields the kaoliang was knee-high, the cotton ankle-high. We were thinning the cotton rows to single stands. Hua did not even welcome me back; he was working his jaw muscles over the eight rainless days we had had. He shouted at us to hoe the soil toward the plants. I worked wondering if the day before, the day of my wedding, had passed in a dream, or in delirium. Nothing at all was changed.

⟨[Married Life

If there was change, it was for the worse. For all concerned. I was in a continuous fever of wanting to be with my husband. "You are useless," said Hua, furious at me for my begging of chits, his eyes drought-ravaged like the brass sky we had been having.

Dolphin refused to come to Hua's. "Hua is like a badger. He smells like a badger," Dolphin said. "I can't stand his gut-rot smell."

"You don't want to be with me," I said, and I hated myself for whining.

"Here I do. Or in the fields. Not at Dirty Hua's."

This meant that I saw him less than I might have.

Our work was scraping and irrigating. The cotton plants were as tall as small dogs. We hoed the channels between the rows, leaving water furrows, and we hauled at the lifting levers of the scattered wells until our arms ached, but still the plants seemed parched. Hua ran to the temple every day to demand rain.

As summer moved on, Dolphin, besides scraping for Sun by

day, was assigned on rotation as a nocturnal crop-watcher. In the sixth month, when table vegetables came to harvest in the rich man's vast gardens, the temptations for both slaves from neighboring farms and poor yellows from the countryside to steal good food in a dry season were curbed by Sun hogs' standing guard. The vegetable fields were dotted with small booths, which had walls of reed matting and each contained a light wooden bench-like litter covered with a layer of kaoliang stalks.

Dolphin gave me notice of his watching duties, and these shabby booths became our "homes."

What frenzied nights we had in our "homes"! With utter hopelessness we poured out to each other on the rustling litters the full intensity of our feelings—our violent lusts that seemed our only escape from slavery; a crushing occasional tenderness which, when it welled up in Dolphin, so that his hands played on my cheeks with a trembling touch, reduced me (for he was usually so selfish, so callous) to awful hacking sobs; jealousy (was I the only one who helped him guard the fields?); and, now and then, a clawing at each other that took the place, I suppose, of our destroying our yellow masters.

One night he had a jug of millet liquor.

"Where did you steal that?" I asked, delighted. We'd make our "home" shake *that* night.

"I bought it," Dolphin said.

"From your *money belt?*"

"I earned the money. You turtle-daughter!" Dolphin suddenly blazed up. "I get up before the dawn gong to weave baskets. I made eight mats. I'll spend the money any way I like. It's nothing to you."

"Yes!" I said. "Get rid of the money! Piss it down the latrines!"

"All right," Dolphin said, tight as a well rope lifting a full bucket, "just try to get your Dirty-Hua-sow mouth around this jug neck! Not a drop for you. This is *mine.*" At that he took an enormous drink; I could hear bubbles gurgling up into the tilted earthenware bottle.

But this was strange! I knew what the little hoard in the money belt was for. Dolphin had more than once called it his "mountain-climbing money." I had hated the money. It might have meant the end of me—the removal, I mean, of the vessel of my passion, my obsession. Yet here I was in an uncontrollable fury over his spending a few coppers for some stomach-dissolver.

"You selfish beast!" I hissed in his face. I grabbed for the jug. Roughly Dolphin snatched away his hands, with the liquor safely in them.

"So you want my money, you little pig whore!"

"Have you forgotten that I brought you money—*gave* you money?"

I closed my eyes. I began to shake as a terrifying thought battered at the back of my eyelids: that perhaps I *wanted* Dolphin to go to the mountain. Did I love him so much I wanted him to be free—but so little, too, that I wanted to be rid of him forever? Now suddenly I yearned to make peace with him, but I heard curses still streaming from my mouth like blood from a wound. I had not yet stemmed the flow when I felt the bottle thrust into my trembling hands. Silence. We were both panting. I drank. He drank. I again. It all happened in a flash. We laughed at our own, and each other's, rages. We lay down together, and our connection was ferocious. Afterwards we fought again on exactly the same topic.

It was as if we could not steer our poor selves.

All through these days I was in terror of a separation more complete than that of Hua sow and Sun hog—in terror of the mountain; in terror, too, lest Sun, who knew no names of his slaves, only statistics, accountings, might sell Dolphin away. Until, one evening, Hua gave me a surprise with some wild hope in it.

In small and absurd matters the Huas liked to pretend that they were wealthy slaveholders. They insisted on petty forms: we slaves had to address Barley Flower with the honorific "Kuniang," or "girl lady"! From the rafters over their k'ang Hua had suspended a kind of swing, and as the hot weather progressed and swarms of bluebottles and gnats invaded the house, Jasmine's ten-year-old son Bargain was placed in the swing with a pretentious fan of peafowl feathers in one hand and a donkey-tail fly whisk in the other, and it was his duty to fan his master and mistress and whip at the swarms of insects.

We were at an evening meal. The dry weather was still on us, and Hua was in a vicious mood. The leaves on the cotton plants were limp, the irrigation wells were almost dry. We slaves, eating in the work space, kept a somber silence, knowing that our master was near his wits' end.

Suddenly we heard him roaring for Jasmine. But Jasmine was at the cookstove at the most delicate stage of quick-frying some white cabbage; she poked her head around the divider and whispered, "White Lotus! Go see what he wants."

I saw, the moment I entered the Huas' chamber, what was wrong. Bargain in his fanning cradle had fallen fast asleep. His donkey-hair whisk was hanging loosely by a looped thong from his limp left hand, and its long ass hairs were hanging down directly in front of Hua's wife's face. The ends of the peafowl feathers on the long-handled fan were dipped in a bowl of chicken broth. The Hua children, awed by their father's massive wrath, were struggling not to titter.

Seeing me, Hua grew still more enraged. "I asked for Jasmine! Where is Jasmine! Why did they send this weed-back?"—an expression for a slut who would lie down to either whites or yellows in the open fields. "You!" he said, addressing me with a penetrating stare; this look suddenly had in it an element which, fearful as I was, puzzled me—a glint not merely of rage and frustration but of something else far more disturbing. Occasionally a man can be seen suppressing an up-bubbling smile when he is saying something sad, bitter, cruel, or outraged; Hua's mouth showed such a struggle. "Get the boy out of here and then come back. I want you to listen to speech."

I wakened Bargain; now the Hua children laughed openly, until Hua's wife, resonant with echoes of Hua's smile-fumed anger, cuffed Barley Flower. All, including Bargain, began to weep. Hua roared for silence, causing the children to raise their voices to howls. I took the fan and whisk, lifted Bargain down, and hurried with him from the room.

The bedlam—but not its basic emotions—had subsided when I returned to the room. Hua, cross-legged and arms folded, his neck tense, his mouth still twitching with inappropriate delight, was waiting for me.

"I'm sick to my heels of your running off to that hog at Sun's. I know what you do at night. Did you really think Daddy Chick would hold out on me? Listen to speech, you filthy weed-back. I am going to put an end to your being so tail-tired all day that you can't lift a hoe. I'm not going to write a single chit more for you." He waited, savoring my terror, and then, with the smile now daring to emerge openly under the false colors of a new idea, he said, "I'm going to trade. I'm going to get that pig of yours over here. Then you won't be running off every night. I'll trade Lank off for him. What's his name?"

"Dolphin."

"I'll teach the turtle to work. Those Sun hogs don't know what it means to be slaves."

The disturbing look on Hua's face was now fully open, like some poisonous flower, and I understood it. It spoke of debts. I owed Hua for my marriage; now I would owe him for the man-trade.

But I was so overcome with pleasure at the news just thundered at me that I ignored the look; I even failed to wonder how Dolphin would like the idea of being traded off to the badger, Hua.

(Stripping Day

On an agreed day in the seventh month each year, according to an unwritten law of East-of-the-Mountains Province, whoever chose to do so could go into anyone else's kaoliang fields to strip the lower leaves up to a man's height. This was supposed to allow the stalks to "breathe." The leaves made fine fodder and had almost as many secondary uses as the stalks.

The whole countryside descended on Old Sun's estate on stripping day. Hua, who had carefully defoliated all his own kaoliang, left Daddy Chick and Grin to guard his acres and took the rest of us, including his wife, with huge cotton-lint baskets, to garner what we could from Sun.

Hua put us to work. Then he said he wanted to talk with Venerable about the trade of men, and he went off.

Lank was as excited as I. The prospect of getting away from our master's squalid farm, and of change for its own sake, had this morose gambler in a state bordering on agreeableness.

Soon Hua returned. His wife, who also wanted the trade, because she had seen what a powerful hand Dolphin would make, in place of bony Lank, asked what luck he had had.

"Ayah!" Hua said. He seemed to be licking his chops. "Old Sun gave me a dressing down! Said I was far too lenient with my pigs. He said his father was the same way—too kindhearted. He said his father was too religious, had too much devoutness in him to keep his hogs down in the wallow where they belonged. He said I had yet to learn the first rule of hog-taming: Overhaul every one from time to time. Give him a good raking. Then he'll stay where he belongs, in the mud by the trough. Old Sun says that's what *he* does. Ha-ha-ha-ha!"

"And what about the trade?"

Hua looked at his wife, then at me. "He hasn't decided. He says he must discuss it with One-Eyed Chang." This Chang, who had two keen eyes but was so stubborn, and therefore so narrow-visioned, as to have earned this nickname, was Hua's successor as overseer of all the Sun slaves.

"One-Eye will never do *you* a favor," Hua's wife said.

(A Question of Face

Two afternoons later Hua received a curt message from Old Sun which made him feel so much loss of face that he shut himself up in his room all one day.

One-Eye had told Old Sun that the hog Dolphin had refused to be traded; said he would kill himself first.

Hua, determined to recover face, went to the rich man again. He returned swaggering. He said Old Sun himself had talked with the slave Dolphin, and Dolphin had agreed to the trade on condition that Hua would build a separate hut for Dolphin and his sow. To this, Hua reported, he had said, "Keep your filthy proud pig, Venerable. I cannot afford to build him a private mansion."

At this Old Sun had laughed until he got the hiccoughs, clapped his hands for One-Eye, and commanded that the trade (*hic*) be consummated on the following (*hic*) day, whether the what's-his-name hog (*hic*) liked it or not.

(Snake's Blood

Dolphin arrived on the bed of a cart with his hands and feet all tied together with one knot of rope behind his back. Daddy Chick, who had gone with Hua to deliver Lank and collect Dolphin, said it had taken four men to truss Dolphin.

Just as Hua and Daddy Chick, with the rest of us for audience, were murmuring at the main gate about how to unload Hua's writhing acquisition, and whether to untie him or let him remain bound to think awhile, a hullabaloo approached along the sunken road from the direction of the district town.

Though I had never seen such a sight before, I knew at once what it was: A runaway slave had been captured.

The noisy party consisted of a professional slave-hunter; his squad of three "boar-chasers," athletic young yellow roughnecks of the poorest class, in ragged clothes, loudly arguing in transit with the hunter about their wages for this capture; a pack of yelping wonks, like emaciated yellowish wolves, in a large bamboo cage on a cart; and, tied to the cart tail, with a heavy wooden cangue locked on his neck and wrists, the quarry of the chase, stumbling along half dead.

It was not hard to see why the hunter had so far underpaid his "boar-chasers." These hunters with their packs of vicious trained wonks were customarily paid in full by the owners of runaways only if they brought in the captured slaves unmarked by the dogs. In this respect the hunter had not been successful this time; crimson tags of flesh hung from the staggering white man's forearms. The hunter might not get much for this botched job.

Here is the scene at the fruition of my daydreams—the arrival of my beloved husband to share my (somewhat overcrowded) k'ang:

Dolphin, who yearned for the mountain, lying on his side on Hua's cart bed, his back painfully arched, his extremities cuffed behind with a raveled length of hemp, his furious eyes suddenly melting into a look of astonished compassion when he sees the lurching bloody captive; the children, both Hua's and Grin's, rushing merrily out to the road, as if this were a sideshow at a temple festival; my owner in a state bordering on paralysis, not knowing how to deal with the massive rage on his cart; Moth, impervious to the boiling emotions on every side, nudging me and giggling about how busy a certain little mouse will be from now on; and I, weeping because I think that Dolphin thinks that I planted the idea of the odious trade in my master's mind, and trying not to be seen weeping . . .

The procession passed.

Hua, confronted by the certainty that he would never master Dolphin if not now, stepped forward with a wan face and untied the bonds.

Dolphin gave his master a surprise: sprang from the cart, suddenly cheerful. During the rest of that day, Hua laughed loudly at everything Dolphin did, too loudly.

We went to the fields. During the afternoon Daddy Chick gave Dolphin a trivial command—to start a new row.

"Are you the overseer?" Dolphin snarled.

"You must get something straight," said Daddy Chick. "You're lucky. You have a good master."

" 'Good' and 'master' don't fit. Your face is soiled off his behind."

For the most part, however, Dolphin went about his work with energy and an indifferent attitude. By day he ignored me; at night he took me off in the fields, and nothing was either better or worse.

He started right in working for coppers on his own time, mornings and evenings, making baskets, mats, mule collars, chopsticks, birdcages, and hoe handles.

One day he told Hua that a certain task on the cotton rows was done in a better way at Old Sun's, and he offered to show how it was done.

Hua became quarrelsome—called his new slave insubordinate.

Another time Hua flew into a rage at Dolphin. Dolphin came in from the fields carrying a black snake by the tail. He said he had broken the snake's back by tracing a cross mark in its track and spitting in the juncture of the cross.

Hua shouted, "You idiot of a turtle! Don't you know that a snake's track in the road will bring rain?"

Dolphin remained polite and cheerful; this was what truly angered our drought-parched Hua.

In our slave hut that evening Dolphin cut open the snake and dripped some of its blood into a little bowl of millet liquor, which he had poured out from a bottle hidden in his bedroll, and he drank it—"to get strong. I'll do more work than all of you put together."

Next day came the first real impasse. We were scraping. Hua came storming along the rows. "Move faster, you white shoat," he cried at Dolphin.

But Dolphin did not move faster. He began, with shocking deliberateness, to move much slower.

([A Living Cloud

For a few weeks, until the calamity happened, I suppose my lot could have been called happy. I remember, at any rate, many moments of heightened perception, when, with a keenness of vision and depth of feeling that I could hardly bear, an isolated instant's joy would become fixed in my mind like a perfect swift sketch on a scroll.

An example, somewhat ironic:

Hua's wife believed that our swine could be protected from hog cholera by attaching a small piece of red cloth to a stick and placing it at the gate of the sty, and she had commissioned me to make and to fly this antiseptic banner. I did. The moment I remember is that of standing back, seeing the long-tailed triangular pennant I had made whipping its vivid bamboo-copperas red against a sky which, having had several weeks to dry out, was the pale blue exactly of Dolphin's eyes. He and I had coupled, with extraordinary peace of heart, in the burying ground the night before. Now the brilliant sunny scene—the mud fence of the wallow, the pigs dozing, a willow beyond brushing at the morning in the breeze, the beloved sky-eye blue, the small sanguine banner—filled me with the greatest pleasure a slave could have: for a second forgetting that he, too, was a pig, pig, pig.

Two full moons had passed with but two brief squalls of rain—quick downpours of huge drops which scarcely dampened the skin of the ground. Of Hua's ten irrigation wells, nine had gone dry.

As Hua watched his cotton plants shrivel he became more and more religious, which seemed to mean: somber, depressed, punitive. He took us in a party every day to Limestone Hill Generous Temple to pray. Other masters were also herding their slaves to the temple, and poor yellows flocked there, too. The crowds milling about the hill above the quarry were larger every day.

Hua became increasingly precise in his rituals, and more and more harsh toward us.

I began to see religion as a suit of clothing, covering naked barbarity. At the temple pigs talked to other masters' pigs, and it was our common understanding that the more religious a slaveholder became, the more malicious, violent, vindictive, and deceitful he became. Piety and cruelty were mask and face.

In Hua I saw something else. He began to look at me, whenever Dolphin's back was turned, with an expression I could scarcely misread, of overt lechery. Always behind his surreptitious looks was a creditor's arrogance; I was not to forget my debts to him.

Then disaster fell on us out of the arid sky.

We were all scraping one day in what Hua called Giant Toad Second Field, for weeds grew in the dry dirt even if cotton stood

still. Dolphin and I worked shoulder to shoulder, and I was churn-
ing with the most complicated feelings. On four separate occasions, recently, Dolphin had disappeared after the evening curfew
gong; he had told me, the following mornings, with sour wine on
his breath, that he had gone to see his old hog friends at Sun's—
he missed them too much. Was he meeting some sow in the
graveyard? We were all physically exhausted; the daily hike to
the temple and back came on top of our regular work. I was
growing afraid of Hua. My dear friend Moth was doing her best
to seduce Dolphin before my very eyes. I hated the idols in the
temple; I hoped the cotton leaves would curl and die. I brought
my hoe down with bone-jarring conviction.

Dolphin beside me seemed cold. I had learned to my joy that
he was capable of deep feelings, but I also knew that he was able
readily to close them off altogether. Far, far away was the
haunted, wild, bloodshot-eyed Nose of the Capital, devoted to mere
desolate badness as his answer to the masters; far remote too,
was the equally haunted visionary Peace of South-of-the-River,
trying to organize revenge. My husband seemed dispassionate; took
slavery, marriage, hoeing, whiteness of skin, lovemaking by grave
mounds—took everything as a matter of course. Was this what
his bonds had done to him—flattened him out? Or—a comber of
panic surged over me—was he calm because he had made up his
mind for the mountain?

"Dolphin." Crut. Crut.

"What?"

"Dolphin. If you go to the mountain will you take me with you?"

"Hush, baby. Take it easy. You're going to kill your luck with
that hoe."

"Will you?"

"If the badger hears you, you'll get beaten and me beaten. He's
getting to be a snake. Watch your words."

"Will you?"

Now *his* chopping is hard.

"You don't go in pairs."

"Why not?"

"Anyone knows that. There never has been a slave reach that
place except alone."

"You'd leave me?"

"Who said I was going?"

There was a dry, rustling whir at my ear, and downward across my field of vision slanted the air-fanning flight of a grasshopper. I saw the green papery insect land on a brownish leaf of cotton, and my eye stayed on it as it began, with a voraciousness that only a slave could understand, to clip at the edges of the leaf with its ravenous little mandibles.

A few hoe strokes later I saw another come down. Dolphin also saw this one. He put down his hoe, stepped to the row, and with hands making two cups trapped the insect. Carefully taking the sawlike lower joints of both the great jumping legs between a thumb and forefinger, he carried the little creature down the line to Hua.

I saw the storm come up across Hua's face. He began to scream, "Kill it! Kill it! Were there any more? Ayah! Ayah! Kill it, you white turtle!"

It was a locust.

At this knowledge I felt a surge of triumphant malice, and hastily I searched along the stunted, drooping plants for the first of the insects I had seen. I found it with barely room left to stand on the leaf it was consuming, and, imitating Dolphin, I caught it, pinched its hind legs, and carried it without a word to Hua. I felt the wildest pleasure at the sight of the consternation on his yellow face, and when he looked at me, and I saw a flicker of his eye that responded to my awful delight with a much more awful threatening anticipatory delight of his own, I turned away, with renewed shouts from Hua, this time of desire thinly wrapped in alarm, at my back, and I ran in fear to Dolphin, reaching out the insect for him to kill it and somehow protect me.

Hua, however, turned his mind from me and forthwith adjourned our scraping and herded us off to the temple, where we found half a dozen excited masters and their slaves already gathered, crowding to worship the plaster idol of Ch'ung Wang, god of insects.

These farmers, or their slaves, had all seen locusts. One of the yellows told Hua the locusts were coming from the district to the west of ours; it was a punishment, he said, for our magistrate's not having attended the funeral of a deceased warlord of that district, Ch'i by name. Hua shrugged.

Hua hurried us back to the farm. We saw no more locusts that day, but the next day they came in squads, like groups of scouting outriders. We spent the entire day spotting them and killing them.

The third day the insects fell like light snow. Hua divided his inadequate force into noisemakers and beaters. Half of us pounded on gongs, pans, and an old peddler's drum Hua had once bought for just this purpose, and shrilled and whooped, too; some of the insects, perhaps scared by our clanging and booming and shouting, swooped up and flew on. The rest of us thrashed with spades, boards, brooms, and bundles of willow twigs at insects that had landed. Dolphin nailed an old shoe sole to the end of a stick and wielded this swatter with great effectiveness, leaping here and there, roaring, making a jamboree of this macabre sport.

I spent the forenoon with a gong, the afternoon with a broom, and the whole crazy battle seemed to me an uproarious joke— though I dared not, of course, show this on my face. Hua was being ruined! His gaunt face, ravaged now by a total loss of sleep, seemed so funny to me that I had several times to turn away to keep from laughing. Yet I was uneasy, too. Would we have enough to eat? What if Hua failed altogether? Where would I be sent? Would Dolphin and I be parted?

The fifth and sixth days were the worst. The insects came in such masses that we abandoned trying to kill them one by one. We dug trenches across the fields and drove them with noise and brooms into these ditches and buried them wholesale. We stayed up the entire fifth night, setting fires whose light attracted the grasshoppers, thousands of which flew straight into the flames; thousands of others, alighting near the fires, were easy prey for our beating tools.

Long since, the mad joke had palled; I was horrified. The creaking, rustling creatures crawled in my hair, tickled my arms. I half expected them to turn their insatiable hunger against me. And Hua, looking more and more like a lightly framed locust himself, seemed unable, in the midst of his feverish despair, to take his eyes off me.

On the sixth afternoon a visible cloud of the insects came from the western horizon like a summer squall. Crossing the sun their transparent wings made at first a terrible, tremulous, vibrating shadow on the ground; then the cloud thickened, until at last we could not see the sun at all. The sky resounded with a great dry whisper of millions of wings.

Hua simply bolted. He ran off in a panic toward the temple.

Had it not been for Hua's wife, who stood beating a gong with a steady forearm, as if convinced that she herself would drive away the living storm, we pigs could simply have walked away into the chaotic countryside. Somehow the stolidity of our mistress, in the ever-darkening shadow of the plague, her sad but by no means resigned face, her look of contempt for gods and insects and husbands alike, roused some measure of feeling in me, whether of pity or admiration I could not have said, and I joined in the noisemaking at the top of my lungs.

Whatever the reason, it appeared that the main cloud was flying over and beyond us.

Dolphin, indifferent now as ever, said the locusts knew that Sun's crops were tastier than Hua's.

At this Hua's wife unexpectedly broke into strident laughter.

Hua, returning at a run from the temple, could not credit his eyes when he saw that only stragglers from the great cloud had landed on his farm. I think he believed his praying had done it, and once, after dark, when with the very last of our strength we were trying to annihilate the locusts that had fallen like trailing fringes of rain from the cloud, I felt a religious hand on my buttocks. I swung my broom swiftly around and struck my master hard on the arm and chest. What a surge of joy I felt at that blow! Hua drifted away into the shadows without a word.

On the seventh day the worst seemed to be over, though we could not be sure that the main cloud of the plague would not double back and attack what was left of green on Hua's acres.

That afternoon Hua took us to the temple to thank Ch'ung Wang for having sent the cloud farther along.

As we approached Limestone Hill we saw a large crowd milling around outside the temple, and coming closer we saw fists plunging and we heard angry shouts. A regular riot was in progress. We broke into a run. At the edge of the crowd, which seemed emotionally spent when we arrived, we learned that two boars had dug a tunnel from the shrubby slope behind the temple into the central hall, and they had made themselves a snug secret sanctuary under the banked-up stages on which the gods reposed; one of them was said to have made his nest right under the form of Ch'ung Wang, who was in charge of insects. The boars' asylum had been discovered only that morning. This desecration was clearly the cause of the plague. The riot was now already abating, we were told, because the two boars had some time since been beaten and stamped to death by—I almost fainted when I heard it—by a mob of frenzied slaves whose masters had hysterically threatened, in the excitement of the discovery, to kill all of them. The infestation, the masters had shrieked, had been brought on by white men. To save their own lives the hogs had kicked and trampled to death two of their own kind. I wondered if the boar I had seen under the bush had been one of them. Had I thought the plague a monstrous joke?

(The Master Collects

It was now Jasmine, to the surprise of us all, who emerged as leader of the whites on Hua's farm. This quiet, gentle mother, who had seemed engrossed every minute with the care not only of her own four children but also of Hua's little yellows, and who, cooking for our owners, had seemed so anxious to please them, saw that our master was on the brink of collapse, and with appalling ferocity, hidden always under a calm, obsequious manner, she began to devise ways of pushing him over the edge.

Hua, surveying the state of his farm, walked about with head hanging and face as dry, rutted, and depressed as the miserable highway in front of his house. Four cotton fields were a total loss; three might pull through with mediocre crops if rain came soon; five others had got off lightly and might do as well as drought-starved cotton fields could. The kaoliang was ruined, the millet was not bad, the table vegetables were a mixed lot, some capable of regeneration, some killed, some disfigured but alive. At best, Hua could hope for half a crop all around, except in precious all-purpose kaoliang, which was quite lost.

Hua was in a punitive temper with us from dawn till dusk— perhaps his increasingly fanatic mind had begun to believe the screams of the temple rioters, that white pigs were the cause of all his troubles. Jasmine taught us to act humble, apologetic, hang-dog to his face, but to work for his destruction when out of his sight.

One method was to break tools. In this the men, on account of their physical strength, were the principal agents, and Jasmine rode herd on the crudity of their approach. Neither Dolphin nor Grin had much enthusiasm for this campaign (Daddy Chick could not, of course, be enlisted), but if it was to be carried on, they wanted to be thorough, quick, and manly about it: smash them all. Jasmine showed them that they must be slow and subtle;

everything must appear to have been accidental, and the master's torture of anger and worry over this attrition must be prolonged. A hoe one day. A plow stock three days later. The bottom out of a vegetable basket. Three bean poles knocked down. Another hoe, broken in another way, at the throat. A hammer, hard to come by, left out in the fields where the plow stock was fixed.

Jasmine's patience was rewarded. Hua did not see the "accidents" as purposive, but only thought hogs infuriatingly stupid, careless, and lazy.

We began to get rain, a single shower in the morning three or four days a week, and broken clouds the rest of the time; the winds were no longer baked airs from the Gobi Desert but soft maritime good wishes from the east. These rains, rather than cheering Hua, put him in a greater knot than ever, of wanting to save every leaf of every plant. He rushed around like a worried barnyard fowl.

I kept my distance from him. The more gaunt he became, the more he stared at me with his mad rooster eyes.

Dolphin, in these days, continued bland, unfiery. He humored Jasmine but teased her, too. Sometimes he deliberately failed to follow her instructions; he seemed just as amused by her dismay as by Hua's. He was delighted, too, by Daddy Chick's puzzled rages over our breakage. I was angry with him for this perversity myself, and he laughed me down. Grin, who hero-worshipped Dolphin on account, I suppose, of Dolphin's marvelous physique, his throat's tolerance for freshets of *baigar*, and this fate-defying indifference of his, followed suit.

Thus all the more it fell to a woman, Jasmine, to lead the way. Moth and I may have giggled a lot, but we were solidly with her.

I believe it possible that Hua, even though he did not yet realize that a planned campaign of sabotage was being carried on against him, dimly sensed a conspiracy of sows against his dignity.

Hua and his wife were now working as hard as their slaves, probably harder, considering that Jasmine had us malingering whenever we could. Even the two oldest children, Hua's Barley Flower and Grin's Perfection, were put on half-hand tasks; Hua's wife took the other children to the fieldsides to play, so an adult would not be tied down to watching them; these little children were supposed to keep an eye on Moth's infant, who remained wrapped in cloths in a basket.

One day Hua's wife ordered me (only later did I realize that

Hua had put his wife up to this command—that indeed he must
have dimly half planned this entire performance) to remain in
the work space in the main house mending a canvas donkey
harness that had been "accidentally" ripped in two places a few
days before. Seamstress again! Everyone else went out to the
fields. I took my own good time about the sewing—partly because
I knew Jasmine would have wanted me to, partly because this
chore kept me out of the fields.

Late in the morning—so late that the others were doubtless
eating the noon meal they had carried out—I began to hear
strange noises somewhere near the compound. I ran to the door
of the house, and I heard Hua shouting furiously and a kind of
whimpering—was it Moth's voice?

The sounds came closer. I made out now that Moth was in for
a bambooing.

I was paralyzed. I wanted to run out of the compound gate and
intervene in some way, but I knew that that would not rescue
Moth and might indeed earn me my first beating. I stood like an
anchored post and listened in horror to what followed.

"Come around here, you pork bait," Hua's enraged voice said.
I could hear the two going around the outside corner of the compound wall.

Hua had given a picture of himself as a reluctant chastiser,
who thought corporal punishment a mean business, to be performed out of sight and sound. Ostensibly this was why he was
going around to the far side of the compound: to be well hidden
from the rest of his force, who were working, in any case, in a
distant field. (But he must have known all the time that I was inside the compound.)

"Get down."

"I beg you, Venerable!" Poor Moth, trying by the use of an honorific title to get herself off!

"Come on. Down, down, down."

"Have you forgotten everything, Master?"

For Moth's sake I wanted not to hear her. But I could not move.

Then it sounded as if Hua's throat was almost splitting open
with fury. "Silence! You filthy field whore. You think you can use
that bastard turtle baby to get off work?" (I heard later what had
happened: that Dolphin had—deliberately?—ruined a whole
series of cotton plants by under-hoeing their roots, and Hua,

having railed at Dolphin for this offense, then spotted Moth sitting under a locust tree beside the field, her back comfortably reposing against the trunk, with her baby cradled in her arms, her face tenderly bent down; for some reason the baby had been crying, and she had gone to comfort it. Hua had run over screaming that she was not due for a feeding until after the midday meal. Moth, failing to rise out of respect for her master, had mildly answered back—the baby was suffering with gas; something of the sort. Hua, really angry at Dolphin, had flown out of control at Moth's effrontery and had taken her off for a thrashing. We had a saying, that the pig is whipped oftenest who is whipped easiest.) "You think you can get out of hoeing on account of that little slug?"

"Master!" Her tone of voice seemed to mean: You are the baby's father!

This appeal only threw Hua to the extremities of blind rage. "Get down!" he roared. "All right. Pull up your louse-bedding. . . . Farther, you whore. . . . Now. From now on you think about *working* for Hua."

I heard the first whirring stroke, and the blow. There was not a sound from Moth beyond a sharp intake of breath. The second. I could not stand Moth's control. I threw my hands over my ears and I ran inside the house. I waited, with my palms pressed to the sides of my head, minutes. Then I had to know that it was over, and I took my hands down. Silence. I stepped to the door of the house. I heard just beyond the wall Moth's labored breath.

"Enough?" Hua said. "Do you understand now?"

Moth remained silent—whether through defiance or defeat I could not tell.

But Hua apparently felt it was the former. "So you haven't had your lesson yet? Good. I'll teach you, you sow. Turn over on your back."

Now I heard one horrified word from Moth in a barely audible tone. "*Master!*"

"Be quick about it. Gown up. Now."

I heard the renewed blows. Even though I covered my ears I could hear Moth's cries. "No, Master! Please, Master! I'll work, Master! No, Master! No, Master! Please, Master! Ayah! Ayah! Ayah! Ai, Master! No! . . . No! . . . No! . . ."

At last it stopped. I took down my hands and heard a shudder-

ing low guttural moaning from Moth, and I thought I heard the
master walking away *toward the gate of the compound.* I ran into
the house and with shaking hands took up the harness.

Hua came into the doorway of the work space. I realized that
tears were coursing down my face. I daubed at my cheeks with
the crook of my right arm.

"How long do you think you are going to take on that harness?"
Hua asked with glittering eyes.

I could not bring myself to answer.

He took a step forward. "What did you think you gained by
hitting me with a broom?"

Then I knew what was in store for me. My master was going
to collect his debts.

He came toward me and stood over me. There was no mistaking
his intention. My feeling, at that moment, was of a total numbness. I was somehow beyond disgust, fear, hatred, outrage, sadness, loathing. I was far beyond dealing with Hua by screaming or
scratching. I was numb. Was *this* what was wrong with Dolphin?
—this white-skin numbness? Had I at last reached the final lot
of a slave—to be filled with and enveloped in *absolute nothing-
ness?* Was my heart beating at all?

As Hua began to bend forward toward me I said (the sensation
was of shouting into an impenetrable fog), "What if the mistress
comes in?"

Hua still did not speak. He firmly pushed my shoulders back
and down. He began to yank at the hem of my gown. Now the
numbness had poured into every reach of me, and Hua, fumbling
at his pants, was about to mount a kind of cold, cold corpse.
Moth's low moaning beyond the walls served as a perfect dirge
for this dead body of mine being claimed by its owner.

([Asses' Laughter

Before that day was over Hua's wife, fifteen years older
than he, was fiercely jealous. She understood, with her powerful
intuition, exactly what had happened. This was the beginning of
awful times on the farm.

Hua began to see impudence in everything: now in our answering with one tone of voice, now in our answering with another,
now in our answering at all, now in our *not* answering. We had to

wear blank faces—until blank faces were thought impertinent. It mattered how we inclined our heads; how we raised our hands; how we stepped out—all might be thought insolent.

At the same time, our sabotage began in earnest. The gate in the wall of the swine run was left open, two donkeys were brutalized till they hauled up lame, the plow stock broke again (this was rash), plants were trampled in the dark, a cart axle gave way right under the master. We became artfully plausible, assuring Hua that a task was done when we had only skimmed its surface, and in cases of "accidents" making excuses that he was obliged to accept though he knew them false.

The mistress treated me like an infected prostitute, with utmost scorn and distaste. I took tender care of Moth's cuts; she seemed to understand, without being told, what had happened to me. In fact, I felt that everyone but Dolphin knew what had happened. Even Daddy Chick was unusually kind to me in his pottering way. Dolphin, however, was unchanged: impassive, aloof, cool. Did he have most of the time that horrible sensation of numbness?

Hua and his wife were in an agony of despising and needing each other, but their misery gave us slaves no comfort because they poured their bottled-up rage at each other onto us.

The two donkeys that had been lamed now sickened. The braying of Hua's four asses had always seemed to me the purest expression of hopelessness I had ever heard. Those hee-haws, half screamed mirth, half bawled sorrow, spoke for us who were white-skinned with an open grief, touched with insanity, that we could never dare express. And now, when one of the creatures, then another, fell ill, growing thinner, staggering in their mud-walled stalls, their sobbing cries seemed to me almost unbearable because so faultlessly true to my feeling.

One day, while we were working in one of the table-vegetable fields nearest the Huas' main compound, Bargain, Jasmine's second child and oldest boy, a lazy, cheerful child of about ten, began tormenting the Huas' third, Stone, who was well named—round, hard, old-looking, dirty, and stubborn. As often happened when the children began to roughhouse, laughter spilled over into tears —this time from the yellow-skinned child. Jasmine, having no time for investigative justice, ran over and gave Bargain a hard blow on the side of the head and told him to treat Master Stone with respect. This was a perfunctory command of Jasmine's, but Bargain chose this occasion to take a formality literally. He saw

no reason why he should kowtow to stupid Stone. Jasmine hit him
again.

"I'll run away," Bargain suddenly screamed. "I'll go to the
mountain."

Where had the child heard this expression? I felt gooseflesh
creeping down my arms.

Aghast, looking at Hua's wife to see whether she had heard
(she obviously had), Jasmine clapped her hand over Bargain's
mouth.

I had heard Jasmine say, "You dirty little shoat, you don't know
what you're—" when suddenly the two sick donkeys began to bray
in their stalls not far away, drowning out all speech. This time
the braying sounded like heartbroken laughter.

Jasmine pushed Bargain away from her, and the boy, exagger-
ating his mother's roughness by several fold, fell to the ground,
though he could easily have kept his balance. When he arose he
limped, to show that his own pig mother had crippled him. Offstage the crazy guffawing of the donkeys' abject misery rang on
and on.

Where *had* Bargain (who was soon racing around without a
trace of hobbling) picked up this idea? We had lately been having
more news of the anti-slavery movement in the core provinces,
but we whispered it to each other, far out of hearing of the little
ones, when it came. I had, in fact, in recent days, acquired from
a sow belonging to Sun a broadside from the Uncage-the-Finches
Society. I had folded this paper into a tiny wad and had hidden it
in a chink of our k'ang; one day, with mad daring, I carried it in
the tiny tobacco pouch on the string around my neck that contained my mole paws of good luck. These paws themselves had
taken on new meaning, for we had heard at the temple new
whispered stories of the Kingdom of the Mole. From time to time
we had also heard, however, chilling tales of runaways being
caught: just two days before, of a hog found drowned in Gray
Pearl Pond, his hands and feet in chains and his skull crushed.

Hearing these stories filled me with fear—though on some
days I felt waves of the numbness sweep over me, washing away
fear with every other emotion. When the numbness receded I was
afraid of not being afraid: terrified of betraying to the yellows,
through not caring, some secret that might mean safety and
freedom for a runaway hog. I suppose that it was a numb day
when I wore the broadside in my neck pouch.

It seemed to me that Hua watched me closely, perhaps for a giveaway opening in a moment of this non-feeling. I knew how practiced his eye was, at probing out slaves' unguarded moments. Could he possibly want my lifeless body again?

He wanted us to talk while we worked. He could not stand a silent slave. "Make a noise, make a noise," he would say. "Bear a hand, you pigs. Let's have some chatter."

On the fifteenth day of the eighth month, the Moon Festival, when most farms granted a three-day holiday, we worked straight through. We had a barren feast of a scrap of pork, noodles, fruit, and moon cakes, and with a begrudging stiffness Hua gave each of us a miserly basket containing a couple of sugared millet rolls, a few grapes, a piece of moon cake, and a cheap woodcut of the rabbit who lives in the moon. He had already set up in the dirty courtyard a table with an incense burner, a clay rabbit, some moon cakes, and some peaches as offerings to the full moon which bathed the scene in its cool light by the time we set out for the slave hut and sleep.

Passing the sacrificial stand with his basket in his left hand, Dolphin casually trailed his right hand across the table and came away with a peach, which he swung into his basket.

Now Dirty Hua was a poor farmer, and glass was a frightfully expensive item in East-of-the-Mountains Province, but our owner had bought and set one small square pane of clear glass low in the paper window by his k'ang for the obvious purpose of keeping a sharp lookout for his interests. And now he must have seen the slave's hand skim across the table.

He came roaring out. He counted the peaches. "You turtle excrement! This is the last from you! I am going to sell you!"

([Acquiescence

Heat. Dolphin and I were seated alone together under a black haw during the noon break. On stifling days Hua gave us a long recess in midday—not out of any mercy but to get more work out of us the rest of the afternoon. We two were the only slaves awake. The rest had lain down in the shade and were napping, with the shallow cones of their sun hats, of a sort we wove for ourselves of reeds, tilted across their cheeks to keep the light out of their eyes. Hua was fanning himself in a crop-watching shelter; a slave-watching shelter, now. Hua's wife had taken all the children back to the house.

During the noon meal I had told Dolphin I wanted to talk with him. I was excited and anxious; he was impatient—wanted his nap.

"All right, baby."

"You call me 'baby.' You could have a real one on your hands."

"What do you mean?"

"I am pregnant," I said.

A familiar chill swept through me, one I had suffered many times in recent days—as if I were sitting in a draft of numbness-wind. What would Dolphin do to me if the baby turned out to be a mix, like Moth's, by the same father? Dolphin had taken my body a hundred times; Hua once. Could my luck be that bad? Ayah, could a slave's luck be anything but bad?

Dolphin was staring at me with a horrifying expression—nothing about it had changed in the least. No surprise; no pleasure; no displeasure. Nothing. The same look of annoyance and indifference as before; wanted his nap.

"I'm pregnant, at least I think so," I said; perhaps he had not heard me. Was Dolphin himself numb through and through? Had he taken seriously Hua's threat to sell him away? Did he not care where he slaved, or for whom, or beside whom? Sometimes in the nights, these past few, when I had missed my period and waited and waited to make sure, and had grown sure, I had wakened swimming in sweat in certainty that Hua had indeed meant his threat to sell Dolphin, and I had been doubly frightened by it because I sensed it had vaguely to do with me. But at other times I had thought it simply a stock shout of meaningless warning, such as owners and overseers often threw at their pigs, as ignorant slave mothers used threats of dragons and witches to silence their children.

Dolphin stirred slowly. A momentary flicker of some sort of confusion sped across his face. Then he said, "I have to tell you, baby. I won't be here to see it."

"You're going off. I knew it."

"Hua says he wants to sell me. I can't stand around and wait for that."

"Maybe Old Sun would buy you."

"What good would that be? He uses the bamboo like any other yellow man."

"But you won't take me with you?"

"I'm going with Grin."

"With Grin! I thought you had to go alone."

"Two *men*, baby. That's different."

Why was I so attracted to a totally selfish man? Why couldn't I even feel any anger?

"Does Jasmine know?"

"She'll have to know now."

That thought made us both look along the shadows of locusts and black haws down the edge of the field, at the human lumps, sound asleep. I suddenly felt drowsy myself, as if drugged, overcome with a fearful yet sweet lethargy such as is supposed to sweep over one who is freezing to death. The terrifying news I had just heard made me, of all things, sleepy. Looking at the sleepers, I envied them. The yellows, citing deep naps like these taken anywhere and anyhow, called us lazy, shiftless, spineless, sluggish of blood; the expression they used for us was *huai-le,* meaning "bad," "spoiled," "broken," "out of order." What the yellows had not the capacity or sympathy to know was that sleep was our freedom; we ran away into it as into ownerless country. It was the peaceful mountain available to each of us without danger of slave-hunters, wonks, starvation. Frightened to my very marrow by Dolphin's words, I yawned.

Dolphin, however, was apparently thinking of the new situation that was created by my knowing his and Grin's plan. He got up, went down the line to Grin's limp form—legs drawn up and hands tucked under the chin like a baby's—and woke him by shaking his shoulder. Grin sat up. Dolphin beckoned to him and came back to me. Grin arose, fully awake at once, and came to us.

"You'll have to tell Jasmine. This one got it out of me."

Grin was outraged. "How's that? I thought you said not to tell them until the day before we went."

Dolphin replied in the same bland, unconnected tone as he had used toward me. There was a kind of magnificence about his detachment; he must have been the Emperor of the Not-Carers. "She got it out of me."

"How 'got it out of you'? Did you have to answer her?"

Still utterly indifferent: "She's pregnant."

"Oh."

"Not saying by whom."

A rich blush sped up my neck and across my face. "You turtle!"
I said, but my voice was not strong.

"I had to tell her."

"Could she keep it from Jasmine for a while?"

"Why should I?" I said.

"You have to tell her," Dolphin said.

"Ayah," Grin said. "That's not going to be easy." But Grin was
suddenly sunny. "Listen, Dolphin," he said. "I had an idea. We
ought to take rope bridles with us. Then if any yellows see us
while we're getting away, and ask us, 'What are you doing here?
Why don't you have chits? Are you boars?' we can say, 'No,
Master, we belong to Hua next to Sun, we were leading his team
of donkeys in this evening, and a hare jumped out from under a
bush and the donkeys ran off, and we took out after them. Have
you seen two donkeys? One of them has a black streak down his
nose.' We could say something like that."

Dolphin was smiling, but the smile was grotesque, because his
eyes were dull and humorless. It was as if he had been told to
smile. "That's beautiful, Grin," he said. "We'll do that."

Then we heard Hua's shouts. "Tumble up! Tumble up, you
pigs, and to work."

I supposed that Jasmine was informed of the plan sometime
that day, but closely as I watched her I could see no change in
her. Perhaps she thought of Grin's plan as something every hog
should try; perhaps she was tired of him anyway. We slaves had
had plenty of practice in acceptance of daily horrors, and perhaps
Jasmine's reaction was simply the norm of slave behavior:
acquiescence in the inevitable. What could one really do but take
things as they were? Grin was the father of Jasmine's three children; for reasons good or poor, he had stayed on with her for a
long time. Yet the news that he was to go apparently struck her
as not worth fighting. I felt, watching Jasmine, as if the white-
skin numbness was gradually overcoming us all; that soon we
whites would be exactly what the yellows wanted—dead souls in
living bodies, automatons, walking and working hypnotics.

Yet in the days that followed we four were, at times, remark-
ably buoyant. Now that Jasmine and I knew the plan, Grin and
Dolphin spent more time with us than they had been spending.
Sometimes we softly sang hopeful slave songs with cryptic lines:

Discarding my sash I put on a coat lined with mountain-goat skin;
Discarding my ankle bands I wear shoes with magpie wings,

and we played games of secret words. In the fields, before Hua himself, we used simple everyday words, which we had coded to mean things important to us, but in which our master would hear nothing out of the ordinary. By stealing, buying, and sewing, Jasmine and I helped assemble sets of clothing Grin and Dolphin had never been seen to wear. Daddy Chick remarked to Hua, before us, that it had been long since he had heard so many joyous exclamations around the farm.

As for me, no matter how heartsick I might be, when Dolphin touched me I felt the numbness drain away. The graveyard was still our favorite place. Under his body, between two memorial mounds, my body responsively moved; his excitement spoke to mine; the throbs of his final gift each time shook my whole body in a long, slow, almost unbearably happy unstringing, and I knew afterward, with tears on my cheeks, that the waves of numbness that flowed over me and through me many times each day meant less than I had feared, because I was surely alive.

⟮ The Kite

On ninth ninth, the Ch'ung Yang Festival, it was the custom to ascend to the highest lookout in the countryside—in our case Moon Wall Hill, across a valley from Limestone Hill—and there, enjoying wine and special cakes reserved to that day, to gaze at the view. This was supposed to promote longevity. Our master led us all out in the early morning, with two hampers of wine and cakes, one (capacious) for yellows, the other (small) for whites.

As we set out, Dolphin had under his arm a large and elaborate kite, which over recent days he had made himself, out of materials he had bought from vendors from his own money belt. He carried the kite covered, and therefore hidden, by a wrapping of cheap rice paper. He had allowed no one to see it as he made it.

The morning was fine, a north wind blew. Dolphin, more animated than he had been for a long time, said we would see a vision on his kite string.

The Ch'ung Yang Festival inaugurated the kite-flying season in East-of-the-Mountains Province. Moth had told me all about this soulful sport, and I looked forward with childish delight to the display. From now on for several weeks, she had said, the sky would be tenanted by the most ingenious kites—dragons with great wings, segmented centipedes, butterflies, frogs, flying tigers, bees, eagles, all sorts of vivid and horrid creatures. Most of them would have been made by slaves, who competed with each other in sending up fantastic contrivances, many of which, Moth said, proved, because of the simplicity of the art with which they were made, comical beyond words; while others, made by kite geniuses, white men, were breathtaking in their beauty. Many of the creatures that leaped in this way into the blue would be agitated, Moth said, by the wind—would roll their eyes, flap their wings, ramp with their paws, swing their long tails, or, best of all, growl, moan, mew, whistle, roar.

So we walked out to Moon Wall Hill in gay spirits.

The highest part of the hill was of course reserved for the yellows; a stripe of powdered lime, girdling the summit, marked the contour above which slaves were not permitted to climb. And so below the hill's nipple of yellows we whites gathered, in exceedingly large numbers. It did not take us who were Hua pigs long to drink the wine and eat the cakes from the master's parsimonious slave basket; nor did we need long to contemplate the landscape—to us, an expanse of dirt furnished and curried by our own hard work which would certainly not give us long life.

We kept teasing Dolphin to launch his surprise.

"Wait!" he would say, with a glassy look of the wine bottle already glinting in his eyes. "Gaze at the view! Suck in old age through your eyeballs! Come on, Daddy Chick. Look out there: ten thousand years just lying in wait for you."

Daddy Chick was the only one who took seriously the inscription Hua had pasted on the doorpost that morning: SEE FAR, LIVE LONG. The oldest of us all, he was squinting and straining, with his hands outstretched in the wonder he wanted to feel, looking like a man trying to make his way across a dark room.

Soon, from here and there in the lower circle on the hill, kites began to rise on the steady breeze, and at each one a murmur of admiration, or a ripple of laughter, or (in the cases of flying monsters) a shout of mock apprehension would go up.

"What's the matter, Dolphin? Won't your kite fly?" Grin asked.

Grin's latter question had double meanings, because among themselves whites used the expression "flying a kite" for a man's having the stiffness of desire, and, indeed, some of the squeals of laughter on the hillside that had been saluting the taut going up of the many kite strings had been allusions to a pleasant sport which was not, like this one, seasonal.

"Don't worry yourself, Grin," Dolphin said. "It will go up when I tell it to."

"You have it trained?"

"No. It wants to go up all the time."

"What are you waiting for?" I asked with a suitable lift of my voice.

Dolphin smiled and patted me on the shoulder as a reward for one side of my sally.

"I think there had best be a crowd of kites up before this one flies," he said.

More and more kites were strung out, and they were making all sorts of funny noises in the air. It was a glorious noontime. We were surrounded by whites; the sky was the blue of a respite from moisture, not of drought, a kite sky, a sky for these paper jokes and casual works of art with strings attached. I slipped my hand into the crook of Dolphin's elbow. I did not yet know what he felt, if anything, about the life that had taken root in me. For this day I was feeling flippant, Moth-like, and sun-warmed, though underneath this light mood lay a pit of uneasiness. Dolphin and Grin had not set a date for their running away; they drifted along, making plans so desultory that it seemed the whole idea might pass. On the other hand, I knew I might wake up any morning to find Dolphin gone.

With his elbow he squeezed my hand against his rib cage.

"Wait till you see it," he said, winking at me.

Finally, in one sweeping motion, Dolphin uncovered his kite, drew it over his head planing on the wind, and paid out string. In a few moments it stood high above us, yawing back and forth as Dolphin let out more and more scope. He fetched up near the end of the string and there in the sky, blinking its eyes, was a yellow man's face.

It was Hua.

The kite was an unmistakable caricature of our master: sad, dogged, lewd, pretentious, seedy, drought-haggard. Hua's unkempt queue was the kite's tail.

Near us I heard Sun hogs whispering, "It's Hua. It's Dirty Hua."

Laughter broke out around us. I saw guffawing slaves pointing at this kite among the others. I looked back, half expecting the real Hua to be rushing down the hill at us, and saw that a similar commotion was stirring the yellows on the hill crest—of pointing and laughing.

I began to be afraid. Dolphin's face was bland—no particular signs of emotion. Now and then an old friend of Dolphin's from the Sun force came over to him and jokingly congratulated him for his astonishing recklessness. "He's going to tickle your backsides," Quart said. Dolphin unconcernedly nodded. I feared far worse than that.

I wondered what Hua would do. I realized he could not come down the hill to order Dolphin to strike his kite and take us home, for that would only call attention to this scandalous act of derision; Hua would lose too much face. But what would he do later? He had ordered us to rendezvous with him "before the noon hour"—meaning, whenever the gathering would begin to break up—at the stone-lion marker at the corner of the Cheng farm at the foot of Moon Wall Hill.

When the general adjournment came, we waited for some time at the marker. Dolphin had the kite under his arm. At last Hua and his wife came along, in company with some other inferior yellow gentry; they were all carrying on a lively conversation, the Huas laughing and chatting with the cheeriest of them. The Huas were in their best holiday clothes, which looked shabby enough. Hua pumped his chin at us as the party passed, signaling us to follow.

We fell in behind this group. Slaves belonging to other yellows in the gathering joined up with us, and all of them steered significant looks at Dolphin, but he seemed oblivious; cheerful, unexcited, armored in some sort of seashell calm.

The informal procession reached our farm, and we fell out. The Huas called polite farewells, bowing and dipping their fisted hands to their friends. We slaves started for our hut, but Hua shouted to us to go into his courtyard and wait for him.

When Hua strode in to us his face was still masked—or perhaps bandaged—in the sociability he had been keeping up with his companions on the return trip. "Now!" he said. "We have all had a pleasant morning. Now let's go out to Sixth Low Field for a half task of scraping. Get your hoes. Be brisk!" This was all correct and usual: too much so. "Daddy Chick, lead them out and get them started while I get into my work clothes."

We went to work. It seemed to me that Hua was a long time

coming out. When he came, he had changed into more than his work clothes: he had changed—but it was not any more a laughing matter—into the creature on the end of Dolphin's kite string.

He walked straight to Dolphin. His face was drawn and miserable in its hardness. He spat out: "I thought I told you to repair the door of the vegetable pit."

"Yes, Master," Dolphin mildly said, "I fixed it."

"How fixed it? It came off its hinges when T'ai-t'ai tried to open it."

"I hadn't finished it. It was all finished but the fastenings."

Hua walked back and forth; he was obviously seething. "I gave you the task a week ago."

"Yes, Master," Dolphin said. "You told me you wanted to buy some new hinges next market. Or that you wanted to think about buying them."

"I said no such thing."

Dolphin shrugged, as if to say, "It's your word against mine, and a slave is always wrong."

Hua looked for a moment at the hoe Dolphin was holding. It had been broken at the throat, and had been crudely repaired— the handle chopped off, whittled to a point, reinserted, and hooked in place with a bent spike. Hua walked to Dolphin, kicked the hoe violently, so it flew out of Dolphin's hand, and in a passion shouted, "Turtle! Turtle! I told you to fix these hoes smartly."

Dolphin said, "That one is only temporary, Master. We needed some new handle stock. Daddy Chick said—"

But Hua broke in with a flood of curses. Then he turned and ran toward the crop-watching shelter beyond the next field, and in a short time he was back with his beating rod—a billy of bamboo as thick as a thumb and long as an arm, its joints, like little knuckles, blackened with the blood of previous punishments —Moth's blood?

When I saw Hua striding back towards us, I felt as if he were coming after me; he was like a punitive figure in a bad dream I had often had, beginning in the Northern Capital. I wanted to run. Hua walked up to Dolphin and said, "Take off your tunic."

Dolphin's eyes wavered for a moment, and I could see that the thick impenetrable varnish of indifference that Dolphin had lately been wearing was cracking and scaling off him.

"Big Master Hua," he said in a voice that was suddenly trembling. "I will not take it off."

"You *what*?" Hua stepped a pace closer to Dolphin.

"I will not be bambooed again by any man. I've decided that. If you beat me, Master, or if you have me beaten, I'll never do another day's work for you or for any other man."

Hua was now shaking all over. He could manage nothing with his voice except to repeat what he had said before: "You *what*?"

"I'm not going to stay here and be bambooed. You said you were going to sell me. I wish you would. I don't want to stay here with you."

For Dolphin to suggest that he *disliked* Hua both as master and as man—this was too much. Hua lunged forward, seizing Dolphin's throat with his left hand and raising the rod with the other to deliver a blow across Dolphin's face. But with the agility I had seen in the boxing matches at Sun's, Dolphin ducked sharply to one side, so the whirring rod missed him completely, and at the same moment he reached down with both hands for Hua's left knee and lifted it so fast and so far that Hua, losing his grip on Dolphin's throat, toppled over backward. Twisting Hua's leg at the knee, and bearing down on it, Dolphin placed a cloth shoe on Hua's neck and held the master pinned tight to the ground.

All this had happened so quickly that there had not been time even to realize the enormity of Dolphin's self-defense. And now that Hua was down, there was an appalling moment, for me, of knowing that Dolphin had made his final choice; a moment at once replaced by another, just as awful as the first, of feeling trapped, like a fly in a drop of amber I had seen on a brooch at a guest's throat once in the Capital. None of us would ever be able to move; Dolphin would have to keep his foot forever on Hua's neck; we could neither return to the world we had lived in before nor go forward into the unimaginable hell that must follow.

But Dolphin simply took his foot away and dropped Hua's leg, which fell like a length of wood to the ground.

In an instant Hua was up. His face was orange as a dust cloud coming down the sky from the Gobi. He turned and ran. We saw him go past the compound walls and into the sunken road and along it.

"He's gone for help," Jasmine said. "You'd better get out."

"No!" Grin said. "If Dolphin runs they'll kill him."

Dolphin was standing there with a glaze of indifference—the numbness?—over his eyes again.

Daddy Chick, shaking his head like a mourner, said, "I have never in my life seen such a loss of face for the white people. We'll never live this down."

"Be still, you fool," Jasmine said.

"The abbot," I said. "Couldn't we get the abbot at the temple? You know, Old Whiskers? Perhaps Hua would listen to him."

Grin had run off toward Limestone Hill Generous Temple for the old monk before I had even finished speaking.

We had then the most terrifying wait, and we passed it in a curious way. We hoed. Upon a routine call to work from Daddy Chick—"All right! Stir yourselves!"—we chopped like an orderly gang of dutiful slaves at the earth along the rows. Dolphin did his part as if nothing had happened. I felt, besides a grief muffled by waves of numbness, a sharp pain at the root of my belly.

Grin and the crown-shaven, white-bearded monk in yellow robes returned first. After each of us (even Dolphin) had fallen to his knees and kowtowed to the abbot, we gathered around him all (except Dolphin) babbling at once. The old man looked at us with an expression of sweetness and tenderness, of an inner peace that seemed to glow in his eyes; and my heart leaped with joy and hope at the sight of his benign calm.

"I have no right to come here," he said in a quavering voice, and with those words I knew—as perhaps I should have known all along—the foolishness of my hope that Hua's religious fervor might have been appealed to by this apparently saintly man; for religion here in slave country was nothing but a justifier. "I have made a pledge to myself," the crackling voice went on, "never to visit a farm without permission—I came this time because this white man told me with great sincerity that one of his companions was being killed. Where is this victim? Listen to me, children, I have nothing to do with the working life of you whites. I will hear no tales from you about your masters or overseers. I am no party to your quarrels. It is my task to cultivate justice, impartiality, and universal kindness." These qualities shone on his good face, but I knew there was nothing behind the look of love and blissful gentleness but empty words.

Hua and four yellow men came across the fields. I recognized the others. They were struggling third-rate farmers like Hua; three of them had been in the party walking home from Moon

Wall Hill, and the other was a nasty fellow, owner of a large pack of wonks, who occasionally hired himself out as a slave-hunter. These four approached with an almost comical wariness, on springy knees, as if they were placing themselves in great danger.

On seeing the priest they all kowtowed, and had we been led and resolute this would have been our moment to jump them.

But Dolphin was in his shell. He seemed not to care what happened. We all stood around waiting.

The yellow men scrambled to their feet. With exaggerated caution they approached Dolphin. He either had decided that resistance would be foolish or, in regaining his unconcern, had lost the drive to protest. The abbot stood by watching; the men had not spoken a word to him. The men grabbed Dolphin's arms, tied his hands, and wound a rope several times around his chest, binding his arms against his sides. They walked him away from us.

An hour later Hua sent Grin and Daddy Chick out with a cart to fetch Dolphin's unconscious body from the pine tree beyond the Goat Field irrigation well where it was hanging by the hands.

❪ "Are the Cloth Soles Firm Enough?"

Nothing was said; no signal was given. But Jasmine and I understood now that it was only a matter of waiting until Dolphin's bamboo cuts were healed.

I felt a constant pain in my vitals, which I interpreted as an agony of fear, of anticipated loss, and of overwhelming disappointment at the way things always turned out for one who had white skin. It seemed to me that the pain was held at bay, in the area of my body where a new life was trying to establish itself, by the now familiar numbness, which inhabited all the rest of my body and pushed at the pain from all sides, making a tight sphere of it.

Dolphin recovered with surprising rapidity. As the day of escape approached, Grin developed cold feet.

One day in the fields, in the presence of Dolphin, Jasmine, and me, Grin announced that he hadn't the nerve to go. "I had a dream last night," he said. "I dreamed I was in the work space, and I heard a strange rushing or roaring sound. I ran out to the gate and there in the road was an army of wonks—just a river of yellow fur; the fur at the necks was bristling, and the roar was a snarling of all those dogs, a river of wonks, Dolphin. The dogs were all different sizes. They were running toward the east— toward . . . toward . . . I couldn't think of the mountain in the dream, I just knew they were running toward something frightening. Then I think I was hiding under a pile of kaoliang stalks, and I could still hear a noise like a wind, but now it was a sniffing sound. This wind of sniffing sucked at the kaoliang stalks, and I could feel the stalks stirring, and I heard the rustling noises as some of the stalks were sucked off the pile by that gigantic sniffing. I tried to be smaller and smaller. . . . I can't go, Dolphin. I want to go but I . . ."

Perhaps it should not have been a surprise that Jasmine was deeply disgusted by this turn of Grin's. As for Dolphin, I saw relief on his face: *He wanted to go alone!*

"It was a going-to-sleep dream, Dolphin. You have to be careful about a dream at the beginning of the night. There's something to it. There really is, friend, I'm being honest with you. Really, friend, watch out for a dream that tries to tell you something when you're dropping off." And Grin went on, at great pains to justify himself.

I could tell when the final day had come by Dolphin's manner. He was suddenly restored, for that one day, to his true self—the indifference all shucked away, full of jokes and bravado, his braggart manner thinly concealing a sweetness, at least to me, that drove both the dead feeling and the pain out of my body. He called me "monkey," "dearest," "little cat." He teased Jasmine all day about her program of sabotage. He persuaded me to write characters on a slip of paper which, when Hua was out of sight, he pinned on his hat, turning the sense of Daddy Chick's hat sign, of which the old slave was so proud, inside out:

DO NOT TOUCH THIS TIGER
OR HOG WILL EAT YOU

He was exceptionally tender with Grin; many times during the day he put a hand on Grin's arm or shoulder, expressing without words his love for this friend who had gone weak with funk.

To me the day—despite the shadow of irrevocability that lay over it—was one of the happiest of my life. I was puzzled and even, at times, chagrined by my lightness of spirit. I felt everything so strongly! My laughter was genuine, I appreciated my friends. And Dolphin's touch, whenever he brushed against me or caressed me, as he casually did many times during the day, caused surges of feeling to flow through me that reminded me of the period when I had first fallen in love with him.

After dark Dolphin took me for the last time to the Sun grave-yard. By that time apprehension and desperation had begun to crowd aside the delightful feelings of the day, but I nevertheless felt, as we merged ourselves, an abundance of yielding fondness, of fierce pride in Dolphin's manliness and courage, and of joy. I realized that my happiness all day had been an aspect of my sur-render to him, of the first selfless and altruistic love of my life: I was deeply happy for Dolphin that he would soon be free.

Afterward Dolphin took some dust from one of the grave mounds and put it in his shoes. "Wonks can't track you if you have grave dirt in your shoes," he said.

As we walked back arm in arm to the slave hut we heard Daddy Chick, still up, playing on his fiddle the tune of a slave song whose words were:

> The fruit on the branch is ripe;
> The climb is steep.
> Are the cloth soles firm enough for ten thousand li?
> Ai! See the sunset's streaks beyond the heights!

I felt my flesh crawl with fear and excitement, and I said, "Do you suppose even old Daddy Chick knows you are going?"

"Of course he knows."

"Aren't you afraid he will tell Hua—or has already told him?"

"Never! He's an 'old good.' Listen! He wishes he could go himself."

It was true. There were sounds in those harsh fiddle strokes of ineffable longing—the longing in the heart of every white man who lived in slavery.

Late in the night Dolphin changed into the unfamiliar suiting Jasmine and I had made for him.

All of us, including Daddy Chick and except for the children, were still awake.

I heard Dolphin clap his hands onto Grin's and his anxious whisper, "I have a queer feeling. Hua knows. I have a feeling he's waiting for me."

"Ai, man, that's strange!" Grin whispered. "I just thought I heard something."

"Daddy Chick . . ." Dolphin began in a suddenly threatening tone.

"Huh? What's that? Did someone call me? . . . Hrrumph. . . . What was that?" the old man jabbered, perhaps pretending he had been dozing.

Then I saw Dolphin's form in the doorway, and suddenly the barely visible rectangle was empty. He was gone. He had not spoken a single word of goodbye.

For four nights we knew that Dolphin was lurking somewhere around us. At times Grin went out and met him, according to plans they had had, quite near the cabin. Dolphin came nightly to the Huas' drinking well to fetch water in a cedar bucket Grin had stolen for him. One night I heard the well arm squeaking; I had to bite my hand as I lay on the k'ang to keep from calling out.

On the fifth night Grin stayed in, and I knew that Dolphin had left.

On the eighth day a messenger came from the slave hunter Hua had hired, saying that the hog had been caught but that the dogs had killed him. The body was lacerated almost beyond recognition. Did Hua wish to have the corpse as proof?

Hua said no, let the wonks have the remains.

The pain in my womb began to pulse, and I miscarried.

(The Salt Inspector

As I slowly recovered I found that my main struggle was not against physical weakness but against the numbness which more and more seemed to blank out all my feelings. There were times when I could not, for the life of me, have said that I missed Dolphin. I grew fearful that I would become like Moth— who lived for the mere physical sensations of each moment, and whose apparent gaiety was trivial, insensitive, and absurd. I let Grin, who flew kites like any other man, take me to the graveyard one night, and (to show how involuted my feelings had become) I did not like it that my body was *not* numb under his yet I felt totally numb just before and just after our joining. Hua appeared to be relieved, and at times I would even have said that he was immensely buoyed up, by his loss of Dolphin; he began, as soon as I was on my feet, to ogle me, and I found myself more than once wondering whether he would find me lifeless if he tried me again. Each time I had such a thought I raged at myself, not because of any sense of moral right or wrong, for I had no use whatsoever for a baggage of ethics, but simply because I felt I was going the way of the enslaved white man: that I was losing my sense of myself.

My inner battle, then, was to find some way of taking hold of my worthless life. In this battle I was aided, as the picking season began, quite by chance, by a visitor.

For several years the Emperor's Ministry of Salt had been shaken by scandals. The trade in the life-giving stuff had been riddled, all the way from the administrative chambers in the Forbidden City in the Capital down to the most humble bowl of *mien-fan* in a mean house like Hua's, with graft, bribery, squeeze, false measurements, crooked weighing, adulteration, loose packing, thievery, syndication, poisoning, murders, and whispering in insiders' ears. The Emperor had set up an elaborate machinery of surveillance; no one knew whether His Inexpressible Perfection had done this in order to clean up the foul business or in order to insure that all dishonesty should lead to exclusively Imperial profits. At any rate, a Salt Inspector came in the tenth month to our district.

Whatever progress was being made otherwise in the elimination of the scandals, one minor piece of graft was still strictly honored. This was a convention that the farmer in whose house the Salt Inspector lodged should lend this dignitary the maid service of his female slaves during his stay, in return for which hospitality the Inspector would see that the farmer was amply provided with salt throughout the subsequent year. This was called, by slaves, in their secret language, "pickling the white mice."

One would have thought that under these circumstances the Salt Inspectors would have elected the richest farms, best stocked in likely sows, such as Sun's. But not at all. In recent years the rich farmers had been striking such hard bargains for "annual provision" with the Inspectors, and had by collusion with each other so universally agreed not to pay surface bribes, the purpose of which was the non-reporting of subsurface bribes, that the Inspectors had decided rather to profit piecemeal at the expense of the smaller gentry. "Ten thousand caraway seeds are worth more than one watermelon."

So it happened that Salt Inspector Feng came to stay twelve days with us. Jasmine, Moth, and I were assigned, on daily rotation, as his maidservants.

Our first impression of Salt Inspector Feng was that he was a younger son of a wealthy family in North-of-the-River Province who had failed in the court examinations, and who was, like many such failures, cynical, dissolute, and inclined to accept a rather seedy way of life. His attitudes were, from our point of view, insufferable. At meals (while we crouched on our hams in the work space, hearing every word) he talked loudly, usually with a mouth crammed with food, about hogs, pigs, sows. He told stock jokes about the laziness of white men and the promiscuity of white women.

That first night he started talking about runaways, and Hua told him he had lost a slave to the wonks only a month back. "Gar-r-r," Salt Inspector Feng said, choking down too big a mouthful, "there's nothing more stupid than a hog when the dogs are on his trail. You know a story they believe? They believe a hare can shake wonks by doubling around to its starting point, and there it jumps very high in the air and licks all four paws before it comes down again—goes off in a new direction and the wonks can't follow. Ha! Ha! Ha! They really believe that. Try to pretend they're rabbits themselves. What? Oh, friend, that's good wine. Just a half a cup. Did you warm it enough? Another belief: They believe that if they sprinkle some grave dust in their shoes the wonks can't smell their footprints."

At that Hua roared with laughter, and even at such a great distance as the opposite end of the house I felt a fiery blush of anger and hatred suffuse my face.

Moth was his maid that first night. We made up a bed by laying boards across the loom. The maidservant was supposed to fetch and brew tea and carry toilet water, to undress and dress the man, massage his legs if he had had much standing about during the day, entertain him by singing or telling some of our slave tales, and bear in mind at all times that a year's supply of salt was at stake. The maidservant was provided with a bedroll in a corner of the room.

The next day I could get nothing but giggles from Moth. She seemed to be suggesting, by her airy-fairy laughter and her batting eyelids, that Salt Inspector Feng was a most peculiar man, whose

demands were bizarre, to say the least. It was also possible, however, that Moth was trying, above all, as she often did, to make
herself seem mysterious.

That night Jasmine was on duty. In the morning, as Grin
crowded in hungry for bad news, she shrugged and said Salt
Inspector Feng was not an objectionable man. He had not touched
her, she said.

"Hai! You expect me to believe that?" Grin squealed.

"Think what you want. The camel thinks the horse has humps!"

I believed Jasmine.

During the day, when he was in the house, Salt Inspector Feng
continued his loud, loathsome talk, yet Jasmine reported that he
had been mild and considerate of her. Apparently he was a man
of some inner contradictions. Could it simply have been that he
thought Jasmine unattractive? She was older than Moth and I,
her nose was sharp, deep lines were incised in her forehead, yet
she had liquid brown eyes, thick lips, and a sturdy, youthful
figure. The hogs at Sun's always flirted with her; this made her
proprietor, Grin, strut, though I suspect she may have deceived
him many times.

After dinner on the third night Daddy Chick entertained the
household and its official guest with tunes on the Tartar fiddle.
The recital over, I withdrew to the work space to puff up and
spread out Salt Inspector Feng's quilts and to set his tea water
on the fire. He talked awhile with the Huas and drank some wine
which Hua's wife warmed for him. I heard his vulgar outbursts
and Hua's deferential guffaws.

When Salt Inspector Feng came in to me he was flushed and
seemed drunk. With a clatter and a fuss he pawed over his heap
of paraphernalia—his scales, weighing baskets, official weights,
sampling bottles, and all the gear for his inspections—to make
sure nothing had been stolen. He spoke not a word while I undressed him. My hands trembled with both nervousness and, I
must admit, curiosity. Beneath his official uniform his under-
clothes were elegant and expensive; he was a young yellow man
with a soft body—I was used to slave flesh. He was careful to
be modest. His night robe bore an exquisite peony blossom embroidered over his heart.

He sat cross-legged on his crude bed on the loom. I gave him
a bowl of tea and bowed to him. He startled me by bursting out
in his ugly loud voice, which could easily be heard by the Huas

at the opposite end of the house, "Bring me paper, brushes, and an inkstone. I want to write today's reports. Hurry up, you sow."

Had I been so badly mistaken? Had he found Jasmine attractive (her serenity in the morning!), and was he finding me just the opposite? I hastily dug out the writing materials he wanted.

"Turn up the lamp, you little fool, or I'll go blind."

I placed the coal-oil lamp beside him on his board bed.

He hawked and spat on the dirt floor—and then was suddenly transformed. He looked at me with a puzzling sweetness and silently he beckoned to me. I warily approached. He began to write, and with a pointing finger he directed my attention to the characters he drew. He had a hasty hand; the strokes were slurred, but I could easily read them:

"I know that you can read and write. Read this carefully. I want to play a game with you. Get up and sit beside me. When we have finished writing, turn out the lamp and lie down beside me."

I boldly reached to his hand and took the brush from him, and in my precise, rather tight characters I wrote: "A game is for two or more. Your game can only amuse one person."

He took the brush and wrote: "Except for your face I will not touch you."

Then I wrote: "A young boy's promise."

He wrote: "That is not the game I meant. Let us play conundrums. I want to see how clever you are. I will start." He took a fresh piece of paper and wrote:

> *He contains the thread that will contain himself.*
> *See! I SET HIM FREE in order to contain myself.*

I seized the brush and wrote: "Silkworm."

My heart was beating hard, because there could be no doubt that Salt Inspector Feng had written four characters deliberately larger than the others.

Salt Inspector Feng took the brush again and wrote: "Excellent. You are quick. Another." He wetted his brush on the inkstone and wrote:

> *Pine seeds in his beak; a bamboo prison.*
> *If he is heartbroken, how can he sing so sweetly?*

This time my hand was certainly shaking as I took the brush and wrote: "Finch."

Salt Inspector Feng then wrote: "You are too quick. Why are
you not afraid of me? Now do what I wrote at first."

Why was I not afraid? Was it because I could be excited and
not care at the same time? Was curiosity all that mattered to me
now? I took the lamp off the bed and turned down its wick until
it gave off only the dimmest glow. Then I climbed up on the
quilts and stretched out on my back beside the now reclining man.
In a moment I felt his warm breath at my ear, and he began to
whisper.

"Listen carefully to what I say. You are a wonderful woman—
just a child—so quick. Do not be afraid of me. Trust me. . . . I
know about your husband—where the dogs caught him, how he
looked. He only made twenty-seven li in three nights. Why did
he try to go alone, without help? I have selected you. I am going
to open the cage and show you how to fly. Your man was a fool
—he must not have really wanted freedom. Listen carefully to
everything. I am to be here nine days more, all the details will be
arranged. Our people will see to you. . . . You lie very still. Are
you not thrilled? You will need steady nerves. Are you wondering
why I do this? Have you wondered that?" A tension had come into
his whispers, a tremor. "Perhaps I do it"—I felt his lips against
my ear—"just to be able to breathe into an ear like yours." Suddenly he blew gently into my ear, tickling me; but I was horrified
and rather than laughing I lay limp and waited. There was something disgusting in this strange, tense playfulness—maybe Moth
had not been self-glorifying, after all, in her giggling hints at
perversion. *This man was yellow.* Why *did* he do what he was
doing? *Could* he be trusted? Was he only playing with me, like a
kitten—or a pet finch? I remembered the trained bird on a
string at the New Year party at Sun's. Perhaps these thoughts
produced a coldness in me which Salt Inspector Feng could
actually feel; he changed his tone just then, at any rate. "Tell no
one. You must not trust your best friends here. No one must
know. The woman who was here last night—Jasmine?—she may
seem sound to you, but she might tell her husband. You must tell
no one—especially not that first girl, who is really broken-
spirited. Do you want to know how it's done? Why don't you
respond? Aren't you excited?" That tremor again.

Placing one of my hands under Salt Inspector Feng's chin I
turned his head, lifting his lips away from my ear, and I twisted
myself and whispered to him, "If you blow in my ear again I will

tell Hua that you are a member of the Uncage-the-Finches, that you have been trying to get me to run away. I'll tell him." Then I resumed my former position and waited for his whispers.

"Ayah! You chilly little sow. But don't bother yourself. . . . Usually, you know, we take men out. I have to work then through their women. Do you think I could do that and offend the women? . . . Never mind. . . . You'll have to be patient—wait a month after I leave. We don't want them to see a pattern. We will set your leaving in the night before a temple day—perhaps double eleven —that usually gives a night and a day and a night for a start while everything official is closed. Do you want to know these things? What is the matter with you? You're like a dead fish in a market stall. Was I wrong to choose you? Do you have the white man's dead-head?"

My heart began to pound at this last question. Was my intermittent numbness a slave's well-known failing, illness, corruption, surrender? Again I exchanged our ears and mouths, and I whispered: "Yes! Sometimes I do! Will you let me go anyway? I want to go."

When we had re-turned, Salt Inspector Feng sighed into my ear and whispered, "That's better, child. I'm glad to hear a little eagerness. Only, be on guard. When you have the dead-head you must fight every minute to hold your tongue. . . . Listen. There are two most dangerous parts: the first three days, till you get out of range of the wonks, and two days beyond the border in the first core province, because of the Clip-the-Wings Edict. You'll be in a party of four: three men and you. For the first three days a wild boar will lead you. Then you'll be in charge of a yellow man —he'll be your 'master,' going home from a pilgrimage. Beyond the border the moles will pick you up and pass you along. . . . We'll have plenty of time to plan . . ."

⟨ The Pilgrim

Our "master," the pilgrim, boldly set out with us in broad daylight. How frightened I was! Everything was so bewildering: We were traveling *away* from the sacred mountain, T'ai Shan. Our pilgrim was ostensibly returning home, but I could not tell whether he had actually been to the mountain. He seemed truly holy, steady-eyed, stringy, and quite sure of himself. My companions—three strong white men named Bang, White, and Horsehoof, all freed by Salt Inspector Feng—and I were dazed with exhaustion and fear; we had had four moonless nightmare nights, led by a ragged, hairy, amber-eyed boar from filthy temple haven to damp cave to hollowed kaoliang rick to burrow under a pagoda, following Tou Mu, the North Star (how glad I was I had always bowed to her idol!), now through a country of estates, now through a region of scrubby farms and poor people in the dusty bed of the former course of the Yellow River, famished, with the tracking cry of wonks (or imagined barking) ringing in our ears, not even daring to pause to steal raw turnips still left in the ground, afraid to drink from wells at night because of a terror of killing the well-guarding frog and therefore going blind, too excited to sleep as we hid pressed to each other by day, nourished only by the wild-animal nerve and the unbearably sweet and civilized selflessness of our tattered guide, the boar.

Our new "master" had met us at the pagoda platform before dawn, as the boar disappeared wordlessly in the shadows; "Master" had fed us and cleaned us up as best he could, and now we were making our way along a sunken country road (we might have arrived right back at Hua's for all the countryside showed) in a party of two great-wheeled north-country wheelbarrows propelled in rotation by Bang, White, and Horsehoof. "Master" rode one and I was carried on the other; I felt a heavy burden to my fellows.

These three men, sampling brief tastes of a freedom they had as yet by no means attained, asked our "master" forward questions, and we began to learn things about him which, far from pleasing us, had us by the first nightfall thoroughly alarmed.

He was a dealer in provisions for poultry. Nothing wrong with that.

He had promised his life to the cause of freeing slaves. "I am," he said, with a strange vehemence, "*ashamed* of my yellow skin." He said he felt the burden of the cruelty of his race.

When we stopped under a willow tree for a frugal noon meal, it came out that he was a convinced vegetarian. More than that. It trickled forth that he was a member of the Total Abstinence Society, offshoot of the White Lily Sect; he had never in his life touched alcohol, tobacco, ginseng, pepper, ginger, mustard; he had never watched a theatrical troupe, he had never played at cards or jumping sticks; he had never burned incense or offered sacrifices; he had never owned a dog, or a cat, or a chicken. I felt my first real lick of fear of him when, with an eye which burned for all the world exactly like that of our perfect sweet-hearted life-lost wild boar who had led us past the wonks, "Master" said he had never read a poem, because poetry was "lasciviousness."

Tucked in a sleeve he had a Buddhist prayer wheel, and before he set out he uttered prayers which we clearly heard.

One of them went like this: "Patient Buddha, gird us all to do valiantly for the helpless and innocent. Bless those who die in the harness of a mule and are buried on the plowed field or bleach there."

Bang, gripping the handles of "Master's" barrow, heaving, with the shafts hanging from a white cotton hauling strap slung over his shoulders, grunted out a question we all wanted answered. "Will we reach the border? Isn't this a dangerous way to travel?"

"Son," our "master" said, "there are dangers all about us: less for you than for me. They would simply take you back—for me, much worse. I forgive in advance yellow men for their curses and stones; I am *ashamed*."

At the same time, he voiced a genuine humanitarianism—a decent pity and concern for us.

But in the afternoon I saw "Master" reading a book. He had no way of knowing that I could read, and during a halt, while Horsehoof was relieving Bang, I, on a pretext of stretching my legs, approached closely and saw the cover: *Book of Martyrs: How One Thousand Stepped Lightly to Death.*

I need not, it turned out, have sneaked to find out the title, because before long, in answer to Horsehoof's (by now rather anxious) question, "Why do you do this for us?" he openly said, "I am *ashamed*, I have told you that. I must purify our record. I have had to settle with myself: Can I clasp the faggot, dear friend? Can I lie and have my legs cut off without flinching?"

And later he said, "I am reading a book here about men who suffered that their stories might move others. Shen of Plum Garden who gave his life to save a temple from the army of the Western Kingdom. Heroic names, fiery names. Fu. P'an. K'ung. Kao. Many, many. Our yellow race must cleanse itself. P'an said, 'The blood of martyrs is the wine of serenity.'"

To rescue us—or to risk us? We began to see the chances "Master" took. He had us wheel our tiny caravan straight through the gates and through the heart of a district town; with the gendarmes at the gates he was haughty, reckless, and stingy in his squeeze money. "Those guardsmen," he later said, "are my tormentors. I pray for them."

It began to seem to us that he was taking chances with us that he need not have taken. After each narrow-eyed scrutiny by toll-house guards or by Imperial cavalrymen at yamen gates, he seemed to be transported into an almost trancelike religious ecstasy.

At other times he was considerate, gentle, solicitous of our weary bodies and frayed nerves.

With glances—easily understood—Bang, White, Horsehoof, and I agreed among ourselves that this man was extremely dangerous to us; at the same time, no one else could save us.

Thus we traveled for three days in constant and extreme anxiety. On the third day "Master" indicated to us that we were approaching the Wei River at the point where it crossed into the core province of North-of-the-River, and that here for six hours we would pass through a border area teeming with adventurers, slave chasers, guards, corrupt revenue agents. "Master" was exhilarated. At every challenge he shouted and arrogantly waved his credentials as a pilgrim. We kept going after dusk. It was quite dark when we turned off into a deeply rutted side road. "Master" kept praying in a low voice. "Give me strength, Buddha, not to run until I have been beaten with the heavy bamboo as often as K'ung—eight times." Then at length he had us hide the wheelbarrows in a hazel thicket and we went on, walking. It was the dark of the moon—an inkblock night.

At our sides, the tremolo call of an owl! Ah, it was "Master."

Another owl answered in the distance. We stumbled forward. I felt mud sucking at my feet.

A loud whisper: "What do you say?"

"Master": "O-mi-t'o-fu."

At this password a shadow materialized. There were whispers. The shadow embraced "Master." A hand took my arm. Something hard—gunwale of a sampan. A grating sound as the men pushed off; dripping of a single oar. Why did I feel so light of heart? I had escaped from "Master"! That was all!

A sheet of stars on which we glided.

In the distance, ahead, a lantern.

◖ The Kingdom of the Mole

We had reached, in dead-flat country, "the mountain."
We were now in a core province, where slaves were supposed to
be free, yet we were told that we were in the zone of maximum
danger. This was on account of the Emperor's Clip-the-Wings
Edict, which His Sweet-Smelling Sublimity had promulgated for
reasons no one seemed able to understand—perhaps to appease
the powerful landowners of the slavery provinces, in order the
more easily, one day, to swallow them whole. We were told that
he was preparing a war against them. At any rate this edict levied
an Imperial fine of two hundred taels—several times the price of
a prime hog—for harboring escaped slaves or preventing their
arrest. A "master" or his "agent" could seize a runaway and procure from a magistrate a chit proclaiming the chattel's return.
Proof: the "master's" word. The danger zone near the border was
accordingly filled with shiftless flesh-speculators, armed to the
ears, who pounced on any white-skinned creatures they saw,
dragged them to magistrates, and obtained papers of extradition.
White skin must not be seen.

Bang, White, Horsehoof, and I were in firm hands. We were
hidden by day in "burrows": in packing boxes in a godown, in a
rail pen covered with straw, in a cellar connected with a root
cellar. We were moved along "the mole run" both by day (in a
train of four carts with false bottoms, in a load of kaoliang
fodder) and by night (afoot, reverting to the nightmare time with
our boar guide). Some of our guides were yellow, some white.
One night, in a dark back room of a rich farmer's compound, we
had a glimpse of "the Queen of the Moles," a former slave woman,
tiny and frail, said to suffer from dizzy spells, who, we were told,
had returned into West-of-the-Mountains Province seventeen times
to lead out fellow slaves, and who was now on her way back yet
again.

Through all this I felt, above all, a great uneasiness. What made
these yellow people kind to such worthless white nonentities as
we? What caused that sickish sweetness in their behavior—the
insatiable *suffering* in their eyes as they looked at us? What did
they really want of us?

Later, as we moved out of the danger zone, we traveled more
freely, on our own, and my lungs filled up with air that tasted like

something I had read about in one of the books Old Uncle had given me: perfect thirst-slaking nectar that had been made by melting a queer late snow from the petals of peach blossoms. There really did not seem to be any slavery here.

The "moles" gave us directions. I carried a note: "Rap at the gate of the first house after passing a place where pomace is sold from a large cart in the street."

The Number Wheel

❰ An Elegant Life

FREEDOM! We four furnished our minds, Horsehoof, Bang, White, and I, as we trudged towards Peking, with all the joys of our new state. Remembering the Shen mansion, I told my friends of the elegant life ahead: carved marble spirit screens, goldfish drooping with shot-silk veils, chopsticks tipped with filigree. Which of us would be the first to ride, one day, in a mandarin's green sedan chair *borne by four yellow men?* Horsehoof kept saying, "I have a friend. Wait and see. He'll set us up." This friend, a runaway slave named Jumping Stick now living in the Northern Capital, was going to be our patron, with nothing to do but show us the way to satin, and in truth as we walked and talked he developed magical powers.

We arrived at last and decided in cheery spirits to enter the Tartar City by the Gate of Unmixed Blessings.

A bannerman stepped from a wooden booth. "Your gate chips."

Bang said, "Gate chips?"

Little bamboo counters, we were curtly informed by the yellow guard, that were issued to whites as passes. Finding that we had none, he ordered us in sharp tones to go down to one of the gates of the Outer City.

At the Eastern Wicket Gate to the Outer City a guardsman took down our names (we gave false names) and issued us single-entry passes on slips of green paper, and he told us to register with the Red Banner Corps within the city.

Horsehoof, adopting the humble, appeasing manner of a rural white slave, asked what gate chips meant. Why were passes issued to whites? Why registrations, if it wasn't rude to ask, Venerable?

The yellow guard seemed irritated, not by Horsehoof's questions but by his obsequiousness; perhaps the bannerman knew that it was a stale pose. "It's because of the Number Wheel," he said. "Move along." He waved us peremptorily through, so we could not ask more questions.

Upon passing through the gate, we were beset by a flock of white beggars flapping and clucking like fowl at feeding time. What could they hope for from us?

There was a subdued atmosphere, a strained quiet, in the streets. White workmen were at the same old slavey tasks, free men carrying baskets of night soil on shoulder poles, hauling water carts, pushing wheelbarrows overloaded with roof tiles— but instead of being in colorful uniforms they looked drab and foul in faded blue cotton tunics and trousers.

Horsehoof asked a water cartman if he happened to know a big wonk of a white man named Jumping Stick.

For answer the cartman only threw back his head and laughed.

Four times Horsehoof reaped this same scornful laugh, then he began to ask in a low voice where newcomers should go in this city.

By stages we were directed to a section, north of the Altar of Agriculture, where, in a maze of narrow, twisting alleys, a mixed population of poor yellows and poorer whites lived in inexpressible squalor.

We spent three nights in a foul doss house; men and women slept like tossed burdens on the floors of the rooms on three sides of a courtyard in which, by day, bricks were manufactured. Clay dust was ankle-deep. At night the coughing around me was worse than the worry of country dogs at the full of the moon. Freedom! The mountain for which I had yearned so long! How I wept!

⟨ The Pigeon Cote

By the fourth morning panic was coiled in my belly. The string of cash the moles had given me had all been spent long

since, and I had not eaten for two days, and my clothes were
a hostel for lice which I had time, but no heart, to pick. Horsehoof's great friend Jumping Stick was nowhere to be found. No
prospect of work: wherever I begged for work I heard, besides
repeated noes, mumbled complaints of the Number Wheel, which
seemed to have run over and crushed all vitality in the city. I
understood nil, for no one spoke to me.

These stinking alleyways housed a cooliehood of both whites
and yellows, and I sensed a standoff, misery envious of wretched-
ness. Poor yellows walked one side of the midstreet ditches,
poorer whites the other; scowls and sullenness.

Threading the lanes of the Outer City on the hopeless hunt for
work, I wandered into a hutung, Glazed Tile Factory Alley, and
found myself in a fairyland of open shops where old books, pictures, and curios were sold.

I stepped into one of the shops, intending to tell the owner
that I had some learning and could do any work he wanted. A
yellow youth, livid pimples and frog eyes, came at me with a
feather duster, shaking in my face a cloud of potential sneezes
and snarling, "Out! Out! No sows allowed in here!"

I backed into the street with my arms folded above my head,
and I turned to run through the crowds, with remembered lines
from *The Happy Mean* ringing their ironies in my aching head,
and I bit my lip to quiet the throbs.

But my desperation wound down, I slowed my pace, and I saw
ahead of me a yawing spine, a hobble-walk. I hurried abreast.

"Mink!"

At first the face that swung toward mine was blank, then
recognition foliated in it. The cripple embraced me; incurious
pedestrians jostled our mismatched hug without second looks.

"What are you doing?"

"Doing? I'm a runner for a prick of a merchant in cloisonné
ware."

"Are you all right?"

"Jobs don't last forever. What slanty boss wants a white with a
bad back? It's very off-and-on. You?"

"Ayah!"

"I know." But there was no vehemence in this Mink; I remembered the tartness that had made him a scourge to Peace. There
was a thin screak of self-pity at the edge of his words.

How had he come here?

He told me this brief story: From the Yens he had been sold, through a slave agent, to a miser of a grain factor, the very sort of niggardly hunks who *would* buy a bent-backed slave on a glut market; but the sweet thing about this cheese-parer was that he lived in Tingchow, and when slavery had been abolished in the core provinces, Mink said, he had simply obtained his freedman's papers and hopped off to here. "Where nothing is any better."

"But, Mink, what is this Number Wheel?"

"It's on account of the war."

"*War?*"

Ai, this was freedom for a white nonentity: Walking all those weeks, I had heard nothing, and no one had had a tongue in the doss house. I was in a dark box of ignorance. A war had been started, core provinces against outer provinces, and all this time no one had told me a word of it. Mink said it twice over, I shaking my head. What was it about? About us! About hogs in the hogpen! No! Don't tease me, Mink!

"And the wheel is a lottery for conscripting soldiers. The slant-heads are out of their minds about it. They blame everything on us. The drawing begins in a few days."

I told Mink I was weak with hunger, he shouldn't hit me with bad jokes.

Mink veered off at my word "hunger." He put his face close to mine, at his lower level, and I had strongly the impression of a wire, behind the eyes, that had been kinked and might part if pulled too hard. "Where are you living?"

In a few words I told him my plight.

"Wait, wait," he said. "I know a yellow woman—takes roomers."

"But I haven't a canary's tooth to my name."

"She's used to that. She gambles on us."

So he took me straight along. On the way he told me about the woman. Fat, and jovial, but her laughter was like boulders rolling down a mountain in a landslide: watch out! She was called, not without sarcasm, "Dowager."

"How many boarders does she take?"

"Not many, not more than three or four at a time. Just now I know of a professional beggar, named Groundnut, and a man of odd jobs, Rock. Ayah, that Rock! A quarrelsome hog. You'll see."

"How do you know her so well?"

"I've stayed with her—it's not a first-class inn, you know."

Indeed it was not. Dowager Chu lived in a hovel off an alley down whose center ran a sewage ditch, and her whole home consisted of three spaces at the south side of a narrow yard, most of which was filled by a pigeon cote and by a tower of bamboo poles lashed together, with a ladder up one side and a platform at the top. On this stage, higher than the roof ears of the house, two men stood when Mink and I arrived, and one of them was coning in wide circles a long bamboo pole with a yellow-and-green pennant at its upper end; in circles in the air, as if towed by the pennant, went a whir of nearly a hundred pigeons. The courtyard, the walls, and the roof were stippled with white droppings.

At the foot of the tower stood a fat yellow woman, looking up, gurgling joy at men and pigeons.

Mink made a loud motorish pigeony sound, and Dowager Chu lowered her eyes to us. "Ai, to see the little flag suck them down!" She clasped dimpled and fat-braceleted hands.

"I've brought one in for your coops." Mink meant me.

Dowager blinked. The dimples and bracelets shifted. An arrangement was soon made: As a favor to Mink she would charge me only forty per cent interest on the rent I would be unable at first to pay. That was good for a jolly laugh.

The men were climbing down from the bamboo tower; the pigeons whirled down a vortex of fanned air to the cote.

Dowager asked Mink to stay and share a rice bowl, and at the word "rice" her eyes danced in their prison of fat; but Mink said he must run his errand.

Dowager took me into her hutch: a k'ang in each end space, a cookstove in the central one. She said I could choose my bed—with the hogs (what a merry lilt she gave that hateful epithet!), with her (suppose she rolled over on one in the night!), or on the floor in the cook space. I said I would spread a mat on the brick floor by the stove.

The men came in with a basket of washed rice, and what a meal! Rice—delicacy in this millet-growing region—and pigeon eggs beaten and folded into a crisp roll with sautéed onion and bean sprouts! I tried to pretend I had eaten once that day, but I could not help moaning over the egg roll.

"Blaaah," the man Rock said, twisting his full mouth toward a pretended retch, but his eyes laughing, "wait till you've eaten them every day for a month."

⟪ Mercy Errand

Had anyone ever heard such boldness? Rock said that the war, which had erupted during the time when I was walking upcountry from "the mountain," was going badly, and the population of the core provinces was apathetic. The Emperor had soiled his breeches (Rock's effrontery!) because he had had to thin out the banner guards of the capital so he could send more troops to the various zones, and the city was becoming disorderly. And now he'd announced that civilians would be chosen by lot to swell out the Imperial army. This was to be by the Number Wheel, and this was supposed to be a liberalization—selecting men by drawing numbers instead of shanghaiing them—but soldiering was the lowest form of life, a louse-infested, mud-soaked, running-away sort of life, and the yellows in the capital were seething. Especially the poor yellows. For one thing, the decree exempted any man whose number was drawn who would pay two hundred taels to buy a substitute. But worse than that, the poor yellows, who had to compete for food bowls with freed whites, resented the "Grand Harmonious Mercy Errand" of the war, as the Emperor kept calling it—the goal of freeing the slaves in the peripheral provinces. Everyone knew that this cause was a filthy rationalization: that the Emperor, who had scooped the floors of the Imperial coffers building new palaces in the Western Hills, wanted to get his shit-smelling hands on the outlying farm lands, for their revenues. (Hooo! I shuddered at Rock's recklessness.) Rock and Groundnut were outwardly cynical about the issue of slavery in the war, saying that it brought down on our white shoulder blades the sanctimonious "kindness" of upper-class yellows and the frank hatred of the poor; yet by some clue, some tremor in Rock's snarling voice and Groundnut's sarcastic but milder tones, I sensed that they were inwardly attached to the Grand Harmonious Mercy Errand all the same—indeed, that it meant so much to them that they were forced for self-protection to turn their feeling inside out, into sneers and railing.

Rock said the registrations for the great lottery of human beings had already begun, and he had heard that the enrolling officers were to come into this district in a few days.

◖ Looking for a Food Bowl

Learning that I could read and write, Dowager said that I must make every effort to "save" myself—get work in one of the inner cities, Tartar or Imperial, away from the miserable swamp of poverty all around us.

My first task: acquire a gate chip. Gate chips could only be procured at Red Banner headquarters in the Tartar City; one needed a gate chip to penetrate the Tartar City at all; ergo, one could not get a gate chip!—except, as Groundnut pointed out, by buying a counterfeit. Dowager provided the money and Groundnut provided the corrupt man; and soon I had the oblong bamboo domino of legitimacy.

Miraculous! From a trunk Dowager produced a dingy gray silk gown which fitted my body and made me feel like the best pigeon of all.

I had no trouble getting through the Hata Gate, under the Fox Tower of shivering memories. A tall bannerman took my chip in his hand, flipped it over, and tossed it back to me, saying, "Hai, little fox! Would you like a nice skewer of Tartar lamb?"

In a fury at the soldier's foul mouth, I hurried into the inner city.

Such a whirl of responses to all that I saw! Nightmare memories, yet a strong fondness for the best of the past: a catch at my bowels at the thought of carrying out Big Madame Shen's dirty bath water, yet a sweet weakness, as if my limbs were drowsy, at recalling the revels at Chao-er's.

I saw that in my aimless meandering I was following old paths. Everything was altered. I came to the place where the noble gate had stood: HARMONY IN ALL THE COURTYARDS!—now a cold entrance to a warehouse where the flags, catafalques, sedans, liveries, and drums of one of the Boards were stored. The old vegetable market—now the site of a bannermen's barracks. An alley, Chao-er's tavern—now a school, chanting children's voices. The great temples, the purple inner walls, the curfew towers, the Coal Hill, the white dagobas, the golden roofs—all the signs of yellow mastery remained; what was vague, what seemed to melt before my eyes, was any image that attested to my own change of condition, to my freedom now as a human being. I began to feel

the sensations of that horrible numbness I thought I had left behind forever.

Then I was in the plaza leading to the Meridian Gate, and
before me was a cluster of white men, free men, playing a game.
They had formed a circle, and they were tossing from one to another a large polished ovoid granite stone into which a metal handle had been studded. The stone was a load—must have weighed
twenty catties. Yet flinging it in arcs and catching it always by
the handle and swinging it round for new flights, the men made
it seem grasshopper-light. They never missed. While the stone was
leaping among them, they started up as well a foot shuttlecock,
which they bounced from one's side-flung heel to another's, so
they had two timings to follow, of granite and pinfeather. Their
adroitness and grace were breathtaking. Their cries of mutual
admiration and delight were like sounds in fruit groves long ago.
No yellows were watching; no yellows were tossing coppers. I
could no longer tell which object was heavy and which light. My
spirits began to jump with the stone and the cock, and my incipi-
ent numbness gave way to something akin to excitement, an
impulse to laugh, a flicker of hoping that freedom might mean
something after all. I felt as if freedom had at least kissed me on
my eyes and ears.

I was supposed to be searching for a food bowl.

I winched up my courage and applied at an imposing gate—Imperial Horse Department. I got no farther than the gate guard.

My manner was slavish, I spoke with dipped shoulder and
slight humble whine—any work for a clerk? copyist? recorder?

I got, for my effort—besides an air of irritation which responded, I sensed, to my ritual white meekness—nothing but a
transparent formula.

I tried that afternoon half a dozen great gates of bureaus and
boards—for I wanted no more housework. I tried a more arrogant
bearing and only earned an even greater irritation. No, nothing,
move on! I needed some key to these gates.

My free mood that the playing whites had given me was
evaporating. But I summoned up a thought of that contentious
man, Rock, who was simply not satisfied with anything, and I
did smile thinking of him.

The sun was plummeting, and I was fearful of being caught
within the Tartar City by the nightly closing of the gates, and I
ran a long distance to get to the Hata Gate; so fast did my worry

carry me that the sun was still on the afternoon's hip, above the western wall, when I reached the portal.

Around the foot of the Fox Tower swarmed white beggars, some lying in the dust, legs drawn up in fetal self-satisfaction, seeming to sleep, others plying their trade.

As I approached the guardhouse of the gate, a cringing creature, a man as short as I who made himself smaller, came up to me and began to croak, "Ayah, T'ai-t'ai, save me. Send me down some money. I'm hungry. My hunger hurts my belly." This monster, the remnants of a white man, was so hideous that one could not give him alms in pity; rather one paid him to go away, to remove his revolting person—a caricature of suffering humanity—from one's sight. The murmuring was on a dirgelike monotone, a sound of self-mourning: "Hunger is eating me. T'ai-t'ai! Hunger bites my belly. Ayah, T'ai-t'ai."

Three quarters of the beggar's crown was covered with a white cap of fungoid rot; one of his eyes was filmed to blindness with a greenish mucus. He limped; he shuffled; he leaned.

Something about this figure haunted me. What dim memory did he evoke?

"T'ai-t'ai, T'ai-t'ai," he wailed. "I pray for you. I kowtow to you, Ta-niang. Save my life! My pain is unbearable."

I had no money. What could I do? His clawlike hand plucked at my sleeve. I looked at the face as I wrenched my arm away. There was a ghost of a smile around the filthy lips. Those lips, that smile—vaguely familiar. What *was* I reminded of?

I myself was hungry; I had had nothing to eat all day. I began to tremble. Was this some kind of supernatural visitation from the past that kept up its moaning appeal? "Ai, ai, my hunger eats me. Send down money, T'ai-t'ai. Save me, save me."

The claw was on me again. The decomposing face came closer. The lips were bent to a grin. In my ear the wailing voice: "Give me money, White Lotus!"

I was so startled at hearing my name that I almost dived into the face; our noses nearly touched.

"Ha ha ha ha ha! I knew you had no money, child. Dowager sets limits on her generosity. Listen. Wait a few minutes. Rock meets me here. We'll go home to our palace together."

It was Groundnut! I had never seen him go off begging. He always left before dawn, to be at the gate for its opening rush. What a foul mummery!

At last I could speak. "Groundnut! How disgusting you are!"

"Am I not a masterpiece?" he said, as if my revulsion were the sweetest of compliments. Then, to frighten me further, he resumed his mendicant groaning. "T'ai-t'ai. T'ai-t'ai. My hunger burns. It's like fire. Ayah. Ayah. Help me!" He laughed then. Even though I knew that all his agony was just as counterfeit as my gate chip, and that his diseases were disguises, I could not look at him for fear of becoming sick to my also-hungry stomach.

"Come over here, pretty flower. We can sit on these kegs while we wait. There! Don't look at me. Watch the camels going through. Now. Did you find a food bowl?"

I told him about my day. Groundnut was gentle and solicitous, and soon—being careful not to look at him—I was comfortable in his company.

"Your friend—what was his name—Mink?—with that lovely twisted back—it's like a whirlpool dragon's back: I could make a Hata Gate beggar of *him*."

It seemed that the Hata Gate beggars were the aristocrats of the profession.

"Speak to him," Groundnut said. "I'll be his teacher."

"He's too proud," I said, though I was not really sure that was true.

"What does a white man have to be proud of?"

"What is the matter with Rock," I said, "if not pride?"

"Ayah, Rock!" Groundnut said. "He has a snake in his guts."

I found that I wanted to talk about Rock—that my desire to talk about him amounted to a kind of vehemence, and that it was somehow connected with the new feelings I had had after watching the white men playing toss-stone.

"Really," I said, "what's wrong with him?"

"Wrong with him? He's argumentative. Anyone can see that."

"I don't mean that."

"What, then?"

"What's the name of the snake?"

"Who knows? Maybe it's Envy."

Hooo! I felt something like a tug of desire at that word. Yes! Envy! Sometimes known as a yearning for *their* freedom. Real freedom—which means: mastery, power. I laughed aloud at the knowledge that we whites were far from "free." Only the powerful are "free."

From where we sat we could see the sun being shut out of the inner capital. Just as the teeth of the distant city wall began to bite into the orange circle, a single deep clang sounded overhead. I jumped in alarm away from the kegs.

"It's the closing gong," Groundnut said. "Come and watch."

He led me a few steps away from the gate and pointed up to the lip of the wall beside the Fox Tower. There stood four huge Tartars with heavy wooden mallets. After the last of the reverberations from the great gong had died away, one of the giants swung his maul. Clong! So the strokes followed one another, at first with massive deliberateness, then merely slowly, then gradually pulsing faster, until, when the sun was down and the clashing had gone on for nearly a quarter of an hour, the pounding of the four hammers made one long sound. It was the sound of power, a clanging indistinguishable from what we used to hear in slave days. Suddenly the hammers stopped. In the tunnel of the gate four other bannermen now began a series of warning cries. The sleeping beggars stirred—a rush of last-moment squeaking of barrows and carts, a bedlam of brayings, carters' shouts, and gate guards' commands. Groundnut looked about anxiously for his friend. The gates began to close with orotund groans from the old ironbound timbers.

At the last moment Rock came running up, and showing our chips on the trot we slipped through the closing gap.

"The turtles!" Rock said, cursing the guards and yellows in general.

I remembered the white men standing in a circle arching the heavy stone and the feather-tailed cork bird, and now my own spirits soared again in response to Rock's incautious vitality. Envy! Yes!

Up on the walls bannermen hooted a chorus of long-drawn howls, expressive of the yellow power we hated and envied, meaning, "The city is safe! Safe! Safe!"

⟨[Thieves of the Sky

The moment we reached Dowager's courtyard Groundnut began to shed his loathsome gear. In one sweep he tore off the scab of fungus from his crown; he scooped the pus from his eye— it was all makeup. Beeswax, silk, suet, pigment. Dowager had a wooden bucket of hot water waiting for him in the yard, and splashing and blowing he made himself over into a sound young man. He changed from his tatters into decent padded cotton clothes.

The pigeons in their cages of bamboo wattles welcomed Rock and Groundnut—filled the air with their purring, jumped like impatient children, beat up a rustling storm of feathers. While Groundnut cured himself of his beggary, Rock went to the cotes, lighted several lanterns against the dark that had not yet come, and busied himself with the birds.

Knock at the gate. Groundnut ran and opened it to a yellow man in good dress who appeared to be a merchant—in fact, a collector for the beggars' league to which Groundnut belonged. Hayah, even white beggars were under the thumbs of yellow profiteers.

Groundnut undid the cinch of his voluminous trousers and pulled out, from within, a cloth bag of coins. The collector slipped an abacus from under his gown, and the two squatted on their hams and counted, with clinks and clicks, the day's take and the league's squeeze—forty per cent, Groundnut told me later, a standard rate, he said, for self-respecting extortionists. Fifty per cent meant insult; thirty per cent meant something too easy like kinship. The two men had a brief argument, wild and scurrilous, a matter more of ceremony, I gathered, than of substance; then the collector left, and Groundnut, rubbing his hands with satisfaction, joined Rock at the cotes.

The dusks of those dry early-summer days in the Capital lingered on and on with a kind of reluctance in the pure sky, like a glow of youth in a happy woman's skin. The bamboo tower stood stark against the pale-peach-colored expanse, its segmented round legs and braces gleaming like gold tubes lighted from every side.

As Groundnut and Rock bustled, the pigeons grew more and more eager to be on the wing in that lambent air.

The men threw up the lids of the cotes—what an uprising! I could feel the wind of the wings on my cheeks. The flock circled once and flew off northeastward.

Walking home from the Hata Gate the pair had told me that they would show me this evening "the secret of the pigeons." Now, eyes sparkling with mirrored lantern flames, they whetted my curiosity by unfolding to me one phase of their secret—told me they had, with patient work over months, enlarged the crops of their pets by forcing marbles down their throats and later causing them to vomit the crop-stretchers by manipulation. Rock ran inside to fetch these objects for me to see: marbles such as boys had used back in Arizona, glassies, agates, sparklers, tiger's eyes, twisties, steel bombs!

The pair spread a sheet of cotton cloth on top of the cotes, and they filled several shallow bowls with water and placed them at intervals on the cloth. I saw Rock sprinkle some kind of powder in the bowls. Every bird would drink on the flock's return, Groundnut told me; the pigeons had not been watered all day.

We waited. Light ran down the sky's drains. The two men climbed the tower, Groundnut carrying his pole, at the end of which, in place of the pennant, he hung a flickering red paper lantern; Rock took up a flute.

The lantern began to fly in circles, and I heard from the flute a low, mournful, steadily repeated figure, in tone halfway between pigeons' speech and the sound of the sad whistles I'd heard these birds sometimes carry on their tails.

Soon: the fuffuffing of wings. Around and around till the men were satisfied that all had come home. Down men and birds came then.

By lanterns the pigeons drank up. The powder, Rock whispered, was alum. The birds began to throw up what was in their crops.

Rice! Surprisingly large piles of rice from those marble-enlarged crops.

Now it was Groundnut and Rock who behaved like excited pigeons. As each bird emptied itself a white hand would gently lift it and put it in the cotes by lower doors. Soon all were unloaded. The men lifted the ears of the cotton cloth. With frugal care they transferred the rice to a basket, and weighed it. Nearly twenty catties! They washed the grains by dipping the basket over and over in a large tub, and they took the haul to Dowager, who had a caldron boiling and something savory sizzling in oil.

We had a feast of carp, stolen one night by Rock from the sacred fishponds near the Temple of Heaven, and of rice—stolen, I was finally told, by our heavenly thieves from the Imperial granaries in the Tartar City, near the Gate of Unmixed Blessings, where they had hungrily gorged themselves on the wastage in the yards, among the wicker scoops, in the carts, from the weighing sheds, from stored baskets, and had brought it all home to vomit out for us.

Over this repast Rock and Groundnut openly expressed their delight at cheating, with this beautiful ruse, the most powerful yellow creature of all, the Emperor. How grandly they masticated their sweet little sample of revenge!

Dowager, promiscuous in her jollity, laughed hard (watch out!) over the idea of our kind besting her kind.

Groundnut said, "Dear pigeons! Could there be anything freer than one of these birds going up there? Think of these friends of ours shooting up to the granaries. Or a hawk! I wish I were a hawk, to soar and soar. I wouldn't even object to being a crow. Ai, I'd flap over this city shouting filth at those turtles down on the ground. Cawr-r-r! Cawr-r-r!"

But, I thought, you've made slaves of these pigeons you say you love so much.

It was Rock who, after our rollicking supper, took heaping bowls of cooked rice out to reward our providers. I heard him clucking over them. Where was the brutal arguer?

❲ Registration

"Hai! Hai! Hai! We must see the fun," Dowager cried, waving her great arms helplessly, to indicate that she wished to be cranked to a standing position.

The enrolling officers for the Number Wheel had come to our alley.

Rock and Groundnut grappled at Dowager's vast armpits, and with curses, groans, and laughter assisted her to her poor little feet.

Out we went, and we found an unpleasant scene. A squad of bannermen backed up with matchlocks a white-button who, at a table straddling our vile street gutter, was setting down the names of men eligible for enumeration.

From a hard pack of yellow men of the rottenest sort the white-button was receiving a shower of abusive language.

The bannermen, huge fierce Tartars, made sallies into the crowd and hauled men forward one by one. The white-button asked each a series of questions.

We had been watching only a few minutes when the Tartars, skidding aside, as it were, suddenly seized Rock and began hauling him out.

What an uproar of arms, legs, and maledictions! I heard Rock spew out a series of foul objections to the Number Wheel. Why, I don't believe he had thought that whites were to be registered at all—this was a yellow man's war. I felt that I heard the sound of tearing in his voice, of some fabric in him being ripped—his feelings about the Mercy Errand, about a war that was "for" faraway whites, his being roughed by the yellow soldiers, his hearing obscenities hurled at him now by the yellow men in the alley.

The white-button quietly persisted, the Tartars held his arms, and to get out of their hands Rock gave a fictitious name and a false address.

Groundnut, with much less fuss, did the same when he was taken out.

How Dowager's laughter pealed out as we went back to our pigeon-muted yard!

(Bad Hog

That same afternoon they spiraled up a plan, Rock and Groundnut—to buy and train a fighting cock. More than that: a white cock. Show the yellow bastard bettors in Fighting Cocks Pit Lane that the color white was not to be given laughable odds. How they savored this scheme!

They began independently to scour the city, and a few days later Rock found a healthy yearling white-pile cockerel, which had a few yellowish-red feathers in its hackle and tail but otherwise was white all over. Groundnut, who had an earthenware crock of cash buried in the ground under one of the dovecotes, approved the bird and bought it. They named it—to lengthen the betting odds—Bad Hog.

Now serious training began. Groundnut, with a genius for making birds understand his wishes, instilled in Bad Hog an obedient ferocity, while Rock invented clever hobbles and hindrances, little weights and clumsy shapes, which, when fastened to the rooster's legs, wings, or head, helped to strengthen the muscles of self-assertion. They fed the cock, besides regular millet feed, helpings of cooked rice and chopped hard-boiled pigeon eggs. They even bought and gave it what we never ate ourselves, bits of mutton and beef. They plucked every off-white feather; trimmed the slope of the wings; reduced the rump and hackle; inhibited the comb.

They massaged it under the feathers—summit of self-denial!—with *baigar*, the liquor they loved, to toughen the skin.

When we could, we three went to the cocking mains to pick up pointers. Rock and Groundnut were expert to a degree, having long been devotees of the fights, as were many of the harder sort of whites. These whites attended, I suppose, in order to experience, now and then, vicarious revenge; they invariably bet on the less-favored bird, and if it lost they shrugged, but when, as sometimes happened, it killed the stronger bird they took their money silently and left, and then, having put a distance between themselves and the cocking yellows, hooted in the streets, danced about on light feet, pounded each other with fervid congratulations, and got weepingly drunk—over such trivial, if rare, victories. This kind of pleasure was not for me—women prefer genesis to cockfights; I went only to be beside Rock.

White-owned birds always lost. Why? We saw that they were deprived, by tacit agreement among the yellow trainers, of at least two stages in preparation for the fights: Yellow trainers were given time and place in the pits to hold almost-ready birds within close sight of each other, goading them to fury so that their maddened efforts to get at each other would add extra strength to their muscles and wills; and later yellow-owned birds actually sparred, with leather caps on their spurs. Birds belonging to whites were denied these refinements.

To compensate for these denials, Rock made, with great patience, realistic dummies of adversaries for Bad Hog, mainly from pigeon feathers which he dyed various colors, to simulate, in the finished models, some of the famous breeds: Soochow Duns, Southern Capital Topknots, Supreme Black-Reds, Red Quills, Tartar War Ponies. These dummies could be attached to a long bamboo pole with levers which tucked under the wings, so, hidden behind a screen, Rock could enliven the pretense and fill the air with flaps of his own suppressed anger. Bad Hog was white and reacted to these machines with a frustrated rage that we, being white also, understood all too well.

(Dutiful Beneath the Skin

Mink came to see me from time to time, and during one visit he said he knew of a food bowl that I might get, in the Tartar

City, as an attendant in an asylum for abandoned bastard white children. He had worked there awhile and knew the superintendent, and he said he would take me to see the man.

A few days later, when Mink had time off, we set out together. Summer was on us; the air was like goose down.

On the way Mink said, "When I was a slave my curvature had a definite value, because, you see, I knew I had been bought and could be sold for very little money, ayah, I was a bargain, and so whatever value I gave in work was a kind of quick profit—I was always able to give my master a pleasant surprise. But now my cheapness belongs to no one but me. Hai! I'm no bargain to myself."

I remembered how Gull had seemed to adore Mink—for his bitterness, his wit, and for a piquant force in him that lured her to the sedan shed those many afternoons; and I recalled, too, the electric bolts of his cynicism with which he kept trying to shock Peace, and the dead aim of his hard little eyes. This new note of self-pity repelled me; I had to remind myself that he was being kind.

I noticed also that Mink was obsequious to yellows; he craved their love, it seemed.

A stately gateway in a hutung in the eastern part of the city. This was, Mink told me, the former mansion of a young Imperial favorite who had had his head cut off. In a decade this young man had built himself a huge fortune and vast power in the Court, and then, in one instant of one evening, under moonlight, on the Pavilion of the Soaring Phoenixes on the bit of land called Posturing Terrace Island, in a lake of the winter palaces, he had made his fatal move. Conversing with the Emperor's then third-favorite concubine, Round-faced Beauty, this glorious youth, intoxicated by brazen advances that she was unmistakably making, and forgetting that some women have a forked need—to be fondled and to talk about it later—surreptitiously and ever so fleetingly pressed his hand into the soft Y at the lower front where her influence with the Court lay sweetly couched. Thus his estate became available for an orphanage.

The gateman knew Mink and let us in at once. He told us that the superintendent would be found in a side chamber of the second courtyard.

All about me within these walls I heard, like a delicious rain, the splashing laughter of children. In the second courtyard we saw a

score of white boys about ten years old walking on tall stilts—
their feet were above my eye level. Some had drums attached to
their belts and were beating out martial rhythms as they marched
on their heron legs. Others had gongs. One was hopping on a
single stilt, holding the other upright behind his back. A pair was
running a race. The boys' faces expressed a perfect tension between gravity and joy—mouths twisted in concentration, eyes
like wealthy mandarins'.

We knocked at a double-leafed door. An attendant led us around
a folding screen into a spacious chamber, and there, sitting in a
carved ebony chair, like a prefect in his yamen, with his hands
drooped on the ends of the chair arms, sat a round-bellied white
man in a fine silk gown. I noticed—the frill of his hands on the
arms made me think he wanted this to be seen first—that he had
long fingernails, in the style of idle yellows.

Ayah, he was lofty! His name, Benign Warmth. He nodded to
Mink, squinting with what appeared to be suppressed distaste. I
had the impression, when he reopened his eyes, that he was either
so nearsighted or so self-centered that he could not delineate us
clearly, and that he took what he perceived of Mink's infirmity
for an appropriately respectful cringe.

Mink said, "This is White Lotus. I thought perhaps . . . as she
can read and write . . ."

The superintendent nodded again, his mouth a tight little bag
of patience.

"I thought you might have work for her."

"This institution," the superintendent said in musical tones, "is
the charitable good work of certain mandarins' wives. They are
remarkable women, Small Mink." (Hai! The hog! Using the contemptuous diminutive to a white person!) "They give freely of
their time and of their husbands' money. Let me tell you a story.
One day Big Madame Hsüeh" (Hoo! Delicious! The in-between
turtle turns around and uses a magnific title for a yellow person!),
"wife of Hsüeh Li-fang of the Censorate, a lady of great refine-
ment, came to see me about the refurbishing of our refectory, and
I was saying to her" (So! It is not a story about the generous
grandam at all, but rather about what *he* was saying!), "I said,
'Hsüeh T'ai-t'ai, there is something I want to tell you about the
white race. Do you see these children playing in the courtyard
here? Do you see that urchin we call Tiger Ears? The one with the
devil's top? Perhaps you'll say he looks irresponsible. He does.

He looks like a bad boy. He is. He *is* a bad boy, I admit freely. But underneath—here's the point, T'ai-t'ai, this is something you may not know about the white race—underneath he has a sense of duty. He'll grow up into a dutiful man, a *white* man. This is our claim to merit, Big Madame. This boy, this Tiger Ears, *knows the difference* between yellow and white skin. He needn't be taught that, because it's instinctive in him; he understands what the Master meant when he said, "Lizard, do not leap, you will never have feathers." ' "

"Yes, Big Venerable," said Mink, out of habit.

After much more of this I was hired at a paltry wage, not for my reading and writing but simply as a servant-attendant. I was to live in the orphanage.

Having no property, I did not even return to Dowager's but asked Mink to tell her, when next he saw her, that I would pay the rent I owed her as soon as I earned it; and to tell Rock where I was.

I was given a slice of a k'ang in the nurses' quarters. The orphanage was housed in ample grounds: five courtyards, each with its hall and side chambers, verandas and terraces—a jewel of a moon bridge swooped over a tiny pool where goldfish philosophized under floating lily leaves. The beams of the main rooms were decorated in the vulgarly ambitious taste of the late owner.

The asylum harbored three hundred white children of unknown parentage, all under twelve years of age. Upon their actual or estimated twelfth birthday, a matron told me, they were promoted like young scholars—turned loose, that is, to survive or starve in the chaos of the Capital. For every orphan who turned twelve and was spewed out, twenty other younger ones were at large in the city waiting for admittance. Why so many bastard white children? Because among whites marriage (Dolphin! My husband! Poor selfish Dolphin!) was a travesty—had been ever since the first days of slavery, when marriage had meant merely a master's blessing on fornication, or his urging his chattels to breed.

For our three hundred children we had a staff of five matrons and a dozen attendants, all women but for the gate guard.

Most of my work was, after all my effort to avoid it, domestic labor: sweeping, cleaning ashes from k'ang ovens, passing food in the refectory, and washing bowls and kitchen utensils. But I was at least serving whites, and I had, each morning, a saving hour with the children at play in the courtyards.

One day I observed the "bad" boy of whom Benign Warmth had spoken, named Tiger Ears, and I saw that his "badness" was a state of being, a quality that the pompous superintendent would be quite incapable of tolerating: elusiveness.

We were playing a form of tag, and I called out once to warn him, "Tiger Ears!" The urchin seemed not to hear me, but I could tell that his unheeding was put on. I swooped close to him and repeated his name.

He looked straight at me and said, "Whom do you want?"

"You."

"You have the wrong name." (A glint of excitement was embedded deep in the aspic of his eyes.)

"What *is* your name?"

"White Lotus," he said.

This took my wind. I had no idea he had even noticed me. "How did you know my name?"

"It's my name."

"You don't look like a girl."

"I'm not." (Indignantly.)

"White Lotus is a girl's name."

"So? You said it was your name."

"You just said it was *yours.*"

"You're confused," he said, and I was beginning to be.

Tiger Ears' elusiveness, I soon found, had a theme. It was that Tiger Ears was not only not Tiger Ears, he was not anybody. He was, accordingly, unknowable, unpredictable, unaccountable, unpunishable; and although he had a round face with prick ears, sturdy legs, chapped knuckles, and wobbly wrists that could belong to only one personage, he was, in sum, unidentifiable.

He was quick and clever, and I think he had sensed that if he could avoid being anybody until puberty, then, as a white man, he might easily sail through the rest of his life incognito, so to speak, and therefore unnoticed, untouched, and irresponsible. A paradox: In his shrewd and premature assumption of a grown white man's basic cipherdom he had made himself into a vivid child rather than a nonentity, a scourge to Benign Warmth, who, to avoid trouble with the mandarins' wives, wanted his charges to be genuine nothings rather than counterfeit nothings.

In the women's quarter, the main hall of the fourth courtyard, I shared a k'ang with a matron named Belted Persimmon, "a settled person," I heard her called one day, a woman who could not have worked anywhere but in an orphanage. She believed, in the face of daily proofs to the contrary, that every human being (even yellow) was good and kind. When some of us laughed to her face at her sentimentality, she put her hands up to her cheeks and wept with pleasure at what she called our wonderful love of life, which produced such happy laughter. She was really a fool! The children, however, flocked to her as chicks to a hen, and most of us were secretly jealous of her spell over them.

After my exchange with Tiger Ears I talked with Belted Persimmon about him.

"I wish you could have seen him," she said, "when they announced the Number Wheel. They've set up the big wheel for the selections, you know, in the Board of Rites, only a few streets from here, so we had a lot of chatter about it among ourselves. Tiger Ears has big ears; listens to everything. He was thrilled— wanted to be a number and ride around on a wheel. For days you could only get his attention by shouting numbers at him, and he had the idea that the Emperor was going to win the war with arithmetic—yang numbers were stronger than yin numbers, he said."

One of the other matrons, named Hemp Hands, said, "It will take more than an abacus to win this war."

Everyone except Belted Persimmon was gloomy about the war.

The Seditionists of the outer provinces had pushed a force into South-of-the-River Province, and the yellows in the Capital, growing fearful, tended to turn snarling on the whites as being the cause of it all. There had been several ugly beatings. Belted Persimmon remained blithe. "The Emperor's decency will win the war," she said. "The justice of his Grand Harmonious Mercy Errand will win it."

"Ayah," Hemp Hands said, "we'll all be slaves again. You'll see."

The company of such women depressed me. I was lonely. In time the bubbling cheer of the orphans got on my nerves, and I felt as if I myself were under durance within locked gates.

One afternoon the gate guard came running to the kitchens, where I happened to be working, and said there was someone to see me.

I went to the outer gate. It was Rock!

"Come for a stroll," he said.

"I can't. I wouldn't be able to get permission."

"What do you need with permission? Just leave the place."

"It's my food bowl."

"Find another! There are plenty of ways to eat."

Ai, Rock's surly face, his frown and hard mouth, lifted my spirits. I asked him how the pigeons were.

"I've left that fat yellow bitch," he said. "I have a hole here in the Tartar City. When can I see you?"

"What do you want to do, Rock—stretch my crop so I can steal rice for you?"

"Not a bad idea!" He smiled; a sudden thaw.

We arranged to meet on my next rest day.

(Rock

He came early, while the city's myriad crows were still shouting to each other the astonishing news that another day had dawned, and when I reached the gate he said, "Hurry! Something to show you."

"But this is my day off, this is my day not to hurry."

"Wait. This will interest you."

When we set out, he said, "First I want you to see the hole I live in"—though this was not the main sight he meant to show me, he added—and at a pace which gave me a stitch in my side he took me to it.

He had called his new place a hole, and it was just about that—less a residence than a burrow. In the western part of the Tartar City, in a crowded region of stables, abattoirs, carters' inns, and mat-weavers' shops, stood an abandoned lamasery now serving as a warren for too many whites, and Rock's room was a former cell of a monk: a man's height squared, without a k'ang or even a chest. The floor was dirt, the light was dim. Camels were tethered in the courtyard, and a heap of Mongol imports lay under perpetual guard—salted carcasses of sheep and of a species of deer with twisted horns; bales of felt; vats of butter which tasted, Rock said (having stolen some from under the guards' noses), like cheese and rancid suet mixed.

Rock asked me to brew a pot of tea on a little tripod brazier he had, and in the half light we acted a domestic scene—sat and sipped with nothing to say. Rock brooded; I waited for him to make some move. But he wanted nothing more just then of me than tea, it seemed, and when we had finished he jumped up and led me out.

He would not tell me what we were going to see. When I asked, he opened his eyes wide and round, as a juggler would who was about to set a pair of plates spinning at the tops of slender wands.

Here was Rock as we walked: a big man, keyed up, pumping shallow sighs out of his chest; with a tuck in his upper lip which was like a little purse for sneers, in case he might need to spend one in a hurry; muscles for a certain squint, expressive of suspicion, of skepticism, around his brown eyes, so often used as to have formed tiny ridges and wrinkles which also served for ambiguous smiles; deep lines around his mouth that seemed to have come from biting back hasty words.

We came to a crowd that had clotted all the way across a wide street, both yellows and whites, and Rock wedged a way into its center, pulling me after him.

And there, deep in the open yard of the Board of Rites, I saw on display, right where it would soon be put to use, the big wheel itself, the Number Wheel.

Even before I could look at it closely, I felt the stretch of tension in the crowd. Rock must have felt it, too, for he had a noisy spell—spoke and laughed in tones that were surely provocative to these yellows with parched eyes.

"Off an elephant cart," Rock said with that metal burr on the edge of his voice.

The wheel was indeed enormous, and it may well have been taken from one of the elephant-drawn land vessels in which the Emperor had used to voyage to the Temple of Heaven. Three or four mandarins were walking back and forth on the platform on which the wheel stood, evidently trying it out. The metal tire had been removed from the perimeter, and it appeared that hundreds, perhaps thousands, of small slits had been cut into the wheel's felly, and the mandarins had wedged little bamboo slabs, like gate chips, into the notches. After a while they turned the wheel, which rolled heavily on its supported hub, and the bamboo slabs made a whirring noise against a pointer, or stopper, at one side, and we could see that when the wheel ran down and the whirring ceased, the pointer lay against one of the slabs: this would be some man's number, and he would be chosen for the war, when the selections began.

Up to this time the wheel had been imaginary, legendary as it were, just an idea, just words in announcements and a thing for

us to talk about. But there it was! Varnished wood, scores of
spokes, a huge circle. This was the wheel the yellows throughout
the city considered a threat and an insult, and seeing its actuality,
seeing the mandarins rehearsing its use, seeing one of the grandly
dressed gentlemen on the platform put a hand again to one of
the spokes to start it up, hearing the whirring, the yellows here in
the street became, as we could feel, sullenly furious.

But the fury was static. Nothing changed in the crowd. Small
clumps formed, chatted in murmurs, dissolved, re-formed. We
found ourselves at one point in a group of about a dozen whites
of both sexes. Some of the white men were joking about the
wheel under their breaths.

When we had listened for a while Rock said with ill-suppressed
vehemence, not trying as hard as he might have to keep his voice
down to the range of the white circle, "We all should go and fight.
It's our war. It's about us. It's shit-mouth cowards like you," he
said to the last speaker, "who have us where we are."

But Rock, you gave a fake name to the registrars! I remembered
Rock's and Groundnut's sarcasm about the Mercy Errand—but I
recalled, too, the tremor of voice underlying their jibes—the
hidden attachment to the Emperor's grandiose professions. Hope
for freedom! Mockery of hope! This was the horrible double knot
with which we were always bound. The yellows called us simple,
but nothing could ever be simple for us, nothing could be unitary.
Idealism and foul reality; hope and hopelessness; trust and suspicion; self-reliance and humiliating dependence—every thought,
every act, every desire of ours had its own reciprocal lodged in
its heart. Was this the source of Rock's quarrelsome posture?
Were these what attracted me to him—the altruism couched in
his selfishness, the honey in his bitterness, the pity in his anger?
The pulls between the Peace and the Nose in him, the Gabe and
the Dolphin?

I had a flurry of my own with him: about Groundnut. This was
odd. We stood around talking, as the yellows also did. *Whir*. And
again, *Whir*. The glistening spokes revolved and slowed. We stood
talking. The yellows' anger was constant, and nothing seemed to
change. The yellows themselves were chatting, as the wheel
revolved and revolved, winding something up in all of us.

"What about your friend? Is he still with Dowager?"

"Groundnut? He has to stay in that neighborhood—the beggars' league."

"I can see your leaving Dowager. Could you just walk out on him?"

Bang! Off went Rock's brass cannon! Friend? What kind of friend was Groundnut? He would steal the toenails off your toes. *Whir.*

I was beginning to know this quarrelsome Rock, and I said quietly, "The way you say that makes me think you're sorry you left Dowager's."

Well! Such fireworks! Groundnut was no friend—a cheap parasite; and worse. Qualities for which everyday adjectives would not suffice, and which could only be bounded by the vagueness of obscenities.

Then: "And what do *you* know about friendship? Didn't you just walk out? You didn't even come back to tell us you were leaving. You sent Mink. I'll wager you haven't paid back a copper of what you owe Dowager."

I had not. With little to spend money for, I was saving most of the pittance I earned. I felt myself blush, because I had just about decided not to honor my debt to Dowager. I justified cheating her of the principal by the fact of her having demanded a cheating interest.

But I saw what Rock was doing, and I quietly persisted. What had estranged him from Groundnut?

Rock calmed down and told me that their break had come one night, in a violent argument, when he had tried to persuade Groundnut to stop being a beggar. With an air of put-upon decency, Rock said he had tried to make Groundnut see that begging strengthened the yellows' hands against us—that in his daily disguise Groundnut was living proof of the yellows' view of us. I sensed something hollow in this report, something held back, but with a sudden feeling of boredom I decided not to pursue the quarrel any farther.

Now, at the height of a whir of the wheel, I got a jolt.

"Come and live with me," Rock said.

So this, rather than tea, was why he had wanted me to see his monk's cubicle! I looked at his face. I cannot say that it was broadcasting any messages of deep emotion. He looked as bleak as the sky.

"I have a good solid food bowl at the orphanage," I said.

Now his feeling came tumbling out—abuse. I heard the singing of the wheel behind his sharp talk—mixed up with it. Where was my spontaneity? Why did I behave like a slanthead? Why couldn't I just do whatever I wanted? Why did I have to calculate every-thing—forty per cent interest here, just like Dowager, and forty per cent squeeze there, like the beggars' league?

I must admit he got under my skin—under my sensitive flea-pierced white skin; and I descended to: "What if staying in the orphanage is exactly what I want?"

Whir. Tall bannermen were beginning to thread through the crowd; their faces were grim, they would brook no trouble.

For some reason the sight of the bannermen caused me to break into tears, and I heard myself saying that I would ask Benign Warmth's permission to work in and live out.

Rock patted me on the shoulder and said, "You won't be sorry."

A bannerman, passing, jostled me hard. Rock's hands flew out and shoved him away. It then appeared that the one thing a white man may not do is to lay a finger on a bannerman. In an instant four of them were closing in on Rock, their jaws pushed forward like steel wedges.

Here was a ring of demons. We needed and hated these Im-perial guardsmen. I knew how Rock despised them. They were the only force for order in the city, and in many a scrape they were the only ones who would stand up for our rights—or, rather, make up for our lack of rights. But they were yellow men, and they clearly loathed their stinking duty of taking the part of whites, and whenever one of our race was in the wrong he caught ten times his share of the cruelty of those who had the power to keep the so-called peace.

I saw Rock hold firm. Then, as the four uniformed men pushed their net of ribs closer and closer to him, I saw a white man's pain-learned patience seep into Rock's stance. A slight shift, a giving of a toe's length. A sheepish grin that I knew he did not like to wear. A mumble about clumsiness—his own. An acknowledg-ment, by a dipping of the head, of yellow power. A spendthrift honorific title offered to all. A blush seen by them as shame, but by me, Rock's new concubine, as no more than a hot-skinned con-cession to time.

(The Cubicle

To my surprise, Benign Warmth made no difficulty about my sleeping outside the orphanage.

He was a practical man. "You have a lover?"

"Yes."

"If I refused," he said, speaking as if chewing hot rice, "you would bribe the gate man and sneak out nights."

He was right about that.

"Be here no later than the crows' cawing in the mornings."

So I moved into Rock's cubicle. This dark box of squalor and filth proved to be the happiest home I had ever had. We lay together, lanternless, on mats of woven reeds in moldy-smelling quilts, and we gorged ourselves on each other's desires like famished wolves. This man, so pusillanimous by daylight, made aggressive demands in the dark which ripened me, in a few short nights, from a cautious used girl into a wanton. There was no mention of marriage; I had tried that, and so had he. Except when I sensed that he needed to stretch his wits, we seldom quarreled, for I think I was the first girl he had had who saw some sense in the marvelous tension in him, and he was the first man— or white person of either sex, for that matter—whom I had ever known whose anger at the yellows was hitched to steep demands on the self. With all his growling he expected a great deal of his own whiteness. I came to see this. Perhaps exposure to this bitter optimism in a white gave me my first taste of freedom as a white, of inner freedom. We shared our miserable pasts, and he told me to beware: Often he had had this apparent harmony with a sow, such as he had with me, only to have it slip away into dreary bickering, discontent, and finally staleness like that of hard old bread. "I'm never satisfied to leave a stone where it is," he said, "or a flower on a branch, maybe I should say," and with that he grasped my chin and held it for the longest time, as if suddenly afraid of losing me. He would not say that there was anything different about me from the others, but as weeks passed I could feel our love holding ground from night to night to night. That was enough.

⟨ The Date Is Announced

Rock was working at odd jobs, mostly ugly and menial, and his summer days were full of conflict; he quit often and was dismissed more often. The irregularity of his life, which he liked, meant that he was usually able to be free when I had a day off, and we began to move around the city together.

One day while we were walking I had a thought. "What about Bad Hog?"

Rock had forgotten all about the fighting cock, he started as if he had been poked with a camel herder's prod. "We must go and see that turtle Groundnut."

So we did, late in the day, at Dowager's. We reached the fat woman's hovel before Groundnut arrived home from begging.

The cotes were still full, but pigeon droppings were scarcely to be seen. Dowager told us that Groundnut had found he could sell the dung to a vintner, and that in the courtyard he constantly carried a basket and a spoonlike scoop with a long handle; she showed these implements to us.

I was fearful of a tongue-scourging from Dowager for not having paid what I owed her.

All she said was: "Ayah, you little whore, you're like all the other whites, aren't you?"

"I have it saved up," I lamely said. "I've been meaning to bring it down."

"Too late, too late!" she said, dismissing me with a dimpled hand. And that, I knew, was the last of the debt; I would never pay her.

Groundnut came in encrusted in his vile disguises, and Rock embraced him. It was as if the two men had never quarreled, never parted. At once they were on their old footing—conspiratorial, full of whispers, muted chuckles, mysterious frowns.

And what about the cockerel?

At this question Groundnut croaked with excitement: Splendid! A real dragon! Almost ready!

Groundnut fetched Bad Hog's ample cage from beside the cotes. Between the spindles the bird blinked at Rock an eye like an ember.

"Ai," Rock said, "the bastard looks love-starved. I'll have to come over and shake some of those dummies at him. See if he thinks they're hens."

"He'll tear your dummies to pieces," Groundnut said.

So Rock began to visit Dowager's nearly every day to resume his part in Bad Hog's training, and when I could I went with him. The bird had grown into a prodigy of pure meanness, and it did in fact destroy Rock's dummies, one by one. How Rock's eyes lit up at the white bird's burning viciousness!

One day on the way home to the lamasery from a training
session we noticed that a new *Gazette*—the vehicle for Imperial
proclamations—had been posted on billboards scattered throughout the city, and I read the announcements to Rock; the first of
which was:

*Drawings from the Number Wheel will commence on the morn-
ing of seventh month, eighteenth, the day following the Spirit
Festival.*

Rock was much distressed. This was bad, he said, this was
very bad. This might lead the judge of the cocking mains to refuse
to allow a white-trained bird, and especially a *white* white-trained
bird, to enter the pits.

Ai, how I laughed at Rock!—and wanted to weep. This was an
edict that would change the basis of our lives, and he fretted about
Bad Hog's credentials!

❰ Fowl-Soup Fight

Rock and Groundnut decided to risk Bad Hog at once,
for we could feel a rising surge of rage among the yellows after
the announcement of the date of the drawing.

On the next market day we took the bird in a cloth-covered
basket to the mains. In the oval pit in the mat-shed hall I saw
more than the usual number of whites in the crowd; our boys had
passed the word about their white wonder, it seemed.

The judge, a wrinkled autocrat, Old Hsing, whose decisions at
every step of wagering and of the fights themselves could not be
questioned, unless at a risk of permanent banning from the premises, was at first scornful of my friends. He waved them and their
hooded basket aside. Did I imagine that there was anger in his
look—Number Wheel anger?

But when Rock tilted the lid of the basket and Hsing saw the
glistening creature within, flashing its never-to-be-cuckolded eyes,
the old judge nodded.

This nod produced an inexorable sequence. Keepers plucked
Bad Hog from the basket and weighed the bird; an official measured the steel spurs that Groundnut produced from a velvet-lined
box; the cock was held aloft and announced; his adversary was
displayed and announced—an Eastern Shawlneck named Odor
of Gunpowder Smoke; the betting clerks began shouting back

and forth with wagers and tossing their small bamboo tubes
to gather and hold the cash of those who accepted the offered
odds, which were, it goes without saying, insulting to our bird.

The betting was closed. The cocks were held at opposite sides
of the pen. I had never felt such silence in the bowl. We were,
for once, in the front row.

The cocks were introduced. Old Hsing tossed them a few grains
of incitement. Then hackles went up, a moment's incredulous
staring passed, and the cocks flew into a death struggle—over a
half dozen miserable seeds.

Rock started to bounce about as if manipulating his pigeon-
feather dummies, and I heard beside me the falsetto commands
that Groundnut had devised. I felt, myself, a deep, inexplicable
sadness.

After the first few flurries I wanted to look away. It seemed to
me that Bad Hog was being overpowered—how could my friends
have miscalculated so badly?—and that if I watched I would
only see a re-enactment, in a swift sharp-spiked dance, of *our*
lives as the outmatched of the world.

I was dimly aware that my two friends were not discouraged.
But it was clear that the white cock had been early and badly hurt,
and that it was merely carrying on in the grip of an automatic process—an unswerving, mechanical, instinct-fueled fury.

Once the Shawlneck had gained an advantage, it seemed that
there could only be one course: a widening of its advantage. And
so it happened, but with an agonizing slowness. Rock and Groundnut gradually became less animated, as the roaring among the
yellows in the crowd grew triumphant.

Then, as sometimes happened, the almost beaten cock, enraged perhaps more by his down-dragging pain than by his opponent, staged a rally. With a series of flapping leaps Bad Hog
rose higher and higher, until the Shawlneck was kicking from
beneath. In a single flashing stroke of steel the white cock put
out one of his enemy's eyes.

The Shawlneck in his turn climbed to a new ledge of rage, and
once again the white cock appeared to be getting the worst of it.

But the gap had been narrowed, perhaps even closed, and I
could feel the hope flooding into Rock and Groundnut again. Yes,
we could see the white cock, grown crafty, saving its strength,
evading, pouncing only when it could strike. It was gaining. I

remembered reversals of this kind that had proved decisive. Shrilly I shouted.

Then Old Hsing pulled back a sleeve and made a chopping motion with his right hand. Two attendants with sacks leaped out and captured the birds. In a cracking voice the judge declared the contest at an end, the Shawlneck the winner. Bettors on Odor of Gunpowder Smoke would be paid. It was, he ruled, a "fowl-soup fight"—one bird had an advantage so decisive that it must lead in the end to the death of the other, but the inevitable might take long to unfold; this would curb the program of fights to follow; it was the judge's right to end the match; the losing bird must be destroyed—hence, "fowl soup."

Rock and Groundnut stood with mouths gaping. They looked as if they were roaring, but no sounds were emerging. Then at last the protests did leap out, like water gushing from culverts.

Twenty white men were suddenly clustered around us.

Old Hsing stood up. This was the peremptory command from the ruler of the pit for silence. But a hush did not ensue. My two friends kept shouting, and an ominous, low, humming, stuttering growl began to come toward us from the yellows massed in the bowl.

Next I saw that the whites had gathered about us for a purpose quite other than I had thought. They laid hands on my friends, and on me, and they dragged us out of the pit into the street. All the while Rock and Groundnut bellowed.

In the street those who had hauled us away from the yellows, to save their own skins as well as ours, now flailed around us shouting their remonstrances against the obvious unfairness of Old Hsing's judgment. Then, when everyone's breath gave out, we disbanded in silence and went our ways.

(Rock's Ambition

Rock was not easy to live with in the days that followed. Unfairness! This was almost a new idea to us. When we had been slaves the question of equity had never arisen. Rock was exhilarated by the concept of unfairness, and, as always, high spirits produced in him a torrent of rudenesses; he set about cheating the yellow cheaters in every way he could, and if frustrated by

them he turned on me, whom he loved. Our close box of a home
resounded with his bad temper and my (I must say) bold self-
defense. Rock had another bitter squabble with Groundnut on the
topic of beggary—and now Rock's motive for urging Groundnut
to give it up, accounting for his peculiar manner when he had told
me of his earlier break with his friend, came out for me to see:
He had all along wanted Groundnut to cease begging in order to
join him in a pickpocketing team. Begging, even with its guiles
and disguises, was a cause for shame; jostling yellows and slitting
their purses would be a matter of high honor! So Rock argued.
And so I began to understand the source of the dim, shapeless
optimism I had always felt under Rock's rough manner: His ambition was to be some kind of hero, even if a fumbling one, or indeed a criminal one, of whiteness.

Groundnut, however, was unshakable. He said he had a pot of
good money buried in the earth under the pigeons, and was filling
another. He was proud of his talent. He was never in trouble with
the bannermen. And, he argued, what better way than begging
of reminding yellow men of their guilt toward our people?

"No! No!" Rock shouted. "You disgust them."

(The Eve of the Drawings

In most years the Spirit Festival yielded an evening of
magical beauty, honoring and appeasing the spirits of the dead.
Benign Warmth, corked in his bottle of pomposity, was vapidly
unaware of the stirrings in the city over the coming conscription,
and he decided to allow the older children, the tens and elevens,
to march out as usual and watch the spectacle on the banks of
Ten Temples Sea in the northern part of the Tartar City. I had
been assigned to their escort. For two reasons I could not bear to
be separated from Rock on that night: because I wanted to share
the famous sight with him, and because I was apprehensive over
the yellows' ugly arousal; and departing for work that morning
I had asked him to meet me at the orphanage gate at the time of
the Drum Tower signal of the delaying, for this evening, of the
curfew. He had agreed.

So now we set out, forty-odd children, half a dozen matrons
and attendants, and incongruous Rock, just at dusk. Each of the
children carried a homemade lantern that was capable of floating.

We had spent days fashioning these lights in the shapes of boats, lotuses, fish, water lilies. In the streets were many yellows carrying such lanterns.

Rock walked beside Tiger Ears.

"What's your lantern?" Rock asked.

"A lantern," the boy said.

"Yes, but what's it supposed to be?"

"A duck. Are you blind?"

"Why a duck?"

"Because it's a spirit."

"A spirit? A spirit of what? Of a person?"

Long pause. "Of air."

"How can there be a spirit of air?"

"Where else would a duck fly?"

"Why a duck?"

"You're an old stupid."

Rock liked that frank non-answer, and he laughed with his head thrown back.

After a time Rock said to me, "Ayah, I wish I were an orphan."

"Aren't you?" I said.

When we reached the shore of Ten Temples Sea a crowd of several hundred had already come. Our children launched their lanterns on the still water. All around the lake a border of floating lights—which in time became thousands—was drifting out from the banks. Most of the lanterns were in the form of lotus leaves and blooms. "It's all for you, White Lotus," Rock said, on an unexpected note of gentleness. I noticed drawled shouts and slurred laughs; many men in the crowd seemed to be drunk. Sometimes I felt Rock beside me stiffen. The dreamlike beauty of the scene—the sparkling luminosity of the lantern-spangled lake, the children's eyes like tiny skies of stars: the sights seemed the more lavish because of the tautness, the expectant and reckless mood, of the yellow crowd.

All this broke open when a force of the Blue Banner Corps, garrisoned in that part of the city, carried to the edge of the lake a huge papier-mâché junk, thirty paces in length, with a full complement of paper crewmen, and with rows and rows of lighted candles. They launched this vessel. Drums, gongs, cymbals, and flutes played music expressive of a grateful Emperor's pride in the spirits of those who had died in battle for him—the many candle flames. At first the crowd greeted this ship, re-

minding them of the war and of the drawing on the Number
Wheel to come the next day, with silence. Then a murmuring
began, a desolate low sound.

After the vessel, which capped the breathtaking scene on the
lake, had drifted about for a time, a bannerman rowed out to it
and set it on fire, in order that the spirits of the dead might return
to their dwelling place by the light of the lotus lanterns. As the
flames grew into a floating bonfire whose reflections made the
water itself seem to be on fire, the grumbling of the crowd grew
into an angry babble.

We were suddenly conscious of a pressure of yellow men
around our island of white children. Above the mob-noise we
heard abusive shouts aimed at us. What were these little pigs
doing here? What right had they to praise the war dead?

We were surrounded—in a pigpen of mad drunks.

Then I heard some of the men railing at Rock, who was one of
the very few white men by the lake.

Rock firmly told the senior matron to start the children away
from the shore, and then he did something so wise, for him so
controlled, that I, though my heart was freezing, almost wept with
surprise, gratitude, and love.

He moved to the center of the clump of children. By this act he
isolated his own provocative anger from that of the shouting
yellows, and he made himself a stone pillar of the greatest
strength of all, which is restraint, in the middle of our flock of
now bewildered children. We women pressed at the crowd, which
uttered fumes of millet liquor in our faces, and gradually, with
painful patience, inspired by Rock, we managed to drift our
charges away from the lake and out of the crowd and into the
streets. We fled to the orphanage.

After we had settled the children for the night, I went home
with Rock. The city was restless and full of sound at that late
hour—seemed to be talking in its sleep, to an evil dream.

❴ The Wheel Turns: First Day

It was a dawn of the kind Dirty Hua used to call "under
the toad's belly"—dark and damp, with a low, solid, warty sky
pressing down overhead, so you didn't know, as Hua had put
it, whether you'd be squashed or pissed on.

As I turned into Hata Gate Street, on foot to work in that first gray, I dimly saw, at a distance up the way, the entire wide expanse of the avenue blocked by some barrier, like a low dam. The darkness of night, as if it were a heavier fluid than the light of dawn, seemed to have settled in the street and was still standing there, held back from draining off by that obstruction ahead. It was not until I had approached quite close in this murk that I made out the nature of the dam—a crowd of people. So many so early!

Then I realized that the crowd abutted the grounds of the Board of Rites, where Rock had taken me that day—where the Number Wheel had been set up, and where it was now to be turned to choose soldiers at the gong of the first quarter of this morning.

Chilled though I still was from our scare by the lake the previous evening, I was nevertheless drawn forward now by a perverse desire to press myself into this throng, and when, close at hand, I sensed that the crowd was orderly, half awake, passive, and sluggish, and that there were a few women among the men, a few whites among the yellows, I felt emboldened; I would weave my way slowly through the assemblage, see what was happening, then pass on to the orphan asylum.

But one thing happened as I moved along to change my plan: I encountered Mink.

The crowd was actually not thick. I could tell that some of the yellow men had been up all night and were still drunk—but they were fuzzy-headed, subdued, and quiet along with everyone else. No one bothered me. You could hear murmuring, that was all. To the right, in the open yard of the Board, I could just see the ghostly circle of the wheel; spectral figures, probably of guards and mandarins, moved on the wheel's platform.

"White Lotus!"

I turned my head, and yes, even in the dimness it was certainly Mink, straining on tiptoe to see as much as he could.

"Are they going to pick your number?"

"Ai," he said, "I have no number. I tried to give the registrars my name."

"Tried?"

"They don't want a crookback."

Mink urged me to stay and watch awhile, and I thought: Why shouldn't I? I could excuse myself for lateness: been held up by the crowds. Mink seemed to be having a good time, as he chatted with the yellows around us, joked about the wheel, made it clear

that he shared the yellows' feelings about authorities who would
set up a cruel lottery like this. He was soon something of a pet
to our early-morning neighbors.

But then light began to drench us. Faces developed hard lines,
eyes came forward out of black sockets and glinted with signs of
a feverishness that the earlier gloaming had hidden. I did not like
what this prying brightness brought out.

Now we could plainly see the wheel. Mandarins bustling. Uniformed men at tables with papers.

And up like a waking henroost's bedlam came the city's day
sound, a vast fabric riven by barkings, screechings of hubs, tinklings, hawkers' cries that sounded like the appeals of drowning
swimmers. Having grown more alert with the light, I strained
to hear the special message of the city's voice for this day: Was
its timbre different from that of other days? Was it oppressive,
like the weather? Quieter than usual? Just the same?

There were the drums for the first quarter! Now it was nearby
sounds that mattered, as the crowd around us, which was constantly thickening, stirred with expectation: this was the announced hour.

Of course there were delays: the wheel stood up stark, the
mandarins played their hands on it, bannermen pomped here and
there—but nothing happened. We waited and waited, and this
was not good for the feelings of the rabble.

I kept thinking, "I should go. I'm late enough. I should run
along." But I was rooted in the paving, I could not break away.
Was it Mink who held me there? Mink's excitement?

Then for the first time it came through to me that almost
everyone in the crowd had some sort of tool or staff in his hand;
many of the women in this throng that had seemed so orderly
were carrying chunks of brick or shards of roof tile.

I whispered something about this to Mink.

He raised his hands for me to see. Each held a stone.

"We're going to make them feel it!" he said, and I saw that *his*
eyes were hot like all the rest.

At that I had to know that I myself shared in some way the
pressure that was building in the crowd as the delay continued.
I felt the wheel now as a taunt, and the mandarins up there as
men who would have to shoulder responsibility for *my* griev-
ances. I saw that the whites in the crowd were rather numerous,
and that their faces were all on fire. I swelled up with an un-

familiar strength that derived from an unexpected common cause.

Deep in the first quarter of the morning a bannerman on the wheel's platform struck a gong, a mandarin grasped a spoke, and the wheel turned.

At once there was a total hush, and distinctly I heard the *whir* of the bamboo slabs against the fateful pointer.

For three or four numbers, as the silence held, it went like this: The wheel turned, the slabs whirred against the pointer, round and round till the rolling stopped, and a blue-button took out the chip against which the arrow rested and bellowed out a number, and maybe we would see some poor fellow near us in the crowd go pale, and his wife would let out a wail, and the registrars rattled through their flakes of papers and called out the name that went with the number, and the bannermen took the fellow away if he presented himself—or if he did not, a squad went off to his home to pick him up; and they gave the wheel another spin. They had greased the hub; the wheel turned perhaps a dozen times for each number, to an awful whirring from the bamboo chips which had the sadness of a pigeon whistle moaning in the sky.

After the first few numbers an eerie droning started up from the crowd around me, a murmur of pain and anger—a blending of hundreds of voices, speaking low, saying "Ayah," or "Hai," or "Look at the sons of turtles up there in their silk," or "Let them fight their own war"; sighs and grunts and protests all blurred into an unearthly grunting sound.

All the same, I felt happy in some way. I heard Mink growling beside me. I grumbled, too. I felt as if all these yellow men and women were my companions in resentment for once. We were all together. I was part of a vast potential.

Mink and I were in the forepart of the crowd, which now had a much thicker mass than when I had arrived. Many toward the back began to shout:

"We can't hear!"

"Louder!"

"What number?"

We began to feel a forward pressure from those at the rear, and the whole assemblage began to bulge into the great plaza of the Board.

One of the mandarins on the platform, reacting to this heavy wave, raised his hands in a gesture of pushing us back.

He may have meant these motions as a plea, but his manner

was unfortunate—imperious and (worst possible tone on this occasion) military. *I* felt angry at the sight of his fluttering palms.

A half brick flew from the middle of the press, and with a fortuitous dead aim struck the wheel. One of the spokes splintered. The sight of the broken spoke—the perfect new wheel flawed —the fragments of the spoke splaying out at queer angles: it seemed the Emperor himself had been defaced; I felt a jolt of elation; this simply released a jubilee in the crowd. With one throat it gave a whoop—such a delighted whoop! And it—*we*—surged forward.

Ai, I wanted something in my hands! Mink and I pushed forward shoulder to shoulder.

Ahead, men climbed on the platform. The wheel tottered and then fell over backward, and a loud cheer burst from *our* throat. Bricks and tiles and stones began to pelt on the more distant roofs and against the latticed paper windows of the Board of Rites. The bannermen—there were no more than a hundred on hand, a ceremonial guard and squads to fetch selected registrants—were overpowered by the human flood before they could even level their silly gilt spears.

I was caught up in the joy of the thing! I could feel it in my throat. I had no idea any more what this was about, I was simply swept along in a common cause that had no shape or name.

I got my hands on a bannerman's tunic—*we* tore it off his back —it tore like paper!

In the distant background I heard the deep gongs and drums of the city's gate towers commence their accelerating announcements of the shutting of the gates. So soon had the authorities taken alarm! But far from staying us these warning sounds inflated our—my—desire for revenge.

We reached the tables and got our hands into the heaps of records: names and addresses and numbers for the wheel. The papers began to flap wings. Whoosh! Shooo! Some of the men with tools broke the wheel all to pieces, and armed themselves with the spokes. Then one of them with a huge bottle of some inflammable liquid—tung oil or pine spirits—scattered it about on the platform and set it on fire, and the crowd stood around throwing the Number Wheel records and bannermen's uniforms and officiating mandarins' hats into the flames.

In a short time fire broke out, no doubt from the same cause, in one of the buildings of the Board of Rites. This sobered me:

this was getting to be a good time of an order I hadn't foreseen.
I clutched at Mink's shoulder, wanting to back out of the crowd.
But the mob was suddenly bored—here everything was wrecked.
There were shouts off to one side that I couldn't make out, and
a big part of the horde surged out of the plaza. Mink's face was
red, he took me by the hand like a lover and towed me along. I
had no idea where we were headed; nobody seemed to know.

Soon I saw. We were going to the Straight-Toward-the-Sun Gate
—the one in the south wall reserved for the Emperor's processions
to the Altars of Heaven and Agriculture—and it was obvious that
the leaders of the mob had in mind *capturing* the gate, so it could
be opened and unlimited numbers of the poorer classes of people
could come in from the Outer City to take part in this . . . this
celebration! Quickly done. The guard of bannermen was come
upon utterly by surprise—never expected such boldness.

The gate swung open.

Ai! Listen to this! I was a useless white girl and Mink was a
hog with a snag in his back—and we ran back and forth, hand
in hand, three times through the sacred gate that is supposed to be
reserved to Old Dragon-Face! We *all* romped through and back
laughing and embracing each other! Yes, even yellow men hugged
me! Soon hundreds of poor people began pouring through from
the Outer City, all grinning and cheering.

But then: Down from the direction of the Forbidden City we
saw a sedan chair coming—eight bearers. Official. A mandarin
stepped down about fifty paces from the edge of the crowd. This
was surely a messenger direct from the Emperor—to order us
to clear his gate.

I saw the front edge of the mob open up like a mouth and just
go out and bite the mandarin into it. I was wildly happy. I saw the
man's silk gown tossed in the air, and a knot in the crowd up
there was bending down and dipping—and then that was over,
but something new was coming: a squad of bannermen with
jingals.

Ayah! I tell you, the gala feeling, the sense of redress—suddenly
rather thin. These soldiers with their two-man guns came swinging down. Halted. The first line of muzzle-bearers knelt with the
barrels on their shoulders, the stock men knelt behind. The mob
was simply frozen, you just couldn't believe that the celebration
had turned into *this*—until someone half-screamed a curse on the
Emperor himself and a shower of brickbats flew at the banner-

men. Mink and I took one look at each other's face. We knew it
was time for whites to be unseen—to go—to dissolve. We cut
into Water Gate Alley along by the wall. On the run. We had only
gone a few paces when we heard the first volley. After it there
was utter silence—the quietest quiet I ever experienced—nothing
but the sound of our cloth shoes on the ground.

Near the orphanage we were winded and we slowed to a walk.
Mink, his chest a forge bellows, laughed. Panting, he spoke of his
joy. "We—gave it to them—all right!"

That "we"! I thought that this Mink who spoke of elation looked
bleak, and I felt the mob spirit draining out of me with alarming
speed.

By the time we were inside the orphanage and Benign Warmth
had begun to question us right at the gate—we were disheveled,
I needed no excuses, he had heard the city gates closed and
wanted to know the reason—I began to face with astonishment
the feelings I had so recently, and with such abandon, harbored.

Mink, less quick to react than I, spoke of yellows and whites
surging forward *together,* and Benign Warmth broke in then,
speaking to his matrons in a tone of simple confirmation—a
man who is always right cannot lower himself to the point of
sounding triumphant. "It has nothing to do with us, as I told you."
He could not stop at that. "Hai! You see? You people came in here
last night high-tailed as Mongol ponies. Wood Pillow and Snow
Bug"—two of the senior matrons—"were hysterical all night.
Belted Persimmon was the only calm one. We have nothing to fear
from the yellow race. We have a special position here. Do you
follow me, Small White Lotus? Why, at the slightest sign of
difficulty I would send a messenger to Big Madame Hsüeh or Big
Madame Huang, and *i-ko lang-tang*"—the yellow magician's mys-
tical formula, *presto!* "Do you realize that Venerable Hsüeh Li-
fang is a member of the Censorate? And that Venerable Huang
Fu-ju is on the Board of Punishments? They'd have the Banner
Corps around here in a blink. I have a clean table. I'm astonished
at you people."

I burned with a blush, for I felt then the whole shame of my
having let myself be carried away. I felt no less the shame of
Benign Warmth's inanity. I had thirsted so long for something, for
something—and now that I had tried to slake my thirst the taste
in my mouth was bitter, bitter; nauseous; perhaps even poisonous.
What was so strange on the air? I listened. The entire city seemed

to be partaking of my shame. A dead hush. All the usual sounds
—of drums, cock crows, sellers' chants, notes of flutes and fiddles,
advertisements of storytellers, barking of dogs, beggars' and argu-
ers' urgencies; and the undertone of contentment, games, family
peace, innocent playing of children—everything in the city that
bespoke life and a love of life was stilled.

❨ The Wheel Turns: First Evening

But the hush was no more than a lull; it hung over the
city like smoke till some new gust of trouble blew it away. The
urban roar rose again, and in it we could hear unfamiliar crack-
lings of anger and havoc. At times through the afternoon we
heard ominous sounds in the middle distance—crashes, splittings,
rumbles. Once we heard a fusillade—jingals again? Three times
the brooding air near us was shaken by a surge of voices and
hurrying footsteps, as a seething crowd swept past the asylum,
sounding like a whooshing flock of jackdaws on its way to raid
a heronry. Where were the mobs going in such haste? The gate
gongs, and even the Drum Tower and Bell Tower whose signals
usually marked the parts of the day, were silent; the city remained
shut.

Benign Warmth, who kept repeating that the disturbances had
nothing to do with us, nevertheless had the prudence to order
our gates double-barred.

I worried all day about Rock, who was, at the moment, out of
work. Would he be able to resist running with those packs?

In the evening Benign Warmth gave me permission, in view of
the turmoil in the streets, to leave for Rock's cubicle before the
children were settled for the night, while there would still be
plenty of light left for my passage across the city.

I hurried along. I was astonished by the extent of wreckage
in the main streets: crushed carts, staved-in store fronts, smashed
house gates, crumpled sedan chairs. Signs of looting and arson.
As if overhead, as I hastened, the chatterings of a roused city flew
in waves from here and there, and I began to feel, against my will,
some of my excitement of the morning. The memory of the bannerman's tunic ripping under my hand! The sense of revenge!
We—the poor of the city, yellow and white—pouring out our bitterness against the authorities!

And so when, in a mouth of a hutung just below the Imperial Ancestral Temples, I came on a wild crowd that had a mandarin of the Blue Banner Corps cornered, I felt a renewed flood of triumphant vindictiveness. I set my teeth and pushed into the edge of the crowd. There were whites in this pack—this was all aimed at those in power.

One of the rabble's leaders was there; I was not far from him. He was a tall ugly yellow cock on a military mule, a banner-corps animal, and he was wearing a banner-corps officer's helmet that he had stolen, with ear and neck lappets shining like a whore's gold chains, and he was swinging a spoke of the Number Wheel around his head, and he was shouting like a madman.

I heard what he was roaring. His filthy tirade pierced me— punctured me—let the joy of revenge out of me like the air out of a child's pig bladder—*pshshsh!* Hai, had I felt a "common cause"?

"My fellow free men—we're free men so far—but maybe they want *us* to be slaves like the hogs now—I hear that's what this hog's war is about—but you're free men and women still: You see that mandarin turtle pizzle cringing in there against that wall? Are you going to let that turtle's son of a hog lover go free to run in and set up another wheel to put dirty numbers on for their pig lovers' war? See this spoke here? They're not going to use this piece of wood to bring up *my* number for their pork war! All right, boys. Keep your eyes on the dirty hog-loving sow-screwer."

I was hypnotized; I wanted to run from this horror but I could not. I hung at the edge of the mob—in terror now but paralyzed by a need to watch, by some lingering grip of mob fever, unable to run away before I saw this bad dream of the truth of these riots played out.

The mandarin made a scramble deeper into the hutung to a mansion gate and went to his knees and pounded with his fists on the leaves of the door, and just as the mob closed in on him the gate flew open, he threw himself inside, and the gate slammed shut. What followed did not take long. The rioters found a saw-timber and broke down the gates and burned every hall and side chamber of the place, and then they broke into the next-door mansion, and they were for no reason setting fire to it, too, when I finally fled.

I made my way somehow to the lamasery. Rock was not there. I lay huddled in his cubicle, unable to flush my burning eyes with tears, until, long after dark, he came in. I soon heard that he understood the truth I had learned.

"I tried to go over to the orphanage—started in time to get there at dusk—to intercept you, White Lotus, to tell you to stay there. I couldn't make it. The mobs—there were herds of them running every which way—I think most of the yellow turtles from the Outer City had come inside the big wall—ayah, I came up to one of these packs on the way over there, and I could smell the blood thirst on the bastards as if the whole mob were one big slaughterhouse armpit. Hooo! They were burning a tavern near the Temple of Double Pagodas, and they had vats of *baigar* and *Shao-hsing* and they were slobbering it down cold, using their cupped hands for wine bowls. You know the cattle market in behind the temple there? It had been shut down for business all day —all the shops everywhere were boarded up as tight as their owners could shut them—but this crazy mob broke into the cattle pens and turned the animals loose in the streets. Just now, coming back, I had to swim my way through a milling panic of bullocks and goats and sheep and pigs, and then it began to rain tile shards! I was in the middle of a storm around Heavenly Peace Gate—the maniacs wanted to get into the Forbidden City. You think they wanted to go after the Imperial family? Ha! Listen— all they wanted was permission from some palace-household eunuch to turn around and kill pigs—kill every one of us, every single white hog and sow that they blame for the war—what they call the hog war. It's going against us. It's *us* they want."

"I know, I know," I moaned.

(The Wheel Turns: Second Morning

There seemed to be another lull at dawn—perhaps the mob-tongued beast was taking a nap. Rock and I decided to try for the orphanage; we might be safer there.

We were about to start when a friend of Rock's who lived at the lamasery, a little slinker named Cricket, came in from outside, pale as rice, shaking all over. He told us the bad part had started.

"They were out all night," he said, "breaking into taverns and getting drunker and drunker." Suddenly he was on the verge of blubbering. "Ayah, Rock, they're after us whites," he said, leaning against a wall as if about to crumple.

"Haven't you known that?" Rock said. "What did they do—announce it in the *Gazette*?"

"It's no joke," Cricket said. "We've got to get away."

"Pig shit," Rock said, violent in his disgust with Cricket. "When was it ever a joke? What did you see?"

"I was trying to make my way up to the northwest quarter, Rock. I have a woman up there. I came on a crowd that seemed to be getting a good laugh out of some high official's sedan chair. But I saw they had four white men on the shafts—four stupid bastards who'd been playing along with the crowds. They were all drunk, the whites, too. They had a big pig, I mean a porker, Rock, a real animal, in the sedan, jogging it up and down. It was giving them some abattoir squeals for their fun. But then one of the whites on the lifting poles lost his temper over something, and he snatched a staff from a yellow man and cracked his head with it, and the man went down. You know hog luck! This man's mother, the mother of the man he'd hit, was right there in the crowd, and she began to wail, and the white fellow ran for it, ran toward his home, which wasn't far off, but they caught him at the gate and got him down and jumped on him and pounded him with stones till he was certainly dead. They began to sing, 'Hang him up, hang him up!' and someone came in with a rope, and they strung him up from a tree by the feet—sliced his fingers and toes off first. Hacked the body. Then they put the sedan chair right under him where he was hanging and set fire to it with the pig still in it. And they burned the house where he lives in and all the whites' houses around it. And some woman shouted about the houses and former monasteries down this way where she said hogs live. They're on their way here, Rock. Burning as they come. And killing if they can."

"All right, Cricket," Rock said. "Stop your tongue and start your feet."

And we, too, got out.

It was not easy to move now. There were barricades across the bigger streets, of broken-up carriages, furniture, barrows, sedans, split gate planks, all sorts of trash and rubbish heaped up shoulder-high. Ayah, the wine-soaked monsters! Had I felt a common cause with them? I blushed as I ran; I'd been unable to tell Rock of my real feelings the previous morning. We dodged around through side streets; some had dead ends: Turn back! Try another! We were keeping away from the knots of people. At a distance we saw a spear charge of bannermen, and we skirted a cackling crowd of yellow boys of about fifteen or sixteen who were sacking the mansion of one of the royal princes, Ch'en. Mobs had been ripping down the boardings of shops and gutting the stores of their goods, some of which lay like vomit in the streets. We went along under the Tartar wall near the Gate of Peace and Harmony for a short distance, and some invisible malevolence up there showered down bricks, chunks of wood, and even things like kettles, but luckily nothing hit us. Bannermen up in the tower at the next gate were singing out an impotent proclamation from the Emperor.

We reached the orphanage gate and both of us pounded on it with our fists. Through the gate tube we heard scurrying within— a pause—then someone puffing right in the tube—then Benign Warmth's voice: "Go away! Leave us alone! We are all peaceful here! All this has nothing to do with us!"

I could hear Rock's hoarse fractiousness rolling into the tube mouth: "Open up, you turtle dung! I have White Lotus here. Open up!"

Thinly through the tube we heard a hesitant discussion within. A voice that sounded to me like Belted Persimmon's spoke of Rock's good behavior beside the lake, the night of the Spirit Festival.

We heard the gateman lifting out the timber locks.

At last we were inside. The timbers were replaced.

Rock faced Benign Warmth, and he said, "May I stay here?"

All Benign Warmth could do was clear his throat.

"Will you allow me to stay here?" Rock asked again.

The superintendent tried to wrap his lips around a refusal. "This is," he said with a laboring tongue, "an orphanage—"

"You're going to need some grown men," Rock said.

Then Benign Warmth's face suddenly cleared. "You may stay," he said, "as my messenger. You must go to Madame Hsüeh's. I will tell you where she lives. . . ."

⟨ By the Postern: Second and Third Days

Within a few hours Rock had become more than messenger. Three times that afternoon he risked his life in the streets, to carry Benign Warmth's supplications to Madame Hsüeh,

Madame Huang, and Madame K'ung. The answers came back in identical terms: "We are deeply concerned. Lock the gates. Take good care of the children." In other words: Expect nothing from us; you've grown dangerous.

Before nightfall of that second day of the rioting Rock had taken over, in effect, as superintendent of the orphanage. The more absurd Benign Warmth's faith in his yellow patronesses proved to be, the more desperately he clung to it. He kept telling us that the bannermen would be coming any moment to escort us out of the city.

Rock told him roughly, at last, to go and swill some tea behind the silk-glass screen in his reception chamber, and Benign Warmth, trying to clothe himself in a few last tags of pompous dignity, withdrew. Rock set about preparing a plan for the protection of the three hundred children. The matrons acknowledged that Rock had taken charge. Toward evening Benign Warmth, openly sulking, had evidently suffered a kind of collapse, a deflation, and he was happy to be treated like an orphan himself.

As for Rock, I saw, beneath his moves, a firmness and serenity that spread about him like a radiation, calming us all. This was the man I had watched irritably rattling the dummies of roosters on the end of the long pole before Bad Hog!

While the children were having their evening meal and so could be left more or less unattended, Rock, having inspected every court and corner of the orphanage, called together the whole staff in Benign Warmth's reception chamber, and he spoke to us—bursting, I could see, with impatience at his own awkwardness, his inability to convey his real feelings:

"The yellow people have turned on us—we won't ask why it was the Number Wheel and not something else that started them off; there isn't time to wonder. When I was in the streets yesterday I saw a crowd of yellow women drag an old white woman, a white-haired white woman, from a courtyard gate, and they beat her about the head until she fell. Why? Why? We have to think of the children here in this orphanage. I remember that as a slave, when I was a boy, on a tobacco farm, I never knew my father, I used to dream of having a father, a man who'd take my part when things were bad. He would keep them from beating me. I imagined him always beside me. When they punished me, I called, 'Father! Father!' There's a boy here I've talked with, Tiger Ears. Every time I speak to him, he lies to me. I'm not surprised at that. I grew up arguing and I still argue. He will always lie—I don't blame him. I'm trying to say . . . Now listen to me. It's only a matter of time before the mob will remember that there is an orphanage for white children here. . . ."

And then he outlined his plan. We would brace the gates with shores as well as we could, but of course that would only delay the mob when it decided to enter—they could break any wooden thing down, or burn it. Rock said he had found the place where the drainage ditch from the kitchens and baths and urine pits evacuated—a tiny water gate under the rear wall that went out into the stinking ditch in Golden Cloud Hutung, behind. The hole had a hinged wooden screen to keep wonks and cats out, and when the time came he would open that. All the children and most of the women would be able to escape through that little passage; so would Wang, the gate boy. Only Wood Pillow, Belted Persimmon, the superintendent, and he himself were too bulky to be able to squeeze out that way; he had found places for those four to hide inside the asylum. Those who took the children out would have to rush with them to the headquarters of the Bordered Red Banner Corps—not far, around by the hutung against the Imperial Canal. With only this tiny culvert for escape, our people must be in order at every step. Youngest first. Snow Bug would assign matrons and helpers to each year group. With the children we would have to make a game of it. If we were lucky, it would be daylight. . . . "Now you had better go back to the refectory."

I ran to Rock and begged him not make me go through the gutter gate but to let me hide with him.

He shook his head. "The piglets need you."

I began to weep. "Show me where you're going to hide."

He refused. "I'll get away," he said. "They'll find the children are gone, and that will take the fun out of it for them, and they'll leave."

"They'll burn everything."

"I have a nice cool place."

In his self-possession Rock was remote, and I had a moment of thinking I might arouse the familiar quarreling roustabout in him by cursing him, but I could not. I felt instead a flow of mild happiness that surprised me, for it seemed ill-timed and even improper. I went back to my duties, and the perverse good mood lasted.

Early the following morning, the third day of the rioting, there

came an urgent thrumming of fists on the compound gate.
Through the peepholes our gate boy, Wang, could see that some
whites were seeking refuge; they had a wheelbarrow carrying
all their goods—but where flee, with the city gates locked? They
had thought of the orphanage, and their pleas for shelter, which
they wailed at the cracks of the gates, seemed a plaint we had
heard for ever and ever—the lifelong cry of our cursed race.

Rock had the shores taken down and the gates opened. There
were six, a family. All were small of frame, small enough to escape by the drainage-ditch postern, and Rock ordered that they
be admitted.

Others came during the morning, and they were accepted or
turned away on one basis only—their size. To those few who were
too large and had to be refused, Rock explained the reason. To
those who were allowed to stay he laid down the rule that, if the
storm came, the children and their caretakers would be the first
to escape, and they the last. By the middle of the day we had about
forty of these refugees camping in the courts.

Their eyes were the darting eyes of mice in the shadows of
hawks' wings, and their cracked lips told us this:

The mobs, possessed of the energy of madness, ran through the
Tartar City day and night. Sometimes an exhausted cluster of
rioters could be seen in broad day sprawled in widespread disarray
in the archery grounds of the Central Park, resting heads on one
another's thighs, snoring, pale, their faces wretched in repose;
but they would start up after an hour and go baying off. The mobs
had coagulated; on the first day they had roamed in packs of low
hundreds, whereas now they were joined into sluggish throngs
of thousands. The Emperor had caused them to smart, and they
were chary now of attacking his properties, for one crowd, approaching the gates of the winter palaces, had received canister
shot from a great brass howitzer, and it was said that twenty-two
had been left dead and scores had been hurt. Accordingly the
rioters had turned more than ever against the easier mark—
against us. Whenever a pack stalked down a person of white skin,
whether man, woman, or child, it sank its fangs in the helpless
victim. A hutung in the quarter of the Examination Halls where
many whites lived had been scoured, and every white had been
beaten to death. A dozen white men had been decapitated. Several
had been bambooed until their ribs were crushed. This wolf mob

was insatiable—each taste of blood increased, rather than slaked,
its thirst.

Late in the morning some of us realized that Benign Warmth,
Wood Pillow, and Belted Persimmon, the three large ones who
were going to have to stay behind with Rock, had disappeared.
Someone asked Rock: Had he hidden them already? All he would
say was: They were—and would be—safe.

The children, aware of our icy calm before them, behaved,
that morning, rather well, though one could see a suppressed
excitement in their eyes, an innocent anticipation of some kind of
outing they dimly sensed they were going to have: Would it be
like the walk to the lake on the night of the Spirit Festival?

I saw Rock near the screen at the main gate, and I ran to him
and begged him to tell me where he planned to hide. "I want to
be able to picture you as safe."

"I'll be safe, White Lotus," he said, and he put a hand on my
shoulder. "I'll join you afterward at the Banner Corps compound"
—spoken with arrogant assurance.

I felt at once, again, that upwelling of some aspect of happiness
which I had experienced the day before, and which had puzzled
me then by its apparent inappropriateness. Now, scarcely daring
to believe my good fortune, I put a name to it: courage, given
me by this rough Rock. Courage was new in my life. In slavery
there could have been no courage, only desperation, a degraded
drive for revenge, a search for a means of escape, a hopeless
desire for change. But this, pouring into me from that hand on my
shoulder, was of a different order—of an order beyond daydreams.
We may be low as dirt, the grip of the hand seemed to say, but
we are talking in hushed voices about the *future*. . . . I felt that I
could face separation, anxiety, uncertainty. . . .

At the middle of the day we fixed a meal of millet gruel; the
children grumbled.

In midafternoon we heard new knocking at the braced gates.

A white man—one of those, too large, whom Rock had turned
away!—had come to warn us: He cried at the crack of the gate
leaves that he had been scouting, and he had seen a large crowd
turn down Hata Gate Street in our direction. Four or five thousand,
he thought. He did not know their plan. . . . Then he was gone.

Yes: courage! A courageous man without even a name!

Rock decided not to wait for the mob to arrive. He called Snow

Bug to have the children lined up by ages, and he ran to the rear wall and opened the little postern.

I had a double assignment. I was eventually to be with the last group, the elevens, but I was detailed to help at first with the infants, who would have to be passed out through the low culvert from hand to hand. We had about twenty of these little helpless bodies; the plan was to lay them down in the hutung outside while the older children scrambled out, and then, as the groups made off for the Bordered Red Banner Corps barracks, the accompanying matrons, the women attendants, and the gate boy—we were fifteen adults altogether—would each take up one or two little lives and carry them along in arms.

All the babies soon were howling; we gave them dusty sticks of malt to suck. Snow Bug was first to go out, and the gate boy, Wang, knelt inside the postern and handed the wriggling infants through to her. I was one of those who relayed babies to Wang's skinny hands. The ditch smelled. The city outside was so far no noisier than usual. With a sinking heart I saw how long it was going to take to get all the orphans out through the one foul hole; I was to be in the last party.

The older year groups were being assembled in the various courtyards, and when the infants were all out I went to the peony garden, where the elevens were herded.

The earlier buoyancy of the children had faded now to a mood of hesitation.

Tiger Ears, the boy who wanted to be nobody, came up to me and said, "Where are we going?"

"We're going to join the army."

"Will they give me a number?"

"No doubt."

"Good."

We would have a long wait. I persuaded him to help me line the others up in pairs and number them off; in this way they would march through the streets.

Now we began to hear, crescendo, the mass cry of the rioters pouring down Hata Gate Street: a strained, dry-throated, never-to-be-satisfied yearning of many voices. What *did* the yellows want of us?

The militancy drained out of our little regiment of elevens when they began to hear this noise. They must have remembered the hostility that night by the fire-spotted lake, and they flocked around me now, begging to know what was happening out there—the great roar had reached our block.

The nines and tens were in other courts of the orphanage, and I had no way of knowing how the escapes were getting on. I did my best to return my small soldiers to their ranks, with a minimum of explanation.

At the main gate we now heard a single shrill voice dominating the mob sound. Ai! A speech! With all my heart I was thankful for the peacock in some men that makes them spout oratory at opportunity. The hum of the crowd abated as the man's voice fanned out in an ecstatic display of hatred. This stupid vaunter would give us time!

Rock, coming through the garden, said the line at the postern had reached the eights.

Over the renewed racket of the crowd, which was now responding to questions from the ranter with swift barks of assent, I heard Rock say, "I'll see you tonight, or tomorrow at the latest, my flower." Then he said, "Better move this group to the rear court now." He turned as if to walk away but then hesitated, swung back to me, and—I craved another word of recognition—he merely said, "Better get them through as fast as you can."

By the time my elevens were double-lined at the rear wall, and the last of the tens was on hands and knees in the gutter, we heard a roar go up from the crowd—more distant now, as we were at the far side of the orphanage from it, so the roar was dull, round, and off-trailing like faraway thunder. The speech must have been over. A few stones clattered on our roofs. I started my youngsters through. I heard a thud—a battering ram? My hands turned to ice. I called to the children to hurry. Then, as the refugees crowded behind me, fighting to be the first of the last, I fell to a crawl and then stretched out full length in the putrid ditch. The odor was horrible—everything disgusting and corrupt about mankind seemed to have found its way into that miserable channel, and it was all I could do to keep from retching. As I wriggled through the confining hole I felt the wetness reach my skin all along the front of my body.

I was through. I jumped to my feet. Tiger Ears—his eyes shone; he had lost his human tag; he was Number One—had put the line in good order on either side of the hutung's filthy sewage ditch. From the tiny water gate the refugees popped out and ran off.

One infant was left on the ground in the lane—a pink mouth

contentedly folded around a candy nipple; I picked the baby up
and clutched it to my piss-wet heart that might break for Rock.
We ran off. Behind us we heard a faint crash and a mob's orgas-
mic *Aaaah!*

⟨[With the Banner Corps

At my first knock the gate flew open. We were beckoned
inside by urgent yellow-skinned hands.

All but Tiger Ears, who loved his martial role, my children were
tight with dread, but now something remarkable happened: Half
a dozen yellow men, bannermen, took me and my orphans in
charge, and as they led us through three outer courtyards they
were courteous, gentle, and respectful, even toward eleven-year-
old white bastard urchins. These were keepers of the Emperor's
order, and for the first time in my life under the yellows I realized
that law *could* be impartial.

The bannermen led us through, at last, into the great parade
ground of their compound, where hundreds of white refugees
were already herded. Many were crumpled on the ground like
lifeless parcels; most had taken flight, as we had, carrying nothing
but the burdens of their hearts.

Against a far wall I saw our orphanage crowd, and I asked the
soldiers to take us to it.

A surprise as we approached: Here were Benign Warmth, Belted
Persimmon, and Wood Pillow! I learned that Rock—and with this
my fears for him pumped harder than ever—had slipped the big
three out the orphanage gate the previous morning; he had done
this in secret, letting it be thought that they were hidden, in order
to forestall others of the staff from wanting to flee then also. He
was back there alone!

Benign Warmth was comfortably in command again. All had
turned out as he had predicted; thanks, no doubt, to his patronesses, the Emperor's bannermen were taking good care of us.
We were safe. Every single orphan. Every member of the staff. He
puffed his cheeks and wagged his head—and acted as if Rock had
never existed.

Near the end of the afternoon a field kitchen was rolled out onto
the parade ground, and the multitude was fed—polished rice!
Ayah, I had not tasted such rice since the feasts brought us by

Rock and Groundnut's pigeons! With continued firmness and correctness, the bannermen kept the famished refugees in order, fed our children first of all. My clothes were still damp and foul, and the clinging odor and my concern for Rock choked my appetite. The children ate like gulping puppies.

In the milling about the field kitchen I saw a stooped figure: Mink—Mink who had been so thrilled by the opening passages of the riot, and whose thrill to my shame I had shared. I had lost track of him since our escape, and I was glad to see him, and told him so. He looked up at me from his crouch with hard eyes and said, "Help me get a bowl of rice. They won't let me close enough. People don't understand what it is to have a bad back."

Stunned by Mink's self-absorption, I said, "Have you asked a bannerman to help you?"

"Hai! They'll jump for a soft girl—do you think they'd lift a finger for *me*? Slanthead bastards!"

A bannerman standing close to us heard Mink spit out this epithet, and first I saw a flash of astonishment on the tall yellow soldier's face, then I saw an abiding loathing lurking behind the propriety that the man pulled with visible effort, like a split-bamboo awning, back down across his face.

With alarming suddenness it was dark; I had lost all sense of time.

The orphans, blessed with the suppleness of innocence, fell fast asleep on the ground. Some of them started up from dreams and cried out, but with caresses and murmurs from us they melted again into slumber. Best and most profound of the sleepers, however, was Benign Warmth; he slept the sleep of the justified. The smell of the ditch was in my nostrils; I could not drop off. Rock hid in my mind.

Late at night—in what quarter of it I could not tell—I heard, first as a distant growl, then swelling like the oncoming edge of a rain squall beating on dry earth, the same mob noise as had borne down on the orphanage in the afternoon.

Soon, in response to the unmistakable approach of this muffled roar, the large crowd of refugees on the parade ground was stirring—except for the oblivious children—and we heard bustling, stamping feet, and orders being shouted in the outer courts of the bannermen's quarters.

I had a bad thought: Was the mob only now coming away from the orphanage?

In a short time the noise had risen to an ominous din—greater, it seemed to me, than we had heard at the orphanage—which was centered at the gates of the Banner Corps compound. We could only guess that the rioters, enraged by the thought that whites were being shielded from them by the Emperor's troops, intended to try to ravage the place.

Then I heard—once, twice, three times—like a huge slow drumbeat, the pounding of a timber butt against the gates.

But three times was all. A burst of explosions! The bannermen were firing! The throat of the mob outside uttered a cry of frustration and despair, and then we heard the great hiss of its flight, like the sound of a spent wave pulling sand and crunched shells back down a beach.

At that a new voice made itself heard—that of the press of refugees in the enclosure, which, though it dared not openly cheer, gave out an eerie whispered sigh of relief, surprise, and half-believing satisfaction. But I—I was weeping for Rock.

The night persisted endlessly, as if it were a fever that would not break from my forehead.

When at last an inapt rosy dawn came seeping up the sky, I felt drowsy, but the stirring and groaning of the refugees prevented me from drifting off. I leaned against the wall with a foggy mind, trying to summon back the courage which had so elated me the day before; but it would come no more than sleep or wakefulness.

For perhaps a long time, as half thoughts lurked behind my hooded eyes, I half watched two men sitting at some distance in the throng talking in earnest. They half seemed to be dear friends to each other, and perhaps even to me. One's head was strangely streaked and smeared; the other, three quarters turned away from me, was stiff-necked, and his gestures were a farm boy's, of grasping tools, weeding, and striking a stubborn donkey's flank. They fascinated my half attention, those two; there was some dim pull for me about them. A whisper came sweeping across the parade ground, of unknown authority, that the rioters in the city were flagging; there were no more whites at large to catch and kill; the mobs were scattered, sleeping like wild dogs in the streets; their rage was spent—so the whisper said, but the report swept across an indifferent me and flew on. I lay there dazed, staring at nothing —a nothing centered on the two men, who were arguing.

Then, having a dawn of my own, I stirred, felt my mind swept clear, looked more closely across the way in the growing light, sat up, heard a cry of surprised life in my own throat, and then was on my feet staggering and sobbing through the jammed yard in a rush toward the two men.

They were Rock and Groundnut.

❨ Our White Way

I threw myself down and grasped Rock's knees, weeping. His trousers were filthy and sour. He greeted me as casually as if I were coming home to him from work at the orphanage and we were alone in his lama's cubicle. "Hello, sweet girl."

I wept harder at the sound of his voice; in time I recovered some composure and sat up.

Groundnut was dressed in his beggar's pickings, and the smears on his head were of his vile cosmetic ills, partly pulled and wiped away. He had been earning his rice bowl at the Hata Gate when the riot had begun, and at the closing of the gates his curiosity— together with a white man's hope that a public disaster might bring change, which could not be for much worse and might be for better—had made him decide to stay in the inner city.

I urged Rock to come and join the orphanage party and to tell us what had happened after our departure.

He refused. "I might kill that pompous mandarin's wife's pap-kisser."

"Then tell me."

"There's not much to tell. I hid. They came in and tore the courts apart. Then they left. I waited a good long time and came out and ran over here—that's all."

"But tell me more. Where did you hide?"

"You wouldn't want to know that."

Ayah, this was my old Rock back. I had to pitch in. "What makes you think I wouldn't want to know this or that? You arrogant rogue hog. You white bastard. I'll give you a fingernail if you don't tell me."

Hai! His eyes began to dance with pleasure. "Listen, sow," he said. "You come over here interrupting a perfectly good quarrel I'm having with Groundnut, and begin telling me what to say and do. Hold your tongue! What'll we do with this saucy little sow, Groundnut? Shall we crank her tail? What? What do you say?"

Groundnut laughed. "Ai! He's a bastard, all right," he said to me. "I'll tell you where he hid: He hid in a night-soil jar—just where he belongs."

And at this Rock laughed, too. Indeed, this was exactly where he had hidden, he now told me. A perfect place, too.

The latrines at the orphange, for defecation but not for urination (which latter was done if possible into pits draining out by the postern of our escape), consisted of brick-lined wells, into which huge jars, high as a man's chest, were lowered to catch the inmates' excretions, so precious to outlying farmers that it was bought by honey-cart drivers for good cash; slabs of slate with raised foot-shaped standards, straddling ample holes, covered the jars. In the time while we had waited for the mob's approach, Rock had scoured an empty slop jar standing in one of the orphanage's storage rooms at the back, and had lowered it into one of the vacant toilet wells.

"And when the mob broke in," he said, grinning, "I let myself down into the jar, and pulled the slab over me, and I was as safe as a turtle in his shell. Ahai! I took one of those peony plants in the garden out of its glazed urn, and I wore the urn on my head down there, just in case some filthy rioter—but I was lucky. Not one! I even took a little nap after the mob left. It wasn't bad at all."

And what had happened to the orphanage?

"Ripped open, sacked from corner to corner—the only thing I could find was one of those cloth shoes for a baby made with a tiger's face on the toes that some son of a turtle had dropped because his arms were too full; it was lying in one of the courtyards, just the one solitary shoe. They burned whatever they could. The place is a shell." Rock suddenly looked glum. "The only thing I regret," he said, "is that I let that wind-filled superintendent slip out yesterday morning. I had a jar knee-deep with orphan dung to put him in."

I asked then if those two had decided anything.

They had agreed, Rock said, to get away, to leave this garbage city as soon as the gates were opened. "You can come, too."

To where?

To anywhere. Anywhere away from this war and this Number Wheel. "The war," Rock said with one of his sneers, "stinks to the sky."

Where was the man who had saved us all? Where was the courage I had felt under that firm hand on my shoulder? I did not

need it; I felt a glow of comfort. I had Rock. The sound of the mobs
was dead in my ears. Ai, I agreed with those two. We would take
care of our own skins: if too hard to stay, we would leave; if too
hard to fight, we would adapt. This would be our white way.

(【 The Double Edge of Memory

   Three days later the gates opened and we left. We became scavengers, we *avoided* the war. The sound of cannon fire,
wherever we heard it, drove us on the veering course of hares
across the countryside with many others who were playing the
same thin game. We went hungry dodging battles. And in a ditch
one day, after many months, we heard of the Emperor's victory,
and of the death of slavery in all the provinces, and we guessed
that the greatest flux would be in the outer provinces, and we
headed toward them. Our passage was a slow one. Even within the
core provinces the roads were flooded with restless yellows and
whites: home-going soldiers, soldier-searching relatives, and people simply moving on—all those bitter dreamers who imagined
that a change of era and of air might produce a magical change of
self. The farther we walked toward the provinces of the defeated
Sedition, the deeper into chaos we felt we were plunging. Dis-
possessed yellows sat on the gate steps of ruined houses with hollow eyes; swarms of refugees pecked and scraped in lawless packs;
yellow profiteers wheeled about like buzzards; freed slaves roamed
in a delirium of self-importance that was quite mad, absolutely
unreal; the riffraff of disbanded armies of both sides stayed on in
old camps. Hungry, tattered, and dusty-haired, we went from city
to city, from camp to camp. For a time we lived in a palisaded
enclosure, once a Sedition camp which had degenerated into a
filthy, anarchistic, disease-ridden village of torn tents where former soldiers of both sides, freed slaves, uprooted widows of war
dead, children of murdered slaveowners, nondescripts of every
kind, indeed anyone who could bear, or after a war craved, utter
degradation, half-lived in a hopeless wait for the Emperor to come
to their aid; and in this mire Groundnut was ecstatic, for the whole
world around us was a-begging, and he set himself up as a professor of begging, with all the kudos and perquisites of the chief
of an academy—no more need of disguises.
   But Rock grew restless in that fenced-in mudhole. He was still

obsessed by the Number Wheel riots, in a double-edged way—on the one side by the memory of the sounds of those hate-poisoned crowds, and on the other by thoughts of the brief chance he had had to *do* something for a handful of his race. At his urging we left the camp and drifted on, deeper and deeper into the outer territories; every cart wheel and barrow wheel that Rock saw started him nattering about that other, larger, more fateful wheel of death and opportunity.

The Lower Hand

BOOK SEVEN

⟪ The Headman

WE STOOD WAITING in the village headman's courtyard. A little boy with a shaved crown and a milky walleye had run to the fields to summon his father.

Rock and Groundnut, both wearing queues (as did all white males in the postwar period, for it was an assertion of freedom to dress the hair in the style of the former masters), looked haggard, weatherworn, dirty, sullen, and rather dangerous, after our long period of vagabondage.

With nods, chin thrusts, and thumb pokes, we silently pointed out to each other the signs of the leaf-thin frugality of this headman's life: a scrawny vegetable patch, one pig in the sty, a stack of corn roots saved for fuel, a conical pile of human manure outside the shoulder-high walls of the open latrine.

Hai! This village was where we had drifted, and this was where we would stay.

Here the man came. I felt, and suppressed, an impulse to laugh —not at him but at ourselves. Seeing the actuality of this white village headman, I wondered whether we had become drunk on an idea—of settling in the worst place of all, in the so-called Humility Belt, which lay like a scalp infection across Hunan, or South-of-the-Lake Province, having come on strangely mixed motives, for we wanted to live in a society crowded with whites where nothing mattered, where we could be weeds among the rankest weeds, yet we also wanted to do what we could to raise the level of the poorest whites' lives. Rock's experience in the riots lay at the root of this idea; and I could read and write. We were hardened whites, we had a road-weary arrogance, we thought we could teach some of the world's better ways to the people of our race in the Humility Belt, of whose sorry condition we had heard so much.

But here one of them was. An instant's picture, as he burst in at his gate, panting: warm, shrewd, adaptable, superstitious, loud, and not to be cheated. Raise *his* level? Ha! He would sooner depress ours.

"Go, go, go!" he said, waving us on backhanded toward the house for cups of tea before our talk, whatever it might concern.

There had been rain. On a mild surge of playfulness I placed my worn cloth shoe soles, step after too long step toward the house, in the soft-dirt footprints of my Rock, who walked ahead.

From behind, the headman banged my shoulder. "Watch yourself. Walking in another person's tracks will give you backache."

Dark within—an impression of an immaculate chest on a matted platform, its old wood gleaming with tung oil, its brass hinges and corner bindings brightly polished.

The headman's wife—we had not seen her; she had been lurking inside the house; she had already steeped some tea—was a mix, with "good" eyes having heavy overfolds, a broad nose, and straight black hair. She was silent and deferential, but I could see by her bearing that she had a certain power. Was her husband headman because of her?

While we sipped at our tea, spied upon from behind his mother's legs by the walleyed boy, Manager Wu, as this white headman called himself, rambled on a note of off-business politeness. We were town-bred? A joke about a man who was cocksure in the city but was an easy mark in the country. A recent escape from an embarrassing predicament, involving yellow landowner. A grimace and groan, a rupture suffered lifting a cart tongue three months before. A remark about some deep thought, and a gesture to go with it, betraying a belief that the stomach was the seat of the intellect.

Then Manager Wu's tea bowl went down with an emphatic clink, and we knew that we could raise our question.

"Can we settle in your village?" Rock asked.

"What's to stop you? We're all métayers here. Get a tenancy and build a house. Who's to prevent you?"

What a letdown this flat indifference gave us! We had wandered as vagrants for many months, and at last we had come to this village in a valley, in the heart of the Humility Belt, where tea was grown, and table foods, a double village, with the yellow section at the "upper hand," placed more favorably from the point of view of geomancy, according to certain mysterious influences of wind, water, dragons, spirits, and land values, immediately to the northeast of the "lower hand," where the whites lived as best they could, as free men and women. The village was in a swarm of similar villages, but for some reason it had struck us, when we came over a rise and saw it early in the morning, as precisely the one we wanted. We expected our arrival to arouse some feeling; after all our months of walking here and there we wanted a welcome, even an angry one. The least the headman might have offered us was hostility, but he neither rejected us nor accepted us.

"Go to Old Lung, he's the provisioner for this area, he lives in Wang Family Big Gourd Village. See if he will arrange you a tenancy and furnish you. Don't let him take more than half your crop, the turtle."

I saw that Rock did not like this advice. "We heard that you could claim a few mu of land from the former plantations."

"Those old promises! Go up to the provincial yamen—see what good it does you! No, we farm by rack rents. And not so well at that. You'll have to have what we call a 'second,' if you want to eat every day. Hairlip Shen" (all the whites in this area, it seemed, had taken surnames of former masters) "makes bean curd and vends it in the neighboring villages. The Lin family makes spiral bean cakes. Rich Shen has one son who's a carpenter, one who's a roof-mender. Many of the women make shoe soles. Strong Ma works certain days on the provincial road. The Changs have a son who is effeminate—they send him fishing for carp nights. Do these people sound hardworking? Ai, they're all lazy! But you can't manage on tea farming; nobody can. You have to have a 'second.' "

I said, "What if I started a school?"

Manager Wu looked at me severely. "You? A *woman* teacher?"

"What difference, when everything is confused?"

Manager Wu did not answer me but carried on the thought he had begun. "Lazy? Not exactly. They're shiftless—don't care. You won't either. I saw Hairlip Shen leaning on the wall of his pigpen

saying, 'Don't grunt so, old hog!' They all have to pay me squeeze
to pay Provisioner Lung, who keeps some and gives some to Magistrate Su, who keeps some and passes some along, and so on up to
the top, wherever that is. All those officials are criminals! You see,
we *lost* the war out here. The yellows they put in charge—ignorant
scoundrels. I was a slave to Big Venerable Cheng: a hard man,
but educated, alert—you couldn't get squeeze out of him, and he
wouldn't take it, either. He's gone. All the masters were killed or
run off the land. Start a school for the yellow turtles in the 'upper
hand,' Mei-mei. They need it. This village is on one little corner of
Old Cheng's place. He had thirty thousand mu of tea plantations
—beautiful! Ayah, how are you ignorant city pigs going to learn
how to crop tea bushes, make withering tats, roll the leaves? These
are skills. *You* want to start a school? Pfui. I don't care. You can
starve here as well as anywhere else."

([Being Furnished

What a happy surprise is Provisioner Lung! How gracious he is! He greets us at the spirit screen of his courtyard, by
doffing his enormous, wire-rimmed spectacles, waving them about,
and putting them back on again. Once they are fastened behind
his ears, one can see, looking into his gentle eyes, that the lenses
of these glasses are simply circlets of windowpane, with no magnifying power. He is a yellow man in his seventies, I would guess,
with a clean, long, and unusually full white beard. Courtesy,
manners, graceful gestures. "Come along, come along." In the
courtyard, slung from the branch of a cherry tree, a bird cage.
Groundnut the bird fancier exclaims. Provisioner Lung pauses to
show Groundnut his lark. For five "feathers"—moltings, or years
—he has exposed the bird to the classical repertory, and with a
little kissing sound the provisioner starts the singer off: the merchant names as we hear them the thirteen cries of the wood sparrow, black warbler, red warbler, magpie, cat, flock of chickens,
swallow, eagle, yellow finch, wild pigeon, partridge, cuckoo, mating widgeon. Groundnut is ecstatic.
"Ayah, the three 'mouths' of the eagle were the hardest to teach.
I had to take him all the way to the provincial capital, to Bring
Larks Restaurant, where the proprietor keeps roosts out over the
water of the lotus pond there, meat-baited roosts, and eagles come

screaming in there. You should have seen my good boy—head on one side." Whipping his beard, Provisioner Lung turns his head and becomes a lark listening, trying hard to remember. "I had one other lark before him, for seven years. He died, and the very next time I went out walking a dog bit me."

He leads us into a modest room, and, being white, I have my first suspicion. The modesty is too perfect, too discreet, too shrewd —no profiteer lives here! A woman enters with tea, and with a vulgar pride Provisioner Lung tells us she is his concubine—the only concubine, he boasts, in Wang Family Big Gourd Village or, for that matter, in all the seven villages closest at hand. Since his wife's death the year before, Fragrant Dew—she is wizened, and her mouth is all drawn up in wrinkles, like a newborn puppy's, and her gown is as plain as mine—has been his only company. She moves about silently, serving us. Provisioner Lung says he bought her thirty years ago, "the same year I bought these," and he holds up a pair of polished mountain walnuts that he rolls in one hand to calm his nerves and promote circulation.

Does he have to tell three vagrant whites such things? Everything about him is counterfeit, second-rate, and his "style" would certainly not have been tolerated when his social betters were around to keep an eye on him.

He lifts a tiny corked vase from a table, pours out some snuff into a little brass bowl, and with a forefinger lifts some of the dust to his nostrils. *Harrcha-a-a!* A peasant sneeze!

The cups are empty. So. Rock speaks. We have talked with Manager Wu in the Village of Brass-Mouth Chang. We wish to arrange a tenancy. Be furnished in tea and food crops.

There are spikes like those of a thistle on Rock's voice.

Now we learn about the whole thieving process. The tenancy, on land with several mu of "somewhat neglected" eight- or nine-year-old tea bushes, will be arranged with the landowner, who lives in the provincial capital, Changsha, or Long Sands, on the river below the big lake. The bushes are guaranteed to bear the first season. We give as rent a percentage of the tea crop only; no percentage of food crops. Do we have a donkey and a cart? No? Provisioner Lung will furnish them, on chattel mortgages. Seed and a half month's rations will be forwarded on credit, against eventual payment in food crops. When the first flush is ready to pick, another mortgage will be given on the tea crop, to pay for monthly provisions, which may be picked up at each new moon:

twenty catties of fat side pork, a half picul of rice for the three parties. Also, clothing and shoes, farm quality. Medicines. Shoeing for the donkey. Harness. Tools. All to be provided in exchange for small food-crop percentages.

Rock sharply says, "You mentioned 'somewhat neglected' tea bushes. What does that mean?"

"It means that tenants come and go. You will be taking up where someone else left off."

"It's a swindle!"

I see behind Provisioner Lung's windowpane spectacles a fleeting look: strange! Can that have been, in the eyes of a man who is in absolute control, a look of anxiousness? But the look is gone. The merchant shrugs. He is now staring at Groundnut, at the top of the shrug, which he holds a long time.

Groundnut, who has been a beggar, and who knows that beggars do not trump up moral arguments against those on whom they fawn, is grinning, and he imitates the provisioner's shrug.

"You come from the core provinces, yes?" Old Lung asks Rock.

"We do."

"I could see that. You don't know tea."

Rock is bristling. "I've learned harder things than tea."

"I have no doubt of it. And I see that you're not like most of the hogs around here." Rock jumps a little at that insulting word. "These people need a creditor to sharpen up their heel bones. You came from Manager Wu in Brass-Mouth? Look, he talks like a lion, he's the headman of the lower hand over there—but he's like the rest of those shiftless hogs. This is what I have to deal with. He has no idea of time. 'Tomorrow,' he promises—that day never comes. He won't work if there is some way of getting out of it: came running from the fields to see you, I'll wager, plenty of time for a cup of tea, plenty of time for complaints about Provisioner Lung. Right? That's all time away from paying off! He's a sort of clown. Dirty and smelly, hoo, garlic! Doesn't know the meaning of chastity, modesty—watch out for him, girl." The merchant looks at me, and I have an impression that he is somehow inwardly uncomfortable. "He doesn't know the value of a copper—spends it on foolishness, gambles it away, then comes sniveling to me for side meat for his children: he's the one with that cock-eyed boy, isn't he? Gullible! His villagers take advantage of him every day of the year. All right. He goes to the temple, knocks his forehead on the bricks—but he believes in ten thousand ghosts, spirits,.

charms, demons. He has a mind like a child's—shallow thinking. He'd steal the underdrawers from your dead mother. Has no respect for property or morality or manners or for life itself—*can't control his impulses,* that's the underlying trouble. And this is what they're all like. You think I *want* them in debt? I never get mine back. They break my tools, destroy my carts, lame my donkeys. They pick my tea at night and hide it. Pay me debts? 'Tomorrow, Provisioner Lung! Tomorrow! Tomorrow!' But tomorrow they abscond."

I keep wondering about that look in his eyes. I think I will give him a tiny shock. In a half-theatrical voice I say, "The Master said, 'Extravagance leads to insubordination, and parsimony to meanness. It is better to be mean than insubordinate.'"

I hasten to explain that I have concluded from what the merchant has been saying that Manager Wu appraises himself wrongly—as white people are liable to do, I add as a sop. It seems that the headman thinks himself grand, but all the time he is mean. I hide the sarcasm from my voice, a cultured flute swaddled in rags. But perhaps this little experiment in veiled effrontery has been a bad mistake, for now I see distinct annoyance in Provisioner Lung's eyes. He does not like the thought of a bedraggled white person with some learning. He is deficient in it himself.

He turns to Rock and curtly says, "All that matters to you is: Am I good for what I promise? Come with me."

He leads us through a series of courtyards, giving onto storage rooms, and we see an appalling wealth of carts and plows, shoes and clothes, barrels of salt pork and sacks of rice, seed and manure, dried fruits, and peppers, and cabbages, and umbrellas and pots and hats and jars of herbs.

"You see," he said, having led us around again to the spirit screen at his front gate, "I am good for my word."

Rock says, "Yes, but we haven't talked about something else that matters. The percentages."

"They're the usual. For rent, sixty per cent of the tea. For monthly provisions—"

But Rock explodes. "Sixty is *not* usual." He turns to Groundnut and me. "Let's go."

Quickly Provisioner Lung says, "You don't know tea."

Now Groundnut comes in for the first time. "But we know bad bargains."

"I am the only merchant who furnishes for Brass-Mouth."

"There are other villages," Rock says. Again he says to us, "Let's go."

The merchant sighs and comes down to fifty-five per cent. It takes a quarter of an hour to get him down to fifty. All the other percentages and charges require long haggling. The lark sings in the background, intermittently pretending it is an eagle. We stand the whole time at the spirit screen; amenities have been forgotten.

(Our Own House

We were building a house. Ever since the meeting with the provisioner, Rock had been in a wool-gathering mood, and he was behaving like an "old solid," one of those whites the yellows preferred, of the type that appeared to be gentle, tractable, peaceable, and possibly stupid and easy to best. He was also distant; he would not tell Groundnut or me what was on his mind. I had the feeling he was storing away his bitterness against some future need.

No one would take us in, and while we built our house we slept in the open, on the ground, as we had often done on our travels. We lived sparely on Provisioner Lung's rice and fatty side meat, which we cooked over open fires of dried grasses and twigs.

Manager Wu had assigned us a location for our courtyard, at the bottom of the village, on low ground, a poor place, and for some time we had been making flat mud bricks, a thumb's length in thickness, a foot wide and two feet long; we made them in wooden molds, grudgingly loaned us from the communal village supply by Manager Wu. Groundnut cut the mud and mixed it with dried reeds that we scavenged from a nearby swamp, I filled the molds, and Rock tamped the matter into the flat boxes with a heavy stone rammer.

Groundnut, with the brashness of a beggar, poked about in the village more than Rock or I, penetrating into courtyards asking questions of the hostile population, and one day, seeing on his return a wise-cat look on his face, I asked him what he had stolen.

He pulled out from under his jacket a pamphlet bound in brilliant yellow paper and handed it over to me. It was entitled *Almanac of the Year of the Tiger*. I flipped through its pages. Ayah, it was made for ignorant people, all, save the simple numbers of the dates, in pictures!

"You can't piss in this village without getting permission from the almanac," Groundnut said. "Every question I ask, they go to the book and look at the pretty pictures. I thought we'd better have one."

"Look up housebuilding," Rock said. He was perfectly bland and serious, and for a moment I had to restrain myself from teasing him: we had planned to educate and elevate these benighted whites, and we were letting ourselves, instead, be stupefied by them.

Here! On third third, the Spring Festival, soon to come—one could see a picture of graves being repaired, blossoms, a man planting a tree. Marked by the yang, the sign of the male, light, positive, benign principle of life, were those things it was auspicious to do on that day: offer sacrifices, pray for wealth, visit friends, walk in fields, take baths, cut fingernails, cut out clothes, cure the sick by acupuncture, put money by, and what we meant to do: raise king and queen posts, lift up ridgepoles. Under the forbidding yin: undertaking mercantile dealings, weddings, making wine, sinking wells.

So we waited for the holiday, and on it, while the yellow villagers from the upper hand strolled in the countryside gazing at the flowering trees and darting warblers, and the whites from the lower hand dozed by their compound walls, chatted, gambled, got drunk, argued, or crouched on their hams sullenly watching us, never once offering to lend us a hand, we erected the frame of our single-space house.

Fortunately, Rock knew what he was about, or we would have been heartily laughed at.

There was one man, however, who could not resist telling us that we were doing everything wrong. His name was Bare-Stick Wang; Groundnut had heard and told us about him—the village firecracker. He came forward from the circle of our audience of squatting villagers. A big man, he wore a cloth cap at a studied angle on the back of his head, and his light-brown hair, which had a slight curl, was braided into an unkempt loose queue as thick as his forearm. Most of the village men were fastidious about looping up the flies of their outer gowns to their necks, but Bare-Stick wore his unbuttoned nearly down to his waist, revealing a deal of dirty white undershirt. His shoes were down at the heel, showing—the aggressive man's little surprise—elegant embroidered silk socks. He carried a snuff bottle on a string from his

waistband. Groundnut had told us he had a reputation for setting
fires, destroying crops, and informing on his fellow villagers at the
yamen of the district prefect; he would also hire himself out to
settle scores.

"Hai, hambone!" Bare-Stick called to Rock: a way of calling
Rock a white pig.

Rock, lashing the notched ridgepole to the king post with raffia
cord, looked affably at the big man and asked him what he wanted.

"You a city man?"

Rock knew enough not to answer such a sparring question.
"Why?"

"You have that turtle-screwing rope on backwards."

"What do you mean, backwards?"

"You're winding it south-east-north-west; it ought to go south-
west-north-east."

Rock did not answer, but went right on binding the timbers in
the same direction as before.

Bare-Stick moved a few steps closer.

"Did you get permission from the lids to move in here?" "Lids"
was secret white-talk for the yellows—standing for eyelids, their
folded eyelids.

Now came this surprising "old-solid" behavior of Rock's, which,
it seemed to me, simply fed the braggart's fire. "We arranged
things with Manager Wu," Rock politely said.

Bare-Stick spat and moved yet closer. "You'd better make yourself known to the upper hand. If you don't you're liable to have
visitors from The Hall some night." He rolled his eyes in a mysterious way. "That is, if this house of yours stands long enough for
you to spend a night in it at all."

Rock went on with his work. Bare-Stick, obviously displeased
with the newcomer's silence, turned on Groundnut, who was handing materials up to Rock. "Did I hear that you people are button-
kissers?" This was the derogatory term that had been used by
yellow Seditionists for their enemies from the core provinces—
"button" standing for the Emperor's mandarins, who wore colored
buttons on their hats according to their rank.

Groundnut had the beggar's instincts: appease, whine, flatter;
and besides, Bare-Stick was a big man. "Whom-kissers?" Groundnut asked in a high, squeaky voice with a nervous laugh.

Bare-Stick wrinkled his nose in disgust at Groundnut and addressed himself again to Rock. "What's your 'second'?"

With a forbearance and sweetness that seemed absolutely genuine to me, Rock, looking straight into Bare-Stick's eyes, said, "We're going to start a school and teach the classics."

At this Bare-Stick gave out, first, a single bark of laughter, then two barks, then a half dozen. Then he began doubling over, pounding his knees, rearing back, mouthing great lumps of laughter; his face grew purple and tears started in his eyes. He turned and staggered to the silent circle of squatting onlookers, and we could hear him, half choked with his guffaws, shouting a report to them. "Classics! Classics!" we heard him cry.

A few young boys in the watching crowd laughed halfheartedly. But for the most part Bare-Stick's uproar was greeted by silence; the eyes were as sullen as before.

Within a week we had finished our house and built a courtyard wall.

The day before we were to sleep for the first time in the house, Groundnut announced to us that he was not going to live with us, for he had found a snug corner, he said, in a more or less abandoned temple at some distance from the Village of Brass-Mouth Chang—ayah, the rendezvous, no doubt, of white thieves, beggars, conjurers, ruffians.

Rock said, "We've built you a bed here." But it seemed to me that Rock did not really press Groundnut to stay—even though the pair were true friends, and even though we would badly need Groundnut's two hands to help make a living from our tenancy.

It was just this last that Groundnut himself had realized, and he said now, with a sheepish smile, "You know me, Rock. Honest work is bad for me. Helping you build this house has knotted my hands all up, like fish netting. I wouldn't last a week on the tea bushes."

Rock seemed not the least upset. Somehow he procured colored pictures of Ch'ing Ch'iung and Yü Ch'ih, warriors of darkness and light, and he pasted them on the two leaves of our courtyard gate, to ward off thieves. On the mud wall of the empty pigsty he affixed an untrue notice on red paper: FAT SWINE ARE IN HERE. Provisioner Lung furnished us a crude chest, and by the two locks Rock pasted red papers with these inscriptions: GET MONEY AND RECEIVE PRECIOUS THINGS and TEN THOUSAND OUNCES OF GOLD. On the door of our simple chamber he pasted a picture of the fertility god, riding a unicorn and carrying in his arms something

Rock apparently wanted as much as he wanted an end to wandering—a boy child.

⟨ The Village

The Village of Brass-Mouth Chang lay in the played-out valley of the Box River. It was closely crowded by Hsing Little Village, Ma Family Graves, Seeing the Horse Village, Mud Bridge, Hot Pepper Village, Wang Family Big Gourd Village, Tiger-Guarded Village, Liu's Dog's Tooth Village, and the Village of the Benign and Loving Magistrate.

Since the war the countryside had changed. The great slave-economy tea estates had been broken up; the population was growing; freed whites abounded, in many places outnumbering the yellows; a rash of divided villages like ours had erupted all across the area known, from the poverty of the inhabitants, both yellow and white, as the Humility Belt.

In the upper hand of our village were nineteen gates, altogether one hundred and three yellow mouths; in the lower hand, sixteen gates, counting our new one, with one hundred twenty-eight white mouths, counting Rock's and mine.

Now that our mean house was finished, we felt free to move out into the lower hand of the village. In the lengthening evenings we put on the new clothes Provisioner Lung had supplied us, and we went strolling. It seemed that in the pleasant hour before sundown the villagers, who formerly had seemed so forbidding and resentful, could not help being cordial. We sauntered along, and the white men hailed Rock: Talkative Chang, Rough Ma, Hairlip Shen, Ox Yang. We stopped to chat; Rock was an "old solid," agreeable to all questions. Suggestive jokes flew my way, and I felt that the men were excited by the arrival of a new young woman in the village. We paused at the communal well with its semicircular wall against dust and evil emanations, and a gossip, pointing to a compound gate, told us about Suspicious Chang, the old founder of the village; his cow had sickened and died, his son had run away to the city, and thieves had stolen the brass clock from within its glass case on a chest on his bed. The empty glass case still stood on the chest, bearing witness to that outrage. Old Suspicious seldom came outside now; he locked his compound gate, wore a ragged beard, peered with care at strangers on the few occasions 'when he walked. "He will hear about you," the gossip said, "and he'll blame everything on you." We learned, too, about Rich Shen, the most prosperous man in the village—at that, he had only thirty-seven mu of tea bushes, of which he owned but twelve and farmed the rest on rack rents like everyone else; his riches were his two sons, carpenter and roof-mender, and they were said to be quarrelsome with him. Though the men rolled their eyes at me, a new female, there were, in fact, too many women in the village, which some considered to be under a spell. War, disease, and cities had taken off young men, and even in childbirth the village was luckless—thirty-two girls to twenty-four boys.

We saw some of these boys, oblivious to the village curse, if there was one, beside the common grindstone spinning a top with a whip—a game they called "beating the button-kissers."

We were warned against intruding into the upper hand of the village. Manager Wu was the only white who was supposed to go up there. The yellows there were poor—"not so poor as we, of course," the villagers said—and they were somber, vindictive, joyless. *They* never strolled in the evenings; every gate was double-barred.

Our white lower-handers were, indeed, adept at the art of enjoying themselves. "Ai," they said of anything unpleasant, "toss it on the compost pile," which in every courtyard consisted of human manure. Life was cheap, crime was easy, a joke cost nothing. Why hurry? What's the difference? A man who was careful was called by our villagers a "tight bowels."

Conversation by the curving wall of the well in the twilight hour was fluent and witty, and much of it was detractive. No one said anything good of Manager Wu's mixie wife. The women considered her sheepish; her beautiful hair they called "the black willow tree," her good eyes were "steamed meat dumplings." Manager's ruptured groin was material for much speculation and snickering, and the men said Manager was quick to tell jokes about the yellows but whenever he went to the upper hand on business he came away with an empty basket.

In general the Box River valley, with a leached-out soil for tea, rice, wheat, kaoliang, peas, and peanuts, was no worse off, and certainly no better off, than most of the Humility Belt. Whites shared with yellows the psychology of defeat. Political corruption was widespread. At the end of the war the Emperor had sent forth a locust swarm of bureaucrats, yellow men, of course, mostly inexperienced, who had tried to take up the government of the Sedition provinces where the now destroyed educated class of former slaveholders had dropped it. These men had tried at first to put the remaining yellows and the freed slaves on the same footing, but quickly they had seen that peace of soul lay in squeeze, and they had settled down to a life of extortion. Upon the shoulders of our tormentor, Provisioner Lung, sat one of these grasping bureaucrats, Magistrate Su. Yellows and whites alike called him and his kind "weasels"—after the biggest thief among the animals.

At the wellside we heard whispers of a shadow that lay over the lower hand: the yellows' band of "visitors" from the mysterious organization called The Hall. "Stop-Wind and I and the children were asleep on our platform. Somebody lammed at the outer gate with a staff or a knife handle, it might have been. Stop-Wind whispered, 'Run hide in the storage hole, they won't hurt me.' I said, 'They'd find me there, kill me sure.' I went out and opened up the gate. They walked right past me, inside. Had warriors masks on, hooo! They pulled the quilt off her, looking. She sleeps bare but they didn't say a word, flung the quilt back on her. They lifted the plank off the big jar in the corner, and I said, 'That's fat-meat, that's all.' One of them said in the mournful voice they use, 'We come from Hell-Beyond-the-Mountain, we don't look for dead meat, son.' Said they were looking for Stop-Wind's brother. He lives forty li downriver. Said he'd done something or other."

Dusk was settling down. The children were away, and voices were low. We heard itinerant vendors, poor white men, each with a distinct chant or signal, still hoping to eke out a transaction before pitch dark: the vegetable-oil-seller with a hollow wooden block, toc-toc, toc-toc; the seller of women's combs, thread, soap, powder, hair oil, with a middle-tone snakeskin drum on a handle, thrum-a-num, thrum-a-num, thrum-a-num-a-num, going farther and farther away; the cabbage-seller, his empty-purse chant on a dying fall; the tinsmith with a deep, deep drum; the man who made little rice-dough effigies, hooting his last on a two-toned flute.

Then a cymbal's clash from the upper hand. Curfew for whites. We hurried home.

([Our Scattered Strips

Neglected in truth our tea bushes were, and partly under cursory instructions from our neighbors, who did not seem fiercely eager to have newcomers succeed, and partly by watching them closely and imitating what they did, we began to prune the shrubs and to cultivate between the rows. Our tea share consisted of three widely separated plots, the largest comprising some thirty rows, a quarter of a li in length, the others much smaller, with bushes of varying ages. All three plots were set without hedge or fence into a huge area of similar plots—quite simply the less desirable stretches of the great tea plantation of Manager Wu's onetime master, Cheng, broken into strips. Yellows owned or rented the richer soil and the better bushes. Our tenancies were marked by numbered corner stones. We had, as well, two food-crop strips, also far apart, and we planned to place a garden of greens in our courtyard.

Rock and I worked endless hours, which in the good weather seemed swift, and we ached and stiffened. We had not much left over for reflection, and the days ran like empty-headed hares.

How sweet the blossoms on our shabby tea bushes!—white, with anthers of a buttery hue; they were like little wild roses.

([Groundnut Finds a Food Bowl

One day Groundnut sought us out in the tea plots. His face shone with happiness, and his whole pate glistened from a recent shave. He had found a brimming food bowl, he said: and indeed, he had brought us presents—three fat white cabbages and a bottle of vegetable oil. He did not offer to help us work but stood between the rows praising his own alertness and acumen.

"The bird makes his nest by going and coming," he said, "and by keeping his eyes open."

A small distance from our village, he told us, partway to Mud Bridge and not far from Seeing the Horse Village, there stood a temple, Restful Thoughts, that even after the war had served the yellows, but it had gone sour, and they had abandoned it. Geomancers said that the establishment of a new graveyard to the west of Mud Bridge had disturbed the local dragon; this had changed the wind-water of the temple, so its idols were impotent. Also, a slaveowner's son had hanged himself from its rafters. Its images were badly flaked, dust mantled the gods, spiders were doing good business. White riffraff slept there and moved on. Young white lovers sometimes crawled in behind the statue of Buddha to wrestle a few minutes. Otherwise abandoned, proprietorless. Groundnut had observed that the roof was sound; the idols, though degenerating, had been well made; a sweet-water spring was nearby; pretty birds were plentiful; and the view from the gate was splendid.

In short, Groundnut had carefully focused his eyes on a good living, a beautiful swindle, and a humane service. Why not become a priest?

A priest of what? A priest of Everything.

"These hogs around here," he said, "are starved for conjuring. I had a white tea tenant come in (they *flocked* to me as soon as they heard a priest had come)—said he'd been riding his cart along a sunken road, and a chinaware washpot jumped right off the tea field beside the road onto the wagon behind him. The lid rattled at him as if trying to say something. Frightened him—but his wife wanted to use the basin. Asks me: Should he let her?"

And so Groundnut would bring comfort to those with fears, would barter counsel for eatables. He would preside over thieves. He would manage crude justice, as between white and white, through omens, oracular pronouncements, and conjurations. He would be a politician, a mumbler of wisdom, a boss, an intriguer, a receiver of stolen goods, an idealist. He would be a spiritual juggler, too, keeping earnest good faith spinning in the air along with tact, kindness, understanding. All this, of course, as Rock and I understood without being told, would not entail betraying his basic craft—of cheater, beggar. He would leave teaching to us; as for him, he would play on ignorance.

How could we be disgusted with Groundnut for being himself?

There came a day when Rock and I could bend our backs no more, and by way of easing them we went to visit Restful Thoughts Temple and its self-appointed priest.

The walled grounds were spacious, the buildings shimmered in the sunlight with an unassailable grace of proportion—of perfect curves resting on slender columns, roofs of heavy tile seeming to float on misty air. Within, an atmosphere of gloom, hopelessness, benign faces crumbling, birds nesting on beams.

Up behind the main altar in the first building rose a once gilded Buddha, his fat pocked with faults, so one could see he was made of humble earth bound with swingling tow; his set grin was flaky, one eye had fallen out. Sitting in an orderly row beside the Buddha were nine figures of elderly men, once richly dressed, in dusty-elegant tatters now, their benevolent expressions rendered sinister and hypocritical by the cracking and spalling of their painted clay flesh; one of them was patting an earthen dog. In the second building three female idols stood, each with an altar crowded with dust-caked vases, candlesticks, and incense burners, relics of long-dead hopes. The figure in the center held an ancient infant, fissured and chinked, in her arms; the two on the sides, seated on huge lotus leaves of corrupt gold, had many arms, and they held in their many hands net bags of many hundreds of artificial eyes, offered in years long past by yellows who had pleaded to be cured of in-closing darknesses. In the wings once malignant-looking divinities stood robbed of most of their evil by the fearless chippings of neglect, yet perhaps the more horrible in being, in their ruined state, facetiously stern and cruel.

A sort of suppressed terror hung about us in these chambers, yet Groundnut bounced beside us, in grotesquely shabby crimson robes, winking and grinning, happy as he had used to be when he cooped his rice-robbing pigeons in Dowager's gate yard. While we moved about, a few miserable whites, suffering over this or that, and having heard that the temple was alive again, drifted into the buildings; they kowtowed before the figures, muttered prayers, and left humble offerings, some of which, edible, Groundnut snatched away from the altars and popped into a basket that he carried before the worshippers had even turned their backs.

He was not at all ashamed, because, as he whispered to us, "I have something of great value to give these poor pigs: a path to resignation. I've taken a hint from the yellows—let these miserable people be interested in the only thing that can give them hope, which is death. Since they haven't kept track of their dead ancestors, let them worship dead-looking idols: I don't plan to renovate here. Do you see? The trick is to get their hopes up over their *next* life. If a pig has no hope of happiness in this world, he can find comfort in thoughts about another; he can hope that maybe he'll come back to this one another time as a more fortunate being. If he's really lucky he may come back as a yellow! I'm *helping* these ignorant people, and I mean to keep them ignorant if

I can. You want to teach them, White Lotus, but I know that my
power depends on mystery, darkness; I want them ignorant. Eyes
on death! Look, this is not at all selfish of me. It helps them. They
find strength by denying any meaning or importance to the 'facts'
of their daily lives. The things they can see and touch and smell—
their tea bushes, their hard sleeping platforms, their compost
heaps—these are illusions, just shadows of dreams; the only
substance lies in the spirit. Observable facts and truth have
nothing to do with each other; 'truth' is an inner matter. You
see, Rock? This eliminates despair, which comes from the unbearable realities we see around us."

Into the offering basket went a reality in the form of a good-
sized turnip. Catching the offerer's eye, Groundnut nodded curtly
to him. The worshipper, a young white farmer, fell to his knees
and kowtowed to the priest of Everything, who was giving
him surcease from the pain of facing life.

❰ Wisdom and Setting Hens

After this I could not wait to start my school. Once late
at night I was wakened by an owl. I quickly turned over three times
on our platform.

Rock, rousing, sleepily asked, "Is anything the matter?"

"I'm making a wish: I heard an owl."

"Ayah. What now?"

"That I can prove Groundnut wrong. I mean, through my
school."

"It's just a rice bowl for him. Stop fretting. Go to sleep."

When we had finished planting our food crops I called on
Manager Wu and asked permission to take pupils, and though
he frowned and huffed, he finally said I might go ahead, providing
I would confine my tutelage strictly to the *Tri-Metrical Classic*,
that I would rely solely on rote memorization, and that I would
not strain the children's minds by teaching them to read and
write. The following day he procured for me a single withered
copy of the *Tri-Metrical* from the schoolteacher in the upper hand,
and that evening I posted on the circular wall by the village well
a notice, which read, *School will begin on the tenth day of the
fourth month. It will be at Rock Liu's house.*

Since no one in the village could read, except Manager Wu,

Rich Shen, and Suspicious Chang, and those three did not stroll in the open at evening time, the villagers had to ask me, when Rock and I went walking, what the notice said. They knew that I had put it there; a woman had seen me do it. I read it to them. There were some snickers; no other response, no questions.

I had some days to wait. What if no children at all came to my school? Manager Wu's disapproval and indifference! Those hand-covered giggles and snorts when I read my notice to the villagers!

The morning of fourth tenth came. Rock was away early to the tea bushes, and I dressed myself in Provisioner Lung's gown, and put some morning-glory blossoms in my hair, and waited. How long! The sun climbed. I kept thinking that even if pupils came, I would have spawned a folly. The ponderous ignorance of these people—and the incredible task of learning. Had it been Peace's "brother" Smart or the Old Uncle at Hua's who had told me the number of characters in the great K'ang Hsi dictionary? More than forty-four thousand! Unthinkable! Impossible even to make a start!

Then within a few moments, as if they had hung back all together, eight fathers entered our courtyard with eleven children—seven boys and four girls.

I bowed to the men and quoted Confucius to them: "Beyond a small material gift I need nothing; and even the one who gives no gift I shall teach."

Some haggling followed—between the men, who ignored me altogether—and finally one of them, named Horse Hsing, said that for each child they would give me five catties of rice a month.

I followed the forms—said I was unworthy. They insisted, unable, however, to hide their inner doubts and unspoken parsimonious regrets at having offered so much—though what they had proposed was, in truth, not much.

Now I was in for a shock. Having set me up as a teacher, the men concluded at once that I knew everything. A man named Nimble-Hands Chao said, "Horse Hsing and I have been having a disagreement, teacher. You see, it is time to set hens. Horse says, if you want pullets, then a woman must carry the eggs to the nest in the lap of her gown, but if you want cocks, carry them in a man's hat. I say, set the hen in the morning for roosters, and in the afternoon for pullets. Which is right?"

I said, "Excuse me, neither one."

"Then what's the way?" Nimble-Hands asked.

"There is no way. No matter what you do, you will, in the long run, get just as many cocks as pullets. Not in one setting, mind you. But if you keep track of the next one thousand eggs you set, you'll see that I am right. Half hens, half cocks. More or less. Within a few."

The men were exceedingly displeased with this answer, and they glowered and shook their heads and grumbled, so that I was afraid they might withdraw their scholars forthwith.

Nimble-Hands said, "Horse Hsing thinks he knows all about chickens. He says that if you go to the roosts at exactly midnight, you will hear the chickens sneeze. He says that in the core provinces they tell time this way, by chickens' sneezing."

"Untrue," I said, as forcibly as I could; then I thought of Groundnut's shrewd synthesis, for the consumption of these ignorant whites, of yellow doctrines: that there was no link between observable facts and "truth."

Apart from Nimble-Hands, who enjoyed Horse's discomfiture, the men appeared to be angrier than ever at me.

Horse Hsing cleared his throat and said, "What is the best way to keep the hawks from stealing your chickens?"

I realized from the way the men thrust their chins forward that they were by now rather doubtful about this teacher's wisdom, and that I might indeed lose my school on its founding day if I did not watch my words. In despair, with a feeling of being dragged down, I said, "A way my old yellow master Hua used to do it—it worked well for him—was by threading eggshells, that chicks have just been hatched from, onto a piece of straw. Then hang the straw in the chimney. That worked very well for my master."

At this the men sighed, as if greatly relieved about me, and nodded their heads with satisfaction. They pushed their children toward me. Horse Hsing slapped his son across the crown and said, "Do as your teacher tells you, you little thief."

(A Wedge

School lasted only through the morning, and in the afternoon I joined Rock in what he called the lower crop field. I told him about my exchange with the fathers.

"You did the right thing. With these stubborn hogs around here, you have to give way a little."

"You never used to give way, Rock. Why do you say that now?"

"Life here isn't easy. We can see that already. I can see it, can't you? Everything seems to come at once. While you work at our 'second,' I have to work alone on the tea bushes, or here in the crop fields. The millet already needs hoeing, so do the bean rows. The melons are coming up. The first flush of tea leaves is beginning, and before long we'll have to pick—you'll have to close the school while we pick—and then we'll need help from someone with experience for the withering and rolling and fermenting and firing, or else the crop will be worthless. You know some of the classics, but you don't know tea—and you're not a great scholar of chickens, either, for that matter."

"Is not knowing tea a reason for giving way to worse ignorance?"

"We have to eat. That comes first."

"Groundnut eats. He's going to be as fat as Buddha."

Now I saw some of Rock's old quarrelsome side smoldering behind the face of the "old solid." "Groundnut is a louse. Lice live on others' blood. We can't live that way. Ai! We came here, don't forget, because of our anger at what the yellow people have done all these years to us whites. We thought this would be a place where we could do something as whites and for whites. I couldn't go around with that offering basket snatching the food those poor fools lay on the altars."

"Why didn't you say some of that to Groundnut?"

"He's a white man. I haven't the time of day to be against him. I'm against Provisioner Lung."

"If you want to eat, you'd better not be against Provisioner Lung."

"I *am* against him. From dawn till dark, every day. He is the biggest louse, and he's a *yellow* louse. Some of these villagers say, 'Stay away from the yellows. The village is divided into two hands. Just stay down here where we belong and there won't be any trouble.' But we can't stay away from the yellows, because they're in every corner of our lives. Provisioner Lung squeezes our stomachs every day. I intend to fight him all the way."

"Can you live off him and fight him, too?"

"I can try."

"But how?"

"Look, I'll fight him by driving a wedge in him. There's a crack in him—right in the best in him, and that's where I'll split him. Between the practical good and the spiritual good. Between the Confucian and the Buddhist in him. Remember about the disciple asking the Teacher what he would do first, if made Emperor? And his reply was, 'Straighten out names,' and when they said that that was silly, he answered that good government came when the ruler was ruler, the magistrate magistrate, and when the father was father and son son; when things were really what they were called. Dominance is for the ruler, husband, father, elder brother; submission for the subject, wife, son, younger brother. These slantheads have added four more 'names,' no matter the war and the Mercy Errand; master and slave, yellow and white. To keep everything in order, rely on the essential goodness of men and the benign example of those who are dominant. So all the practical-good side cares about, really, is man in this life, and his duties to other men—'While respecting matters of the spirit, keep aloof from them.' But on the other side, the spirit is everything: We are born to pain, which is caused by craving—of the passions, for existence, even for nonexistence; and the only way to end pain is to end craving, so as to go quite outside practical daily life into a spiritual state of utmost peace. One must hurt no living creature, forgive enemies, be friendly to every being. But you cannot live by both goodnesses. You cannot, in *this* world, dominate as ruler or master and not hurt others. You cannot consider pain a noble truth and be predominantly benign. You see, Provisioner Lung, on his decent side—on his lark-training and sweet-manners side—tries to go both ways: Man dominates singing bird; rich yellow is humbly kind to starving whites. And then switch those pairs! I tell you, White Lotus, I'll split him on his good side. His evil side is solid, I can't crack that. But his goodness, instead of being his strength, is his weakness. I'll pry him wide open from that side."

"What about your good side, Rock?"

"When I'm my own man it will be time enough to be good."

⟨ Bare-Stick Takes a Canter

On fifth fifth, the day of the Summer Festival, we hung mugwort and willow twigs over the doorway and pasted red papers shaped like gourds on the walls, and, as the first flush of tea leaves was ready for picking, Rock said he thought it would do no harm to walk out to Groundnut's temple and perform a kowtow or two before the idols.

I put a fragrant sprig of mugwort in my hair and wrote the character for "tiger" on a circlet of red paper and pinned it to my gown—to bring me strength on the Summer Festival day—and off we went in a holiday mood.

A large crowd of whites swarmed around outside the temple, and the air of easy sociability raised our spirits. Everyone seemed to know everyone else; strangers spoke to us as if we were friends.

Near the gate the braggart Bare-Stick was talking with his donkey voice.

We entered the temple, and we saw Groundnut, in his filthy red robe, upbraiding a middle-aged tea tenant for spitting on the temple floor near one of the altars. "The only place to spit is under the big bronze bell," Groundnut was crying, with a show of anger. "If you spit anywhere but under the bell, your teeth will all loosen. Truly. Be careful."

Groundnut was nearly delirious over this rush of business. His basket brimmed, and he danced about snatching offerings from altars as the outstretched hands of ignorant worshippers were still poised over their gifts to the gods.

Rock made him an ironic obeisance, and Groundnut received it straight-faced, as something due him.

We went through perfunctory motions of worshipping certain idols. Groundnut had made the poor tenants believe (and perhaps Rock and I half believed it) that two of the shabby gentlemen near the Buddha were "tea spirits"; we bowed to them, and Rock also wanted to pay respects to the fertility goddess in the second building. As we kowtowed I kept thinking that there was a wide gap between Rock's mood of revenge, his determination to bring down Provisioner Lung, on the one hand, and the air, on the other hand, of passive submission that even Rock wore in this depressing temple. These sweet and gullible whites! How they seemed to yearn for the false peace that Groundnut offered them —of resignation. If they could but achieve it, then shiftlessness, squalid human relationships, indulgence of every sensual pull, laziness as a virtue, crime as a substitute for effort—everything would fall into its comfortable place, and one could give up trying.

That this was precisely what the yellows wanted seemed to occur to no one; if Groundnut understood it, he did not care.

Now Rock paid tribute to Groundnut's new-found power.

"I want to get someone to help me treat the tea leaves after we pick them," Rock said to him. "Look around and talk around today, Groundnut, and find me someone."

"I already know your man," Groundnut said. "The noisy one. Bare-Stick."

"You turtle! That bullfrog? What do you take me for?"

"Wait, I know him," Groundnut said. "He is up here all the time. Underneath all that shouting he keeps a little self that isn't so bad—don't forget, it's the feathers on a fowl that make it big. Let me tell you a story I've heard. Bare-Stick's father, called Cudgel, was a slave to Old Cheng, whose former land you work, you know, and they say that he, Cudgel, was one of the best white men in the whole Box River valley. He was in charge of treating the tea crop after the picking, for the entire Cheng plantation, and they say he was no toady to the yellow man: he was expert, and he was stouthearted. And he had one pride, his son, this Bare-Stick. He taught the boy everything he knew, including how to be both white and manly. But it seems that an evil spirit began to seek out the father—it would flutter at the window, would blow out the lamp, and once it slapped Cudgel's face. One evening, at dusk, this fine man and his little boy were walking along the road back to the plantation from Long Sands, on the river, where they had gone on a market day, and the spirit appeared in the form of a cow with a single horn standing out from the middle of its forehead. Cudgel said, 'What do you want of me?' The cow said, 'I want your boy-child.' Cudgel said, 'You can have my girls, I have three girls, you can have all three. This is my only son.' The cow tossed its crooked horn and said, 'No. The boy.' Cudgel groaned and asked, 'But why?' The cow said, 'I am the Spirit of the Fermentation of Tea Leaves. I have worked for you at the plantation for many years. Now I want your son to work for me.' The father bellowed, 'NO!' and summoning all his courage and strength, he grasped the cow by the one horn and *lifted it off the ground*, and the spirit cried out in pain that it would not take Bare-Stick altogether, it would only ferment the boy a bit. The father then dropped the cow, which vanished, and the good man died within a week. They say Bare-Stick began talking loud from that night onward."

"Do you believe that story?" Rock asked.

"I believe that Bare-Stick talks loud," Groundnut said with a half smile. "Anyhow, he knows all about withering, fermenting, and so on—learned it from his father, or from that one-horn cow. Get on his right side, he'll rescue your crop for you."

Outside the temple Bare-Stick was still blatherskiting at the center of a rowdy circle. We joined in. Bare-Stick was saying, "I don't mind sucking dry yellow tits, if it gets you what you want. Ayah, if you flatter the lids, in a certain way, you can go a lot farther than they ever dream a hog will get. I just make it a joke. I act like a powder-nose—a clown. And I usually get what I'm after. I don't care how much the lid I'm sucking insults me so long as he gives. If he lets me stay near him and keep talking, I'll find his sweet side. I say 'master' and 'venerable' and 'teacher' and 'old uncle'—whatever he wants—pretty soon I'm cracking his walnuts! It's easy!"

Rock listened to all this and much more in silence. He seemed to me to be taking Bare-Stick's measurements.

There were pretty girls in the circle, and the sunlight was like wine. The men and girls were approaching each other and withdrawing—playing the endless warm-weather game of trying to touch and tease. I felt the lazy warmth spreading in me, too, and I saw that big Bare-Stick's eyes were like clumsy bumblebees droning from one peony to another on a hunt for any honey-pollen at all, even if left over from another. He looked at me. I stared back boldly, on the theory that this might be a help to Rock, and deep in the braggart's eyes I thought I did see a small boy much impressed by a cow with a single horn.

Along the road toward the crowd of whites outside the temple came three men riding fat ponies. Their arrival provoked hasty whispers, then an unnatural silence.

The three men were wearing papier-mâché masks, representing ancient warriors—faces of such exaggerated ferocity as to break through beyond being comical into the dark unreality of folk-tale fear.

I heard a young man near me mutter, with a kind of gasp, that the men were members of The Hall out by day!

The men drew up their horses at the edge of the crowd of whites, and we heard one speak in strange, lugubrious tones, muffled by his mask. "What are you pigs doing here?"

There was a long, long silence. Several men and girls in our circle looked at Bare-Stick: *he* knew how to suck hard yellow tits!

At last, indeed, his was the voice that answered. In the hush of the crowd it crackled louder, perhaps, than he had intended. "Been worshipping."

The yellow man—the hands on the reins were yellow—who had spoken from behind the mask wheeled his round little horse suddenly toward Bare-Stick, and we heard the cavernous tones again. "Worshipping here in the road?"

Bare-Stick alone of all the crowd laughed. "That's a sharp one, Venerable."

"Answer me!" the hollow voice commanded. "What are you doing here in the road?"

"Talking. Just talking awhile, old uncle."

The masked man spurred his pony straight into the crowd, toward Bare-Stick, and the other two followed.

"You pigs know that you are not to gather in crowds. After worship you go home, or there'll be no worship. And you, talker! You'll canter home ahead of us and show these other hogs and sows how to get there."

Bare-Stick's face was as white and waxy as a wave-worn seashell. He turned and headed out from the crowd to the middle of the roadway toward our village. The three ponies followed him. Bare-Stick broke into a run, and the ponies started stiff-leggedly to trot right on his heels. Soon Bare-Stick began—undoubtedly at the urging of that awful voice—to run with uneven, rocking steps, imitating as well as he could a four-legged creature's canter.

⟦ Advice from Bare-Stick

Some of the sunset idlers were leaning on the semicircular wall by the well, and some of them squatted on their hams.

Bare-Stick was louder than ever. Far from having been abashed by his absurd trot home in front of the ponies of the riders of The Hall, he was glorying in it—in his having been singled out, in his having been the only man in the crowd at the temple with horse hooves, as he put it; he meant, the only one who had dared speak to the masked yellows.

Then Rock, in his style of a mild-tongued "old solid," asked, as if really interested, "Were you winded?"

At once Bare-Stick stood straight, making himself as tall as he could, and he said in a put-upon tone, "How 'winded'?"

"I mean when you reached the village."

"Why should I be winded?"

"It was a long run." Rock's tone was ambiguous: admiring, yet also seeming to leave something unsaid, as better left that way.

Bare-Stick gave himself away—moved a step closer to Rock. "Why are you interested in whether I was winded?"

Rock drew in the lure. He shrugged. "I was just wondering."

"I have good lungs."

"So I hear." Rock's manner—his bowed head, mild voice, modest eyes—suggested the innocent reading of this answer: that Rock had heard from a villager of Bare-Stick's prowess as a runner. But Bare-Stick caught without a doubt the possibility of another construction: that Rock's ears told him that Bare-Stick used his strong lungs for too much talking.

"I didn't hear you talking back to those pricks from The Hall," Bare-Stick said.

"No. And I walked home. And wasn't winded."

"What's all this about being winded?"

"I just asked a friendly question."

"Friendly? Whose friend do you think you are?"

"But you haven't told me whether you were winded."

"What business is it of yours?"

"You were making this trot everybody's business."

"It's not yours, button-kisser."

"I was wondering, though: Were you winded?"

Several of the men who had been crouching stood up. No one laughed, but I could see devils dancing in many of the watching eyes.

Rock had reached the trigger in Bare-Stick, who now was inching by tight little steps toward his provoker. "Suppose I was! What is it to you?"

Now Rock stretched his words out in a countryman's drawl. "It seemed to me—I just wondered—maybe you could tell me— wouldn't a man running on horse's hooves—I mean, hooves are heavy—wouldn't a man's legs feel heavy?—get winded?—long trot like that? I mean, it seems reasonable."

Upon the emergence of the naked mockery, embarrassed laughter broke out around us. Bewildered, Bare-Stick whirled away from Rock and faced the laughers. But further confusion! Their laughter was not cruel; their faces were now innocent; they wanted no particular resolution of the duel between the two men.

After a moment's hesitation, Bare-Stick himself broke into guffaws, which were as powerful as they were insincere.

The storm had passed. Bare-Stick seemed irresolute at first, then soon he became positively pleasant to Rock and me, behaving as if he owed Rock money.

Taking advantage of this turn, Rock said that he and I were ignorant about tea, and that we had heard that Bare-Stick had learned the most expert tea-treating from his father. Would he help us? Just with this first crop?

Bare-Stick blustered. Had a tenancy of his own. Wife pregnant. Couldn't go around withering and fermenting for anyone and everyone.

"Five per cent of the crop?"

"Ayah, Rock," Bare-Stick said, suddenly in the best of humors, "you're a turtle and a son of a turtle."

As things turned out, Bare-Stick could not do enough for us. Rock had apparently reached his innermost soft spot, and I allowed Bare-Stick to have goggle eyes for my body. He inspected our tenancy, showed us exactly how to crop the bushes. Promised to loan us his withering tats. Said he would let us use his ovens for the final firing, then Rock could build our own later.

One evening Bare-Stick brought us a wonk puppy, a squirming ball of orange fur, and he said our compound could not be a real home until it had a watchdog. To prevent the wonk from becoming a wanderer, he said, we should cut off the tip of his tail and bury it just outside the door to the house.

We did this. Was it to please Bare-Stick, or because we were beginning to think we could not survive without following the absurd rules of folklore? This question depressed me, but the puppy—by night panting and yipping at the loss of its mother and litter mates, but by day racing about gnawing at every worthless and valuable object, playing with shadows and blown dust—made me, and my pupils, too, laugh with a rippling sound that expressed, better than words could, our pathetic eagerness to accept the rotten bargain of our lives.

Up until then, I had been excited by my school but was far from being made happy by it. The children had no interest in learning, and I felt the heavy drag of their resistance to the masters and to me. What could "piety" and "correct knowledge" and "the proprieties" mean to these hungry scurfy urchins? Why, for that matter, should earnestness and yearning impress them?

I was, besides, physically tired all the while, and sometimes ill-tempered. It was clear that even with the school as a "second" we were not going to have much to eat, and it was Bare-Stick who —having warned Rock that our tenancy, though more than we could properly till, was too small, too small—introduced me to some supplementary labors, working at hire for *other* whites' 'seconds,' making bean curds and noodles, spinning, sorting miserable pig bristles by color, length, and thickness. My eyes watered, my fingers were like twigs.

One evening Rock, Bare-Stick, and I were in our "kitchen"— one end of our single-space hut.

"You haven't enough," Bare-Stick said. "This tenancy of yours is a flea-bitten wonk. It's the same one Provisioner Lung strapped on Simple Hsi's back—Simple was starved out in two years. Moved up the valley."

"Is it the poor soil—or is it just too small?"

"Some people say it's the wind-water. Others say Simple didn't know how to do things. You have to wait till you're angry to plant peppers; if you're planting large vegetables, plant in a squatting position and walk away without looking back. Simple ignored things like that. They say Simple didn't do anything right—but I think it was the tenancy. Before Simple Hsi it was Hook Wang. Before Hook, another man who even had a son to help him, I forget his name. Two or three years, each one. It's a wonk. You ought to go to Provisioner Lung and have him change it."

"What's Provisioner Lung's weak spot?"

"He doesn't have one. We've all been looking for one with both eyes open."

"I'm going to find one."

"Don't try to kill him. If you kill a lizard you'll grow ragged."

"I'm ragged already."

Bare-Stick began to huff. "Don't try to kill him, Rock. Don't try to be a boar. We don't need a big-prick boar of a race hero around here. I mean it, Rock. You'd spoil life for every mourner in this valley." ("Mourner" meant white person—white was the yellows' color of mourning.)

"I don't mean to kill him."

"What do you mean to do?"

"I don't know. Just look for a weak spot, I guess."

"All right. Get him to change this wonk of a tenancy. But don't meddle with the rest of us. Cut your own mud."

I was worried about Rock, and I had more and more strongly
the feeling of being dragged down, down. Rock was thin, and
he was playing the "old-solid" part with too much conviction; gone
was the arrogant, quarrelsome, care-nothing air that covered
caring too much. It seemed to me that his fire was banked and
burning low. I could not tell what he was thinking, and he took
my body infrequently and with a passion that seemed as weary
as my poor frame. Was he to become a kind of automatic man,
propelled through life by superstitions—*when planting a tree,
name it for a tall person, and it will grow large*—and was I to be
a pig-bristle sorter the rest of my days?

Yet how I laughed when the puppy wonk came wriggling to me!

❲ Provisioner Lung's Counter-Probe

Once again Provisioner Lung was all charm and form;
it was as if we had never haggled like vulgar chaffers over percentages. He wanted us, as honored guests, to inspect his beautiful
set of the game called "house sparrow"—its ivory-faced tiles
engraved with flowers, cranes, circlets, and characters, the hard
tusk incised as if by delicate brush strokes. In a mumbling voice
I read on certain tiles the colors of the dragons and the compass
points of the winds, and Provisioner Lung complimented me on
my culture as effusively as if I were a laureate of the Imperial
examinations.

"I understand that you have a tasteful school. *Tri-Metrical
Classic*. Most impressive for a white village."

Nor did Provisioner Lung's compliments end there. He praised
Rock for the soundness and modesty of the house he had built.
Humbleness was a quality he admired. " 'He who walks with his
head too high slips on the mudbank underfoot.' "

At this Rock showed a moment's spark. "Meekness," he said, "did
not prevent me from slipping more than once when we were
cutting the mud to build it."

Provisioner Lung laughed heartily. Humor was another quality
he cherished. Especially earthy humor. Ha-ha-ha! Earthy—mud:
Did we catch his intention? Ha-ha-ha!

As the merchant's withered concubine, Fragrant Dew, passed
bowls and poured steaming jasmine-flavored tea, we traded laughs.

Ai, how pleasant we were! Yet I knew that hatred for this man was in Rock's bowels; Rock yearned to find his weakness.

"I hear," Provisioner Lung said, "that you have a frisky house pet."

So! Now his prying compliments were intruding within our courtyard gates. Provisioner Lung must have had contracts with five hundred tenants in the villages all about, yet he knew—and by his pretty volleys he was letting us know that he knew—every detail of our lives.

And next, a discreet rap on our knuckles: Did we have any idea how much a full-grown dog would eat?

A long silence after that. How could we answer such a question? The tea was too hot to sip. But Provisioner Lung did not let his chance pass. "Speaking of eating," he said, "I know why you have come to see me. At least, I can guess why you have come. And I am full of admiration for you, Rock Liu, for coming to me—for not waiting until it was too late. You're a superior hog, young man. You're a hard worker. I saw when you first came to me that you might not be like most of the pigs hereabouts. You want to improve yourself—and considering that you two have a school, it seems you want to improve your fellow pigs, too." The repetition of the insulting term was all that we needed to grasp the warning undertow that was now flowing beneath the smooth surface of Provisioner Lung's praise. "It is a pleasure at last to see some enterprise from clients of mine. Listen: The only way to deal with the shiftless pigs that stayed on in this valley after the war is by debt-slavery. Listless men without a grain of ambition in them have to be kept under pressure, *for their own sakes*. I doubt if you will accomplish much with your school, T'ai-t'ai"—what a load of irony that honorific bore when he tossed it at me!—"because these pigs have atrophied brains. They couldn't learn anything even if they wanted to. But I'll say one thing—perhaps you've observed it: These white pigs, who aren't nearly so clever as you are, Rock Liu, have one amazing talent. It's a talent for being happy in the middle of the most sordid surroundings. Laughter in squalor! It is wonderful! They must be children of nature—born of crickets and dung beetles!"

Now Provisioner Lung sipped his tea, with the ferocious slurping sound the yellows affected. The expression on his face, as he set down his tea bowl, was serene and gracious.

"By the way," he said, "at your house, did you remember to leave a little hole in the paper window? You ought to have a little hole in the window until the first of the tenth month—that's when ghosts and spirits are shut away for the winter by Ch'eng Huang, you know, the wall god. When you built your house, you may have trapped someone's malign spirit inside, and if it couldn't get out by that little hole, it might cause you all sorts of trouble. The reason I'm saying this to you is that I believe this is what happened to the hog named Simple Hsi, who had your tenancy before you. He only lasted a year and ten months. I think a ghost soured him. It is easy to take this precaution. All you do is to wet the end of your finger and apply it to the paper window from the inside, the unshellacked side. A tiny hole the size of your index finger is all you need."

"Might it be," Rock asked, "that Simple Hsi failed on the tenancy because the tenancy can't support a family? The upper tea plot—"

"—'has crabbed bushes! The lower-middle plot is sour-soiled!' " Behind the windowpane glasses Provisioner Lung's eyes were so gentle, so sympathetic, as Rock visibly started, hearing Bare-Stick's exact words! "If I am not mistaken, you have been listening to Bare-Stick Wang. Bare-Stick's father, Cudgel Wang, was one of the finest slaves in the valley, but this boy—something went wrong. They say—but that's a long tale. . . . In him there is a Law of Opposites. He goes around shouting. *Every white man for himself. Do not interfere in another man's life. Cut your own mud.* At the same time, in practice, this magpie meddles in everyone else's courtyard and neglects his own."

The accuracy of Provisioner Lung's shots simply dumfounded Rock, who had come to call on the supplier partly to ask for a larger tenancy but mainly, I thought, to probe for the Provisioner's vulnerability, whatever it might be. To the contrary, what was happening was precisely that Provisioner Lung was probing for Rock's undefended point. And perhaps he had even found it. Perhaps Rock's weakness was that he might allow himself to see his fellow whites as Provisioner Lung saw them, with such apparent accuracy—shiftless, double-visioned, dry-brained, foolishly laughing progeny of dung beetles—until, in the end, Rock might come to see himself as just like all the rest of them.

"But you," said the Provisioner to Rock, as if he had just read *my* mind, "may be different from these other pigs. It strikes me that you may be. You haven't come out and said so, but I assume that you want to ask for a bigger tenancy, and a more fertile one. I'm interested in you, Small Rock, and I have a proposal. Let's wait a short while and see—see whether you really are different. Let's wait until after your first cropping, at least, and let's see then what we'll say to each other."

⟪ A Study of All Things, One by One

My schoolchildren at their games made our dingy courtyard echo with delight. Some of the boys kicked a shuttlecock; others played a game of nimble fingers called "catch stones"; three girls whirled in a wild dance with interlocked legs, called "linking and framing."

I clapped my hands. Time for recitation!

It took a while, as for a coltish wind puff from the north to peter out, for the squeals and laughs to die down. Then I was seated behind my "desk"—a plank resting on two stacks of mud bricks— and the children were seated in rows on the ground before me. I was oppressed by a feeling of futility—where, among these eyes looking into mine, were the appetite, the urgency, the yearning I had felt so long ago under Smart's teachings in the soot-stained smithy? Here they squatted, sullen after the interruption of their play. Old Tiger, Little Fat (who was thin), Little Stupid (scholar's name!), Little Third, Little Root, Straight One, Little Maid (a sickly boy), and the girls, Big Phoenix, Persimmon, Little Duck, and Precious Necklace. They did not seem to want what I had in my heart and head to give them.

"All right," I said. "Little Root. Come forward."

I saw the flush of agony at being singled out spread with astonishing speed across the boy's face, but I was counting on him, for he was the brightest one, and in him, every so often, I had thought I had seen a flicker of desire, of ambition; and, yes, I was counting on him, not simply to recite well for his own sake, or as an example to the others, but also to raise my own dead-weight spirits that morning.

He stepped to the plank. I had the old book, with its page corners perfectly expressive of intellectual wilt, spread out before me. The boy's eyes evaded mine, and his hands twisted the ends of the dirty sash of his trousers. He stood for a reluctant moment facing me, then turned his back on me, tilted his face to the sky, took a deep breath, and began to howl, with great rapidity, and in a bawling tone, like that of a mule crying either in pain or in some sort of protest at his own endless muleness, all the wisdom he had memorized: " 'If men want their country well ruled, they should first bring order to their families. If they want to be in charge of their homes, they should mend their own deportment. To have good behavior, they should whet their consciences. To repair their consciences, they must be sincere. To gain in sincerity, they should gain in knowledge. To get knowledge requires a study of all things, one by one. . . .' " The high-pitched, unchanged boy-voice wailed out these great assumptions as if they were descriptions of aches and pains. Little Root's memory was sharp; his indifference was massive. I began to feel angry, perhaps with myself, and I ordered the boy to face me and started questioning him about the couplets.

We came to the line *kou pu chiao*. I asked Little Root to paraphrase it. He began speaking gibberish. Something about moonlit nights, robbers in the streets, a courtyard gate unbarred.

Then the key to the riddle came to me. The proper translation for *kou pu chiao* was: "if one is not learned," but the phrase was a homophone for something else a village urchin could more readily grasp: "if dogs don't bark." Then courtyards carelessly barred will be robbed! Little Root hadn't the faintest conception of the precepts that he had, with such harrowing diligence, recorded in his aural memory.

I found myself weeping. Little Root staggered backward, as if bodily affronted by my loss of control. He ran and sat down in his place, himself beginning to whimper.

Soon in command of myself, I made a decision which I suppose had been forming for some time. For days that classic line, "a study of all things, one by one," had been beating obsessively at the back door of my mind. I left my place behind my desk, and I went around to the children and sat cross-legged on the ground, and I gathered them close beside me. I told them that we would continue with the *Tri-Metrical,* which I dared not abandon, but that I was now also going to begin to teach them to read and write the names of the things around us. Paper and brushes and inkblocks the upper hand would not allow us to have, I said; dust and our forefingers would have to serve as writing materials. In fact—I spoke with all the gravity I could amass—*the yellows must never hear about this part of our schooling.*

In the few seconds it had taken me to say these things I had, I could see, stirred my miserable ragged scholars for the very first time. Conspiracy! There was a fire in Old Tiger's eye, Little Fat had stopped chewing his sleeve!

Within a week the dirty childish fingers flicking the courtyard dust had begun to trace, with a wild assurance, the shapes of names for *mud, millet, corn roots, manure, almanac, bedbug, pickled radish, fox.* . . .

⟦ Harvest of Defeatism

The first flush of tea leaves was more than ready for cropping, but we were obliged to wait for Bare-Stick to finish his own, so he could help us treat our picked leaves. One evening Manager Wu asked Rock when he planned to take in his harvest, and Rock flew into a rage. "You know that's an unlucky question! Are you trying to conjure me? Take your dirty owl eyes off me!"

Manager Wu shrugged and said, "Ayah, listen to that turtle-mothered hambone! You'd think no one in this valley had ever cropped a tea bush before."

All the same, Rock had a right, on the level of the paralyzing nescience all around us in the lower hand, to be angry, for he was reacting to an honored superstition, of which Manager Wu was assuredly aware: that a man should never pry into another man's crops.

At last, one night, Bare-Stick told us he would be ready to help us on the following days.

At dawn the next morning, Rock took me to Groundnut's temple, where we burned paper money and incense before the figure—one of those skin-cracked, tattered gentlemen sitting in a row—which Groundnut had quite arbitrarily designated as that of Shen Nung, god of agriculture. Rock traded with Groundnut a half catty of side meat for a string of firecrackers, which Rock took to the tea strips and set off there before we began picking, to drive away evil spirits.

As we started our work, each dragging along a large basket, pinching off only the delicate bright-green new leaves, I thought, with a feeling of deep melancholy, of another first picking, in another crop, with Moth, at Dirty Hua's, so long ago—the day she told me, framing her pouting face in the foliage between us, about the faraway mountain. Was I any better off now? Was I any more my own agent than then? Was there any mountain to run to from here? Could it be that the fight against the yellows for freedom was so far from won that it might indeed only be beginning? I remembered once having decided, "Only the powerful are free." I felt just now so weak!

Hooo! This was unrewarding work! What a small volume of leaves came, at last, from each bush!

"Who's that turtle lurking over there in Ox Yang's strip?" Rock asked me under his breath.

"He has a white beard," I said. "I can see the beard when he looks this way."

It did not take us long to figure it out: Provisioner Lung, spying on his own tenants.

This infuriated Rock. "That's one devil the firecrackers didn't drive away," he said between his teeth.

Provisioner Lung, apparently realizing that we had seen him, arose from a squatting position and came into our strip, cheerily waving his spectacles at us and murmuring good wishes and blessings on our crop.

When he bent over and closely inspected the bushes we had stripped, however, he frowned. "You're scanting a third of your crop," he said, shaking his head. "Come here. Watch me. Use the fingernails! Pinch. Pinch. Pinch. Like that, you see? Pinch. Every bit of the leaf."

"I was told to be careful not to take off too much. They said I'd crimp the buds of the next flush."

"Hai! The flush will come. Don't worry, Rock Lui, the flush will come. The point is, *this* crop is worth something."

"To whom?" Rock asked with a bitterness that was all the more poignant in being subdued, under control.

Provisioner Lung peered in Rock's basket and glumly shook his head but said nothing more and walked away along the tea rows.

All day Rock cropped tea in silence. I was low; I did not feel that I was exempt from his anger, which seemed to have spread out in all directions.

Late in the afternoon we returned to the village with the baskets of our crop loaded on the donkey cart that Provisioner Lung had furnished us.

Bare-Stick was waiting at our gate. When we unloaded our

harvest, he said, "Is that all? Have you cropped your whole tenancy? Is that all you could get?"

"That's every leaf," Rock said.

Bare-Stick said we would never make it on that sort of crop. "Ayah, the turtle!" he broke out in his loud braggart voice—and we understood well enough whom he meant to curse. "My own crop is thin again this time. Every flush, I think, this time I'm going to be able to crop more than enough! But what happens? The bushes shrink in front of my eyes! The bastard leaves get smaller and smaller!"

Bare-Stick had brought with him, rolled up under his arm, some coarse jute mats on which to spread the leaves for withering, and stakes to make frames on which to stretch the cloths. We worked until well after dark, by lantern light, setting up the tats in our courtyard and spreading the leaves out on them. Bare-Stick, aware of Rock's fuming, reacted to it, opportunistically, by flirting with me, and I was so heartily sick by then of Rock's wordless anger that I, with a feeling of reckless gaiety-in-despair, joked and played with Bare-Stick, leading him on and behaving as if Rock's silence were his total absence. My behavior did not improve matters, but Rock and I were too exhausted, when our work was finished and Bare-Stick had left, to fight with each other, and we lay down on our hard sleeping platform without eating and without speaking, and plunged into a sleep of bad dreams and groans.

The next day was sunny, and Bare-Stick came in midafternoon, and we took the leaves in baskets in our cart to his courtyard. This was our first sight of his home; it gave me a new chill of despair, a new feeling of living on the edge of quicksand, for it was every bit as barren, as mean, and as raw as our own.

We began to roll the leaves by hand on well-worn wooden rolling blocks, crushing the flesh of the leaves and freeing the pungent juices. Bare-Stick's wife, whom we had frequently seen at the well and at the temple, helped us. The braggart's wife was partly deaf, and she was obviously strong-minded and shrewd, though perhaps rather stupid. Broad-cheeked and broad-mouthed, she was ugly and at the same time fresh-looking, or restless. Her hips were too wide, she waddled; Bare-Stick had said she was pregnant, but that did not show.

Perhaps to punish me, Rock opened up to her, babbling senselessly about the past—about the "fun" of avoiding the campaign at the Yellow River, and the "thrills" of the Number Wheel riots. I had a feeling he was somehow mocking himself, in his utter discouragement.

The rolling took us several hours, and then Bare-Stick fired the leaves in his oven, and when we were finished—again, long after dark—Bare-Stick said we had a small crop, but well cured.

We carried it home in our cart, and we found Provisioner Lung waiting for us at our courtyard gate. Hai! He was not going to let us hide part of the tea before he took out his percentages! He looked in our baskets and shook his head in the same glum way as before, in the strip. When the weighing and dividing were done, he said, "I'm disappointed in you, Rock Liu. I thought you would do better for me than this."

"How could I have gotten more? Could I have *begged* the bushes to give more?"

Provisioner Lung said, "You asked me to furnish you with a larger tenancy. I can't do that on the basis of this showing. What I would be glad to do, Rock Liu, is to increase your credit. I will lend you one half of my share of this crop, which you can sell in the tea exchange, against an additional ten per cent of your food crop, plus an extra ten per cent of your next tea flush, some part of which I will make available on a similar loan. . . ." And so on and so on, far beyond the point where I could follow him, weaving a glistening spider's web of credits, loans, percentages, rebates, forfeits, advances, shares, penalties.

Later, when Provisioner Lung had left, Rock sat on the edge of our bed, and his tongue loosened; he talked to me for the first time in many days. It was as if a sluice had been opened, and a flood of defeatism poured out.

"Maybe we came to the wrong place, baby. This place is a real pig wallow. These hogs around here—*your* friend Bare-Stick!—they're rolling in stupidity. Bare-Stick! What does he know how to do, except to shout? Does he think the whole world is deaf, just because his wife is? Look closely at him: He has no courage. Can't think ahead. He knows tea inside out, but what has he made of himself? That courtyard of his! Hooo, baby, the white man out here has been held down so long he can't get up. I tell you, these hogs haven't a chance. They're just no good. Ah! Sometimes I think white is *evil*. We're in it with the rest of these imbecile pigs. We're no better than the rest of them, and we're right in the pen with them. We're just as spineless and stupid as they are, and we're never going to get out of the wallow. Ai, baby, the yellows are smarter than we are, that's the trouble. The white man hasn't a chance!"

What could I say, whose need it was, and inclination, too, to agree with him?

⟪ A Decree on a Scroll

On a dry-sky autumn day, some weeks later, one of my little scholars, Old Tiger, was reciting to me from the *Tri-Metrical*. Mechanically he sang out the lines. There was a sharp knocking of hardness on hardness, and I sent Little Root to the gate to see what it was. Old Tiger howled on. Little Root swung the gate open.

Before I could see what or who was outside, Little Root came running toward me, a hand at his mouth. He veered around the end of my plank desk, and as he hurtled toward me he cried out twice, "The Hall! The Hall!"

At that, all the other children arose from the dust and ran around the desk and threw themselves on me. Those who could not directly grasp me by the waist or legs reached through for a grip on my gown. They were whimpering and senselessly babbling. How often they must have been sent to bed with a threat of visitors from The Hall if they didn't behave!

And now three men were standing inside the gate. Two, in peasant gowns, wore ferocious warrior masks, and the third, in more elegant clothes, had on the mask of a wise Emperor of old times, with huge black brows and a long white beard. I saw that they had great old swords in their yellow hands.

They came across the courtyard. I did my best to silence the terrified children.

One of the peasant-warriors stood awkwardly before the desk, as if ready to recite, and asked me, "What do you teach these shoats?"

"I teach them humility, reverence, and gentleness."

"What texts?"

"We are struggling with the *Tri-Metrical*."

"What else? What others?"

"That's all, Venerable," I said. I hated myself for spending that honorific so cheaply, but I was very much afraid.

With a peremptory gesture the peasant-warrior before me com-

manded the others to conduct a search, and the children and I remained in breathless silence while the men did their thorough
work. I heard our locked chest broken open inside the house, and
the sounds of things being overturned and smashed.

While the men were combing the courtyard, I caught a glimpse
of the Emperor-face in profile, and I saw, under the beard of the
mask, another separate white beard, and a familiar one at that.
O-mi-t'o-fu! Provisioner Lung—and taking orders from a yellow
peasant! These visits, then, I deduced, were far from impromptu,
far from spontaneous. They were made, surely, at the command
of a dark organization which, cutting across the yellows' own
social structure, must keep even themselves in awe and dread!

The rooting about having been finished, the spokesmen stepped
again to the desk, and he said, "We will have an examination.
Who is your best pupil?"

Frantically I tried to think which of my pupils had not the
quickest mind but rather the toughest fiber, and I settled on the
thin urchin named Little Fat. I patted him on the head, and when
he looked at me, first in surprise at being designated brilliant, and
then in realizing fear, I said, with love, "Do your best, Little Fat."

He stepped around to the other side of the desk, chewing his
sleeve. The peasant-warrior said in a far louder voice than was
needed, "BEGIN!"

Little Fat turned his back on the terrifying specter, threw his
face up, and, with veins standing out on his forehead, his shaved
crown, his temples, and his neck, he cried out, as if summoning
distant help:

> "Man at birth is good;
> Men seem alike but differ . . ."

Little Fat had recited only three or four lines when the spokesman shouted, "Enough! Turn around."

The boy, his eyes like full cups of hot tea, turned slowly toward
the apparition.

The peasant-warrior roared, "Crouch down and write in the
dust with your finger 'mud brick.'"

I saw Little Fat shudder, as if indecision had momentarily
rattled his wits, then he said in a shouting voice, almost as loud
as the masked man's, "I don't know how to write, Venerable."

Oh, my Little Fat! You heard me call the man Venerable! How
proud I am of you!

"Crouch down and write the word 'pig.'"

"I can't write, Venerable. I tell you, I can't write! We study only the *Tri-Metrical* here! We play games and study the *Tri-Metrical*."

Little Fat was beginning to cry, for evidently he had reached the outer border of his courage; but the appearance on his face was of vexation. The visitor was precariously close to losing face. He turned, spoke quietly to the Emperor-Provisioner and the other peasant-warrior, and the three men left.

It took Rock and me the better part of two days, in times that we could ill spare from the imperatives of our lives, to clean up or repair the wanton breakage the men of The Hall had accomplished in their swift search—and we could not fix the chest, the front face of which was badly splintered; Rock would have to scavenge, perhaps for months, for a pair of cedar boards with which to remake that box.

On the third morning, while my children were again reciting, there came another knock at the gate. So solemn were the children's faces at the sound that I decided to go myself.

Manager Wu stood outside, holding in his hand an official scroll tightly wound onto a pair of wooden spools.

Following the forms, I invited him in for a cup of tea, but he was brusque, and even angry, and he said, "You broke your promise to me. You told me you would confine yourself to the *Tri-Metrical*. You have made the entire lower hand of this village eat loss." And with that he swung his right hand, as if with a magician's flourish, and the scroll licked out full length from one of the spools. It hung there, trembling slightly with Manager Wu's agitation, for me to read.

It was, quite simply, a decree from the district yamen, citing the authority of a law which predated the Seditionists' War by a decade, and which prohibited any education whatsoever for white children: to the effect that any schools that may have been established within the district for the purpose of teaching white children were hereby pronounced illegal, and were to be closed forthwith by the proper authorities.

At the foot of the decree were many chops and seals, in red, blue, and black inks, impressing upon the miserable document the many jealous authorities who hovered like hawks over our lives, all down the skyline to Manager Wu.

When I had read the document I simply turned away, leaving

the headman as bereft of the forms as he had me. The gate stood open. I returned to the children, who had, in the absence of my discipline, resumed their usual harsh crow song and cricket talk.

I took my place at my desk, and, not knowing or caring whether Manager Wu was still standing in the open gateway, I continued the recitation where it had broken off.

Then, when it was over, I told the children that the yellows were closing our school.

Ayah! My children were white children, indeed! Not a sign, not a sigh. No emotion whatsoever. Guarded, cautious, hooded eyes. No comment, no protest, no questions.

My own heart was in such pain that I was starved for some show of grief from them, but they gave me, as they would give every authority, nothing, nothing.

The girl Big Phoenix said, "Do you want us to go home now?"

"No," I said, "we'll finish out this morning's time. You may play now."

Out in the sunlight at the center of the courtyard, soon, the children began a game called "bow to the four directions." They formed a circle about Little Root, who was wearing, that day, funny striped cotton trousers. The circle began to turn. Little Root slowly turned in the opposite direction, bowing, nodding, shaking hands with himself. The children whirled around, faster and faster, and their shrill laughter was no less gay than on any other day. Little Root in his striped trousers sang out, in a voice as loud and doleful as that with which he had so many times recited to me the wisdom of the masters, a queer, queer song about a wedding, the depths of which I was sure they understood no better than they fathomed my biting my quivering lip:

"Bow! Bow! Bow to the four directions!
You men from the four directions, give the bride two gifts:
Two gifts and two gifts, they'll be gaudy.
The groom rides a fine horse, his hat is a new one.
Change the new hat! Wear a fur hat!
The fur one is fur, and the sky is gray.
The sky thunders, dogs bite the thief.
The pomegranate girl and the vegetable snake enter the bedroom.
Hair oil, laurel string,
Things in the bowl and things in the jug;
The fragrance is strong.

The girl moves one step, tap tap.
When she moves a second step, see her silk trousers with the
  design of the golden duck egg on them!
Blossoms lie in the stream and fall in the stream:
Who knows whether you have stolen anything from the room?
We know not, we don't know.
So give some money to buy air in your stomach!"

⟪ Careless

In the autumn weeks that followed Rock and I became
—in many ways—careless. We were so discouraged, so put down
by Provisioner Lung, so deeply disheartened by the indifference
to their own face and interest of our fellow whites in the lower
hand of the Village of Brass-Mouth Chang, and by their abject
helplessness, that we slipped into being heedless, inconsiderate,
rash, slovenly, imprudent, loose, listless, indiscreet—and, yes,
even singularly elastic, buoyant, and lighthearted in the most
bitter way. We did not actively desire our own and each other's
destructions; we simply did not mind what came along.
Rock was unfaithful to me. I let him be and went my own way.
It seemed that we had tacitly agreed to get the most we could for
the senses out of each moment. The verb of our lives: to take.
That was all.
Rock did not sneak. Neither did I. The bad faith was all right
out in the evening street; whoever lounged by the well could see
Rock make his approach, first to Ox Yang's unmarried daughter,
who was at sixteen a laughingstock on account of her promiscuity
—would trade her mouse, the women said, for a garlic bud, for a
broken comb, for a pin with a paste-pearl head. Rock blatantly
told me to run on home, he would be home later. I got a laugh
from the bystanders by asking Bare-Stick, in a low voice which his
deaf wife could not hear, to carry me home on his back—for, I
said, I was tired out from running home so many nights. Bare-
Stick the blusterer did not have the gall to escort me home then
and there, but as soon as he had safely seen Rock drift off with
Ox Yang's daughter, he came trotting around and knocked softly
(the shouter's muffled knock!) at our gate, and in no time, instead
of my being on Bare-Stick's back, I was on my own, ayah.
Rock aimed himself at more and more difficult marks, and I

soon guessed that he was climbing up a valley of thighs to those of Manager Wu's mix. I understood that this ultimate goal was not set because the headman's wife was partly yellow; it was because she perched alone at the social apex, for what *that* was worth, of the white part of the village; because she was a powerful personality; and because she was inaccessible and so maybe exciting: Manager Wu did not air her in the street, and he barred the gate of his courtyard. (A jar of cash was said to be buried somewhere in it, but I think that was a myth, spread perhaps by himself to hone the edge of his bargaining power.) The headman's wife was twenty years older than Rock, and if he ever got in a position to flirt with her, this fact would be his shame, or else his joke, and her temptation.

So, having in the course of time frittered my favors on various brave hogs of the village, Rough Ma, Talkative Chang, Horse Hsing, and others (but I drew the line at Hairlip Shen), I decided to go after Manager Wu—not, I swear, as a competitor with Rock, but for my own reasons. To erase, above all, or perhaps to avenge, the chagrin of standing limp at the gate when the angry headman had unrolled that vile scroll. Avenge, by giving idle pleasure? Yes, in the sense that he would not be able to condescend to me, but would beg, beg, beg for what I could let him have or not as I chose!

It would be easier for me to snare the headman than for Rock to gain access to his mix, and I must be careful only to see that my assignation with the husband did not prove to be the occasion for Rock's with the wife.

Before the next new moon the thing was done, on my side— and, if village gossip, which was always laced with malice, was to be credited, on his, too. For my part the business was all too easy and, like everything else in our lives, not worth doing. I visited Manager Wu on a pretext of requesting permission to reopen my school, and right under the half-yellow nose of his mix, dutifully pouring tea, I gave him vague signals as to possibilities.

He followed up the very next day with an errand to our courtyard to report an invented interview he said he had had with certain parties in the upper hand. Purely imaginary "negotiations" on the reopening were now undertaken, and these required numerous conferences between the headman and myself. (Of all the miserable doings of that hollow time, this shadow-acting about my lost scholars was probably the most disgusting.) One day Rock was away and thoroughly accounted for, and Manager Wu duly begged, and when the begging had gone on long enough to have been recognized by him for what it was, the thing was accomplished with little pleasure and no remorse, so far as I knew, for either party.

How or when Rock flew his wonderful kite for Manager Wu's wife, I did not know, or care to know.

All this was a product of our rope-end frustration. Rock and I knew that we had more joy of each other's body than of anyone else's; we were hopelessly careless. We had foul fights, which enlivened the dullest periods of all.

Often heart-free and fiercely gay, I also wept often, trying to figure out what was happening to me and to my Rock—ai, yes! I still thought of him as mine. Besides his philandering, Rock was spending much time gaming; he gathered with others at Hairlip Shen's to play a card game called "palm leaves" and a sort of dominoes, which, because the counters were made of horn, was called "pushing the cow." Groundnut had told me long since that Rock was not a true gambler, he must simply have wanted to pass the time, to lose money we did not have, and thus to ensure beyond question our utter penury.

Every day we cursed the yellows, and most feelingly on the days after we had been unfaithful to each other—until, finally, we had persuaded ourselves that the yellows' grip on us was not only responsible for every one of our personal failures but even excused them and demanded new and worse ones. Thus we became, on top of all else, complacent and self-pitying. This was even more demoralizing than the discouragement that, not long before, had led Rock to conclude that the white race was good for nothing. What of it? The yellows were to blame.

❨ Drinking the Forfeit Cup

What a school for priests is beggary! Groundnut was already a power in eleven villages, and at a new low point in our general lowness we went to see him, on the chance, I think, that with his help we might be able to bring to bear against Provisioner Lung some form of destructive magic. In an antechamber of the temple's main courtyard, Groundnut had devised a room for consultations, where everything was, as throughout the temple, pur-

posely shabby, except for a single piece, the center and focus of
the room: a fine wooden chair for himself, a kind of throne which
he must have hired or bullied skilled white artisans to make for
him, brilliant with designs of herons and pheasants against
backgrounds in crimsons, yellows, and blues more lurid than
even an Emperor would dare or care to use. There were, as well,
grouped around this throne, a half dozen birdcages, containing
siskins, canaries, and larks. Was it Groundnut's ambition to out-
lark Provisioner Lung? When Groundnut was seated in his high
chair, and we before him on a low and rotten bench, the effect
he gave off was of a startling grandeur of spirit. We knew him
through and through; we knew his sharp ways. Yet—perhaps
the utter vitiation of our own morale allowed us to be hypnotized
by his spread sleeves and his dream-dimmed eyes—he now gave a
powerful illusion of being wise, decent, and in a position to intervene with authorities. His birds sang his praises.

Rock spoke in a dispirited voice. "It's Provisioner Lung—the one
who furnishes us, you know. I feel as if he has me in a box, or,
let's say better, a real pigpen. I asked him to improve my tenancy,
and instead he 'improved' my credit. He's like a rodent that sucks
bird eggs. I've been trying to think of a way . . ."

"When you see a bad man," Groundnut said, "examine your own
heart."

I couldn't help coughing up a laugh at that. "You've learned
your words well," I sarcastically said to Groundnut.

He waved a hand as if warding off the painful thought I had
thrown like a dart at him. "You are unkind, White Lotus. You
have always been short on self-restraint. Without due self-
restraint, courtesy becomes oppressive, prudence degenerates into
timidity, valor into violence, and candor into rudeness."

Ayah, how deeply he had embedded himself, like a frog in a
mudbank to get through freezing weather, in the majesty of priesthood! He almost seemed willing to pretend that we had never
known what he was really like. "No," I said, "I am sincere. You
are so convincing that you have begun to believe yourself."

"Be quiet, White Lotus," Rock said. "Let me talk to the man. . . .
Listen, this lid spies on me when I'm picking my tea leaves. He
stands at my gate when I'm curing them to make sure I won't
hide a single leaf from him. He charges . . ."

"Rock! You are not yourself! Where is the 'old solid' you have
been? The higher type of man is calm and serene; the inferior

man is constantly agitated and worried. Now. This Provisioner Lung. Pity him if he is bad. All men are born good; he who loses his goodness and yet lives is lucky to escape. And remember, it is at least better to be niggardly than to be arrogant."

Groundnut spoke with a deep and apparently heartfelt sadness, as if he were carrying on his weary shoulders all the woes of all the whites in the eleven villages.

"Hai! It's all very well for you to talk about pity," Rock said. "You're getting as fat as any idol on the offerings up here. We have to think about eating."

"With coarse food to eat, and little of it, with water to drink, and with the bended arm as pillow, a man can still be happy. Compare, my friend: Compare the lower hand of any village in this valley with its upper hand."

"Do *they* pay you to say that kind of thing?"

But Groundnut could not be ruffled. He seemed truly to have imbibed the tranquility of the sages; there was something more than glibness sitting on the ornate throne before us. "Why do you have such a strong wish to overcome, to grapple? If a spirit of rivalry is anywhere unavoidable, it is at an archery contest. Yet even here the refined man courteously salutes his opponents before taking up his position, and again when, having lost, he returns to drink the forfeit cup."

Archery! "We assume," I could not resist saying, "that the white man always drinks the forfeit cup. Is that so?"

Groundnut ignored me. "Do not do anything rash," he said to Rock. "Think before you carry your anger into action, but do not paralyze yourself with thought. Chi Wen-tzu used to reflect three times before he acted; when told of this, the Master said: Twice would do. Look for the better side of Provisioner Lung. The nobler sort of man emphasizes the good qualities in others, and does not accentuate the bad."

Yes, Groundnut did seem to believe his own words—or the Masters', when, like the thief he was, he stole them and made them his own—and there was so much manifest human decency in these words that the rising anger I felt, and that I saw swelling the veins on Rock's face, was puzzling to me. But then Rock cleared away the puzzlement, and I was simply angry. "You're asking *us*, your old friends, Rock and White Lotus—you're asking *us* to suck the yellow tit."

"The nobler sort of man," Groundnut said with unchanged tone,

"is accommodating but not obsequious; the inferior sort is obsequious but not accommodating."

"But we can't accommodate! If we give in to the lids all along
the way, we die!"

"No, son. Make the best of life. Do not be blind to the good
things around you. It is only when the cold season comes that
most people know the pine and cypress to be evergreens. And,
at any rate, having heard the True Way in the morning, what does
it matter if one should come to die at night?"

"Ayah, ayah," Rock said, "how can *you* be on the yellows' side?
My old pigeon friend! Don't you remember Bad Hog?"

But now Groundnut had, as it were, lost touch with us. His voice
began to drone. "The nobler sort of man pays special attention to
nine points. He is anxious to see clearly, to hear distinctly, to be
kind in his looks, respectful in his demeanor, conscientious in his
speech, earnest in his affairs, careful to inquire when in doubt,
alert to consequences when angry, and mindful only of his duty
when offered an opportunity for gain."

Rock and I left the room, but not without a bow toward the
priest mumbling yellow-man's "truths."

(Dunned

Time runs fast when life is very good or very bad; when
it is bad enough, one is constantly on the move, as is a métayer's
thin hen scratching first the seedless dust, then its own mite-
infested feathers. So the end of the yellow year was on us before
we knew it. We had harvested a second flush, and though we had
succeeded in gathering and curing more than the first time, our
outlook had become, if possible, worse than ever.

A few days before the yellows' New Year, Rock and I, having
visited Groundnut's temple, were walking home along a path that
cut shorter than the eleven-village cart road, which veered from
the temple to Seeing the Horse Village to Mud Bridge and back to
Hot Pepper Village before it swung around to reach ours. It was
an afternoon hour; a gray sky lay low over the valley; a dull chill
was on the air. We were going through a declivity, a freakish cut
in a limestone ledge, on a path that yellows must have used for
centuries, since long, long before they had any whites under their
knuckles—so long that there were places where cloth shoes had

worn the stone smooth! Here in this cut I always had a disquieting thought: How had the yellows kept up their self-esteem without the whites to tread underfoot?

Rock and I, just at this time, were more or less at peace with each other—a weary peace of inuredness rather than understanding; we were simply tired of being upset by each other, or by anything at all. We chatted with each other in a friendly way, and there, dropping down through the stone-flanked cut, we happened to be talking about Provisioner Lung. Was he richer than he seemed to be? Could there be a paradox so cruelly funny as that furnishing and bleeding the miserable whites was, after all, unprofitable? I was in fact half laughing at this mad idea exactly when, coming around a limestone shoulder darkened with the skin oil of centuries of hands that had groped for support just there, there, and there, I came suddenly face to face with the man himself. Provisioner Lung seemed to jump out at me as from a stone-fort ambush. I stopped so short that Rock, watching his own footing, bumped into me from behind.

At once we were at the usual disadvantage: It must be the yellow man who would set the tone of the contact. He could greet us or ignore us, stop to talk or hurry past, bring fists together and pump out a show of humility, demanding reciprocity, or keep them tucked in sleeves, demanding discreet reserve. The initiative was always the yellow man's, his to choose the degree of intimacy or impersonality of each social moment, and he invariably kept us teetering off balance by unexpected turns in his mood. Our being in a heap, on account of our near collision, increased the disadvantage.

This time Provisioner Lung promptly signaled two things: there would be no ceremony, there would be some talk. He did not whip off his glasses and oscillate them cheerily in his customary greeting. He barely nodded—and how was a white supposed to respond to a curt nod?

"I'm glad of this meeting," he said. (But had he in fact been climbing up the cut, or had he, as I now distinctly felt, been lurking behind the boulder in order to *make* a meeting, or a series of them?) "I've been wanting to see you two."

"We're always glad to see you, Venerable," Rock said, with precisely the same amount of emphasis as the Provisioner had put into his greeting—in other words, tendering a prudent echo.

"Have you a moment's time?"

"Most of the moments of every day of my life belong to you, Venerable." With the echoing tone of his voice, and with that final honorific, Rock took all the bite out of that retort and even turned it into vague homage.

Provisioner Lung laughed, but his laughter was cracked, as if his throat were irritated by dust. "I wanted to see you because the New Year is approaching."

"We were just saying, coming along, that time goes very fast."

"It does. I make new contracts at the New Year. You're a good hog—and your wife is a good sow—and I intend to increase your rent lands, as you asked me to do."

Rock wisely waited, and did not explode into pleasure. "Venerable knows what's best," he murmured, a routine formulation of thanks, expressed for the giver's pleasure in terms of the helplessness of the recipient.

"But as a condition, I want to clear the debt for the current year." Here was the thunderclap! "As you know, the twelfth month is the time of debt clearance. I'd like to have everything wiped off the chip during this month."

"But the spring food crop was definitely reckoned—"

"Borrow against it."

"But from whom, Venerable? You're my credit."

"Ai, Rock Liu, you've been through other twelfth months, you weren't born this year."

That was true enough. Even in slave years there had been debts to pay in the last month of the year—and how? By borrowing. In the twelfth month every pig was a borrower and probably a lender, too. Every white owed every white and owed the yellow man, too. No one ever paid full cash unless pushed to the wall. Pay a part, promise the rest! By third third, by ninth ninth, I promise the rest! But the yellow creditor was a hater of promises, he spat on the ground when he heard promises. And sometimes, all too often, he had the means to push the white man's shoulder blades hard against the wall.

"I'll see what I can do," Rock said with a too bland voice.

⟨ The Monkey Myth

Just before dark that evening Manager Wu knocked at our gate, and I thought: Ayah, more trouble. Since the encounter in the limestone cleft Rock had been in a silent rage of such a depth that I had dared not go near him, much less converse with him, and when I answered the gate and found the village headman there I tried to get Manager Wu to tell me his mission, but he insisted on seeing the head of the house.

I led him inside. Rock was sitting cross-legged on our platform. I offered to prepare tea, but the headman waved me off.

He had come, said Manager Wu, to levy a tax. He knew, he said, that ours was a poor village, but we were confronted with a struggle for pride with other villages that were no less poor: The lower hands of the eleven villages in this part of the valley were going to collaborate in putting on theatricals during the last three days of the twelfth month. A mat shed would be erected on the threshing ground opposite Restful Thoughts Temple; a company of white strollers from Long Sands had already been bespoken. Each village had been assessed a share of the basic cost. It was his duty to spread our assessment through the village, according to gates and mouths.

O ominous Rock! How sprightly you reacted to this news! You asked what our share was, and when Manager Wu named a figure, in cash value, to be paid in either money or crops, you knew that he had overassessed, in expectation of bitter complaint and argument on your part, yet you nevertheless said you would not only be delighted to contribute the share he named but would try to give more—and would also certainly give time, mats, and raffia cord for the construction of the stage shed.

What a perverse man! Were you simply determined to strip yourself of the least possibility of paying your debts to the provisioner?

No, it seemed to be that, yet much more than that, because when the headman had left, your anger—at Provisioner Lung, at the world we lived in, at me, at yourself—seemed to have vanished like steam from the spout of a kettle; it was quite gone into the air.

And in the days that followed you were at the very hilltop of your manly best. We were not happy, by any means, but I would say that we reveled!

You rushed about offering your services and your worldly little to make the theatricals a success. The charm, energy, and male sweetness that had won you access to many a mouse now won over, wholeheartedly, in turn, the cuckolds you had made. The entire village said, "That fellow Rock Liu is a cheerful donkey, isn't he?"

Then why did your behavior give me chills?

All eleven villages were aflutter with anticipation. Satin ribbons were dug out from chests, visits of relatives and friends from distances were arranged, and chickens were given extra feed that could not be afforded.

The day before the arrival of the troupe of players the valley seemed to turn upside down; the river ran across the sky, the hills pointed down, and, antlike, whites scurried all about the unders and overs of this disarrayed vision of pleasure.

The focus of all the activity was the level field across from Groundnut's temple. To this center the métayers from the whole cluster stretching from Tiger-Guarded Village at one end all the way to Ma Family Graves at the other carried, with self-endangering improvidence, contributions of reed mats, bamboo poles, sheafs of rice paper, planks, bundles of cord, tea bowls, and all sorts of things that were not even needed, such as strings of dried peppers. It goes without saying that Groundnut wound up as custodian of all edible overage.

Rock sped here and there like a nest-building hare. Men from all the villages noticed him, and I lost for a time the unaccountable feeling of dread his high spirits had been giving me, and I gave way to simple pride in him.

In a day the barren place became an ephemeral settlement, fabricated of bamboo and reeds and paper and cord. For the theater itself Rock and many other volunteers erected a large framework of bamboo poles, to which they laced a sheathing of reed mats; at one end of the shelter a rickety scaffolding was raised for a stage. And all about the theater and the temple, flanking the road and, in some places, encroaching on it, there sprang up scores of small mat sheds, for cook shops, tea houses, wine stands, gambling booths, and all sorts of vendors' huts. Within the span of an afternoon, the area became something like a lively fairground.

The performances began early the next morning, and lasted all day—and so for three days.

Rock and I were there in plenty of time. A vast horde had gathered: eleven villages, to the last man, woman, and child, and many from farther away, too. Among the mob there were sure, Rock said, to be a large number of sharpers, pickpockets, and persons whose nasty little vices would flourish, like crawling insects, in tight-packed crowds. He told me to hang my pathetic purse within my inner gown, and to keep to old acquaintances. This last sounded like notice that he would be drifting away from me—and this, indeed, he did do. I took up with Bare-Stick and his deaf wife. So early in the day Bare-Stick was showing signs of having been drinking. I kept looking about for Rock; his restless exuberance worried me.

Now came a surprise. Large numbers of yellows began to arrive, and in the mat shed they were placed along the two sides of the theater. The yellow intruders faced us whites, not the stage. There was Provisioner Lung among them. Ayah, they had come to watch the spectacle of the white people enjoying themselves!

No matter. We did enjoy ourselves. I stopped worrying about Rock. The interminable drama was woven about the myth of the monkey who became a god—the perfect, hope-giving tale to spin out before poor whites. It was all crude. Beyond the substance of the lines chanted in a wild falsetto by the actors, the illusion was entirely evoked by costumes. There was no scenery; except for weapons, of gilded and silvered wood, which seemed to abound, there were no properties. But the costumes! Dragon robes. Serpent robes. Double sets of inner garments brightly embroidered. Suits of papier-mâché armor. Ceremonial gowns of scholars and ministers. The dress of high-born ladies, mandarins' wives, concubines. And best of all, the rags and lumpy quilts of the "flowery-faced ones," the clowns who were also villains, whose cheeks and brows were plastered with chalky powder.

Yes, the villains, the shabby ones, the earthy ones, the comical ones—they were unmistakably white, whiter than white.

And how we laughed at the monkey's foibles and trials! The Conscience God had provided him with a Head-splitting Helmet, which would tighten on his skull whenever he was tempted to sin, and he was so tempted, deliciously and uproariously, at every turn. Ayah, yes, the yellows must have laughed at our laughter! There were no separate acts or scenes; it was all one sweet and endless dream. When a new character appeared, and when his costume or his pantomime was not enough to identify him for us, we hooted, and he turned to us and told us straightly who he was, and what he had lately been doing offstage in the myth, and, like as not, what he was about to do before our eyes.

Bare-Stick's wife, who could hear little of it, laughed as hard as I. We were all pressed together tightly. Bare-Stick gave me squeezes, transferring his appreciation of the drama to various parts of my body. I yielded to every influence, and wept as I laughed.

Hai! Chu Pa-chieh, pig fairy, with your muck rake, sturdy ambassador from the realm of the coarser passions, how we adore you! You mirror! We are you, you are my inner self, pig, pig, pig.

And Priest Sha! How weak you are, how human! You need praise and encouragement to stiffen up your watery knees every time you come near these rough beings.

And you, monkey, discoverer of secrets! If only *I* could have an iron wand like yours! The gold-banded iron wand of all my desires!

Then into the edge of the dream comes an oblique, flashing thought: If I had the wand, I would . . . would *dispose* of Provisioner Lung.

Where is Rock?

For a moment I look around for him—but there is Lung Wang, the Dragon-King of the Eastern Sea. . . . I am transported again. . . .

Sunset outside the mat shed and a cold wind ranging from the faraway loess highlands, rather than a dramatic moment on the stage, decreed a halt for the night. I went home with Bare-Stick and his wife, and all the way, breaking out peals of renewed laughter, we reminded each other of superb moments. Bare-Stick said, "I liked that part where the pig fairy was getting ready to mount the Pearly Emperor's daughter—the way he snorted and rolled his eyes!" We laughed and I said, "And when the monkey made his wand so small he could hide it in his ear—but it pricked him there!"

Rock was not at home when we got there. He came in late, drunk, and poured out onto the platform from a leather pouch a mass of cash—a fortune! He would not say where it had come from; I assumed—I hoped—he had been gambling.

"Enough to pay back Provisioner Lung and have some left," I breathlessly said.

But Rock sprawled on his knees and greedily raked in the copper circlets with their little square holes and he said over and over, "Never, never, never, never, never." He tied the purse, when it was full again, to the cinch of his trousers, and later, drowsy from his drinking, he said, in a kind of growl, "I saw him there. Laughing at us." Those were his only words to me that night.

The next night Rock did not come home at all.

I stayed up late, waiting, and heard a whippoorwill's endless keening. During the small hours, having dozed off, I wakened in great fear, with a vivid feeling that I was being ridden by an evil spirit; my neck had been saddled, a witch-steel bit was in my teeth. I dared not get up to light a lamp, and indeed I could not move at all. After a long time I went galloping off suddenly into a swamp of dreams. When I woke up in the morning the corners of my mouth were chafed, as if a real bit had been pulling at them, and cold sores were beginning to form there; my neck and back were weary and stiff.

When I went out in the yard I found that our single hen had been stolen—presumably by some of the scum that the plays had attracted.

I set out for the theater, asking of acquaintances if they had news of Rock. No one had seen him. In the theatrical shed Bare-Stick took me under his heavy arm again. Feeling lead-limbed and full of apprehension and foreboding, I could not help telling him that I had had the feeling of being saddled during the night.

Bare-Stick's blustery reaction was somewhat reassuring, for he took my night burden as a commonplace that every white bore sooner or later.

"Put a sieve beside you on your platform tonight. Those spirits can't resist counting, something makes them count. They'll be kept busy counting the holes in the sieve. Or do you have a book? Almanac? Set it out. They'd have to count the characters and pictures."

"Does it have to do with Rock?"

Bare-Stick reduced his blaring to a murmur that his wife could not hear, and with a highly inappropriate naïve beaming expression he said that if Rock stayed away that night, he would sneak out and visit me.

The players' antics that day seemed overdrawn and chaotic to me; I could not follow the action. I was distracted. I kept looking for Rock. Bare-Stick's great mule guffaws beside me only irritated me. The sores at the corners of my mouth stung more and more.

I did not see Provisioner Lung among the yellows in the great shed.

Where was Rock?

Immediately after the plays adjourned, men began to untie the mats and tear down the sheds and shelters, in order to reclaim the materials they had contributed. Rock, so active in the raising of the structures, was not to be seen.

Gradually I heard reports. He had been caught the previous evening trying to steal a suckling pig in Liu's Dog's Tooth Village. He had been seen drunk in the lower hand of Mud Bridge. Attempted with the crudest methods to seduce the headman's wife —a woman over fifty years old—in Hot Pepper Village. Rampaging, roaring, cursing up and down the valley. The story that caused me the sharpest fear was that he had been heard in Wang Family Big Gourd Village railing with a foul mouth against Provisioner Lung.

I considered going to look for him but decided against it. If I found him, this would cause him to eat loss and would only make him wilder than he already was.

It turned out that I had no need of searching, because he came in that night, and I saw at once that the rumors had been well based. Haggard, three days unshaven, his clothes and even his queue muddy, the money vanished, eyes red-rimmed, with a breath like the vapors of fermented pig swill, he talked in a rushing, stammering torrent about the woebegone valley in which we lived; he sounded not so much drunk as . . . as . . . *O-mi-t'o-fu!* . . . as ridden by a witch all too familiar to me. I trembled on a corner of the bed to hear him.

Very late I drifted off to sleep still hearing him rattle his crazy speech, as unceasing as the previous night's melancholy whippoorwill.

Several times in the night I was wakened by his stumbling around the house and yard, cursing, rummaging, busy in the dark.

Once I awoke to a horror like that of the night before, hearing a terrible metallic screaking—and I realized that in the pitch blackness he was sharpening a knife on his flat grindstone.

Unafraid for myself but filled with a kind of folk dread, I called out to him, to try to get him to settle down. But he seemed to be beyond communication.

With daylight he appeared to be somewhat calmer, and I even succeeded in persuading him to take some tea and a millet cake.

It was the New Year morning—time for visits to friends. I wept. Rock dozed off sitting up.

Then Bare-Stick came whooping in with an earthen jug of millet liquor, and his noise made Rock open his reddened eyes.

Bare-Stick ogled me and said he had come to see whether the wanderer had returned. I saw Rock stiffen at this oafish declaration.

Bare-Stick said, "Hai, Rock, I've seen a sight this morning that you would have liked. You know how Old Provisioner Lung was at the plays and around the sheds these last days trying to collect the year-end debts? He dunned me five or six times. His period for collection was supposed to be up at dawn this morning. Just now, in broad daylight, some of us saw him walking along Eleven Villages Road with a lighted lantern—his fiction that the night isn't over yet, so he can still collect a debt or two! Wouldn't you have liked to see that?"

Rock stood up. He looked like a mastiff. He roared, "I'll pay him, I'll pay him," and snatched up the knife on which he had been working in the night and ran out at our gate.

"Ayah," I said after his back, but of course he could not hear me. "Be careful."

Bare-Stick promptly started pawing me, and he tugged at the cinch of his trousers to loosen them. I slapped him hard, and he left, carping at my want of New Year spirit.

I sat down, unable to think, not daring to venture out, my blood a-throb in my ears.

The day was cold and clear. I was vaguely aware of the sunlight creeping across the papered window.

It must have been after noon when Manager Wu and three others—Hairlip Shen, Ox Yang, and one of Rich Shen's sons—dragged Rock in, his elbows pinned together behind his back and bound with cord. There was blood on his quilted jacket. The panting men blurted out that Rock had been seen running up and down the whole valley, cursing and shouting, and that he had come back to our lower hand and had stabbed Bare-Stick six times in the chest and abdomen, to the edge of death.

I shrieked. Had I shrieked words, they would have been, "But that was not the man he meant to kill!"

❨ The Stripping

Manager Wu and the others left. Having delivered Rock home, there was nothing more they could do; Manager Wu was not empowered to make arrests, or to judge, or to punish.

So I was left alone with my man. I knew that I would have to try to rediscover him now—and rediscover myself, for that matter, if I could.

I untied his pinioning, took his jacket from him, and set about washing out blood. We did not speak. Rock went out into our courtyard to do some chores, as if this New Year's day were any other day.

Shortly I sensed his standing behind me as I bent over the caldron, at work on his coat.

"Where's the hen?" he asked.

"Stolen."

"Is anything else gone?"

"Not to eat."

"What do you mean?"

"Where's the money you had the other night?"

"What money?"

I stood up and faced him. His eyes were, of all things, defiant. "Are you trying to tell me you don't remember that you had a leather bag full of copper cash after the first night of the plays?"

"I've been drunk. . . . Why didn't you take it away from me?"

I turned back to the caldron. "Why don't you sleep it off?"

Rock did not answer. He stretched out on the platform and in ten breaths was snoring. I pulled off his shoes. He slept all the rest of that day and all that night and until well after noon the following day.

Late in the morning, while Rock was asleep, I went to the well for water and learned that Bare-Stick was still clinging to life.

There was a crowd loitering at the curved wall, for our villagers were taking full advantage of the yellows' tradition that the first days of the New Year, up until the Lantern Festival, should be set aside for visiting, gambling, gossiping, and a general lay-off. Approaching the idlers, I was apprehensive. How would they treat me?

Ai! They greeted me as on any other day. Indeed, there seemed to be a new note of something like respect in the men's voices. I was given a full account of Bare-Stick's condition—dips of unconsciousness, delirious mumbling, weeping, great lassitude because of loss of blood. There were hints of gratitude to Rock —perhaps for dealing Bare-Stick a reckoning that other men had not dared give him, perhaps simply for bringing some excitement into the village.

I went home fairly skipping. Why was I so lighthearted? Was it because of relief that the whites, at least, would not punish Rock? Was it because Bare-Stick was alive and Rock had not killed a man? Was it because I realized that the crime had to do with *me*?

When I reached home Rock was awake. He seemed cheerful and said he was hungry. I fixed him an enormous meal, of side meat and millet cakes and rice and white cabbage and tea. He smacked his lips, nodded at me with his mouth full, and belched in resounding appreciation of the feast. It appeared that without the intervention of words something had been settled between him and me.

He received the news of Bare-Stick without comment and without visible emotion.

"I had nothing against him," Rock said.

I laughed, and Rock asked me what struck me as so funny. "You have nothing against him," I said. "That's an odd thing to say about a man you nearly killed. He may die yet."

"Don't try to make me say I'm sorry," Rock warned me.

A few minutes later Rock said, "You tell me there's a crowd up at the well? Let's go up. I'd like to get in a game of 'palm leaves.' I feel restless."

And so we went, and the impression I had gained was amply borne out, that Rock was not going to be blamed by our lower-handers, and might even be regarded as some kind of new petty white mandarin.

He was soon squatted on his haunches in a card game near the public grindstone, and I heard bouts of laughter from the men who were playing and from the men who were giving the players unwanted advice.

Manager Wu's wife, who seldom stirred from the headman's courtyard, appeared that afternoon at the well, and, apparently stimulated like everyone else by the news of the stabbing, she spoke in a most friendly way to me. I suppose each of us had heard from the village magpies that the other had seduced, or been seduced by, her husband; this was now an absurd bond between us. I think we knew that such games would not be played again on either side. I had a wild thought that one day Rock might succeed Manager Wu as the head of the village. What a pleasant afternoon!

Late in the day one of my little scholars, Straight One, came running like a blown leaf to the well, straight to me; he was panting, and his eyes were pools of that particular gray liquid that filled white children's eyes whenever they felt they should not commit themselves in any way.

"There's a cart," he blurted between gulps of air, "three slanties, teacher—three yellows with a cart at your gate—big oxcart, double-yoker—they're taking out your things—loading the cart—"

"Provisioner Lung?"

Straight One nodded.

I ran to the card-players and told Rock, and we dashed home. We arrived just in time to see a large cart drawn by a pair of oxen pulling out onto Eleven Villages Road. The vehicle was top-heavily loaded, and we could see that our own donkey cart was on it, upside down, and our short-legged donkey was tethered to the tailpiece and was trotting double-time to keep up with the stolid ox pace; and we could see our chests, our pots, our tools, our bed mats and quilts; and we noticed a huge earthenware jar with a lid, so big a man could stand in it; and we saw baskets brimming with the poor turnips from our root pit, and with the stalks and stubble we had garnered for fuel. Everything, everything. Rock, who knew futility as well as any man, did not run after the cart. This was his punishment; he knew it, and I knew it. We turned inside our courtyard. It was stripped. Every removable object was gone. Every grain of rice was gone. Our chopsticks were gone. Our spare shoes, so dearly bought, were gone. And in truth—ayah, that great earthen jar!—our compost heap was gone, for Provisioner Lung, stripping us barer that bare, had taken away even Rock's precious excrement, and mine.

(Double Man

Having slept unquilted on the dusty earth of our bed platform, we started out next morning to consult with Groundnut, to try to make a plan for our future, and, if it must be known, to beg a present meal from him.

Rock voiced the possibility that Groundnut would take us in at the temple—to housekeep for him, sweep the brick floors, clear away incense ash, dust the idols.

"No," I said, "he has become too important to let anyone take care of him. He's a great official of the valley now. He can't have anyone encroaching on his place. Besides, he wants the temple dirty. Especially the idols. You know that."

Strange! Emerging from the limestone cleft where Provisioner Lung had accosted us, and coming out onto a high point of Eleven Villages Road, we could see, ahead, that a crowd was already gathered at the temple gate. There must be some new sensation in the valley to have convened our parliament of gossips so early in the day. We lengthened our pace.

Yes, as soon as we arrived at the edge of the circle a group formed around us and pelted us with a score of questions about the stripping. We were a bit pleased, having the impression that we were the cause of the convocation.

It was some time before the hubbub died down enough for us to learn what really was new: a sensation, indeed, for us.

Ours was not the only compound that had been scraped clean.

Provisioner Lung and his assistants had had a busy day, for they had despoiled at least a dozen homes scattered through several villages. There had been strippings before—Simple Hsi, our predecessor in our tenancy, had not only been stripped; his house had been leveled to the ground. But never had there been a dozen in a day!

So this had not been a punishment of Rock's crime at all! At least, it had not been the yellows' requital for Rock's use of his knife, and if it had been a chastisement, it had been, rather, for the crime of failing to pay debts.

Then I realized—and the recognition gave me anger rather than relief, demoralizing anger, degrading anger—that the yellows had no interest in the hurts that whites gave whites.

Later we learned, indeed, that the white victim might be a "criminal" just as much as the white assailant. Bare-Stick's place was one of those that had been denuded. The big, noisy man had, it seemed, grown careless, or improvident, or both, and he had fallen behind in his percentages. Provisioner Lung's men had lifted Bare-Stick up off his platform and pulled the mats right out from under him. It was said that Bare-Stick was nearer death than ever—unconscious most of the time.

We heard a report that Provisioner Lung had taken away even the hot poultices of bran and ground pulse that Bare-Stick's wife had put on his wounds.

Ox Yang was standing by when this detail was served, and he clapped Rock on the shoulder and cheerily said, "Then if Bare-

Stick dies, it will have been Provisioner Lung that killed him, not you, old turtle-suck!"

Ayah, we could, in the end, blame the yellows for everything, everything.

We went inside, and Groundnut, who had already heard of our misfortunes, took us to his throne room and asked us to tell him the whole story. I say throne room, but the elaborate chair was gone—in its place a simple bench. Groundnut seemed distracted, and he was markedly more gentle than the last time we had come to see him.

Giving an account of the stabbing, Rock said, "You told me, you rabbit of a priest, to think before I acted. Don't you see that that was my trouble? I'd been thinking, thinking, thinking, day and night, and I couldn't stand it any longer."

"But why Bare-Stick, son? Why not the yellow man?"—surprisingly honest query from Groundnut.

I expected, perhaps I half hoped, to hear Rock say: Because Bare-Stick had taken to fumbling at the mound of my wife's privacy.

But Rock said, "I don't know. I haven't anything against Bare-Stick. But I think it was this: I think I saw that I was turning into him. I was becoming exactly him. That may be why I wanted to get rid of him. Isn't that a good enough reason?"

"There is no good reason for hurting any living creature," Groundnut said; this was not quite the old voice that was unconnected with any reality whatsoever.

I had been right: no mention of our moving into the temple grounds, even on a temporary basis.

Now when the question of eating came up, Groundnut did provide for us, but not without a deal of unpleasantness. It seems that a beggar, being begged of, cannot resist mimicking all the rebuffs he has suffered over the years. The pupils of his eyes become little pinholes out of which distaste squirts, his hands flutter high about his neck to avoid poverty's contamination, his face is like an abacus ticking off the calculation: How little can I give and yet discharge my responsibility for the inequities of human life?

Still, I was curious about Groundnut's manner through all this habit-ingrained chariness: he kept glancing over his shoulder, as if expecting someone in his quarters, and twice he excused himself, hurried from the room, and came back looking preoccupied.

Rock surprised me—for I had thought him wholly absorbed by
our own fix—by saying, "What's gnawing your liver, Groundnut?
You're in a condition."

Down came Groundnut from his loftiness with something like
a rush of pigeon wings, and in a confidential voice he said, "Another priest has moved in with me. To stay."

Rock guffawed. "You'll be paying squeeze to a priests' league
soon—you'll find that the yellows squat on all the temples!"

With a perplexing sincerity Groundnut said, "This man's an
old good. I want him to stay."

"You mean he'll draw business."

Groundnut blushed. "I want you to talk to him about your
trouble."

He trotted out, and soon he was back with another man. "This
is Runner." And to the other: "I've told you about Rock."

Runner was older than the rest of us, perhaps in his late thirties.
He wore dirty red robes like Groundnut's, his head was shaved,
his face glowed with a health of frugality and kindness; one could
see at once that he was kind, that he had an inner strength, an
armature of experiential iron supporting this outer warmth and
giving it a firmness that was not sickly or false at all. I saw in a
first glance why even Groundnut was impressed by him.

Rock was diffident, perhaps suspicious at first of the very things
I had seen in the priest's face, so Groundnut told him parts of
our story, and his response seemed to me electric. His questions
were all about Provisioner Lung. I felt that his mind was leaping
ahead. I wanted to linger and talk with him, but Rock grew irritable, said we had to leave.

So, with appeased stomachs and heads quite empty of prospects for the next meal, we went back out to the crowd in the road.

But we did not leave; indeed, where for? I stood by Rock. The
whites by now had chewed and swallowed all the bitter details of
the strippings; there was a kind of communal satiety, a dullness.
Rock, the stabber, provided a new center of interest, and people
gathered around him. O my tiger! He held his head high, and I
thought he was talking too loud. Double man! What he uttered as
modest disclaimer emerged as inside-out boast. His guilt was his
release from guilt; his crime had been a positive act. I remembered our original two-sided impulse to come and live in the
Humility Belt—to be absorbed into the mass of whites, but also
to help raise the level of the poorest whites. Here was my Rock,

caught in that ambiguity: triumphant, at one with the ignorant crowd, admired, probably disliked because he was admired; and yet also aware of his helplessness before the yellow power, pessimistic, bitter, suppressing his feelings until they drove his sharpened tongue to bragging, or his sharpened knife into the wrong body. Double vision; double values. Torn, he veered from shrewd calculation to animal impulse, from forms and proprieties to cheating and plotting, from kowtowing to sneering, from sacrificing at chipped idols to spitting in the priest's footsteps, and from honoring his wife to philandering in beds of ashes. How I loved him at that very moment of seeing through him! White man! Ayah! Was Rock to be a mere firecracker? How scornfully he put down Ox Yang and Hairlip Shen, his fellow villagers!

Now came one of those nightmare repetitions of life under the yellows, a refrain of unpleasantness; one of those events that could no longer evoke protests because it evoked only the cry, "This has happened to us before!"

Three scourges of The Hall rode up. One of them asked in a mask-damped roar why we were congregated so. Those who had been put down looked to Rock. I saw his bare-stick eyes. At last he said, "Worshipping, Venerable."

The familiar exchanges, then Rock being ridden down, then a command for him to hoist his hooves for home.

But Rock said, "I have no home."

The mounted man nearest him gave off a muffled explosion behind his mask—a warning against being clever.

"But it's true," Rock said. "The yellow man who furnished me took everything away yesterday. He's driving me off my tenancy."

One could see the quandary of the man on horseback, feel the pause of moral hesitancy. Then he said, "Aren't your villagers going to take care of you?"

"No, Venerable."

Then one of the other riders edged forward and impatiently said, "Is your house still standing?"

"It stands empty."

"Then that's where you belong for now. Move along, hog."

I saw a look of despair and fear on Rock's face, and I understood it—not fear of the yellow men hiding behind papier-mâché masks, but fear of what he was degenerating into: the village braggart, the bully, the stabber, the one who would always be singled out to canter home with yellow men at his heels.

❪ Under the Steerage Chains

When I walked into our gutted house, Rock, sitting on the barren earth bed, looked up and said at once, "We have to get away from here. This place is no good. There is no way here. I have to get out of this valley right now. If Bare-Stick dies I'll have to take his place in the village, and I am not really like that. Do you understand that? Sometimes you get into a kind of pen, or trap, and the confinement takes ahold of you and turns you into a stranger, even to yourself. Do you understand that?"

"Ai, I do, Rock. I know you. You aren't Bare-Stick."

Rock suggested that we go to the coast, to the great modern city, Shanghai, Up-from-the-Sea, about which we had heard encouraging rumors. It was said that whites could make some kind of life there.

"But how will we get there? How will we live?"

Rock did not answer me but went to the wall of the house, near the stove, to a place at the height of his mid-shin, and scraping with a fingernail he cut through some thinly plastered mud until, in a few moments, he had exposed a loosened section of mud brick. He drew this out and reached into the hollow space behind it and pulled out the leather purse full of cash that, drunk, he had showed me the first night of the theatricals.

"You think your own wife would steal from you, don't you?"

"She might," Rock said. "To get away from me." But Rock was grinning.

We left straightaway, without even telling Groundnut. We walked, lying in fields overnight, to Long Sands, where we embarked on a lake boat, a steam paddle-wheeler, that carried us out to the Great River. At Mouth-of-the-Han we took passage on a cargo steamer downriver, and our quarters, we learned, were ones set aside for whites: the rearmost section of the afterhold, an area unspeakably filthy with coal dust and grimy rags, cluttered with ship's gear and with the baskets of the white beggar-vendors of the river, who were called "musk shrews"—after ratlike water animals that were notorious for their rotten odor. The great steerage chains clanked and rattled over our heads day and night, the propeller thumped directly beneath us. No fresh air could penetrate our miserable den. Some twenty whites, most, like ourselves, quite without baggage, sprawled on the rusty metal decks. As we

traveled, well-dressed young yellow men came into the compartment ostensibly to drink and to gamble but really to try to find a
way under the gown of a likely-looking white girl. I received some
exploratory attention along these lines, but opportunely, from
time to time, my powerful Rock would loom up out of the shadows
and speak to me, and how the little yellow spaniel heat-sniffers
would scatter! I found myself thinking sometimes about Runner,
the priest—the first pair of eyes I had seen in a white face for
almost ever that had nothing to hide; eyes of a giver without limit.
In eight days we reached our destination.

The Enclave

BOOK EIGHT

(The Envious Shroff

CITY OF WONDER! City of modern times! For three sunny winter days we lived on the coppers in Rock's leather pouch, at ease, walking about. This great port of ocean commerce seated on a curving riverbank, Up-from-the-Sea, was a far cry from the Northern Capital. In the prosperous part of the port, called the Model Settlement, were buildings that loomed up from the ground two and three storeys high and even, in the cases of some of the vast white-walled mercantile hongs along the Bund, laminated skyward five and six floors! Enormous crimson or black characters, names and claims, on hanging signs. Globular electric lamps on brackets out from shop fronts, sparkling polyhedral lamps with tassels of crimson cord hanging down. Tea shops, their upper faces adorned with storytelling woodwork, carved, lacquered, and gilded. Shops of healers of sick rich men, stocked with ginseng, angelica, licorice, and powdered deer antler. Pawnshops—hope for thieves! Caverns of grass cloth, silk, satin, brocade, and embroideries whose intricacies whispered in sybaritic tones of the ruined eyes of a generation of white needlewomen.

And the traffic, the crowds bustling for profit! Two-wheeled conveyances drawn by white men: rickshas, everywhere. And on the thoroughfares named for provinces and for other cities, several of the smoke-breathing, glistening motorcars of which we country tenants had heard but distant superstitious rumors. And thousands on thousands afoot, whites mingling without fear with yellows.

By night we crawled into a woebegone unheated flophouse for migrants (one copper per night per chill-racked body) in the huge white area of the metropolis. This district, called the Enclave, was the ancient walled city, a circular urban sore, once historic and all yellow, then gradually encroached upon by, and finally totally abandoned to, the myriad white migrants who had streamed into the city of freedom and hope. The old area's physical walls were down, but it was, if anything, more sequestered than when it had been girdled by stone: the color line was drawn around it. It teemed. Coming from the sparse lower hand of a deep-country village, Rock and I were strangely elated by this crowding of the whites—for we knew that, much as the yellows used and needed us, they really wanted us to vanish from their sight; they would have liked to have us altogether eliminated— by some respectable and possibly miraculous means, of course— and so we perversely delighted in our very numbers, which were getting beyond any possibility of liquidation. Besides, these whites who jostled us in the narrow hutungs of the Enclave seemed to us, after the country-village cross section, to be clear-eyed, energetic, bright—the cream of our kind. And indeed these were the best: these were the restless ones from downcountry, who had developed an itch for vertical mobility, those who had managed to educate or somehow sharpen themselves and run away. And here were half a thousand thousands of them, jammed with us into the Enclave.

In those first days we felt free. Change is itself an illusion of freedom, but we felt more than mere escape, mere motion. Despite our having to return to the stable at evening, so to speak, we roamed at large all day, filling our eyes, as if they were our purses, with the city's riches, and no one stopped us to identify ourselves, no one gave us patronizing looks that demanded bows or stepping aside.

Rock and I had each other, too, in a sense that had never obtained before. We were coupled in a new state of mind. Rock's outburst in those awful days in the village had cleansed him. Not that all of his frustration with life, by any means, was discharged; after all, he still did not know whether he had killed a man—a white man, at that. But Rock was freer than he had ever been, in the inner sense; he noticed things he had never seen before, delights both to the eye and to the mind, and it was he who kept insisting that some new sort of firmness was visible among the whites in this free city. It struck me, even then, that this new quality, whatever exactly it was, may have been his to see because it was in him rather than in them.

On the afternoon of the third day of our aimless luxuriating in the city, we were standing in the street in our rude quilted country clothes—all we had left from the bounty of Provisioner Lung —staring into a treasure cave of an open-fronted shop on West-of-the-Mountains Road, where were sold headdresses, tea-root figures, combs and fans and pearly pins, ear guards, purses dripping with silk fringe, painted umbrellas and embroidered shoes, and many other toys of vanity, and we noticed that there was one white employee: the shroff. Very few whites worked in the Model Settlement; we had seen a handful of shroffs. This one sat within a little cage, and at each transaction, after the yellow cashier had ticked up the sum of the purchase on an abacus, and after the yellow clerk had accepted some well-dressed yellow woman's money, the coins were slid along a board into the cage, and there, with a juggler's flowing fingers, the white shroff tested the coins. He would balance them one by one on the middle finger of his left hand, and with a sound coin riding free on a fingertip of his right hand he would strike the two together, an ear bent down to the sweet silver chime or copper plink they made, and then he would feather-lightly place the coin in a certain slot in an intricate little scale, and then he would lift it waferlike to his mouth and click his teeth to either side of it—all with such lightning speed as to make the whole trial seem only one floating wary gesture, as of caressing a cat. Virtuosic performance! And how often (there must have been many a patient cheat in this free world) he rejected a coin!—shaved, debased, flawed, tapped, leaded, clipped. . . . We had stood gaping at the man's swallowwing dexterity for some time before I began to be vaguely uneasy in watching him.

Then my heart was hammering, and I gripped Rock's arm. The shroff was Top Man—the slaveherd from the Yen family farm. He was wearing a black skullcap and a gray silk gown, and, what with his yellow-shop-clerk dress and his astonishing skill, he had a suave and cosmopolitan appearance, which the slaveherd had certainly never worn. But no mistake: Top Man.

I hurried Rock down the street away from the shop and told him
who the shroff was.

Now Rock and I had often discussed former times that we had
not shared, and he knew very well my assessment of Top Man—
a yellow man's white man; how hard the slaveherd had tried to
please Overseer Li and the young master and the Matriarch, yet
how pathetically in the last days of our planning he had tried to
enlist with Peace. Shame-faced bearing. Big-chested false show of
authority. Guilty instrument of punishment. Craven before the
yellows. Ayah, how I had despised him! And yet . . .

Yet how thrilled I was to have seen him now! And Rock, too,
was excited. I am sure that our sudden feelings of cordiality toward Top Man were as alloyed as some of the coins that he, with
no sign of emotion, had slid back along the board from his money
cage: we must have realized at once that he might be useful to
us. But there was, as well, for me, a genuine joy in having seen
Top Man again. Perhaps it had to do with a stirring up of the
past, which, though miserable enough, had attained a fierce value
merely from being gone. Perhaps it had to do with the exaggerated, automatic closeness a white person felt with any other white
whom he had ever known; we were all fellow members of a league
of underdogs.

Rock and I decided at once that we dared not go into the genteel
yellow store in our filthy peasant clothes and make ourselves
known to the shroff; free as this city was supposed to be, such a
trespass might be a misdemeanor, and it would at best cause Top
Man to eat loss, at worst to forfeit his valuable job. We agreed that
we would wait outside the store, perhaps a little down the street
from it, until its closing time, and waylay Top Man when he came
out to go home—for his home was sure to be in the Enclave.

Dusk fell while we waited, and the hanging shop lamps along
the street came on, picking out rills of gilt and glints of red lacquer
along the store fronts; we could see our breath fogging as the
night's sea-damp seeped along the streets—and through our
sleazy quilts.

At last the heavy plates of barrier planks were carried out and
were upended and were locked in place, and, as we moved closer
in the shadows, we saw at "our" store a metal net rolled down
over the planking as a redoubled precaution against burglars. It
was quite dark. Figures began to emerge from a gate at one side
of the building, and I was suddenly afraid I would be unable to

recognize Top Man. I lunged forward toward this and that striding form, and recoiled again and again at glimpses of yellow cheeks in a pale lamplight.

Then there he was. That slaveherd pace, that same over-assurance of the unsure. He had changed from the gray silk gown—perhaps it belonged to the store—and seemed to be in a long quilted winter gown probably of cotton; it had no sheen under the shop lamps.

This time I tugged at Rock's sleeve and set out in certainty. Following at a distance far enough to be well away from the store, I then trotted a few paces, and in a soft voice said, "Top Man!"

Our quarry whirled. A lamp was shining full in his face, and the source of light must have been behind Rock and me, so that Top Man could only see our outlines; I had chosen a poor place to accost him. His face was congealed in its old familiar look—noncommittal caution. Were these beggars? A woman with a strong-looking male accomplice—knockdown cutpurses? How had the woman known the name?

I quickly said, "I am White Lotus. From Yen's farm. Do you remember me? Do you remember 'the woman of Sorek'?"

I have to say that Top Man's reaction was immediate, spontaneous, and quite without stint. He stepped forward to me, clasped my shoulders in his hands, and greeted me with—it is true, for I saw the icelike flashes of reflection of the lamp in the overflow—tears in his eyes. I introduced Rock, and at once Top Man said we must come along and have a cup of tea with him. Not a meal, a cup of tea; but the invitation was hoarsely issued, with a push of sincerity.

We walked along toward the Enclave. "Oh, yes," Top Man said, as we spoke of the new sense of ease we had felt in Up-from-the-Sea, "I can move about as I wish, I don't have to stroke the lids at all. You saw the job I have—clean work. I can speak out, and I can speak on my own side. There's money here and there are ways to use it on yourself."

And he told us that this was a city in flux, with open gates, a city of kite-flying and "the pipe" and sports according to choice. Top Man's speech was peppered with a terse argot, apparently of the Enclave, yet he had also developed a certain pomposity, a largeness of tone, to which Rock, I could sense, did not respond well.

Now a minor surprise and shock: Top Man took us, for the tea he had offered, not to his home, but to a seedy, crowded teahouse on a narrow street. Had he, under some lamp, taken a close look at our tenant rags and suddenly become ashamed of us, of me? Did he want to avoid a continued relationship? He treated us, all the same, with something like warmth, though there now seemed to me some stiffness and caution in his cordiality.

Then I saw his caution, as well as his kindness, as a sort of insurance—against exulting over my bad lot compared with his easy one; there came into my mind, from a past so dim as to seem a dream, an Arizona proverb: "The reason the sheep has a split lip is that he laughed too hard when the goat fell down." Top Man would be careful not to laugh at me, though he surely must have remembered, with thanks for the irony, his abject humiliation before the moral superiority of such as I on the day before Peace's doomed rebellion. Now we were another way around.

The Yen place? Broken up, after the war. The Matriarch had died of a ruptured purse, the young master had fallen in love with a rich boy from the Northern Capital and had wandered off. The place—the area—all gone to seed.

The girl Harlot, from the Yen farm, said Top Man, was somewhere here in Up-from-the-Sea. He had seen her. Yes, she was doing rather well. This was a good city for a mixie woman.

He talked to us about the Enclave. It had the Model Settlement on one side, where whites could wander freely enough, but better not go off in the other direction, where lay a swarming nest of poor yellows, known to the whites as Fukien rubbish, vicious, spiteful, and dangerous people. The only other place where whites could live, besides the Enclave, was a satellite enclave of foul huts in the southwestern section of the city, inhabited mostly by the white scum who pulled rickshas.

"White scum"? This sounded strange on Top Man's white lips.

If there were poor yellows in Up-from-the-Sea, why couldn't whites find new places to live? Why couldn't they break out from the Enclave? Couldn't they rent space outside?

Key money. The device of key money stopped them, Top Man said. To consummate the agreement for a rental, a tenant anywhere in the city was obliged to "hire the key" by putting up a sum of money. Whenever a white tried to rent property outside the Enclave, no matter how mean the hovel, a sudden mountain of key money would be required.

Ayah, the Enclave was the city's night-soil heap, where the

yellows dumped their poorest merchandise, their vices, lusts, and perversions, and their third-rate yellow city officials—their tenth-rate policemen.

As Top Man started to pour out his resentments and complaints, his grand manner began to decompose before our eyes, the patrician affectations that we had seen degenerated into envious whining, the tight control of his exquisite shroffing gestures gave way to nervous motions of chopping, punching, and stabbing with long-nailed forefingers. And I thought: Ai, he hasn't changed. He has tried to train himself, but he's the same man.

"You want to know why we're embedded in this cesspot of an Enclave? It's not key money. It's our own out-fronters—our priests, our chinkties, our hong men, our little stuck-up white mandarins. They want to keep us right where we are—right in their sleeves. Do you remember big Duke, the Matriarch's Number One Boy? Ai, yes, he's here, too. They're *all* here. Duke—ayah, that tiger thinks he's the next thing to a lid himself. Hooo! What a chinkty he is! He? Duke? He's some kind of comprador for the Forgetfulness Hong—that hong runs everything in the Enclave: the lottery, the pipe dens, the provisions shops, the mousehouses. Every tiger in Ivory City who's on the pipe has to pay squeeze to some miserable Forgetfulness Hong runner. The hong owns all the street vixens, and it runs all the gambling holes. It has every man in Ivory City right by the eggs. Duke stands around—you should see him!—in a black satin gown; he's grown fingernails like long drips of snot. Hai! Parasite! But listen, White Lotus. If you think *he's* bad, have you heard about Old Arm? He's the big race man, the boar of boars. He's going to right all the wrongs, lead us out of Ivory City, put us all on even terms with the lids. He feeds us on promises—how he'll humiliate the lids. *He's* rich—and how do you think he got all the rice? He pretends to be for the race but he has sold out like all the rest of them, and what makes you despise him is that he didn't get rich from selling out; he got rich off his own white people and then sold out to the lids for a stingy potful of pork chitterlings. He's puffed up just like Duke, only worse. I tell you, White Lotus. The mourners in this city have nobody but their own turtle-screwing out-fronters to blame. . . ."

On and on he went, spewing out envy and spite. After a time he suddenly jumped up, paid a waiter for the tea, and left, and only then did Rock and I, who still sat on at our tiny table, realize that Top Man had talked so long and so fast that we had not been able to ask him any questions that mattered—about how to live.

The waiter came to us and curtly said he needed the table because there were customers in the outer room waiting to come inside.

As we were making our way across the room to the door I heard a tinkling, feminine splash of laughter that was so familiar that I snapped my head about to see from whom it had come.

There sat Moth, from Dirty Hua's, with two men's arms around her.

❪ The Puzzle Box

As in the old days, Moth had a little porcelain pitcher in her heart, full of emotion: she poured it out, put it back, and—hai! *i-ko lang-tang!*—it was instantly full again, like the slopped-out bowls in an itinerant white magician's water-bowl trick. She sat us down in her company and bathed Rock with modest-lascivious looks. Her two "tigers," as she called them, were of an unemployed type we had seen standing around in knots in the alleys of the Enclave. One was named Old Boxer. He wore, as "tigers" were somehow able to do, a new and well-made quilted jacket with exaggeratedly long sleeves, and his gesture of shooting his hands out, ruffling the sleeves up around his elbows, holding a fist up and shaking back the cloth around his wrists—all was done with such a cheeky look on the face, such cool loose-jointedness, such a straight bearing of the back, that I had the impression that indifference, nihilism, selfishness, and contempt for all striving had achieved almost perfect expression in him. The other, named Ox Balls, was a sparse, thin, short, sniveling, sneaky-eyed fellow, who looked like a pure opportunist with a sharp nose for meat, a bedbug of a man; he kept his hands clasped within the long sleeves and appeared to be cold through and through. Besides these two, Rock, who was by no means a tenderfoot, looked stolid, prosperous, and even complacent—whereas only a few minutes ago, seated by Top Man, he had seemed haggard and all played out.

I asked Moth, "How is your little boy?"

"Fo-o-o"—she made a kind of spitting sound. "Dead. Bad lungs." And for as long as it would have taken to wink she gave me a look so bleak that I was reminded of the numbness—"the white deadhead," the salt inspector had called it—which I had felt in those awful days at Dirty Hua's; but her recovery was disconcertingly swift, and her eyes sparkled again with a thoughtless frivolity.

I asked her then, "How do you live?"

"On the chits, sweet, the lottery chits. And on my tiger friends." She patted a pillar of support on either side of her. "Listen, sweet, for a girl there are only two things the lids will let her do—she can work as a silk-reeler, but that's too *hard*, ruins your eyes, boils your fingertips all day, f-f-f-f! Or else they don't mind if you want to sell your mouse. But I always say"—and Moth gave out a trill of her marvelous laughter, a dumpling sound, a filling of peppery disenchantment wrapped in a steaming dough of innocence—"I always say, Why sell something it's so nice to give away?"

"Do you mean they won't let a white woman work at anything else but reeling?"

"Reeling or whoring," Old Boxer said. "Either way they make a wonk of you, dear. I mean either way they screw you till you're nothing but a wornout old wonk."

So this was the great cheat that lay hidden like a fruit worm in the "free" city! Of course there had to be one. Rock asked what about men, and little Ox Balls said, with a sneer, that a man had a *big* choice, he had *three* kinds of work to choose from—"Tit-Suck, Haul-Ass Number One, and Haul-Ass Number Two"—which, when translated by Moth, turned out to mean house servant, wharf coolie, and ricksha boy. A man could get a permit to be one of those. That was all.

But what about Top Man? We told about his work as a shroff, and that he seemed well off, and the answer was that there were a hundred men like him in half a thousand thousands in the Enclave—a very few who had picked up a specialized and needed skill, such as shroffing, that the yellows for some reason seemed unable to perform, or perhaps had not the patience to learn.

There was, to be sure, a certain amount of "clean work" within the Enclave, but according to Old Boxer you had to either pay squeeze to the Forgetfulness Hong or (he pointed to a teahouse

waiter, who looked pale and harassed) "swallow your own puke"
—by which he meant, it seemed, hide your shame at the double
debasement of being white and working for whites. *O-mi-t'o-fu!*
How we had become infected with the yellows' attitudes!

I was so angry, so let down, that I could not help asking—the
question came out in a low, trembling voice—why so many whites
living here couldn't *do* something about the work situation.

"Ha!" It was Ox Balls, rodent when laughter pulled back his
lips. "Ha-ha-ha! Listen to the little lady boar."

Then Moth said to me (and her voice was low and vibrant, too,
but not, I thought, with feeling about what we were discussing
so much as with simple loyalty to me in the face of her tiger's
ridicule) that Old Arm—had we heard about Old Arm?—he was,
she said, the closest thing to a race hero in the Enclave—Old Arm
was said to be planning a huge Give-Us-a-Rice-Bowl campaign in
the late spring. Some said it could only lead to a bloody riot—
and at this Old Boxer and Ox Balls began to make gargoyle faces,
pantomiming delightful violence, drawing sword fingers across
their throats, poking lance fingers toward each other's eyes, looking cross-eyes, gurgling, gritting their tobacco-stained teeth; until
Moth, giggling, slapped at them both.

With a prickly stiffness Rock asked, "What do you turtles live
on?"

The reproach for their clowning that seemed implicit in Rock's
tone only fed the prankish nihilism of the two tigers, and they
began to give each other heavy, significant glances, shooting up
their eyebrows, looking ludicrously earnest, mocking all soundness of mind.

I knew that Rock did not like to be laughed at. He sat up
straighter and pulled back the slingshot of his voice and fired
out, "What do you live on?"

Old Boxer looked straight in Rock's eyes and said with unfore-
seen honesty, "We live on the edge, brother."

Rock was suddenly satisfied; he seemed to understand exactly
what the man meant. And the tigers made no more fun of him.

I could see that this excited Moth. "I have a *feeling*," she said.
"I have a feeling *here*"—she pointed to her stomach—"that I'm
going to hit the chits today. I have a *sweet* number. I'm on a chit-
clue book—it's the one called *Water Spirit's Sister Flies to the
Moon.* It has a code, you see, that gives you outer numbers and
inner numbers for each day's lottery, and I really believe I read

the code in the proper way this morning. I won last week, but it was only a first-outer-number win, a four-for-one. . . ."

She babbled on, her eyes darting now and then to Rock, and afterwards, each time, to me.

I wanted to ask about silk-reeling; I wanted to be alone with Rock and to talk with him; I wanted to shout my disappointment and anger at this "free" city.

Moth asked me, with an indifference too thick to be anything but studied, "Where are you living?"

I told her about the flophouse.

She bounced up on her chair then and said with a young girl's fresh enthusiasm that there was a room free in the "puzzle box" where she and the two tigers were living; a woman had stabbed her man with a wharf-coolie hook just the night before, and he was dead, and she had disappeared, and Rock and I should move in right away. Boxer and Ox Balls thought this a splendid suggestion and they began pounding Rock on the arms, urging him to agree. Rock began to laugh, and this made Moth giggle like an unstoppable wren.

So off we went, through a series of alleys that grew, one after the other, narrower and dirtier and more crooked and more crowded with children running in packs, until we came to a certain gateway, exactly like every other one of the ten gateways on the dead-end alleyway on which it faced, and one of the tigers drew a large brass key on a filthy string out from the inside of his trousers and pushed it through a hole in the thick gate leaf, and let us in.

"Puzzle box"! Rock and I saw soon enough what that term meant. We crossed a narrow courtyard, its winter-dirt packed and dusty, a country-style open privy with shoulder-high walls odoriferous in one corner, and we entered the shallow front room of the lower of the house's two storeys. Here lived the tenant agent for the house, and his family of wife and five children. Why was the room shallow? Because the landlord had erected a partition, making what seemed to be a second narrow room at the back; but when, having passed diagonally across the tenant agent's room and gone through a doorway to some steep stairs, we ascended past this cut-off space, we found that the rear space, in turn, had been cross-partitioned *both ways*, horizontally and vertically, making four windowless compartments in back, in each of which a household of some sort was established. None of the sections was high enough for a well-made man to stand straight in. The second storey was compartmented, too, by dividers, into eight of these miserable cubbies, and the former kitchen, at the back downstairs, Moth told us, had been turned into a joint home for two families, and the loft over the kitchen was yet another crowded room. Fourteen assorted groups; the landlord had distributed six charcoal braziers for cooking—sources of incessant bickering. One privy; a lean-to room off the kitchen with a huge hooped wooden knee-tub for anyone who dared wash himself in such cold weather.

Yes, the partitioned house was much like one of the clever little puzzle boxes, made of sandlewood, with sliding sections and false backs and a carved ivory ball to be moved about within, which one could buy from any toy vendor for five copper cash.

The stabbed man's body had been removed and had been put in the street to be taken away by a benevolent burial society. The tenant agent had put down a new piece of reed matting to cover the dried blood. We agreed to take the dark hole, and Moth and I, capturing a brazier, set it up on a stair landing to prepare a supper for our men.

And who were our nearest house mates? A woman whose husband, named Blinker, had lately been jailed for breaking into a store at night; a former cook in a yellow sports club who had been fired for stealing face cloths and was now a bowl-washer in a drab Enclave restaurant, living with a silk-reeler; a "she-ram," who was, Moth said, trying to get her hands under every girl's gown in the house, and was causing a deal of hysteria among both males and females in the puzzle box; a pair of teen-age tigers, "with sleeves down to their knees," whose section was a meeting place for an astonishing number of young boys and girls, sweepers, apprentice thieves, semi-prostitutes, peddlers of stolen goods—unripe and gangling adolescents—who pooled their little money, cooked up pots of pork culls, and spent afternoons smoking dross-of-dross, drinking yellow wine, and making love in groups; and sundry decent wharfmen, purse-snatchers, families trying to live clean on reelers' wages, an Enclave street-waterer, three menservants living together—a collection of the poor, the unstable, the striving, candidates all for arrest on "suspicion."

Our white cabbage, quickly cooked in sizzling peanut oil, was delicious, even if it had to be eaten to the sounds of a screeching argument between two women in upstairs-lower-left-front.

❮ A Brief Career

Rock said, "The first thing I will not do is to become a donkey and pull a ricksha. The second thing I will not do is to become a dog and work as a houseboy. That leaves only one kind of work to do."

He went off to the wharves one morning, and he did not come back for three days, so I began to think he had tired of me and had skipped away to some city vixen.

Late the third evening, however, Rock returned to our puzzle box with a rope shoulder sling, a nasty-looking hook, seven coppers, and a good temper.

For two days and nights, he said, he had moved slowly up what we called the Greater Queue—a line nearly two miles long, from the Garden Bridge well out into the district called Yangtszepoo, of men waiting for work. There were two tens of thousands of wharf coolies in Up-from-the-Sea, he had learned, and thirty tens of thousands of unemployed men: men who *wanted* to work, not counting beggars, tigers, idlers, and men who lived "on a string"— by flying their kites, trading a living for the reliable servicing of employed women.

The work on the wharves, once he was hired, Rock said, was at least not monotonous. There were many "skills" to be mastered: lifting, hauling, pushing, ayah, tugging at rope falls, pulling carts, rolling kegs, hooking bales, shouldering poles, prying levers, tilting boxes. And, above all, grunting. Ai, there were so many tones of grunting to learn!—almost as artistic as learning to play the flute.

This good mood, ironic as it was, and a product, I think, of those seven coppers carried home, did not last any longer than the money, which was gone the next day.

The third evening after work Rock said, "I saw Old Arm today, the race hero that Top Man told us about—said he was so rich, so puffed up, remember? He's a wharf coolie, like me! He may be rich at night but he wears rags by day and works at Haul-Ass Number One. I talked with him—or rather, I sat on my hams listening to him during our midday rest. He's shrewd, very clever —and he dampened me. Ayah! He's a man who'll never have enough. He had a circle around him. At first he was talking about the squirrel wheel we whites are in: how the yellows' ideas about us—that we have undersized brains, that we're shiftless and dirty, that we're incapable of learning to read or of running machines—how all these ideas are given proof, as the squirrel wheel turns, by our shirking, our lying, our going on the pipe, our squalid kite life, our breaking everything, our not wanting anything beyond today's bowl. The lids 'know' that the hogs are never going to better themselves because they 'see' that the hogs are stupid, lazy, unambitious, and (here is where those huge round eyes of Old Arm's began to glint!) cowardly. He's a short and slight man, with an almost comical ridge of bone running down the center of his crown, which is shaved, and he has a weak chin. But he has huge eyes, like an owl's, of a hazel shade that seems not to reflect but to suck all images into his head, and a voice that growls like a charcoal fire in a deep brazier when you blow on it. He has heat, force, plenty of it. I suppose his smallness is the wellspring of his power, and his power seems greater because he's small. Ai, 'cowardly' was the word that set him going, and this was the part I didn't like. He milks hatred. He talks about the Give-Us-a-Rice-Bowl campaign, but the tone of his voice says, '*Take it!* Take the rice. Don't let them call you cowards. Hit them. Use knives. Use wharf hooks. Use bamboo shoulder poles.' I had to ask him a question, I became upset and had to ask him: 'Have you ever killed a man, Old Arm?' The moment the question flew past my lips I wanted to eat it, get it back down, because this Old Arm was both arrogant and elusive; I could see he would put me in the wrong, he would make it seem that I had misheard, misconstrued. And he did but he didn't. I mean, he just stared me down, he made my question seem a squirt of impertinence that was somehow disloyal to the white race, but at the same time he did nothing to answer me—he did not by any means deny the imputation of blood hate and blood lust. I had the most peculiar feeling—that he would never forgive me for that question. And in the end I felt torn and depressed—perhaps because the man *I* had killed, or may have killed, was *white!* I think about Bare-Stick often—every day—you know that. And it's true. That was a *white* man I stabbed. I didn't hate Bare-Stick as much as I hated any yellow stranger in the upper hand. My instinct now, much as I hate every yellow turtle I meet in the streets, is to be against a policy of stabbing him with a wharf hook—against what I thought I heard in Old Arm's voice—"

Suddenly Rock began questioning me: Had Bare-Stick ever taken me?

I told Rock that I had never asked him for a list of women who'd got his kite up.

He pressed me hard, and soon we were in the midst of a shouting fight of a sort that seemed quite at home in the strife-packed puzzle box; and I ended it with a cruel line which subdued my Rock: "What are you trying to do, Rock—justify stabbing Bare-Stick?"

When Rock came home the next evening he told me this story:

At the end of each working day on the wharves, the coolies formed lines, at the wharf sheds of the various hongs, to collect the day's wages, and immediately beyond the cashiers' cages swarms of white human parasites descended on the newly paid coolies, competing with every wile for a share of the few coppers each man had just received. Beggars begging from beggars! Opium-dross providers, sellers of fried beancakes, pimps, lottery-chit-runners, wine-peddlers, thieves, younger brothers of volunteer whores. An impression, Rock said, of a gnat cloud of white men. There was a wild excess of white men in the city: thousands of tenants who had left their wives and children on the farms while they went up to the famous city of freedom to make their pursefuls; herds of idle men—last hired, first fired. Drifters: never able to earn enough to settle down, never able to learn enough to have an inner value, they had first been driven into a pattern of restlessness and then the restlessness had developed a pulse of its own, so that now wandering itself was the only pleasure in life. Scum, Top Man had called their betters, the ricksha boys; so these must have been the sub-scum of white humanity. How superior we had thought all the whites in the city to be when we had first arrived!

On being paid, Rock slipped the nine coppers of his day's sweat into a cloth bag and tucked the bag inside his trousers, where it could not be slit or pilfered, and he was elbowing his way through the eddying clamor of wheedlers and leeches when suddenly he was confronted by a stooping, twisted figure holding up a rack of brightly printed lottery chits. It was Mink. Rock recognized him at once and spoke his name, but for some time Mink could not seem to focus his eyes on Rock's face. He was as thin and limp and pallid-gray as a newborn field mouse, and his eyes looked

lost in a feverish dream—the pupils were constricted to tiny black
awl holes. And when Rock had at last put across his identity,
Mink's joy at the meeting was generalized, indiscriminate. Ayah,
he was on the pipe! Rock heard in Mink's droning, whining tones
of happiness the opium-smoker's deep indifference. Yet Mink
clung to Rock's sleeve, begging him to buy some lottery chits, in
a way that seemed to Rock to be something more than an appeal
for needed cash for the needed drug.

"Do you remember," Rock said to me, "Mink's thrill, the first
day of the Number Wheel riot, at the idea that he and the yellows
had a common cause? I had a strange feeling that his pawing of
my arm was saying, 'Please forget that. I wasn't myself then. I
was mad then, but I'm sane now!' What he was actually saying
was: 'I have good numbers. I have good inside numbers. Ask
the regular players. They all know that Mink has the best inside
numbers. Rock, my friend!' Then it seemed that he had recognized me on an entirely new level, as if the door to a new room in
his head had just opened up. And he began to weep. I tried to
persuade him to come home with me—to see you. Floods of tears
when I mentioned your name! But he said he had to sell his
chits, muttered something about the Forgetfulness Hong. I asked
him where he lived, and he gave me the name of a 'basket'—one
of the lottery pickup stations in the back of a shop here in the
Enclave—where he said a message would reach him within six
hours on any day, because there are two drawings daily. Look, I
bought two outers from him—he said they were just right for
you."

Rock held up two slips of cheap rag paper on which were
printed double pairs of numbers—on the upper one, 37-52—and
over the numbers little woodcut pictures in red ink, the codes
of the day: a wolf, a cormorant, a peony, a lotus for me.

I heard myself asking in an angry voice, "How much did they
cost?"

Rock made me bite my tongue. "Two coppers for a friend," he
said.

Next morning I took the slips to a lottery basket near our house
and checked them against the posted lists of winning outers of
that forenoon's drawing, but wolf and cormorant didn't even
figure, to say nothing of lotus.

Four days later Rock lost his job. He and three other coolies
had been assigned the unloading of a dried-hemp junk and they

had taken up the loose deck planks from the forward cargo compartments and were beginning, two by two, to hook up the fragrant bales, when Rock examined his partner for the first time —a short keg of a fellow in shameful rags, with eyes of an intelligence that seemed to forswear the rags; he almost seemed an actor in costume. His name was Gentle. Generally Rock had little to do with scurfy partners that he drew by chance for the wharfside labors, and he put down an impulse to speak to this one. Better simply do the work and not get involved. They carried two bales down the ribbed gangplank and placed them in the marked area on the asphalt Bund, alternating rear and front positions. For the third bale Rock was in front, holding the handle of his hook with both hands behind him. Halfway down the plank he felt a sudden jolt at the backs of his legs, and, about to lose his balance and fall forward, he felt the hook handle twist out of his hands. Stumbling forward from the plank onto all fours on the dusty asphalt, he heard a splash, and he was about to turn, rise, and curse his partner when he looked up and saw the thick little man already standing over him and pouring abuse on his shoulders. Then the hong's yellow comprador was standing there, and before Rock could stagger to his feet the short man had clicked out a lying story that Rock had for no reason let go of his hook and caused the fall of the bale. The comprador, who seemed on familiar terms with the heavyset man, would not even listen to Rock's side of the story; he took him to the wharf shed, then and there, gave him six coppers, and told him to be off. Rock raised a noisy fuss, and he stayed by the hong's wharf shed until payoff time, hoping to persuade the other two men in the hemp detail to be witnesses of his innocence, but he found that he could not recognize them among all the coolies being given their coppers. Afterward, in the crowd of paid men and urgent parasites, he saw the thick bullet who had been his partner and accuser talking with another man just as short as he, and much thinner—Old Arm. They were laughing.

(A Whitelist

We had to eat. Rock returned to the wharves and learned, after having stood in the Greater Queue two more days and nights, and then after he had been turned away by hong after hong, that all along the wharves his name was on a whitelist of coolies with bad records; in short, no hong would hire him. Baffled and bitter at the thought that he had been trickily punished by the whites' race hero for having done nothing worse than to ask a heartfelt question—*Did you ever kill a man?*—he refused to seek work as a servant or as a ricksha boy. We had to eat; I knew what I must do.

([The Filature

Early on a cold gray morning I walked along the Bund of the Model Settlement and over the Garden Bridge and out to the crowded industrial section called Yangtszepoo and took my place in the Lesser Queue, the line of women seeking work in the silk filatures.

As I moved slowly up the line during the day I saw on either side of me the dreary long narrow sheds of the filatures, their walls of prisoning brick, the northern slopes of their roofs sheets of wire-meshed, grime-filmed glass, every vent and fissure issuing into the winter air cheerless plumes of yellowy steam.

None of the women near me in the line had ever worked at reeling before, so I could learn nothing of what lay ahead.

When dusk fell the filatures all shut down—not, I gathered, for humanitarian reasons but because the work of reeling could only be done under light of day—and I found myself a scant fifty bodies away from the top of the line, which now also stretched a long distance behind me. Some of the waiting women had brought small round baskets of rice, which they consumed without sharing, but Rock and I had no rice; we had eaten only a single small millet cake a day for three days. To keep my place in line, I lay down in the dust, and I managed to sleep a good part of the night, though chilled to the marrow.

In the morning, after the alto whistles all along the narrow sheds blew the dawn call to work, I was readily hired, and soon I found myself inside one of the filatures, being led to my station by a white instructress.

Ai, what a sight! Along the entire length of the corridorlike building was a double series of copper basins connected to each other by steam pipes; there must have been three hundred pairs. On the one side stood a row of little white girls, beating at the boiling water in their basins with small reed brushes, and on the other, separated from the girls by a wire-net partition, were seated the white women reelers, dipping up cocoons from their basins and making swift motions with their hands and working treadles with their feet.

The air was hot, and the light pouring down from overhead was steam-dimmed.

Pipes clanked, the basins hissed and bubbled, the treadles clattered, the girls and women kept up a hum of talk.

My instructress, a narrow-shouldered, broad-hipped white woman who by her tucked upper lip and her flared nostrils made me feel like spoiled and wormy meat—ayah, how much haughtier and more condescending than any yellow she had become in her superior position!—led me along behind the row of reelers' basins to an empty stool. She sat down, placing me directly behind her, and, with a sniff of disgust directed, I supposed, at my presumed inability to learn anything at all, told me to watch with cat eyes.

Standing opposite, beyond the wire mesh, stirring cocoons in her basin of boiling water, was a girl perhaps ten years old, with lumpy features and a look of stubbornness and of middle-aged weary-wisdom. As soon as the instructress took her seat, the girl rolled a cocoon up the side of her basin with her reed brush and, balancing it against the brush with a fingertip, passed it through a small window in the wire screen and dropped it into the shallower reeling basin; then she passed through another and another, until there were six on our side. The instructress, with fingers apparently hardened to all feeling yet as sensitive as butterfly probes, plucked one cocoon after another, up to five, from the steaming basin and somehow found strand ends and with pinching motions attached them to a thread, itself finer than a human hair, which ran up through a system of brass rings and tiny pulleys back over her head and mine to a reel in a box on a high rack. By working the treadle she wound the five-strand thread up and back onto the reel. As the thread moved she dipped out the sixth cocoon and held its strand end in readiness to be attached to the thread the moment one of the other strands broke.

Within a few minutes she changed places with me and watched over my shoulder, breathing condescension and disapproval into my hair as I tended the thread.

I felt at once that she was right in her wheezing disparagement. I would never learn. I would fail. I would be dismissed. Then what would Rock and I do? The water and the steaming cocoons scalded my fingers. I could scarcely see the ends of the strands lying against the tawny cocoons, and my stinging fingertips seemed far too gross to pick them away. From time to time tears flooded my eyes, and I could not see whether a strand was breaking. I perspired in the air heated and moistened by the pipes and bowls.

I was aware of a new pair of eyes. I glanced up, and beyond the mesh, beyond the girl, I saw the face of a yellow woman staring at me. Then I heard my instructress and the yellow woman, who was evidently a section overseer, talking to each other, and by the time I realized they were discussing me it was too late—some sort of appraisal had been made, and I had not heard it.

For an interminable half morning the instructress stood back there watching me, sighing, hissing contemptuous instructions, reaching over my shoulders and slapping aside my parboiled hands when I made a mistake, and mending the errors with a dexterity that was itself a rebuke. I felt that if only this brooding lump of disdain, the more cruel in being white herself, would go away, then suddenly my fingers would be cool, they would fly, they would be pincers of perfect delicacy. Instead I grew clumsier, hotter, more tearful, and more fumbling.

Then, unexpectedly, she was gone.

I asked the girl, "How long was this seat empty before they brought me in?"

"Not long."

"What happened to the one who was here before?"

"She didn't mend the breaks fast enough."

"Was she awkward?"

"To be sure."

"More awkward than I am?"

"I don't know."

In spite of her guarded answers I felt that this snub-nosed girl, who told me her name was Pigeon, was in truth my partner and even (I had a moment's fantasy) a co-conspirator in some vague plan for a less bad world.

After a short time she whispered to me over the hissing of the steam pipes, "Watch out for Old She-Frog"—and the child jerked her head toward the yellow woman, the section overseer, who was at the moment moving away from us up the line of girls' basins.

In time I felt able to look around me. Two seats away from me on one side was a nursing mother. Her baby lay on the cinder-covered ground by its mother's treadle, wrapped tightly in blue coolie cloth, and remaining silent, as if instinctively knowing that if it cried and kept crying the mother would lose her job.

Once I saw Old She-Frog punish a negligent child, two or three stations from ours, by plunging the girl's hand in the bubbling basin that she was supposed to be tending. The child not only did not scream; she suppressed any show of feeling whatsoever. I glanced quickly at Pigeon's bumpy little face, where I saw only a half-formed frown, apparently of concentration.

Breaks occasionally did occur in the filaments that I was reeling, and watching for them, particularly when Old She-Frog happened to be passing, made me nervous. My instructress had told me that a good reeler would supply a reserve strand to the compound thread within two spans of a break, and she said that an unmended break would produce a thin spot in the thread and an off-shade line in the finished fabric.

This made me think of the elegance—the glossy perfection, as of the skins of plump washed grapes—of Big Madame Shen's many gowns hanging in their fortlike armoires in the house in the Northern Capital, and I thought of the night when I had tried on those dresses one by one: how beautiful, how beautiful I had been! And how many years had how many reelers spent making the threads for that one woman's wardrobe, and for me to have that single hour of radiance?

For some reason I was suddenly drenched by a melancholy longing for Rock—but for a Rock who was more than Rock, perhaps.

"Is it always so hot in here?" I asked Pigeon.

"They can only open the ventilators when there's no wind," she said. "The wind would break the threads."

At the noon rest Old She-Frog came along the aisle behind the reelers' basins and stopped at my station, and my heart pounded with fear.

But she was on a strange educative mission. She had in her hand a "book" of finished thread—a bundle of skeins removed from the reels and twisted into a packet of a certain classical shape. She reached it out to me and said, "I want you to feel the thread you're making. It is standard Tsatlee, Chop-Three quality. We have every new reeler examine a book of what she is making."

Taking the book in my hands I understood why. The silk thread, aggregated this way, was of the purest white color, and it had an iridescent luster, a luminosity, as if it were a source rather than a recipient of light, and it had, too, a body so resilient and nervous that it seemed almost alive in my grasp. I felt, for a moment, a paradoxical surge—of both humility and pride in what seemed a unified emotion.

But as I passed back the sweet fruit of my colleagues' work I remembered that the yellow hand into which I put it belonged to a creature nicknamed, in disgust and dread, Old Frog.

During the afternoon I talked more easily with Pigeon. She was, she told me, the third of seven children born to one mother by a team of fathers—there seemed to have been no exact census of the fathers, none of whom, in any case, was presently in evidence. Four of the seven children now worked, three girls in filatures and a boy, the eldest of the seven, named Little Lizard, her hero, as a sorter of chits in a lottery basket. Pigeon had worked in the same filature, at this very station, for more than a year. How many reelers across from her had come and gone? "I don't know," she said, "about a hundred." Uncomforting round number! Pigeon sniffled constantly; she was outwardly an ugly child, but I was deeply impressed by her stolidity, her inner strength.

"You must have a number-one mother."

"She's on the pipe."

"Who takes care of her?"

"The smaller ones."

"Where do you live?"

"On the run. We're always trotting." Pigeon's eyes sparkled as she said this.

By midafternoon I realized that, although it would take a long time for me to become truly skilled, I was going to pass muster as a reeler, for I had sharp eyes and reasonable dexterity, and I began to relax. Soon I was chatting with the women in the neighboring stations. Aural acquaintances! I could not study the faces of these women, because the single requisite of reeling was a fairly constant and intense concentration on the strands before one's eyes, yet from their voices and from what they said I had clear pictures of them: Left was sturdy, overblown, genial, but lacking in self-love and constantly half apologetic and half begging for agreement; Right was also physically rather powerful but a put-upon personality, rude, self-centered, and unkind.

They and I, as they and their neighbors and all the reelers, no doubt, were also doing, passed the time "riding our tongues to the palace"—taking out our frustrations in talk. We talked of the Enclave, of Fukien rubbish, of chinkty snobbishness, of Old Arm's coming Give-Us-the-Rice campaign, of puzzle-box landlords, of Old Frog and the invisible management of the filature, of prices and rents and fares, of our unemployed men, and of the only foods that whites could buy: culls and windfalls, honeycomb gut lining and tail bones and feet and maws and hocks, fruit with livid bruises and greens with limp and brown-edged leaves.

The day was too long. Pigeon, who must have started walking to the filature from home, wherever it might now be "on the run," at least an hour before dawn, had begun, by the second quarter of the afternoon, to sway on her feet, and though she was skillful at keeping her fingers out of the boiling water in her basin, they were dead white and loose-skinned, and her face was blanched, and her clothing appeared to be soaked with perspiration.

I, too, felt finger-wrinkled and damp from the steam and heat, but in my case weariness took the form of complacency, an easing of vigilance, and before I knew what had happened, I was suddenly the object of a torrent of scathing abuse from Old Frog. I had only four strands going onto my thread! Old Frog could see this from beyond the wire netting, from beyond Pigeon's back! She began to ask me cutting questions. I did not answer; I made myself too busy to answer. And I thought of Peace, in the great prizing barrel in the tobacco shed, when the young master had asked him questions about the work he was doing—and how he feigned a jaw-sagged and stammering stupidity. I could not pretend here to be an idiot, because that would surely cost me my job; but I could follow the same principle—safe silence.

The storm subsided. I tried to redouble my attention to the tiny spider cables, but my eyes began to fog and burn; my fingertips were numb.

At last, at last, merciful dusk closed down the filatures, and in my place in the long line of reelers filing out I soon had eight thrilling coppers in my sweaty palm!

The air outside was like the edge of a knife.

⟨ One of Two Consolations

On my third day at the filature, before the opening whistles in the dim light of dawn, in the waiting yard, I found myself suddenly engulfed in an embrace by a sputtering woman who, as I momentarily drew back in her arms, appeared to be yellow. Horrible! A *yellow* she-ram, lurking around this pen of white ewes? I fought to get away from her.

Then it came through to me that my assailant was Harlot of Gaza! Top Man had said she was somewhere in the city. Ai, sweet mixie friend from long ago! Now it was I who hugged.

How we babbled! She worked, it turned out, for the same filature as I, but not as a reeler; she was a sorter. All she had to do, she said, was to eliminate doubles—cocoons made by two silkworms at once—and pierced cocoons and those that were too tawny or malformed. I did not speak the thought, but I wondered if she had stepped up to this obviously privileged job on the strength of the yellow blood she owned. As the day lightened and I was able to search her face, it seemed to me that she did look more like a yellow woman than she had in her slave rags on the Yens' farm.

"Have you gone through the needle's eye?" I asked her. This, or "threading," was our euphemism for mixes' posing as yellows.

"Do you like my hair this way?" she answered. "No, I only thread sometimes at night."

We laughed together at this, but there was constraint on my side, and at once I wondered, with a flick of annoyance at myself, whether this holding back might have stemmed from envy. Did I *want* to be yellow, or at least a little bit yellow? I could certainly be excused for wanting to be a sorter.

The whistles, usually so welcome, were hateful that morning. We arranged to meet at the hong's outer gate and walk home to the Enclave together that evening.

I was light-fingered and clear-eyed all day, for the sight of Harlot had raised my spirits. Moth and Harlot, my dear consolations from the past! I decided during that day, as I thought about them, that it wouldn't do to try to bring them together. They wouldn't get along—and besides, I wanted each of them for myself, for different sides of myself! It seemed to me that Harlot was perhaps the more important to me, and perhaps precisely because of the tension in her between the advantages and disadvantages of being a mixie. She was more complex than Moth; one part of her could become a priestess, one part was grasping, one teased, one was selfless and capable of self-denial, one grieved at the tie with the master color, one took advantage of it. Moth was more spontaneous, impulsive; shallower; more simple fun; and more dangerous to one's man—or, on second thought, was she? Could she not be forgotten by a man as easily as he could be tilted onto her hip bones and shoulder blades? Two tigers at once!

Harlot and I walked home together in the dark. With Moth, who lived for each moment as it came, there seemed no need to fill in the past; now, with Harlot, there were so many questions to ask each other! Had she been Top Man's woman after I was sold away? How long had she lived in Up-from-the-Sea? Was Top Man's account of the decay of the Yens accurate? Had she ever heard or seen more of Auntie? . . . And all my life with Rock to pour out.

We dealt in fragments—half-answered queries and unfinished thoughts. Indeed, it was the eager and affectionate speed of our exchanges that mattered, far more than their actual substance. We promised each other that we would have plenty of time to delve, that on other days and nights we would tell out each happening to the end.

Then Harlot asked me, "Have you been approached by a hall?"

At first this question gave me a stab of fear, as I remembered "The Hall" of the Box River valley, the organ of punishment, vengeance, and yellow discipline.

"I think there may be an opening in mine," Harlot said. "There's a girl named Wood Mist—none of the rest of us can stand her. She puts on chinkty airs—wants us to kowtow to officers as we enter meetings. And then she turns around and cheats at house sparrow! She doesn't know the fundamental rule of gossip, that whatever you say bad about a person flies like an arrow, with your name on it, to that person; so that we're *always* hearing disgusting things she's said about the very people who are supposed to be her best friends. We have her maneuvered around now to the point of resigning. When she does, I'll let you know, and I'll get the others to look you over."

The Enclave, I gathered from Harlot, teemed with "halls"—small social circles, of twelve to fifteen members, mostly either all men or all women, who met frequently, transacted with great formality bits of meaningless business of a "charitable" nature, ate a modest feast, and then played various upper-class yellow parlor games. The halls were obviously a force for respectability; as Harlot put it, "We stand for bettering the race—by which I mean, if you stay with a man, you should be discreet if he isn't your own man, and

you shouldn't shout and be coarse in public places; things like
that. We have a list of strict rules. Our motto is, 'Heart as pure
as the carp pool.' By that we don't have to be prudes, you know—just
not public nuisances! Our hall flower is the persimmon blossom."

"What is the name of your hall?"

"Did I forget to tell you that? Ayah, those filthy cocoons rustle
around in my head. We call ourselves the Pavilion of Phoenixes.
Isn't that good and chinkty?"

"Are you mostly mixes?" Why was I so anxious as I asked that
question? Did I hope so fondly that they were?

"About half, dear."

"I'd like to come."

❡ The Good Life on a Day Off

The filature gave its reelers every tenth day off, on rotation, with the option, however, of working anyway to earn extra
coppers, and I was determined to take no rest days—but I made
an exception of the first that came up, for it happened to fall on
third third, the Spring Festival, the annual occasion, in rustic
areas, for cleaning graves and walking out to see fruit trees in
bloom. How would the city celebrate?

I was nervous about my extra coppers. On full hours I earned
twelve a day, and Rock and I subsisted on seven or eight, and I
had coppers hidden in crannies, in matting, in folded clothes, all
over the tiny space in which Rock and I lived. I was afraid of
thieves; I was, to be honest, afraid lest Rock and the money, both
idle, might venture out together in search of entertainment. I
proposed depositing the surplus, about twenty coppers, with
Silverfinger, the famous white moneylender of the Enclave, who
borrowed, too (at interest rates at least better than the yellow
moneylenders), and Rock agreed.

We set out in a mild morning. The streets of the Enclave were
crowded—with white shoppers streaming in and out of white-
owned stores, lottery-chit-runners, itinerant barbers, street vendors of candied apples and trinkets and artificial flowers, and
always, in the offing, murmuring beggars. At the street corners
stood yellow policemen, reminders of reality. To my eyes, which
in daylight hours for ten days had strayed from the delicate filaments of silk only to peer through steam-fogged air at the two

long rows of static figures at their copper basins, this scene danced. The entire Enclave seemed to me to be some great fair or celebration; the whites milling in the streets appeared to be gay and reckless, out to spend, flirt, take chances.

And what a feeling, here at the crossing of Four Rivers Road and Dog Road, at the very heart of the Enclave—what a feeling of white grandeur! There on the corner was the largest white-owned clothing store in all the yellow provinces. An exclusive teahouse, where, they said, you might find one of the three white men who had risen to the yellows' Provincial Council, or a brace of our foremost white poets, or a famous white woman dancer who could nightly express, with motions of her ivory limbs, all the yearnings of our race. A few doors away, behind a spirit screen carved from greenish jasper, an elegant tavern where the rich white henchmen of the Forgetfulness Hong often gathered to drink millet liquor. And, clustered within a radius of half a li, the white-staffed Enclave hospital; the Moon Garden Compound, made up of former palaces of yellow nobility, now chinkty apartments; the expensive hostelry ironically named Forbidden City; Silverfinger's establishment; five upper-class temples; and, best of all, the dazzling Good Life, playground of whites rich and poor. Under the skin of this splendor, tucked away out of sight but everywhere easily found, were the commonalty of lottery-chit baskets, shop-back temples, pipe dens, mousehouses, gambling halls, cheap tearooms, one-copper dosshouses, and everlasting puzzle boxes.

It was I who said on a sudden impulse, "Let's pass by Mink's basket and see if he's there. And maybe buy an outer or two."

"Ai, why not?" Rock said. "We'll never get rich on reeling."

The lottery basket was in the rear courtyard of a grease-spattered shop where twisted bean crullers were fried in deep peanut oil and sold, two for a single cash, to the poorest whites—who seemed to be the most avid players of the lottery. The word "basket" was figurative; it stood for a large room where a brass-keyed orderliness was encapsulated within a disarray that must have shaken the confidence of many a poor white chit-buyer. Old lottery chits were strewn everywhere, on tables and floor, in piles and swirls; old notices of drawings were stabbed and hung about the walls on spikes; chit boys sat on their hams slurping tea; players leafed through dog-eared chit-clue books searching for magic numbers. There was a constant chatter of accounts. At the middle of this chaos sat three white men like weasels, sorting, receiving, issuing, conversing with players in melancholy tones, keeping track of every rag and tag, imposing a discipline of mystery, hope, and surety on the entire scene.

We edged up to one of them.

"You have a chit boy named Mink with a bad back," Rock said.

"Yes," the basket man said with a courtesy most surprising in such a rat-clerk of the underworld. "He's one of the wharf boys."

"When does he come in here?"

"Before each drawing. About an hour before each drawing. He plays the chits, too, you know."

"I can imagine why."

The clerk gave Rock an odd look, as if to question whether Rock was Mink's provider, whether Rock was after Mink for opium money, whether he should protect his chit boy. But I saw the look fade, as, examining both of us, he saw us for what we really were —specks of dust blown in from the city streets.

"He may be late today," the clerk said, "on account of the killing."

"The killing?"

"You haven't heard? What damp stone have you been under? The whole Enclave is talking about it. Down on the wharves along Whangpoo Creek."

"What happened?"

"A yellow comprador caved in a coolie's skull with a bamboo mooring spar. Not just any miserable hog: this was one of Old Arm's fingers. Named Gentle. The whole Bund and both creeks are in an uproar."

"*Gentle?* What did he look like?" Rock's question was sharp.

The pale, long-nosed man, habituated to emotional chit-players, looked down from Rock and began shuffling papers. He had apparently cut off the interview.

Rock leaned forward and put a hand on the weasel's shoulder and shook it. "What did this Gentle look like?"

"Can't you see I'm busy?" the clerk said—but glancing up again into Rock's eyes, he evidently saw something that made him turn to his colleague weasel at the next desk and say, "Hai, this dung beetle here wants to know what the fellow looked like who was bashed. Did you hear anything?"

The second clerk looked at Rock: these men were obviously

bored—with their work, with the pathetic white vermin who were addicted to the chits, and, worst of all, with themselves.

"Some pig was in here saying the fellow was built like a dock bollard. That's all he said. That's all I know."

Rock was now agitated. "That's the one! I know that turtle. I'm *glad* they gave it to him!"

The clerk with whom Rock had been talking was, to all appearances, back at work; the second weasel, who had given the description of Gentle, was looking up at Rock. Rock was red. The third clerk asked the second, "What's going on?" The first weasel gave out a low whistle, forced out through the generous gap between his two front upper teeth, and in an instant a half dozen chit boys, who until that moment had seemed almost inanimate, crouching in a corner and against one wall with bowls of tea and a quilted pot, some fishing at their teeth with straws, were suddenly erect and picketed in a circle around Rock and me. The clerk with whom Rock had been talking arranged the papers on the table before him with a deliberation like that of a weighed judgment; then he stood up and walked around to the cluster of men, and the circle of chit boys opened to let him in. The pallid basket man barely came up to Rock's collarbones.

"What did I hear you say?"

Rock, I could see, was in one of his furies that might, at any moment, become all too rashly articulate, and I pulled at his sleeve and said, "Come on."

"Not so fast," the rat-clerk said who had started out so politely. He faced Rock. "Repeat what you said."

"What's caught in *your* throat?" Rock insolently asked.

The clerk stood in silence a long time, then said in a voice of such studied calm that its trembling seemed deliberate, "We don't allow any remarks in this basket about Old Arm or *any of his people*."

And with that the circle of chit boys, enclosing us more tightly, began to move toward the door, and Rock, who could count, simply turned his back on the clerk (and on me), and walked out as though by his own will, as though the cordon of disreputable toughs were nothing more than the circumference of his own splendid personality. I tagged along behind like a sheep.

Outside, gnawing at a bean cruller, Rock was ready for a wild time. I couldn't tell whether he was elated by the news about

Gentle or was merely responding to the first excitement he had had since he had lost his job on the wharves. He proposed that we go to the amusement grounds called The Good Life.

"I have to go to Silverfinger's first," I said, and I spoke firmly, because I knew that if I failed to lock up the extra coppers at once, they would all go off like a string of firecrackers before the day was over.

Silverfinger's Provincial Money House was the pride of the Enclave—soaring flights of column and beam, coruscating panels of lacquer and semi-precious stones, subtle screens and hangings, and glimpses of silver ingots and of cylindrical parades of copper coins! It was all a vision that might have floated like dream smoke up from the richest reaches of the Model Settlement, yet it was all right there, solid and palpable, in the white Enclave, and it was the lair of a white money-prince. With this opulence Silverfinger had hit upon a valuable hypnotism: in his halls poor whites felt vicariously rich at the very moment when he was fleecing them.

Shuffling on our hushing cloth soles across the polished stone floor toward one of the usury tables, we almost bumped into a huge white man who by his conceited bearing, his beard that had been thinned out to resemble the scraggly growth of a yellow elder, his silk gown with the nacreous sheen of a sunset on still water, appeared to be closely connected with all the money in this palace.

His glistening balloon back had scarcely been revealed when— thunder in my ears!—I recognized him. He was Duke, once the Matriarch Yen's Number One Boy who had decided I would not do as a miserable seamstress!

I ran to him. He recognized me, I could tell, yet he looked down his nose at me. "White Lotus? Hrrrmm. Ah, yes. One of the field slaves. I remember, I remember."

Ayah, Top Man had been right. What chinkty airs! Now Rock was standing at my elbow, breathing through his mouth like a stupid tenant—on purpose, I felt, to express some sort of inside-out hostility. Duke looked down at him as on a flea.

Angry, I found that my own tongue was unbridled. "We saw Top Man," I said. "He told us you were here in the city—said you'd grown grand. He said you were a lick-spit for the Forgetfulness Hong."

"Top Man—a syphilitic shroff. He's *trying* to grow grand." Then Duke was annoyed with himself for having reacted to my jibe, and he wanted to shake us off before he lost any more composure and face. "Excuse me, we're being rushed off our feet. There seems to be a mild money panic on account of the killing."

"Why a panic?" Rock asked, and Duke could not turn away from that skeptical voice with a ring of elation in it.

"Some of this white scum"—Top Man's phrase!—"seems to be afraid that Old Arm will break loose with his rice-bowl campaign."

"Why should that cause a panic?"

"Because thin hogs scare easily, that's all."

"While fat hogs get fatter."

"That is correct," Duke said, now in command of himself.

I could see Rock's perverse high spirits dancing in his eyes, as he said, "What will we find in our rice bowl when Old Arm gets it for us—Silverfinger's chestnuts rolled in deep-fried lottery chits?"

Duke became white as wall chalk and he said almost in a whisper, looking to right and left to see if anyone might have overheard what Rock and I had been saying, "I'd advise you pigs to watch your tongues. You're talking"—Duke's vehemence grew —"like lids." Duke turned and walked away.

So this was Old Arm's moral blackmail—anyone who was against him was against the white race.

Rock spat on the polished stone floor in Duke's wake, and, deciding to spend our money rather than save it, to put a punk fuse to our miserable little string of coppers and let them make what noise they could, we left.

At the geographical center of the Enclave, The Good Life lay close also to the seat of its paradoxical good cheer—for as the fecund horse and donkey breed the sterile mule, so poverty and misery in the Enclave often produced together a hybrid without a future: a powerful stubborn exuberance. We had it that morning. Entering the amusement ground through its ornate gate, we saw before us every facility for spending our coppers and our shallow joy: a wide park, a jubilation of new-decked trees and brick-edged paths spreading out lavishly in the vitals of the congested Enclave, a water-lily-lidded lake, a games ground, a temple, and a large octagonal hall, The Good Life itself, where at any hour of the day one could watch boxing, theatricals, magicians, jugglers. Over this area thousands of whites teemed, and all of them, whether splashing with sculling oars in sampans on the lake or shouting at pitchpot or kissing on the ground in the shade of trees or simply strolling arm in arm—all of them

seemed, like us, to be in the throes of bursting good humor. Among
the yellows in this city the overriding urge was not, as it had
appeared to be in the Northern Capital, to become learned and
influential; it was frankly to grow rich. But what with the job line
whites could never begin to mimic, or even to caricature, this
yellow ambition, so whites had learned to live for the present
moment. If there were any thoughts for the future, they were
fantasies of reincarnation in some other form than that of white
human beings. This day's hair decoration, this day's bad joke,
this day's crackling of the bed mats under the struggles of a
dalliance, this day's millet cake, this day's sight of a prestidigita-
tor pulling an endless string of colored pennants out of his mouth
—these were all that a white wanted.

We bought some peanuts and watched some boxing in the
great hall, and I had a picture in my mind of the Drum Tower
Boys "boxing the board" in a faraway marketplace, long ago, and
of Nose spinning with me in his arms; I responded to this memory
not with melancholy but by guffawing like a prostitute at the
slambang match here in The Good Life, and clutching tight at
Rock's arm.

Then we floated on the lake. There were so many sampans hired
out that we could scarcely move, and for a time we hung alongside another boat, wale to wale, and talked with a pair of young
lovers. They were adolescent and outwardly hard, and they had a
revolutionary zeal; they thought that after this killing Old Arm
was going to turn the world on its ear. Rock was twenty-four years
old, and scoffing he seemed middle-aged alongside these little
urban fanatics, to whom nothing had ever happened. The beard-
less boy grew angry, fancying that Rock was challenging not so
much his radicalism as his manhood, and even his very whiteness,
and he tried to push off with a commotion of waves, but Rock
laughed at him because we were in such a press of boats that he
could not put any water between us.

Later, at the food stalls, we bought some bean curds and a
bottle of raw wine, and Rock grew noisy and playful.

But I said to him, "Be careful, Rock. That arm they talk about
is long."

Rock said, "What can anyone do to me? I have no work. By
this afternoon I will have no money—and what I pretend I have
is yours anyway. I have nothing to do with my days. I'm nobody.
I'm really as hollow as a bamboo stick—nothing there, nothing at

all." Rock uttered these self-negations with the greatest of good
cheer.

As the hour of noon approached, when the first lottery drawing
would be made, we decided to go back to the basket to find Mink.

Beggars swarmed around the gate of the amusement ground,
and one of them came up to me and spoke my name. *O-mi-t'o-fu!*
It was Jug, the young Yen's body servant, who had been a handsome house slave, a mirror to his epicene master. Horrible! Now
he was a leper. The disease had not progressed far, but the skin
about his nose was discolored, and pits and nodules had formed
on his nostrils and lips. How he had used to swagger! I told him
I had encountered both Duke and Top Man, but Jug was not
interested in anything outside himself. Rock gave him a large
part of our remaining wealth—two coppers—and we hurried
away, both from him and from thoughts of him.

Rock strode into the back room of the lottery basket with a
sneer and an extruded jaw, as if expecting, and half hoping, to
be thrown out again, but a drawing was imminent, and the room
was packed, and when Rock deliberately forced his way to the
table of Weasel Number One and asked for Mink, the clerk appeared not even to recognize him, and with the sweet, courteous
tone of his first answer to Rock said that Mink had, yes, come
in, and he was probably with the numerous chit boys squatting
in the tea corner.

So we found him. Though pale, he was alert and cheerful, for
he had high hopes that with *this* drawing he would scoop up
money enough for a year of pipes. He recognized me at once and
seemed glad to see me, though he was undemonstrative.

We waited for the drawing. Mink's numbers were worthless,
and he suddenly went almost limp with moroseness. Rock persuaded him to come to our puzzle box and spend an hour with us.

At the house we went to Moth's compartment, where we found
her "living the lids' life," as whites called idling, with Old Boxer
and Ox Balls, and with the street-waterer from upstairs-lower-
right-front, named Round Knees, and his girl, a hard little piece,
Trumpet Flower. With our arrival, we were eight bodies in the
stuffy cubicle, and there was barely room for us to lounge about
the floor.

Moth was exercised about a woman downstairs who had been
arrested for whoring. "It isn't as if she were just an 'easy time' "—
the phrase for amateur street pickups, bed-mat enthusiasts of

the Enclave, who, having given themselves at no charge to men, would graciously accept tidbits of money from them as "gifts" of appreciation. "She makes a full-time career of it. She practically lives in Old Barrier. They had her in there for a month, and the day she was released she went out soliciting again, and now she's back in. She's really shameless. Works alone, doesn't even work under a whore matron. I think she needs a *tai-fu*, too—she has some queer-looking pimples. Dirty thing! Why does she do it? I wish she'd move out of this puzzle box. She's always stumbling in here at any hour of day and night with some clappy ricksha boy."

How prim was Little Moth, mistress to two tigers! I suspected her of wanting to seduce my Rock, and the only thing that protected and comforted me, on this point, was that Rock thought her a female clown. Moth was not quite an "easy time"; she was just a natural girl. In her, generosity and selfishness were indistinguishable, for they worked toward the same delightful end, where men were concerned.

Now she fetched a garlic bud and a knife and with deft strokes of her petal hands she diced it, and she passed the bits around, and we all took some. Thus did Moth act the hostess. Garlic! How raw and hot our pleasures had to be! Some whites considered garlic healthful—ward against head colds. I believe, though, that Moth thought it aphrodisiac, and considered that, sweet hostess, she was dispensing, in those burning little white cubes, good times for the very near future, which she might happily share with one candidate or another.

The street-waterer, Round Knees, began to rail against a yellow shopkeeper in an Enclave food store who had, Round Knees felt, pushed his prices beyond the boundaries of fairness and reason. The man was, of course, a Moslem. Three quarters of the merchants in the Enclave were yellow Moslems, and much as the minority of white storekeepers railed against whites' buying "sheep-eaters' stuff," the population kept on going to Moslem shops; and now Round Knees was complaining of this. "They think it's chinkty to buy from a yellow man, they want to feel important. Lots of them go in there because it makes them feel big to have a yellow man wait on them. But all the time he's giving them the old turtle head right between the legs. Ayah, I hate those yellow mutton-eaters."

Mink sat leaning his twisted back against a wall, and now and again tears came in his eyes, possibly when he thought of the un-reasonableness of the lottery; he slaved for it day after day, and it would not give him a grand reward. Or perhaps he was feeling the pain of his need.

Rock, who was beside him, asked Mink if he had been nearby on the wharves when the killing had taken place, and Mink replied in a meandering yet alert and pointed way, going straight to the center of Rock's unbending position.

"You whites," Mink began, as if he were not one, "do you think you're going to get out of this turtle-screwing Enclave by com-plaining about Old Arm? That he pretends to be a simple dock-man, and he's ten other things? I know what you say! That he'll put you down like a mandarin at the Jade Table or any other restaurant or teahouse? That he's ruthless—that he didn't weep like a woman this morning when they knocked Gentle over like a bale of goods? Who else is there to help us? Who else is working for us? Who else cares? Who else cares what happens to a useless chit-trotter who's on the pipe?" Tears were suddenly dribbling once more down Mink's nose. He paused. "Yes, I was nearby—at the next hong's wharf. But I didn't see anything, until a crowd gathered, and I didn't think much of *that,* either. There's always some argument or accident that will draw eyes. But then I saw Old Arm walk over to the group—someone was with him who had run to fetch him—and I made my way over there. I never found out what the argument had been about, but it must have been some money problem: a dirty yellow comprador wouldn't kill a wharf coolie over anything but money. The compradors all along the line knew Gentle *very well.* Anyway one blow had done it. And I saw Old Arm stand there as if he were looking at a dead wonk. All right, Rock, I grant you: that turtle is a cold one, he won't let anything get in his way, least of all loyalty to a friend. But what of it? *He's for us.* That's the way I see it. Well, Old Arm didn't try to get the police after the comprador, I guess he knew what a farce that would have been. He just told some of the white coolies there to heave Gentle's body out on the Bund roadway, so that a benevolent burial society would find it and cart it away. And he went back to work. That was all there was to it. But within an hour we began to hear definite reports that Old Arm was putting out instructions to get everybody ready for the rice-bowl campaign."

"When is the campaign supposed to begin?"

"Ai, I should think it would take two or three months to get the whole Enclave worked up. Sometime in the summer, I guess."

Then Rock—casual Rock!—spoke in a way I had never heard from him before. "I agree with Mink, that Old Arm seems to be for us, and that there doesn't seem to be anyone else. But listen: while I was working the docks I sat with him. He talks reason but he has blood in his eye. You know me, Mink, well enough to know that I won't hold back from a quarrel or even a real fight over something that matters, but I don't think Old Arm has the right way. When it comes to the lids his way won't work—his way, as I see it, being to ask for what we want and then, when they don't give it to us, as they certainly won't, to resort first to strikes and then to letting things just get out of hand, in rioting and running wild. But *they* can run, too. Remember the Number Wheel, Mink? Ask White Lotus here sometime about Peace's revolt—it takes more forethought than Old Arm has in his head to organize for blood, because when bloodshed is in prospect, men start behaving in unexpected patterns, brothers go back on brothers, and the ones who have been brave talkers suddenly turn into bad-breath informers. But it's more than that that worries me. Something happened to me on the docks, at the hands of this very fellow Gentle, because I was indiscreet enough to speak out against Old Arm, and that experience made me realize that what Old Arm wants more than anything—more than jobs for white men—is power for himself. I tell you, Mink, I'm ready to try to *do* something about being a hog in a lid world, but I have to be shown a selfless white leader, a man who lives with all his heart for the race and for that alone. And one who has a better way than Old Arm's, though I've no idea what that could be."

During this speech of Rock's, Mink seemed to fall farther and farther into the agony of his craving for a pipe; his face became pasty, he began to perspire. And all he said when Rock had finished was: "You'll never find such a man."

He left to return to the wharves.

Later Rock and I decided to go out for a walk. Ai! Strolling in evening streets! *This* was what it was to have a good time. We sauntered along through the shopping areas of the Enclave, stopping now and then at a buzzing, chuckling group where I might spot an acquaintance from the filature or Rock a wharfman he had met; and there we would become friendly at once with other strangers. Flirtation was open, and one had a sense of adventure, as if taking a trip far from one's dull home. We would move on, stop while I read aloud to Rock the bill of fare of a restaurant out from whose swinging gates savory smells would float, and then we would find another group and pause to joke and to appreciate handsome faces and flashing eyes. Gradually with a queer sensation of wading into deeper and deeper waters, we wandered into the more pretentious quarter of the Enclave, where the chinkties lived behind high walls in wide streets. And here, walking in the evening shadows airing a siskin in a bamboo cage, came Top Man alone. He did not seem displeased at meeting us, and I made a good start with him by saying that we had encountered Duke that morning at Silverfinger's, and that we had found him just as Top Man had advertised; I said he looked "too fat for satin and too sleek for silk."

Then Rock joined in, saying he had been exposed to Top Man's "other dear friend" about whom he'd spoken to us—Old Arm. Top Man snorted. Rock then openly told what had happened on the wharves. Top Man was delighted. He raised the birdcage to his face and made kissing sounds and said to his pet bird, "Did you hear that, darling, about that turtle Old Arm? What did you think of that?" I could see on Rock's face that he was already wondering why he had confided in this foolish shroff, and rather mischievously I said, "After his job campaign, we'll all be testing coins, Top Man! You'll have to look lively to keep your position."

The shroff humorlessly said, "Nonsense. The campaign will fail. I'll tell you something. The white race will never get anywhere by forming mobs. Individual effort—that's the only way. Each man must set himself a goal—as I did, mind you: I practiced ten hours a day, and it wasn't easy for me to get the coins to practice with, I'll tell you that. I had to get my hands on perfect coins and defective ones, too. It wasn't easy. And shroffing itself isn't so easy—though I won't complain, it's a good rice bowl. Every white man for himself, I say, but it takes work. Patience, silence, swallowing puke. It takes time and work. And I don't know whether your typical white scum can ever bring himself to work hard enough. He'd rather sit around and listen to Old Arm and dream about great days to come. . . ."

We parted on better terms with Top Man than we particularly wanted. As we walked home, Rock said, "I can't stand doing nothing."

(A Story of Sleeping Birds

One evening when I returned home from the filature Rock was not at the puzzle box. I saw that he had not brought in the day's rice allotment—for as an unemployed male he was on the municipal rice lines and was entitled to one tenth of a catty of cooked rice a day, which he and I stretched to serve two. There was no stigma attached to being on the lines, but Rock, whose only wealth in those days was time, hated the cost of a half afternoon he had to squander getting through the long line. I reasoned that he must have been out most of the day, at least since noon, and as I had lately been worrying about what he would begin to do in his idleness, it was with an anxious mind that I set about stripping a head of white cabbage for frying. I did not cook it. Rock still did not come in. I looked in at Moth's compartment, but he was not there. I went back to wait for him. Tired and finger-sore from my day at the boiling basin, I began to doze, struggling against my weariness and having a feeling of being jostled by whispering figures in crazy half dreams.

Then I heard a clatter in the puzzle-box stairwell, an everynight sound of homing drunks, but as Rock had not touched spirits for a long time (for he had not the money with which to buy them), I sighed and turned on my side on my mat.

Our door, bursting open, struck my foot, and I started up into sitting position to see two big men looming over me. One had his arm flung over the other's neck.

"Hey, you bitch fox, look what I found!"

O-mi-t'o-fu! It was Rock and Bare-Stick!

I jumped to my feet and, in my surge of relief at the thought that Rock had not killed a man, I flew into a smothering hug of both men.

"Want to see my scars?" Bare-Stick asked in the friendliest way.

"No no no *no!*"

Bare-Stick, pummeling Rock for my benefit, said, "I love the son of a turtle. I've forgiven him."

And Rock said, "But I haven't forgiven *him*. I told him that if he laid one night-soil-filthy finger on my woman again I'd inscribe him again with a pork knife—only this time I'd do the job right."

Rock protecting me! Was he being ironical? I chose to think not.

Rock had forgotten, or anyhow failed, to get the rice ration, so we had nothing to eat but white cabbage. I commandeered a brazier and fried some, searing the pale chunks swiftly in hot oil and turning them out into bowls crisp and underdone.

Bare-Stick had been in the city only two days, and he was still in that bemusement of the first exposure that we had also felt. Freedom! Superior hogs! He had his little bag of copper coins, just as Rock had had, and they were going fast.

As Bare-Stick asked questions about the city, I watched Rock for signs of the immense relief I supposed he must be feeling at the knowledge that he was not a murderer. Instead I saw short-ness of temper, irritability, and hints of a greater frustration than ever, until—

We asked about Groundnut, and Bare-Stick told this strange story:

Provisioner Lung was the scourge of the lower hand of every village in the Box River valley. Whenever tenants fell behind in the payment of their extortionate rents, they would be tormented by visitors from The Hall, and at last their homes would be stripped, as ours had been, and Bare-Stick's, too. When he had recovered from the stabbing, Bare-Stick had made an entirely fresh start—had reborrowed and rebuilt, and had quickly fallen behind again in his debt to Provisioner Lung. Indignation grew among the whites at Provisioner Lung's ruthlessness and the severity of all the yellows in "keeping the pigs penned," as they put it, but at the decrepit temple Groundnut and his new col-league, Runner, kept cautioning against attempts at overt re-venge. "They are more cunning than we are," Runner said. "They are cats, and we are thrushes." The two priests talked much this way, of thrushes, and pipits, and magpies, for they seemed to have the winged creatures of the region under a spell. The temple had become an aviary. Groundnut was a natural warden of wild birds; Runner seemed to be profoundly their companion, directly in touch with them. A wild bird, a palpitation of color, was always to be seen on Runner's shoulder or perched on a forefinger; the flocks of heaven had whitewashed the temple roofs with their droppings. Runner and Groundnut had come to be known throughout the valley as the Bird Priests, and now it was that Runner drew an inspiration from his air-beating friends. News came one day of the final, insupportable hardship: Pro-visioner Lung had announced that he was raising all his rents, of every sort, by five per cent. A crowd of white villagers swarmed to the temple, and it appeared that this time there would be no way to curb their rage. Runner spoke to them, with blackbirds circling around overhead unafraid of the grumbling people, and said he would like to lead a troop—a "flock," he called it— of ten men to go to Provisioner Lung to try to make him change his mind, and when Runner said he wanted ten of the strongest men in the valley to go with him, the mob cheered, because it seemed he had come round, at last, to the use of force as our only means of defending ourselves. Bare-Stick volunteered, but Groundnut rejected him, as not yet fully mended from the "inscription" Rock had incised in him. Off Runner and Groundnut went with their sinewy delegation, early the following morning, and with many others Bare-Stick waited at the temple for the group's return. But they did not come back all day, and those who waited feared that they had been killed by yellow gendarmes or by The Hall. At the last of dusk those at the temple saw the "flock" winding its way back down the valley road, and when the strong men arrived at the temple it was nearly dark, but it was easy to see that they had not been in even the slightest physical scuffle. They were in a daze of weariness and befuddlement, as if the priests had them, like their wild birds, under a charm. Runner announced that the flock would return to Provisioner Lung's at dawn; then he sent everyone home. What buzzing there was in all the lower hands that night! It came out that Runner and Groundnut had led their men to the gate of Provisioner Lung's great commissary palace in Wang Family Big Gourd Village, and Runner had directed them to "perch" in a group, each man to stand on one leg, with the other leg drawn up, "like a bird asleep." It had been painful work to stand that way, the men of the "flock" reported. Provisioner Lung's gates had remained barred all day. No one had emerged; no one had entered. The villagers were astounded by this account. How had the men allowed themselves to be used in such an absurd way? "Wait," the members of the flock stubbornly and repeatedly said. "Let's see. Give it some time." They were certainly hypnotized. And indeed the curiosity of the villagers was powerfully aroused. The next morning several additional men pressed Runner to allow them to join the delegation; they wanted to see for themselves. Runner took them, and the flock swelled to nineteen. All that day the men stood in silence, each on one leg, outside the merchant's gate. A handful of yellows came to stare at the sleeping birds for a time, laughing at the idiotic behavior of the whites, and once Provisioner Lung himself came to the gate and peered out and slammed it shut again. On the third day, still more lower-handers volunteered, and this time Runner accepted Bare-Stick among others. Nearly fifty men "perched" that day. Yellows came to watch, and this time they did not laugh; Provisioner Lung's gate remained locked. On the sixth day, Runner allowed some women to go. By the tenth day a crowd of three hundred poverty-stricken white tenants went to stand, each on one leg, outside Provisioner Lung's compound, and a large crowd of yellows, too, turned out, and by this time the upper-handers were surly and disapproving. The Provisioner's gate remained closed. By the fourteenth day the yellows were openly angry. Runner had daily instructed his flock what to do under every circumstance, and on the fifteenth day the sleeping birds were tested. A ceremonious troop of five masked men of The Hall rode up. They asked who the leader was. Silence; perching. Runner was buried in the flock. They repeated their question loudly several times. No response. They rode into the flock, which simply parted; those who were jostled put down their raised legs and moved aside and then resumed their perching. One of the masked men, in a fury, dismounted and began rushing at sleeping birds at the edge of the flock, pushing them, and knocking them down. Quietly those who were felled stood up and perched again. The men of The Hall rode off; their fiction may have been that they had not lost face because they were masked, but all the same they slapped their horses' reins and kicked their ribs. The next day a large mob of yellows, risking bitter loss of their bare faces, rushed the flock, hurling stones and swinging staves. Several of Runner's by now faithful followers were badly bruised and cut, but with a courage bred of lifelong suffering they managed to repress every sound and sign of pain, to recover balance, and go on and on and on and on with their quiet perching. The fury of the mob broke into shame. One could see the effect of years of mouthing the precept "Hurt no living creature." These pliable one-legged things were as helpless as wingless birds—shame! shame! The yellow mob ebbed in silence. Afterward Provisioner Lung came out and glared at the big flock for a long time. Once he croaked, "Go back to work. You're all getting farther and farther behind." The flock perched silent; many of the sleeping birds had closed their eyes.

Provisioner Lung soon returned within. The next day there was a sign on his gate: *Who started the rumor that rents were to be increased by five per cent? It is not true! It never was true! Go home!*

❨ Idle Rock

Rock began to lead an irregular life, independent from mine. This was what I had feared. Sometimes he was missing for two days at a stretch; often he came in late at night, after I was asleep. What strange reactions he was having to Bare-Stick's return and to the story of Runner's "perching"! I could tell that he had been stirred by Runner's bizarre success, if it had been that, against Provisioner Lung; when we were together he kept reminiscing about Groundnut, not the priest but the beggar. Yet in his own life Rock seemed to be moving away from hope and determination.

One evening I heard quarreling in another quarter of the puzzle box, and among the loud shouts I thought I distinguished the voices of Rock, Old Boxer, and Ox Balls. I was about to investigate when Rock irrupted into our compartment carrying a bundle—a large, dirty piece of coolie cloth slung baglike by its corners, containing a good rounded weight. He put it on the floor and untied the corners and opened out the cloth—a heap, a month's heap of rice! The grains were dirty. "Wash it carefully," Rock said. "There may be mule dung in it."

"Did you steal it from the rationing godown?" I could put no severity into my question, for I felt a surge of senseless pride in whatever outlawry against the yellows Rock had conspired in, and with the hollow of hunger that seemed always to be in me, I was *glad* to see the rice.

"Remember Groundnut's pigeons?" Rock said, and he gave out a deep-throated chortle that had in it the pleasure of the afternoon's badness, whatever it had been, as well as an exultation before me, a youthful showing off, and even some of the harsh aggressiveness of the quarrel (the shouting I had heard) over the spoils. "I've been thinking about those pigeons—thought about them all afternoon. All that game with the pigeons was Groundnut's invention, I suppose you knew that. Do you remember, did you ever watch, his hands around the body of one of those birds?

Like nothing more than warm air on their feathers, his hands."
And so he went on about Groundnut; he did not speak Runner's
name.

I asked him where he had stolen the rice, but at first he would
not tell me.

"Wash it and cook it and we'll eat it. Don't stint me. There'll
be more."

He waked me up in the night, however, to tell me about the
theft.

It had been a so-called sweeping. A group of five had been led
by one of the teen-age tigers who lived in upstairs-upper-back-
right: the leader, named Storm, and Rock, Old Boxer, Ox Balls,
and another youth named Gate Boy, all long-sleevers save Rock.
"These young shoats have thick bristles," Rock said. "They don't
care for or about a single thing in this world. They're pure city
stock of whites—never noticed a leaf, or what's in a human eye,
for that matter. Ayah! What cold little eyes *they* have—pipe eyes.
They're getting on the pipe; smoke a little but aren't hopelessly
caught yet. But they already have that faraway look that I think of
as three-quarters dead, though *they* speak of hogs who try to live
clean as 'the deads.' They think they're the only ones who are
alive. And ai! They *were* alive this afternoon. Made *me* feel alive!"

At near midday the five made their separate ways, each by each,
Gate Boy alone on a bicycle, the others afoot, to one of the busiest
commercial intersections of the Model Settlement, the crossing
of West-of-the-Mountains Road and Southern Capital Road. Here
traffic from the Bund, cargoes of all sorts loaded onto heavy carts
and flatbed motor trucks, was creeping toward shops and godowns
away from the river, at cross purposes to a swarm of smaller
vehicles, wheelbarrows and donkey carts and rickshas and bi-
cycles, traversing the noonday city. Horns, bells, cries of warning
and alarm! On a railed pedestal at the center of the intersection
stood a splendidly uniformed policeman with crossed white shoulder straps and three clinking medals. This satrap sawed at the air
with his pure-white gauntlets, and made gestures of refusing,
punching, tickling, beckoning, swinging as if at enemies, and
swatting flies that were not there, all the while twirping at a brass
whistle and swiveling on paramilitary hips now to the city's
longitudes, now to its latitudes—ai, dancer of the law! But futile.
He made no sense of the onrushing vehicular floods. He was in
a bad temper. Coolies, drivers, cartmen, cyclists, ricksha boys—

all were in the same vile humor of haste and near-catastrophe.

Just as the four pedestrians were arriving at the crossing, walking separately on either side of Southern Capital Road, approaching West-of-the-Mountains Road from the direction of the river, and bracketing the main flow of Bund traffic, in the throat of which, just then, there happened to be three large motor vans in tandem loaded with great hills of burlap bags filled with rice— just at that moment there was a tinkling crash on the far side of the intersection, followed by a chorus of abusive shouts and a sharp trilling of the traffic policeman's whistle. A crowd rallied at once, of pedestrians, drivers, carters, ricksha boys, and passengers. The street was blocked. The shouting rose on a crescendo like that of a quarrel of many curlews. The policeman leaped down from his stand and stormed upstream.

It seemed that over there a stupid cyclist (our Gate Boy) had cut sharply across the bows of an oxcart, causing it to veer one of its massive hubs into the headlight of a motor truck. The two vehicles were now mated in a shameless public embrace.

As soon as the policeman was swallowed deep into the swarm of onlookers, the team of four pedestrians on the river side of the intersection darted out into the roadway. Knives twinkled out from beneath their tunics. Five strokes of four blades, twenty slit bags. A pretty rapids and fall of rice onto the street. Now clever Gate Boy, who had taken a moment of wild argument between the drivers of the miscegenating oxcart and truck to duck out through the audience, bike and all, joined the others. Next to where the rice showered two men spread cloths, the other three used the heels of their hands to sweep heaps of grains onto them. They filled five cloths, tucked them up, and scattered swiftly in five directions.

"Now I know," Rock said at the end, "why they call themselves tigers. They really are."

He stretched luxuriously, yawned, and fell asleep, and I was left awake to think about the direction in which my energetic Rock was moving.

Rock sold some of the rice, and he hid the money. Said he was going to buy a long-sleeved tunic when he had saved enough.

Another evening, coming in late again, he was in a talkative mood. "I'm attracted to opium," he said. "I was with Mink this afternoon. We took a walk down along the Bund. What a crowd of boats in the anchorage! Beggar boats and fishing boats were

swarming along the edge of the embankment. Out in the center
of the stream the junks were anchored, tier on tier of them. Mink
knew them all: The plain ones from right here in Up-from-the-Sea
with brown oiled wood. Foochow junks—high sterns with gay
paintings in primary colors; they had masses of long poles slung
outboard at each side—how could they steer at sea? Ningpo junks,
with sinister black hulls, and red and green paintings on the top-
sides—little eyes painted on the bow. But Mink was taking me
along through all this to show me something else farther along:
four unsightly dismasted vessels anchored in a row, well out. The
opium hulks, he said. They're a safe place for opium to be kept as
it's imported, registered, taxed, and bonded. The *Monkey*, the *Dart*,
the *Valiant*, the *Fair Wind*. He said the *Valiant* had been a trading
junk that had been dismasted off the Saddles. They had to use
hulks, Mink said—if they tried to bond the stuff ashore the customs shed would be burgled, stormed, set fire to! I wish you could
have seen Mink's eyes when he was gazing at the barges. What a
look of love! I envy a man with that much passion. How wonderful to believe in one thing, and one thing alone, with every fiber
of your mind and being. He told me about what it's like to get a
lamp on—the animation, the sense of kinship with the man on
the next divan, the suspension of time, the sweet talk, all pain
gone, hunger gone, poverty gone, whiteness gone. Mink is thin;
the pipe takes the place of food for him. But he has a sweetness in
his eye now—he has no shame about foolish things he did in the
past, he just floats along from pipe to pipe. His eyes looking at
those ugly hulks anchored out there in the brown water! I tell you,
I envied him. I'm attracted to it. I am."

I had been cooking Rock a late meal, squatting. Now I was on
my hands and knees, facing him. "Don't you dare even try it! Not
once! Never! It washes all the guts out of a man. *Be like Mink?*
You're a *man*, Rock!" I was screaming at him.

He spread his hands out to stop my tirade. He was smiling like
a grandfather at a grandchild's tantrum. . . .

There were nights when Rock did not come home at all. What
sleeping I did on those nights was alert; I started up from oblivion
at the slightest sound. My worrying and my weariness were at
odds all the time.

Then there came a stretch of several days—no Rock. I had no
daylight during which to hunt for him, and I could only wait.

On the fourth evening when I came home from the filature he

was there. His face was a pulp. Both eyes had been blacked. His cheek was bruised. His lip was cut, but he managed to smile, and he said, "What you see isn't all, little mouse."

"Who did it?"

"Turtle police."

I undressed him. There were horrible bruises all over his body. A woman weaver lived in the former kitchen downstairs, and I went down and begged some flax tow from her, and I made several cold compresses for the worst of Rock's black-and-blue welts. And I felt a familiar anger, and with it the same tender unskilled nurse-love as once long ago—for Dolphin in the slaves' sick-house, with the ancient swindle of a priest lounging in the shade by the door. I had no time to regret the past; I could only suffer it as a reinforcement of the present: I was most angry now, and most tender.

It had been folly, Rock admitted—but fun, too, at first. The idea had been Gate Boy's. It seemed that some gangs of yellow youths, Fukien rubbish who lived near the south flank of the Enclave, had been stealing vegetables from white truckers who had their stands in that quarter of the white section. Gate Boy suggested setting an ambush for one of those raids. Seven tigers, including Old Boxer, Ox Balls, Storm, and Rock (yes, he called himself a tiger now, though he still could not afford a long-sleeved tunic), had picked their station and with the grateful blessings of an often victimized trucker had tucked themselves into blind spots near the open display. They had had to wait overnight. The second afternoon the yellow robbers came—five gaunt, dirty yellow boys, about twenty years old. The tigers jumped too soon, for they could not wait to see the trucker hurt, and the rubbish ran and it was only outside the Enclave that the tigers caught them. They began a thorough dusting. "I cannot tell you," Rock said, "what the sensation is, exactly, when you smack a yellow face with your fist. It's very queer. I wonder if this is it?—you're letting a whole lot of *time* out through your skin. Not exactly time. Some kind of pressure. Has to do with time, though—something that made you old long before you should have been." (But, Rock! Rock! Were you not against Old Arm? How did you get into this senseless fight?) Rock said that in the melee he felt twice as strong as ever before. Then—another swarm. Police. An alarm had apparently been raised in the Enclave, because these turned out to be dirt-of-dirt—Enclave policemen. The public show was a model of yellow propriety: the fight was stopped, the tigers were all arrested, the rubbish were all released.

"They took us to Old Barrier House," Rock said. "You've seen it, haven't you? No? It's a bold building made of stone, thick walls— out in the Model Settlement, *on their ground*—with Moslem arches and a central tower from which guards can watch every wink and gob of spit in the whole compound. They took us in past the iron exercise cages where, it being afternoon, the prisoners—almost all hogs—were being aired; and how they jeered us: for getting caught! Ayah, the turtles 'questioned' us. Ayah, yes. . . ."

But Rock did not describe the beatings, he talked only about one of the policemen who had taken part in them.

". . . For some reason he concentrated on me. He was fattish— but one of those fat men who remain strong without keeping fit; and he had a broad face with beads of sweat popping out on it. The harder he worked on me, the more friendly and *merciful* he looked. I kept up my courage by thinking about him. I tried to see things his way: 'Look,' I said to myself, 'he's been brought up to think all whites are swine. He's had no education. He sees plenty of whites, but they're all thieves, street vixens, whore matrons, pimps, cutpurses—"that's what pigs are like"—I can hear him. At best he's had dealings with some of their "good hogs" —the squealers, the slimy cowards who inform on their fellow whites, and most of *them* are shadies who trade informing for free passage. "So"—says my friend—"give this pig a pounding: this'll teach him about crime. This is the only way to keep the pigs in their pen where they belong. Jail," he says, "won't correct anything. Ai, pigs *like* jail. Old Barrier means roof and steady rice and jolly company. So, let me give it to this dirty pig. . . ."' But after I tried to see things his way awhile, I thought, 'Who *is* this bastard of a turtle? I wonder what made him want to be a police-man in the first place. No doubt he was Fukien rubbish, or the next thing to it, to begin with—listen to the turdy grammar he uses—and now that he's big he has the authority to swing one of those, one of those . . . Ai! The bastard is paying off his own fear —that's what the sweat is about—*he's afraid of me*. The miserable son of a turtle. Look, he can't stop. He's started on me and he can't stop. Shall I say something? Threaten him? "I'll get you when I'm out of here." No. That would only stretch it out. Look at those pressed lips! Is the bastard trying to squeeze out a smile? . . .'"

I said to myself: I will have to take Rock in hand. No long
sleeves.

(At My Expense

I held the purse strings. One evening when I came home
from work Rock, now recovered from his police markings, was
waiting for me, and there was what seemed to me a forced cheerfulness in his greeting.

"Let's go out and have some *chiao-tzus*," he said. "I could put
down some dumplings."

His tone made me uneasy, and I had a hunch I should check
some coppers I had hidden among folded clothes in the crate we
used for a chest, and I said, in a hard voice, "You mean you're
sick of rice and white cabbage, and you're sick of this flea box.
You're sick of the miserable food I cook after I've worked eleven
hours at the basins."

Then I had a terrible moment of feeling that *both he and I*
barely managed to avoid adding: And he was sick of me.

"All right," I said, with a precipitate change of attitude. "I'll
have to get into my gown."

Changing gave me an opportunity to fumble in the crate. My
coppers were gone. I said, casually, "I'm pushed over on my
back. This is the first time you've asked to take me out since—
ayah, I can't remember."

"Hai," Rock said, "you're the big rice bowl around here. It was
just an idea."

"You mean," I said, coming to what appeared to be a full stop
in my changing, "the silk filature is taking us out to eat? I thought
you were inviting *me*."

"It was just an idea. If you don't like it we can stay here. I've
eaten plenty of white cabbage in my time, and I can eat some
more. It's nothing to me."

"I misunderstood you," I said. "I thought we were going to eat
an inch off those sleeves you're saving for." But by this time I
had solidly intuited that my money had already been spent, and
that Rock's sleeve money was gone, too. Was he gambling? At
this moment he was not in a position to decide what we would do,
and I was, and I could not resist enjoying my having undone his

male control. Thus, with the power of a little money, I would manage him, subtly if possible, bluntly if not, and I would insulate him from becoming a ruffian, a jail louse, a mass of bruises. I resumed changing, and said, "I'll gladly pay. My mouth's watering, Old Rock."

"If you want to go, it's all right with me," Rock said, as if he were now being somewhat forced to go.

So out we went, and I paid. And before the evening was over I wanted Rock to make love to me, and here was where I began to feel as if my purse strings were tied around my gullet, choking me. If I wanted Rock, all of Rock, on our bed mat, I would have to accept him on his terms: I could not have command there. When he did take me, I still felt, at the end, a gnawing need, a yearning; it seemed to me that his side of our love-making had been perfunctory. My yearning cooled into suspicion. Had he, during recent days, spent his coppers on vixens? Or as "gifts" to easy-timers? Moth? Did Rock stay with me only for the money I brought home?

"Ai, Rock," I said, "I feel as if you'd been making love to a reeling basin. Don't you want *me*?"

But Rock seemed lazy and cheerful. He slapped his bare belly. "Those sweet-sour pork hocks were good."

(Dream Court

One dawn at the filature Harlot invited me to a meeting, three evenings away, of her hall. The Pavilion of Phoenixes, she said, had managed to freeze out the girl everyone disliked, Wood Mist, and she, Harlot, had told the members about me, and they were eager to meet me. I dreaded an inspection, but I found that I hungered for the respectability, the safety, the exclusiveness, the being an insider, that one of these small clubs could offer— especially a hall with several mixie members.

Before the whistles, on the morning of the meeting, I spotted Harlot from a distance, and I saw that she was not in her drab everyday tunic and trousers but was dressed in a clean blue gown. That evening after work I rushed home to our puzzle box and went straight to Moth's compartment and with tears of embarrassment in my eyes begged her to lend me her best gown, which was green —a glazed cotton. Moth's two tigers were not at home.

"Ai," Moth said, "are you going out with the owner of your filature?"

Before Moth I was ashamed of the idea of joining a hall, and I pleaded with her not to ask any questions. This made her certain that I was involved with a man.

She paid me off for being glad to let her think this, by frightening me a little. "So Rock will be free tonight!" she said, rubbing her hands together.

I had not even told Rock about the meeting. He had long since stopped accounting to me for his absences; why should I tell him my plans?

"He'll be as free as the wind," I said.

"The same wind as raises kites? Look here," Moth said, as she handed me the gown, "are you trying to let me know you *want* me to tell Rock you borrowed my gown and went out?"

"May I change here?" I asked. "Tell him what you wish," I said. I was blushing, and I decided to let things stand where they were; I knew Moth well enough to guess that she would read my coloring in her own shrewd way, no doubt accurately, and that she would say nothing to Rock.

Harlot had given me an address in the northern part of the Enclave, and I knew that the alley she named was somewhere near the border line of the chinkty, or more fashionable, district. I found that the house was, at any rate, on the poorer side of the dividing line, and that it was a mere puzzle box, though roomier than mine, and that the meeting was to take place in the large main front room, for one of Harlot's fellow Phoenixes, a mixie, was the wife of the tenant agent of the house.

My gown, or Moth's, of fake satin and garish green, was all wrong, as I sensed in a flash. It was a man-getting gown—for getting a certain low type of man, at that. I saw Harlot look at it with surprise. Four of the girls were in the plain work clothes of silk-reelers, not much better than what I had been wearing all day. There were ten girls, counting myself, and only three, as far as I could see, were mixies. They greeted each other, and me, with yellow-genteel courtesies, bowing, pumping up humility with joined fists.

Harlot, my sponsor, tried to make the most of me. "I hear you have a *fierce* man—is that right, dear? Is he beautiful?"

I was in the sky, and I talked too easily. "I'll let him love me as long as he behaves. But the minute he starts kite-building while

I'm off at work, or anything like that—out! I'll kick his shuttlecock right over the wall."

Harlot in this circle was a stranger to me and a darling of strangers, and when the attention of the circle had moved away from me, as it did with alarming swiftness, I looked at her at the center of the group, and I was rather sad. I felt we would never enjoy that time we had promised each other, of raveling out to the end of the thread every scrap of our experiences. I began to feel self-conscious, tongue-tied, and pushed aside. What a flood of chatter and laughter that had nothing to do with me!

A formal meeting began. It seemed that we were in a little imperial court, and every member of the hall was an official. A girl named Feather was "Empress Dowager"; Harlot was "First Crimson Button"—which meant that she handled the money. Some business, meaningless to me, was transacted with much argument as to formal procedure; one of the girls, named Brass Beauty, was "Custodian of Rites," and she kept cursing and shouting like a harridan at breaches of protocol and punctilio by others. So bewildering was the etiquette of the meeting, so many were the squeals for attention, the shrieks for order, the catcalls of rebuke, that I was quite caught by surprise when Harlot, coming over to me, asked me for three coppers, my "tax"—I had, at some point, been accepted as a member!

Then there was a great deal of talk about raising money for Old Arm. An appeal had gone out to all the halls of the Enclave for funds to support the job campaign. As the girls gabbled and squabbled—arguing not whether but how—I began to think about what Rock would want me to say, and what he would say himself, about all this. Was he against Old Arm simply because he had been the victim of the vicious and ruthless side of the race hero as a man? Did Rock really oppose the idea of organized resistance, which might lead to violence, against the yellows? What of his exuberant account of the battle against the Fukien rubbish? I was suddenly on the edge of tears, as I realized the depth of Rock's feeling about Runner's awkward country tactic, so courageous, so stubborn, so humane, and so effective; and as I realized, too, that I had somehow lost touch with Rock. I had no idea, any more, what he wanted, either of me or of life. "I'll let him love me as long as . . ." Hayah! I ached suddenly to leave, to go home, and I felt smothered by the cackling of these light-headed girls.

But the formal part of the meeting was over, and a brazier was glowing, and food came out from under damp cloths, and soon I ate the best meal I had had since . . . since slavery!

Afterward we played house sparrow at two tables: I had to be instructed, and Brass Beauty swore at me for not moving the tiles in just the right manner.

I walked home in a pleasant inward fog; much about the evening had seemed to me false, squalid-elegant, and imitative of the yellows, but I had had a happy time. The girls' acceptance of me had seemed to be quick and complete, and what I saw as pretentiousness, now that I had left, had, at the time, made me feel rather high in social tone; the dream of a court of which we were the nobility had seemed, as it passed, intense and sweet.

But when I entered our poor cupboard of a home the dream burst before my face.

Rock was furious with me. Why had there been no hot meal waiting for his return this evening?

Then his eyebrows shot up. What was I doing in that vixen gown?

Then he reached out a hand, palm up. I fumbled for my purse, unslung it, and put it in his hand. He loosened its neck and poured out the contents. Nine coppers instead of twelve.

"Ayah," he said, "don't tell me you're one of those vixens who pay instead of being paid."

But in the end it was the want of supper that enveloped the whole of his anger. If I wanted to be his woman, he said, I'd better keep track of my duties.

I did not make excuses; I did not mention the mad fantasy of a ruling court, the "Empress," the numbered "Crimson Buttons," the abusive guardian of formality; I certainly did not give a picture of myself, with a tile of the green dragon poised above the game board to add to my pattern and my score.

❰ The Madak Room

Dutifully I fixed a hot meal the following evening, going to unusual expense and trouble to procure some tripe and to cook it in a savory oil with bamboo shoots and bits of water chestnut. But Rock did not come home to eat.

Nor was he there the next night, nor the next, nor the fourth. On the sixth evening Old Boxer told me that during the afternoon he had seen Rock "with that lottery-chit boy with the bent back," floating along Foochow Road—where the large opium taverns were clustered—looking, the tiger said, as if they both had a lamp on.

My free day was to come three days later. I dared not miss a day at the filature for fear of losing my basin and never getting it back. I marked the time of those intervening days with sighs.

On my off day, when at last it came, I waited until the time-keepers' gongs had struck the half-morning watch and then I went to the bean-cruller shop and through it to Mink's lottery basket behind. Mink was not in the chit boys' corner. I edged to the desks and asked Weasel Number One whether the chit boy Mink, the one with the bent back, had been coming in regularly.

The clerk merely shrugged; he was adding a mass of figures and closed his mind to me and to everything else beyond the desk.

I waited through the noon drawing, and Mink did not come in.

As the chit boys in the corner stirred to take out the chit books for the next drawing, I moved among them asking one after another if he knew what pipe tavern the man named Mink frequented.

Suspicion and caution clothed these miserable peddlers, and most of them simply turned away without answering me, but at last one of them, touched perhaps by the urgency of my appeal, said, "Try the Golden Herons, on Foochow Road. Beyond those three big Cantonese teahouses with the carved fronts—do you know where I mean?"

"I think so," I said, having no idea, and sped away to the Settlement.

When, after much wandering and inquiry, I found the Golden Herons, I thought the chit boy must have been playing a malicious joke on me, because the place obviously catered only to the most wealthy of yellows. Beyond a row of crimson columns and flanking a gate studded with bronze conch shells were two bas-reliefs in lacquered wood, in a style that was elevated yet commercial, betokening high prices within; picnic scenes of philosophers, noblemen, maid servants, deer, acacia, and gilded herons flying across broad reaches of lapis-lazuli sky.

But I was on an urgent hunt, and timidly I pulled open the doors and edged around a carved spirit screen within.

A yellow attendant in a figured-silk gown rushed at me raising his hands and pointing his long, curved fingernails at me as if to lacerate the eager question on my face, and he said in hysterical yet hushed tones, "Back door, you sow! Go around to the back where you belong. Out of here before you're seen! Out, out, out!"

This errand meant everything to me, and I did not intend to be rushed, and I asked, "How do I get around to the back?"

The attendant was so taken aback by my equanimity that he began to explain, rather politely at first but then with a growing anger at having been taken off balance, how to thread my way through a complication of side alleys to the pigs' gate. . . .

And just then one of his distinguished yellow customers pushed open from within one of the several side doors off the central hall where I stood, and the customer, in an ecstasy of waxen animation, turned to chat a moment with someone inside, and as he held the door I saw a magnificent room. It contained several groups of padded divans clustered about brass lamps set on pretty tripods, and on the divans I saw richly dressed yellow men reclining, some busy cooking pellets at the lamps, others smoking and chatting with neighbors with an appearance of casualness and cheerful friendliness. Beyond, at tables, sat other rich yellow men playing games or toying with delicious snacks for which they had no appetite.

The customer, with eyes sleepy but for the fierce and bottomless little apertures, like ant holes, of the pupils, dreamily came out into the hall, letting the door close behind him. On light feet, as if lazy-skating along on a cushion of scented air, he came up to me, and he said, "Delightful! Delightful!" He rubbed the backs of his knuckles on my cheek. The attendant was frozen in a noncommittal attitude. With all my anxiety, I nevertheless enjoyed this moment: the officious yellow underling not only interrupted in his contempt for me but, as it were, countermanded from it by a man of superior taste. The customer floated around the spirit screen and out. The attendant flew at me now, closing his claws on my upper arms and rushing me backwards toward the door. I flung up my arms with all my strength and threw off his stinging grips, and I turned and ran out at the door.

I made my way through a maze of dirty alleys to the back, or pigs', gate of the Golden Herons; the only decoration on *this* entrance was an outline drawing of an opium pipe. The spirit screen was of double-thick brick, for the evil ghosts of hogs and sows, addicted perhaps even in the grave, would most crucially have to be kept off the premises.

Here at the back there was no silk-clad attendant but instead two armed yellow policemen.

"Work or smoke?" one of them curtly asked me.

"I'm looking for my man," I said.

"Make no noise or fuss," the policeman said, and turned back to conversation with his companion.

"Where are the smoking rooms?" I asked.

A thumb pointed over a uniformed shoulder, and I pushed open a wooden door.

My first impression was of a sickening, sour odor—of humanity rather than of the habit. Ayah, the number-two facilities were less elegant, by farther than far, than those I had glimpsed off the front hall. Here there were no divans; the smokers lay on mats on the floor, crowded side by side. Men outnumbered women, ten to one. Tattered whites! Some reclined on their sides, holding up their heads with forearms propped on elbows, heating over the lamps' flames little balls of dross—lumps of prepared opium that had already been smoked once by the yellows in the number-one rooms out front—impaled on metal stylets with bamboo handles; others had pushed the heated dross balls into their heavy pipe heads and were drawing smoke into their lungs, holding it there, and slowly and reluctantly blowing it out, then talking with animation with their neighbors, or lying back, eyes open, on the headrests provided here for the clientele: bricks wrapped in rags. The faces, as I looked about for those of Rock and Mink, did not seem to me to be pathetic or wasted or sick: to the contrary, there was an atmosphere, here, which rather frightened me, of something like true freedom, and these bodies between which I gingerly stepped belonged to whites remarkable for seeming to be pleased with absolutely everything. Could I begrudge Rock such a deep and still sense of well-being as these forms seemed to be enjoying? Could there be anything wrong with his having such pleasure except that it was a pleasure that had nothing to do with me?

I had scarce begun to ask myself these questions when I concluded that Rock and Mink were not in the room.

There were nearly two hundred whites on the dirty floor of this room—as compared with perhaps thirty yellows on their divans in the number-one accommodation that I had glimpsed earlier—and I decided to go round once more, to make sure that I had not missed Rock and Mink.

This time I heard snatches of the smokers' talk, which was

commonplace, lucid, and euphoric, and I was surprised to hear how many of these men and women, prostrate with their habit, were speaking of Old Arm and of his coming campaign. Then I realized the absurdity of my surprise: What better forum than this for hope?

I had not missed them. They were not there.

I had some coppers with me. I felt a surge of temptation: if I could lose every worry, every pain! Be non-white for a few dreamy hours! One pipe would not make a habit.

My eyes swept once more around the room, and, pulled away from the temptation by a thought of Rock, I inwardly murmured envious congratulations to these happy few whites and then went out in the hall and asked the policemen if there were any other number-two smoke rooms.

There were not.

The policeman had spoken of work. Where was the work done? The thumb again.

Now, little knowing where I was going, I entered the regions of the damned: a series of small rooms where bands of whites, obviously all on the pipe, worked at various stages of preparation of the drug for smoking, in order to earn the coppers they needed to smoke themselves. In each room a single process was carried out by perhaps a dozen whites, working under the ever-sharp eyes of four yellows, including a policeman, to make sure that none of the opium would be stolen. They worked, further, with their forearms protruded, and firmly strapped, through small holes in a wire mesh that stood guard between themselves and the precious dream stuff.

I hurried through the rooms, checked at each entrance by that room's policeman, who in each case repeated the admonition of the officer in the hall. "Make no fuss." "We want no disturbance." *We? Policemen?* What unholy collaboration between the famous Forgetfulness Hong and the municipality had I stumbled upon? I grew angry, thinking of Rock's fat policeman, perspiring and growing more and more "merciful"—yes, Rock had said "merciful"—as he increased the force of his interrogatory blows. The hypocrisy, not the truncheon, must have been what hurt.

Dead silence in these rooms, the boiling room, the chandoo room, the madak room. Here the whites were not pleased. They were haggard, skinny, cadaverous. They seemed overcome by the most painful of lassitudes, at the edge of utter prostration, incessantly yawning as they struggled to shorten the hours until they would have earned enough for a pipe. Their eyes watered and their nostrils dripped. Occasionally a mouth would pull, as if for speech or a groan, but no sounds could be heard.

I found Rock and Mink in the madak room. They were sitting side by side. I saw at once that Rock was not like the others, for there was flesh on his face, and color in his cheeks, and his eyes did not seem to be made of convex fish scales with pin pricks in the centers; Mink, on the other hand, was ghastly thin, pale, and watery. Was Rock simply nursing his friend through a crisis? I suddenly wanted to draw back. Had I made a terrible mistake in coming here?

And Rock had already a certain skill. I saw him diluting purified opium with chopped grass-cloth root and tobacco, and rolling the mixture into pipe balls bound with gum arabic. Perhaps he was happy here, rather than across the hall—this was his first productive work in a long time. Again I felt that I might have been disastrously wrong to come here.

He had not seen me. He looked, now and then, at Mink, and spoke softly to him, apparently murmuring encouragement. The rest of the time he paid close attention to his work; he was accomplishing far more than the others.

Then I remembered why I had come: I wanted Rock back. And no sentiment about nursing his friend, honest work.

I went straight to his seat and spoke his name.

His head spun about, and seeing his eyes close to mine I knew, or firmly believed, that he had been smoking opium with Mink, and suddenly my commands grew bitter and harsh, though the thought of all those policemen kept them to a whisper.

"Go home," Rock said in a hushed but angry voice. "I'm *Rock*."

What did he mean? That he was trying to hang on to the last shreds of himself?

I lost all hope, and with it all control. I tangled my fingers in his hair, and I tugged and let out a wordless caterwaul of despair. Rock could not disengage his thick wrists from the straps in the little gates in the wire mesh, and he writhed from side to side and roared, "Go home, you bitch wonk! Leave me alone!"

A policeman and a yellow attendant were at my arms. They unclamped my fingers one by one and dragged me away. In my horror, outrage, and utter sadness, as I was pulled away kicking and trying to bite the hand that covered my mouth, I had room nevertheless for one startlingly clear impression: Mink and all

the other wretches working in the room did not even look up, their
eyes remained bleary with the one dim, dim idea—*continue with
this agonizing labor, for it will lead at last to freedom.*

([A Walk to Work on a Gray Day

         A late-spring morning, yet I felt chilled. I had just set
out for the filature. Even in the dimmest pre-dawn light I could
tell, from the clothlike weight of the wet air, that this would be
a gray day. I saw something bright on the dirty paving of the
narrow street—a coin? Could one afford not to make sure? I bent
down. I picked it up; it crackled in my hand—the discarded outer
scale of a garlic bud. Pungency and filth! Ayah, my poor laughing
fellow prisoners in the Enclave! Pellagra, syphilis, bad lungs. Bad
luck. Worthless lottery chits. Restless loins, malicious tongues.
Rock! Rock! Ai, Moth had approached with such sympathetic eyes,
such friendly and gentle eyes, irrepressibly sparkling, however,
with her eagerness to see me wilt under the hot blast of her information. "I have news for you," she had eagerly said.

     I usually valued the walk to work along the Bund. What was it
about the first of morning that imposed a hush on the outpouring
of workers from the Enclave? Thousands walked along the asphalt
towpath, and on the street itself before the row of impressive
hongs; in the noonday light this scene was a bedlam of bells,
creaking hubs, horns, whistles, gongs, and tongues, but now in
the first light the only sounds were the whisper of myriad cloth
soles and the gurgling and sucking of the leaden river about
anchor rodes and the flanks of junks and the stones of the embankment. None but whites were moving yet. Was it the yellows
only who made the noise of the world?

     It had been ten days since my visit—the thought of it caused a
sudden ache like a fever chill—to the front and back rooms of
the Golden Herons.

     Had Moth's two tigers shared in the malice?—certainly that
bedbug of an Ox Balls had, with his wrists thrust into opposite
sleeves, hugging himself on account of his own inner frost; he had
been sitting there, ostensibly waiting his turn at palm leaves with
Old Boxer, but I had seen the twinkle!

     Surely I had not driven Rock away! I had not wanted to bind
him with my purse strings, nor to change him. All I had wanted
was no change—for things not to get worse.

What had changed him, what had snatched him away, was the intractability of the yellow power, its inflexibility, its standing there like a great stone wall.

Along at the left, looming as dark solid remnants of the night, were the cavaliers of that wall—the Merchants' Hong, the Telegraph Hong, the Up-from-the-Sea Club, the Chartered Bank—then to my right on the riverbank the Customs receiving shed; and in the river the trading junks, and (shivers) the opium hulks, named like fighting ships: *Monkey, Dart, Valiant, Fair Wind.*

What could I do alone? My heart started beating faster, as if I were already putting into pounding feet my sudden desire to run away, to run back to the country village and stand on one leg for Runner and the white race.

Could I work for Old Arm? Could I work for someone Rock had despised?

Here was the hated police-court building—I saw as if on a scroll in my mind the fat, perspiring, "merciful" face—and soon the charming public gardens: glass hothouses with flowers for every season (for sale to yellows), walks (for yellows) under pine trees, artificial bridges (to carry yellows) over pretended rills, and a pavilion for open-air theatricals (yellows only). Charming? It was in these gardens, triggered by an alleged trespass by two white male prostitutes, that the frightful Up-from-the-Sea race riot of six years before had started.

Moth the actress! She comes toward me across the room. "I have news for you." Gentle eyes, signaling information of a most ungentle sort. Then a long rigmarole about how she has happened to hear what she has heard, seating me, with her, at the opposite side of the cubicle from the two men playing cards. "Hai, White Lotus," says Old Boxer. "Where have you been?" Ox Balls' eyes dance. Moth allows time for soakage. I cannot bring myself to say what she wants me to say: Hurry, hurry up, if you're my friend. She offers me tea, relents, says it: Rock is living on the string with a reeler who has a puzzle-box room on the other side of the park and grounds of The Good Life. Pause. I cannot ask what this woman is like; those purse strings are choking me. Moth says, "I didn't learn much about her—except they say she has a rather ordinary face." Moth's own face looks devoid of mischief, though this last item has had the effect of reddening mine. "Maybe," Moth adds, by way, I suppose, of intended mollification, "she has something else to offer. A face isn't everything." Moth is not smiling. . . .

I crossed Hongkew Creek by the Garden Bridge and started out the broad thoroughfare of Yangtszepoo Road. So Rock had left me to go on a kite string with another woman—giving her, as he had me, the use of his body in barter for food and shelter. Hadn't he, in reality, been living that way, "on a string," with me? But with me this had been too shameful. Why? Because he had not been dependent on me in other times and places? Whereas, starting fresh and frankly with some other woman, this subservience could be stomached? What a revolting power twelve coppers a day could have! My miserable little money power had driven Rock away; yet this other woman had attracted him with money—and something other than a pretty face.

I was just then passing the great cotton spinning mills out Yangtszepoo Road, the locus in fact of the anger of all the whites in the city—for in these wonderful mechanized mills only yellows were hired. Just now only whites were walking past; the yellows went to work two hours later than we. Soy Chee Mills, Lao Kung Mow, I Wo, Yah Loong. Each one with forty, fifty, sixty thousand modern spindles, entirely tended by yellows, who earned thirty coppers a day at a minimum. The Central Kingdom Spinning and Weaving Company: broad roofs, stately godowns. Whites could be hired for less than half the wages of the yellow workers in these magnificent plants—but, as the word went, "It takes two and a half pigs to do the work of one yellow man." Also, "A white man just *destroys* machines." "They're born lazy." "They don't work for you, they work against you." I felt, almost as a presence walking beside me, Rock's old anger against these yellow clichés, his ruffian anger at injustice, great or petty. What had happened, after all, to Rock's capacity for indignation? It had simply raveled like the sleeve of a coolie coat worn too long.

I tried to imagine Old Arm's coming demonstrations against these fortresses of yellow economic power; tried to imagine a revivified Rock taking part. A stone in his hand, a yell swelling the veins in his neck. The picture would not come clear.

Then I was in a torment of blaming myself. Why had I been so prudent, so hasty about finding work myself? Why hadn't I been able to live more in Moth's slipshod mode, letting each day bring what it would? Rock could have done *something*: he might have kept his self-respect by sneak-thieving, or pimping, or becoming what I had determined he should not become, a true tiger to live

by wits and for laughs, often hungry but seldom bored and never
ashamed.

It had been I who had wanted to live by the grubby yellow pattern: earning, saving, climbing; when I knew that whites could
never, as we put it, "reach home by that path."

How could I reproach Rock, who had a so much freer soul than
mine, for wanting to live as a man, a *white* man?

And now the filter beds and pumping stations of the Up-from-
the-Sea Waterworks, managed, crewed, maintained exclusively by
yellows. The I Wo Waste Silk Mill. Dan Too Oil Mill. Grand, capacious, modern; for lids only.

I would go on the lottery. I would get a chit-clue book. *Water
Spirit's Sister Flies to the Moon.* I would change my ways now. . . .
Perhaps I could buy chits from Mink; perhaps he would be able to
tell me. . . .

And at last a kind of petering out of civilization: mat sheds
along one side of the road, dirty shops on the other; a view of
willow trees, tilled fields. Yes, the sky was gray, sullen, and stuck.
And ahead marched the grim parade of filatures.

Then at the side of the road there was a strand of fragrance
that made one's mood take off, like a finch off a branch into the
sunlight: of sweet chestnuts roasting over a charcoal brazier. I
went over and bought a copper's worth, my breakfast and my
lunch. A group of little basin girls was clustered around a pair of
tomboys who were—as if grown-up tiger men—having a mock-
earnest match at boxing, their fists like little half-opened tulips.
Reelers, cracking the chestnut husks and biting into the too hot,
mealy meat, were greeting each other with garbled, full-mouthed
noises, and with the never dying cheerfulness of white working
women.

A chestnut warmed me. I began to feel more alive. . . . I must
go across to one of the booths over there and purchase a chit-clue
book. . . . But Harlot! There was Harlot!

She was buying a cup of tea, for a cash, at one of the roadside
booths. I hurried to her; she put down her tea bowl and embraced
me with her always overflowing warmth. I bought a bowl of tea,
and told her about Rock's having left me.

"You have to have a man," Harlot said. "Right away! And I'll
help you find one, dear. You want one with some money. That
scum like the one you had—they're always restless. Look, there

are plenty of white men in the Enclave who can give you a good time—in the best places, too. We'll find you a man, I promise you, White Lotus, and a real chinkty one, at that."

When we had finished our tea we walked on toward the waiting yard of our filature. Harlot pressed her promise on me; she really intended to settle me with a man like her own. "He never runs with other women, he really doesn't. All right, maybe he'll curse at me and slap me if I give him reason to; but he won't grouch when he's sober, and he simply wouldn't think of putting my life in danger in any way when he's drunk. He never carries a knife or anything like that. Hooo! He's too lidsy for anything so vulgar. You should see the clothes he gives me. Very quiet, very good taste."

"Where does he get the money?"

"He's a tax collector in the Enclave, works for the municipality, and for the Forgetfulness boys on the side, I guess—though I don't ask questions."

"But if he takes such good care of you, why work out *here?*" On that stress of mine I put a load of feeling about the filatures.

"Ayah, darling, don't you see? I'd lose my self-esteem if I didn't work. I mean, I just couldn't hang around him all day long. He'd dump me in a hurry."

Harlot fortified her promise by asking me to come to her puzzle box that very evening after work.

I had tender feelings all day toward my little basin girl, Pigeon. Her family had had to move again—into a mud hut at the edge of the ricksha-pullers' area. But she seemed to be quite without distress; her eyes were lights in the steam. She had grown fond of me, and we laughed that day as if our miseries were hilarious.

(On the Far Side of the Mirror

Harlot lent me a gown and took me into a world that was new to me. We were going to a reception for a white storyteller, the famous Dogtooth, she said, in the chinkty district, among the upper-class whites.

Walking from Harlot's puzzle box through the evening streets, we came to a subtle dividing line, where the strolling crowds abruptly thinned out, the street-facing walls became more imposing and were tipped with fragments of glass to ward off burglars, and a thick hush, which was somehow genteel, unreal, off-white, like a mountain mist in a painting on silk, hovered over the neighborhood.

We arrived at our destination—the Moon Garden Compound, whose many courtyards had once comprised three palaces of yellow nobility, all three premises now girded by a single wall. Here the "best" whites lived, Harlot said: there was a waiting list ten li long of whites who were rich enough, but perhaps not "nice" enough, to get in.

I wondered: Were there so many wealthy whites?

We were questioned at the gate by a guard, a white man in a uniform patterned on that of the yellow municipal police.

Harlot said that we were going to Old-Third Kung's party for Dogtooth.

The guard saluted us with the full honors of an old-fashioned bannerman's salute—the drawing and shooting of a nonexistent crossbow: left foot slightly advanced, seat well protruded, aim taken, a pull of the imaginary trigger pump, hind foot briskly closed up, right arm swung out and held in an attitude; all done with a superb swagger.

As we walked through the quiet courtyards, with potted fruit trees, marble lanterns, tiny soaring bridges, Moth said, "There are sure to be some unattached men on the prowl. Keep alert."

Sounds of a subdued camaraderie; a glow of an open door. Then we were plunged into a hall with brilliant beams and a crowd of beautiful people. Harlot had me by the hand. As we moved through the press of guests, many nodded to Harlot, or fluttered at her; I saw that she was known and liked. There were numerous mixies as young and as pretty as she.

A man coming toward us greeted Harlot with yellow formality —a bowed head and peace-pumping fists. Harlot's face flushed, her eyes gave gifts of open pleasure. Ai, this must be her man! She introduced me: his name was Pride. I was surprised. He was middle-aged and dewlapped, and his head was shaven, and when he turned to lead us to his circle I saw three fat-creases at the back of his neck.

I had another surprise in store for me: I saw ahead that Duke was in Pride's group of friends. Hai! What was thought of him? This encounter might mark me for good in the chinkty quarter. Should I claim Duke effusively for an old friend, or should I pretend I had never seen him before?

Duke took the choice away from me. He knew Harlot, of course, and bowed to her, and when I was presented to him by Harlot's friend, Duke spoke to me as to a stranger: not to freeze me, I quickly realized, but simply to erase my past as a field slave from this brilliant chamber whose society could not tolerate thoughts of such lowness—though there may have been a deal of it in light disguise around the room. Duke was, indeed, cordial to me, and he allowed not the slightest suggestion, on his part, or admission, on mine, of the chasm in rank that had once separated us. Perhaps he played his game too well; he raised his eyebrow in a stiff signal of willingness to flirt. I turned away, thinking of Rock spitting in Duke's footsteps on Silverfinger's highly polished stone floor.

People stood around chatting. Tea bowls were passed.

Hooo! The attitudes of these people! When they spoke about race problems, they tended to blame all the woes of the caste system not on the yellows but on the low standards of behavior of the poor whites. A pretty girl on their own social level was spoken of as having jade-white skin or, in the case of a mixie, ivory; but the common whites of the Enclave drew the scornful epithets invented by yellows: pigs, moonlights, smalls, fogs, whitewashes, tuskers. They criticized the bizarre clothes of tigers, the raucous noises made by wharf coolies, the shame of hogs on the pipe.

Duke spoke of the Garden Riot. "There wouldn't have been any trouble," he said, "had it not been for your tenant trash—the peasant whites, you know, who flood this city, because they think they can be just as shiftless here as they were down on their tenancies and still make a good living." Duke was looking at me. Did he know about my life in a lower-hand village? Was he taking his little revenge on me for my having turned my back on him? "Those migrant farm pigs were the ones that caused the trouble."

"I've heard about the riot," I said, "but I heard the yellows started it because white prostitutes walked in the Garden."

"That's just the point," Duke said. "That is the way it started. The problem was that the yellows *wanted* our prostitutes to walk in the Garden, but only so far. They wanted them available but not obtrusive. There was an imaginary line from the peony beds to the pine grove on the river side of the pavilion—white prostitutes were not to go beyond that line. But your dirty migrant farm prostitutes: they were the ones who had to 'dare' to go a little farther. They're your pushers. Especially the male prostitutes—they were all farm trash, anyway. You don't have male prostitutes coming from city stock. And if you remember, the actual rioting started around a pair of male prostitutes who had crossed the line."

"I see," I said. I refrained from asking Duke if almost all the whites in the whole Enclave were not essentially of farm origin—as he was, and I.

How agreeable I was! How eager to please! One thing I noticed here was that these chinkties and would-be chinkties had yellowy intonations, and their speech was largely free of the Enclave's argot. The Enclave was basically a community of illiterates, and I could see that to be at the top, one must be, or seem, educated. Casually, as I was engaged in talk by Pride, I dropped an aphorism from *The Doctrine of the Happy Mean,* and ears pricked up around me, and Duke and Pride leaned toward me to catch more of my delightful conversation.

"Is it true," a girl of jade-white skin later whispered to me, "that Harlot is the daughter of a big slaveowner?" Harlot had spoken of me as an old "core friend," meaning from the core provinces and so, euphemistically, a former fellow slave.

I saw the interest and envy in this girl's eyes. "Yes," I said, "it's true enough. She was the young master's half sister. So I understood."

"Was it an important estate?"

"Huge."

Too soon I felt too much at home. How easy it is, I thought, for someone bitterly poor to change his clothes and modulate his speech and pass as a chinkty. Thinking that, I proceeded to make a gaffe that must have exposed me as an outsider.

I spoke—and striking a chance lull in the babble of our group my voice clattered out with startling loudness—of Old Arm: for some reason, obscure to me as I did it, I praised him.

The faces around me slammed shut like the house gates in an alley at an outcry of "Thief!" or "Mad wonk!"

I saw at once that I had hit the bull's-eye of social error. These people wanted to hear and think as little as possible about their own responsibilities, if any, as whites; their wheelbarrow was well packed and they didn't want it overturned.

Amid the rustling gowns and the sounds of the yellow-style slurping of jasmine-fragrant tea, I thought of Pigeon, and of her mother, drugged on dross opium paid for with Pigeon's coppers, in their new home, a mud hut in a miniature city of mud huts, the

notorious ricksha-pullers' quarter. How much really separated me
from that existence? Could I forget the hovels Rock and I had
shared?

I moved about in the elegant crowd with Harlot and Pride,
studying (often asking) who these people were. They were petty
officials, customs clerks, tax collectors, government messengers.
They were managers of yellow Moslems' shops within the Enclave,
bookkeepers, shroffs, messengers, recorders. And some were
"slugs," as the more cautious and less well-to-do whites referred to
employees of the chit-lottery syndicate and of the pervasive Forgetfulness Hong. Thus our high society—parasites and underlings
to the yellow world. How haughty some of them were! Having
frequent touch with wealthy yellows, our bona fide chinkties had
learned to mimic the mannerisms, the gestures, the graces of the
true lights of the yellow world. But this I quickly saw, too: any
white person could learn these moon-terrace tricks, and in the
chamber were many sweet-mannered people, especially girls, who
were not proper chinkties. The hands told all. Real chinkties had
"clean work" and soft hands. Girls who reeled for the filatures put
make-up on their hands, to hide as well as they could (and as I
had not known enough to do) the reddish boiled hide of their
fingers; but a close look was enough to detect the counterfeits. So
I had not needed to speak of Old Arm to reveal myself as an inter-
loper. Yet even the shams were accepted and honored if they had
a certain over-all style; not what one did but how one did it set his
rank. Modest clothes; a light patter about the game of house sparrow but ignorance, real or feigned, about another game, vulgar
palm leaves; avoidance of the loud, high cackle ("Will they eat
me?"); attendance at the accepted temples. Woman-beating, de-
sertion, bastardy (except where yellow semen had swum astray),
sweeping the street for rice from slit bags—Hooo! Never! It all
struck me as pathetic, yet I acted my part as hard as I could. I
amused myself by trying to work out the hierarchy. At the very
top, by repute, were two chit-lottery "princes," a certain prominent
tax collector, a family said to have inherited a fortune in cotton
from a by-the-way yellow father, and two manufacturers of fans
and hairnets. I supposed that below these standouts, government
couriers were nearest the top, for they had affluence and stability
—their income was steady, their conceit impenetrable. They wore
uniforms; that was a stunning advantage. Then bookkeepers and
clerks were very high; they were indeed "clean," they had to be

literate, they enjoyed financial credit at their own shops. And down, down, down, the route from this room—to wharfmen, ricksha boys, chit-runners, and, down down dizzy down . . . to those who put their wrists through the tight slots in the wire mesh at the opium-cooking benches in the back rooms. . . .

Rock was at my mind's elbow all the time, and I saw that he had the wit to be able to take his place anywhere he wanted up and down this pyramid. Why was his drive to move ever downward? I could not help giving him the benefit of doubt: Was his the only honest way?

Ai! How long did it take me to realize that a handsome boy had adhered to me? His smile was like a theft from a silk purse: clever, swift, rewarding. He entertained me, for he was at least cynical. He was quite frank in telling me he was "a Hong man"—in other words, that he worked in some way for the Forgetfulness Hong. A slug. His name was Lacquerer.

He took me off to a side pavilion, where we found cushioned chairs beside a once prim little rockery that was now dusty, cracked, plantless, and carpless.

" 'Forgetfulness,' " he said, "is not in the sense of absent-mindedness but rather of sweet oblivion. The Hong sells dreams. Chits, vixens, the pipe. All those things that lie *on the far side of the mirror*. As you know, whites can't organize into *real* halls or gangs; our slugs are lone wolves. There are ten here tonight who are the biggest men in the Enclave. Hai! No! I'm not one of *them*. I'm just a little nuisance. The big ones are race men, or want to be. They want to advance the white race—without jeopardizing their own position." Lacquerer knew I was a stranger, a novice, but he did not condescend to me. He spoke to my curiosity. Perhaps he saw possibilities in me beyond the simply sensual; I saw that he saw the latter, at any rate. He dangled new activities before my gaze. "The parties they have—not at all vulgar. On their tables you'll have Peking duck and sharks' fins and pomegranates. They go to the races—I mean at the Race Club, the lids' Race Club. Horseback riding. Endless games of house sparrow. They have summer compounds up at Kuling. Scrolls, classics, instrumental music. And they also collect good-looking women—not vixens. The fast girls who work in some of the chit baskets. The best and the prettiest. Easy-times—some of them here tonight."

Ayah! How much was swiped suddenly from the silk purse with a beaming smile!—a hint that with respect to the best and prettiest

girls at least, Lacquerer felt himself the match of the biggest Hong
men of all.

Why should this surprise me? Conceit was far more common
currency than copper among hogs. What hackles were to a rooster,
conceit was to a yellow-ridden white man: an illusory show of
being huge, fierce, and dominant.

How could I help comparing Lacquerer with Rock? Rock in his
less subtle way was conceited, too; my folly and crime had been
to try to pluck his hackles one by one. Rock on his downward path
was honest, for he would not give the yellows even the satisfaction
Old Arm was about to offer them, of showing them his feelings in
a big way: until he could show them to some effect. Whereas this
Lacquerer was smooth—meaning, totally lacking in any feelings
at all, beyond those a baby has when he wants to take suck or to
void his inner pouches. Lacquerer, I could guess, was one of those
white strivers and strainers who wanted, more than harmony of
soul, a "best and prettiest" woman, a fine home with scrolls, brocade, brassware, cloisonné, horn-sided lanterns, who wanted to be
tended by servants of his own, who wanted to be an "old comfortable"—who wanted to be excellent by outward yellow standards.
I could guess further that Lacquerer did his buying in the Model
Settlement; would prefer suffering humiliations from yellows to
trading in an Enclave store owned by whites, where the merchandise, he would say, was "imitation." He was the ultimate
snob: he had contempt for the reality of himself. And with all this,
he was beautiful, charming, quilt-warm, and equipped with teeth
as square as house-sparrow tiles.

As a matter of interest, I questioned Lacquerer about Old Arm.

"Hai! What a swindle that one is. He pretends to be a race man,
pretends to be a ragged wharf coolie: but, ai, he has satin fingertips. I haven't seen him tonight, but he comes to most of these
receptions, White Lotus—expensive clothes, all from Lin Yi, that's
the *big* yellow tailor on Soochow Road. And where did he get his
money? He's sold out just like all the rest of them—this famous
rice-bowl campaign will be a farce, the yellows know every move,
he *tells* them. But what's disgusting is that he didn't get the money
for the Lin Yi gowns from *them;* he sold out to *them* for bean
sprouts. He got all his money by milking the poorest whites—his
own wharf men. It makes an honest Hong man like me sick to my
stomach to see the way some of the best people at these receptions
kowtow to him."

Almost Top Man's very words. So this was the chinkty line about the race hero. I wondered how much of this venom was justified by truth. I trusted Rock's instinct about Old Arm, but his was a far different concern.

When we returned to the main chamber, it was much more crowded than it had been.

"It must be almost time for Dogtooth to come," my young man said, and he began to point out personages. "Look! There's Honey Lung—she's the second daughter of the Lungs who have all the cotton money. *There's* your Old Arm. The short one with the shaved head. In the green gown. And over there, the tall osprey with the beard—that's Printer Wu, the first white man to be put on the Provincial Council. The poet Earthclod. Silverfinger—there. And look, Old Churn—he's the priest at Ta Kuan Miao, the temple where all the 'best bacon' goes to worship. And there's Southern Peony—you've heard of her—she does Annamese ritual dances at the Silver Pavilion, with no clothes on."

"Isn't that a lid with her—or is it a mixie?"

"That's a yellow man, one of their mighty mouse-hunters—but don't worry, White Lotus, he'll pay taels for peach pits. The money will pour out of his ears, and he'll get nothing. Southern Peony is clean, she's kind of a race heroine for it—famous for leading them on. Her nickname among the Hong men is Dying Wind: as soon as the yellow kite gets up, she sees to it that the wind gives out. They never know the whole Enclave is laughing at them."

I was astonished, on looking around, to see numerous yellows in the crowd, both men and women; they seemed to be onlookers, they had come to watch us be ourselves.

A murmur, a clamor. The storyteller had entered the hall. We saw the crowd parting deferentially, and Dogtooth made his way to the raised dais of a heron veranda leading off the main chamber. There he turned to the crowd and waited, a hand on one hip, for silence.

Dogtooth's face was itself like one of the myths that, I had heard, he often told: a tight-packed assemblage of supra-life-sized entities, scooped and split and time-smoothed, as it were, out of hard old beliefs. Grossly ugly in repose, it achieved, as soon as it moved with his speaking, a mesmerizing beauty.

He first made an announcement, in a flat voice: "A true story of our people."

Then he began his narrative in a deeper tone. "Once, long ago, in the bad time, there was a strong white man who slaved in South-of-the-River, as tall as a gate, with matted hair in seven braids, and with a scar like an inch of surprise over his left eye. . . ."

I began to tremble. Peace! The story of Peace's rebellion! How would he tell it all? All: the soot-blackened smithy; riding the mule-towed canal barges to the city to enlist men; the brilliant banners, the trail of goat droppings up the steps to the beautiful yamen; the secret meetings by the waterhole—Dogtooth seemed to know all those things, all, all, and he swept me, with the others in the room, along on a great stream of emotion.

But soon I began to have queer feelings of riding two carts at once: Dogtooth's and my memory's. All the pictures were there in Dogtooth's singing, booming account, yet everything was, or seemed, out of focus. Could I say for sure that his tale was wrong and my memory was right? Perhaps I, just as much as literary necessity, had distorted the reality. Perhaps what he was telling was "truer" than what I now thought had happened.

But Dogtooth's road and mine diverged more and more. What was wrong? Had I been so blind to happenings all around me?

Ayah, what power in Dogtooth's narrative! I found myself wanting to believe him, deeply aware of my own fallibility. The crowd was with him; I wanted to be with them.

Suddenly, as he came to the eve of the war itself, as Peace made scythe-swords and the last recruitments were reported, I realized what was wrong: Dogtooth had left out God—the old God with a white face, the visions, the prayers, the secret names. Dogtooth's was a story of men alone rising against men, of lonely human courage, hope, loyalty, and love—and, in the end, of mere human betrayal. There was no hurricane at the end of Dogtooth's story, no lightning, wind, rain, flood. There was no abandonment of the white man by his white God. Dogtooth's story ended with the treason of their race of True and Brass, Ma's slaves, who had informed their master of the whites' plans, so that a yellow force had come, rather than an all-obliterating storm, and scattered the rebels.

At first I was overcome with uncertainty. *Had* it turned out that way? Had there been only, perhaps, a light rain that night and such confusion in our hearts and minds that we who were there had seen the end all wrong? The crowd in the hall was swarming toward Dogtooth. I saw tears running down white cheeks. Yellows

who had come to watch wore quizzical smiles—at the emotional-
ism of these pigs? And by chance I saw, for an instant, the face
of Old Arm—blanched, pale, not at all carried away with feeling,
for Dogtooth's version of Peace's rebellion was surely a kind of
warning to Old Arm.

I pretended to have entered into the heart of the story. I made
a show with Lacquerer. When the fuss died down he asked me to
sup with him the following night—I had a man, if I wanted him.
He did not take me home, for it was understood that I would be
embarrassed to show him my poor circumstances.

In my room, on my mat, now seeing Dogtooth's story as a
parable of caution, an artful chinkty warning to Old Arm, a yellow
man's errand beautifully run, but then again thinking my memories deluded, the "truth" revealed in art, and my whole past in
doubt, I lay in an agony of conflicted shame and defiance. Then
later, when I was calmer, I ended by being mildly glad that I had
a man of sorts and something to do ahead. Thus I felt, dozing off,
irresolute. Could I believe my own view of anything that had happened to me?

⟦ An Arrival

I began to lead two half-lives. I was a reeler who lived
in a puzzle box on the edge of hunger; and I was a guest in the
parlors of the somewhat rich. By day I cooked my hands in a brass
basin; by night I whited them with a talcum of maize starch
dusted on a base of scented sheep fat. By day my tongue rolled
the poor-white argot; by night I quoted the literary masters. I had
two kinds of friends: Moth and her tigers and their set; and
Lacquerer, Harlot, Pride, and, for the tarnished side of my pleasure, even such pompous fools as Duke.

Lacquerer continued to be what he had seemed at first; enter-
taining. He offered me much—good food, good times—and asked
for little. He took my body now and again (a kind of rent I paid
for an illusion of living among "the best people"), but his demands
were mild, even perfunctory, a matter of form. He was a cold,
ambitious slug. I saw that he wore me as a sort of decoration; my
not-bad face, my clothes, which improved under his guidance
(after I borrowed rather heavily from Silverfinger), and especially
my education, which was better than his—made me a passable

facet of his conceit, and a tool of his desire to be one of the more
splendid polite criminals of the Enclave. I didn't mind. He opened
doors for me.

All I thought I really wanted was to have Rock back. I told myself that in going with Lacquerer I was simply keeping from being
alone. But was I beginning to like the chinkty life?

Lacquerer did not require my company every night, and one
evening I went in my work clothes to see Moth and her men. The
street-waterer from upstairs-lower-right-front, Round Knees, and
his girl, Trumpet Flower, were also in Moth's compartment.

The moment I appeared at the door the two tigers, Old Boxer
and Ox Balls, stood up and began to mince about, greeting each
other over and over with dandy manners; then they pretended to
notice me for the first time, and they approached me with a flood
of caricatured chinkty affectations and effusions.

"What a sweet moon-dragon pattern on your gown!"

"You look the soul of health!"

"Ten thousand years of happiness!"

"What delicate hands, my dear!"

Ayah, the bastards. Had they seen me going out one evening
with my powdered hands?

I passed off their teasing with as good humor as I could. "I eat
well, thank you," I said.

Moth questioned me with wide eyes about my adventures, but
the company was quickly bored with the topic of someone else's
good fortune, and talk turned to other matters.

Round Knees was playing up to the tigers. The street-waterer
was a timid man who submitted himself every day to the most
painful of physical labors, hauling a water cart, as a donkey might,
through the Enclave's alleys. He apparently envied the tigers' un-
trammeled spirits, and he put on, to try to impress them, a disenchanted manner. He scoffed at the very things he seemed, when
he was not with them, to believe in most. He was a frequenter of
temples, a believer in magic, a respecter of yellow power, but in
the tigers' presence he made the sounds of a fierce cynic. But the
tigers only abused him. The more he tried to please them, the
more cruel they were to him.

"Have you heard about the Bird Priests?" he asked his heroes.

"Your fingers stink of temple incense punk," Old Boxer said.

"No, this is really funny. This is a pair of hairy country priests
—just came to the city a few days ago. They've rented a shop-

temple and set themselves up. I heard about them and went to see them. It's something to see. You really should go. They have the back courtyard of a cloth-shoe shop on Third Smaller Lane off West-of-the-Mountains Road. You go in there, and the place is filthy—they have some old cracked and dusty images, but the point is, the courtyard is full of birdcages *with their doors open,* and there are scores of birds flying around one of the priests—on his shoulders, on his head. Buntings, pipits, larks, shrikes, cuckoos, ousels, crakes, stints. Every kind."

I could hold myself back no longer. "I know them! They come from my old village. One is called Groundnut—a thousand-year friend of Rock's."

"I don't know their names, they're just the Bird Priests. That's all anyone calls them."

"Have you heard what they did in the country?"

"Yes, that's the real oink of it!"—the heart of the joke, he meant. He turned to the tigers. "They tell a story about how they led the poor farm hogs in their district against their landlords by having them pretend to be birds! And it worked, too, they say it did. They got what they wanted. By pretending to be birds. Did you ever hear anything so funny? Ha-ha-ha-ha—human birds! To frighten the lids! And now they've come to the city to show us poor pigs in the Enclave how to fly—something like that. Ha-ha-ha-ha-ha."

I saw that beneath the street-waterer's "real oink of it," beneath his gargle of mocking laughter, there was already some hope that the Bird Priests' magic might work here in the Enclave.

The tigers had begun to hop around flapping their long sleeves, cawing like crows and singing, "Cuckoo! Cuckoo!"

(On the Chits

I yearned to see Groundnut, and I thought often of those sapphires of calm in Runner's eyes, but I could not bring myself to visit them. I did not even know where Rock was! I could never have swallowed loss of face to the extent of admitting such a thing to Rock's old friend. I found out exactly where the Bird Priests' shop-temple was, and several times I skirted near it, and once I went so far—heart hammering—as to ask the price of a pair of shoes I did not need in the shop in whose rear courtyard Runner and Groundnut housed their birds, their cracked idols, and their burning idea.

In the same furtive way I flirted with seeing Mink but avoided it, too. I was now heavily on the chits. The interest Silverfinger charged for the money I had borrowed for gowns suitable to my life with Lacquerer was so burdensome that I wanted to pay off my debts at one stroke, if possible through a single sunburst of luck. I traded at Mink's chit basket, but I went there only in the evenings or, on my off days, at hours far from those of the drawings, when I believed he would not be there.

As to the chits, Moth was my monitress. I knew the fundamental rules of the drawings—that each day two double-digit numbers were drawn, the first an "outside" number of two digits, on which the odds were low, the second, "inside," valueless unless paired on a chit with the day's "outside" number, and so carrying much higher odds—but Moth introduced me to the entire mythology, the cult, that had been built on the chit lottery: the symbolism of animals and flowers and birds connected with inner and outer numbers, the chit-clue books exploiting this intricate set of images, the "books of dreams" which related the stock nightmares and wish dreams of poor whites to the symbols on the chits, the seedy seances of "number-spirit women" who for fees consulted various occult authorities for predictions on proximate drawings, the ways of studying the techniques of the drawings themselves for guidance in buying chits, the cultivation of clerks in chit baskets who happened to have tongues, the superstitious sweetening of the white mandarins of the chit lottery by contributions to their various race causes. Ayah, it all kept us busy if it did not make us rich. We won just often enough on cheaper numbers—two-to-one and four-to-one on single digits ("outside-outsides")—to feel that the big strike might be within early reach.

For me there was an added, private magic in the chits: On the day when I made my hit I would also get Rock back.

(An Innocent Stroll

But now the strangest event in all my life took place: I fell in love, or thought I did, with a yellow man.

I met him—his name was Han—at one of the chinkty receptions to which Lacquerer took me. He was, at first, simply present, in a chatting group, behaving with reticence and dignity. The party was for the poet Earthclod. Han modestly advanced the view that Earthclod's work was too imitative of that of Fu Tun and Chao Tsu-ping, two "modern" yellow poets who happened to be in fashion in Up-from-the-Sea at the moment.

This criticism by a lid of our white guest of honor was received in our circle with a frosty silence, but I, who hadn't the slightest basis for judging the worth of the comment, admired Han's forthrightness, at least, and his refusal to be intimidated by the suspicion with which his very presence at the party must have been greeted. I had felt this suspicion myself on seeing yellows at these receptions. What were they doing there? Were they merely watchers? What was it in us at which they wanted to peek? What did they have, as we said, on the other side of their fans? What were they really after? I remembered the pilgrim who had conducted me from Dirty Hua's to the mountain: "I am *ashamed*." Did these guests want to atone for something?

Then Han was talking to me. I felt at first that I wanted to shield myself from the reflector-lantern gaze of this yellow man, and I was painfully self-conscious at having been singled out by him. Was everyone looking at me? Lacquerer, as it happened, drifted away—was this a rebuke?

Han was at my side for only the briefest time, and he was quiet and friendly, though I thought that I was aware of constraint and hesitancy on his part, which I could have read as signs either of a sensual eagerness held in rein or of insincerity.

On the whole, I told myself, the encounter was faintly unpleasant for me. Lacquerer said nothing about it, after all, and may not even have noticed it. . . .

One evening shortly after that Lacquerer took me to the Silver Pavilion, a peculiarly white institution, an amusement house open only at night, where tea, wine, and cakes were served, and where brief entertainments were offered, ranging from readings of verse by young white poets to the nude ritual dance of the famous Southern Peony. Among wealthy yellows, who set such a value on modesty that their women used a kind of drop cloth to cover their bodies even while making love, these dances seemed a pagoda-peak of perversion, and the Silver Pavilion, though deep in the Enclave, was much visited by parties of upper-class yellows on the sniff for sensation. And Han was there that night. Indeed, when Lacquerer and I were first led toward a table, I saw him,

seated with yellow friends several tables away, watching me;
then when we were placed, he arose and made his way to us. He
greeted me with elegant manners and, unaware of his shocking
rudeness, quite ignored Lacquerer. His eyes glittered with messages I was unprepared to decode. Lacquerer good-humoredly
asked Han to sit down, which he did, in an empty chair that he
pulled from another table. No sooner had he settled himself than
a white magician appeared on the stage, to cymbals, and we
could not talk. During the performance Han was sitting close to
me, and I felt that he was leaning toward me, pressed by the
intensity of some powerful obsession; he was like a child in the
openness and awkwardness of his yearning. I was conscious of
the radiating heat of his arm close to mine. I had strange, confused feelings, and wondered, above all, "Why me?" As soon as
the magician had finished, Han arose, bowed blushing, and left us.

The third time we met, Han came across the room to me like
a hurled stone, again, and he seemed feverish. "I have to see you,"
he found a chance to whisper to me. "Meet me at the Three Kingdoms on Foochow Road tomorrow night, at the first-quarter gong."

I nodded and quickly assured myself that nothing but curiosity
had led me to accept.

I was curious, and I was in spite of myself thrilled. To go to
the Three Kingdoms, fashionable among the upper lids! I thought:
Han must see me as special; it seems he would not be ashamed to
appear there with me.

But one thing I had forgotten, as I discovered on my way to
meet Han the next evening: to walk to the Three Kingdoms I had
to pass the Golden Herons, the opium tavern in the back rooms
of which I had found Mink and Rock. Suddenly, when I saw those
lacquered picnic scenes beyond the crimson columns, I had a
vivid impression of Rock's face, as it might have reacted to the
disclosure that I was going to meet a yellow man in a yellow
eating house. Then my reaction—shame copulating as ever with
defiance!—as I heard myself murmur out loud, "Rock, Rock, you
turtle, you've done this to me."

Only with the greatest of efforts could I haul myself past the
mouth of the alley leading to other alleys that led to the pigs' gate
of the Golden Herons. Could Rock have been inside?

Then I was with Han. Here, on his own ground, his demeanor
was calm; his fire seemed ashes. Was he disappointed in how I
looked, away from the mysteries and perversions (as he doubtless

saw them) of the Enclave? On my part, I hardly noticed him for glancing around.

Hoo! I had arrived! This was what the chinkties mimicked. Linen brocade on the tables; booths with beaded cords obscuring the openings. *O-mi-t'o-fu,* I was to be served by a yellow man. I was to be served by a yellow man. I was to be served by a yellow man.

We were seated in a booth. There was a tightness in my throat, and I put my hand in Han's. My emotion, having to do with the waiter, with how the yellow waiter was going to abase himself before me, struck Han as a tribute to himself, and I saw that he was perhaps slightly let down and further cooled by this, having possibly hoped for much greater difficulties. I was soon composed.

With respect to my race, Han was a proud liberal. One thing one had to say about Up-from-the-Sea—said he—was that there was no social problem as to color. It was wonderful that a place like *this* made absolutely no fuss about serving whites. (I did not say, as I might have, that he was making quite a fuss about the no-fuss. Was it in the very nature of yellow liberalism to be insensitive, since its mission was to call attention to injustice and to itself? And to its own virtue; also its refined taste? Would I have shrimps with a Cantonese sauce? Bean sprouts with tarragon?) But as we went along I found Han sweet and easy. There was a steadiness about him. . . .

Then I realized: I had never since childhood been in any relationship but one of subservience to a man who was, or seemed, in control of his own destiny. Yes, he was rich indeed, for he could afford to be definite. Assurance, generosity, and arrogant tactlessness! The care of such a man made a woman (white-skinned) feel both relaxed and wary.

Ai ai, Rock, you turtle!

Then came the first of the savory dishes, and at once I noticed something peculiar—as Han, it seemed, did not; at least, he said nothing about it. Instead of serving the courses in common bowls from which we would both help ourselves, the waiter brought separate bowls of each food for Han and for me. I let the matter pass. Probably just a question of form where mixed parties of yellows and whites were concerned. How I was looking forward to this feast in the famous Three Kingdoms! I tasted a nip of the sweet-mustard pork. . . .

Pfoo! My tongue curled and shriveled. The sauce? Was *this*

what the yellows called delicious? I tried the shrimp. Hai! Hai!
The same knife-edged stringency. The beautiful egg roll: the same
foul fire.

Then I waked up. It was salt. All my dishes were steeped in salt.
*There was no social problem as to color. A place like this made
absolutely no fuss....*
"What's the matter?" said Han.
"I'm not hungry."
"Eat, eat! You don't come to the Three Kingdoms every day."
"That's just it. I'm too excited." I reached a hand out for his
again—this time I was mobilized. I would not let myself be surprised again by deep feeling. I sat and watched him eat. We
talked. He was a nice man. He asked shy questions about my life,
and I decided to tell him the truth: I was a reeler, I worked ten
hours a day, my man had left me.

I determined not to ask Han, "Why did you invite me here?
Why do you go to the Enclave? What are you searching for among
white people?" I remembered meeting a young prostitute in Moth's
compartment one evening, a hard white child, Snow Pollen, who
said with numerous curses, "They"—meaning her clients—"all
ask, 'Why do you do this? Why are you a whore?' They ask the
question *after they have given it to you.* They never ask before."
I felt a delicate tension in Han. He was not a ruffian. He told me
that he was the second son of a textile merchant. His father and
his older brother were men of great force; there was no room
for him in the hong. He had wanted to be a scholar, but in the
commercial society of this city, scholarship was felt to be effeminate and backward-looking. His parents had arranged a marriage
to a girl of "good family" but bad blood—she and her kin all had
warped jaws; she was interested in amassing a collection of T'ang
Dynasty sculptures and did not mind what he did. Ai, I was
wary, I saw how my friend Han was building a picture of a man
starving for understanding, sympathy, fondling. He was putting
out his gossamer net.

Yet something strange was happening to me. I was coming to
know a yellow person, as I had never known one. Always I had
seen yellows as if from below—with perhaps a helpless child's
uplooking foreshortening: balloon legs, tapering torso, little head
aloft. I had at last become, I realized, thoroughly insulated from
the yellow race. I lived in the Enclave and worked in a row of

white women. Old Frog at the filature was the only yellow I saw in all this city as a human being, and even she seemed a kind of mechanism, an instrument of the plant for which I worked and she policed. Yes, the only yellow role I really knew with intimacy was the police function.

Now I was being offered new intimacies. Han was a person. When he spoke of himself as a son he was already no longer part of the institution of yellowness. His father was a fiercely acquisitive man and had no patience with a son who was pale and stayed up all night reading *Water Margin*, sometimes called *All Men Are Brothers*. Han told me about the morning when his father, ready to go off to his hong, had found him with the novel and had become enraged.

A carriage was waiting on Foochow Road for Han, when we left the Three Kingdoms, and he took me riding in it. He grew quiet and pressed his upper arm against mine. Once I felt his palm on my thigh. His hand began to move, and I lifted it off and away. That was all; he took me to the edge of the Enclave, and we got down, and he walked with me partway to my puzzle box: but not beyond Dog Road, for that would have taken him into a crowded area where it was not quite safe for a yellow man to be seen walking after dark with a white woman.

As we parted he asked me to join him again the following evening: He would meet me in his carriage at the Bund, across from the Telegraph Hong.

Now began a series of adventures which for me were all new. Han, touchingly infatuated, gave me glimpses of yellow life. He showed me the Settlement, both its night side and, on my days off, its sunlit streets of shops—a glitter of curios, a hong where lacquered coffins for the very rich were made and sold, a display of scrolls with paintings of mist-touched mountains that could only loom in gifted dreams. Little surprises: he gave me one day a pet live dragonfly leashed by a thread to a wand, its blue veins breathtakingly netted in its iridescent lantern-paper wings. Hai, he bought me a purse the shape of a fat little tiger in the shop where Top Man was shroff; Top Man, sad white snob, seeing that I was with an upper-class yellow man, came fluttering out of his cage to attach his recognition to me. Han took me to Chang Su-ho's Gardens, where we rode the water chute and watched the cyclists racing, and late at night fountains of fireworks sprayed the sky in what seemed an effort to hang new sparks in the highest constellations, the Bushel, the Mansion, the Throne of the Five Emperors.

In all this time Han treated me with utmost respect, never touching me except shoulder-to-shoulder as if by accident when we rode in his carriage, and I became filled up with an emotion which I confused with gratitude. He (yellow) was so kind to me (white)! He (man) was so considerate of me (woman)! I suppose my murmurs of thanks began to be touched with a slight scent of venery, but at first I did not realize any such thing.

He took me to gatherings of young people in private houses out on Bubbling Well Road, and these seemed to me the most elegant yellow society I could imagine, though I came at last to understand that the women were of the demimonde; a few white girls were usually present.

One girl who was on hand for a number of these evenings puzzled me, for she seemed white, but her hair was black and her eyes had the epicanthic fold; I assumed she was a mixie. Her name was Snow Peach. She quietly taught me manners and tricks. Then one night it came out that she was white through and through, she had had her eyes "pulled." She urged me to do the same. She knew a yellow surgeon, a skilled expert in this operation—two tiny incisions, a tug of skin, a suture. One had merely to disappear from circulation for a few days and then emerge remade, so thoroughly changed that with a little make-up you could even thread the needle. "You'd be amazed," Snow Peach said, "how different the world looks when you get good eyes."

I said I would think about it. . . .

Han had been taking me out for about a month. It was my day off. We stood in the square stone enclosure of the famous Bubbling Well, a ridiculous muddy spring charged with chokedamp gas. It was something to see once, he had said. We returned to his carriage. The coachman, a white servant who never looked at me, closed the curtained door. We were in a dim, private place. Han's face swam near mine, and he said in the voice of one at the boundary of his strength, "Come home with me."

I was flooded with recognition—of the real nature of my aching gratefulness to this sweet man. "Your wife!" I said, giving notice through this protest of my acquiescence, and even, I think, of my yearning.

"She has gone to Woosung to view a figurine she wants to buy,"

Han said. "Anyway, I've told you, she doesn't care." After a few moments, he added, "We have a number of courtyards." Another pause and then, "There are such things as locks, you know."

I lowered my head. Han rapped on the forepart of the cab; the coachman jumped down and opened the door, and Han said the one word "Home."

I caught a glimpse of the white coachman's face: it was porcelain.

Han's home was on Horse Road, near the Loong-fei Bridge. We entered it by a postern gate from an alley barely wide enough to accept the carriage. It seemed that the coachman knew the rules.

Han led me to a small room in a side court, perhaps a maidservant's room, with red-papered windows. He barred the door. He wanted to talk awhile. The platform was deeply quilted, a scroll hung on the wall:

> *The sun of spring touches the branches,*
> *Petals open like pale white fans.*

Han took me in the late part of the afternoon, half undressed, and I was overwhelmed. Where was the stereotype at which we laughed in the Enclave?—the yellow man fumbling at his silk underdrawers, unsure of his powers, sputtering off like a silly fingerling firecracker on a short fast fuse. No. Han was not like that; he was deeply sensitive, moreover, to any shame that I might have on account of his color. Before, I had been full of desire; afterward, I was in love, or thought I was—was there any difference?

We held up our arms, side by side. My white skin was coarse, tiny brown hairs leaned from the great pores; his yellow skin was smooth, close-pored, shiny, delicate. Each said he liked the other's better.

Then what was the matter with me? Full of love, I was blurting out some white "secrets." Yellows play a white person cheap, I said. Then they start asking you questions, and, Han, do you know that you'll get lies or silence, one or the other, in answer to those questions? Whites don't like to spill their entrails in front of yellows—do you know that? Because they don't like to have what they say twisted around against the white race. Whites are *always* suspicious of yellows, even when there's not the slightest ground for suspicion, why don't yellows seem to realize that?

After that came a surge of remorse—for what? For speaking

this way to gentle Han? For giving away what I over-regarded as
"secrets"? For having given away much more than that—myself
—to this man whose skin was different from mine?

Hai, was horrible Rock riding my tongue?

That night Han was possessed to run a tour of the crazy pa-
vilions and courtyards of the Enclave. His interest, as he made out,
was more or less sociological. Southern Peony's naked dances were
only the start. Opium divans in the chinkty quarter. Homosexual
nests masked as taverns and clubs. An exhibition of flagellation in
the back court of an elegant white teahouse: the punisher, a
white woman; the punished, a perfectly delighted yellow gentleman. Han took me to such spectacles as I had never heard of.
I was wild and proud and took the tour as a matter of course.

On days that followed I loved him, or thought I did—and what
would be the difference? He, too, was surely in love with me. The
signs we spoke of—melting touch, pangs seated in the chest.

We walked along the upper Bund on another of my days off,
oblivious to the honking and shouting, and into the Garden. There
we walked arm in arm, our heads inclined together. I remembered
the stage, when Gull was teaching me the yellows' tongue long
before in the Northern Capital, at which I suddenly stopped trans-
lating and began to think in the new language; so, now, I found
myself beginning (with caution, and in spurts) to accept Han
as a man, rather than as a yellow. Then (in other spurts) Rock's
damnable quarrelsome state of mind took hold of my head, and
I was white rather than a woman. Now in the Garden we were
very close, man and woman.

But as we walked on the shaded paths I began to feel a vague
undercurrent of uneasiness. I could not have said at first what was
wrong. Could it have had to do with Han? It seemed not, for he
was squeezing my hand and murmuring. Yet I felt somehow on
guard.

We crossed a pretty arching bridge over an artificial stream. I
looked back along the way we had come, and I saw four young
yellow ragbags—Fukien rubbish for sure—with their eyes on us.

Then I realized with an instantaneous clarity what was wrong.
We had crossed the line, from the peony beds to the pine grove on
the river side of the pavilion, beyond which white prostitutes
were not supposed to walk.

The four men were close behind us, and they had begun a kind
of muttering which seemed ominous. Han, besotted with me,

seemed to be unaware of their presence. Their remarks became audible and unmistakable: they were addressing Han.

"Did you ever hear of the riot, brother?"

"Keep to the river side of the line, you crotch crab."

They rushed forward and tore Han from my side. I saw the look of amazement on his face before I turned and ran for a policeman I had seen near the theatrical pavilion.

I told the policeman a yellow man was being attacked by four robbers up beyond the bridge.

The policeman looked me over and asked me what I was doing in this part of the Garden.

I thought with despair: What use for a white woman to say she is not a prostitute? I wept and said a yellow man was being killed —wasn't he going to do anything about it?

Slowly he started along the path. I could not bear his deliberate pace, and hoping to speed him up I ran ahead.

When I reached the place, Han lay unconscious on the ground, his face bruised and bleeding. The four men were fleecing his purse and exploring his garments for secret pockets. At the sound of my footsteps they straightened up.

"How about a dip of fish?" one of them said to me through gaping teeth.

Another said to his companions, "Who goes first with her?"

The policeman came around a curve in the path. The rubbish did not run away but stood ground, and soon I saw why. The policeman sided with the roughs, chiding me with scathing coarseness of language for having crossed the line. The fun seemed to be over; the four hoodlums sauntered off. As Han recovered consciousness and sat up, shaking his head, the policeman bent over him and told him roughly to keep out of this part of the Garden with white whores; then he, too, left.

Somehow Han seemed just then immensely more valuable to me than ever before.

("We Will Catch Up with the Lids"

One evening when I arrived home from work Bare-Stick was in the courtyard of our puzzle box waiting for me. I took him up to my cubbyhole. He sat cross-legged against one wall.

What had my times with gentle Han done to me? I saw Bare-

Stick now as prickly, dirty, oafish, and disgusting. Would Rock seem that way to me, too?

"Where is Rock?" Bare-Stick asked.

"Why should I care?"

"I wish you would tell me."

"The last time I heard," I said, "he was tickling the mouse of a plain-looking woman who lives beyond The Good Life."

"I know. I found her. He's not there."

"Then you know more than I do. So why do you come to me?"

"I thought he might have run back to you."

"What makes you think I'd let him?"

"You would, that's all."

To hide my reaction to this, which was inwardly an angry grief and outwardly a blush, I turned away and went to the crude box that served me as a chest and pretended to look for something in it.

"I have another man now," I said, in case Bare-Stick might get impulsive ideas of taking Rock's place in my life and making me happy again.

"So I hear!" Bare-Stick said, with a rising inflection of sarcasm which suggested that he knew I was going with a yellow man.

I turned back to Bare-Stick and with forced cordiality changed the subject. "How are you living?"

"I work for Runner and Groundnut."

"I heard they'd come to the city. Is Groundnut eating well on offerings?"

"He's changed, White Lotus. You wouldn't know him. Ever since the beginning of 'the method.'"

"Method?"

"'Sleeping birds.'"

"Are they really serious about all that?"

"Runner is serious, ai, he's serious. Look, White Lotus, you know there are—how many temples in the Enclave—five hundred? Every shading. Buddhism, Taoism, Lamaism, Confucianism, and all those cults—Californian Amitabhaists, White Red-Hat Sect, all those. Four fifths of them have crawled into shop-back holes. There's not one of those holes I'd choose over Runner's. The reason I like it, and so many poor hogs and sows like it, is that Runner makes us feel that we have found a future, a *possible* future. The place is dingy and small, like the traps where most hogs live; we're at home with Runner—his serene face! Beggars swarm there: Groundnut welcomed them to begin with, and Runner has given them hope of a new life. A lot of your friends"—that sarcastic tone again; he'd heard of my chinkty nights; who could have secrets in such an envious, gossipy city?—"would make fun of the place, because *they'd* belong to one of those ornate temples that used to be mosques, and the Moslems who sold it to them on mortgages charge ten thousand taels a year interest, and your friends will be paying off for the rest of their lives for their fancy temples."

"I have no concern with any of that," I said. "I want results here and now, not when I come back as a water-buffalo cow next time. I know, the shop-backs are supposed to be the woman's world. There we can knock our heads on the bricks to the proper idols and get rid of stealing, adultery, palm leaves, the pipe, puzzle-box quarrels, husbands who don't come home, cheating in the market, dirt, fleas, lice, fighting with one's man, drinking, backbiting, whoring—every evil stink and sore and grunt that makes us white people seem like pigs. Only it doesn't work that way, does it, Bare-Stick? The evils run the streets all the same, the yellows go right on using us. Groundnut used to say, 'Keep them ignorant'—meaning his own people. I don't trust priests."

"Groundnut doesn't say things like that any more." There was a stupid sincerity on Bare-Stick's face. "Runner keeps saying things to encourage us, and Groundnut says them now, too. 'The race is advancing.' 'We'll catch up with the lids.' 'We must be better than they are in their own terms.' But Runner can't just promise, he has to have a plan. He has to fight the job line, and he has to fight our being shut up in the Enclave, but at the same time he has to tease and prod and criticize the whites themselves for their laziness, their slackness, their lumpishness, their not caring. It's not easy. You tell people they're lazy and they turn away to some other more flattering hope."

"The idols only lull them all the more," I said.

Then Bare-Stick gave me a start. "Rock has been to see Groundnut."

"He should. They're old friends."

"He came once. I didn't like the stare he was wearing—same look as before he inscribed me. But Runner wants to find him again. They want his help. They're looking for strong men."

"To be birds?" I asked on a derisive note.

"Maybe. Would you like to know someone else who has been to see us? Old Arm himself. Look, he warned Runner not to start any sleeping-bird demonstrations here. Think about that! What does that mean?"

"Perhaps it means that for men to act like birds is silly, in a city."

"Don't mistake me, I admire Old Arm. I like an aggressive race man, one who has no fear of the lids. I don't care what his motives are, or whether he takes money, or likes chinky mice at night. Our white leaders are like the yellows', they're men, they're human, they want position and power, and maybe they want squeeze and cumshaw, and maybe one or two of them even make a big swindle out of race. We have so many bad leaders—I mean manipulators. Silverfinger—he's supposed to be a big race man. Boasts about how he picks the yellows up with his little bamboo chopsticks. 'Make your lid feel he's a big man'—this is what Silverfinger says—'and you can pick him right up with your chopsticks.' I don't care how 'bad' our leaders are, if they're really strong, too, if they can get something for us. . . . But Runner is different—he's pure, I really believe he's pure. I didn't like the way Old Arm came in there with a squad of his bullies to tell him not to try his method here in the city. Only one thing I liked about it: It showed that whatever Old Arm had heard about Runner had made him take Runner seriously. Very, very seriously."

What moved me so about the way this big, clumsy, wonk-witted man talked? Was it the mentions of Rock? The stirring up of so many memories? I could not help saying, "You've changed too, Bare-Stick."

"Working for Runner fills you with a feeling of closeness to all the ragged, miserable, louse-bitten men and women who come in there to kowtow and to watch the birds and listen to Runner talk. You feel like one of a big society, a secret hall, of sufferers—and that makes you stop worrying about your own face. About your own endless eating of loss in front of the lids."

"I have to get ready to go out," I said, suddenly wanting to cut off this talk of sufferers. "I have to change my clothes."

Bare-Stick rose to leave. "If I find Rock, do you want me to tell you where he is?"

"No," I said. "He's out of my life."

When I met Han, later, he asked me at once why I had been weeping.

¶ When Time Would Not Stop

Han took me to the races on one of my off days. Imagine
the thrill I felt when Han's coachman pulled the carriage off Bubbling Well Road in to the stately gateway of the Recreation
Ground, the sacrosanct demesne of the highest yellow society, and
the armed gate guard, responding to the casual salute Han gave
him—a tap of his closed fan on his oyster-gray silk skullcap—
called out to my escort, "Pass in, Elder-born Han!"

We were early. It was a good form to be early, Han said. The
coachman put us down at the steps of the Race Club pavilion, and
we began to stroll about the vast grounds. Young yellow bloods
greeted Han, and one asked, "Where have you been keeping
yourself?" The sky was a brilliantly polished vitreous bowl. I
was wearing a new Lin Yi dress that Han had given me, and I
felt the envious eyes of Han's friends on me. Surely I was at the
pinnacle! How could a poverty-stricken white girl be carried any
higher? To think of the number of *yellows* who would never worm
their way inside these walls! Han held a parasol to shade me from
the sun; the Recreation Ground seemed to be a wild-flower bed
of brightly colored parasols. "The Archery Club," Han said, pointing to a pavilion we were passing. "And there's the Swimming
Bath. The Kite-Flying Grounds beyond." This last he said with a
twinkle in his eye, for I had told him what kite-flying meant in
the hogs' under-language; we shared many darkened-room secrets!
"There's the Fireworks Stand: we must come some night to see
the display: they hold it at the black of the moon. That pavilion
belongs to the Walking and Talking Club. I've never joined. They
have an artificial wilderness, beyond there where you see the
cypresses, and they walk around on sand-covered paths. Truly.
Does it sound absurd? Ayah, it's frightfully serious." I was aware
of Han's boyish pride, both in me and in being able to show me
these yellow wonders. "The free grounds, outside the racetracks
and between these various clubs, where you see the low fences—
they're allotted by the Recreation Trustees to the many foot-
shuttlecock and stone-tossing clubs of the young gentlemen in the
hongs."

"Strange," I said, "the gents playing at poor men's games."

"They believe in keeping fit," Han said. "You should hear them,
sometimes, at the best receptions, rehashing their boring games.
By the hour. They remember every detail."

It was nearly time for the first race, and we sauntered back toward the Race Club. Hai! There was Harlot in the crowd! Not with Pride but with another, younger yellow. I saw her eyes on mine, yet she showed nothing. I began to lunge forward, thinking to call her name; she looked away. Then I realized: She was threading the needle in broad daylight. Her skin was exquisitely made up, yellowed. I thought, with a secret laugh: More power to her!

We climbed into the upper part of the Race Club stand and sat on satin-cushioned, squarish chairs. There were several white women with young yellow men in the crowd near us, and I recognized a number of white men, too, in a large all-male party— they were the "bigs" of the Forgetfulness Hong whom Lacquerer had pointed out to me the night of the reception for Dogtooth.

Before us spread the great irregular curve of the track, which was pear-shaped rather than oval. The dusty bed of the track had been sprinkled by water carts and leveled with harrows; the fragrance of the damp earth rose to our level, and the pattern of the running harrow teeth was sharp in the sunlight. A gentle breeze. The wafted colors of silk gowns, the lazy flags of the stable owners, the sweet undulations of the chartreuse skirts of the weeping willows beyond the course!

The first race, Han told me, was to be a mile-and-a-quarter run for griffins—untried, newly broken Mongolian ponies that had never raced before. How jolly these griffin races were, Han said. These ponies were immensely strong. Sometimes they swerved and bolted. Threw their riders. Could not be stopped and ran round and round the track for twenty miles while everyone laughed his head off!

Now the nervous ponies—shaggy, short-legged, round-bellied beasts with powerful shoulders and thighs—were being walked out on bridles held by riders on lethargic lead horses. The jockeys, all yellow boys, were dressed in silk tunics and trousers exactly like some of the old-fashioned slave uniforms of the Northern Capital. The Race Club's gambling brokers, in crimson gowns piped with black, circulated in the crowd taking bets, and Han put down five taels on a chunky filly named Water Song. The colors, Han's flashing eyes, the murmur of anticipation all around—how lucky I was to be alive at precisely this place and time!

The ponies, shying and snorting, were held at the starting post by grooms. Water Song—the brown-and-white one, third from the right; the rider's colors, silver and blue.

The starter's banner drops! The pack leaps forward. One pony rears high, spins around, and runs the wrong way. The jockeys' glistening tunics flap in the wind of speed. Water Song is caught in a press of the leaders. Leather Fetlocks is ahead. Han is holding both my hands. Ha, the crowd shouts!

At this moment I have a wish, the burning intensity of which is as powerful as the most urgent wishes of my childhood: that all this could stop exactly where it stands, be frozen in its uttermost brilliance, never change, never fade—an eternity of beating heart and tingling skin. Ayah, I wrench my hands away from Han's and close my small fists and beat against the speed of the race, try to stop it, stop it, stop it. But the ponies fly, the breeze snaps the flags, the throat of the crowd roars for victory. . . .

It was all over before my wish had time to fade. How did it come out? What horse won, Han? Where was Water Song?

Han was disgusted. His filly had finished in the ruck.

A laugh from the crowd: Here at last came the horse that had caracoled and started in the wrong direction.

But my wish had been denied me, and I did not feel like laughing. I began to see certain things with a sunstruck clarity—that there were upper and lower sections in the Race Club pavilion, divided by a wide aisle, and that there were distinctly two qualities in the crowd. Below the aisle, not a single white. There below the aisle were the really rich, dressed in perfection of the sort that only good money could buy, the owners of ponies, the owners no doubt of filatures, too. Up here was a shadier class. I could see that. I recognized Snow Pollen, known to me as a prostitute, with a young yellow man, not far away. And there in the distance was Duke—where was his haughtiness, as he played lapdog to some underling of the Forgetfulness Hong, running here and there to place a bet and buy a bowl of tea for the man? And Han?—a discarded son of a powerful father who was above going to the Race Club. Ai, ai, why had everything not stopped in all its vividness in the midst of the race?

After the second race the entire pavilion emptied as the crowd went out for a ritual of leg-stretching. While we were descending the Race Club steps I began to hear a wild altercation ahead and below. A white ricksha boy, who had brought a latecomer to the races, was raising the usual howl for more money. This was standard practice. There were no set fares, there were not even "understood" fares, for ricksha rides in Up-from-the-Sea. The passenger merely gave the ricksha boy as much, or as little, as he thought he should, or could. The coolie always cried out, with a show of outrage, for more, trying to shame or embarrass the client into a grudging extra copper or two.

There was a raw stridency to the ricksha boy's protests that troubled me. I looked away but could not shut out the disturbing sound. I felt, for a moment, mortified at the thought that a white was making such an unseemly racket at this of all places; then I was angry with myself for wanting the white man to be satisfied with the cheating pittance he had doubtless been given, for it was well known that the richest yellows paid the meanest fares. How, after all, did the rich get rich? I saw the ricksha; it was a brown beauty with highly polished brass fittings—suitable for dignified entry to the Race Club steps. How that voice haunted me! The coolie was following the passenger up those steps, plucking at the man's gown, calling out in an appalling wail against callousness, unfairness, inhumanity.

Then my heart plummeted. I looked right at the ricksha-puller for the first time and saw that sweat was pouring down his face, and that he was Rock.

At that moment I saw where I was. I saw that I had been dragged down to the lowest class of human beings, the class of the scum of the Enclave, of the dirty shop-back temples, of second-hand stores, taverns, cheap theatricals, boiled hands, overcrowded puzzle boxes, the class—ah, yes—of pimps, cutpurses, pipe addicts, and whores. How was I not a whore? Did it make any difference whether Han paid me in cash or in Lin Yi gowns? Snow Pollen and I at the races!

I turned, fearful that Rock, even in his furious preoccupation, might see me, and walked up the steps again. I held myself back from running; he would be all the more apt to see me if I ran. Han hurried up after me, and when we were safely out of sight, and when at last Rock's abusive, whining shouts ceased, I turned. Han's kind face was drawn, and he gently said, "Is something wrong? Did I say or do something wrong?"

I put a hand on his arm and said, "No, Han, I just wanted to get out of the sun."

"But I have the parasol. Why didn't you tell me the sun bothered you?"

([The Uses of Selfishness

At the filature the next day I had a feeling of coming back from the moon. My little colleague Pigeon, beyond the wire mesh from my basin, suddenly seemed the truest person I knew, and when I thought of her stanch fidelity to her worthless mother, who was fast wasting on the pipe, and her adoration of her older brother, the chit-sorter, Little Lizard, and her endurance and unwavering courage and astonishing accommodation to me— always standing there, frail stalk, respectfully waiting for me to make my mood felt before she would form her own for the day—I wanted to ask her forgiveness for my folly of recent weeks, my unfaithfulness to all that she meant to me, and was in me. I had tried to lead two lives. That was over. I had vomited all night. I had spit up salted food, spit up gentle Han, spit up Lacquerer, spit up pretending to yellow standards. And I knew what I must do at once, that very day if I could find a way: I must go to Runner.

"Tell me another story about Little Lizard."

With what clarity Pigeon responded to my revived interest in her life—and, it must have seemed to her, in my own! For a long time I must have been taciturn and moody at work. Off she brightly rattled:

Ai, the other day Little Lizard had told a falsehood in the form of a maze. It seemed that he was a master liar. It was a commonplace thing to deceive the lids—every white had to do that every day. But Little Lizard even loved to lie to his own kind. On a sharp-breezed occasion a few days before, he had wanted to take a part of the afternoon off to go with a friend to the piglets' kite ground, a barren field beyond the ricksha-pullers' mud city, and he was obliged to lie himself away from work at his basket. Little Lizard worked at one of the larger baskets, and his job was to count the blocks of not-yet-sold chits as they arrived from the Forgetfulness Hong printeries; at this basket were eight clerks, three counting boys, and twenty chit-runners. Seeing the wind whirl the dust off the bricks in the courtyard of the basket, Little Lizard could not wait any longer to fulfill his desire, and he went to the Number One Clerk and told with prodigious rapidity a lie that, being a puzzle and offering numerous alternative paths to solution (and escape), was actually a maze.

"My count is off. On this afternoon's goat block the count is off by nearly forty chits. Maybe I've counted wrong, but I've counted four times. It's possible that part of this pad of the goat block was put in the wrong consignment at the printery, because when my first count was wrong I asked the printery cart boy, and he said the sorter over there—this sorter's wife has a wen on her neck, and the cart boy says he's worried, makes all sorts of mistakes—the sorter might have confused goat and lamb; but the cart boy said his donkey was bitten on the ham by a mule fly, on Southern Capital Road this side of the granery, and the ass kicked the cart and some of the chits might have been shaken right out of the box, though he doubts it, but when I came in this morning I saw one of the runners, I don't want to name him to you, Old First, because I might be wrong about this, but I know what district he works—I thought he was fumbling around the new consignment while the cart boy was unloading it; you know how they'll steal chits if they can. When the consignment was divided for delivery to the sub-baskets and for doling out to the runners, this part of this pad might have been sent over to the sub-basket at Hat-head the carpenter's, or it might have been sent back to the printery by mistake with the unsold returns, and the sorter with a wife with a wen might have caught it and set it aside, but this pad is double-inside, so the chits are highest value—you follow me?—and so they should have been stacked at the left rear of the locked room, but I remember when I came in this morning that you told me to take the front right-hand stack—do you recall? So maybe . . ."

On went the swift flood. I was giggling. Pigeon's eyes flashed as she told about her brother, the genius at twisting his tongue. At last the chief clerk had started flapping his hands and Little Lizard had begun asking what, beyond one further recount, the clerk wanted him to do—run to the printery and check up on the sorter?—search Hat-head's basket?—find the suspected runner in his district and see whether he had any of the missing chits? —find the cart boy to see if they were still on his cart? There were a dozen ways to turn in the maze.

In short, Little Lizard went kiting.

(He enjoyed it, too, complacent in the knowledge that all the time the count had been square; the chits were in the locked room; he would turn them up, triumphantly, on his return.)

The value of this story to me was that it made me realize I

must lie to Old Frog by midafternoon, in order to have time to go to Runner and Groundnut. I could not wait ten days, for my next holiday, to see Runner. I must lie well, too—well enough so Old Frog would keep my basin for me overnight and not hire another woman to take my place at once.

Over the weeks I had come to see that despite her bluster and primitive cruelty Old Frog had a picture of herself as a sentimental matron; the little girls standing at the long row of dissolving basins were all her dear children. Every stroke of Old Frog's harsh discipline was followed by a series of loving pats; the time for me to catch her for my purpose was right after one of her shocking punishments. Fragile Pigeon was one of her special favorites. I had watched the shrewd child, more than once, ask Old Frog for advice on some matter having nothing to do with the work at the basins, some home crisis; Old Frog had responded with an excess of feeling, a grotesque yet touching mock motherliness.

So I asked Pigeon's help and made a plan with her.

Old Frog gave us our chance in due course. Near us she slapped a careless child, then made her way toward us.

What a little devil of an actress Pigeon was! By the time Old Frog reached our basins Pigeon had somehow worked herself into tears. She turned her streaked face to Old Frog, who put a hand on her shoulder and asked whatever the matter was. With a catch in her throat, Pigeon pointed to me and asked Old Frog to talk to me.

Old Frog leaned forward to the mesh and asked me what Pigeon's trouble was.

Pigeon's mother, I said (knowing that Old Frog knew she was a hopeless pipe case), had been evicted from a hut in the ricksha mud city. Pigeon must find another hut for the family before dark; I wanted to help her do it. Pigeon was loyal to her basin—she had been at the same basin for more than a year—and she hesitated, I said, to ask Old Frog for the rest of the afternoon off for the two of us. Could she let us go?

Old Frog gave me a piercing look, but a well-timed sniffle from Pigeon drove thoughts of possible deceit from Old Frog's mind. She said we could go.

I cleared my throat. (We needed insurance against Old Frog's regretting her softness and giving our basins, forever, to others.) Even in ricksha town, I said, the landlords demanded key money. Not much. Usually thirty to thirty-five coppers. I said I had promised to give Pigeon my wages for this day, but my twelve and her seven would not be enough. Would she be an old good and let us each have the next day's wages in advance, to piece out the key money?

I believe my saying that I was giving my pay to Pigeon was what pushed Old Frog over the edge, against her natural feelings, into generosity. She was a little jealous! She not only excused us; she let us have the advances.

Ai, this was splendid: I was free to go to Runner; Pigeon had the rest of the afternoon off; and Old Frog, having staked us to the next day's pay, was committed to keeping our basins for us.

I told Pigeon, as we parted outside the filature, not to throw her coppers away; there'd be no more the next day. And I asked her how she managed to cry so easily at a moment when tears had such value.

"By imagining that what you were going to say was true," she said. "It was easy to believe, you know."

I feelingly thanked her, and she, using the genteel yellow formula, told me not to behave like a guest.

I hurried to the Enclave, to the shoe shop behind which Runner and Groundnut had their temple. I went around back, through filthy alleys. There was no mistaking the postern gate of the temple, for it was surrounded by a swarm of beggars. Ai, yes, Groundnut the beggar, the beggars' patron! Jug was there, the leper. He approached me, whispering. I remembered, in the Northern Capital, Groundnut's scabrous crown, his oozing eye— but Jug's disease was surely not a sham; one could add to his face but he could not *take away* from it. I drew back from Jug in revulsion and guilt, for I had two days' pay in my purse, and I dared not give Jug a copper for fear of showing the other beggars how much I had.

As I turned away I heard Jug murmur, "Ayah, I was a house slave and you were a field slave"—meaning by this to ask me: Are you so hard that you can't forgive the distant past? Hooo—I *did* remember the ugly way the dandy Jug had teased Moth and me by the stone washtubs in the house slaves' compound that day long ago at Yen's. How hard was I?

The temple within was just as Round Knees had described it: shabby, unkempt, in tune with the sorriest puzzle boxes. Birds were nesting among the idols in the first room I entered; a few ragged women were worshipping—as well as, to my surprise, a trio of glossy-coated tigers, who laughed between kowtows in a merriment of embarrassment and ill-hidden hope.

I found Groundnut in the second chamber. He gave a kind of bounce at seeing me, folded me in an unpriestly hug, and led me for a private talk to the tiny room where he slept—a barren bed and a score of cages. He lived, no doubt of it, in utter simplicity. I found the many birds oppressive: the chippering, the odor, the click of claws on perches, the many glittering eyes.

He asked me why I had come. Bare-Stick had told him about his chats with me.

I said I wasn't sure what had made me come.

"Are you looking for Rock?"

"No. Why? Is he looking for me?"

"He's looking for trouble, if you ask me. He came in here one day—low."

There were pouches under Groundnut's eyes; he moved his hands to a cage and adjusted a cuttlebone. Something languid had crept into him—perhaps it was the seriousness of which Bare-Stick had spoken—and I felt that a scrofulous beggar was no longer cringing and whining so close beneath the cheerful skin. He began to talk about Runner and "the method," and Groundnut's pomposity that had so crushed Rock in those last days in the village seemed quite gone. "Look at the whites here in this Enclave. They're never going to get any betterment that they don't win for themselves." He gave me an extended narrative of the flock perching at Provisioner Lung's gate. He was sincere, to be sure. I remembered the single-mindedness with which, upon taking up priesthood, he had carried on his blatant drive for edible offerings, his "Keep them ignorant," his essential selfishness. Now his tone was altruistic and brotherly—for the race, for the poor, for the helpless beggar, for the workman without work, for the lame and weak—and I had a strong sense of his moral debt to Runner.

I asked if I could talk with Runner, and Groundnut took me to the entrance to the courtyard beyond, and there I saw the other priest airing a pair of pipits. He was holding the cage high and getting the birds in a mood to sing by making a squeaking noise with pressed lips. The birds flashed from perch to perch. Runner's face, tilted up to the cage, had that look of inner quiet I had seen on our first meeting, the after-waves of which had come over me, from time to time, ever since. He opened the door of the cage and the birds darted out, and up, and climbed into the sky on the delicate spiral silver ladders of their joy, and Runner gazed up at them, as if the notes of song condensed in the air as the birds uttered them and fell back in a cool rain on his face.

I stood beside him for some time, then he turned to me. He recognized me at once. "They'll come down," he said. He spoke of Rock. "He came to see us. He seems to me to be *ready*. There's a wonderful power in that man that makes me want to find him again."

The full force of this man's confidence in his poor fellow white soul struck me, and I had to take a deep breath. Bare-Stick had thought Rock in a dangerous mood, Groundnut had called him "low." But this man saw some sort of readiness, and strength!

"My life is empty," I said, "and I want to work for you." For some reason I did not say "for the race." I said "for you," and perhaps meant "for myself."

(A Word on a Grimy Slip

On an unswept wharf at the bottom of the Bund I found him, the white man named Marvel, whom Moth had urged me to consult. His famous flag of bells, making the morning glisten with its fine tinkles, had attracted a crowd of both yellows and whites, and he was ready to commence. Moth had told me there would be feats first, then fortune-telling. Marvel wore ragged coolie trousers belted with sea rope, and his ribs made steps up his bare chest to his bony shoulders. His head was shaved; his eyes flew about for a moment like two bluebottles, grotesquely independent of each other.

He placed six agate marbles in a pattern on a plank and using three inverted bowls began to shift the marbles in a dazzling confusion of appearances and disappearances; he kept uttering incantations. He held a marble against a winked eye and made as if to strike it with a fist, and—*i-ko lang-tang!*—the marble was tucked under the closed lid, the orb beneath seemed swollen by the blow; then he held up both arms showing empty coppices of hair in his armpits, whereupon the swelling vanished from his eye and he took the marble from under one armpit, and after it many others—more than had been on the plank—out from both armpits. He swallowed the marbles and excreted them from a nostril, pushed them in the other nostril and drew them from an ear. He swallowed a spherical donkey bell, of a walnut's size—I could see the lump go down the thin neck among the netted veins —and began to leap, a warrior with a heavy sword, a monkey, a stiff-legged manikin, and with every jump we heard the bell inside him. He made vociferous demands for cumshaw. Then, coughing, gulping air, grimacing, crossing his eyes, turning a somersault, wheezing and coughing again, he vomited the bell. "Ayah," he cried, slapping his shelved chest with his skinny wickerwork hands, "I've lost my food. I'm hungry." He drew a seemingly endless breath, and all his guts seemed drawn up into his chest, and his abdomen was a cavern—skin against backbone; in this skeletal state he strutted about. Then he exhaled and drew in air deep once more, and this time the bellows in his chest descended to his bowels, and he became a balloon, as weirdly round as he had been concave, and strutted again. Then he took nine porcelain bowls, squeezed one under each arm, held one in his mouth, and fanned three out in each hand, and he whisked in a sudden effortless backward flip head over heels in the air, then flung himself in a forward flip, and not a bowl was lost.

Coppers splattered on the Bund, and Marvel said he would look into the future for any who cared to know what they were about to do. "Yellows first, whites after."

I stood in the long line. I badly needed to know what I was about to do; ever since I had seen Runner I had felt unable to guide myself.

Runner had welcomed my offer to help him and had suggested two possible courses: I could spread the news of Runner's "method," preparing the path at my filature for understanding and eventual enlistments; or I could go and live at the temple and directly proselytize worshippers there, as "sleeping birds."

Could I risk giving up my job? Throw away a sure living? Abandon Pigeon, who had trusted and helped me? Did I really believe in Runner's "method"?

Events of the past few days, since my visit to Groundnut and Runner, had made me wonder whether Old Arm, after all, might not have the better way.

A new Municipal Council had been installed, under the chairmanship of a prominent yellow banker, Fu Lin-chia, who believed that the solution to all problems lay in the use of police. A sudden storm of police severity had fallen on the whole city, on Fukien

rubbish as well as on the Enclave, on yellows as on whites—but
with a special virulence on us. Council Chairman Fu called it
Scrubbing Clean.

Thinking one evening to talk with Mink, half hoping that he
had seen Rock, and to get his advice, I went to his basket at
drawing time. I found the place in a state of frigid propriety.
Mink was there; his head was clear of opium fumes but he was
in a panic. The whole chit lottery was getting a scrubbing, he said,
and while this basket had not yet been raided, a police visitation
was expected at any minute of any hour. What were they after?
Nobody knew. They would come into a basket and rip it apart—
breaking into locked rooms, scattering priceless bundles of unsold
chits, beating up clerks who were mere employees. The Forgetfulness Hong still paid squeeze to the police. Mink's fright was for
his habit. Where would he get the money for it? Where would he
smoke? The police had scoured the Golden Herons—cleaned out
the back smoking room, that is; but hadn't touched the workrooms
or the big front chamber. Some people said Old Scrubber Fu was
a little on the pipe himself. It was all capricious and mad. Far
from getting counsel myself, I ended by urging Mink to go and
see Groundnut and Runner.

On my day off I went to Silverfinger's to pay interest on my
borrowings—loans for gowns that I no longer used. Hai! The
lovely palace of usury was shut tight. Six yellow policemen stood
guard at the door. A crowd of depositors and borrowers had gathered. There was no disorder. A grim silence hung over those who
had entrusted their meager savings to the great Silverfinger—
and even over those, too, like me, who had taken and used his
money. I asked neighbors why the place had been closed. No one
knew. One man whispered, "Old Scrubber wanted those ingots
we used to see stacked up behind the velvet curtains. He stole
'em." The man nodded, as if this speculation were known fact.
I had had no love for Silverfinger, nor for Duke, who worked
here, and I supposed I was free of my debt now, yet still I felt
a shock to my pride, an anger. This had been a *white* money palace; the shroffs who had issued me loans had been my own kind.

The next day at the filature I heard an alarming report: the
previous evening the police had dealt a beating to Old Arm himself. It was said that a squad of the so-called Special Detachment
—being a pack of tall, burly mercenaries from the northern
provinces, notorious brutes of the force—had hung about the

wharves at payoff time, and, on hearing some sort of minor quarrel among the white coolies, had used it as a pretext to swoop in, seize Old Arm, who had not even been involved in the quarrel, and to administer to him a clubbing that left him unconscious and bruised from head to foot.

In the late morning a message came along the line of reelers: Old Arm could be seen in person in the filature's waiting yard during the noon break, for he was making the rounds of the city to display, in his resilient person, the works of yellow brutality.

Of course I went out to see him. He came round in his wharfman's rags, stripped to the waist, a mass of black-and-blue welts.

I felt, and shared, the surge of anger among the women of the filature.

Old Arm spoke a few sentences to us—a call. His voice was low yet wildly inflammatory. "Why is it you who have to work? Why can't your men find work? Why can't your men get jobs, as the Fukien rubbish does, in the match factories, the flour mills, the enamelware works, the paper plants, the printeries, the rubber-goods factories and leather-goods factories, the foundries, the food plants, the cotton mills? Why are our men restricted to housework, ricksha-pulling, and wharf labor? As soon as I am strong again, we are going to begin. Be ready. Do not worry about secrecy. I *want* the yellows to know that we are coming—with bamboo and stones, and knuckles, and pieces of pipe, and bricks. I solemnly promise to give back every bruise on this body. We know what we want and we mean to get it. Be ready."

He hurried off to visit other filatures.

The Enclave that evening was electrified. At every turn one saw groups buzzing. I myself was caught up in the general air of expectation and excitement. With incredible folly the authorities had made a hero, a near-martyr, of Old Arm; I felt his pains in my body, I felt I had been passive too long, I was restless and angry.

I went to see Moth. Her tigers were in a half-drunk ecstasy of boastfulness and loudmouthing. They flapped about the tiny compartment, cutting the air with their hands, raising their knees with force; they had engaged to go out with one of Old Arm's flying squads. . . .

I was near the top of the line moving toward Marvel. He took only one or two minutes on each fortune. He had put on a scarlet tunic, and he was sitting cross-legged on the ground behind a box

covered with a dusty square of velvet; from the box he took an
endless series of talismans, bits of paper, magical signs. I saw
that for some he waved and kissed a symbol of the nearly forgotten religion of the white God—an ivory cross. He spoke rapidly
in a murmur which only the one person seated opposite him could
hear.

My turn came. I sat in the dirt. Marvel never seemed to look at
me; his eyes were hooded and veins stood out on his forehead.
Fumbling and handling his shabby charms, his wonder objects,
he began speaking to me in a babble, giving me by his clairvoyance one astonishment after another. "Your filature . . . I see that
you want to stop reeling, you will stop reeling. You are not alone,
child. The bruises were shocking, you have seen signs of worse—
bamboo—a broad back. You miss someone, you search for someone. A long absence. You will work for the race. . . ."

I felt as if I were being rushed along by an irresistible wind. My
chest ached, and I thought I would sob. For the race! Yes! I
would work for my white brothers and sisters, and for the one I
missed after a long, long absence. That wild wind roared in my
ears. My eyes filled up as if smarting from its cutting force.

Marvel took a small square of paper from his covered box; a
pen and inkblock were beside him. He wrote a character. Blinking
my blurred eyes, I saw it. It was "temple"! Had he divined that I
could read? After writing the character he struck his foreteeth
with the fingernails of his right hand three times, and said, "The
sun rises bright and large. This paper will banish doubt and mis-
fortune. From my mouth I will spit true fire. In my eyes are steel
darts. I call on the god of the pig. Who guards the temple? When
the spirit enters the eighth quarter the answer will come. Place
five copper coins in my right hand. Take this paper. Walk twenty
steps to the northeast and swallow the paper, and you will know
what you must do."

I paid him and I did walk twenty paces in a direction which I
thought to be northeasterly, but when I looked at the paper in my
hand it seemed trivial and grimy to me; I could not put it in my
mouth. I knew, anyway, what I must do.

⟨ A Comb of Mud Cells

I moved to the temple. I moved that very evening.
Groundnut, who seemed to be in charge of the practical affairs of
the shop-back, gave me a litter in the windowless storage space

where odds and ends of ritual and housekeeping were kept—
bundles of incense punk, stacks of paper cutouts of cash and
sacred symbols, brooms, buckets, baskets; and I lay there warmly
clothed, for the first time in my life, in a sense of self. This was
the first room I had ever had to myself! This was the first important decision about my life that had not been forced on me; I had
made a choice. But what about Marvel, with ribs like winter
branches and his piercing mind? I told myself, at this distance,
that Marvel's "clairvoyance" had all been mere observation or
coincidental guesswork, that he had known me for a reeler by
looking at my hands, had guessed that, like many reelers, I had
seen Old Arm's bruises and yearned to work for the race—he could
not guess how; his word "temple" had probably come from an assumption that I was, like the rest, superstitious. Yes, I told my
newly seen self, *I* had chosen: *I* had decided what path to take!

Runner had received me, too, with a delight that made me feel
I was a separate and valuable entity. He showed me every corner
of the temple, every birdcage, the idols, his own room, the watchman's cubby by the postern gate where Bare-Stick lived. Bare-
Stick hugged me with impressive sincerity; he had been doing
the temple cooking and was very glad to see me.

As I lay on my litter, full of myself, I began to wonder where
Runner would lead me after all.

Runner was disturbed by what he had heard about the storm
Old Arm was stirring up. He was opposed to Old Arm's blustering
hints of violence, mainly because he felt that the use of violence
would be a hopelessly dangerous means of trying to get what we
wanted, for surely the yellows would not only overpower Old Arm's
flying squads and strikers and "spontaneous" rioters; they would
as well punish many an innocent and still docile white. Besides,
Runner was being unduly rushed by Old Arm, who was starting
his campaign too soon; Runner wanted time to gather forces for
a trial of his method.

And now the ebb tide from my sense of myself to self-indulgence
was streaming fast, and in the name of wanting to help Runner
I made a decision that filled me with such selfish delight that I
laughed out loud in my own dark room.

The next morning I told Groundnut (not quite daring to tell
Runner) that I must do some personal errands that might take all
day long; once these were taken care of, I would be able to settle
into wholehearted work at the temple. Ai, I thought, I have a surprise in mind for you priests!

I hurried along the Bund to the hemp wharves, and there, as I had hoped to do, I found Mink peddling lottery chits.

Mink looked sick. He was thinner than ever, his face was greenish, he perspired, he kept wiping snot on his sleeve. He told me in a weak voice that since the scrubbing of the Golden Herons he had been having great difficulty finding pipes, and had only been able to smoke irregularly; he was in pain, and was afraid.

I said I needed his help. I wanted to find Rock.

What a sunburst on Mink's gray face at those words of mine! It was as if I had offered him some magical salvation, some swift cure—or, indeed, a pipe.

"Ai, we'll find the turtle," he said. "We'll go to his ricksha concessionaire. But I have to get rid of these chits first."

"I'll help you sell them. Give me half."

And I did very well as a chit-vendor, too. One almost never saw girls running chits, and I suppose I was a novelty for the wharfmen. I flirted with them and made them feel that my chits would open the way to mysterious pleasures. I sold twice as many as Mink, even though he had his regular customers. We were done long before the noon drawing. Mink carried the cash to the basket, and then we were free.

Rock's concessionaire was the Swift-as-Seasons Company, which had its grounds on Horse Road—a large walled lot capable of holding nine hundred rickshas, where, when we arrived, there were only a dozen vehicles, disabled with broken springs or shafts, or bent mudguards, or flat tires, being worked on by grease-streaked white mechanics, while across one half of the lot clotheslines were strung on which hundreds of ricksha coolies' company coats were being hung out to dry by white washerwomen running back and forth from huge laundering caldrons.

We went to the concessionaire's office, a shabby mat shed where two hirers and a half dozen cashiers, all yellows, sat swilling tea; along one wall were the cashiers' cages where the pullers turned in their fares and drew their percentages.

One of the hirers thought twisted Mink wanted to work as a puller, and he broke out laughing. He flapped a hand toward Mink and said, "Get out, man. We don't hire grasshoppers."

Mink said with flesh-crawling humility, "We want to find one of your pullers, Old Good. Where can we wait to meet him when he comes in?"

"They don't come in till dark. And some don't come in then."

"We can wait. Where would you like us to wait?"

One of the cashiers spoke up. "What's this turtle's name you're looking for?"

"Rock Liu."

The cashier turned to one of his colleagues. "Rock Liu? Isn't he one of the ones they took the tin from?"

The second cashier said, "That's right. Last week."

The first said to Mink, "He doesn't work any more. They took his license away. You won't find him here."

I said, "What did he do? Why did they steal his bowl?"

The hirers and cashiers all laughed—at the note, I suppose, of indignation in my voice. Then the hirer who had first spoken to Mink shrugged and said, "Police."

Out in the street we decided to go all the way to the ricksha-pullers' mud village on the long chance of finding Rock there. We had a two-hour walk, through a wide district of middle-class yellow shops, past the many splendid plants where yellows could work and whites could not—printeries, foundries, factories for small goods—and through a respectable residential section; until at last we crossed a creek and, penetrating a thick screening hedge of clumped bamboo, we came to a scene of squalor and desolation that froze my heart—a great plain where, it seemed, a crowd of creatures had encamped while waiting permission, or opportunity, to become human. There were hundreds and hundreds of mud huts like the earths of dirty foxes. No streets, or even alleys, marked off this swarm of hovels. Paths of packed dirt led every which way. Scraps of salvage, broken tiles, bits of corrugated tin, rotten boards—the huts were patched and bandaged with whatever might be found or stolen. Worry-ravaged women and filthy half-naked children were to be seen working and playing.

And so we began what seemed a hopeless task—finding one soul in this great comb of mud cells. We began to ask. Rock Liu? A man called Rock? Head after head shook us wordlessly away. I thought once of Pigeon: her home was one of these huts, her family lived here, she slept here in this hell at night—and how cheerful, how responsive, how sensitive, how steady she had been by day! Who was sitting at the basin opposite her now? Did she miss me? I felt a pang of guilt at the way I had used her that last day and then abandoned her.

Rock Liu? Rock Liu?

Then I thought of a moment with Han—a gown of Lin Yi silk

next to my skin, the heel of my hand on the velvet nap of the carriage seat, vine leaves incised in the glass of the carriage window, a view beyond of the flags of the Race Club pavilion, and the gentle-hearted yellow man beside me, who never did me a moment's harm, murmuring something about its being good form to arrive early.

I thought, Rock is lying somewhere here, perhaps unknown to any neighbor, an absolute zero of a man, in one of these awful dens.

Then suddenly we found him. A small bare boy with his little tag of maleness hanging at the base of a dirt-caked belly led us to him.

Ayah, Rock, how undignified! Asleep on a pile of moldy straw with your mouth open.

Mink waked him up. Rock was quite cheerfully glad to see us, but it was clear that he had no need of my dramatizing sympathy. Nor did he jump up into my arms; not at all. He stretched and yawned. He was obviously, sleekly, full of food. He had stolen a tunic of the Swift-as-Seasons Company, and it was newly washed. He was clean-shaven, chin and crown.

He made no secret of his good fortune: He was being "kept alive," as he put it with a flick of one eyelid to Mink, by three girls who lived nearby, women of ricksha-pullers. They fed him by turns. One of them had kindly laundered his coat. Another had paid a mud-city barber a copper to shave him. They were good enough to see that he had all conveniences; I thought he needn't have laid such stress on "all."

Indeed, Rock sat us down (on the dirt floor) and offered us yellow wine, straight from a half-full bottle he pulled from under the dirty straw.

At first I felt a stir of anger, then abruptly I was inclined toward laughter. Yes, what a joke on me! I had expected a scarecrow— Rock three quarters starved, desperate, suicidal. Ai!

Something had to be said, so I asked, "How did you lose your license?"

And off he charged with his old zest. "Ayah! That! Well, you see, from the very first I was a good coolie. When they said, 'Chop-chop! *K'uai-k'uai-ti!*' I flew—swift as seasons, according to the characters on the back. I didn't mind. I liked whooping along through traffic, shouting to every lid and wonk to get out of the way. What beautiful swearing the ricksha boys have! I was a good

coolie, and I brought in the coppers for the company. Pretty soon
they let me have one of their sweet little brown number-one jobs,
the kind the rich boys insist on—varnish—filigree—brass-tipped
everything—it is well known that the coolies who pull the number-
ones for Swift-as-Seasons have brass-tipped you-know-whats in
their trousers! I earned more yet. Only trouble is, the police are
rough on number-one pullers. They don't like coolies to 'get big.'
And when the scrubbings began they had no mercy. I had heard
that was going to happen, I'd been warned, but you know me,
White Lotus—ayah!—you know me, I had no intention of going
prudent. So there I was, hooting and swearing along Southern
Capital Road when a stupid wheelbarrow man cut left in front
of me, and I pulled up short as I could, but I couldn't stop in time,
so over went the wheelbarrow with a load of wooden shutters,
down went the wheelbarrow man, backward went my ricksha, and
out onto the road, tail over top, went my gent. He had a white
beard; that was bad for me. I was the only thing standing, so of
course the bastard police slipped my little tin plate out of the
grooves on the back and told me to crack off to the yard. That
was it."

As Rock finished his exuberant tale, poor Mink was wheezing
with what passed with him for laughter, and he said, "Ai, you
brass-tipped turtle-head, you *would* be the only one left standing
when everyone else is flat on his ass!"

Rock shrugged. But I was looking now into the deeps of Rock's
casual manner, and I saw a sign I had seen before—that the rims
of his eyes were discolored, as if bruised; I got a strong sour-wine
whiff of the Rock in the tenant village, just before the stabbing.
Low; dangerous mood. Then I clutched at what Runner had said,
that a marvelous strength was ripening in Rock, and that he
seemed "ready." For what, for what?

Rock said, "Where do we go from here?"

"To Groundnut," I said. "We're going to live at Runner's temple."

There was a long silence. I felt that the name Runner had exerted some sort of physical push against Rock's face; his head
recoiled from the word, and he raised his hand holding the wine,
and his mouth and the mouth of the bottle briefly kissed each
other.

"Are you staying at Runner's?"

"Yes. Bare-Stick is there. Groundnut, of course. Runner wants
your help."

Another silence, another sip. Then Rock spurted off in a new tone, seeming to talk to Mink. "Can you worm in with some of the hong slugs and get my tin back—my puller's license? I want to work. I have to be working. Old Arm has a grip on these men"— with a gesture Rock indicated the waste of ricksha-pullers' warrens all around us—"and no wonder. It was easy enough for me, alone. Some of these fellows have three, four children. Seven coppers a day, if you work hard. Most of them have rackety hearts and putrid lungs—this weather's one thing, but you can imagine what it's like in winter: you have just the single thin tunic, and you run two miles, with the yellow bastard back there on the seat in a temper shouting, '*K'uai-k'uai-ti,* hurry hurry,' and you work up a sweat, and then you're idle for a long time waiting for the next fare, and there's a wind like a butcher knife, or maybe a cold rain. You bring the miserable seven coppers home, and the whole family crawls into one of these mud boxes, and the tobacco smoke and charcoal fumes start everyone hacking and weeping, and the worst of it is, you have a hard knot in your belly, because you know that the only way to get your seven coppers the *next* day is to go right on licking the lids—be ingratiating, call every yellow prick an old good, run your head off for him, run till you think your heart can't take another jouncing step. Each ricksha has a name. Steadfast Righteousness. Eager to Fly. Respectful Son. Ayah! There's only one way to do this thing: Shame them. *Shame them.*" Rock pounded his fist on the straw-covered floor. "I've seen the shame on their faces when I've shouted at them for cheating me on fares."

Would I ever be able to tell Rock that I'd heard him shouting that way one day—and that for a moment *I* had felt shame over a white man's making such a disturbance?

"Ai, Mink," Rock went on, "we've all made a lot of mistakes, haven't we? The bastards force us into mistakes. I went to see this Runner once. I haven't been back. Groundnut—so mandarin! My old-time beggar-louse friend! But I've been thinking about your Runner a great deal." He threw that "your" at me; his voice was rising. "About him and Old Arm. He may be right, and Old Arm may be wrong, but Old Arm is the one who has all these ricksha boys tied to the roof by the pigtail. They don't want to shame the lids—they want to give it to them in the groin." Rock's abrasive shout suddenly trailed off into a gentle whisper. "Yes, let's go, Mink. Let's go live at Runner's."

Mink was weeping—as much, surely, from the exertion of our long walk and from his deprivation as from emotion. Sniffling, he asked me, "Did you mean to include me?"

Before I could answer, Rock said, "Of course." Rock was grinning, blustering. "Runner needs our help. Haven't you heard, Runner is *ready*, Mink?"

Rock's giving back that word to Runner made me start.

Mink wiped his nose on his sleeve and weakly said, "How will I get pipes?"

"You filch me a tin, I'll find you a couch," Rock said. . . .

When we arrived at the temple, Runner took Rock's arrival as a matter of course. What an infuriating letdown! Runner seemed distracted. Groundnut, who was subdued, made arrangements: Yes, of course Rock should move into the storeroom with me. Mink could go into the postern-gate room with Bare-Stick. (Did Bare-Stick's face fall at that? Not at all! Someone to put down!)

Runner moved off into the courtyard and began cleaning and filling the water pans of the many cages there.

Then he was back again; a mynah was muttering on his shoulder.

"Old Arm begins three days from now," he said. "We just heard. It's definite—a wharfman told us. He plans to stir up a mob at the gates of the big match factory on Soochow Creek at Four Rivers Road—right at the edge of the Enclave, you see. We'll have to make a move of our own there somehow. Think about it, Rock."

Rock said nothing, but I felt *his* readiness, whatever for, rising in him like a fire forced by bellows.

⟨ A Parcel of Shame

I had Rock back. What riots, what demonstrations, what boons to the white race, what loosening of tight strings all had their place in the storage room that night! Starving? Suicidal? Ha! Ho! Ai! Rock!

During the next two days, while we waited for Old Arm's first trial, the tension among us at the temple was like a palpable liquid. Particularly between Runner and Rock did I sense flashing looks, an electric touchiness. Rock's reaction to the priest fascinated me. Nothing seemed to rouse Runner from his steady, opaque serenity; not even Rock's show of bottom-touching badness

—for since he had left me Rock had indeed gone from outward
bad to worse to white man's worst. I remembered Top Man's word,
"scum." Was Rock now part of the scum of our race? But Runner
had seen in him some potential force that he, Runner, wanted to
enlist. I could see bursting through Rock's apparent indifference
to everything his strong desire to impress, and even to please,
Runner, so more and more that deep potential came out to be
seen, and more and more I felt what I had vaguely guessed at in
the past: that underlying Rock's long descent into the scum there
had been a perverse idealism, a defiant honesty, an unwillingness to
pretend, a refusal to accommodate. In the light that shone from
Runner's face I could see the strength in Rock's rottenness; I could
see the strength that Runner had seen, and I knew why Rock
meant so much to me.

On the second evening of our wait, Rock told a group of us a
story of ricksha-pulling. Really he was telling the tale to Runner;
he delivered it into Runner's ears and eyes.

"I had a fare one day—a soft-spoken yellow man—who left a
parcel in my ricksha; I found it later. I kneaded it with my hands,
but I couldn't tell what it was, and I didn't dare break the seal on
its wrapping. What should I do? Try to find the man and return
the parcel? Pawn it? Turn it in to the concessionaire? I would
run risks whatever I did—if I tried to return it, of being accused
of thievery in the very act of being decent, or if I pawned it, of
being betrayed by one of those dirty pawnshop informers.

"In the end I decided to do nothing—just delay. I put the parcel
in the box under the seat flap where I kept my polish and rags and
I finished out the day, and then I trotted round to the Swift-as-
Seasons yard.

"I was ahead of the rush, because it was far from dark yet. I
had good earnings; I liked to cash in before the place would be
swamped. I intended to leave the parcel in the seat box overnight.

"When I walked into the cashiers' shed I heard a man shouting
at the two hirers and at the top comprador. The man was my fare!
I backed out before he saw me. The walls were only matting; it
was easy to hear from outside. Did I say my man was soft-spoken?
He was screaming. The concessionaire was a thief, to hire dirty
pig thieves. A quiet question from the comprador. Then the strident voice described me to a hair—from the rear. Ai, yes, my fare
had known he was being hauled by a man and not a donkey. He
described my loping run—I think he must have run a bit inside

the office there, to illustrate. My shaved head, the ridge at the back of my skull. I could tell that the Swift-as-Seasons people weren't interested in anything but what was in the package. My man didn't want to tell, but his excitement suggested that whatever was in the parcel was valuable. The comprador tried to cool him off, without success. In fact, my soft-spoken chap began to threaten lawsuits. At last he gave his address, in case—not likely! —the thief turned the parcel in.

"I ran to my ricksha and skinned out of the yard before the man emerged, and I ran to the address he had given, in the wealthy section out beyond the Recreation Ground and the Horse Bazaar —I Wo Terrace.

"I was there waiting at his spirit screen when he pulled up in another ricksha—another little brown number-one; a fellow I knew was pulling it, named Rogue. He tried to argue for more money and nearly had his head bitten off.

"How my fellow started when he turned and saw me! I held the parcel forward in my hands, and I was half crouching, half crying. 'Venerable,' I said in a slimy voice, 'ten thousand apologies. I didn't know until my next fare showed me. I'm an honest man. I had the greatest difficulty tracing you.'

"My yellow friend stood there swallowing. Ai, yes, he was forcing back down his gullet all the filthy things he had said about me and about ricksha boys and about thieving pigs and lying whelps of wonks and bastard whites and sneaks and—best of all —dirty pricks who have no shame.

"Then, as soon as he had the parcel safely in his hands, he began to cover up. Yes, he began to try to hide his own shame, and he became really funny. Gruff praise. 'Good boy.' He had been saying at his hong that afternoon that ricksha boys weren't as bad as some people thought. Finally he went groping in his leather purse, and out came the price of shame—four coppers. 'You're a good boy.'

"I refused the money. Ha, no! I couldn't take money for being dutiful. Now this made him truly angry, and we had the argument of my life! He ate and ate and ate his loss. I pushed the air with my hands. 'No, Venerable.' Ai, he wanted to curse me, but he couldn't—because of his shame.

"When I had shown him the true meaning of humiliation, I took the ten coppers he had worked up to, and I left. I never knew what was in the parcel."

Rock's eyes were sparkling—with desire for a word, a nod, a smile from Runner.

"We will see," Runner said, in a tone that was noncommittal and cool, "about this matter of shame. Day after tomorrow."

I felt, with a flash of anger of my own, the thrust of Runner's challenge to Rock.

⟨ A Childlike Child

Little Pigeon was on my mind, and with Runner's permission I started out before dawn for my old filature, to see whether Pigeon would come to the temple to help with our cooking; the work would be much easier for her than standing at the steaming basin all day.

It was not yet fully light when I reached the waiting yard, and I was ahead of most of the reelers. Autumn was on the air; before I could distinguish the faces of the women and girls as they arrived I could see the plumes of fogged breath leaping from their mouths and nostrils.

Groups formed. I heard from one clump the phrase "give it to them." I moved closer. The women were talking of Old Arm. Here, as throughout the white community, there was great excitement about what was to come the next day—and wild rumoring. One woman said Old Arm was going to burn down the match factory; another spoke of "ten thousand wharf hooks." The minds of our miserable white people seemed, like this chill-edged morning, to be crepuscular, dim, mist-smudged. Even where their own deepest interests were involved, these women seemed to get things all mixed up: These who had jobs felt that Old Arm's campaign had nothing to do with them. I heard no word of Runner, or of "sleeping birds." I fought down both my anger at the absurdities I heard and an impulse to break into the chattering circle and tell the women about the difference between Old Arm's violent approach and the strange serene power of Runner's unhurtful method.

It was growing lighter; the horizon was kindled. I began to see faces, and I hurried from child to child, looking for my frail partner of the basins.

A woman stopped me. "Hai! You again! Coming back to work?" It was the reeler who had sat next to me on my right, the put-upon woman, so insensitive, self-centered.

"No," I said, eager to get away from her. "Just looking for someone."

"You should see the fox who has your old basin!"

Not finding Pigeon, I began to be anxious. Had Old Frog fired her, after I had failed to show up, because of her complicity in my stolen day? The whistle would blow soon. I began to run here and there, and I felt foolish.

I did not see Pigeon; Pigeon saw me—shouted my name and flew into my arms. She began to sob in her happiness at having found me again, and I wept, too, relieved at last of the sharp guilt I had felt over abandoning this stolid and loyal child.

I asked her if she would like to come to our shop-back temple to help with household work. We would pay her what the filature did. She could sleep among the idols whenever she wished.

She jumped and squealed with a delight like—I was going to say, "like that of a child."

As we started away, I told her that at this temple we were working for the white race, and I spoke of Runner and Groundnut and the cages with open doors.

"Do you mean," Pigeon said, with another spurt of that pure delight, "that yours is the temple where the Bird Priests are?"

I felt a sudden lift at hearing that this alert child, at least, knew about something more than Old Arm's knuckles.

We walked along the Bund. Up strode an ox of a sun; it was going to be a warm day after all.

(Birds of the Dust Storm

We were on hand in plenty of time. The Immediate Flash Match Works, lying on the banks of Soochow Creek and facing Four Rivers Road, provided an ideal locus for Old Arm's first show of strength, because the factory's lumber yard and waiting area were surrounded by a chain-wire fence rather than by a brick wall, so anything that might take place inside would be visible from the road, and vice versa; besides which, Four Rivers Road, debouching from a shop-lined bridge over the Creek, was wide here, affording room for many to muster. It was past noon on a gray day. Over the area lay a stench of sulphur which forever drifted into the Enclave beyond the Creek. Gradually Old Arm's force, mainly dock coolies whom he had pulled off the wharves after the midday break, assembled, drifting into Four Rivers Road in groups of five or six at a time.

I stood between Rock and Runner; Groundnut, Bare-Stick, Mink, and Pigeon were with us. We did not yet see Old Arm.

Runner, in his red priest's robe, wore the look of a man who knew something the rest of us had yet to learn; perhaps this would turn out to be his plan for the day, for none of us were even aware that he had one. Groundnut had tried to persuade him to recruit "birds" for this occasion, but Runner, unperturbed by Groundnut's nervous eagerness, had quietly said we would have to wait and see what Old Arm intended to do. I had the feeling that Runner expected a great deal, though I could not imagine what, from Rock.

Rock at my shoulder was as tense as the spring of a heavily loaded ricksha. As I wondered what we could do, in the face of this growing mob of Old Arm's, with our mere handful of adherents, it suddenly occurred to me that Rock *was* ready, ready to act for himself and for all of us—indeed so ready that he might do anything he was asked to do, even by Old Arm.

By the middle of the afternoon Four Rivers Road was quite full. The wharfmen were cheerfully on edge. I dare say these roustabouts were in earnest and believed what Old Arm had told them about themselves, but they gave the impression of being merely bored young ragbags needing to let off steam.

Indeed, as Old Arm postponed later and later his arrival on the scene, boredom seemed to have become the sole theme of the day, until it was dangerous in itself.

Perhaps this was just what Old Arm wanted; he may have been starving his hounds to make them sharp.

Inside the wire fence, from time to time, yellow men could be seen stepping out from the factory buildings to look with anxious curiosity at the crowd in the street, then going back indoors.

A large number of white onlookers, including many women, had come across the bridge from the Enclave to see what was doing.

Our group was standing in front of the crowd, near the wire fence, not far from the Soochow Creek bridge.

I noticed in Rock, besides his tenseness, a willingness to bide time, a patience within impatience which seemed new in him—something he had found, perhaps, between the shafts of his ricksha. In other times he would have covered his restiveness with a stream of mocking comments, teasing Runner or Groundnut for teasing's sake. I knew how he had felt all along about Old Arm; but I knew, too, how he had felt about white men being restricted to the three servile labors: of house servant, wharfman, ricksha boy. He must have been torn, and I felt torn. What were we to fight for—or against? Surely our adversary was the yellow man's power. Yet was it? Was it Old Arm, a white man? What did Runner want? Did he after all know?

There was a stir at the far end of the crowd, which now fed some distance beyond the match-factory grounds along Four Rivers Road. Old Arm! Old Arm standing on a donkey cart which was being pulled through the crowd by a "flying squad."

A roar went up from the wharfmen.

Inside the yard several yellows came flapping out from the factory doors to see what the noise meant; then they ran back inside.

The flying squad pulled the cart through the eddying wharfmen up to the main gate in the wire fence.

Old Arm held up restraining palms, and the clamor died slowly down. In a piercing high-pitched voice Old Arm began to shout what was probably the first open, public incitement of whites against yellows in the history of Up-from-the-Sea, or of any other yellow city.

Ai, what a turmoil his speech stirred in me! All that he said about the yellows was true, was straight from my own memory stock. He knew how to speak to my deepest resentments, he stirred my anger. Yet there was something nagging in his voice which roused the crowd in an ugly way and frightened me. His words did not go so far as his tone of voice did. His words urged only "frowns," "shouts," "let them know how we feel." But the whine, the snarl, the grunts, the snuffling—these came from the throat of an enormous cat of hatred, and they worked a primitive, claw-unsheathing stimulus on the men packed in the roadway mob.

I looked at my companions. How frightening was Bare-Stick's face! He was with us, he was one of Runner's pillars, yet in response to Old Arm's volleys he was nodding, running his thick tongue over his lips, scowling, letting out yelps of concurrence like the rest of the mob, and his face seemed to be lit up with a yearning for a roughhouse. And I could see that even Rock was on the edge of being carried away by the torrent of the speech. Old Arm was evoking our sufferings, and Rock, too, had suffered.

Rock wanted to be against Old Arm, but now and then a flicker of frustrated rage, as of approaching lightning, would fleetingly twitch his face. Mink was in a state of bliss; Old Arm had captured the whole of his attention, so for a few minutes he had lost sight of his pain, as if the speech were almost a pipe. Pigeon's eyes were round and solemn.

Runner seemed not to be listening at all. He was staring upward, and following his line of vision I saw a huge bird, perhaps an osprey, in flight toward the ocean, alternating the clumsy, lumbering flapping of its heavy wings with a marvelous patient soaring toward the edible fish of the sea. But as I looked again at Runner I saw that he *was* listening—with a taut inner attention; he was listening as a hawk watches.

Old Arm's speech was accelerating, the yips and bellows of the crowd were growing more frequent and more insistent.

At a moment of fierce opportunity when Old Arm had just bitten off a kind of peroration and the mob was on a nervous razor's edge, the day's-end whistle of the match factory gave out its long, shrill cry. It seemed a provocation; the mob howled at it.

Then the factory's doors flew open and yellow workmen began to stream out into the wire-fenced yard.

The yellows must have been hearing the crowd's roars from within, and they were curious, excited, and, upon seeing the actual assemblage of whites, angry. They wanted to go home. But they were disadvantaged by being enclosed, and it was easy to see that they were also nervous and probably afraid.

A group of the yellows came toward the main gate, perhaps with the intention of trying to open it and force a passage out. The mob outside bellowed and pressed forward. Then some yellows—evidently some of the factory's supervisory staff—came running out of the factory doors toward the advancing group of employees and turned them back. This prudence brought a new roar of confidence from the whites. The bosses shouted and gesticulated to the main body of employees, and they all retired to the rear portion of the waiting area.

The withdrawal, bringing with it a suspicion that the yellow workers would escape through a rear gate, broke whatever restraint was left in the white mob.

On his cart at the gate Old Arm himself was making wild gestures of interdiction which somehow had precisely the opposite effect on the men near him. They seemed to take his pushing motions for beckoning; perhaps he subtly meant them as such. The men surged forward. They tried to open the gate, but it was stoutly locked. They swerved to our side of the gate, quite near our group, and grasped with their hands at the wire fence. Some climbed on others' shoulders and grappled at the crest of the fence with wharfmen's hooks, and suddenly from nowhere coils of sea rope appeared, sisal lines of a sort the wharf coolies daily used, and were knotted to the hooks, and a half dozen hauling chains were formed. We heard now, first from the men on the lines, then, with an eerie effect, from the entire crowd, the heartbreaking gruntlike heaving chants of white men on yellow-owned docks. The ropes were all hooked to the fence within a narrow span, near us, and soon the fence at that place began to bend and to give out metallic screeches. The crowd interrupted its chants to cheer each yielding of the strong fence.

Within the yard we saw the consternation of the plant's supervisory people, who ran here and there like ants when a great shoe has stirred the hill. The workmen, now thoroughly aroused—both alarmed and furious, it seemed—stayed at the rear part of the yard. Either there was no rear escape, or they chose not to make use of it.

A heave! A bending of the metal! A roar of delight!

What was Runner thinking about, with that faraway look? Bare-Stick was oafishly cheering with the roustabouts. Mink was almost asleep in his interested peace of mind. This seemed to me a moment of terrible danger, inviting a whole epoch of retribution from the yellows. What could this crowd do in its excited folly? Surely the municipal police would arrive with their clubs, and even guns, at any moment. I was unable to think in any new way; it seemed to me that the white mob had quite lost its head and had put us all in worse jeopardy than ever.

And Rock? Rock was watching with a deeply troubled look in his eyes; the muscles of his jaw were working, as if he were chewing some last morsel of bitter hope.

Then a stretch of the fence gave way with a tearing sound. So sudden was the collapse that all the men on all the lines fell down backwards, and at this the enraptured mob gave in to laughter. A tornado of laughter!

It was Rock who led us in. Rock had the presence of mind to take advantage of the slapstick moment. He snatched at Runner's sleeve, and he beckoned to the rest of us, and he jumped up on the sagging curve of fence and danced down the bouncing wire slope into the yard. He ran forward four or five paces and stood on one leg; he was a sleeping bird.

In a rush we were beside him. Pigeon was agile, and even Mink moved with a clearheaded alacrity. There were soon seven of us, sleeping birds, within the fence.

At the sight of the fall of the fence and of Rock's hurdling within, the crowd of yellow workmen had surged a few steps forward. But Rock's sudden assumption of the awkward pose, and our joining him—even a woman and a little girl!—caused the workmen to stop. What was this?

And on the outside the white wharfmen, too, were caught for a while by astonishment, and the laughter, which had been caused by the collapse of the heaving lines, persisted.

I distinctly heard Old Arm screaming, "No! No! Don't let them! Stop them!"

Ahead of us the yellow workmen held their ground, waiting to see what would happen.

With a pounding heart I heard the metal fence behind us creaking as someone leaped on it and ran down it. I expected the human flood to overwhelm us first from that direction. After that I could hear that another man was on the fence, and a third.

Then I saw a new arrival take his place on the end of our line and lift one knee. It was a beggar!—one of the crowd of beggars from the postern of Groundnut's temple, surely. The second man, another tattered scarecrow, joined us. Now others were coming across the fence. I dared to look around. Out from the huge crowd —how had we not seen them there?—was it that they were only one remove in shabbiness and degradation from the wharf coolies themselves?—were coming first a handful, then a score, then a huge flock of beggars. They crossed the bowed-down fence and came to us and stood as sleeping birds. Scabs and tatters, feigned and real. Jug, the leper! Maimed men, figures of hunger and loneliness. Here came one, helped by two others, who only *had* one leg. More beggars than I had ever seen in one place. Bedraggled birds! Birds of the dust storm!

My glance brushed across the faces of my companions. Ai! Groundnut! What a look of a man who has had a good meal! On Rock's face, something I had never seen there before—a serenity to match Runner's.

As neither crowd, neither the white nor the yellow, could seem to bring itself to stir, but held back in amazement, amusement, or perhaps even some sort of respect, I felt a sudden flow of the greatest joy I had known in all the time since the day my friends and I had been marched like goats from our Arizona village—a joy of triumph. There was still great fear mixed with this exultation, for I expected that the joy would be as short-lived as it was incredible.

No, it was not simply triumph. I had a sense so new that it was not easy to put a name to it—perhaps of dignity. These wretched companions were good company—eloquent, eloquent. We all stood on one leg, with bowed heads, peaceable, vulnerable, utterly reproachful.

Ahead of us there seemed to be a new mood in the crowd of yellow workmen—yes, a peculiar bewilderment, and shame, and anger that must follow shame: The workmen were grumbling, slowly advancing.

And behind us I could hear Old Arm's screaming commands to his flying squads to cross the fence, push the birds—he called us birds!—aside. What was to take place beyond that he did not specify. But Old Arm had apparently lost his own men; there was a lull behind us.

Now the supervisory personnel came at us in outrage, shouting that we were, of all things, trespassers.

This flurry of the bosses seemed to have an immediate effect on the mood of the yellow workmen, who stopped advancing and fell to looking at each other with baffled faces.

No one among us answered the employers. They could not shout long at dummies. They stormed off toward the gate, perhaps believing that we had been sent in by Old Arm, and they began to call through the wire to him.

Then I heard once again the creaking of the fallen fence behind us as someone—then several weights of men—landed on it and jounced forward toward us. For a moment I was terrified: Had the lovers of violence finally recovered their impetus? Would we be attacked, first from the rear and then from the front?

But something happened now that none of us could have imagined possible. Some of Old Arm's wharfmen—hard-eyed, disillusioned, tested beyond bearing by the miseries of their lives— joined us; they ran up to us and stood each on one leg. The first to do so caused a flurry of excited chatter in the crowd in the street—for it was surely a courageous commitment, entailing, with its defiance of Old Arm, an almost certain loss of work on the wharves. Then a dam of caution broke, and with shouts of reckless gladness, and with laughter, more, many more, many many more men jumped on the fence and ran to us. Scores of dirty wharfmen came up. I saw men in the tunics of ricksha-pullers. Some were well dressed—were shroffs with us, too? Now women began to come. Soon we were pushed forward; the yard was filling. I turned my head and saw that Old Arm was no longer standing on the flat-bedded cart beyond the gate; instead, there were half a dozen men balancing as sleeping birds. The street outside must be filled with sleeping birds! Thousands of whites standing as sleeping birds!

Once as we were jostled forward by the growing flock within the yard, Rock gently took my hand, and the full intensity of my emotion poured out from my throat in a groanlike shout, as I realized what had happened to me, at last, at last. I was free!

Somewhere in these confused actions I had come to realize that freedom could be felt at best only for moments: that even for the powerful, even for yellows, it was inconstant, elusive, fickle, and quickly flown. It turned out to be an experience rather than a status. Ayah, much needed to be changed in our lives, to give us, not freedom, but mere humanity. Freedom was not to be bestowed but grasped—and only for a moment at a time.

This was such a moment. What a catch of exultation at my throat!

Yes, this was my first moment of freedom. I felt it pouring into me, like a pure, cool stream slaking my ancient thirst: I had a picture in my mind of the perfect crystalline pool that I had seen on the day of the yellow masters' picnic, after Nose's death, at Jade Springs Hill, where cresses and water snowflakes and floating hearts swayed in the greenish depths. I drank till I was cool and peaceful.

I was full of it, and I recognized it.

I looked in Rock's eyes, and I saw *them* brimming with it, too.

Then I discerned, ahead, through and beyond the still-benumbed crowd of yellow workmen, reality walking into the yard, in the shapes of a squad of municipal policemen. There must after all have been a rear gate to the factory compound; police were streaming into the yard now in large numbers.

I should have trembled but I was calm; I felt Runner's calm and

Rock's strength, and I felt, above all, the cool sweet draughts of freedom in me that I had just drunk.

They were approaching, armed with thick bamboo clubs. They knew what they were doing, and their first phalanx came straight at Runner and his nucleus. We still perched. In a moment my sense of freedom deserted me, as I saw frail Pigeon bowled over. Some brave defender of the yellow order had picked out a tender target. She went down with a twisted mouth and eyes full of disbelief. How could such a thing happen? I felt the absolute horror of a world in which a strong human being of one color was driven to do this to a weak human being of another color.

But then, miraculously before I myself was touched, I saw another thing. Two yellow policemen jumped on Rock, who, having no square footing, fell at once to the ground. The men ran over him and rushed a beggar. Then Rock—my quarrelsome, powerful man, Rock of the orphanage, Rock the trainer of Bad Hog, Rock who liked to give as good as he got—quickly rose, and with a look on his face of great determination, equanimity, and joy, he raised his left knee and stood quiet again. I knew then that I had been right to think of what I had felt as a moment of freedom, and that now we could not be stopped.

Virtuous Wisdom, Gentle Hand

⟨[The Silence Is Broken

WE TWO, at the center of the reviewing ground in a silence that is like a chambered privacy, are locked in a dialogue of eyes, and I have long since been forced to realize that my earlier guess was correct: Governor K'ung is simply going to wait me out.

I feel resourceless; with recollections of the past I have deferred trying to think what I can do to counter him.

How much time has drifted away? Excellency K'ung stands motionless and mute, his sword pointing forward, parallel to the ground. The sun shines on the fortlike yamen. The dog has not come back; there is no more laughter. The vendor lies off to the left among his scattered belongings, and the Governor, I still feel sure, is unaware of him.

It is as if we were in a room alone, yet here we are on a public square surrounded by a crowd of onlookers.

I am used to him now, standing in front of me; I feel so familiar with him that it is only with an explicit effort of will that I can remind myself that he is a monster.

The sun has moved, or he has turned a little, and I can no longer tell from the glints on the sword whether the man is still trembling. I doubt it. He is as used to me as I am to him. The idea of an insurgent white race has been reduced in his eyes to the form of a woman whom he can think of ravishing. He has thought of it. I have seen those looks of sensuality, those little ocular stumbles, more than once.

My thoughts of the past have given me strength. I know the enormity of this despicable fat man's debt to me and my people; I feel a strong tide of inevitability—we *cannot* be stopped. At the same time, I am caught here in this impasse. Try as I will, I cannot call up now the rapture I felt that day in the yard of the match factory, the flashing ecstasy of knowing that I was free, truly free, if for only a moment. This eludes me now. It seems to me that something new is needed, to break this lock. The Sleeping-Bird Method has reached the limit of its power; something new is needed.

Something beyond shame is needed. What I am doing here requires that shame must come into play—shame so crushing as to cause a moral retreat. But what if my adversary is no longer capable of shame, or is so inured to it that it does not deter him— may even, in fact, stimulate him in some awful way?

Why do I feel that this silence is so heavy, so threatening—this deadness of the air not only between us two but also hovering over the whole crowd?

I see some sort of shadow crossing Excellency K'ung's face. There is a disturbance in his chest, a swelling, and the little slit of a mouth flutters with a long exhalation. I think that was a sigh. The sensual glow had died out somewhat from his eyes, and there is an inward-searching look.

He is beginning to be weary! He has had an inspiration, he has invented a really brilliant answer to the sleeping-bird tactic, but carrying it through is tiresome. He sees that he may have to stand here all day.

To dominate is hard work! He really is squirming with annoyance and sheer jadedness, as he sighs again and shifts his weight on his feet. The trouble with "Only the powerful are free" is that the powerful are enslaved by their own power. They have to tend it, be clever for it, and sometimes even wait patiently all day for its sake. It may drive them to crimes they dread committing; it may bore them at the very brink of murder. Looking down, I see that the Governor is in fact no longer holding the sword parallel to the ground. The blade is drooping. His hand must be tired; lassitude is a component perhaps of prolonged vigilance. I can imagine that the tip of the sword will soon be resting on the ground.

It may be that the first gradual declining of the blade, perceived at the outer edge of my field of vision as I scanned the Governor's face, may have brought this life-saving realization into my mind: He will not kill me now. At least I believe that.

But is that enough? I grope blindly for the something new that I need to break this deadlock.

Some other thought, or some impression, is trying to force its way into the front court of my mind—I feel this as a vague uneasiness, a readiness of some kind—but I am so saturated with relief at the sight of the sagging sword that for the moment I cannot admit any interloping image or sound or idea.

The Governor looks as if he might be biting back a yawn. What a grotesque little zero that mouth would make if it were stretched into a yawn!

What is it that I want to think about, to know? Something seems to push at me, something painful that paradoxically stirs hope in me.

Now I hear a hint of this something. From a great distance, as if from the faraway edge of night, I hear a low sound. I think it is like a formless, meaningless groan in a dream of waking.

Suddenly I am a-tingle with awareness. It *is* a muffled groan, and it is off to my left. The vendor is alive! It must surely be he!

The sounds come at intervals, and it seems that with each outward breath of his still mostly unconscious body the vendor must be trying to shape an utterance that is halfway between a protest and a cry for help. This ambiguity is what makes the groans so eerie, so stabbing. This is the innermost sound of the white race. This is Rock's never-uttered outcry, my unscreamed screams, our stifled white moaning of anger and need, and at its tolling as I hear it now the gooseflesh spreads all over my body.

The crowd is silent; there is not the least ripple of mockery or enjoyment—or distress—or anything. It is a thoroughgoing silence, a cautious holding back, a waiting to see; a massive response to just what this crowd deserves—a shock.

The groans are louder now, they are so intrusive that the focus of interest on the wide reviewing ground must certainly have moved from the two figures at the center, from Governor K'ung and me, to the prostrate form, perhaps writhing now, off to the side.

But the center of interest for me is still right here: it lies in the Governor's eyes.

He has heard the sound. This is not simply a deduction on my part, from the volume of the groans I am hearing: this is something I see for a fact in the bird-snare eyes across from me. Gone now the boredom; the eyes are alight. I am thankful for the brilliance of mind I thought I had seen behind those brown pupils, for it enables me to do some reading now: most importantly, that I had been right in assuming that His Excellency had not seen the vendor or been aware of him in any way. These sounds baffle him. The remarkable presence of mind the Governor showed me when the laughter broke out at the wandering dog is not there now. He is so surprised and shaken by the groans he hears that he has, for these few moments, begun to lose sight and thought of me, and thus for the first time the advantage in our duel has started over to my side.

I see again the tiny dartings of the pupils which seem to be tugging at the Governor's will; the dark, shining circles may tear themselves loose now and look aside, whether he permits or not.

I can imagine, from the depth of my own desire to turn my head and confirm what my ears and guesswork have told me, how powerfully the Governor wants to look in the direction of these unexpected sounds of pain, aggravation, and consummate bewilderment.

It seems to me that the Governor hears these groans, as I do, as *white* sounds, for his ear is sharply attuned to white entreaty and even more finely to white outrage. He cannot imagine that there has been, all along, another white person, besides the sleeping bird, out here on the open ground; much less one who has come to such grief.

He must see a possibility of miscalculation—that all that was so certain a few moments ago may now be slipping out of hand.

His self-control breaks. He turns his head, on the poise of his huge neck, to look.

I see one eye now from the side, and through its refracted intelligence I take in the scene: Fifty paces away, a few feet this side of the edge of the crowd of yellow ruffians, on the ground, a number of things lie broadcast as if by a fury of wind—a white man on his back, with matted hair, in ragged clothes, his face as pale as barley flour, his forehead bloody, his mouth stretching one-sidedly with grisly sounds that no man ever wished to utter, and near him, various smashed and battered objects, bits of curved varnished wood, a brass canister, parts of an ash-colored brazier, an iron bowl; and scattered charcoals, still steaming, and a dark stain of oil on the ground.

The voracious eye-in-profile, the leaping full brow above it, the twinging membranes that pass for lips—the face that has been so impassive is electrified by rushing thoughts and feelings. Among them I think I see two that help me: anger at yellow citizens for having taken initiative into their own hands, and, far more important from my point of view, contempt for his own kind, fully as powerful, for a moment, as any he could possibly feel for mine. There are as well a thousand alarms and annoyances that I cannot yet decipher, for it seems that he himself cannot sort them out.

He is so used to being in charge that I see him tempted to walk away from me to this new center of interest, and there peremptorily to deal with it. I also see the flicker, toward me, of remembering that he has undertaken something here that he cannot abandon.

The fullness in my throat which comes from the feeling of the flow of advantage toward me, is so strong now that I think I am going to have to speak. I cannot help myself; I am going to break the fundamental rule of the Sleeping-Bird Method, I am going to utter words.

I do now quietly speak the first words that come into my mind: "Virtuous wisdom, gentle hand."

These are the words I saw inscribed in the memorial arch that spans the parade ground. Governor K'ung must have seen those words many a day.

My voice is not at all loud, but the effect is that of a gunshot. Back comes Governor K'ung's face with a startled snap of the great neck.

He is appalled at what he now sees on my face: a desire to speak further to him. I want to tell him the whole terrible story. I want to make him listen. Perhaps I even want to ask him—when I have finished speaking—what can possibly be in his vile mind.

Yes, this may be the new thing we whites have needed to break the basic deadlock into which we have fallen: speech. Silence is what has shackled us so neither side could move. Our white demonstrations, our silent mimetic acts of protest—these led only to further and deeper silence, which the yellows in turn answered with silence—blows, a sword—and these led to today's confrontation of silences here on the parade ground.

Oh, none of us has lost his tongue in these recent months; neither whites nor yellows have lost the power of speech. It is just that we have not spoken to each other for a very long time. We whites have been issuing statements at large, and so have the yellows, but these peremptory utterances on both sides have amounted to nothing better than silences. It has been a long time since we have spoken to each other and longer since we have heard each other's words. They will not listen to us; we think we know the lies and hypocrisy they will spit out. Yet now at last I have had the urge to convey something directly to a hateful yellow man.

Here on the reviewing ground the vendor's groan first broke the silence; then my words shaped a thought.

And a violent change has occurred. I have a powerful fantasy that Governor K'ung and I have changed places.

I am in charge. He is utterly demoralized. He does not know what I am going to do with him, and I have not yet really decided.

I had no time to plan what to say, and those words from the inscription on the archway simply sprawled into my mind. Apparently those words, together with the vendor's moaning, and the sight of the vendor and his kitchen strewn on the ground—these disarmed the yellow man, stripped him of his power, and turned him over to me. In my mind it seems that we have changed places.

But now this impression begins to slip away from me. I am aware of the sword, which is being held again at the ready position, parallel to the ground. I look at the sharp tip of it, and I am easily able to see, without the sun's help, that the hand that holds the sword is trembling again. Rage? Fear? The rage that feeds and is fed by fear? I can well imagine that my power was momentary, and is surely ended.

To see where I stand I look up at the eyes. Such a change has taken place in them that I wonder whether Governor K'ung, in the moment of hearing those few words from my lips, felt on his side a slight draft of thralldom. Did he get a glimpse of what it is like to be white? Did he, too, have the sensation of changing places?

The look of implacability is gone. Of course the sensual glint has been driven out. I still see hatred, and yes, I guess there is rage. The something new that I see looks to me like uncertainty. I see fear, too.

Could it be that Excellency K'ung with the neck of a ram does not know what he should do?

It is obvious to me that he must act, and soon. In the circumstances the K'ung Method is turning into a fiasco; he cannot wait me out now. The entire multitude of yellows, and our band of whites where Rock stands, too—all those who hem in the reviewing ground have seen his startled reaction to the vendor's groans. A move is expected of him. To do nothing now would be to lose face beyond recovery.

I am still standing on one leg. I have a burning melancholy feeling at my breast, a fierce yearning—to speak again. But words will not form; because of my own anger and fear, words are lumps that choke me.

I gather, from looking in his eyes, that Excellency is on the verge of a decision. There is a strange hurt look there, as if I, by breaking the silence, have done him an unkindness, been somehow ungrateful, or disloyal, or unloving, or unlike his idea of a full-hearted white woman.

I confess that this look, expressive of a disgusting sense of loss that verges on the sentimental, gives me a vindictive feeling of triumph. I want to laugh in his face, but I am prudent enough to restrain myself.

But the feeling of triumph is quickly washed out by misgivings, as the glint of fear in the Governor's eyes grows stronger. It fills *me* with a reciprocal terror. Of what is he afraid? Does he fear a massacre—the weapons he thinks hidden under white tunics, the weapons that may really be in the hands of some of our hoodlums, our disenchanted tigers, our hardened wharfmen? Is he in terror of the sword in his own hand, the holster on his hip? Of his own impulses, which he has seen reflected in what has felled the vendor? Of speech, which sooner or later must lay bare his (and my) most private and unbearable secrets?

He turns now, looking about. He must have decided what to do.

I put my left foot on the ground, because I know that my perch is over, and I feel able to turn my head and follow what is happening.

First I look quickly to my left, and I get a minor shock, because, while the essential facts are as I had deduced, the arrangement of the details is quite different from the picture I had built in my mind. For one thing, the vendor is lying on his stomach, his arms are gathered about his head, as if to protect himself from blows even in partial consciousness; hence the muffled sound of his groans. His impedimenta are scattered, but not in the pattern I had imagined.

At once I look back at the fat Governor. He is inserting the sword in the scabbard; he has some trouble, in the agitation he obviously still feels, getting the sword's point into the mouth of the sheath. His right hand is held high, his left hand steadies the scabbard, the point waves about uncertainly. There! It is in! He drives the sword home with an authoritative thrust, and I have the malicious thought that he is trying to show that he is still dominant over at least his own blade.

I feel that my chest will burst if I do not speak again. But it is not easy. I feel nausea-like waves in my throat at the effort to convey to Governor K'ung the bare truths of my protest, my yearning, my history, my agony, my needs, my demands, my awful fear of where his fear may lead him. There is such a gulf between us that words have lost their value, yet with all my strength I reach for them.

I manage to say, "I want to tell you something."

But that is not what I wanted to say at all! Why "something"? I meant to say, surely, "everything"!

Governor K'ung ignores me. He turns again and raises his hand, and I see that he is flagging a squad of the most unmartial of all the uniformed figures—the city police. They see him and run a few ragged paces toward him. He wags the index finger of his right hand toward the vendor, and they comprehend: They are to remove the groaner. They trot toward the prostrate figure.

Now the Governor looks around once more; he has to do something about me. He is not, at any rate, signaling to the soldiers with rifles. He spots what he wants, and I follow his eyes. It is another sloppy band of the local police!

And now I see that he is wagging the finger over my head, pointing at me. They are jogging toward us.

He is washing his hands of me, turning me over to mere city authorities!

I look at him, wanting to engage his eyes again. Now I am really convinced that if the deeper impasse that today's lock represented is ever to be broken, we must speak to each other, I to him and he to me, whites to yellows and yellows to whites, openly, in such a way that eventually nothing is held back, each having the courage to hear the most dreadful truths that the other may harbor, for the present, even from himself. I cannot blame myself for feeling that the debt of speech, as of everything else, is very great on his side.

I say, "Can I talk with you?"

His ugly little mouth writhes; I see the light of a guarded wish to respond in his eyes. He is trying to say something to me! I welcome his effort, I want this as much as I dread it. But suddenly he turns and starts marching back to the yamen; his whole satined back jiggles with each step.

I feel put down. I have won today, but we have not really eased our deadlock at all. The hardest struggle is still ahead.

I hear a murmur—is it of disbelief, a grumbling?—from the crowd.

The police, falling over each other, circle around behind me as if I were dangerous. I feel a hand on my arm.

Looking at the retreating Governor's back, I have a thought that floods me, at the very time when perhaps I should be giving way to a blessed sense of victory, instead with a fear as puzzling as any I have felt in all my life up to now:

What if someday we are the masters and they are the underdogs?

❪ A Note on the Type

THE TEXT of this book was set in a typeface called *Primer,* designed by RUDOLPH RUZICKA for the Mergenthaler Linotype Company and first made available in 1949. Primer, a modified modern face based on Century broadface, has the virtue of great legibility and was designed especially for today's methods of composition and printing.

Primer is Ruzicka's third typeface. In 1940 he designed Fairfield, and in 1947 Fairfield Medium, both for the Mergenthaler Linotype Company.

Ruzicka was born in Bohemia in 1883 and came to the United States at the age of eleven. He attended public schools in Chicago and later the Chicago Art Institute. During his long career he has been a wood engraver, etcher, cartographer, and book designer. For many years he was associated with Daniel Berkeley Updike and produced the annual keepsakes for the Merrymount Press from 1911 until 1941.

Ruzicka has been honored by many distinguished organizations, and in 1936 he was awarded the gold medal of the American Institute of Graphic Arts. From his home in New Hampshire, Ruzicka continues to be active in the graphic arts.

Composed, printed, and bound by
THE HADDON CRAFTSMEN, INC., *Scranton, Pa.*
Typography by HERBERT H. JOHNSON.
Binding design by JEANYEE WONG.